I0648023

Persona Non Grata

A Story of Junkture

Stephanie Quinn Jackson

Copyright © 2012 by Stephanie Quinn Jackson
All Rights Reserved
Printed in the United States of America

Persona Non Grata:
A Story of Junkture

ISBN 978-0-9882185-0-5 (098821850X)
Library of Congress Control Number: 2012949787

Cover Design by Adam Taylor
Photography by
Christine Brandigi-Clark/Photos by Digi
"Self-portrait" by C. Berkut
Awesome Posing by
Danielle Turberville, a.k.a. Danger Kittyn

StephQJ, LLC
Atlanta, Georgia USA
www.stephqj.com

This is a work of fiction. Names, characters, businesses, organizations, places, events and incidents either are the product of the author's imagination or are used fictitiously. Any resemblance to actual persons, living or dead, events, or locales is entirely coincidental.

For Jean Burnett,
Because I always said the first one would be for her

Chapter 1

It was raining in my dream. The lush and leafy canopy of crape myrtle, bright pink in deep shadows, caught the shimmering drops, conducting them in offbeat syncopation against the dark and shining cobblestones. He sat on an old brick wall that was slick from the warm, humid air. Dark hair and intense, brilliant eyes, smiling at me, sexy and sly.

He shrugged, slow and exaggerated, his hands coming together and opening fully to reveal their emptiness. Fingers long, palms wide and smooth and a little dirty around the edges. He raised one eyebrow, knowing and suggesting.

The rain began to fall in time to the throbbing between my legs.

The bricks belong in Montevallo, on the university campus where I was first thrust into adulthood twenty years before. The crape myrtle smells like the ones that used to grow outside the last apartment Sam and I shared, before the boys were born. They only smelled like that in October when they put on their last, best show before the dormant winter. The scent staggered me every time I caught it in the autumn twilight. Visceral and genitive. The man, I don't know. I can't make out the face, just his ardent aspect.

I shifted in my sleep, rousing slightly. I calmed my eyelids and tried to drift back into the lingering dream, to keep the consciousness at bay. I didn't want to control it, didn't want to think about it and turn into to fantasy. There was something there, just a moment before, acute, and I wanted it to come back and finish what it started.

It was raining for real. I could hear it falling harder on the roof, dropping from the high branches and the clogged gutters into the drifts of crunched leaves and auburn pine needles covering the ground outside the bedroom windows. I listened instinctively for Sam's breathing, like I did every time I woke. The tell-tale expiration that meant he was still with me. For more than eighteen years that had been the first sounds of my morning.

Sam was pressed next to me, his warm feet against the side of my calf, rough against my freshly shaven skin. His back was bent toward my arm, curving into my shoulder, and I could feel how satiny his skin was still.

I turned my head slightly and fluttered my eyelids just enough to make out the time on the alarm clock.

6:38

Seven minutes.

Seven minutes until the alarm would go off, and I would get up to pee. Eight minutes until I would brush my teeth. Ten minutes until I would feed the cat and wake the children and make their breakfasts. Two hours until I would start the laundry and unload the dishwasher, timing the hot water around Sam's shower before work.

Dull, burning pain was shooting from my lower back and down into my left leg. I tried to shift without disturbing Sam. I wanted to feel his warmth against me, but I needed to move. I felt stiff and sluggish from not moving much in the night. My back and leg had hurt for so long now that I should've been used to it, accustomed to not feeling my toes half the time, to bracing myself before I tried to turn over in the bed.

6:40

Ignore it. Sleep five more minutes.

My shoulders were cold, uncovered and exposed to the draft from the air conditioning vent on my side of the bed. I tried to pull the blankets higher, but they were wrapped under Sam. He moaned lightly, his breathing altered slightly, and turned over to face me, trying to put part of his warm blankets over me. He put his hand on my thigh, sliding it toward my stomach.

I was still throbbing from the dream. Dreamtime was over. I could feel the sun rising behind the rain clouds.

Four more minutes.

An annoying morning DJ's voice screeched into the overcast quiet.

Sam's alarm.

The voice wouldn't stop, talking about all the prizes he'd be giving away in thirty minutes and in an hour and before the morning drive was over.

Turn it off, Sam!

He did, finally. I heard the click of the alarm button, then the sound of Sam's glasses scratching across the wooden nightstand as he picked them up, then the rattle of the frame as he slid them onto his face.

For more than eighteen years, those had been the second sounds of my morning.

He sat on the edge of the bed, taking a moment to wake up. As he stood, the blankets were released, and I pulled them over my shoulders. For a fleeting few moments, I would have the bed totally warm and to myself.

Two more minutes.

Cereal. Sign Tripp's permission slip. Sign Ian's reading log. Check to see if there's email from PTA. We need milk and broccoli for dinner.

Ugh.

The first cramp twinged through my uterus, trickling thick, warm blood inside me.

"Good morning, Atlanta! Coming up at seven-oh-five, we'll be giving away tickets to see Junkture at the Masquerade Music Park on Sunday. Later, be listening for your chance—"

I hit the snooze button.

Fuck, I hate Mondays!

———————

When Sam had first emailed me in August to ask what I wanted for my birthday, I was a little irritated. After nearly twenty-four years in each other's lives, it shouldn't have been that hard for my husband to find something I would like. He'd known me since I was fourteen; surely some gift-giving occasion would eventually come when he could wing it and pick out something nice.

But I knew he didn't want to disappoint me on my special day.

I've never been the biggest fan of myself and always tried to kind of blend into the limelight. Generally, I like to be shiny and special, but it's easier for me to be a *part* of it than to be the *focus* of it. But my birthday is a whole other story.

It's the one day a year when I can be as self-centered and self-interested as I can stand. It's the one day when I can step outside of my normally moody, analytical self and be exuberant and boisterous and just not give a damn what anyone else thinks. I get to be *Tierney-Siobhan-Cavanaugh-Johnson-And-Don't-You-Forget-It!*

So I knew the day was coming. What did I want?

Like so many other occasions, I wanted a CD. And concert tickets.

I love music. I always have. All kinds of music. As a teen, I spent long hours locked away in my bedroom, flipping albums over and reading along with the lyrics and liner notes in time to the music. Music was a big deal in my house from a very early age. I was raised on daily doses of the Eagles, the Doobie Brothers, Elton John, Billy Joel, and Linda Ronstadt. I loved nothing more than choosing the albums for the day at home with my mom, stacking them on the turntable, and singing my little strawberry blond heart out. The first song I remember singing is "Bennie and the Jets", though all I knew was the "B-b-b-bennie and the Jetssssss!" I knew all the words to "Hotel California" long before I ever knew what a colita was.

I spent years in choir, traipsing my Amazonian contralto harmonies around the sweet, tinny melodies of the tiny sopranos. Eventually, I found that singing melancholy songs of teen angst in my bedroom was much more fulfilling to my tortured psyche than any six-part Latin piece would ever be. Bauhaus and INXS and the Doors always seemed to know just what I was feeling. I did a couple of homegrown musical theatre performances and even toyed with the idea of taking opera lessons. It turned out it's really hard to sing scales for hours on end when you're hungover. And nothing will make your tongue trip over arpeggios like cotton mouth.

I still spend hours listening to music, picking apart the bass line, or comparing how the countermelody of the guitar syncs with the singer's voice. For me it's always about the lyrics and the vocals, so intimately tied together, how poignant lyrics can overcome a less-than-perfected vocal talent, *a là* Leonard Cohen or Greg Dulli, both of whom I adore unconditionally.

I have hundreds of CD's and albums and a dusty box of cassette tapes that are the soundtrack to my life.

I'd been a fan of the band Junkture for years. They'd formed in our hometown of Birmingham while I was in high school. Their popularity had grown quickly, and they were rarely still playing hometown shows by the time I was trailing behind their footsteps at the University of Montevallo. After their debut album, *Mantissa*, exploded onto the music scene, their career skyrocketed to international stardom. I'd seen them live several times over the years—in Birmingham and Nashville and Knoxville, even in Atlanta just after we moved there five years before, for one of the last shows of that tour. I'd spent thousands of dollars on tickets and t-shirts and records and whatever memorabilia caught my fancy. But I was never the pushy, sycophantic groupie who followed their every move. I'd never met them, never been backstage, and that was okay with me. Sam and I had been on the front row for shows a few times before our children were born, but then motherhood and toddlerhood and adulthood kind of got in the way of concerts and extraneous entertainment.

My own grown-up life had coincided with theirs. The band had been on hiatus for the last four years. Only the bassist, Max Bennett, still lived in Birmingham. The other members had taken their hard-earned gains and moved around the country. They'd started their own families and had taken some time to enjoy being semi-normal grown-ups. Even though their first couple of records had been outstanding and included at least six top ten singles, the last couple had been panned by the critics and hadn't received much radio play. The Age of MTV was long over, and lots of fans assumed Junkture was, too.

But they'd come back together for a new record. Their new Facebook page listed dates for a forthcoming tour. I wanted the CD, and I wanted to see them in Atlanta, at the Masquerade.

Sam bought me both the record and VIP tickets, which included entrance to an early soundcheck at the venue. The CD sat on my desk for two days, waiting to be opened. I was busy with home and kids and PTA and couldn't get to it right away.

When I did finally tear away the plastic wrapper, I fell instantly in love with it. *Persona Non Grata* was a really fantastic album, not a throwback to Junkture's alternative roots, not aging-rocker adult contemporary—just balls-to-the-walls rock.

I immersed myself in that record. There was something in it that drew me in from the first haunting notes of the opening track, "Before We Start". Every time I listened to it, I heard something new and exciting. It was raw and harsh and reckless, and it struck a chord, something deep and anxious that I hadn't quite known was even there, waiting to be resonated.

All of this was coming on the heels of months' worth of pain and misery, having started in the spring with a back injury. What I thought was a wrenched muscle from moving heavy planters filled with rock and soil turned out to be two bulging lumbar discs. One had a slight tear. I'd had neck problems a couple of years before, but this was way worse. I was in horrible, constant pain. Most days I couldn't feel the toes on my left foot. I'd spent much of the summer splitting my time between my orthopedist's office and my couch.

After the third round of epidurals and weeks of failed physical therapy, I tried a serotonin-norepinephrine reuptake inhibitor for nerve pain, at the suggestion of my orthopedist. I thought I was going to die.

"You'll have to learn to live with the pain," the doctor told me at my last appointment.

Fuck that.

I was shocked to see the scale had hit 298 pounds. That was four pounds more than my heaviest pregnancy weight, and even that had come while I was swollen from pregnancy-induced hypertension.

I'd always been a big girl. I was born a month early and weighed six pounds, six ounces. It's the only time in my life anyone could ever have called me "petite". I was taller than the average kid— I hit five feet by the age of nine—but I was also just bigger. I was a chubby child who turned into a fat, though well-proportioned, teen. It wasn't until a year after Sam and I married that I found out I had Polycystic Ovary Syndrome. It's a complicated mix of metabolic and hormonal issues that causes all kinds of problems. For me, weight gain and substantial fertility problems were the most blatant and difficult symptoms.

Each of our sons had been the product of expensive and protracted fertility treatments. The PCOS had really reared its ugly head during my second pregnancy, and postpartum thyroiditis came ravaging right behind it. Having half of my thyroid removed was just one more excuse for my body to gain weight.

I was beginning to realize how stifled I felt in my life. The year's back pain and illness had left me exhausted, physically and emotionally. I started walking at the park one morning, after the boys were at school. I knew weight loss and restrengthening the back muscles would help alleviate the pain. One mile turned into two, turned into three. I relished the quick, rhythmic movement of my legs, feeling their pumping motion propelling my body temperature and heartbeat away from sedentary. I felt alive and strong, moving. I'd been still and stagnant for so long, and the constant motion was so relieving.

I was feeling better almost immediately but knew I couldn't stop. I logged untold miles while listening to *Persona Non Grata*. I didn't concentrate on anything but my own breathing, pacing it with my stride, and absorbing every nuance of that record. My time at the park with my iPod was starting to heal the psychic damage of self-neglect. For the first time in years, I was focusing on myself for a few minutes each day, after ten years of devoting it all to my husband and children. I was finding this hour a day in my own head to be cathartic.

By the time October 25th came, I was ready for Junkture.

The Masquerade is in a turn-of-the-century building that had begun its life as a mill. It was something of a Franken-building, like parts had been added on over the years, and much of the building was painted a dull, flat black. It stood across the street from a huge, abandoned factory-looking building that looked like it could have been used to process soylent green.

We parked inside a gated lot across a side street from the venue. There was already a line stretching around the corner from the ticket line. Brightly colored mohawks and dyed-black locks topped band t-shirts from all genres. I thought to myself how some of them reminded me of characters from *Mad Max*. I looked at the marquee but didn't know either of the other bands playing on the other two stages. It looked like the Junkture show would be starting first, downstairs in the Hell theatre, around eight o'clock.

Sam and I stood in line, waiting patiently in the warm autumn sunset. Even though we had VIP tickets, we'd been unable to make the soundcheck before the show because our babysitter couldn't get to our house in time. But we filed in as soon as the doors opened, and we took up residence at the front left of the stage, in front of where guitarist Paul Sommers traditionally stood.

I went to check out the merch table and saw that the bassist Max Bennett was milling about, talking to fans before the show.

"Hi, Max," I said, offering my hand. "I'm Tierney Johnson."

He looked at me for a moment. "Tierney *Cavanaugh* Johnson?"

I grinned. "Yeah." *Ha! Facebook!*

We talked for a while about the record, the tour thus far, hanging with Paulie's daughters during the downtime. I told him I was from Birmingham, had gone to Montevallo after they were gone.

"I saw you guys play Springfest a couple of times there, though," I said.

"*Gawd*, we haven't played Springfest in years! We were such *babies* the last time we did it. You know, my house is just a couple of miles from there. *Manuel La Bore.*"

I giggled and nodded. "I think I was at a party there, after College Night, my freshman year. There was a bonfire, and I was dancing around it, and I set my foot on fire."

Eyes wide, Max gasped. "That was *you*! Oh, fuck! That's the night the deck collapsed with, like, thirty people on it."

"Yeahyeahyeah! It dropped, like, five feet. I remember thinking it was good that they were so drunk that none of them felt it."

Max glanced at his phone. "Oh, hell, I gotta go get ready. Let's talk more after the show?"

He went backstage, and I joined Sam by the giant amps at the edge of the stage. He had his own beer in one hand and a Jack and Ginger for me in the other.

The opening bands were fine. Both were entertaining in their own way, and the crowd was ready for more. We watched the techs ready the stage for Junkture, while excited musical butterflies fluttered through my chest. I was firmly planted against the low, wooden wall separating the crowd from the stage. Like he'd done for years, Sam stood behind me, ready to use his six-foot-four frame to block crowd surfers and pushy assholes alike.

The lights went out. One of the new songs, "Before We Start", strained through the dark, loud and overpowering. I watched the silhouettes of the four guys come out and take their places in the midst of the screaming and cat-calling from the crowd. The lights exploded on as Alex Wheeler started singing about lost innocence.

The show was filled with old songs and new. They played the thundering hits that everyone sang all the words to. They slowed the set with the obligatory ballad from the new record, the song that really had nothing to do with sex but that every other fan would get laid to that night. They were engaged with the audience, but also with each other. Alex would sling his arm over Paulie's shoulder while the guitarist sang backup into the singer's microphone. Paulie would cross the stage to Max and do his best to fuck with him and make him laugh every time he acted like his guitar was an extension of his cock. Charlie Taylor pounded furiously on his drums while Alex stood behind him, mimicking his every bang.

And they all made those faces that musicians make. Drummers do it the most, but guitarists make the worst ones. They screw up their mouths and squint their eyes in time to their music, especially when they're *really* into what they're playing. Usually during a solo. And I've always been convinced it's the same face they make when they're fucking. Singers do it, too, though it's usually quicker and over before you can really notice it.

I hadn't seen Junkture, the band of guys, having fun on stage like that in a very long time. I'd never been disappointed with a Junkture show, ever, but this was something different, something easier and bolder than I'd seen from them since their first record. Maybe since my first Junkture show at the Nick, when I was a freshman in college. It was great to see that the four of them were as good *live*, if not better, after all this time than they were on the record.

And I was struck by how they'd matured. They were all a couple of years older than I was, and we'd all passed through the same four years. I knew the changes I'd gone through, so it shouldn't have been a surprise to see them looking a little older, each having passed the threshold of forty during their hiatus. They were no longer the same barely-grown-ups at the height of their career that I'd held in memory for the last decade.

For years, they'd been four all-American white guys with scraggly facial hair under their dark mops. I was surprised to see them all so definitively as *men*, knowing three of the four were fathers. They were still half-shaven, though now it was typically by design. Alex Wheeler had shorn away his long, rocker curls to tight, short waves that barely crested above his blue eyes, shining behind designer glasses. But the presence and the bravado were still there, sexy as hell, swaggering across the cramped stage as if it were a cavernous venue.

Then, there was that opening riff of my favorite song on the new record, "Dollface." It was the best of what I loved about this band. I was dancing and singing and watching everything. Alex moved toward Sam and me at the front end of the stage, and I kept singing along. Suddenly, he was coming to *me*, microphone in my face, and I was singing along *with* him. It happened so quickly that I didn't have time to get self-conscious. I'd never sung from the stage like that, and it was unbelievably fun. He grinned broadly and went back to the show.

Later, toward the end of the encore, Sam went back to the bar, across the room, for another beer. I was planted firmly in the music. Alex started singing "Hot Mess", an intensely sexy new love song. Unexpectedly, he was *back* in front of me with his mic. I just kept singing:

> *You had me on my knees*
> *With your soft panting pleas*
> *And your almost, baby, almost!*
> *So close!*

I stayed with him, breath for breath, my heart beating in time to Charlie's drumming. I could just make out the shape of his eyes, locked onto my face, through the sunglasses he put on for the encore. Alex grinned at me and kissed me on the cheek, going back to finish the set.

After the show ended and the house lights came up, the guy next to me gripped the drumstick Charlie had tossed into the crowd as he took a final bow.

"I've never caught one of Charlie's sticks," I laughed.

"Well, none of the rest of us got to sing with the band," he replied sardonically. "*Twice*."

Half a dozen people came up and congratulated me. Two asked if I knew Alex personally. Sam finally made it back to find me breathless and giddy.

"Did you see me?" I squealed, hands flailing in excitement.

"Holy shit, that was awesome! You sounded great."

I shook my head. "Hardly. I couldn't hear anything any way."

"No, really, but I think I should be jealous. That was sexy as hell. Some chick at the bar asked me if the singer was taking you home."

I rolled my eyes, laughing, and headed toward the merchandise table. The guys were getting ready to sign CDs and posters and the like. I wanted to say hello.

Sam and I stood in line, waiting our turn. We talked to Max again, chatting about the show and who we both knew in Montevallo. It turned out a friend of his had dated my college roommate, Jules, long after both Max and I had dropped out of college and moved on to other lives.

"Hey, singer!" I heard Alex Wheeler drawl. "Come here!"

I peered curiously down the table toward him, a couple of people between us. He was looking at me. He was talking to *me*. He motioned for me to step down toward him, much to the chagrin of the girls in front of me.

He leaned across the table and hugged me, Sharpie in hand. "Thanks for singing with me."

"So much fun," I stammered. "Alex, I'm Tierney Johnson. We chatted on your Facebook wall last week about 'Dollface'. I asked whether or not it was you doing the backing vocals, because it didn't sound like you."

"Tierney *Cavanaugh* Johnson?" he asked.

I laughed. "Yeah."

"*Oh yeah!* You know, saying I sounded like Greg Dulli was the best compliment ever. I fucking *love* him!"

"Me too! He's amazing." I pointed to Sam, standing next to me. "*He* doesn't get my unadulterated superlove, though."

Sam shook hands with Alex and thanked him for singing with me. Alex signed my CD, and we moved down the line. Charlie and I talked about the new record and the crazy year they'd been having during recording. Sam and I talked to Paul Sommers, at length, about everything from parenthood to long-time marriage to the Junkture hiatus. Paulie had a *lot* to say about the somewhat publicized problems within the band, as well as friendship in general.

"I wasn't sure we would ever be back doing this," he admitted. "I mean, we grew up together in this business, and these guys are my *brothers*, but there are days we wanted to kill each other. Usually guys just kind of beat the shit out of each other and go grab a beer. It's over and done! But it took us two years to get together for that beer. We all just kind of went back to our families and went on about our lives. Alex went back to Los Angeles, and Charlie and his boyfriend went and had a baby. Max did what Max always does and waited out the rest of us. I was out in Texas, producing these new artists and wasn't sure I ever wanted to make music again.

"My wife, Sara, she was so fucking tired of having me hanging around the house. It was great at first, when I was home for her and the kids, but after a while we were grating on each other. She'd gotten so used to running the family without me *there*, you know, every day. I was in her way for fucking months! After two years, she told me to call Alex or move into the guest room. She'd had enough of my brooding. How long have you guys been together?"

"Off and on for twenty-four years," I replied.

"*Wow*, that's a long time!"

"We were high school sweethearts for a while, apart for six years, then together now for eighteen." I glanced at Sam and smiled.

"Then you *know* how hard that is, to be together that long. Sara and I have been together for twenty years. There are no secrets anymore, you know?, so being in the same house, all day, every day, just gets to be tedious after a while. There's no mystery left, and I think she was tired of looking at my ugly face every day!"

Paul started to laugh, and Sam and I politely joined in. I wasn't sure if he'd been joking at all and there was a sudden, heavy air of truthfulness. Somehow we ended up on the receiving end of all this energy the guitarist needed to expend. It was unexpected and strangely flattering.

Looking back, I know that CD was the catalyst for so much that would come after. It wasn't the root of anything, but it somehow altered everything, in the most seemingly-minute way. That record was the thing that brought me to the show, which brought me to the next shows, which led me to all kinds of new experiences and people that I wouldn't have otherwise ever known. It triggered in me a deep, visceral reaction, of seeing exactly how numb I'd been for so long— numb to my surroundings and my feelings and my *self*.

In an online interview reposted through the band's Facebook page, Alex Wheeler said the title, *Persona Non Grata*, referred to all of the unacceptable and unwelcomed parts of everyone—the lurid, the shadowy, the hidden, the broken.

"Each of us has a persona, all the time," he said. "I'm one persona with my band, someone a little different with my fans, someone else entirely with my wife and daughter. Sometimes that persona is 'good' and sometimes it's 'bad'. I spent a lot of time exploring the bad sides of normal, everyday people, you know? Not serial killers or rapists or anything. I wanted to look at the things regular people like to hide from the people they know and, most especially, from themselves."

It resonated like a gunshot through my brain.

I had been someone much different, once upon a time. I'd been a wild child who didn't really know what a bad girl she was. Somehow, somewhere I'd lost what made me *me*, squandered away while I fumbled my way through Motherhood and Wifedom.

Where the hell was *Tierney*?

I didn't know, but I had to find her. I *had* to. Inside and out, the persona of *Tierney* now existed only in anecdotes of agony and crazy stories of drug-laden, late-night exploits.

And I was about to crawl right out of my own damn skin.

———————

Monday morning came too early again.
Cat. Boys. Breakfast. Email.
Call Jules.

Julia Jordan McKinnon and I had met the day we moved into Hanson Hall at the University of Montevallo. It was the Saturday before classes started our freshman year. We'd been assigned to each other randomly, based surveys we'd completed during the enrollment process. Someone in Housing had thought we'd be a good match, and they were totally right. We had similar tastes in music, in clothes, and had the same dry, quirky sense of humor.

I was a Fine Arts major, and she was undecided. We had almost identical CD collections and an endless store of lurid limericks. We spent our first Halloween tripping on acid and traipsing around town from party to party in fishnets and not much else. We spent a lot of our two years together stoned and stumbling. It was love.

We hadn't lived together in twenty years. I was in Atlanta, and she was outside of Nashville, teaching English at Middle Tennessee State University.   We emailed and Facebooked regularly and talked every couple of months. We were both busy with life and kids, but our conversations always picked up just where we'd left them last.

"Kitten! What's up?"

Jules had started calling me the Golden Kitten after my ex-boyfriend, Damien, had spent the night in our dorm room. I got him off four times with my hands tied behind my back, literally. "That pussy is golden!" she'd quipped, so long ago.

"So, Sam and I went to see Junkture at the Masquerade last night."

"*Oooooh*, how was that? I haven't seen them in years!"

"It was so good! That new record is so damn good, and they were as good live as I've ever seen them."

"Coolness!"

"And I was talking to Max Bennett before and after the show. He said to tell you hi."

Jules cackled into her cell phone. "How was Max? You know, the last time I saw him was at a party at *Manuel La Bore*, right after he came off tour. Dave and I were there. I think we broke up like a week later."

"He said for you to find him on Facebook. He's still living in Montevallo."

"Fuck, I would still live there, too! I mean, it's the middle of *nowhere*. You have to *know* where the house is to fucking find the place. Dave and I spent half an hour driving up and down the same three miles of that road one night before we finally found the driveway."

Max was a rich kid from Birmingham who'd been orphaned when his parents' private plane crashed on its way to the Caribbean, right after he turned nineteen. He'd spent his teens speeding around the wealthy Mountain Brook suburb in his expensive sports car, snorting his trust fund up his nose. His parents' unexpected death had stopped all of that. It turned out he didn't want to be a useless trust fund baby.

When Max decided to go school in Montevallo as a Business major, he found a great old house less than a mile from campus. It sat on five acres of pasture land surrounded by woods, so there were no neighbors to disturb. He bought it outright with money from his trust fund. It was way more house than he actually needed, and it needed a lot of work. He bartered bedrooms in the house to broke friends in exchange for their help with renovations. He called the house *Manuel La Bore*.

It turned out Max also played the bass guitar, and Junkture was born from the belly of Montevallo. His first roommate was Charlie Taylor. They picked up a singer and a guitarist, Alex and Paul, and started playing local parties. By the time I rolled onto campus four years later, they were only playing the occasional show at the coffee house and local bar in town, having already moved on to bigger and somewhat better gigs around the Southeast.

Two years later they were headlining major tours and selling a million copies of their debut record, *Mantissa*.

"Hang on," Jules said. I heard her typing in the background. "*There!* Friend request sent to Max Bennett. We'll see how long he takes to respond. How are Sam and the boys?"

We spent a while catching up. I told her about my back, about what the boys were doing in school, how Sam was working too damn much.

"That man of yours, he kills me. I don't know how you deal with it. He's always working."

"He loves his work," I replied, "but he's never home. We barely see him. He gets in late at night and is gone early the next day. Mostly it's just me and the kids."

"Well, I think you need to remind him why he should be at home more often. You're the Golden Kitten for a reason!"

"He's gotta pet the kitten to make it purr, Jules. Mostly the kitty gets to lay around on the couch all day, licking herself and getting fat."

Jules cackled mirthfully. "Oh, Kitten! You can do it. Swish your pretty tail and remind him how you like to be rubbed."

Jules and I talked for a while, giggling and bitching until it was time for her to go teach a class. We promised to see each other soon and said goodbye.

There were still a couple of hours until the boys would be home from school. The laundry and dishes were done, and I didn't feel like watching television. I decided to go to the art store.

I'd started college as an Art major, focusing on painting. By the end of my sophomore year, my relationship with Damien had turned so tempestuous and volatile that I'd quit going to class, desperately trying to keep him and my sanity. My professors all assured me I had talent, but I was distractible and did my best to slack my way through my classes. While it was true that I painted some amazing pieces while I was stoned or tripping, I couldn't bring myself to do the other essential work they required. By the end of my second year, I'd lost my scholarship and my boyfriend and decided to leave Montevallo altogether for a fresh start. Not long after, Sam and I were back in each other's lives and had been together ever since.

It had been ages since I'd really put any effort into painting, having mostly done small pieces for myself. Sometimes I would sketch in a notebook or use the boys' watercolors and frayed, oversized brushes to do a quick something. I'd toyed with it, off and on, before the children were born, but there had never been time to go back to it, between diapers and play classes. Now the boys were both in school full time, and painting might prove to be a great distraction from eating.

I hadn't been in an art supply store in at least ten years, and the choices were overwhelming. The brushes and papers and canvases, simple and complicated and convenient like they hadn't been when I was a burgeoning, idealistic student. I spent an hour just looking at everything lining the shelves, politely and quietly declining offers of assistance from the sales guy. With less than thirty minutes until the boys would be home from school, I chose a good studio easel and a sketch board, a sleek artist's lamp, and a handful of synthetic and natural fiber brushes. I grabbed an overpriced box of acrylic paints in a myriad of fantastically-named colors and headed for home.

After slicing apples and pouring cups of milk, I sat down at my computer to check my Facebook messages.

Jules Jordan McKinnon
October 26th 3:45 PM

Max Bennett says he's having a soiree at Manuel La Bore on Saturday, before Junkture plays at Workplay on Sunday. Jason has a soccer game and I can't make it, but he says you should come.

Huh. A party at Max Bennett's house, presumably with the band.

Tierney Cavanaugh Johnson
October 26th 4:15 PM

Tell Max I'll be there.

Chapter 2

"I feel like I'm drowning," I told Sam two nights later. "I need to get away for a couple of days."

I'd spent months heading up a massive PTA fundraising program. It had taken up most of my spare time during the summer and well into the fall. We'd raised nearly fifteen-thousand dollars in six months. It was finally coming to an end, and I was exhausted.

My back still hurt but was getting better. I could stand to walk at least three miles most days, and I'd lost a few pounds. The house was clean. The boys were taken care of.

My new slew of art supplies sat in the corner of the rec room downstairs, piled neatly in the corner in their bags.

Sam was confused, having seen no signs of anything but the lingering physical pain. I seemed to be active and productive and content. The children and the house and PTA were all orderly. He didn't really see anything amiss.

"I just need a couple of days," I said, "to decompress and catch my breath. I need to check out of my life for a little bit."

"What do you want to do?" he asked warily.

"Junkture's playing in Birmingham on Sunday. I could go on Saturday, spend the night and see Frankie. Jules might be coming down, she wasn't sure. I'd be home on Monday before the boys get home from school."

He thought about it for a moment. "Okay." He didn't seem convinced that I needed the time, but he had no reason to fight me on it. "I can't get the kids Monday afternoon, though, so you have to be back in time for the bus."

I didn't want to travel the three hours and try to get time to myself at either of my parents' houses. There'd be all this *chatting*. I needed time and space in my own head, to go and do whatever I wanted without talk of my grandmothers or cousins or ailments.

I made the drive, due west on I-20, listening to the Afghan Whigs the whole way. I checked myself into the Hyatt on Saturday afternoon, a couple of blocks from the Workplay Theatre near downtown. I would be within walking distance of the venue, in case I got as drunk as thought I might at the show. It was the first time I'd ever spent a weekend alone in a hotel.

I unpacked and called Frankie Luna. She was a friend from high school, now married with her own kids, who were the same ages as mine.

"I'm in Birmingham," I said. "It was last minute."

"Are you staying at your dad's? Tell him hi for me."

"Nope. I'm at the Hyatt."

"*Really?* Where's Sam?"

I glanced at the time on my computer screen. "He's probably cooking dinner for the boys right now."

Frankie slid into her sexy bombshell voice, cute and flirty. I'd heard her do it a million times and could picture see her stunning blue eyes sparkling mischievously. "*Oh! So you're here to get into trouble?*"

"I am," I laughed. "Are you in?"

"*Nah*, wish I could, though. Grad school is killing me. I have two papers due on Monday, and I've barely started them. Jay's taking the girls for a while, so I can work."

"That just means more Jack for me!"

"Yep, drink up, sista! I'll have one here while I'm working, in your honor."

I don't know why I didn't tell her about the invite to Max's house. Frankie was living in Montevallo. She was barely five miles from where I would be, if I decided to go. I wasn't sure I was going, though, and this felt like something I wanted to keep for myself.

Am I even going?

Max was great during our fifteen minutes of conversation at the Masquerade. Jules said he invited me to come join then. But this was hanging out with *Junkture*. These guys didn't know me, and there would probably be lots of people there. I would be by myself, probably hanging quietly along the side and trying my best to blend in. The worst thing that could happen would be that I didn't really know anyone and would decide to leave. I could always come back to the hotel and still have a funny story to tell when I got home.

Why the hell not?

I brushed my teeth and fixed my lipstick. I smoothed my long, blond hair, streaked with thick chunks of dark purple. I grabbed my purse and headed for Tootie's, a nearby liquor store. I bought two six packs of Yuengling and a bottle of Gentleman Jack. It would've been rude for me to show up empty-handed.

I picked up I-65 and headed south. Montevallo is a small town built around a liberal arts college, half an hour south of Birmingham. The university was originally a women's college built in the late 19th century but became co-ed in the 1950s. The Education and Fine Arts departments were some of the best in the state, and the small, secluded campus had felt comforting and not overwhelming when I'd visited during my senior year of high school. When they offered me a full scholarship, it was a done deal.

Twenty years before, the eleven mile drive from the interstate to campus had seemed barren. Small, country stores and mobile homes had dotted the wide fields between red brick churches and the occasional new construction subdivision. Mostly there were long stretches of pasture land, sweeping off into the dense, rural darkness that always seemed to separate Montevallo from the real world.

But the area had grown up since I'd last been there. The pastures had been filled with strategically-planned and almost-identical housing developments. There was a new middle school and a dollar store and more fast food restaurants than it seemed one small community could support.

Even rolling into the five-block downtown area didn't look quite the same. Gone was the gas station where I could get Boone's Farm for $1.99. The pizza place Jules and I had ordered from three nights a week was now a real estate agency. Subway had finally remodeled and gotten rid of so much of the *yellow* that had harshly reflected in our chemically-dilated pupils in the middle of so many nights.

There was the cute Victorian house on the corner near campus, still whimsical with its pseudo-turret overlooking town. On the corner near the park was the dilapidated house where Jules had lived with Dave. I'd known dozens of students who'd lived there, a constant rotation of whomever could make rent for more than a couple of months. I'd been drunk or high in that kitchen untold times but had only been back to visit Jules once after I moved to Huntsville to be with Sam. It was a block away from Orr Park, where Jules and Frankie and I had been tripping so hard one night, walking and smoking and laughing until dawn when I was convinced unicorns were grazing in the early gray fog.

That was the park where Damien and I had fought so violently, time and again. In the parking lot or in the gazebo. And the bench, halfway up the walking trail, that was just far enough into the shadows to make it hard to be seen, but close enough to the parking lot that he found it the best place to make me give him a blow job while I was naked, as penitence for some imaginary crime against our love.

I left all of that behind and drove past the small, cobblestoned campus. I was still angry and disappointed in myself for blowing my scholarship and dropping out when life with Damien had become so consuming, and I couldn't bring myself to turn through the huge, iron gates. I slowed on the deserted county road, looking for the small, wooden compass rose that Jules reminded me would mark the entrance to *Manuel La Bore*. It was hard to see in the dwindling light, and I slammed on the brakes to make a sharp left turn onto the unassuming gravel drive.

The house was as large as I remembered, a sprawling rancher with huge windows facing the large, circular drive. Most of the windows were alight, glowing amber against the sunset that swept off into the grassy distance beyond the house. The tour bus was parked dark and silent to the side of the driveway. There were only a couple of other cars.

7:15

Am I early?

Jules had told me seven o'clock. Maybe I was just one of the first ones here. I hated being too early as much as I hated to be late. I felt a little awkward, but I pulled up the parking brake and switched off the ignition. I grabbed the bag from Tootie's and slipped my phone and keys into my pocket as I locked my car, more from habit than fear of robbery.

I could hear music as I approached the front door. It didn't seem to be coming from the house itself, though. I rang the doorbell. When no one answered, I rang it again. Raucous laughter ricocheted from the back yard and across the pasture. I decided to follow the narrow flagstone path around the back of the house.

The deck that had collapsed so many years before had been replaced by a sprawling, multi-tiered thing that cascaded in wide steps down to a broad patio. A high, wooden pergola swooped overhead, covering the outdoor living area with a tangle of flowering vines, speckled with tiny white lights. Far beyond the house stood a barn. The doors were open to the night, and the music and laughter were pouring from inside.

Lighted flagstones led to another patio to the side of the outbuilding. A fire pit was roaring with fresh flame, and Alex Wheeler and Max Bennett were laughing to each other.

"Singer!" Alex stood and stepped around the fire, hugging me. "How are ya, doll?"

"I'm good, thanks," I said nervously. "I brought Jack and beer."

Alex laughed. "That's awesome! Sit, sit!"

Max hugged me and took the bags from my hands. "Glad you could make it. Thanks for getting me in touch with Jules. I haven't talk to her in ages."

"I'm sorry she couldn't make it. Her son had a soccer game. I hope it's okay that I came without her."

Max rolled his eyes. "I *told* her to tell you to come. So come. Sit." He motioned to a camp chair across the fire from Alex.

I smiled politely. "I won't stay."

"Please! Sit down. Do you want a drink?" Alex asked.

I shook my head. "I'm an incorrigible drunk. Besides, I have to drive back to my hotel in a bit."

I didn't go back for several hours. It turned out not to be a party so much as some people just hanging out on the band's off night. We sat around the fire, crew and band members coming and going, talking about everything and nothing. We talked about the record, the tour, the fans. Alex spent some time scouring the internet for album reviews, surprisingly offended that one reviewer accused him of trying to channel Prince, with his falsetto on "Hot Mess."

"At least he's not looking himself up on Groupie Dirt dot com," I said to Max.

Alex looked up from his MacBook, suddenly interested. "What's that?"

"It's this website where women talk about the rock stars they've fucked. They compare them—you know, size and performance."

He started to type quickly as Max snickered.

"He's going to obsess about this all night, isn't he?" I joked.

Max nodded sadly and stood to go into the barn. I could hear drums and acoustic guitar and assumed Charlie and Paul were inside.

"Yeah, I'm not on this fucking list," Alex said finally.

I giggled. "Maybe that's a good thing?"

He glanced up and nodded at me in agreement. "Maybe. My wife would fucking *hate* it."

"But it breaks your heart that hundreds of women haven't publicly testified to the virility of Alex-fucking-Wheeler?"

"*Shit*," he drawled dramatically, "not hundred*szs*. But you'd think at least *one* of them would say, 'Yeah, that singer from Junkture had a big dick and was a nice guy.' I mean, *really*, is that too much to ask?"

"Good girls don't lie, Wheeler." It was Paul Sommers, beer in hand. "Oh, hey, Tierney. I didn't know you were here."

I stood and hugged him. "Hey, Paulie! How are you?"

Paulie was sheepish and a little embarrassed about having unloaded on Sam and me at the Masquerade.

"I guess I had a lot that needed to come out," he said.

"It's all good," I assured him. "It stays between us. I'll never tell Alex the things you told me about him."

Paul laughed as Alex made a face at me.

"Do you want that drink yet?"

I shook my head. "I'd love some water, though."

Alex closed his MacBook and set it on the flagstone next to his chair. He stood and stretched, motioning for me to follow him inside.

"Have you ever been in the barn?" he asked.

"Nope."

"So, when we first started out, the house was a shambles. Max and Charlie and this guy Benny were living here and going to school, trying to fix the place up. We would practice in what used to be the garage, but there wasn't enough room. Max had this thing built, complete with full electrical and heating and air. The stage can be broken down and moved outside. We've done it a couple of times for parties. There's space for rehearsal and just fucking around. You can't really see it at night, but it's bright red with *See Rock City* emblazoned across the roof."

"Like those little birdhouses you see all around Chattanooga?"

Alex pointed at me, his eyes lighting up. "Exactly!"

Some girl, a friend of Max's, was sitting on the edge of the stage with Max. They were close and flirting. Paul was tuning his guitar and talking chord progressions next to Charlie, who was tapping out a rhythm on the rim of his drums. I was watching

Junkture in a completely down moment. I saw their lips moving but couldn't hear a word they were saying over the hum in my head.

Alex handed me a bottle of water. I took a big swig, hoping it would calm my nerves.

"Is this the first time you've done this?" he asked. "Hung out with the band like this?"

I nodded and smiled sheepishly.

Do I seem that nervous?

"So does it change your perception of us, of who and what we are, how we are?"

I thought about it for a moment. "I don't know. I mean... yeah, I don't know yet."

He raised one eyebrow at me questioningly.

"I need time to process it and think about it. I don't know what my expectations of you were, or how this may have changed them. I'll tell you when I figure it out."

"Fair enough," he smiled.

We walked back outside, and I sat in the chair I'd been in all night. Alex moved around the fire and sat in the chair closest to mine.

"You know, you freak me out a little." He shoved his hands into the pockets of his Junkture hoodie.

"*Why?*" I laughed, smiling brightly. I ran my fingers nervously through my hair.

"I used to know a Tierney. In high school. It's not a common name."

"Tierney Watkins?" I asked. Alex looked baffled that I knew her name, and I laughed at his confusion. "I don't know her, but I used to cross paths with her name in high school. You went to Vestavia, right? I went to RLC."

He cocked his head and looked at me thoughtfully. "Yeah. And one of my best friends from high school was a Cavanaugh. Chandra Cavanaugh. She went on and married another close friend of mine. I sang at their wedding."

"So I freak you out because I remind you of two women you knew?"

"Two women I loved. Different reasons, though."

"Are they women you've written about?"

"Songs?" I nodded. "Oh, yeah. I've written three songs about Tierney. In fact, 'Debris'—from the new record?—I didn't even realize it was about her until just recently."

"Really?"

"Yeah." He chuckled quietly, almost to himself, staring into the low flames as if they were fueled by his memories. "I heard from her the other day, too. That's when I realized it was about her."

He looked back to me and continued. "It was on Facebook. She sent me a message. '*How are you?*' I hadn't heard from her in years. She's married, four kids. She was always so *smart*, all four-point-oh through high school and college. She was always *determined*, you know?"

There was something in the tone of his voice, something weighty about *that* Tierney's determination. I half-expected him to tell me her life was a shambles now, or that she'd gone on to rule the world without him and that it made him a little sad. I couldn't tell exactly why his statement seemed so wistful.

Alex put his chin in his hand, propped on the arm of the chair, and looked at me thoughtfully from behind his thick-rimmed glasses.

"Facebook is weird like that." It was the only thing I could think to say.

"I hate Facebook. I hate social media, but it's a necessary evil right now. In some ways, we're like a new band right now, and if we don't engage the fans in this outlet, we're done before we ever start. I've been lucky, though. I haven't had to block anyone or unfriend anyone. But I would, if I thought they'd just gone too far. That's how I am; if someone makes me mad or bothers me too much, I'll just ignore them—won't answer their calls or texts or emails. I'll just *stop*."

"Are you that way with everything? Do you just ignore what you don't like?"

He thought about it for a moment. "Yeah. I compartmentalize everything. I have to, in some ways, being on the road all the time. It helps keep me sane. I'm really good at keeping everything in its own neat, little box, where I can deal with it or not, as I choose. I'm probably *too* good at it."

"I think that's a guy thing," I commented. He nodded in agreement. "I think it's much harder for women to take their feelings out of the equation. Men are much better at tucking their feelings out of the way.

"Obviously there's me," I continued, smiling, "but do you have fans who overstep?"

He told me stories of the craziness of some fans, how they assumed that they knew him well through their limited post-show and online interactions with him.

"This one chick—oh, I have to read this to you!—she messaged me a couple of nights ago after the show in Memphis. '*Hi, Alex! I just wanted to check on you and make sure you didn't do anything stupid with that thing you were flirting with after the show.*' I didn't answer her, I went to sleep as soon as I got on the bus, so she messaged me again a couple of hours later. '*Sigh. I'm guessing since I haven't heard from you that you did something I wouldn't be proud of. I'm very disappointed.*' I mean, *what the fuck?*"

"So is she just a fan? Do you know her well?"

He shrugged. "She's a fan. She has been for a long time. But she's not my *friend* or anything. I didn't fuck anyone—I don't do that!—but it's none of her goddamn business anyway. Look, I *flirt*, sure. I'm sitting here talking to you, and I'm just *Alex*. When I'm on stage, it's a different persona, it's the *rock star*. I'm engaging the audience, and that includes a lot of women. Sometimes when I come off stage, I forget to stop. I'm still caught up in the flirting and the attention. But part of me *needs* that, you know? The temptation is *always* there, but I steer clear of it."

"How does Talia deal with that?"

"She tries to ignore it. She tries not to pay attention to it, but she's always questioning what I do. She knows how I am. I remind her all the time, 'Baby, have you *seen* yourself?'"

I'd seen her stunning picture on his Facebook profile. Dark and petite with a brilliant smile. She was the opposite of everything I was. "She's beautiful. Your wife is fucking hot. I'd totally do her."

Where the fuck did that come from?

I hadn't meant to say it out loud. Didn't mean it wasn't true, just unexpected.

His head shot up, looking at me, piqued. He paused for a moment but continued. "I tell her, 'Baby, look at yourself. If I were gonna fuck someone else, they'd have to be hotter than you. And that's gonna be hard to find.'" I laughed. "I have to remind her all the time, though. She gets really bothered by pictures of me with these women, on Facebook and shit. Mostly she tries to ignore it."

He told me how hard it was to be away from his wife of five years and his young daughter, Amber. The loneliness of the road and missing his loved ones could be difficult, especially when he was constantly moving from one city to the next. Unless he was in a city he loved, like Chicago or New York or London, it was a weird *Groundhog Day* procession of same shit, different day.

"I don't know where the fuck we are most days. We're travelling in the dead of night; everything looks the same from town to town. I wake up, drink some coffee, take a shit, and check my email. I find out what time soundcheck is, and then I take a nap. I make sure the name of the town and the venue is on everyone's set list for the night, and I do my show. We hang after and talk to fans, pose for pictures, and sign some shit. I get on the bus and pass out— usually drunk—and get up and do it all over again.

"And I *hate* being back in Birmingham," he continued. "I *hate* the small town mentality. Everybody knows everybody and they know everything you're doing. It drives me insane. My mom moved to Portland to be closer to her sister after my dad died. I was on the road nine months out of the year, and then I met Talia. She was in Los Angeles, so I moved there to be with her. I could be anonymous there. I can stay hidden, if I want to. Max is the only one still here, you know? I don't know how he does it."

It was late. I was tired after driving from Atlanta. Alex was yawning, and the fire was dwindling.

"You'll be at Workplay tomorrow night, right?"

"Of course," I smiled. "Bells on and all that jazz."

He chuckled and stood. "Thanks for the beer and the Jack."

"My pleasure, Mr. Wheeler. Tell everyone goodnight for me?"

"Of course." He pulled me into a hug and kissed my cheek. "Goodnight, doll."

"Later, tater."

I drove back to Birmingham, blaring *Persona Non Grata* all the way. I wanted to call Jules or Frankie, or Tessa in Chicago, and tell them what had happened. It was late, though, and I wasn't ready to share it with anyone. It was silly and insignificant, but it was mine.

I slept as long as could, though it was no later than I would've slept if I'd been at home, getting up to fix breakfast for the family. I spent an hour sprawling in the big hotel bed, luxuriating in the aloneness. It had been so long since I'd slept in true solitude. It was disorienting and invigorating.

I drove around Southside and ended up at Birmingham Railroad Park. It was a relatively new addition to the downtown area, built after Sam and I moved our family to Atlanta. I was surrounded by ground-level views of the downtown skyline and old smokestacks and the railroad. Families with cavorting children mingled with couples walking their dogs. There were kites and brightly-colored dresses flashing against a cerulean autumn sky and perfectly-manicured grass that was just beginning to brown for the winter.

I took pictures of everything that caught my eye. Scrolling through the images on my camera's LCD display, I was pretty sure there would be something here that I wanted to paint when I got home.

I had a leisurely lunch and went back to the hotel to take a shower before the show.

I walked the few blocks to Workplay from the Hyatt. People lined the block, waiting for the doors to open, and I stepped into the end of the queue.   The Junkture tour bus was parked on the side of the building, a few feet from me.

Ahead of me, a trio of blond twenty-somethings in spaghetti-strapped tank tops and flip flops prattled amongst themselves. Every few seconds one of them would glance longingly at the tour bus, hoping to be noticed and invited inside. There was also a portly guy, a little older than expected, wearing a homemade Junkture t-shirt and trying his best to talk to the girls about the music and which songs they liked the best. The girls were politely ignoring him.

The bus door opened and Max stepped off.

"Hey, Tierney Cavanaugh!"

"Hey, yourself!"

Max hugged me. "Don't stand in this line. Come on."

He took me by the hand and led me in the back door.

I overheard one of the girls gasp, "How did she get in? Who is she? Is she someone's girlfriend or something?"

We found the guys, hugs and kisses all around, and then I told Max to go outside and get himself a girlfriend.

"Or three!" he cackled, walking toward the back door.

"Are you tee-totaling tonight, or are you drinking?" Alex asked.

"Oh! I'm drinking. I'll be incorrigible before the night is up, don't worry."

He led me to the empty bar. I could hear the opening act doing their soundcheck in the main theater.

"Screwdriver," I ordered. "Stoli."

"Never drink Belvedere," Alex toasted with his scotch. "So where's your husband? Sam, right?"

I sipped and nodded. "Mommy needed some *Me Time*. He's at home in Atlanta with the boys."

"How old are your boys?"

"Tripp is ten, and Ian is six. I love them, but they make me crazy. Amber is three?"

He nodded. "Just turned. She's a nut."

"That's a really fun age. They're like these little *people* all of a sudden. The boys were both so independent by then, and so different. They look so much alike but sometimes I'm shocked to find they're related. Tripp is just like Sam. Poor Ian is just like his mommy."

"What does your husband do?"

I braced myself for the explanation. Usually, people will either ask a lot of questions, or they're stunned into silence. "He's in information security. He's a hacker hunter, basically. He works private sector and helps some really huge companies protect themselves from cyber attacks. Sometimes he's conscripted by the government to investigate breaches." I shrugged. "He got to name a couple of viruses. He's been on all the major and minor news outlets. He's kind of a rock star in his field."

Charlie motioned for Alex to come backstage. "Sorry to interrupt—hi, Tierney—but we need you. Now."

"I'm sorry, I have to go deal with this," he apologized, finishing his drink.

"Don't fret it, babycakes. I'll see you out there."

I ordered another screwdriver and took it to a small table inside the theater. Right at seven o'clock, the crowd started to file into the room. I motioned for the waitress to bring me screwdrivers number five and six as I went to take my place at the center of the stage, right in front of where Alex would be.

The opening act was some local guy, added on at the last minute. Max was the only one who knew him. He had a nice, smooth tenor and was adept at the acoustic guitar, but he played a lot of covers and it wasn't what I loved.

The crowd thinned for the bathroom and the bar. I caught the waitress's eye and ordered another double.

By the time the techs were done readying the stage, I was hammered, front and center. Fans were pressing around me, edging me tightly against the edge of the stage. With no Sam to keep people off of me, I slipped into my Purple-on-Blonde-Amazon persona, silently daring anyone to fuck with me and my drunken snarl.

The show was fantastic, as expected. It was the same setlist from the Masquerade. Junkture was just as good as they'd been in Atlanta.

On stage in the bright, colored lights, Alex grinned and winked at me. I sang along to everything, more vodka fueling my love of this band and this music. In my mind, I sounded amazing—sexy and confident in my voice. And in the encore, he was back with his mic, one more time for the chorus of "Hot Mess." I was so drunk, and it was hard to keep up.

I remembered I was supposed to tell Alex if my perceptions of the band had changed. I saw him briefly, across the lobby, as he was talking to some friends. I was busy talking to Max about what made my hair smell so good and that I had great tits. I spoke briefly with Paul and Charlie, killing time and hoping to be able to tell Alex goodbye before they left for their next town. Somehow I lost him in the shuffle and stumbled back to my hotel.

Back home the next day. Back to the same grind. Back to the house and the kids and the whatever. I didn't want to go back to all of that. I wanted something bigger, better, faster, more! I didn't know what it was, but I knew that I needed it. Badly.

"Why don't you come to Chicago?" Tessa suggested during our daily phone call.

It had been a while since I'd been north to visit the Karena family. I needed to see my BFF. We'd been together longer than Sam and I had, and I was jonesing for some girl time. The kids had a few half-days at school coming up, which made it easy for them to miss the time. Sam couldn't get away from work. The boys and I could fly into Midway on Ian's sixth birthday and spend a few days with the Besties.

And it turned out that Junkture would be there at the same time.

Chapter 3

By the second week in November, there was a certain *watershed moment* feeling about my life. All of these things that were seemingly disconnected were converging suddenly. The confluence of urgency and anticipation surrounded everything—my home, my family, my marriage, my self.

I'm a firm believer in Fate. Some things are fated in the sense that there's only one viable choice, based on all of the previous choices you've made. There's nowhere else to go but *here*, because you've come from *there*, and that makes it feel important. But I also believe in Fate as an outside, blinding force. Maybe it's because of other people's choices, maybe it's sheer dumb luck, but it feels like divine intervention, twisting and turning you wildly or slightly. Either way, you can't help but look at what it wants you to see.

There was definitely a feeling of *Fate* in everything that was happening to me.

From: Tierney Cavanaugh Johnson
Sent: November 8th 12:21 PM
To: Alex Wheeler
Subject: Chicago

So it turns out I'm coming to Chicago. Wanna meet up for a drink before the show? If you get this and ignore it, or if you aren't into it, it's no big deal. I saw no harm in trying. Either way, I'm at the Double Door with my bestie that night. And I promise not to get so drunk this time that I try to take Max home in my pocket.

Tierney

From: Alex Wheeler
Sent: November 8th 5:24 PM
To: Tierney Cavanaugh Wheeler
Subject: RE: Chicago

Of course! Come to soundcheck at 5.

A
213-555-1212

The boys and I flew to Chicago on Thursday and spent the first day with the Karenas, which included the world's best cupcakes from Sweet Mandy B's for Ian's birthday. It was the first time I'd eaten sugar in six weeks. I'd known for years that stress eating was a problem for me. The night I ate a low-calorie ice cream cone and it triggered a thousand-calorie binge, I realized there might be more to it. When the same thing happened the next night, I knew I had to just *stop*. I was slowly learning to turn that energy into a workout, most of the time. Thankfully, my body handled one small cupcake, and no binge ensued.

We tucked my boys and Tessa's son and daughter into bed, and then piled up on her couch. The windows were open, and the cooling evening breeze wafted through her old apartment, with its high ceilings and thick, plaster walls. From the fourth floor, the city sounds of traffic and sirens and urban motion seemed so far away.

Tessa's husband, Ed, was working in the bedroom.

"How *are* you?" she asked.

Tessa had been with me since my first days of high school. I'd met her even before I'd met Sam. I was just turning fourteen; she was still thirteen. We were both Virgos, on opposite ends of the zodiac month. We shared the same picky, analytical tendencies. We were both obstinate in our desire to be right. But where I was more overtly emotional and could get my feelings hurt by the slightest things, Tessa always seemed cooler, more detached from the things that were likely to get a rise out of me. To an outsider, she could seem like a total misanthrope. In reality, she was a disillusioned idealist with little patience for ignorance or inefficiency.

I shrugged. "I'm okay."

"How much weight have you lost?"

"Fifteen pounds?"

"I can *see* it, Tierney. You look good." She reached for my hair, much longer than when I'd last seen her in the summer. "And *this* is good. The purple is beautiful."

I smiled at her. Tessa still looked... like Tessa. The same porcelain skin, freckled perfectly. The same dark brows and brilliant teal eyes that sparkled with sometimes perverse mirth. The same breathy, haughty laugh I'd heard so many nights, giggling in the dark in one of our bedrooms.

"So tell me," she shifted, "how the hell did you end up planning to meet Alex Wheeler tomorrow night?" She knew the story but wanted more.

I laughed and blushed. "Hell if I know, Tess. It's *crazy*. I blame Jules."

"Damn Jules. She knows everyone, doesn't she?"

"It's true! Her ex-boyfriend Dave knew Max at Montevallo. I started talking to Max at the Masquerade, mentioned Jules, and *blahblahblah*, I'm going to soundcheck."

"It's crazy, Tierney. I know I keep saying that, but it's *crazy*. Not in a bad way, mind you, just totally unbelievable."

I nodded in agreement. "You're telling me! It seems weird, though, that I've been a fan for this long, have seen them live *soooo* many times, *and* they're from Montevallo. But somehow I've never really met them."

"Even at the party at Max's house? When you were in college?"

"Nope. College Night is huge—it's Montevallo's homecoming. The school is basically split into two teams, the Purple and the Gold. I was a purple. The Purple party was at *Manuel La Bore*. But half the fucking school was probably there that night. I don't think I ever even made it inside the house."

I stood and stretched, turning and twisting, hoping a good *pop!* would alleviate some of the strain on my back.

"Is it any better?" Tessa asked. "How was the flight?"

"It's better. The walking is helping, but sitting for so long is no fun. It *is* getting better, though. Slowly."

Ed came walking down the hall, his bare feet quietly shuffling along the hardwoods. Ed and Sam had been friends since junior high, and Ed had gone on to high school with the rest of us. It seemed strange with only three of us together, and I started to miss Sam.

"I hate that Sam couldn't come," Ed said.

"I know, you feel excluded from the girl talk," I replied. "Suck it up, cupcake."

Tessa stuck her tongue out at him.

He just stood there, shaking his head in incomprehension of our girliness, like he'd been doing for two-thirds of his life.

"I'm going to bed," he said flatly, turning back toward the bedroom.

"Goodnight, Ed! We love you!"

Tessa curled her socked feet underneath her and tucked her hands between her knees. "How are things with you and Sam?"

I exhaled dramatically, sinking back to the couch. "I don't know, Tessa. It's hard. He's working a lot. We never see him. When he's home, he's working. He finishes work and starts drinking."

"How much is he drinking?"

I was almost embarrassed to answer. "At least a six pack a night. Sometimes more."

"*Jesus!* How does he function like that?"

I shook my head slowly. "I don't know. I couldn't do it. He sleeps in a little late and goes to the office by ten. His whole group comes in late, so that's no big deal. But he's up every single night until at least one in the morning." I shrugged. "I spend a lot of time watching television."

"You should be doing something, Tierney. Could you take a class or something?"

"I don't know. I don't really want to. I mean, I know my dad is always telling me I need to finish my degree, but I don't fucking want to do it. I don't even know what I'd wanna do."

"*I* still think you'd make a great attorney," she said matter-of-factly. "But that's because *I* am a great attorney. I know of which I speak."

She'd told me this for years. Before Tripp was born, I'd worked for a boutique financial planning firm and loved my time reviewing complicated legal documents. The more complex they were, the more I enjoyed the challenge of breaking them apart.

"You might be right."

"Of course I'm right. I'm a smart person. Don't you think I'd know if I were wrong?"

I winked at her. "Everything from your mouth is a straight-up fact. It's like the Unbreakable Law of Tessa's Quantativity or something."

―――――――

On Friday, the boys and I went to Willis Tower, to get the expansive view of Chicago from the Skydeck on the 103rd floor. We spent hours walking around the city, exploring small parks and playgrounds, watching the buses and the cranes and the people. I was doing my best to enjoy the day with my children, preoccupied with the evening's plans.

I was excited. I'd brought three different possible outfits and spent an unreasonable amount of time worrying about what to wear. Tessa finally made me settle on jeans and a black lace t-shirt, with thigh-high black suede boots. I walked from the Karenas' apartment to a nearby liquor store and bought a bottle each of Gentleman Jack and Oban 14 for Alex.

We left our four children with the babysitter, and Tessa and I hailed a cab.

Friday evening in the Wicker Park section of Chicago blossomed with a thriving nightlife. There were people going in every direction on the busy streets: couples headed to dinner, friends meeting up for drinks, transients asking for spare change. There was a constant honking of cars and rattling of the L. It was restless and a little bit hectic, and I liked the feeling of being caught up in that momentum.

"I'll see you in a while," she said, hugging me on the sidewalk.

"Have a good dinner with Ed. Is he gonna join us for the show?"

She shook her head and smiled smugly. "It's girlies only. He's going to meet Justin for a drink."

I walked half a block down to the Double Door. The Junkture bus was parked on the Milwaukee Avenue side of the building. The backdoor was propped open, and I could hear the sounds of guitars being tuned.

Their tour manager, Evan, stepped off the bus.

"Alex told me to come by for soundcheck," I explained tentatively.

"They're still at it, but go on in."

Looking inside, I could see that the bar was empty except for the band on the stage and a couple of employees sitting around the bar. I quietly crossed through the club's shadows to the edge of the bar, watching the guys on the small stage.

Alex was slowly working through a vocally toned-down version of one of their songs, though I can't remember which one it was.

"Hey, darlin'."

I smiled at them but said nothing, not wanting to interrupt. Max nodded in my direction when he saw me. He was complaining that his bass didn't sound right.

"Is this floor hollow?" he asked, stomping against the worn wooden planks.

Anton made adjustments at the soundboard near the front of the house. Corey and Ben, the other techs for the tour, moved around the stage, running cables and whatever else needed to be done.

As a fan, it seemed like soundcheck would be really great, getting a semi-private moment with a band you love, to see them do a song or two when no one else does. The truth is, soundcheck is mostly kind of boring. The songs don't generally sound quite like they do when they're performed live. Sound levels are being adjusted, the singer often doesn't use his full voice in order to save it for later. The songs may only be played halfway or at half tempo. There's a lot of silly, inside banter. There's a lot of talking and stopping and starting.

I loved it, though, because I loved watching how the guys interacted. It's part of my deep desire to *understand* the experience. I totally get off on seeing how things work, on understanding the intricacies, and this was prime psychic tinkering time for Tierney. It was a chance to gain a whole new understanding of these guys that I didn't have when I walked in the backdoor. And it was obvious that they loved what they were doing.

When they finished, Alex jumped down the three feet from the front of the stage.

"You wanna go downstairs?"

"Sure."

I followed him through the dim club, down the old, black-and-white tile steps to the underbelly of the Double Door. Small rooms lined the low-ceilinged, twisting labyrinth of narrow hallways. There were no doors, only old curtains hanging in the doorways. Some guy, presumably from the opening act, was checking his phone in a room to my left. On the right was a small, empty room. Just past it was another door with its curtains pulled mostly closed. Alex peeked in past the edge of the faded, stained fabric, finding the anteroom empty, and held the curtain-as-a-door open for me.

Alex settled into a worn armchair at the back corner of the room, dimly lit by a side table lamp. I carefully placed myself on an old sofa adjacent to his seat. I didn't want to look or feel like a fat girl flopping on a couch.

"I brought these for you," I started. "You can share these, or not, as you see fit." I handed him the bag with the two bottles of liquor.

"Oh, wow, thanks!" He held the bottle of Scotch up, checking the label. "Oh, I *have* to have some of this now. You want some? You want a drink?" He opened the bottle and pulled a small, plastic cup from a nearby stack.

"Sure. Normally I'm a vodka girl, but that can wait."

He poured some of the Scotch into two cups and passed one to me. "God, that's what I needed! Thank you!"

"You're welcome!" I laughed, sipping the sweet warmth.

"Are you by yourself?" he asked suddenly.

"Tessa will be here later. She went to meet her husband for sushi."

"Sam didn't come with you?"

"Nope," I said, pursing my lips into a thoughtful scowl. "Work. How are you?"

"Good! Tired. Fucking tour's barely halfway over, and I'm exhausted."

"How was your show last night? Milwaukee?"

He nodded. "Good. Same as every night, you know."

"You don't sound so thrilled."

He crossed his legs and sipped his Scotch. "It's just *tiring* sometimes. I mean, I fucking love what I do. I *love* singing and making music with my best friends, with my brothers. I'm so fucking insecure, and I *need* to feel that *pull* from the fans, letting me know what I'm doing is good. I feed off of that."

"What the hell do you have to be insecure about? You're this incredibly handsome, sexy man." He chuckled and blushed, hiding behind the rim of his cup. "Come on—you know it's true! Everyone in that audience wants to either *be* you or *fuck* you. Some of them want to do both. You're smart and funny, and you have a beautiful family. And you get to do what you love."

"Yeah—and *thank you*—but sometimes it's not enough. There are things...." He paused, mulling. "People don't become rock singers because they're secure in who they are. All of us, all performers, *need* that reassurance for whatever reason. I *need* that energy, you know?

"What is it about that energy that's appealing to you?" I asked.

Alex thought for a moment, his full lips pursed under his dark brow. "As a songwriter, it's amazing to catch a fan singing along to something I've written. There's this give-and-take, of having created this artistic piece that this other person has taken the time to learn and love. I'm singing it to the audience as whole but also to *that* person, who's feeding it back to me with their own voice. It bolsters me as a performer, you know?"

"The reciprocity of that energy...."

Alex nodded at me. "Exactly. I don't get that any other way. I mean, Talia likes to hear the stuff I'm writing, but she's not really a music person, you know? She didn't know who the fuck I was when I met her. She was like, 'Junk*what*?'"

I giggled at the thought. At the height of their career, Junkture had been on seemingly every rock and pop radio station in America simultaneously. They'd toured all over the world and sold millions of records. But that had been ten years ago, and the fanscape had changed dramatically.

Alex's phone vibrated next to him on the arm of the chair.

"Excuse me, just a sec." He scrolled through his messages, typing something quickly. He shook his head, exasperated. "Talia's having internet problems, and she's mad I can't help her. I'm not fucking there! How the fuck am I supposed to know what's wrong?"

"Is she at home?"

He shook his head, sending another text. "She's traveling. She's a designer. She does interior accessories, and she's off looking for materials and fabrics and shit." His fingers flew across his phone keypad again. "*Fuck! I don't know!*"

He locked his phone and dropped it into his shirt pocket.

"Alex!"

I heard a man's voice coming from the hallway and glanced toward the curtain. Paul stuck his head into the room, looking around.

"Oh! Sorry! I didn't know—oh! Hey, Tierney!"

"Hi, Paulie."

He pointed at me. "You're here tonight? Okay. Cool!" He pointed to Alex. "Dinner in five? Investors."

Alex nodded as Paulie backed from the room. "Got it. I'm sorry. We have this unexpected dinner thing with some potential investors in the label. Are you hanging around after the show?"

I nodded and smiled. "Of course! Tessa and I will be up front, like always."

We stood and stepped toward each other, stopping just inches apart.

"It'll be good to see a friendly face."

I smiled sweetly, knowing my dimples were exaggerated like that. "Always, Mr. Wheeler."

He hugged me and turned me toward the doorway, his hand on my back.

I needed to find dinner myself before I met up with Tessa again. I settled on tapas and sangria nearby, plus a little CD shopping at Reckless Records. I stumbled on a hard-to-find Liz Phair EP that I'd lost years before.

Where better to find Liz Phair than in Chicago?

I found Tessa again a while later, outside the front door of the club. As soon as we were inside, I ordered my first screwdriver of the evening. I quickly realized that the Double Door had the worst screwdrivers ever. *Ever.* It was cheap house vodka with orange juice from a can. It tasted like paint-thinner-soaked aluminum. I decided it was best to drink two at a time, to get past the taste quickly, and I started double-fisting my screwdrivers.

When it looked like the opening act was about to start, Tessa and I moved quickly toward the very front and managed to get just to the side of center. The band was good, some female singer with flaming red hair, hanging onto her guitarist a lot. I was eight shots in and feeling no pain.

Tessa pushed her petite body to the bar and back, with more vodka, while the techs shifted the stage for Junkture. I glanced behind me and saw that the crowd had swelled since we'd planted ourselves at the stage, standing against the huge speakers.

The lights went down, the crowd roared, and Junkture took the stage.

The guys were in a great vibe together, and it really showed in their set. People were digging it. It was so loud that I could feel my hair bounce in front of the speakers every time Charlie hit the bass drum.

I flirted and toyed with Max, who came right in front of us to play, his bass and crotch at our eye level. When he leaned down and gave Tessa a souvenir pick that he didn't even use, she looked at me like, *What the fuck do I do with this?*

Standing against the huge speakers, I could feel the beat of the music spreading through me. The copious amounts of vodka had blushed my cheeks. My body throbbed with the rhythm of the drums and the bass pulsing through the amps, melted away with the whine of the guitar, and dripped at the sound of Alex's voice. The music rushed through me, and I grabbed the handle in the top of the huge speaker in front of me and rocked back and forth on my heels, singing and matching every word note for note.

And then there was that opening riff of "Dollface", the scratching rhythm that seemed to mimic my heartbeat. I swooned with joy. I looked over to Tessa and squealed with drunken delight.

"This is for Tierney!" Alex was at the middle of the stage, back by the amps, taking a sip of his drink. Paul and Max stepped up to stage center, playing together, all hats and beards in unison. I looked at Tessa, momentarily flabbergasted, and handed her my camera.

Alex stepped up to the front center and started to sing my favorite song:

> *Pretty little sparkles in the shining lights*
> *Fake and shimmering*
> *Cheap and simmering*
> *Who did you think you could impress*
> *In that tight dress*
> *Showing the world all you have to give?*

He was directly in front of me, sunglasses on, bouncing his mic and cord in time to Charlie and Max's rhythm. The stage lights were flashing and pulsing in time to my heart. The music streamed on, and he retreated to the amps again. Months later, he told me he was sometimes surprised to see how often he does that when he's on stage; it's a way to reset his own energy, to get him back in time to the musical moment. He's also restless, and it helps him burn off his own fidgety nervousness.

Pretty little dancer in the shining lights
Whine and grind
Mute and blind
You don't see them stabbing you
Right in the back
With their sharp, dagger smiles

Alex took off his sunglasses and pointed to me. I blushed and grinned sideways. I motioned him back toward me with the come-hither crook of my finger. He moved in front of me, on his knees, eye to eye with me and still singing. I noticed for the first time that his pale blue eyes were rimmed with flecks of green and gold. Eyes locked on mine, he was in my face, *again*, in my breath, with his voice and his song. *My song.*

Only the mic separated his mouth from mine, so close I could taste his sweet, smoky breath. My voice drunkenly joined his.

Put on your dollface
And your party dress
Cover up the hurt
And pretty up the mess
Hide your scars
Like tattoos of your past
Tell them all your secrets
Even when they don't ask

I knew the song, backwards and forwards, and I popped my voice up to the harmony. Alex grinned broadly, laughing when he realized what I was singing. He fucked with the cadence of the melody, ever so slightly, daring me to notice the difference. I watched the minute movements of his mouth, a breath away from my own, and did my best to keep up with him.

It took everything I had not to put my drunken tongue in his mouth.

He smiled, devilish, and kissed me on the cheek, backing toward his spot. The crowd cheered, and the whole house shook in time to the music.

It's always interesting to be in the crowd at a show like that, whether the performer is Alex or anyone else. When the singer picks someone out of the crowd to entertain personally, it's always crazy to watch. Sometimes you feel like you're intruding on their moment, like an uncomfortable voyeur. The singing fan actually has very little realization that the rest of the house is even still there, that there's anything but them and the singer and the *song*, which is almost guaranteed to become their new favorite.

To *be* that person is *magnificent*. There's an incredible flow of energy that happens between the two of you. No matter how many times you've heard him sing the song, no matter how many times you've sung along in your car or your shower, the singer's *creating* that version of that music in that moment with his voice, and you're taking it in and letting it wash over and through you and feeding it right back to him with your own voice. There are a million thoughts in your head at once, and you're trying hard to remember the lyrics and to remember to breathe. It's intensely intimate and fun and scary as hell, because you don't want to fuck it up in front of this person whose music obviously means something to you.

It's this amazing little moment where you've connected with a virtual stranger. You both *get it*, and—the crazy thing about it— everyone who sees you *gets it*.

So when he chooses to sing *with* a fan during a show, Alex will sometimes sing the harmony, letting the fan stay comfortably in the melody. Again, in my drunken bravado, I thought it would be good to go for the harmony on the chorus. I knew it well and could nail it every time. At least, I could do it sober in my car or in the shower. I sing by ear and knew the *intervals* of the harmony from the melody. I was excited and wasted and struggled to maintain those intervals from where Alex was singing, not hearing that *he* was on the harmony. It was also very, very loud. I couldn't hear details over the guitars and the deep, rumbling bass. I knew my ecstatic voice was off, at least a little. It would be several days before I realized exactly *how bad* it really was.

I sounded like a tone deaf goat.

"Oh, it's horrible!" Alex laughed months later.

I can laugh about it now, could laugh about it when I first saw the video of it on YouTube, shot by another fan who was standing next to me. It *is* really funny, and I'm that kind of self-deprecating girl. But it's also a little heart-wrenching, that I had this moment to shine and barely glittered.

The show went on, high energy and screaming guitars. Toward the end of the evening, during "Mantissa", which was supposed to be the next-to-last song—Paul was doing his thing, slamming the strings of his guitar and making those musician faces. He was totally engrossed in the hard, rocking song and the show, and he stepped to the very edge of the low stage. Some drunken female fan reached up for him, rubbing his calf. Paul looked down at her, his smile polite but a little sly.

She lurched up at him suddenly and *bit* him on the leg.

Max and Charlie were still pounding it out, and Alex was lost is his own vocals, his musical bitching about the screwing of the hardworking American man.

"*What the fuck?*" Paul's yell was barely drowned out by his band. He missed a couple of notes, backing away from her as quickly as possible.

Paulie was at the other side of the stage from where Tessa and I were standing, so it took a minute to realize there was a problem. He tried to shake the pain from his left leg but stumbled and fell backwards onto the hard, wooden platform. He stopped playing and laid his guitar next to him.

The crowd cheered quietly, watching to see what was happening. Ben, Paul's long-time guitar tech, crouched nervously at the edge of the stage, holding Paul's guitar and waiting to see if his friend was okay. Alex paced near the amps again, unsure if Paul was taking a moment to catch his breath or if his band mate was really hurt. The band kept playing, trepidatious.

"My brother, are you alright? Do you need an... do we need to call someone?" Alex asked into his mic. No response from Paul. "Did you break your leg?"

Alex bent down and conversed with him briefly.

"You want the guitar back? Alright."

Ben jumped up and took the guitar back to Paul, still lying on the stage.

"Play through it, my friend!"

Paul Sommers lay on the stage of the Double Door, in obvious pain, and finished a fucking *awesome* performance of "Mantissa." Max joined him, on his knees, dueling guitars under the flashing lights.

As soon as the song was finished, Evan and Ben helped Paul to his feet and off the stage.

"*Goddamn, dude!* That's my boy! I think that might be the end of the show," Alex laughed to the audience.

It was a *show* without question. It was one of those insane rock-and-roll nights that you can never forget as a fan. It was possibly the best ten bucks I'd ever spent.

I walked toward the bar for one last drink, just as Alex was walking out from backstage. I smiled my big, dimpled grin at him.

"Is Paulie okay?"

He shook his dark, closely-cropped hair in amused disbelief. "I don't know. She broke the fucking skin through his jeans! Evan is taking him to get it checked out. Hey, will you do me a favor?"

"Sure."

He grabbed my arm and leaned in toward me, for me to hear him over the noise. "I gotta go to the merch table. Will you *please* get me a drink? Jack and Coke?" He reached toward his pocket for some money.

I shooed his efforts away. "I got it. I'll bring it to you."

"Thanks, Tierney! You're the best!" He turned quickly toward Charlie, who was ushering him toward their awaiting fans.

"The singer wants a Jack and Coke!" I told the bartender. "And I'll get one more screwdriver."

"A double?" she asked, reaching for a cup. I thought for a moment and nodded. "And is the Jack for the lead singer? It's on the house. That show was fucking incredible!"

Her screwdrivers may have been terrible, but she was an absolute delight.

Tessa and I stayed for a while, talking to Max.

"What was with that *fan*?" he crowed.

"Maybe she was trying to give him the Dark Gift," Tessa deadpanned.

"Great! Now just his left leg will be undead," I replied.

"Yep! Four hundred years from now, Paulie will be long gone but his leg will still be dragging his guitar around behind itself."

"Maybe it'll sparkle in the sunlight."

It was late, and our children had been asleep for hours. They would be up early, ready to see more of Chicago. I hugged everyone goodbye, promising Max a drink the next time I saw him.

Alex stopped his conversation with two pouty-mouthed, silicone-enhanced blondes when I stepped close to him. "Thank you, for everything," I said. "Let me know how Paulie is."

"You heading out?" He looked a little surprised.

"Yeah, Hungover Mom Duty will come very early, I'm sure."

"Thanks for singing with me again. Call me on my cell this week and let me know how you are." He kissed me quickly on the cheek, and Tessa and I caught a cab back to her apartment near Lincoln Park.

Chapter 4

I don't know if I actually slept that night after the show at the Double Door. It was hard to wind down from the excitement of the evening. My body rested on the air mattress in Tessa and Ed's living room, but my brain never quite shut down, constantly cycling through the details of the evening from the moment I hugged Tessa goodbye on the street.

The next morning, we were up early as anticipated, the combined giggles and talking of the four children letting no adult sleep past seven. Tessa and I bummed around Lincoln Park with the kids, sampling and snacking our way through the Green City Market outside the Peggy Notebaert Nature Museum, me singing "Debris" the entire time. I probably annoyed the hell out of every passer-by, but I really didn't care.

We sat on a bench, sharing scones from a paper bag, while our children climbed gnarled trees and rolled down grassy knolls that overlooked the small piers and inlets of the Chicago-side of Lake Michigan, at the North Pond.

"Are you ever going to sleep again?" Tessa teased.

"Probably not," I giggled. "I think I'll just be singing for the rest of my days. Should I be so excited? Was it really that big a deal?"

Tessa looked at me, incredulous. "It was a *huge* deal, Tierney. You have loved this band your entire life. In the span of a month, you've seen them three times. *That*'s no big deal, but you've also *sung* with them three times. You've been to the bassist's *freaking house* and hung out with the lead singer before the show for drinks. You have his cell phone number, and he told you to *call* him."

She paused and let it sink in for a moment, the same look of *It-Just-Is* that I'd seen so often since we were kids.

"Tierney, that's *fucking huge*."

I looked at her ardent face, staring back at me as if I should just *know* the truth of what she was saying.

"Are we *friends* now?" I questioned. "I could sell his cell phone number to a thousand women before he could change it."

Tessa laughed over the wind-carried whoops and squeals of our children. "Well *that* would definitely make you *not* friends with the rock star."

I repacked the boys' dirty clothes and small souvenirs, lugging our heavy suitcase toward a cab. I carefully maneuvered the children through the security lines and crowds of Chicago Midway, helping them fasten and adjust the seatbelts against their young bodies. They settled into handheld video games and airline snacks while I let my mind wrap itself around all of it a dozen more times.

Home again, this time with pictures and a story like none other. The horrible video of Alex and me singing "Dollface" showed up on YouTube, but it was a funny counterbalance to the pictures Tessa had snapped, just to my right. They were extreme close-ups of Alex and me, intimately sharing his microphone, just a breath apart, singing and laughing into each other's eyes. Some other fan on Facebook commented on one in particular, asking if we'd just kissed. We hadn't, but it certainly looked like something was going on. Sam politely suggested that Alex was "close enough".

I had so much extraneous energy. I was up to five miles a day, always listening to *Persona Non Grata*. Even such an intense experience of drinking with Alex and singing with him didn't get it out of my system.

But I still needed to *do* something. I waited until the children were at school, Sam gone to work, and I opened the stairwell door to the rec room. The previous owners of our house had updated most of the upstairs, but the basement was still finished with its 1970s goldenrod carpet, worn and faintly stained with years of another family's memories. Rough-hewn cedar planks paneled the walls, dark and strangely warm under the harsh fluorescent lights.

One corner of the room was floored with old, golden-flecked vinyl. The *fleur-de-lis* pattern was warped, stretched decades before over the concrete foundation. Maybe there had originally been plans to add on a bathroom or a wet bar.

I dragged an old bookshelf, taller than I and mostly bare, to the edge of the vinyl, leaning against the cedar paneling. I shoved boxes out of my way, heavy and half-filled with things Sam and I had never unpacked after we moved. I used my hand and wiped the shelves, my palm getting soft and gritty from the dust.

I grabbed the crinkly plastic bags from the art supply store and opened them.

Carefully I laid out the brushes—fan and filbert, round and utility—in different head sizes, some sleek and satin, some silky sable. I lined up the uniform tubes of colors—burnt sienna and raw umber and yellow ochre, cadmiums and carbons and pthalos. A thin, colored strip showed the shade contained within each white tube. I knew them all by heart and could see the exact color of each and how they would blend together in different amounts. How equal parts phthalo blue and pthalo green would make a turquoise. How adding nine parts Hansa Yellow Medium to one part pthalo green would create a bright green that might be too opaque, that might need a bit of transparent gel.

All of this I knew instinctively.

I'd been away from my tools for far too long.

I wasn't sure yet what I was painting. I tore a sheet of canvas paper from the fresh pad and clamped it to the sketch board, propped it all on the new easel. I couldn't see what would be on that page yet, but I could feel the blank, white expanse calling to me, churning with its own creative energy.

I ran upstairs into the kitchen to look for something, anything, to paint. *Wine bottle. Candle. Bowl of fruit.* I grabbed the fruit bowl, thankful that I'd been to the grocery store, and a pair of tarnished brass candlesticks. They'd been a wedding gift from a distant cousin so long ago, and the ivory tapers had never been lit, the wick folded and pressed into the aging wax.

Standing again in front of the easel, I pried open a pack of pencils and flipped to the first page of the unused sketch pad. I moved quickly, a gesture drawing, excited and unexpectedly sure of where my hand was going. It was a bowl of fruit. Nothing especially difficult. But I was surprised to see how easily I could still mold the image from my fingers with so little overt thought.

I looked at my sketch, at the bowl sitting on a small, wooden table that had twice been the resting place for board books and pacifiers in the nursery when the boys were babies. I mixed fresh globs of acrylic on the painter's palette.

Carefully, tentatively, I felt the pristine brush as an extension of my hand, letting it rest light and sturdy between my fingers. *Control the brush.* When I felt myself grasping the handle too tightly, I would relax the intrinsic muscles in my hand until I saw my fingers flex, just slightly, and the tension was relieved.

The first strokes were slow and precise. I wasn't sure if I still trusted my ability to relay what I saw from living space to the flat surface on the easel. It had been fifteen years since I'd done this. Sometimes, when Sam and I were living in Huntsville, I would lay out a plastic sheet in the spare bedroom of our apartment and paint for a few days. The pieces would sit, ever unfinished, for weeks until Sam complained and I packed it all away again, back into the closet. Once we moved back to Birmingham and started trying to get pregnant, the painting became just a distant memory.

"Tierney? Are you home?"

I jumped at the sound of Sam's voice, calling to me from the top of the stairs. I glanced at the clock on the far wall. 3:08 The boys would be home any minute.

"Yeah, yeah! I'll be there in a second."

I stepped back and looked at the painting. It wasn't perfect, but it was good. I was pleased with the shape and form, the shadows. I'd been impatient about waiting for layers to dry before I started adding other colors, and there were places where the hues mixed in inexact ways.

It's okay. It's good enough.

I lidded the palette to keep the paints moist and took the brushes upstairs for cleaning.

Sam came into the kitchen as I stood in front of the sink, swirling the brushes carefully across my soapy palm under a trickle of running water. Over and over, mindless, watching the tinted rinse drain away.

"How was work, baby?" I asked over my stiff shoulder. I craned my neck in circles, stretching the tight muscles.

"Good. How are you?" He leaned down the five inches between us and kissed me quickly.

"Painting," I beamed.

He looked surprised. "When did you start this?"

"Today! I bought some stuff before I went to Chicago, but I didn't open it until today." I glanced toward the kitchen table. "Remind me to bring the fruit bowl back upstairs."

I heard the sudden thundering stomp of little boy feet racing down the driveway. Muted calls of, "Tripp! You don't have to win every race!" echoed off the front of the house and across the cul-de-sac.

"Boys are home," I said wryly.

Tripp and Ian bounded through the front door, carelessly tossing backpacks and jackets and shoes onto the floor behind the couch.

"Mommy! Tell Tripp he doesn't have to win all the time!"

"Tripp, you don't have to win all the time."

"I know—"

"And, Ian, it's okay if your brother wins. He's older and bigger and taller than you. You'll have to run faster to catch him."

The four of us congregated in the kitchen for the afternoon snack of juice and granola bars, recounting the silly and mundane details of our days. The boys were sated and had no homework. Sam was home early and done working for the day.

"Would you mind if I went to get in a quick walk before I cook dinner?" I asked.

"Nope. I'll start dinner, if it helps."

"Whatever," I smiled. "Pasta and broccoli. Maybe the boys will help."

I went into the bedroom and changed quickly into a t-shirt and yoga pants. I grabbed my phone and earbuds and drove straight to the park.

I was still excited about the trip to Chicago, the budding friendship with Alex Wheeler. Was I imagining it? He was nice and quick-witted and smart. He'd been warm and open during our conversations at Max's and at the Double Door. Was it just because I was someone convenient to talk to?

Alex Wheeler
Nov 17th 1:33 PM

> **So is your stage banter totally ad lib, or do you rehearse it?**

Mostly ad lib but if it works in one city I use it again. Shhh. Ancient singer secret.

> **How's Paulie's leg?**

Stitches.   He'll survive.   Fucking crazy!

Fucking's always crazy. ;)

Especially if ur fucking a crazy girl

The best fucks are the ones who don't know they're crazy.
I've been told I'm batshit crazy, but I don't see it. ;P

You are very naughty aren't you?

Why yes. Yes, I am.

Interesting

Why?
Is it interesting, I mean. Other than the fact that I'm a lightly kinked, big-breasted blonde who isn't afraid to try anything once. That's not really a big deal, is it?
Sorry, I'm being inappropriate.

Inappropriate is good
Tell me more

I could say all kinds of inappropriate things. ;)
But I can't tell you all of my naughty little secrets. Not yet anyway. ;P

I'll tell u mine if u tell me yours

I'll keep that in mind for future reference. It will make me feel... inappropriate?

8)

> **Okay, I'm gonna finish my five miles and get back to my afternoon. Thanks for the talk. And the secrets. You've given me lots to think about. :P**
> **Besides, this is just talk. There's nothing wrong with a little talk. Talk don't mean shit.**

I know that you silly thing

:)

I hadn't been that flirty girl in so long. I'd been her for years, fast-talking and acerbic and more than willing to spout off a dirty joke or double entendre without a second thought. When I was with my girls—Tessa and Frankie and Jules—it took almost no time before we were *all* back into our 17-year-old-coquette persona, telling bawdy jokes and flashing our boobs at each other.

The 17-year-old in me caught sight of Alex Wheeler through her eyelash-batting and liked what she thought she saw looking back.

It made me giggly to myself, finishing my trek around the hilly track at the neighborhood park, listening to "Hot Mess." It was a stunningly beautiful autumn afternoon, and I was unbearably happy, moving my energized body and mind through the warm breeze.

I tried not to think much about it, until I woke up the next morning.

From: Alex Wheeler
Sent: November 18th 2:35 AM
To: Tierney Cavanaugh
Subject: Okay here it is

I love anal!

I was floored. It was *hot*—in the sense that the actual deviance turned me on, but also in the sense that this unexpected man was apparently telling me something *very* personal. Damien had been really into anal sex, trying for most of our relationship to agree

51

to let him try it. In my late teens and early twenties, almost none of my friends had done it—or at least they weren't admitting it. All I knew of it was what I saw in bad porn or heard whispered from my older female friends, about how it was kinky and dirty and mostly hurt but how they might try it again one day if they were drunk and in love enough.

As I got older and more adventurous, both with Sam and with myself, anal sex had lost its sense of utter taboo. When my girlfriends and I would talk about sex, that was the one thing that invariably came up as what they most wanted to try. We'd all bought toys and tried every ridiculous position our bodies would allow. We'd all been tied up and tied down, spanked at least once or twice, and some of us had experimentally crossed the bi-line and at least kissed another girl.

But I'd always seemed to be the only one of my friends who wasn't afraid of trying it or talking about it. It was just another natural thing that could feel good in an intimate moment shared with someone you loved.

I sat at my desk, staring at the message on my screen. If what Alex was telling me was true, it was unbearably sexy, and I wanted to run with it. If he was joking, it was funny as hell, and I wanted to flirt back.

From: Tierney Cavanaugh Johnson
Sent: November 18th 9:34 AM
To: Alex Wheeler
Subject: RE: Okay here goes

Wow, what a coincidence—me, too! But I think I have the distinct advantage of being on the giving *or* the receiving end. All the better for me!

Flirty emails flew back and forth, fast and furious, all day long. By evening, they were naughty and explicit recounts of the ways we each loved to come.

From: Alex Wheeler
Sent: November 18th 5:24 PM
To: Tierney Cavanaugh
Subject: Inappropriate?

Attachment: IMG_8025.MOV

It was a seconds-long clip of him, super close-up, using his long fingers to stroke himself.

The video was absolutely inappropriate by normal people's standards, but absolutely *not* by my own.

What the fuck am I doing?!

Within the span of a day, I was having a torrid little *thing* with this man I barely knew, this man who *wasn't* my husband, and I was enjoying the hell out of it. It was naughty and nice. I wondered how far it would go. How far was either of us willing to take this exchange?

I was *on*, for sure. And I questioned it, every second of it. Had we just bonded as flirty friends during our conversations? Was there something more happening? I was *me*—pretty but big, a 38-year-old housewife and mom—and he was *him*—the undeniably gorgeous and sexy-as-hell rock star.

On top of it all, we were both married. I had Sam, with all of our issues just beginning to bubble to the surface after so many years together, and our beautiful boys. Alex had his stunning wife and daughter. He lived thousands of miles away and just happened to be where I was, when I was. I wasn't anything like most of the women he encountered and flirted with, night after night on the road, but he knew that. He'd met me, knew exactly what I looked and sounded like. I knew my fat thighs fit my Amazonian frame, and my large breasts were of interest to virtually every straight man (and a few gay ones) that I met, but there was no reason he would be attracted to me.

But there had been something in those initial conversations. Something just *clicked*, just connected, when we turned face-to-face between soundcheck and "Before We Start." It was like being at a party, packed with strangers, and finding the one person you were searching for, someone you forgot you'd ever met before, and going, "Oh, *there* you are!" I just *knew* him from the moment we met.

Late that night, I was awake, insomnomaniacal. Sam was asleep. Alex was on the road, night traveling in the tour bus. We texted for hours, alternately coy and salacious. It was sexting, undoubtedly, and we both knew what the other was doing, alone in the dark.

Alex Wheeler
Nov 19th 1:18 AM

This feels so dirty. I fucking love it.

> **;) I know. I can tell.**

Talia and I do this sometimes but
it's never so visual.

> **I need to go to bed. I'm tired.
> Someone wore me out. :)**

Go to bed and fuck your husband.

> **We don't do that. We haven't had
> sex in almost three months.**

That's sad.
Really. Why?

> **I don't know. He's just not that
> interested.**

Does he know how naughty you
are?

> **He knows. I just don't think he
> cares.
> He works a lot. My back has been
> a mess for so long. It's just not a
> priority.**

You should tell him to make it one.

> **Again, I don't think he cares.**

So you just go without?

> **I have fingers. I have a ton of toys.
> They'll do when they need to. ;)**

Mmmm. You are divine.

> **I was thinking today that I need a new one. Maybe I'll go to the toy store tomorrow.**

And tell me all about it?

> **Maybe.**

You can't tell anyone about this.
Ever. No one can ever know.

    I knew he was right. While a rocker fucking a fan was nothing out of the ordinary, it took on a wholly different gravity when complicated by a wife and child. Plus there was my own husband and children.

    My attraction to Alex had *nothing* to do with what he did for a living, with the exception of that being how we met. My initial engagement of him was flirty but completely innocent. This was *way* beyond friendly salutation.

    By the next morning, there was a second video, recorded in the tiny tour bus bathroom. *The cum shot.* Though the movie was mostly silent, I could hear him catch his breath as he came, thinking about me and my words. I watched it over and over, making out every detail of his cock, his fingers, the small scar on his hand.

    I was a horny, elated, besotted mess.

Alex Wheeler
Nov 19th 9:34 AM

How's my pussy?

> **It's in bed with my sleeping husband.**
> **And it's warm and wet and tired.**
> **;)**

Mmmm. Very wet?

Let me check.
Yes. Very. And yummy too.

Delicious.

**I'm taking it to the toy store after
I'm awake.**

Buy something for us.

**Ha! I'll send you pics and let you
choose.**

I was surprised by his suggesting buying a toy for "us". Was there an *us*? Was there an intention on his part to really carry this further, at least to the point of an actual, physical hook-up? I wasn't sure what to think about that, so I chose to ignore it for the time being.

But I got ready, feeling pretty and confident, and headed to the Love Shack. I was no stranger to the adult novelty store, but I also wasn't a regular. It had been years since I'd gone shopping for toys in a brick-and-mortar store, having always opted for the ease and secrecy of online purchase.

It was a clean, welcoming store, far enough away from my home that I didn't worry about running into anyone I knew. Staff and clientele were an equal mix of men and women. There was nothing skeezy waiting for me around a dark corner.

The glass shelves and peg racks displayed an enormous variety of toys and games, running the gamut from funny gag gifts to hardcore fuck-anything-and-everything implements that were almost hard to envision. I wandered the rows slowly, looking at everything at least once.

"Let me know if you want to see how something works," the sales girl offered.

I looked at the glass-enclosed display case of expensive toys lined up neatly across folds of red velvet. The molded glass toys caught my eye. Dildos and butt plugs, thin and thick. Hand-blown and twisted into exquisite, artful shapes that were sometimes beautiful and sometimes intimidating when you realized where they were intended to go.

> **Alex Wheeler**
> **Nov 19th 12:57 PM**
> **They don't have the Icicles 24 that**
> **I wanted but they have this.**

I texted him a picture of a clear glass wand, stylized but simple.

Beautiful!

> **Or what about this one?**

I sent a picture of a strap-on dildo, something that I'd never tried and couldn't possibly explain to Sam if he ever happened across it. I knew it would likely turn Alex on as soon as he saw it.

Mmmmm. You can use it on me.

> **And make you come. Hard.**

Yes please.

I bought the simple clear wand and a couple of other small things and returned home.

> **Alex Wheeler**
> **Nov 20th 3:42 PM**

So when am I getting pics? And a video. You owe me video!

> **Ha! I'm home with the boys.**

So?

> **What am I supposed to do? Say,**
> **"Give Mommy a minute so she can**
> **go fuck herself?"**

Yes! Now!

I knew he was jokingly serious. I was excited by the idea of it, but doing it would be something else entirely. Recording my own naked body was a daunting prospect. Regardless of the logistics of doing it with Sam and the kids at home, there was the issue of exposing myself in such a way. It had nothing to do with prudence. The thought of being naked, even partially, in front of another man—especially this unarguably gorgeous man—scared the hell out of me.

But I did it. I slipped away to my olive-and-black tiled bathroom, wand in hand. It was the only place in the house where I could be assured of true privacy, the closed door bunkering me from the noise and distractions of my family. I found the best way to sit on the side of the bathtub, legs spread and feet planted firmly against the wall, and still be able to angle the iPhone, doing what I was going to do. It was just a few seconds, just enough to give him a little show of exactly how the lovely toy worked. I watched it a couple of times, making sure my ample belly and thighs were well-hidden from scrutiny.

Alex Wheeler
Nov 19th 5:12 PM

Ah that beautiful blond pussy!
Delicious!

Yes, it is.

Did you cum?

Yes. ;)

Good girl.

I was standing up when I came, leaning against the wall, and I almost hit the floor when my legs crumpled.

I love that feeling!
Send me pictures of those beautiful
tits!

Seriously?

Yes please.

Sam knew nothing of any of this. He knew I'd met Alex at the Masquerade, obviously, and he knew Jules had sent me to Max's house before the show at Workplay. Although nothing had happened during those few hours at *Manuel Le Bore*, I'd minimized the whole thing when I'd recounted it, glossing over the details. He'd seen the pictures and video from the Double Door but had no idea that I'd met with Alex before the show.

I don't know why I wasn't more forthcoming about what had transpired. There'd been nothing unseemly about any of my conversations with Alex. At least not until after I was safely home in Atlanta. But these events were *my* experience, not Sam's. I wanted to keep them for myself.

Sam was working a *lot*. He was advancing very quickly in his career and making a professional name for himself in a very public way. He worked on major, international computer Trojan cases. He would spend hours that turned into days on top secret investigations of hacking incidents and computer virus outbreaks. There was a constant rotation of interviews on CBS, CNN, FOXNews. He was in *USA Today*, the *Wall Street Journal*, and *The New York Times*, just to name a few.

He would be gone by the time I got home from my morning walks. He would return late in the evening, around the time the boys were already showered and pajamaed, trying their best to negotiate five more minutes before bedtime. He always came home with a six- or twelve-pack of beer that he would slide into the freezer to rechill. Most nights he drank six beers, methodic and routine in how he drank them and carefully rinsed and crushed the cans before depositing them into the freshly-emptied recycling bin. A couple of nights a week he would drink an entire twelve-pack, but never did he drink less than six.

For years, I'd spent my evenings in the den or lying in bed, watching television and often snacking mindlessly. He worked on the other side of the wall, hunched over his computer in the dimly lit office, squirreled away just a few feet from me. We would pass silently by each other for hours, dropping an occasional kiss on the other's mouth. He would eventually pass out in bed, an hour or more after I'd fallen asleep.

I was drinking more than ever. Not a lot every day, but a little bit almost every day. Historically, I didn't drink much at home. If I went out with Sam, I might have a drink or two at most, as I was often the designated driver. But if I knew I was planning to drink, at a show or out with friends when I wasn't driving, I drank to get drunk. Now I was drinking vodka—just a shot or two—almost every night. Instead of watching television, I would drink and sometimes paint after the children went to bed, while Sam was working and drinking, while I was waiting to hear from Alex.

I went through my pictures from Birmingham, from Railroad Park, and found a shot to work with. The downtown skyline of old and new buildings was dotted with defunct smokestacks, across the expanse of greenscape. My favorite was the City Federal building, a neoclassical beauty built in the early 1900s. Its bright, red sign was dark for decades but reluminated a few months before we moved to Atlanta, just as the loft district was beginning to thrive.

I carefully brushed both shadow and light into a beautiful juxtaposition of revitalization in the midst of the decayed industrial spirit that had forged my hometown in the century before I was born.

I was in the throes of an extended period of insomnia. I would sleep for a couple of hours then wake again in the middle of the night. I would unplug my iPhone from its charger on my nightstand and pad across the unlit house silently toward the den. The huge sectional sofa was the haven where I would pile into the jumble of throw pillows, safely wrapped in my favorite old blanket.

I was often cocooned away in the dark by the time Alex was sliding into his bunk on the tour bus. We would text or Skype until we were both exhausted from the culmination of our separate day and collective night. Setting my alarm for a few minutes before Sam's, I would drift back to sleep on the couch where I'd just been with Alex.

I would hit the park as soon as I took the boys to school, walking for an hour or more with my mom friends. Some of them were acquaintances whom I knew only through shared school and kid activities. Some of them were my friends, estrogen comrades who understood that colorful didn't have to be relegated to the past, that we didn't stop being women just because we'd become mothers.

By the time I was finished with the dishes and laundry and errands and whatever else I needed to do for the day, Alex would be up and going, wherever he was in the world that day. He would call or text me as often as he could.

That didn't mean he was at my beck and call. I didn't have the freedom to call him at whim. I had to text or email him first to see if he was available. Often he was busy working or with friends or colleagues, which meant he couldn't pay attention to me. There was a lot of sitting and waiting for my phone to ding. I'm impatient and don't do well to be still, so I sketched or painted while I waited for my next late night Skype session, which was always lewd and exciting.

Alex reminded me, constantly, to delete texts and emails and to clear my Skype history.

Tierney   I know. I will.

Alex   I would hate for your husband to accidentally find this.

Tierney   That would be bad, yes. Though he could always just find the old deleted info anyway.

Alex   ??

Tierney   It's what he does for a living, you know. Info security and forensics. He gets conscripted by the FBI and the Secret Service to do work all the time. He's a hacker hunter.

Alex   Great. Maybe I should never email you again.

Tierney   Maybe you should just *talk* to me on the phone.

Alex   Wish I could, dollface. Other people around, you know.

Tierney   I know. Soon though.

Alex   Yes. What are you doing this week?

Tierney	I'm taking the boys to Birmingham to see the fam before Thanksgiving. Sam has to work, so it's just me and them. Are you going home?
Alex	Nope. Going to see my mom in Portland. Talia's still gone with Amber.
Tierney	So you'll be on your own, and I'll be on my own?
Alex	Yup.
Tierney	And you'll be able to call me and hear me come for you?
Alex	Yup.
Tierney	;)
Alex	I need ur help in dealing with Junkture assholes. Can talk about it while you're in Birmingham.
Tierney	I'm sorry they're being assholes. You deserve better than that
Alex	It's fucked, just ungrateful dickheads. Get some rest

Chapter 5

The boys and I went to Birmingham and made the rounds, visiting with the families. It was two days of driving from one side of town to the other for short, two- and three-hour visits with grandparents and great-grandparents and aunts and uncles and cousins.

"We're fine. How are you? Sam has to work this week and couldn't come with us. No, I'm sorry, we have to be back in Atlanta for Thanksgiving at home for our family. Great to see you—goodbye!"

We settled at my mom's house on Sunday night. It's always strange for me to be in that house. She and my stepdad moved there after my freshman year in college. My things were moved from our old house to the new one, set-up in my room like I wanted, but I only lived there for one summer. Slowly over the years, my things were shoved away into closets or migrated to my now-you're-a-grown-up home, and the bedroom was converted to a cluttered office for the parental unit.

I often find my mother's house to be too dark and too hot or too cold and too busy. They are careful to conserve electricity by using only minimal lights and adjusting the thermostat to better-than-conservation temperatures. The televisions are always playing in the huge, open den and in the master bedroom, never on the same channel. Standing in the dark hallway directly between the two rooms, the sounds of the respective programs reverberate off the hardwood floors and clash in echoes against the walls.

The only place I can find quiet in that house is downstairs, in the rarely used den.

It's a little stuffy and dark with no natural light, but there's an old bed and furniture and a couple of lamps strategically placed around the unused treadmill and rows of dusty, overburdened bookshelves. I always have to turn on a rickety box fan when I sleep there, but it's the one place I feel like I can hide from the family when I need to.

I tucked the boys into bed in the spare bedroom, reminding them to stop touching each other and to go straight to sleep.

"I think I'll run to Target," I said to Mom. "Do you need anything?"

She peered at me from her recliner, over her reading glasses. "I don't think so."

From her tone, I couldn't tell if she meant she didn't think she needed anything or if she didn't think I should go to Target at nine o'clock.

You're thirty-eight years old. You can decide if it's okay to go to the store, Tierney.

"I need to look for something for the boys for Christmas, before I forget about it."

I did go to Target, and I looked at the toys and holiday decorations. But mostly I looked at the spill-proof, insulated cups and the Diet Coke. And I stopped by the liquor store for a bottle of Jack Daniels. Mom and Dan were already in bed when I got back to the darkened house. I quietly filled my cup with ice and went downstairs.

Alex Wheeler
Nov 22nd 10:37 PM
Did u arrive safely?

I did thanks
Passing out

Noooo
You're going to call me
but my tongue is numb

Passing out

Noooooo
Please no I'm so horny

Lol

Do you like to make me beg?
That's so mean to make a drunk
girl beg for cock
I only beg for you, you know

Muah

**Bwahahaha
I can't breathe fucker**

xoxo

Really, my lips are numb

Love

**You could fuck my mouth for days
like this**

Xoxoxoxoxo
Ujjbsmh dkjmdjk nsvo
Sleepy

**What's that Liz Phair line?
Your tip's the perfect suck me
size?**

Trdzi Hajji Fkudnbvy

**Noooooo
Pleeeeeeeeez
I'm so wet**

HWC is Liz Fare

**I was listening to hwc earlier
And watching old footage of your
band**

Hot White Cum

**And thinking, I would totally suck
that guy's cock**

Stoooooopid

Mine?

Paulie was pretty hot ya know
Of course yours, babycakes
Only yours

Paulie who :)

There's no other cock I want
No other cock I would beg for
Only you baby
Right here where my fingers are

Passing out, too drunk

Noooooooo
So mean
You know how bad I need you
I only want you
Only love you
Only need you
Only want your cock ever
Only cum for you

Shut up!
U r lying

Noooooo
I promise

Liar

Noooo
I would never lie to you
Ever

Before I could type the next response, my phone rang.
"Hey," I breathed, drunkenly delighted.
"Hey," he laughed back.
"How are you?"

"*Hard*."

"*Not for long, motherfucker.*"

"Oh, yeah?" Alex challenged. "*Tell me.*"

"Tell you what?" I teased, my voice dropping into fake innocence. "How I'm wet? How all I want to do right now is take your beautiful cock down my throat? How I want to suck it like candy, with your fingers tangled into my hair, squeezing and pulling until I put my mouth where you want it?"

"Yeahyeahyeah...."

"Or how I'll wrap my hand around the base of your cock and squeeze it, just a little, while I swirl my tongue along the shaft? I'll flick it across the head and back down, just a little kiss... until I deep throat you and *suck* your cock as hard as you can stand it."

"I'll fuck your mouth until you gag."

I chuckled throatily. "I don't *gag*, babycakes. I suck cock like a pro. But maybe you'd like it better if I just jacked you while I licked your balls instead."

I heard Alex catch his breath suddenly.

"Oh, you *would* like that, wouldn't you? And should I stick a finger into your ass while I jack your cock?"

"I wanna come in your mouth."

"Not yet," I laughed. I slid my panties down my legs and tossed them to the end of the bed. "You need to fuck me first."

"Do I?" he mused.

"*Uh-huh*. I wanna be on top, so I can fuck you and kiss you at the same time."

"*Oooooh*, and I can suck those beautiful tits while you ride my cock."

"*Mmmm*, I love that! And I'm so *wet* right now. It'd be so easy for me to slide onto you and squeeze your dick with my *tight* pussy."

"Are you really wet?"

I flicked my clit. "*So wet*. These two fingers feel good, but I'm betting your cock would feel better."

"*Do it*."

"I'll be right over you, my tongue in your mouth, and tease you. Just the tip, right inside, squeezing it."

"Your pussy's so hot."

"*Mmmm-hmmm*. I'll slide down, just a little, and back up, almost off, down again just a little more. I'm gonna take my time and feel every inch of you with my pussy."

"Eight inches. Take it. All of it."

I grinned to myself, my fingers moving more determinedly between my legs. "You're all the way in, and I'm squeezing your cock as hard as I can, rocking back and forth. I need to get off, I need to come."

"Make me come...."

"Oh, you'll come. As soon as you feel my pussy dripping down your cock—"

"Down the crack of my ass," he breathed. "*Oh god!*"

"*I'm so close*," I whispered into the phone. "I'm fucking you, up and down, hard and fast. I want you to suck my nipples while you fuck me."

"*Yeah*. Grab your ass."

"I wanna *fuck* you. I wanna come on your cock. Now. Please."

We stopped talking. I dropped the phone onto the pillow next to my ear and turned my face so I could still hear him. Two fingers in me, another strumming my clit.

"*Oh god!*" I moaned. I arched my back as the tingle started between my legs.

"Yeah. Come for me, baby," he urged hoarsely.

Every muscle in my body tensed and released in the same moment, an explosion of pleasure ripping through me as I came, gasping toward the mic of the phone. I heard him gasp and moan deeply as I lay there panting.

"You are *divine*, Tierney! Really, just amazing. You're like my personal sex therapist."

"So...," I twittered nervously.

"*So...*," he mimicked. "What's that about?"

"I don't know what to say now." I was blushing over the phone. Once the moment had passed, I was a little embarrassed about the torrent of naughtiness that had gushed from my mouth. "How long since you've been with anyone else? Other than Talia?"

"Eight years. Mostly." He inhaled and exhaled deeply, trying to return his breathing to normal.

"And how many women have you slept with?"

"Hmmm... maybe... *a hundred*?"

He sounded confident but not bragging. And a hundred women seemed perfectly reasonable given his line of work. Perhaps that should've been a daunting number, but it just wasn't.

"But," he said cautiously, "some of it...."

"Tell me."

"There's not much I haven't done. I'm try-curious, you know? I'll try just about anything once?"

"Are we talking scat? Golden showers? Bodily fluids or animals?"

"*No!* I'm not into that bullshit. But Annabelle, my ex-wife? She had this toy chest. I swear there was a toy for every guy, and most of the girls, she'd fucked. She liked for me to use them on her while she told me about how and when she'd gotten them, how she'd fucked and been fucked with the dildo or the vibrator or whatever. Sometimes, she liked to use them on me. She'd tell me how some guy had fucked her with it... while she fucked *me* with it. She got off on my knowing who and what she'd done before we met.

"And *sometimes*," he continued, "she would take me to these parties or to a club if we were in a big city. She liked for me to watch her fuck someone else. She especially liked to come while getting fucked from behind, so she could see my face while someone else drilled my wife."

I could hear the tension in his voice when he started talking, slowly and evenly stepping through the details of sexcapades with Annabelle, amongst others. He was cautious, obviously unsure of how I would react, but I could tell talking about it was self-mollifying for him.

"Did she include you?" I asked.

"Sometimes. Not always. Usually she liked for me to fuck her after she was done, after someone else made her come. She'd get me to talk to her about how hot it was watching her take some guy's cock or ride some random chick's face."

Alex paused, and I was quiet.

He took a deep, pointed breath, and his voice was taut as he continued. "But then sometimes, she *would* pull me into it. Annabelle would get the girl to fuck me while she fucked my wife. And...."

"Alex, *what*?" I almost whispered. "You can tell me. It's okay."

"Sometimes, not often but every so often, there'd be a guy. Annabelle would be fucking him and get me to let him suck my dick. She said she liked it when I came on their faces."

"Did you ever fuck one of them? Did you ever have sex with another man?"

"Nope. I probably would have eventually, for Annabelle. I would've done anything for her. But maybe for me, too. Is that too much?" he asked apprehensively.

"No, not at all," I assured him. "Why would it be? Who the hell am I to judge anyone else's sexual proclivities? With the exception of children and forcible sex, there's very, very little that I find to be immoral between consenting adults. There may be things that don't interest me, things that either just don't do it for me or that I find to be personally repulsive, but that doesn't mean someone else isn't allowed to be into them."

"Well, it's not... I don't know."

"Alex, it's *okay*. *More* than okay. It's not something you should be afraid of. You haven't told me anything that doesn't play out in untold sexual settings everywhere, every day."

But the tone of his voice told me there was something he found shadowy and base in them, something frightening. He sounded relieved to reveal these raw, untamed acts that had been shared out of love and desire and sometimes desperation.

"And you really want a little bit of that now," I guessed.

"Yeah, but there's no way. Talia, really, would just never get it. It would be too much for her."

"Does she know?"

"*No*. She would never understand why I want to be told what to do, why I *need* to let someone else push me into the shit that I don't even know I want until it makes my dick hard."

"Maybe she might like it. Maybe she might be willing to be there for you, for what you need."

"Nope. Really, she would freak out."

I sat up and reached for my drink.

"Tell me," I said, "about Annabelle."

He took a deep breath, stretching. "I met her at Montevallo. You know I started as a Music major there, right?"

"Uh-huh."

"I wasn't a great kid, but I wasn't horrible. In high school, I started using a little bit of everything. Pot, acid, pills—whatever I could get on the weekends. It wasn't every weekend, and my grades were okay. My ACT scores were really good, so I got a full ride to Montevallo. Everything was okay at first. I made the Dean's list my first semester. I was in the Honors Program. But then I started dating this chick. Annabelle Blue. She was a grad student, a Math major from Mobile with a heavy appetite for drugs and sex and pain. Plus she was four years older than I was, so I was pretty eager to please. I did everything in my power to keep up with her. My grades started to fall. I dropped out and moved into *Manuel La Bore*. The band took off, and we got a record deal. Annabelle was with us through all of that."

"Was that *really* her name? No offense, but it sounds like a stripper."

Alex chuckled. "I asked her one night when we were coked up if it was her real name. She said, 'It is now.' She had her name changed legally when she turned eighteen and got away from her fucked up mother. Even after we got married, she didn't change it to Wheeler."

"So why did it end?" I asked gently.

I could almost see him shrug when he answered, "She was tired of me. I still love her, though."

"When was the last time you saw her?"

"The day we signed the divorce papers, at the attorney's office. I heard a couple of years later that she was dancing somewhere, burlesque, but I didn't go look her up. I can't. I'd love to see her, tell her I hope she's doing well, but I can't go search her out."

Alex had been with Talia, who was eight years his junior, for almost ten years, married for five. He told me how he'd met Talia one night at a bar. She was sitting with friends, drinking.

"Her laugh. It was so good. And her smile. I couldn't stop watching her smile."

With Alex on tour for most of three months, it was a good time for Talia and Amber to be traveling. He Skyped and FaceTimed with them every day. I could tell he missed them terribly, especially his daughter.

"Talia's great," he said. "You'll love her when you meet her."

I think I actually snorted when he said this. *When? How?* I couldn't imagine the logistics of how such an encounter would ever take place, with her in Los Angeles and me in Atlanta, regardless of the weird circumstance of my having phone sex with her husband.

"You *will* meet her. I promise, it won't be weird, and you'll get along great together."

"Because we have so much in common?" I retorted.

As I listened to him talk, I could *hear* that he loved her. I couldn't tell if he was really still in love with her, though. I didn't know him well enough to make that judgment. But there was *obviously* something lacking in his life.

"You know what I think?" I started, drunk and strangely brazen. "I think you love her—"

"I do, yes. I love her to death—"

"—and that she gave you something you badly wanted, maybe that you wanted with Annabelle, that you never thought you'd have—"

"What's that?"

"A child. Amber. You didn't get that with Annabelle for whatever reason, and Talia gave you the most amazing gift. But you're unhappy in that, Alex. Unhappy that you aren't getting what you need."

"I'm not unhappy about anything!" he snapped. "No one's *leaving* anyone here. I—"

"I didn't say that," I soothed immediately. "I know that."

Quietly he replied, "People don't initiate affairs because they're looking for something different. They're looking for what's missing."

For me, really for both of us, the sex was missing. Sam and I barely saw each other naked anymore, and it was flattering and gratifying for me to have an incredibly delicious man describing to me how he wanted to fuck me. Alex was not only away from his wife, he had years' worth of deep urges that he'd denied and repressed, sacrificing his own base, carnal desires for the love of a woman.

But the real attraction wasn't the sex; it was the *truth*. In each other, Alex and I found a safe haven for our secrets and fears and all of the concerns that weighed on us. They were long-pent burdens that had either been dismissed by our lovers and parents and friends, or they were so damn heavy that we never could've asked anyone else to carry them for us.

Each of us had the freedom with the other to explore any memory or feeling or fantasy that we craved. There was never any recrimination or judgment, only celebration of the openness. It was physically safe and satisfying, certainly, but there was an emotional gratification that came with facing the things that scared us the most, the things we'd hidden away from our partners and ourselves for far too long.

The truth was irresistible.

Chapter 6

"You said in Montevallo that you'd do my wife," Alex said to me the next night.

"I did."

"So would you *really*? Are you into other girls?"

"Maybe," I answered coyly. "Do you wanna hear all about it?"

I found my teasing, throaty voice again, whispering coarse and deliciously vulgar things about what it would be like to fuck another woman with him. Lost in the moment, I painted a wickedly lewd picture with a torrent of sexual fantasy.

"Would that turn you on," I breathed, "to watch another girl make me come?"

"I wanna fuck her while her mouth is between your thighs."

I could hear how much he loved it, in every breathy moan. I would say something, leading and building him toward climax, only to pull back and tease him. He would gasp hoarsely and whisper, urging me on.

He gave back as good as he got, and I came twice during that phone call.

Even after the sex, it was strangely easy to talk with him, though sometimes I would get excited and nervous, stammering over my own thoughts. I could hear his infectious smile when he would tease me, "*So. So? So-o!*" intoned in my strange mix of Southern and Valley Girl.

I asked him about his text from a few nights before, whatever the problem was he was having with the band. Paul Sommers, it turned out, was a long-time frenemy. Alex had worked his ass off, had poured his life's savings into the start-up for the record label to release *Persona Non Grata* and risked the constant wrath of his wife. Paul had taken on the role of CEO and was slow to respond to Alex's concerns about day-to-day operations. This loving-but-adversarial dynamic had been going on for years, but the label was in a pivotal position, and Alex was tired of feeling dismissed by his friend and business partner.

Specifically, Alex had been approached about a sweetheart publishing deal and needed the other three to sign off on it. Paul was the only one who hadn't agreed, delaying both with questions and with non-response.

I tried to give him some advice on how I would handle it, how I would approach them if it were me in the situation. My practical and analytical tendencies generally slant toward the obviously efficient, but it wasn't my dogfight.

"That's how *I* would do it," I stressed, "but I barely know him. This is not a business in which I'm well-versed."

"No, I think you're right. You're intuitive and I trust your instincts on this. I'll try to call him tomorrow and see what he says."

I was flattered that Alex had asked my advice about something so personal. Sex was one thing; it was easy to flirt and talk in the quiet dark. But his opening his personal, *professional* life felt different. Talk of contracts and money and revenues meant that he trusted me with private legal information, which was nothing like detailing how he wanted to fuck me.

We chatted a lot about his work, about his history with his bandmates, the ups and downs that had never been covered in the press or on the fan forums. We chatted about what I was doing with the kids and that I was painting again.

"It's scary," I admitted, "finding the difference again in *craft* and *art*. I went to school to learn how to paint, but that doesn't mean I'm an artist. Is it talent, or is it just hard work?"

"It's both. I can sing, and I can write songs, but so can a lot of people. I got where I am because of constantly working. I'm always writing. Almost every day I'm holed up with my guitar, playing and working out something. Sometimes it's good, and sometimes it sucks."

"So what works for you? How do you know when it's good enough to share?"

He was quiet for a moment. "I just *know*. Sometimes I can hear how Paulie's guitar will sound over my vocals, how he'll extrapolate the melody. We've worked together for so long now that I just *know* how he'll run with it."

"Does he ever surprise you? Or do you feel some comfort in that kind of clockwork relationship?"

"He still surprises me. Usually it's when we haven't worked together in a while. Like, he and I didn't talk for almost two years, during this hiatus. *Persona Non Grata* was great, because it was time for us to find that *art* again. It still took a lot of hard work, though.

There were days I wanted to punch him in the fucking face. That's really where the hard work came into play—trying to let go of all the bullshit and just let the music stand on its own. That's how we've had to work for twenty years, though, so I kind of know what to expect and how to deal with him."

I told him about how Sam and I had met, within days of my turning fourteen and starting high school at the county gifted magnet school. After years of not fitting in with my elementary and junior high counterparts, I found myself with a slew of new friends. We were all outcasts of some sort and found comfort in the camaraderie of geeky freakiness. With only about 150 students in the four grades, it was hard to miss anyone in the dank halls, but somehow I managed to completely miss this guy, the older brother of a new classmate, Michelle. A group of us went to the movies, and I met him in the parking lot after the movie.

I remember, very clearly, standing there and someone saying something about Michelle's brother, Sam.

"Michelle has a brother?" I asked.

Just as someone was pointing him out, I looked up and saw this tall, skinny, geeky guy in a black jacket and jeans. He had a bad 80's haircut and black Reebok high-tops. And I swear to God there was a fucking *halo* around the son of a bitch.

I knew in that moment that I would marry him.

We spent a few weeks doing that early high school dating thing, where we were always together or on the phone but couldn't actually *go* anywhere, as neither of us was old enough to drive. Something happened over a weekend, and I came back to school on Monday confronted by the fact that some other girl had done something indiscreet with my boyfriend. The info came down to me from a friend, and I didn't even bother to ask Sam about it. I just broke it off.

I was heartbroken for weeks. Tessa would say it was months, and she'd probably be right. The heartache of shattered first love coincided with normal pubescent melancholy. What resulted should probably have been diagnosed as depression and given the warranted attention. Like so much else in my life, it was dismissed.

Sam and I started dating again a few months after Damien and I finally ended and I'd dropped out of Montevallo. Sam was ending a six-year relationship with one of my best friends, India. Their relationship had run its course months before, but it finally ended when she openly admitted to wanting to sleep with other people. He tried for a while to be open to the idea. He couldn't take it when she started to have feelings for another guy, whom she ultimately married. I was recovering from a rollercoaster four years with Damien. I decided to transfer to UAH to get away from Birmingham and to be with Tessa and India, which meant I'd be closer to my first love and his ex-girlfriend.

By the time I moved to Huntsville that winter, Sam and I were in love again and living together. He was a great, attentive boyfriend. We holed ourselves up, away from the world. We spent countless nights listening to music and talking and laughing, often drunk or high or both. We worked and went to school and didn't want to be apart any longer than absolutely necessary. The neighbors complained that we kept them up at night, laughing uproariously in our bed, writing our own history of inside jokes.

After eighteen months together, we decided to get married. It was a small, lovely ceremony at my mother's church in Birmingham. Sam and I had been married for sixteen years by the time I met Alex.

What I never told Sam—in fact told *no one* until these soul-revealing conversations with Alex— was that I skipped out of that church, hand-in-hand with my new husband and thought, *What the fuck did I just do?* I had a momentary flash of running back inside and saying, "Nonono! I'm sorry, I didn't mean to just do that! Can we have a do-over?" I hadn't had cold feet before the wedding, and I was certain it was just latent fear of the unknown. I choked it down and went straight to the reception, my fears forgotten almost immediately in a buzz of cake and punch and the photographer's constant flash.

Alex and I talked about the difficulties of my fertility treatments, how trying it had been to my body and my head and my marriage. I told him all about Sam's cyclical years of excessive drinking, as well as his complete ignorance of me over the previous year.

We traded more silly and crazy stories from our sexual pasts, in great detail. I'd been with four men for actual sex, but there had been other non-intercourse interludes. There were a surprising number of boys who got their hands in my bra or in my panties with very little effort. And I left more than one teenage schoolboy with a raging hard-on, as I coyly and abruptly ended their hand-job when the bus got to my stop.

I told him about the years of molestation at the hands of my maternal grandfather that had started, as best I can remember, when I was about four. My grandparents lived three hours away, and my parents would send me to stay with them for a week or so, a few times a year. My dad worked full time, while my mom was in school or working. My grandmother was always delighted when I came to visit.

What no one else knew was that my grandfather was happy to see me for all the wrong reasons. He would wait until the rest of the family was gone, or until they were safely occupied on the other side of the house, to touch me in terribly improper and confusing ways.

"Don't tell anyone," he'd whisper to me, his hand on my small, vulnerable body and his eyes trained for the door. I would always hear my grandmother and my aunt and maybe my mother on the other side of the house, talking and laughing. "You'll get in trouble. They'll be mad at you."

I didn't tell anyone, not for years. But I knew it felt wrong. It was wrong to be a little girl and feel that strange tingling between my legs. As I would learn too many years later, it's very common for even a young, innocent body to respond in that way, to feel sexual arousal from stimulation—it's basic physiology.

I told Alex how the feelings of the molestation had come terrifyingly to the surface years later, when I was raped at sixteen. I was at my friend Karolina's house, hanging out with her and her older cousin, Kent, from Mobile. He was very cute and funny, with dimples and great hair. He was interested in my big breasts and laughed at my jokes. The three of us smoked some pot, and then two of us started making out.

I was wasted, though not incapacitated. I knew where I was, and I knew what I was doing. Until he suddenly put his dick in me. No asking, no warning, just bam! I froze in panic. All I could hear in my head was my grandfather warning me to be quiet, not to tell anyone, that I was bad and would get in trouble.

I didn't want this. I didn't ask for this. I didn't want this guy to fuck me.

I was a virgin, and I wasn't ready, physically or mentally. I don't care how many other guys I'd played around with, this was different, and it wasn't okay.

Things were fuzzy and slow, time warping around the sensation of being violated. I don't know how long it went on, how long it was before I finally pushed him off of me. I went upstairs to Karolina's bedroom, shaking and sick. In the harsh bathroom light, I saw the fresh smear of blood on my panties. It had happened, undeniably, and I hadn't said okay, I hadn't agreed. I wasn't asked and didn't have a choice.

"I think Kent just raped me," I said, stunned, to Karolina in the dark middle of the night. I don't even remember if she said anything, though I knew she heard me. I cried and didn't eat for days. I had to go out with her a couple of days later, and he was there. I didn't know what to do or say. It was surreal, and I was numb for a very long time.

I talked openly with Alex about how being sexualized at such an early age had played out again and again, in some particularly traumatizing ways. I delved into dark details of how I'd been lost in my own sexuality, had found reassurance when I spread my legs, counterbalance to my intensely lacking self-esteem.

The worst of it had been with Damien, certainly. As the relationship progressed over the four years, shattered and half-ass repaired a dozen times, his anger toward me would intersect with his own buried issues. Any transgressions—real or imagined—were *always* too great for an apology, no matter how heart-felt I may have been in delivering it. Sometimes just yelling and belittling me weren't enough to pacify his anger. The first time he hit me, I should've run. But I came back, time and again, for more of it. Even when the police had to drag him from my car, armed with a knife and a gun and threatening to shoot me, I searched him out again.

He was always eager to share any craving or fantasy he had, and I'd never been offended by that. Ever. He was the lover who introduced me to sex toys. We tried increasingly complicated and exhausting sexual positions. He was partial to a little light bondage, and I often followed him into willing submission.

But it was his harsh, troubled side that liked to use sex to degrade me. When he was especially angry, he would think of some act that he loved, something he knew I didn't like or was scared to try, and would tell me that I could only make retribution by doing those things. If I really loved him, he said, I would let him use me in any way he saw fit, in any way that made him feel better about the terrible thing I'd done. I performed more uncomfortable sexual acts in public places than I care to remember. There are some things he manipulated and bullied me into doing that I still *loathe* to this day, unable to get past the emotional association of him with those acts.

My parental units—both my mom and stepdad, and my dad—never liked him, though they didn't tell me that until much, much later. Half the time, I didn't like him. He was abrasive and a little controlling, though he could also be gentle and really sweet and caring when he wanted, at least for a while. I was a geeky Amazon with no self-esteem to speak of. It was easy to let him dictate how I saw myself. Somewhere, deep down, I could feel how damaging the dynamic was, but it was only after multiple half-hearted suicide attempts that I finally managed to break away from him.

For whatever reason I had loved him, and my self-respect was defeated long past the point that the love ended. I placidly put up with a lot of bullshit in the name of love.

Even with all the women he'd been with, Alex told me he'd been in love exactly five times. "I've been on both sides of it—of getting my heart broken and of being the one to do the breaking."

"I'm not a casual girl," I told him. "I've never *not* loved my lovers in some capacity, in some way, even as friends. I wasn't *in* love with all of them, obviously. But I couldn't go there without finding *something* about them that made them worth it, that made me redeemable. But *this*.... I'm going to get my heart broken."

"Probably," he replied quietly.

I smiled sadly to myself in the dark. "But I'm all in."

Things were mostly quiet the day before and of Thanksgiving. The boys and I were back with Sam, who was working throughout the holiday week. He was engrossed in a high-pressure project. Even though he was working from home, we barely saw or spoke to him. Sam drank himself to sleep late that night after ignoring me for most of the day.

Coming home to Atlanta and Sam's emotional neglect, juxtaposed with the extremes of this burgeoning thing with Alex, sent my mind churning. I stayed up, drinking Jack and Diet Coke, distractedly trying to sketch what was in my head.

It was dark and quiet in the house, everyone sleeping, and I missed Alex terribly. He was three hours behind me, and I wanted to talk to him. Leaving the lights off, I went into the den and crashed on the big sofa. It was strongly reminiscent of so many recent nights: the darkness illuminated only by my iPhone screen, the silence broken only by the occasional hum of something electronic, the throbbing between my legs when I thought of Alex.

Alex Wheeler
Nov 26th 11:18 PM
It's dark and quiet and I'm alone
and I don't want to be.

Driving. Call u in 20

I plugged in my iPod and listened to Concrete Blonde, "I Don't Need a Hero", wracked by huge, silent sobs in the darkness.

My phone lit up the den and vibrated in my hand.

"Hey."

"Are you okay?"

"No." My voice was weak and tired, cracking under the emotional strain.

"It's okay, Tierney."

Silence.

"Is Sam asleep?"

"Yeah."

"You should be, too."

"I don't want to be. I want to talk to you."

Alex chuckled quietly.

"I want to come. I want to hear you," I whispered.

I sat by the back door, across the house and as far as possible from our closed bedroom door. I leaned against the cool wall, feeling drafts of the approaching winter sneaking in from beneath the door.

"Where are you now?"

"In the den."

"And your husband is asleep, right down the hall."

"I'm being really quiet."

"You're being really *crazy*."

"But you like it that way," I smirked coquettishly. I slid my hand inside my panties. Again.

"Yep. I do."

Neither of us spoke, just did our thing, breathing deeply in a strange and exhilarating and quiet desperation. We both came hard and quick.

"I'll talk to you tomorrow?"

"Yup. Goodnight."

"G'night."

Chapter 7

December was chilly, inside and out. Shrinking daylight meant elongated nighttide and more time for my head and heart to escape into the darkness and quiet. Sam seemed to be mostly uninterested in me, in anything but the extreme stresses of his work. Alex was still on tour, and I was still bored. We texted or Skyped almost every night after he'd settled into his bunk, my chronic insomnia exacerbated by our late night *Truthy Tit-for-Tat*. I loved the singular, intense attention from him, but I knew the tour was almost finished. Talia and Amber would be home before the holidays.

"It has to end sometime," he texted late one night, "but not yet."

Sam and I seemed to be snapping at each other all the time, over anything. We were each preoccupied in our own engrossments. It was difficult to get through a day without one of us griping at the other for not doing something mundane—remembering to get milk at the grocery store or leaving a wet towel on the bed. There was an unabating tension between us, like a cord that was slowly winding tighter and tighter each day.

I was just getting into my car after a late-afternoon walk when Alex called.

"What are you doing?" he slurred.

"I just finished five miles. How do you always know when I'm hot and sweaty?"

"And salty. And sweet. And *creamy*." His voice dripped with dalliance and whiskey.

"Like *butter*?"

"I *like* butter."

I burst with a quick, loud guffaw.

"*So-o-o*," he teased, "what's up, Buttercup?"

Buttercup. Ha!

"Not much. I painted for a while today, came to walk it off. How are you? *Where* are you?"

"Good. Sick. At the venue."

He was somewhere in northern California. It was still early afternoon there, and he was waiting at the bar for load-in to finish and soundcheck to start. His voice was gravelly and congested. He'd been saying for days that he was getting sick, and I could hear the strain of a cold. He started singing the chorus to "White Wedding", playing tinnily from his background, and we both laughed at the ridiculous interruption.

"My voice sounds fucking awesome," he drawled sarcastically. "I'm trying to hang on until I get home."

"How was your show last night?"

"Good! Great, actually! The crowds are getting bigger at each show. But I sound and feel like hell. My middle register is shot. I can hit high and low notes, but the whole mid-range is fucked."

"I'm sorry, babycakes. I'm sure it was still great."

I heard commotion and yelling in the background, then raucous laughter.

"Listen," he continued, "you know I'm going home in a couple of days."

"Yep."

"So we probably won't be in much contact for a while. It'll likely be after the first of the year before I can call you."

My heart sank a little. "Okay, well, I'll miss you?" I didn't really know what to say that wouldn't sound outright sappy and stupid.

"I'll miss our chats, too, *Buttercup*."

I smiled and blushed in the front seat of my car. "Have a great holiday. I'll be painting. Enjoy your time with the family, and check in when you can."

"Will do! Happy holidays, Tierney. I'll talk to you when I talk to you."

I was elated that he'd said he'd miss me, but I knew the crestfall would be coming soon enough.

I didn't expect to miss him so immensely, so soon. It had become natural and commonplace to be in his loop, and I was unsettled when the discourse stopped suddenly. I still woke that night at three in the morning, still went to cocoon myself in the den, but the closest I could get to Alex was his voice on my iPod.

I loved my time with him, *hated* it when it was unavailable, but was thankful to have it at all.

Alex Wheeler had tapped into some long-neglected feelings that I hadn't ever expected to see the light of day again. He made it okay for me to be my basest self and not feel judged for it. He welcomed and celebrated whatever truths about myself I was willing to share. I didn't want to add Alex to the list of regrettable missed chances in my life.

I have one shot at this, and I'd better enjoy it while I can.

I knew he missed his family, and he'd been working hard for weeks. He deserved the break. I still wanted a little bit of his time, though, just to know I mattered. I hoped he would call once more before going home, but he didn't. I hadn't honestly expected him to. His agenda for the last few days of the tour didn't include me.

———————————

After the tour, Paul Sommers posted on his own Facebook wall, asking his friends and fans to give Seth Wiezel's music a shot. Seth was a young singer/songwriter from San Antonio. Paul had produced Seth's first EP, *Outlier*, a couple of years earlier. He was back home in Austin, working with Seth on a new LP, due after the first of the year.

Of course I would listen to it. I was surprised to *love* it as much as I did.

Seth Wiezel's music was nothing like Junkture's. That rock and blues vibe of the band I loved was nowhere to be found in Seth's indie folk sound, regardless of Paulie's influence. He had this booming tenor that could sound so sweet and then turn gritty and sarcastic. There was always something morose hiding beneath his deceptively dulcet tones.

Some passing comment from me on a status update of his turned into multiple hours-long chats.

He was so young—just twenty—but also smart and funny and unbearably wise. He was an old soul hidden beneath a mop of unruly curls and a musician's scraggly beard. His influences were Charles Bukowski and Tom Waits, but he was really a geek at heart. I would often catch him online in the mornings. I would be drinking my first cup of coffee for the day, giving myself a few more minutes before waking my men for work and school. Seth would still be up from the previous night's working and cavorting through his youth. Sometimes we would discuss the intricate connections between music and philosophy and physics. Sometimes we would talk about the bartender he'd gone home with for a while the night before.

Tierney   So how different is the persona of Seth Wiezel from the actual guy?   Alex Wheeler and I had a conversation about this a few weeks ago, about the differences between his onstage personality and *him*. We talked about the role of ego, in a Freudian sense, and how much that pushed him onto the stage.

Seth   Oh, yeah, there's a lot of ego—there has to be—but it doesn't have to be self-involved. I know Alex very well. He acts the same on stage as he does off. We're both very honest, but it's a calculated honesty. Fans think they know you because of how you portray yourself, but it's a false sense of intimacy. On a certain level, you *have* to share yourself. You *have* to be vulnerable. Vulnerability is beautiful—the best works of art are vulnerable and easy to empathize with.

Seth   Seth and Seth Wiezel are two different people, really. They talk about different things. But they share a *personality*, you know? I mean, I have to be open, but I'm not going to share *secrets* with you.

But you do share secrets, don't you?
I knew all kinds of things about Seth that weren't for public consumption. I was both a fan and a friend on Facebook, but our long conversations had opened the door to a real-world friendship for both of us. I'd told him a bit about my history and talked in an unexpectedly frank way about my weight loss and my painting. Seth had told me about his girlfriend of nearly four years and how their often volatile relationship was beginning to unravel.

Tierney   Do you ever find it difficult to leave behind one or both of those, to compartmentalize those persona?

Seth   Yes, very. I don't know what to do sometimes. I get labeled by my peer group sometimes as an egotist, and it's easy to do that. I mean, for fuck's sake, my band name is *my* name, you know?

Seth	But people don't understand. I don't *want* it to be about *me*. It just so happens that my *face* is my *brand*, and it's my brand because I have no other choice. It kind of sucks sometimes.
Tierney	That's funny. Alex said almost the exact opposite.
Seth	Yeah? What did he have to say?
Tierney	He prefers to be the egotist in the room, to have it be about him, musically, and the difficulty of pulling yourself back from dominating it all.
Seth	You know how to make a lead singer better? Step in front of him.
Tierney	Ha!
Seth	It's about ego on stage, it is. But at the same time, we're all there for one thing: to put on a good show. I think Alex and myself are just naturally leaders. We want to lead the band. I don't think it has anything to do about how good you look, but more of what *your* vision is.
Tierney	So what about Paul? He's not the singer, but he's historically been a prominent face of Junkture, whereas Max and Charlie have always been more subdued with fan interactions and the like.
Seth	Paulie's great. I love working with him. He has all of this experience and knowledge, but it's weird because my parents are huge Junkture fans. My dad always talked about what a great guitarist Paul Sommers is. I was raised to basically *worship* this guy.
Seth	But now we're kind of in the same place in our career. I'm relatively new and building this career, but Paul and Junkture are basically rebuilding theirs. The

biggest lesson from Paul is that this is a hard industry. There are all these guys in all these bands. They think they're so talented, and they wonder why they're not selling out every venue they play. They wait for the silver platter to come. I've learned through Paul that there *is* no silver platter. The people who are successful are successful not because of their talent; talent is the icing on the cake.

Seth called me a few days later, to tell me that he would be coming to Atlanta. His manager was based here, and it was time to do some prep work for the new record. He was opening for a modern bluegrass duo for six shows, wrapping up the mini-tour at Smith's Olde Bar.

"I'll bake you a cake or something," I joked.

"Funfetti! That's my favorite!"

"That's my boys' favorite, too. You're just a big kid, aren't you?"

"Yes! A big, overgrown, hairy boy."

I got to Smith's an hour before the show was scheduled to start, two dozen Funfetti cupcakes in a box. I wandered into the Atlanta Room, small tables dotted around the tiny stage. A mop of unruly curls and a devilish grin greeted me from across the room.

"I'd know that purple-on-blonde anywhere," Seth said, hugging me.

I handed the big, white box to him ceremoniously. "These are for you."

"Oh my god! You have no idea how badly I need these!" he said, peeling the paper away from a cupcake. "I'm so hungover. I drove in from Greenville at four this morning. I was probably too drunk to be driving."

He shoved half the cupcake into his mouth, fluffy, white icing smearing across his fingers. "You want one?" he mumbled around the baked sugar.

I shook my head and giggled. "I don't eat that crap anymore. I may be a fat girl still, but there's less of me than there was two months ago."

Seth stepped around a corner into the small room backstage and dropped the box onto a low table. He motioned for me to walk toward the main bar. He led me to a booth in a corner, and we slid across the dark, wooden benches on our respective sides.

The waitress came almost immediately. She was beautiful, with olive skin and long, dark hair. A tiny silver ring was looped through her full lower lip.

"Screwdriver," I said, "with Stoli."

"I'll take a Jameson. Neat."

She smiled and winked at Seth as she turned to get our drinks.

"*Goddamn!* She's *hot*! I have a *thing* for waitresses," he admitted, blushing down at his fidgety hands.

"I take it they don't know you're barely twenty?" I said.

He shook his head and grinned sheepishly. "Nope. That's just between you and me tonight."

"How's your tour been? How were the shows?"

"Shows were fine." Seth leaned back against the high back of the booth. "My girlfriend's pissed at me, though."

The waitress was back quickly with our order. We clinked glasses and took the first sips.

"It's Megan, right?" He nodded. "Why's she mad?"

"I've been gone two weeks. Big deal. Really, it's not that long, but I know she misses me. I miss her, too. But she's frustrated with me, because all we talk about when I call every day is the same thing. Every day is different, but it's within the same mold while I'm on the road. Drive, set up, perform, mingle, tear down, get paid, drive. Every day. And so, like, sharing my experiences gets old."

"Does it ever make you want to *not* do it?"

"Not tour? No way! I *love* touring. My father always taught me that it's all about the journey, never about the destination. The only destination is death."

I was struck, profoundly, by the sentiment of that. So much of my own life had been about getting somewhere and doing something—a job, a house, the kids. Accomplishment was a huge motivator for Sam, but it had never really been that important to me, at least not in the same sense it was for most people. I'd dropped out of college, because it just wasn't as important to me as living the rest of my life, whatever that may have been. I'd enjoyed the jobs I'd had before the boys were born, but not enough to make them a higher priority than raising my children.

My boys were maybe the one exception to my slacker attitude toward life goals. Sam and I had set the goal to get pregnant, which turned out to be much more difficult than we'd ever imagined, thanks to my PCOS. It had taken two and a half years to get pregnant with Tripp, including eighteen months of shots and pills and sometimes painful procedures. All the cycles of the *Pregnant-Not-Pregnant?* game had been emotionally and physically exhausting, and I was still sometimes surprised that Sam hadn't abandoned me when the hormones were making me crazy.

But once Tripp, and later Ian, were born, I'd settled quickly into the adventure of motherhood. I *loved* being a mom. I thrived on fulfilling the implied contractual role of Mom for my children, even with the sleep deprivation and the boredom of days when the only human I contacted for hours at a time couldn't even speak or lift his own head. Even when it seemed like the same thing, day after day, there was always the joy of what new thing my baby had learned or how he'd smiled at me in a wholly new way. And they were incomparably beautiful; I couldn't get past how Sam and I had made such *beautiful* little creatures from our love.

"Are your parents supportive of this?" I asked. "Do they get why you need to do this? I mean, as a mom, it seems like it would be incredibly difficult to watch your child take on a career that's so hard, especially when you're so young. I can't imagine watching your child struggle to do something they love so much and knowing damn well that there are so many things working against them."

Seth lifted his glass to his lips and swirled the whiskey in his mouth for a moment. "My parents are incredibly supportive of me. And not just to be supportive, you know? They actually *believe* in me, which is nice. They believe in me more than I believe in myself."

"And do you believe in you? Do you have days when you think, 'Fuck it, I'm done!' and think you'll just *stop*?"

"I think that *every* day! It's so scary to follow your dream, to dive head first into the water."

"So is there a component of masochism to this job?"

Seth sat up quickly, leaning across the table toward me. He turned animated when he spoke. "Definitely! I want to be the big man on campus, so I have to kick my own ass every day. I have to kick others' asses, too. You have to be aggressive. You have to *take* what you want.

"You know, all guys in bands, we're just a bunch of fucking dorks. Don't *ever* confuse someone in a band as cool."

So I've noticed.

"I mean," he continued, "this is what happens.... You get picked on in school for being fat, so you either start a software company or a band. We're all just fucking nerds trying to prove that our dicks are huge."

"Were you a band geek?" I laughed. I could *see* Seth, sitting in his plastic school chair in a non-descript band room. I'd known dozens of him when I was young.

"Of course! Until high school. I did jazz band. First chair percussion. And I was a fat kid, too, which didn't help. But then I got interested in girls and just lost the weight one summer. But I still think like that fat kid sometimes."

It was hard to imagine, looking at him. He was a little taller than I, normal build. He didn't have the look of someone who used to be fat and lost a bunch of weight. Sometimes it lingers in their face and skin, like the fat kid is still trying to peek out.

"I don't know if I'll ever stop thinking like a fat girl, honestly. It's so engrained in what I do. Like, I don't like to eat in front of people I don't know, because I'm afraid that they're judging me for my food choices."

"You always order salads, don't you?"

"Of course!" I chuckled. "The difference is that now I don't go home and eat a pint of ice cream after dinner. I just try not to eat it at all. I know too much sugar, especially ice cream, will trigger a binge."

"So how much weight have you lost?" he asked, settling back against the dark, wooden back of the secluded booth.

"Thirty pounds."

"Wow. That's impressive."

I shrugged. "It's just what I have to do. I'm still big. I'm still too curvy and just *big* in everything I am and do. That will never change, though, no matter how much weight I lose. I was always Amazonian, but that never stopped me from being loud and bawdy and flirty. Whether because of or in spite of the sexual abuse, I could get guys to pay attention. But Sam and I have been together now for as long as you've been alive, and I haven't been able to see myself as a sexually attractive thing in a very long time."

Not until Alex.

Seth glanced at the time on his phone. He grabbed his glass and turned it up, finishing his whiskey in one, large gulp.

"Come on, Wonder Woman," he said, standing and stretching against his hungover muscles. "I've got a show to do."

I went on about my days, my time, and keeping the family in order. It was the same shit every day, though now I had the distraction of painting while the house was empty. Each morning, I would sidle downstairs with an insulated tumbler of coffee and spend a few minutes looking over what I'd done the day before. So far it was all still lifes or benign memories from old photographs that I pinned to the wall behind my easel.   I was still feeling restless, and *something* was trying to get my attention.

Looking through pictures for new inspiration, I found a crisp photograph that had been given to me by a mom friend at the end of the summer. It was a candid of me and Tripp and one of his friends, taken at the boys' last swim meet of the summer season. Susan had caught us unaware while I was trying to direct the boys to their next event. Judging by the tank top I was wearing and the difficult expression on my face, I remembered that I'd gone that day for the second epidural injection into my back. I was trying my best not to show the exertion of dragging the pain and discomfort with me everywhere.

I was also *fat*.

Not just heavy or big, but engorged to the point that my face was almost lost in the excess. I looked like a girl who'd put on a fat suit for a movie or social experiment to prove the point that obese people are generally miserable.   I've never been especially photogenic, and this was a horribly unflattering picture, but I looked bloated and unhappy and just *fat*.

I wanted to obliterate that image from my mind.

And I was thirty pounds away from that girl. Thirty pounds sounded like a lot, but from the starting point of a size 24, I was barely squeezing myself into a size 20. Some days, though, I felt just a little pretty and confident.

I grabbed my phone and went into the bathroom. I stripped off my pajamas and looked at my body in the full-length mirror. I still looked huge, but I could see the slightly smaller hips and thighs and belly. I could see flaws everywhere: the hips too round, the thighs too thick, though muscular. My shoulders were broad, athletic, and not as delicate as I would have liked. My breasts were okay, heavy but nicely rounded with pale pink aureola and nipples that were almost smooth until touched. I touched them, rubbed them gently then more fiercely. They were suddenly like strawberry gum drops, and I knew exactly which shades to mix to get the desired effect. I held the phone at just the right angle and clicked quick pictures of my body from subtly different angles.

I loaded the pictures onto my laptop and looked at each one, examining the details. How fat did my neck or face or arms look? Did my full breasts seem even and luscious, or just heavy and awkward? I finally chose the one that had the best position and most flattering angles. I sent the image to the printer and took it downstairs.

I tacked the paper to the wall, over an old photograph of my first cat. I didn't start with a gesture drawing; I wanted there to be as few renditions of this image as possible.

But I did start to paint. I hastily mixed paints and quickly drew the outline of my body.

You're fatter than that, Tierney.

I ignored my distorted conceit and reminded my body conscience to be genuine and guileless, to look at the transforming shape with accuracy. I calmed my agitations and let my hand relay the form accurately, without unnecessary emotional distortion. This was only for me, no one else, and I needed to see whether I could find realistic beauty in my body.

In general, it was a nice shape. The curves were well-proportioned—if too big and too sharp for my taste—and I carried the weight evenly across arms and hips and thighs and belly. My Scots-Irish skin was pale but not ashy, with my arms and chest slightly darker than the rest with the lingering tell-tale of too much summer sun. Cellulite dimples and faded, silvery stretch marks were hard to ignore, but I tried not to exaggerate their prominence.

I worked on this piece for days, going back to it each morning as soon as the school bus rambled away with my children safely on board.

At night, I would chat with friends on Facebook or catch up on television shows that were accumulating on the DVR. Occasionally, Sam would join me on the couch to watch something I'd been saving, knowing it was something he would want to watch. Sometimes it seemed to be the only quality time we could manage for each other.

Most nights, though, I was on my own, caught up in my thoughts and missing Alex.

When my dad asked me what I wanted for Christmas, I immediately told him I wanted a gym membership. The walking felt good, but I wanted to push my body a little more, to start to mold it into the shape and size it could naturally be. Having spent so much time looking at my body, I could readily see the easy, natural proportions. I could imagine how the curves would fall and angle around my extra-large, 5'11 frame. I was starting to believe that I could be beautiful as a *fit* girl instead of a *fat* girl.

I found a gym close to the house, one that also had childcare available. There was a special for the membership and five sessions with a trainer. I planned to do the five sessions and get the trainer to write up a workout plan for me, to help motivate me to begin the work by myself. Dad thought it was a good idea and readily agreed.

I left the trainer assignment up to the gym manager. A few days after enrolling, I got a call from Devin to schedule our first half-hour together. When we met face-to-face a few days later, I was surprised at how young he was—twenty-two. He was from California but now living in Atlanta. He had played baseball in college. A pitcher. He was young and built and hot, with bulging muscles and an adorable smile. It was a little daunting, but I figured I could do anything five times.

When I started training with Devin, I was off and running toward a smaller ass, but there was still so damn much work to do. He was sweet and supportive. When I complained that I didn't like doing something, didn't think I could find the stamina to continue, he smiled sweetly and told me to do it anyway. I was paying him to tell me to shut the fuck up and work, and it was exactly what I needed. After our five sessions were over, he suggested continuing the training for another six months, twice a week.

"It's not cheap," I told Sam, "but I like the accountability. It makes me show up and have something to strive for."

"I know," he said a little harshly, "you want to be young and thin."

Young and thin? Where did that come from?

I was thirty-eight and totally okay with that. When I turned thirty, all these people had called and emailed to wish me happy birthday and to goad me into mourning the loss of my youth. I didn't understand it.

But I'd spent my teens and twenties caring what other people thought of me. I'd tried—sometimes hard and sometimes half-hearted—to fulfill the expectations of my parents and my friends and my husband. I went to college even when I really didn't want to. I worked jobs that were mostly enjoyable but not remotely fulfilling. I'd added fitted, tailored splashes of color into my dolorous, frumpy wardrobe.

Turning thirty meant I didn't even have to *pretend* to give a shit what other people thought anymore.

"I don't want to be young and thin," I replied, irritated. "I want to be thirty-eight and *healthy*."

I was beginning to feel stronger and healthier than I'd felt in years, and I wasn't ready to stop.

Chapter 8

Alex messaged me unexpectedly, on Facebook.

Alex Wheeler
December 16th 11:37 PM

I've decided. You're like Julia Stiles, DD!

Tierney Cavanaugh Johnson
December 17th 8:23 AM

What the fuck are you talking about?

Like a bolt from the blue, my phone rang that afternoon.

"*Dexter* is my favorite fucking show. I love it. There's this character, Lumen, played by Julia Stiles," Alex ambled excitedly. "You're so much like her, your mannerisms and your voice. Except with those beautiful double Ds. It just hit me. "

"I had no idea what the hell you were talking about," I laughed. "How are you?"

"I'm good. Glad to be home."

"What else is going on?"

"Nothing. At the mall. Thought I'd give you a call."

"Why are you at the mall?" I had a hard time picturing the rock star cruising the food court like a mall rat.

"Christmas shopping. How are things with you and Sam?"

"They're... *things*."

"You okay?"

"Yeah. Painting. I just finished a nude self-portrait."

Alex chuckled throatily. "Are you using a mirror to look at yourself while you paint?"

Hm. "No, I took some pictures and hung one up by my easel."

"You have naked pictures of yourself, and you didn't share?"

"*Fuck no!* No one wants to see that, I promise!"

"Awww, Buttercup! Not true! *I* want to see that."

"It will be a cold day in Hell before I send *anyone* full body shots of *this*."

"It is almost winter...."

We talked about the holidays, about his being sick after being on the road for so long. He'd kept singing through sinus problems and a sore throat, and he'd lacerated a vocal cord, screwing up his mid-range completely. We talked about nothing, mostly, but it was good just to hear his voice.

"I'm about to lose you in the mall," he said. "So I'll go, but I'll check in soon."

He'd said it would be after the first of the year before I heard from him, but here he was, and he was about to be gone again. I *hated* that it was so quick. I was *thrilled* I'd heard from him at all. It was five minutes of giddy surprise.

"Merry Christmas, Mr. Wheeler!"

"Merry Christmas to you, Tierney. Later."

Alex Wheeler
Dec 17th 1:54 PM

Thanks for calling. I've missed you very much. And I didn't even say one inappropriate thing. ;)

Here's a little tongue for ya, buttercup!
Radio silent

Sam and I were still in the same pattern of pleasantly passing each other in the hall, making sure everything was good with the kids and the house. It was night after night of sitting quietly close to one another, discussing our logistics across a huge chasm.

I was screaming in my head, constantly. I was tired of being ignored. We hadn't had sex in weeks, and I started to think it would just never happen again.

Late that night, Sam was working at his computer, beer in hand, and I came up behind him. I wrapped my arms around his chest and kissed his neck.

"You wanna take me to bed?" I offered.

"Not right now."

It was late, close to midnight. I would have to go to sleep soon, to get up and function the next day. He would go to sleep when he felt like it, get up when he felt like, and work until it all started again.

I was frustrated at being rejected again. I pulled away suddenly, stiffening in my anger.

"You have a box of toys!" he snapped. "Go get it out!"

Now, I was *livid*.

It was insulting. Somehow, somewhere along our way, I'd become unimportant to him. My sexual and emotional needs had been dismissed. I was getting affection and physical contact from the children. I'd been getting intimacy from Alex, though it was never the same as with Sam; they were two very different men, and I responded very differently to each of them. I was learning, slowly, not to fill that void with food, which sometimes left me huffy and confused when I couldn't find a way to make myself feel better. This was one of those nights, when I didn't have Sam or Alex or ice cream to soothe me.

"Go drink your fucking beer and ignore me!" I hissed, turning away from him. "That shouldn't be too hard—it's what you do best!"

"What the fuck are you talking about? I talk to you every day!"

"Yeah, you can say *hi* and ask about the kids, but when was the last time you *fucked* me? When was the last time you got away from that goddamn computer and work and paid some attention to me?"

"You don't mind that my work pays for your trainer or your trips to see bands or nights out drinking with strangers! You fall asleep in front of the television almost every night! You tell me you're sore from the gym or that your back hurts or that the steroids were causing this super long period. It's not always my fault!"

I'd never blamed him entirely. I'd spent months in horrible pain, then had weeks of lingering girlie issues because of the steroid injections, and there would always be fatigue late in the evening when he finally got around to paying attention to me. My day started by seven each morning and didn't end until the boys were in bed after eight that night. If Sam was home, he was still working and couldn't shift his energies to me until after ten or eleven, when I was ready to crash for the night.

"I *know* how fucked up my body has been," I said, trying to reign in my anger. "I *know* how often that's kept me from being naked with you—"

"*Exactly.* Those reasons aren't your fault. Sometimes there are just unpreventable circumstances that you totally discount when you blame it all on my drinking. I convinced myself for a while that I was to blame for our dwindled sex life, but I'm over it. *Lots* of opportunities have been abandoned for reasons beyond my control. Not the least of which is that you can be a complete *bitch* when you want to be. How am I supposed to get it up with you *bitching* at me about it?"

"That's *bullshit*! Half the time you're too *drunk* to fuck me anyway!"

Sam looked bewildered. "That's not true. I may be drinking, but *that*'s not why I don't want to be intimate with you. That has almost no impact on our relationship, Tierney."

The truth was, I didn't like to be with Sam when he'd been drinking. The drinking seemed compulsive, and then his demeanor would often change, even subtly. I'd been so irritated about it for so long that I would clinch up about the time he hit his third beer, which could make me irritable and contentious. It was much easier to disengage, to step out of it and stay away from him, than to watch what happened.

It was an ugly, vicious cycle that we couldn't seem to break. And it was only made worse by the fact that I'd been getting much-needed intimate reinforcement from Alex.

"I can remember *plenty* of times when drinking enhanced our sex life," he continued. "But *now*, sex with you is often a fruitless effort. I don't feel *connected* to you. I feel like a pity fuck, like you feel obliged to ignore my behavior to get my participation in getting you off. I certainly don't feel worshipped or adored—"

"If I forget to fluff your ego, I'm sorry! I have a hard enough time keeping my own self-esteem afloat most days!"

"I don't need you to stroke my ego!" Sam yelled. "I need to perceive basic *respect* as a man or even superficial desires and mechanical participation aren't the least bit exciting."

"*Fuck you!* I completely resent that! I have never been *anything* but willing and adventurous with you, whether or not you've *ever* fully explored that. But the kind of respect you're asking for demands reciprocity, Sam. I rarely feel supported in *any* endeavor I take on that's not first condoned by you. If it's not something that you whole-heartedly support, you're suspicious and contemptuous of it."

"Like what?" He seemed baffled.

"My painting is a prime example! If it doesn't outright include or concern you, it's unimportant to you. When I talk about painting again, there's a sense of utter *disdain* from you about it. I *have* to have a life outside of you and the boys. I *have* to remember what it's like to be Tierney and not just Sam's wife or the boys' mom. I was me long before I met you, and I lost sight of that for a very, very long time."

"Tierney," Sam sighed, "I don't *care* that you're painting again. I mean, I *do*. I'm *glad* you have a hobby. The only thing that concerns me is the hours you're holed up downstairs. I'm not part of it. I don't *know* what you're doing, and you don't share it."

"You ignore me when I try! I *try* to tell you what I'm doing, but you're so busy with work or beer that you don't pay attention. Honestly, I don't give a *shit* about what's going on with your investigations, but I *listen* to you when you talk about it. It's important to you. But all I get from you if I try to tell you about what I've painted is some non-committal, patronizing nod. And I started painting again, in part, just to pass the fucking time while you're working or drunk! I'm *tired* of sitting around and waiting for you to pay attention to *me*!

"I just want you *not* to drink one night and spend that time with *me*!" I exploded. "You can blame it on me, but I come almost every single day! Sometimes two or three times a day! You wouldn't fucking know! You're too goddamn *drunk* to fucking notice!

"And don't think the boys don't know! Tripp complains almost every day about the beer cans in the recycling when he gets up! Ian hears all of that coming from his big brother, and he watches for it. They *both* know you're drinking too much. They're *scared* of you when they see you drunk. You yell at them about everything!"

Tripp would comment to me about Daddy's drinking regularly. He was four years older than Ian and had seen it longer, but he was also one of those sensitive, intuitive kids that could just *read* a person or a situation. From the time he was three years old, he was one of the best judges of character I'd ever known. For weeks, he'd mentioned how abruptly irritable Daddy could be, especially when he'd been drinking beer. Tripp could feel how his father's personality was altered by the alcohol, and it made him tense. Ian didn't say anything, but I knew he was listening intently to his older brother's observations.

I wasn't so simplistic as to think everything disagreeable about Sam was because of his drinking, but I absolutely thought it exacerbated any tensions in the house. I'd openly said for years that I thought he drank too much, usually when he was drinking heavily and we were arguing. He would stop drinking for a while—from a couple of weeks to a few months—then start again one with or two singles each night. After a few nights, the singles would become tall boys, then a six-pack. He would add singles or tall boys *to* the six-pack, which would be about the time he would become most argumentative and difficult. I would be on constant eggshells with him, because I could never be sure what would inevitably set him off. We'd have huge fights, sometimes for several days, and he would drink as much as a twelve-pack for a few more nights, and then stop drinking again. It was a repetitive cycle that had begun long before the boys were born.

He took a deep, angry breath and exhaled his outrage at me. "I'm so fucking tired of you blaming everything wrong about me and us on my drinking! I know lots of people who drink more, regularly, and still function."

"*Really?*" I yelled incredulously. "I know *no one* who can drink a six pack or more, night after night, and not have any kind of backlash in their lives! *No one, Sam!* For fuck's sake, you got *arrested* for a DUI! You got drunk and fucking hit someone else! Do you remember that?" I was condescendingly sarcastic.

It had been almost seven years since it had happened, since I'd gotten the midnight call when he slurred to me that he was in jail. Seven years since I'd called Tessa and Ed in the middle of the night, sobbing that my husband had been arrested and didn't come home to give me the progesterone shot I needed to help protect my fledgling, jeopardized pregnancy.

"Of course I fucking remember! And it was overturned and thrown out of court!"

"On *appeal*," I reminded him. "They lost your fucking records and threw it out when you agreed to go to meetings and stay sober. How long after your last meeting did you start drinking again? I was *pregnant* and you were in *jail* and you still started drinking again!"

"You'll never let me forget this, will you?" Sam hissed. "You'll never forget, so I can never forget! You save this shit up until you're mad and start dragging it out again. You can't forgive *or* forget anything, ever, Tierney!"

He was right. So many times, I'd waited until we were already fighting to bring up other things that had been gnawing at me. Everything I couldn't muster the courage to discuss when we were both calm and sober would become an emotional grenade. I would lob every angry thought and memory at him, no matter how old or minute the issue might've been.

"Knowing how you hold onto everything," he said, "I think your perception of me is so eroded and tarnished by years of dirt. If I can't believe that my mistakes are ever truly being forgiven or forgotten, I can't see any way or reason to change that perception."

"I am *always* willing to forgive, Sam, as long as *you* are willing to ask for it! I can't find it in my heart to magically be okay with things when there's no contrition, and I don't think that's unreasonable. You've never even *apologized* to me for the DUI, for the cost of the insurance and the attorney. You've never once apologized to me for potentially putting my pregnancy at risk!"

"Ian is here! Your pregnancy went fine!"

"No thanks to you! Do you know what that was like? One in the morning, crying to Tessa on the phone, because—on top of everything else—you weren't there to give me the shot in the ass to make sure I didn't miscarry? Do you have *any* idea?"

He said nothing. He stood there with his stoic, steely eyes and said nothing.

"Stop drinking," I said quietly. "Stop drinking or I will take the fucking children, and I will *leave*."

I was exhausted and hoarse. I went to bed, by myself, and did my best to make it feel better before I fell asleep. Sam slept on the couch.

———————————

Sam didn't see the need to ever apologize; he didn't require absolution to get over an issue, even if he was wrong. We'd argued for years that he couldn't apologize without a caveat. He would rather ignore a problem and wait to forget about it than to confront it head-on. I'd spent years detouring around our problems, around myself, and I was read to bulldoze my way forward, no matter the cost.

Even if he *did* ask for forgiveness, was I even capable of finding peace and really letting go of whatever had happened?

I remember all the things people do that make me unhappy. Every little slight, every perceived betrayal, every stab in the back— *it's all here, all the time*, like a laundry list of infractions. Sam had accused me of saving them up and dragging them into the light when it was time to fight. He was totally insane and totally right at the same time. I didn't intentionally keep this ever-growing list of grievances in reserve, waiting for just the right moment to spring them on him. But there was definitely a running tally of issues that had gone unresolved. Until they were addressed or confronted, I could never let them go, almost pathologically.

Sometimes the *not-forgetting* could be detrimental, whether to me or to my relationships, especially with Sam. I didn't know *how* to go about dealing with them. When is the appropriate time to tell someone, "Hey, do you remember that time you were a total ass to me? And you never apologized or told me why? Well, that's still bugging the shit out of me—can we talk about that during the next commercial break?"

I wasn't always cognizant of how these lingering things were bothering me. I didn't always realize that I was worked up about something *until* I was worked up about something else. And it could feel inappropriately good to lash out, to dole out that sucker punch, especially if I was defensive and in danger of losing an argument. It could feel incomparably satisfying to twist my perceptions and misconceptions of a memory to satisfy my ulterior emotional motive.

I was haunted by memories of other people's transgressions, but my own errors and missteps also plagued me like ghosts, rattling the chains that bound me to them. Sam, though, didn't even realize there'd ever been a ghost to give up, so he'd never battled to look at us through its vaporous remnants.

We were in an ugly stalemate. I wasn't seeing making it better as an option. I felt I would have to give up a lot, to sacrifice and compromise and have those regrets I so desperately didn't want to have, including giving up Alex. I was pretty sure it would be a one-way give. I was afraid my marriage was irreparable, that we'd grown so far apart that our best intentions would be for naught.

I don't remember if I emailed asking him to call, or if he just knew, but Alex phoned the next afternoon. He was driving and listening intently to everything I needed to say.

"I don't know what to do. He was such a goddamn dick. It was totally unexpected."

"This is not okay, Tierney. You have to get him into counseling. With you. He has to stop drinking, or you have to take those boys and get out of there. This isn't healthy for you or for them."

"I know it's not. I don't know how to do this on my own, Alex. I don't know what I want. I love him, but I can't take this being ignored and being rejected. I'm so fucking tired of it."

I was sitting on the edge of Ian's bed, my freshly-pedicured toes curled over the thick wooden frame, while the boys played video games on the other side of the house. I sat in the darkened room, peering through the slatted blinds toward the street, watching for Sam's car, expecting him home from work at any moment. Night had completely fallen, and it was raining lightly, blurring the edges of the street lights and porch lights and neighbors' Christmas lights.

"You sound like you're done," Alex said gently.

"How did you know?" I asked contemplatively. "When it was over with Annabelle? How did you know you were finished?"

He was silent for a moment. I could hear the hum of his music in the background. "I just *did*. It was just *time*. And it sucked. I still love her. I dream about her all the time."

"But you didn't have children in the middle of that. I know the day will come when they will get their hearts broken; I just never thought it would be me doing it."

Sam's car turned onto the street, toward the house. He slowed and pulled into the driveway, the beam of his headlights illuminating the cold, winter mist.

"He's home. I have to go."

"Okay. Let me know how you are. It'll be okay, Tierney. You'll make the right decision."

"Thanks for the support. Really. It means a lot."

"Any time. Talk to you later."

I clicked **END** and put my phone in my pocket. I walked into the kitchen as Sam did. Beer in hand.

For the most part, we ignored each other.

Chapter 9

We decided to stay in Atlanta for Christmas Eve, to drive to Birmingham to see the family on Christmas Day. Sam had to work the week after, so the boys and I would be staying with family until New Year's Eve. Man or Astro-man? were scheduled to play at Bottletree Cafe, and we'd gone to high school with a couple of the guys from the band. We hadn't seen them live in years. Sam planned to drive over that night and ring in the New Year with me.

Sam and I were barely speaking. The fight had been truthful and difficult. We were both honest in ways we hadn't been for a very long time, but it didn't rectify anything. We generally found it easy to talk religion and politics and children, but it was almost impossible for either of us to calmly broach the topic of *Us*.

We knew we'd be apart for several days. We were both hurting, badly. I needed him, and he responded. We made love for the first time in a long while on Christmas Eve. Afterward, he fell asleep, and I just couldn't make my brain stop churning.

It was profoundly saddening, and I finally cried.

I wanted to talk it all through with Alex and couldn't, which made me cry more. I was trying very hard to keep all of that separate. I didn't want to fall back on him in a way that made me spin out emotionally. I knew how easy it would be for me to catch myself in my own, luscious trap. When I felt myself needing him, I would remind myself that he was a stubborn, impulsive ass, which sometimes helped. I tried to put him in a little box and keep him away from everything else. If compartmentalizing worked so well for him, I could give it a shot.

Christmas Day was kind of sad. We woke early with the boys and opened presents. I made breakfast and threw some clothes into a bag for us, tearing them away from their freshly-unwrapped toys and loading them into the car for the three-hour drive.

We did our best not to let the children or the families feel the tension. We were affectionate, if quiet. The weather forecast for Birmingham and Atlanta was calling for Christmas snow, which I'd never seen in my entire life. I was worried about Sam driving in that and urged him to go back to Atlanta a day early. The boys and I stayed at my mom's house.

It was weird for me to be there. The last time I'd been there was the week before Thanksgiving, when everything with Alex had blossomed into something darker and deeper than I'd ever imagined. It was hard as hell, being in that bed, in that place where my world had expanded so unexpectedly. And all of the proof of it was gone, which was safer but made me sad.

Boxing Day was cold and snowy, and the roads were closed. I was going stir-crazy. There was only so much Nerf gun and RC helicopter I could take.

Some random tweet from Alex popped up on my phone, bitching about the Cowboys game. I laughed and replied to his tweet.

Alex Wheeler @Junkture:
@TierneyCavJ merry christmas tierney

I missed him badly.

The boys and I made the rounds from one family household to another, visiting friends and relatives. My grandmothers would recount the list of their own ailments and doctor's visits, then tell me about the afflictions of distant cousins and friends of friends. It was a blur of driving and smiling and nodding, of kindly refusing offers of leftover holiday desserts.

We talked to Sam every day, though briefly.

My mom and stepdad left town for their annual post-Christmas beach trip. The boys and I settled at my dad's house for a few days.

Jules was coming into town to see her own family but had promised my dad that she would come to see him, too. When Jules and I became roommates, she was instantly welcomed by my parents, especially my dad. On long weekends and breaks, we would congregate in my dad's kitchen—me, Jules, Frankie, sometimes Tessa or India and Sam—laughing and talking. Dad had been a middle school math teacher for a while and truly enjoyed talking to young adults. We were a constant source of amusement and irritation for him, for years, and he loved it.

Jules and Frankie and I hatched a plan to have a slumber party in my dad's den, upstairs away from the children. Now that we were fully grown, we wouldn't have to hide the Jack Daniels.

"Remind me to go by the liquor store," I said over breakfast.

"I have some stuff here," Dad replied. "There's probably some wine. I know there's tequila."

"Jack and Diet Coke. We're grown-ups now."

"Our dad is addicted to alcohol," Tripp said suddenly around a mouthful of sugary cereal. "Every night when I go to bed, the recycling bin is empty. The next morning, it's *overflowing* with empty beer cans. Daddy's an alcoholic."

"Yeah," Ian chimed in, "our dad is *addicted*."

I was embarrassed and afraid of what was coming, but Dad didn't say anything. We ran some errands with Grandpa and stopped for lunch with the boys, somewhere they could play at an indoor playground, out of the biting December wind. We watched them through a glass wall overlooking the play area, talking about the holidays and the kids and everything else.

"Look," I said, watching my sons bound across the padded floor, "I know what the boys said earlier about Sam. They're not wrong. There are problems."

"I wasn't going to ask," Dad replied gently. "Are you okay?"

I nodded, not meeting his gaze. "Yeah, I'm fine."

"I know there are a lot of reasons people do things, and I know sometimes our kids don't see it right. I just want you and the boys—and Sam—to be okay. I'm here if you need to talk."

I shook my head and smiled. "I don't want to talk about it, but thank you."

We stopped at the liquor store on the way back to his house.

Frankie and Jules came rolling into the driveway that night, just moments behind each other. I opened the front door and bounded down the walkway as soon as I saw their headlights crisscross the front of the house.

"*Girlies!*" I squealed.

We hugged and giggled, the three of us talking fast and loud and chattering over each other animatedly.

"Well, let them come in out of the cold," my dad said from over my shoulder.

"Dad!" Jules and Frankie hugged my dad, everyone saying how good it was to see everyone else.

It was after dark and almost time for the boys to go to bed. We sat in the kitchen with them, my friends talking to my sons about school and video games and what books they were reading. Their children were about the same ages as mine, and they knew exactly how to interact with my kids. The boys loved the attention but were tired and asked to go to bed.

We talked with my dad for a while, who asked lots of questions about what my friends were doing these days, how their kids were, how their lives were. We spent a while with him in the kitchen, when I finally said, "I need a drink!"

Like so many nights of my youth, I was hanging out in my dad's kitchen with my friends. It was the first time I could remember us drinking with my dad right there—at least with him *knowing* we were drinking. He finally excused himself, and we shuffled up the back stairs to the den.

"Tierney, you look fantastic, by the way," Jules smiled in her strong, Southern twang. "What are you doing?"

"Walking. A lot. Careful about what I eat." I shrugged.

"Well, whatever it is, it's paying off. What does Sam think?"

I settled onto the small loveseat, and Jules and Frankie stretched out from either end of the sofa, their legs leaning against the other. The scratchy, striped couches were the first furniture my dad had bought after my parents' divorce. They were worn and dingy, the sagging cushions showing their twenty-five years.

"Oh, Sam...," I sighed. "I don't know *what* he thinks." I took a sip of my drink and set the faded souvenir cup on the floor next to me.

"Okay, spill it," Frankie said. "You've been quiet about it the last of couple times I've talked to you. What's going on?"

I started to talk, explaining about the fight we'd been having for days. I told them how we'd become so distant, how we hardly ever had sex anymore, how Sam seemed to all but ignore me.

"I'm just so *tired* of being what he expects me to be, you know? Mother and wife, always. When the fuck did he stop seeing Tierney?"

"How could he *not* see Tierney?" Jules asked. "You are a beautiful, smart, funny woman who *sparkles*. How could any man not see you?"

"You're sweet, Julesy, but I don't sparkle. I barely glow most days. You know, I used to be this *presence* in my world. I didn't have to be the center of attention, but people at least knew I was there. Now, I don't think Sam knows I exist half the time."

"Oh, Jay's the same way," Frankie interjected. "I finally graduated, while working full time and raising two girls. *Four-point-oh* GPA. Did he even *congratulate* me? Nope. He took us to dinner and reminded me we needed milk and trash bags when he dropped me at the curb in front of the grocery store. He never told me he was proud of me or anything."

Jules shook her head. "That's not right, Moonshine. You worked your ass off. *Congratulations, bitch!*"

Frankie cackled and poked Jules with her foot. "Freak!"

"Something happens, though," I continued. "It's like before we got married. We lived together for a year-and-a-half. We said it wouldn't change anything, that being *married* wouldn't change the dynamic of who we were. But it *totally* did."

"Yeah, it's like people start to look at you differently, now that you're a husband and a wife, and so *you* start to look at yourselves differently." Frankie pulled a throw blanket from the back of the sofa and draped it across her and Jules.

"*Exactly!* And then you become a mother." They both groaned with pent-up gripes about motherhood, niggling at them under the surface. "You can't help but see yourself differently. I mean, you just birthed a fucking baby! Everything changes. But I think women fall into the trap of forgetting themselves after they become moms. You get so wrapped up in being *Mommy* that you forget what *you* were like. The other day, I was talking to Alex about this—"

Jules twitched her head at the sound of his name. "Alex *who*?"

"Alex *Wheeler*. I was telling—"

"No, Tierney, hold up. When did you talk to Alex? In Chicago?"

I shook my head. "No. Well, yes, but I talked to him a few days ago."

"*Interesting.*"

I shrugged. "We became... friends after Montevallo and Chicago. I talk to him pretty often." *Though usually there's sex involved.*

"Wait," Frankie said, confused, "Alex Wheeler? Why do I know that name?"

"He's the lead singer for Junkture."

"Oh, yeah! Okay, continue."

"*Anyway*, I was saying to him that something especially happens with sex. It's like you hold yourself to a higher standard or something, and all the kinky shit you liked before you had the baby becomes *verboten*."

Jules nodded at me in agreement. "I wouldn't let Steve put his finger in my ass again until Jason was two!"

Frankie spewed Jack and Diet Coke all over the blanket. I cackled as she wiped her mouth, glaring at Jules with complete and total mirth.

"*What?* It's true!" Jules pressed, as I laughed harder. "Oh, come on! I know I'm not the only one who likes it!"

I picked up my cup and downed half of my oversized drink. "No, you're not the only one—and that ain't *nothin'*, I tell ya! But the point is, we all just seem to kind of *shut down* that really base, sexual part of ourselves, like it's too dirty to be women if we're also mothers."

"Well, it's not like we weren't women before," Jules answered. "We got knocked up somehow. We've obviously all been into dick once or twice in our lives."

"Once or twice a day," Frankie giggled. "That's the best thing Jay and I have going for us. We still have sex pretty much every day."

I looked at her over my cup. "I'd be happy with once or twice a *month*."

Jules started to say something, thoughtfully, but stopped herself.

"What?" I pressed. "Say it."

"How could Sam *not* want to tap that? I lived with you, Kitten. I know what a freak you are."

I pointed to myself dramatically. "The Golden Kitten is a superfreak, thank you very much. Let's just say that sometimes a finger in the ass just isn't enough."

"So *why* isn't he stepping up to that plate?"

"I wish I knew. He's drinking a lot. He's working a lot. I don't think he likes that I'm starting to do things on my own again."

"It scares him," Frankie said matter-of-factly. "Jay started that when I first went back to school. He admitted, finally, that he was afraid I wouldn't need him anymore."

"But I will always need Sam. He took care of me when I couldn't take care of myself. I can't ever overlook that."

Frankie shook her head. "Being appreciative and grateful are not the same as needing them. They want to know that you would fall apart without them there to hold your pieces together."

"Fuck, I have so many pieces, I need a butler just to walk around behind me and make sure I don't lose any. Maybe Sam is my butler. He butles."

The whisky was making me warm and tingly and mouthy.

"And is Sam a good *but*ler?" Jules teased.

"Again I say, sometimes a finger in the ass just isn't enough."

The three of us stayed up half the night, giggling and drinking and listening to the Violent Femmes, and Love and Rockets, and Siouxsie and the Banshees. We spread the gossip amongst ourselves, silly and lascivious details we'd learned on Facebook about common friends we barely knew anymore. We talked about the antics of our children and how we missed the days of dropping acid all night and walking around Montevallo, making fun of Damien, who was too stupid to get what we were saying.

I left Jules and Frankie to fight over the two couches and crashed in the guest room that would be my home for a couple of nights.

I was having fun, was able to function normally, but there was a constant psychic tug from far away. Alex was always *right there*. Mentioning his name brought him to the forefront of my mind, out of the shadows where I tried to keep him most of the time. Now I was half-drunk, and the night and longing were brutal.

I messaged him quickly on Facebook.

Tierney Cavanaugh Johnson
December 30th 2:13 AM

I'm lying in the dark, fingers everywhere, thinking about how badly I want to fuck you.

After a heavily-caffeinated breakfast with Jules and Frankie, I made it out the next day to see Tessa. The Karenas had flown into Birmingham for their annual post-Christmas visit. Our scheduled visits were barely overlapping, and I only had one day to see her. She and I agreed to meet at our much-beloved Pita Stop for yummy food and girl chat.

She knew about Alex, had known from the beginning. I'd called her the day his email came, hours after I'd already responded. I wasn't sure if he was joking, and I didn't want to share anything until I knew more. She didn't know all of the lascivious details, but she knew enough to know it was intense.

She also knew everything that had been happening with Sam.

Tessa had known Sam as long as she'd known me. Her husband, Ed, was Sam's best friend from middle school well through college. They were both in our wedding. Sam was in their wedding, the one I missed because I was in the middle of losing my fucking mind, holed up in our apartment for months.

Ed did not know everything that had been happening with Sam, or with Alex.

Tessa and I followed the waiter to our booth. The shrimp-colored, vinyl-clad booths were comfortable and fading, like the rest of the restaurant. The Pita Stop had been on Southside forever and was beginning to really show its age. But the food was so damn good, it was worth the dated brass trim and mismatched silverware.

"How were Jules and Frankie? Did you tell them hi for me?" Tessa asked over pita and hummus.

"They're good," I smiled. "It was crazy girl night. So weird to get drunk at my dad's with his blessing. They said hi and that they're sorry they missed you."

"So why didn't Sam come with you?"

"He's working."

"Of course he is."

I relayed the details of the fight from the week before, how we'd been separated since Christmas.

"When was the last time you guys had sex?" She stuffed an olive into her mouth.

"Christmas Eve," I answered, sliding kafta from a skewer, "but before that? I don't know. *Weeks.*"

"That's not healthy, Tierney. Good sex can hide a lot of flaws in a relationship, but, if you're not having sex, that just makes the problems more visible."

"Well, you know, all a girl really needs is two fingers and a Visa."

My best friend covered her mouth full of food, laughing at me.

I finished a bite and turned more serious. "I'm so tired of constantly feeling like I'm expected to fill a certain role, to behave in a certain way, to always be the one to give and not take. I mean, Sam's not a complete dick. I wouldn't have married him and had two amazing boys with him if that had been the case. He's taken care of me in a lot of ways, you know? He can be generous and selfless, but it seems to *always* be about the things that are easy for him to understand. I'm finally stepping out of those expectations, and there's a hefty price to pay for that freedom."

"What is it you want to do that he doesn't like?"

I shrugged. "Breathe?" She made a face at me, telling me not to be ridiculous. "I don't know. I don't think he's come downstairs to see a single thing I've painted. He never asks me how I'm feeling about the weight loss or tells me that I look good. He barely fucking talks to me most nights, Tess."

"You look great, by the way. I can tell you've lost more weight than when you were in Chicago."

I smiled at her. "I feel *so* much better. It's crazy. I feel...strong."

Tessa stopped mid-bite and looked at me. "You *are* strong, Tierney. Don't ever forget that."

We gorged ourselves on tabouleh and falafel. The weather was warming again, more seasonal for Alabama in December, and we decided to walk through Southside. It would be the closest thing to a workout I'd be able to manage for a few days.

"So what do you want?" Tessa asked me pointedly as we walked past one of the buildings at UAB. "It sounds like you're done."

"That's what Alex said, too." I smiled sideways at her. "I want Sam to be okay. I want him to wake the fuck up and tell me he loves me and that he's done drinking. I want him to fucking *fight* for me, to feel that just once."

"And if he doesn't?"

"I told him that if he didn't stop drinking, I would take the children and leave."

"Are you willing to back that up?" Her question wasn't challenging; Tessa was simply asking me if I'd really thought about it all.

I was ready to make the break. I wasn't happy about it, but I couldn't imagine Sam would ever give in and stop drinking. I couldn't imagine that he would get past his own ego, his own ideal of how the life he provided for us should be.

I nodded, shoving my hands into my pockets. "I think I am. But it's scary as hell to think about. I remember my parents' divorce so clearly. I was eleven, you know, when they split. They'd been arguing for my entire life, but it still knocked the breath out of me when they told me they were separating. And they had as amicable a divorce as possible. They were great at modeling an ideal divorce situation. My dad was never late with child support. I never even heard them talk shit about each other until after I got married. In the end, it was the best thing for our family, truly, but that didn't mean it wasn't hard for a while."

I was suddenly overwhelmed by the fear and the prospect of getting divorced. I started to cry and needed to sit down. Sitting on bench along Tenth Avenue, I cried my eyes out, my best friend holding me, shushing me back to calm.

"You can do this. If you decide to leave, you *can* do this."

"I'm not so sure. Is it fair of me to upend the boys' world? Do I have that right?"

Was it purely selfish of me to make that choice? Was it wrong of me to put *me* ahead of him and the boys and this life we'd spent so much time and energy putting together? It wasn't perfect—it wasn't even great at that point—but it usually felt safe and relatively easy. I knew the boys and I would be okay financially with support, but the logistics of a post-divorce life seemed daunting. Living arrangements and custody and visitation. Was it even fair of me to ask Sam to be the one to move out? He was the primary provider for the family, and I knew he would be incensed at giving up everything he'd worked so hard for, regardless of my own contribution to that.

"You have the right to be happy, Tierney, no matter what. And I know that you'll be okay. Maybe not right away, but eventually. And you will *thrive*. I'm not so sure about Sam. It makes me sad for him, but I don't know if he'll ever be okay."

I couldn't imagine being happy again for a long time. I didn't know if it was better to stick with the enemy I knew or to start a whole new battle. I could maintain the status quo, separate entirely with the drama and move on to new drama, or I could push for a weird, "separate but not" option, which I didn't think Sam would ever agree to. If I'd even suggested that, I was pretty sure Sam would've accused me of just wanting the freedom to do whatever I wanted, to fuck someone else, all on his hard-earned dime.

"Goddamn, Tessa!" I unattractively wiped my nose on my sleeve. "I don't *want* to date again! The prospect of looking and starting over...."

"Yeah," she nodded in agreement, "it seems like it would be so *tiring* just to recount your history and the stories of your life to someone new."

"Honestly, I'm not sure my self-esteem can take having to do it all again. I know people do it all the time, and it seems like it would have to be easier at thirty-eight than at forty-eight, but it's *terrifying* to think about. *And* it's not like I'd be leaving Sam *for* anyone else, except myself."

Tessa looked at me intently, her neat little mouth pursed in thought. "How *does* Alex figure into all of this?"

I shook my head. "He doesn't. He doesn't figure into it at all. He has nothing to do with why I'm unhappy with Sam. He wasn't there when Sam started drinking. He wasn't there when Sam decided I wasn't worth his time. He wasn't there when Sam quit fucking me."

"Would you still be in contact with him?"

"I don't know. Probably. He's my friend, no matter what."

She looked at me, pointedly, but said nothing.

"*Okay*," I admitted, "if I got the chance to *really* fuck him, I probably would. Sam or no Sam. Look, I would love *nothing* more than to have some weird, European thing with Sam, where we could quietly have beautiful affairs and still be a functional couple. I would *love* to be able to see Alex every few months and have volcanic, mind-blowing sex for a day and then go back to my happy life. I don't think it's happenin', though."

"Probably not. But that would be so wonderfully French of you." I shot her a grin. "So what do you need me to do?" she asked gently.

I inhaled deeply, feeling my lungs expand and absorb the tension in my chest. "I need you to find me an attorney," I exhaled. "Check around for me?"

"Done. I'll get you a name this week."

I hugged her again, feeling her thick, brown hair against my face. "I love you, Tessa."

"I love you, too. Now let's go walk, so you can work that new, smaller ass."

Alex Wheeler
December 31, 2010 4:17 PM

Are you crazy? My wife has access to all of my accounts, so you probably shouldn't send messages to me like that. I'm flattered tho!

What the fuck?!
The stupid son of a bitch had messaged me about my tits on Facebook. He'd sent me a private Twitter message a few days before, commenting that he wished I was where he was—in Portland, where he was visiting his mom with Talia and Amber. *Now* he had a problem?

It drove me nuts all day on New Year's Eve.

Then Sam called to tell me he wasn't coming to Birmingham.

"I was getting ready to leave, and I got a headache."

He had a history of debilitating cluster headaches and migraines, dating back to before Tripp was born. I could hear the exhaustion and slur in his voice. He spoke carefully, like he was afraid he was going to make me mad or disappoint me.

"I was going to try to come anyway," he said, "but the first painkiller didn't do much, so I have to take another one."

I'd seen these headaches up close so many times. They usually came in cycles of days, three or four times a year. We were at the ER so often during the two years before Tripp was born that we joked about negotiating a "Baker's Dozen" free visit with Brookwood Hospital. The pain could be so intense that only a huge dose of Demerol and Phenergan would take care of it, and he would still be able to walk out of the ER under his own power. There was never a definitive cause for them, even after a hospitalization for a CT and spinal tap.

"I understand," I told him gently. "I don't want you driving like that."

But I was upset. We'd *never* been apart for New Year's Eve. I hadn't *not* kissed him at midnight since I was twenty years old. I'm a strangely superstitious girl, and this was playing into all of my irrational fears.

I went to Bottletree Cafe to see Man or Astro-man? anyway. I spent a long time talking to other high school friends who'd come out to see our classmates and their band. I could see on my Facebook news feed that we were all posting pictures of the same show, taken from our respective angles throughout the small club.

Midnight came with small plastic cups of cheap champagne for everyone. It was great not being home and asleep for the year change, but I had no one to kiss. I felt very, very alone, surrounded by three hundred loud, happy, sentimental people.

Without Sam there, I had no distraction from my thoughts of Alex. I obsessed about his message from earlier in the evening. Yes, I'd been drunk when I messaged him. Hell, I'd been drunk half the time we'd ever talked. I'd sent the first flirty but innocuous text, but he was the one who'd escalated the conversation. From the beginning, I was a willing and encouraging participant.

From: Tierney Cavanaugh Johnson
Date: January 1st 3:11 am
To: Alex Wheeler
Subject: You know what?

FUCK YOU. Seriously. I love you, Alex, (and NOT like that) but you make me fucking nuts sometimes.

You're the one who sent me a Facebook message about my DD tits two weeks ago and then seemed perfectly fine with my responding to you in that venue. You fucking called me that afternoon and didn't say anything about it. You can't go and arbitrarily change the rules of engagement and not tell me, then get mad at me because I don't know how to play your game anymore. That's a ridiculous expectation.

Your gripe asked if I was crazy. That little bit of crazy is what makes me unexpectedly willing to be a total fucking whore for you at the ding of a text. It's what makes me happy to hear your dirty little secrets and crave more. It's what you and I both hate to love about me.

What exactly did you think would happen when we opened this Pandora's box? You, yourself, warned me that the devil couldn't be put back in. This has been on your terms from the very beginning. I recognize that you arguably have more to lose than I do, but you have to be fucking honest and open with me. I spend so much time hanging and waiting to hear from you. If I'm finally in a moment that I'm not consumed by thoughts of your cock, that's almost invariably the moment that you pop up.

Am I just totally making this up? I guess that's my biggest fear, that I am completely and totally alone in the belief that we are at the very least friends with strange, unexpected benefits. In my mind--and PLEASE correct me if you feel I'm wrong--you and I connected quickly and in more than one way. If all that mattered was the fact that I could talk you through multiple jack-offs in an evening, you wouldn't have opened up and told me more. I wouldn't have called on you when I started to watch my marriage crumble.

I hope you know I'm not looking to fuck up your world, babycakes. I am looking for you to clarify my role in that world.

Call me when you can.

Tierney

When I woke the next morning, I was determined to readily embrace the new year, no matter what was coming. I was a little apprehensive about what was ahead for me and my family, but I was giddy in the excitement of my newness, which seemed almost palpable. I couldn't remember a point in my recent time when I'd felt so ready to jump feet first into my life. After years of doing what everyone else wanted, of fulfilling the obligations of life to the point of exhaustion, I was finally devoting time and energy to *Tierney*.

And I didn't care what anyone else thought about it. I'd become all about this idea of *Verisimilitude of Self*, of finding the truths of me and living them. I wasn't rebelling against anyone or anything so much as I was rebelling for myself. I chose to behave in whatever way I found suited my prerogative.

At least on the surface, it was selfish and childish. But I wasn't eighteen doing this. I was thirty-eight, with all of the life experience that came with the extra twenty years. I'd lived through heartache and trauma, experienced life and death in the most profound ways, and seen the worst and best of myself through it all. I was still idealistic sometimes in how I thought my life should be, but that idealism was tempered with pragmatism and common sense.

When I was eighteen, thirty-eight seemed frighteningly old. Now, it seemed as if life was just beginning.

The boys and I went home on New Year's Day. By the time we got in and settled, Sam was feeling better but still not great. I couldn't readily gauge the reason for his somber mood. After the boys were safely tucked into their beds, we settled onto the huge sectional sofa, a million miles of multi-colored fabric between us.

"I can't keep doing this," I told him evenly. "If you don't stop drinking, I'm leaving with the boys. They told my dad you're addicted to alcohol."

He was shocked and hurt. He knew they'd noticed his daily consumption. I'd made sure to yell at him about it during the initial lengthy fight. But this was something else entirely, to hear about their telling Grandpa that Dad was an alcoholic.

"I stopped," he said quietly. "I haven't had a drink since the twenty-third."

I didn't know what to say. I just looked at him across the jumble of throw pillows.

"I don't want to lose you," he continued. "I don't want you to leave."

His words were quiet, but it was the closest to his fighting for me that I'd ever seen.

I was relieved. He would stop drinking, and everything would be okay. We would get back to normal. I wouldn't have to deal with leaving and restarting my life. Things would be better, if only because he wouldn't be drinking anymore.

We talked for hours. I cried. He was worried about where we were headed. So was I.

But we went to bed, together, and I got the belated midnight kiss I so desperately needed.

Was it too late? Was it enough? Would it ever be?

I lay in our bed, snuggled against my quiet and sleeping husband. As I dozed off, I thought, *I have to tell Alex about this.*

Chapter 10

Painting again was key to my finding Tierney. It was a cathartic and productive outlet for this perpetual self-examination I was dragging myself through. I spent hours by myself, in my own head, methodically brushing the color and shade of my thoughts across the canvas. I tentatively posted some quick pictures of what I was painting on Facebook. It felt a little like putting your hideous baby in the nursery and hoping no one tells you it really is ugly. I chided my fears constantly, reminding myself that others had told me, long ago, that I was good, that I was talented, and that I had every reason to believe I had the right and reason to create my version of art.

But the response I got from my friends was overwhelming. I was refreshed and reassured knowing they were with me, supporting me all the way.

There were mornings when I would see my work from the day before and really question what the hell I was thinking when I'd gotten it into my head to paint again. Then I would see something I'd done—some unexpected use of color or brush stroke—and be blown away by how good I thought it was, which both surprised and scared me. It was very difficult for me to see something good in myself, to feel some accomplishment, that didn't directly involve my husband or my children.

My more abstract pieces were the ones that amazed me the most. They were the ones that wrenched the deepest emotion from me, moving me from one gut feeling to another and another as I worked the piece from start to finish. It didn't really seem to matter what I had in mind when I started; those pieces would always take me through some heady emotional issues plucked from subconscious memory, dropping me squarely into some other, unexpected emotional exhaustion.

And just when I thought I'd found a solid landing place to rest for a few days, I was blindsided by my mother.

"I'm cleaning out the office," she told me on the phone one morning, "and I found some old pictures I hadn't seen in years. I'm scanning them and putting them on Facebook."

"Oh, *great*. If there are pictures of me with glasses and braces, I'll retaliate in kind."

She snickered and told me to check online later in the day. She asked about the boys, how they'd done going back to school after the holiday. She caught me up on her ailments and my grandmother's.

I forgot about the pictures until I logged in the next morning. I had notifications that she'd tagged me in a dozen photos. A couple of them popped up in my news feed, and I almost threw up.

They were pictures of young, blond me with my grandfather, smiling painfully against the sun.

I was hurt and stunned. I felt ill.

I'd been thinking a lot about it in the previous few weeks. For years, I'd been able to open up my baggage for almost anyone, matter-of-factly, like a laundry list of trauma. So many things had been unearthed during my conversations with Alex, though, that I had started to think about them all again—really mulling through them to see what I'd forgiven and what I could forget. I'd come to terms with my parents' split years earlier, in large part because of their behavior after the divorce. A chance to unleash on Damien via email, just after he'd contacted me when we moved to Atlanta, had finally given me the courage to stop looking over my shoulder everywhere I went for my abusive ex. The molestation itself had ceased to be a significant, pressing memory when I yelled at my dead grandfather. Rape counseling had been really helpful, but it became much less of an issue when I got the call a few years later that the guy who raped me had died unexpectedly from congestive heart failure in his mid-30s.

After the rape, I told a couple of friends, including Sam's then-girlfriend India. I remember looking at her in the musty, sour-smelling elevator of the Pickwick Plaza parking garage in Birmingham, having asked her to get me away from Karolina and Kent the night I was unexpectedly out with both of them. She stood stock still, gripping the steel handrail and leaning against the glass as we rose five stories. Dark horror and anger consumed her elven face. She'd wanted to kill Kent, to tell Sam and have him do it.

I wouldn't let her. I wasn't so shamed by the incident that I was unwilling to tell someone, but I was still coming to terms with my own culpability. I knew damn well that my being high didn't give him the right to do what he wanted to my body. I just didn't know if I was partially to blame for having put myself in the situation.

I was a mess, for days. I remember standing outside the movie theater where Frankie worked, and calling Damien from a pay phone. I needed his support, even though we were in the middle of a short-lived break-up. I needed him to tell me it would be okay, that I would be okay.

"I was raped," I said, dazed and crying. I stared at my fingers twisting around the shiny steel cord of the phone.

"I'm sorry." He paused. "Look, I have to go. Jenny's coming." His new girlfriend.

I was stunned. I was dismissed. I was hurting like crazy.

The following Monday, I called a former teacher who'd been really great to me. She was the only adult I trusted at the time. It was after school for both of us, but before my mom and stepdad were home from work. I used the phone in the guest bedroom, not wanting to bring the awful energy into my own room if I didn't have to.

"You have to tell your mother," she urged quietly. "Your mom needs to know about this."

So I did. India came over to hold my hand as I sat on the plaid sofa with my mother the next evening. It was surprisingly easy to tell her what had happened, to recount the event and let the words escape into the open. I explained quietly, answering her few questions about what I'd done after and who I'd told.

Did Karolina's parents know? *No.*

Did I want them to? *No.*

She was concerned but not devastated. I don't know if her calm demeanor was level-headed or detached.

"You need to get checked-out. You need to go to the doctor."

I nodded.

"Do you want to talk someone? A counselor?"

I shook my head. I didn't want to talk to *her* about it, let alone anyone else.

No teenage girl who's just been raped needs to be allowed to refuse counseling.

Because it seemed relevant—and because she was one of the only people who knew—India had urged me to tell my mother about the molestation at the same time. My grandfather was still alive, still living nearby, and India knew my constant contact with him drove me crazy. Although the rape was still fresh, it was much more difficult to tell my mom about what her own father had done to me years before.

"I thought something might have happened," she replied.

What?!

I have replayed this moment in my mind a thousand times since that day.

She thought something might have happened? When I was a kid? And she continued to send me back to the place where I was mishandled and violated?

I was too baffled to ask her about it.

My mother did schedule an appointment for me with her gynecologist. She called the school and told them to let me check out for it. I drove myself to Brookwood Hospital, just a couple of miles from my high school, and sat in the waiting room for seemingly ever. Later it would be the hospital I visited hundreds of times during my fertility treatments. It's the hospital where both of my children were conceived and born.

It was scary, to sit there alone, sixteen-years-old, and anticipate what was coming.

The nurse finally called me back and walked me to the doctor's office. I sat on a beige sofa and waited for this woman I'd never met. She came in, introduced herself, and sat in a chair across from me. Dr. Andrews asked me about what had happened, so I told her, trying to be brave through stinging tears. She asked me about my sexual history prior to that night. She told me what to expect in the exam, that they would draw some blood to do some tests, and that I would have to come back for more blood tests in a few weeks to check again for HIV.

She asked if my mom was with me, and I said no.

The nurse led me into the exam room and had me put on a gown and a drape. At the time, they still used cloth gowns instead of the paper ones. That was probably more comforting in a way. Honestly, I don't know if I would've been any more scared if I'd just been naked. I sat on the paper-covered exam table and waited again.

Dr. Andrews and her nurse finally came in, and the nurse pulled up a tray of silver instruments I'd never seen before. I'd let a couple of guys get to third base, but nothing like *that* had ever been inside me. I was scared. No matter how kind the doctor or the nurse were, no matter how at-ease I was supposed to be because of the "Grin And Bear It" bumper sticker on the ceiling of the exam room, there was no way to make this a pleasant experience. I was having my first pelvic exam in the aftermath of a date rape, and my mom hadn't even bothered to come with me to the appointment.

The cold invasion of that first speculum, the sound of the little screws on it adjusting it to open... it wasn't good. There'd been no way to prepare for the feel of that little brush across my cervix, or how violating the doctor's hand would feel after everything that had happened.

As traumatic as the rape was, this issue with how my mother handled the aftermath was so much worse in some ways. The same streak of independence and self-reliance that my parents trusted enough to turn me into a latch-key-only-child at the age of ten, was the reason she assumed I could take care of myself. As strong-willed and mature as I was, I was still a kid, and she'd left to me to my own devices, both in the aftermath of a possible molestation and for the clean-up after a definitive rape.

I learned about periods from *Are You There God? It's Me, Margaret* and a pamphlet my mom gave me about puberty. "Let me know if you have any questions," she'd told me as she backed out of my room.

The closest we ever came to the Sex Talk was when she shook her tear-eyed head, crying at me over and over, "It's not right!", the night I told her I was moving in with Sam.

When I finally went through rape counseling as a freshman in college, my counselor and I talked at length about how I thought maybe Mom had found out when I was about ten but still never asked me about it. The counselor urged me to confront my mother about her statement that she thought something had happened when I was a child.

"It's not my fault!" she cried at me, backing through a doorway. She retreated to the front porch, well in view of the entire neighborhood. "I didn't do anything wrong!"

I was so incensed that I threw a small television at the wall. I never mentioned it to her again.

As angry as I was, still, at my mother for abandoning me in that quagmire of trauma, it occurred to me, finally, that my father didn't do much of anything to help, either. They were long-divorced by that time. He was living across town from her, and me, and only saw me every couple of weeks. I know she told him about the rape. He mentioned it in passing the next time I saw him for my bi-weekly visitation, telling me he was there if I needed him. That was the only conversation we had about it until well into my adulthood.

Alex called that afternoon, while I was crying on the dark blue loveseat in the office.

"Hey," I answered sniffily.

"Hey! What's wrong?"

"My mom's a fucking bitch."

I told him about the pictures, about feeling sideswiped and betrayed. "She'll post about what a great man he was. *He fucking molested her daughter! How the fuck can she say that shit?*"

"I don't know, Tierney," he replied gently. "I don't understand it. I'm sorry, I know that must hurt like hell."

"I know how young they were when I was born. I get that. But that doesn't give them the right to check the fuck out of my life when it was too hard for them. Especially my *mother*! If *anyone* should've been taking care of me, it should've been her!"

I was agitated and started to pace, from one end of the office to the other into the kitchen and back, over and over. It helped to keep the shaking at bay.

"I know, believe me. My mom, bless her heart, she did her best, but she never thought it was enough. I think she was overwhelmed a lot by the four of us. My dad was gone all the time. I was the baby, so she was just *tired* of it by the time she got to me. Talia used to tell me, when Amber was little, that she thought she was a bad mother. There were times I was afraid she would just leave, that she couldn't handle it, no matter how much she loved the baby."

"We all think that," I admitted. "I don't know a mother who doesn't say that, especially during the first year. We have an expectation that we should be a certain way after we become mothers. We feel the expectations of others, certainly, but we really set ourselves up for the biggest fall. I fail at it all the time. Every day, I fail my children in some way, big or small."

"Tierney, you do not!"

"No, listen to me! I *do*, whether or not they even know it. I may yell at them too harshly, or I may not give them the attention I don't realize they're craving because I'm too wrapped up in myself. Or maybe I just forget their favorite snack for that day. All I can ever do, though, is apologize to them and to myself and move the fuck on. I can choose to learn the lesson and live it, or I can bury my fucking head in my sense of failure as a mother and ignore it. But that is behavior I try very hard to model for my children. I will not have them growing into men who refuse to acknowledge their own mistakes or faults and just ignore the truth of their lives because of their fear of accepting responsibility for themselves."

"I'm sorry, Buttercup. I'm sorry this hit you like this. What are you gonna do about it?"

"What *can* I do, Alex? She won't talk about it. She's in total denial about it all, which is fucked up. I mean, my parents have their own reasons for distancing themselves from me and my emotional issues. I'll probably never fully understand those reasons. It's my journey, you know? My parents are on their own journeys. Maybe they should've carried me down my path for a while, but I could never have forced them to do it."

"Your *existence* as their child should've been enough to force them to do it, Tierney. There's nothing I wouldn't do for Amber. *Nothing*. I adore her." I could hear how upset he was getting. He exhaled deeply. "You have the right to heal from all of this. It's been long enough. You have the right to fucking *heal* this hurt."

I sighed into the phone, looking out the kitchen window. "To confront them would make them face themselves, and they won't do it. It would force a bigger emotional wedge between me and my parents. To pick at these old wounds could be damaging to them, especially my mother. Does my right to heal, finally, from all of these injuries trump their right to hide behind their unspoken excuses?"

"I think it does, but only you can decide what's best for you. *I'm* not getting into it with *my* mom any time soon. But *use* it in your painting."

Alex was right. The feelings of dismissal and emotional neglect and abandonment were surfacing anew, and I knew I could explore them on canvas. But I was afraid to dredge up more of myself. It all felt rough and raw again, and I wasn't sure if I was brave enough or strong enough to work myself through that pain thoroughly and not back off at the last moment, leaving me with something half-assed and perpetually incomplete.

"You can do this, Tierney," Alex assured me. "You *are* strong enough to do what you need to do. Trust yourself."

It was boosting to hear him say that. It wasn't the same as coming from Tessa or Jules or Frankie, or from anyone who'd known me for a long time. He knew me intimately and knew exactly which demons I was afraid to battle. Having his reassurance meant a lot.

"And, no," he continued, "I'm not mad at you. I wasn't mad about the message. I told you I was flattered!"

I laughed nervously. "I couldn't tell. It's why I prefer *talking* to you."

"Yes, it's probably best if we stick to phone and email and chat. Things I can control the access to."

"I got it."

"And, yes, you're right. There was a connection when we met. There's more to it than just this sexual attraction."

"Maybe it's the shared Irish blood."

"Maybe," he chuckled. "I may be coming to Nashville, by the way."

"When?" I breathed excitedly.

"The weekend of the fourteenth."

"*God*, that would make me insane if you were that close and I couldn't see you!"

"Maybe you could just get in your car and drive to Nashville. How far is it? About four hours?"

He was right. I could go to Nashville. I could find someone to cover for me—Jules would be an easy alibi. I could go and be with him and *fuck* him, and maybe it would all be out of my system.

"I just might. Where will you be staying?"

"At the Loew's Vanderbilt. But it's a working trip, so I won't be available the whole time."

"I didn't expect you would. It's not like you'd be flying across the country to see me."

"Nope. But I gotta go, Buttercup. I've got a conference call in five minutes."

"Okay," I whined. "Thanks for calling. As always, it was helpful in a lot of ways. I appreciate your advice, Mr. Wheeler."

"Anytime, Cavanaugh. Talk to you soon."

From: Tierney Cavanaugh Johnson
Date: January 4th 5:39 pm
To: Alex Wheeler
Subject: So here's what I'm thinking this afternoon

I really, truly could come to Nashville. The logistics are totally doable, and I could make it happen. I understand that you haven't finalized your plans. I also realize it's a working trip for you, so make sure you have the time to give to me if I make the trek. I don't care about going anywhere, being anywhere with you that doesn't involve your unfettered access to my pussy. I don't want to be an afterthought, either.

My self-consciousness and body image issues are the only thing making me hesitate. I'm in a much, much healthier place than I was even three months ago. I know I look better than the last time I saw you, and you've obviously met me more than once. You've seen the girlie parts in all their glory, which still totally amazes me that I was even able to handle that, truly. But there's still so much to be unhappy about my body, and the thought of being naked in front of you totally weirds me out. I'm me, and you're 14-shades-of-hot, totally-fuckable, amazing Alex Wheeler.

The flip to all of this is that I don't have the weirdness of not trusting you, of being unsure about being open with you. I know I can let go and be me and that you'll take whatever I have to offer. I've been very honest about my overwhelming desire to fuck and be fucked by you. I think it could be volcanic. Whatever I lack in confidence about how my body looks is offset by the knowledge that I am fantastic in bed. I want to be able to take all of that adoration I have for you, all of the love and respect and admiration, and wrap it around your cock and show you exactly how much you and this mean to me.

It's an uncommon and unexpected predicament, and I don't want to put myself out there with you and end up rejected and hundreds of miles from home. I know this probably seems totally ridiculous to you. You know my history and the things that led me to this place of instability with my self-esteem. I'm trusting that, yet again, you're patient and honest with me. To me, it seems like it's kind of a lot to absorb and decide what to do with. You'll respond when you're ready and able. You know how to find me.

XOX

As confident as I was in my abilities to do so many things, I was often plagued by self-doubt. If how I saw myself in relation to my body could bring on so much self-recrimination, didn't it stand to reason that everyone else was judging me by the size of my ass? It didn't matter that I had hormonal and metabolic issues that had gone undiagnosed for years. Since I was eleven years old, there'd been a constant, niggling fear that I simply was not good enough because of my body.

When my pediatrician became concerned about it in my preteens, my mother took me to see a nutritionist. I tried following the diet for a while, or even some other fad diet my mom found in a magazine or a book. Mom would do it with me. But it was too easy for her to slip us back into the habit of "cheating" with food, of having leftover birthday cake and ice cream for breakfast. My dad says he quit asking me about it when I told him I was happy like I was.

No teenage girl is happy when she's fat.

Food began to equate comfort as a young child. It was how most of my family responded to any emotional stimuli. When I was alone or bored or upset, I ate. Between the molestation and the divorce and being a latch-key kid, I had a lot of opportunity to feed my misery.

I'd never felt great about my body. I knew damn well that most grown men like a meatier girl—not necessarily fat, though—and that curves are *sexy*. And I'd never had a problem getting a guy to fuck me. Flaunting my sexuality in rebellion of my past, I'd found comfort in the back seats of cars and the dark corners of parks— places that didn't require me to be naked. That didn't mean I wasn't constantly self-conscious about hiding my numerous physical flaws. The first weekend I spent with Sam, I worked as hard to hide my naked body from him as I did to get him off.

Slowly, I'd learned to draw on his love for me and my imperfections, and let it bolster my abilities as a lover. He'd never *not* known me as a big girl. I was probably a size 14 when we met, and I had gone through numerous ups and downs, culminating in an almost-size 24. From our first time together, he made love to me, touching every curve of my body, all the bumps and lumps and scars, and he celebrated them. I was able to absorb that positivity, let it pass through me and back out to him. All the flaws I saw and felt every day never mattered to him. At least when I was naked and safe in our bed, I could choose to ignore those nagging whispers of self-doubt and drown them out with cries of ecstasy. His acceptance of me, regardless of the size and shape of my body, had allowed me to flourish into an adventurous and willing lover.

All of that was coming full-circle with Alex.

He caught me on Skype a few days later.

Tierney   What are you doing? Where are you?

Alex   Home. Conference call in a bit. Stroking my cock. Thought I'd see if you were around.

Tierney   Ha! For that? For you? Always. ;)

Alex   I can't wait to see that amazing, full body of yours NAKED
And do naughty, dirty things to it

Tierney   Mmmmmm
Like what?

Alex   Like suck those luscious huge tits
And fuck u every way you'll let me

Tierney   Any way you can imagine, babycakes
I'm so wet!

Alex   I'm so fucking hard!
I'm gonna stroke this and think about cumming all over those tits!

We went back and forth, one-handed typing until Alex came and then went.

Tierney   You're leaving me like this?!? I'm a mess!

Alex   You're a hot mess, Buttercup! Sorry but I gotta go. Conference call.

Tierney   You suck, asshat.

Alex   I'm not an asshat. Call u soon.

I was left on my own, a victim of his erratic comings and goings. I knew he was getting in touch whenever he could, but it was frustrating.

I was jonesing for Alex time. I wanted a couple of hours to be able to talk to him, to hear him talk to me. Really, I wanted a couple of days with his tongue in my mouth, but there was still no answer on this possible rendezvous in Nashville. As lovely as our afternoon adventures could be, I missed the great joy of the nights leading up to Thanksgiving. I loved our chats, but I also loved it when he just called to talk to me or listen to me gripe about whatever was bugging me.

And when he said what he did about seeing me naked.... I was so relieved and turned on and even more enthralled with him. He was amazingly and surprisingly sweet. It also did a lot for me to know he'd actually read what I sent. I knew he was often too distractible or occupied to respond, and he generally hated to write even a simple email. I often worried that he hated to see emails from me; I had a lot to say, and I didn't always know that he wanted to hear it.

The forecast for Atlanta and the Southeast was for snow and ice. If I went to meet Alex in Nashville, there was a strong possibility I would be stuck in that shitty weather and not be able to make it home in time to cover my ass. Jules would only be able to be my alibi for so long.

It turned out it didn't matter. Alex texted later that afternoon to tell me his trip was off. He would be going to Seattle instead.

I was irritated but not surprised. It would've been too easy and too difficult if it had worked out. I was bitching to myself when my phone rang.

Seth Wiezel

"Hey!" I drawled.
"Hey!" he mimicked. "How are you?"
"Irritated."
"At me?"
"No, of course not! Someone else."
"Why?" Seth asked. "Tell me."
I couldn't very well just *tell* Seth what was going on. But maybe he could offer some advice or encouragement if he only knew generalities.

"So I have this friend...," I started.

I explained that my friend, whom I carefully refused to acknowledge as male or female, sometimes made our friendship very hard. I could be equally exasperated and delighted when they appeared in my world, but I never really knew when it would happen. They would just *appear* and alter my day as they disappeared just as quickly.

"And I *adore* this person, Seth. Truly and completely. I don't ever want them *not* to be there, you know? So I tend to just accept it. It's difficult, and I wish they would just *be* there if they're going to be my friend."

Seth was quiet. I could hear him smoking a cigarette, somewhere in San Antonio.

"Is this *friend* Alex Wheeler?"

My heart started to pound. *How would he know?*

"Why would you think that?" I asked, trying to sound confused and deflect his attention away from Alex.

"It *is*, isn't it?"

I shushed him over the phone.

"He's just like that, you know," Seth said. "They all are. Musicians, I mean. Hell, I guess that makes me flighty, too."

"Maybe, but your being flighty is something different than his being flighty."

He paused. "What's going on between you two?"

"I can't talk—"

"—*Are you fucking Alex Wheeler?!*"

"Not *literally*, no." *Not for lack of trying.* "But there's more to it, Seth. I can't explain."

"*Ugh.* Tierney, *no*! You can't do that! You're married. He's married."

Did Seth think I'd just forgotten about Talia and Sam? "Believe me, I know. It's weird and complicated."

"Maybe he cares about you," Seth said thoughtfully. "He's not a total ass. But no matter how much you care about him, it'll never be more than a really fulfilling fuck for him."

Wham! Right in the face!

"Your honesty is so refreshing, Wiezel. You're like a hammer."

"I'm sorry. I'm not trying to be hurtful. You just need to know the truth of who he is."

I shook my head at no one. "I know more about him than almost anyone. I know things *no one* knows. And I know you're not trying to be hurtful. You're just walloping me in the face with your big Hammer of Honesty."

"Am I wrong?" he pressed.

"I doubt it. That's why I didn't hang up on you. You're one of the few people who I'd ever let wallop me with the truth when I least want to feel it."

But Seth wasn't telling me anything I hadn't already thought a thousand times. *Why* would Alex Wheeler be *remotely* interested in me? Who was I kidding? There couldn't be anything more to it than the sex, and even that had never come to physical fruition. It was easy for him to picture me any way he wanted when he was jacking off to my distant voice.

I didn't want Seth to be right—didn't want me to be right—so I pushed it away, out of my mind. I boxed it up and shoved it into the darkest compartment I could not-think of and went back to my life.

Chapter 11

The snow and ice started on Sunday night. Four to eight inches of fine, dry powder fell overnight, topped by a half-inch or more of sleet and freezing rain. It was the kind of winter weather event that this part of the Deep South sees every ten to fifteen years. The couple dozen snow plows and graders and salt trucks were woefully outnumbered by the thousands of miles of hilly, often-shaded road. Roads were closed, and schools were shut down.

I was up, drinking coffee and checking email, when I heard Tripp's bedroom door open.

"Mommy? You forgot to wake me up for school!"

I swiveled toward him and peered over the top of my computer glasses. "No, baby, there's no school."

His impossibly beautiful blue eyes went wide and bright. "Did it *snow*?"

I smiled and curled him into a hug. "It did!"

He pulled away and turned toward the hall. "Ian! Ian!" He stopped mid-excitement and turned back to me. "Good morning," he said sweetly. "I love you."

"I love you, too. Now go wake up your brother."

I snuck into the bedroom, trying not to wake Sam as I rummaged through my over-packed closet for scarves and waterproof gloves.

"Did it snow?" he asked groggily from over my shoulder.

"Yep. A lot. The boys want to go out and play. You can go back to sleep for a while, if you want."

"No, it's fine." Sam sat up on the edge of the bed and stretched, putting on his glasses. "I want to go out with them. Just gimme a minute."

I shooed the boys and their rambunctious chatter toward the den, stuffing their bedheads into thermal caps. It was the first year we all had waterproof boots, but I made them wear three layers of socks, just in case the snow snuck in around the edges.

By the time I'd sufficiently bundled the babies and myself, Sam came into the den, pulling his own hat over his freshly-combed hair, video camera in hand.

"I can't stay out long," he said. "I just got an email about an incident, and I have to get on it pretty quick."

I unlocked the front door, and my men poured out into the blinding, brilliant world.

It was the most snow the boys had ever seen. They squinted against the sunlight reflected off the pristine bluish-white. Tripp threw himself ceremoniously into a snow bank, making his first snow angel that wasn't crusted on bottom with dead leaves and pine needles. Ian dragged a long stick, taller than he, from the side of the house and used it as a pole to maneuver through waist-high drifts in the front yard. Sam and I laughed uproariously when Ian fell, uphill, and couldn't climb his way out of his snow hole.

"He looks like the little brother in *A Christmas Story*," Sam joked.

"Well, he is Mommy's little piggy!"

The boys' faces were filled with the wonder of exploration. Brightly-colored coats swished as they ran as hard and fast as they could around the sides of the house, their booted feet trudging unseen through the snow. They glided down the street, on their backs and on their bellies, splayed across old cardboard boxes and trash can lids until they grew tired of lugging their makeshift sleds back up the thick hill. They tried for an hour to build a snowman, determined to conquer the crunchy pack. They finally gave up, their teeth clattering together as they told me they were tired and cold and hungry.

I unwrapped them from their wet clothes, depositing everything in a soggy pile by the washing machine, as Sam layered them in warm towels and fresh socks. They huddled together under a blanket on the couch, watching their daddy build a perfect fire. I brought them warm waffles and spill-proof tumblers of hot chocolate and handed them the Wii remotes.

"Put your dishes in the sink when you're done," I reminded them.

After a shower and breakfast and more coffee, I walked into the office to check on Sam. "So what was the email from work?"

He kept looking at his computer screen, scrolling through his inbox. "Some major websites were hacked overnight. It's all over the news this morning. It's Digital Freedom Front, and I've been asked to look into it."

"TLA?" *Three-letter acronym.* It was generic code for whichever government agency was conscripting his expertise.

"Yep."

"Why do they do this? Groups like DFF? I mean, I get some of the targets. I know they always say they're politically motivated, but their reasons don't seem to make sense sometimes."

Sam looked up at me and leaned back against the high back of his office chair. "Sometimes they just do it because they can. They're constantly looking for information and access. They scrape it from everywhere. They have dozens of people who spend all of their free time looking through mountains of data to see if they can cull anything useful from it."

"But what's useful?"

Sam shrugged. "It depends on who's looking. These guys are so loosely tied to each other, mainly because they're young slackers with skills that let them eke out some money from something shady and easy. Some of them have a vendetta against a company or a person or an organization. They're the digilantes. Some just want to be assholes and prove that they can pown anything they want."

I tried not to pry too deeply into Sam's work. It was often sensitive or even classified, and the less I knew, the better. I knew that he'd received thinly-veiled death threats on multiple occasions, and I'd stopped asking when he gave me a discreet list of TLA contacts, in case he should ever go missing.

"*Fuck!*" he swore. "I need my machine at work to do this."

"The roads are closed, baby—"

"I *know* the roads are closed, Tierney. I saw the news just like you did." *Okaaay.* "You need to keep the boys out of here. They can't be bothering me while I'm working on this." He turned back to his computer.

I left the office, closing the door behind me.

The ice and cold and snow lasted for five days. It was too crunchy and hard to be any fun, and I didn't trust the boys not to lob iceballs at each other's heads. There were lots of video games and movies.

The Snow Madness began on day three. I was restless and bored, tired of napping to the sound of little, mustachioed plumbers banging their heads for coins while trying to save an insipid princess. I plugged in my iPod and hit **SHUFFLE ALL SONGS**.

Depeche Mode. "Enjoy the Silence". *Ha!*

I walked around the house for a few minutes, surprised to find huge sectors of the yard that had been untouched by little boy antics. The ice was smooth and a little slick from the cycle of sunshine melt and overnight refreeze.

I went downstairs and found a long-unused box of tempera paint and dozens of brushes. I filled a couple of small cups with warm, soapy water and took everything outside. I opened the splattered plastic container of deep purple and used a preschool brush to smear a glob of paint across the ice. It froze within seconds, but there was enough time to spread the pigmented goo, if I feathered it quickly. It dried glossy and almost translucent where the ice peeked through the smudgy brush strokes.

I quickly mixed white and black paints and did a four-foot square scene of the Battle of Hoth. *Hothlanta.*

I didn't know what to do next, but I still wanted to be painting in the cold. It was fun and quiet, and I was alone with my thoughts for the first time in days.

What would the Bloggess paint?

Tessa and I had a long-standing love of Jennifer Lawson, The Bloggess. Her blogs about her crazy antics catapulted her to the top of our *Five-Famous-People-We'd-Invite-to-a-Dinner-Party* list.

Snow Patrol. "Crazy in Love."

Cover of a Beyoncé song.

Fuck Beyoncé. I'm listening to Snow Patrol.

Beyoncé.

And there was my answer. I painted a five-foot rendition of Jennifer Lawson's beloved metal chicken, Beyoncé.

By the end of the fourth day, I'd depicted a huge red sled, carefully painting **ROSEBUD** across the end. When I finished Jack Nicholson's face, breaking crazed through an axed door, I knew it was time to stop. If I didn't find a way to extract myself from the house, I was going to film a remake of *Fargo* in my backyard.

All I need is a wood chipper.

There was enough slushing of the long, flat driveway to start clearing it. I found heavy duty gloves and shovels, a push broom from the basement workshop, and hauled them to the front of the house. It was laborious, but I managed to clear an eighth of the driveway in two hours. It was better than any workout I'd had in a while, and it killed time.

Because of a previously-scheduled school holiday, the kids were out of school for ten days, right after the Christmas break. My mom friends and I joked on Facebook about drinking alone while we shoveled our own driveways. As much as I love my kids, being alone with anyone for too much time will make me insane. Especially when they have the social skills of, well, children.

Ian actually *cheered* when we were able to leave on Friday and go to the gym. He was *thrilled* to be in childcare for an hour while Mommy got to work out with her trainer. I was happy to take them with me to the grossly crowded grocery store, though I was so exhausted after an hour there that I stopped for take-out pizza on the way home.

Sam was with us the entire time, at least in body. After the first day of snow-caked house arrest, he tuned the boys and me out as best he could. He was working steadily and needed to be undisturbed. He wasn't drinking, but he was crankier than ever with us, and I did my best to deflect his attention away from the children.

His relentless hours of work were finally coming to fruition, though. He'd worked on some huge cases in the previous year, and this new one was turning out to be bigger than any of those. There was a hefty bonus coming his way in a few weeks. He was a rock star in his own circles, and he was being recognized for it.

It looked like there would be a little additional cash after bills were paid. "Is there anything special you'd like?" he asked. "This bonus is as much yours as it is mine. I couldn't work these hours if you weren't here for the boys."

There were always *things* I wanted—books, music, shoes—but I could usually just go buy whatever small thing I thought might hold my attention for a few days. Sam was willing to spend some serious money on me. What did I want?

"Hardly," I retorted sarcastically. "But I appreciate the sentiment. I'll think about it."

————————————

Alex called on Tuesday after everyone had returned to our regularly scheduled programming.

"How are things with you and Sam?"

"Okay. We were trapped by all of this damn snow for days. He's been an asshole. I swear he's worse when he's not drinking. And I wanted to talk to you and couldn't, which made *me* cranky."

"I know," Alex agreed. "I was thinking about you all weekend. Even when I was fucking my wife."

Huh.

I was excited, knowing that I got to him in his darkest, most private moments, that he was unable or unwilling to totally compartmentalize me all the time. But how would I feel, if I were Talia, knowing that my husband was thinking about another woman while he was inside me?

"We're trying for baby number two," he continued.

What a dick.

"Seriously? You tell me that *now*? That's an asshat move, Wheeler."

"What? How am I an asshat? I can't tell you that my wife and I want another baby?"

Is his head really that far up his ass?

"No, of course you can! It's just...."

"Okay, well, I'll let you go then."

"Alex...."

"Tierney, it's fine. I'll talk to you soon, okay?"

"Yep. Bye."

"Bye."

I was frustrated that we hadn't been able to hook up in Nashville. I was irritated that he could be so close and then still so distant, simultaneously. I was mad I hadn't been able to fuck him yet. The potential of this *thing* between us and the potential baby were suddenly driving a wedge into the middle of this non-relationship.

I knew he was working very hard to make his band successful, both for himself and his family. I knew how badly he wanted to be surrounded by his own large family, like the one he'd been part of growing up. I wanted nothing but absolute, fulfilling happiness for him. Always, and in every way. I didn't want to marry him or have his babies. I was sure that was a perfectly wonderful life, but I had no ridiculous expectation of that kind of future with him.

I loved Alex—though not like that—and he knew it. I didn't want that to make friendship between us hard. I wanted my shot at giving him the kind of fulfillment he and I both knew I could. And it made my heart go all fluttery in those moments when I felt like I was what mattered to him, even when I knew it was fleeting and transient. As much I craved the sexual play and the flirting games, I valued him and his friendship above everything else.

My phone rang a few minutes later, but I didn't recognize the out-of-state number.

"Hello?"

"Hi, Tierney! It's Paul Sommers."

What the fuck?

"H-h-hi, Paul," I stammered. "How are you?"

"I'm good! How was your holiday?"

Why was Paulie calling me? How did he get my number?

"Pretty good. Too much travel to Birmingham to see the family. The boys were out of school last week for all of this fucking snow. I was glad to send them off today. How was your Christmas?"

"We actually got to stay in Austin for Christmas this year. It was nice. I miss so much time with the girls when I'm on the road. I would love to be stuck at home with them for an extra week."

Thanks. Make me feel bad for wanting my family to go away for a few hours. "I love them, don't get me wrong. We couldn't *go* anywhere. And the snow sucked for snowballs and snowmen. Sam was working the whole time so it was just me and the boys. I ended up painting on the ice."

"Yeah! I saw the pictures on Facebook. Why did you paint a giant chicken?"

"Oh!" I giggled nervously. "That's Beyoncé. It's a Bloggess thing."

I could almost hear the crickets chirping as Paul tried to make sense of what the hell I was saying. "Well, they were really good, whatever they were. The Jack Nicholson was fucking awesome!"

Paul Sommers is no Wil Wheaton.

"Thanks!"

Now why the fuck are you calling me?

"What does Sam do again?" Paul asked.

"Information security. He's a hacker hunter."

"Like this Digital Freedom *whatever* that's been in the news?"

"I can neither confirm nor deny, but yes, just like DFF."

"That's crazy!"

"You have no idea, Paulie." I walked into the kitchen for a glass of water. "How's your leg?"

Paul started to laugh. "*Oh my god!* Stitches! Tetanus shot! That crazy bitch fucking *bit* me, Tierney!"

"Tessa and I joked that she was trying to turn you into a vampire." I drank from my glass, calculating in my head how many glasses of water I'd had for the day. "Alex said it took a while to heal."

"Yeah, being on the road, we're not very healthy most of the time. There's a lot of bad food and drinking and never enough sleep. When I got home, Sara got me back to being vegetarian, like I usually am when I'm home. I got better really quickly."

"Wives are good at that. I've lost all this weight now, and the men are still griping because I don't let them eat ice cream every day."

"How much weight have you lost?"

I paused, pretending to be thinking. "I'm down thirty-five pounds. That's probably another twenty since I saw you in Chicago."

"*Wow.*" He sounded genuinely impressed. "That's awesome. I bet Sam loves it."

Does it matter? "He does, I guess. I assume he's noticed."

"Tierney, how could he not?"

"Because you don't notice a lot of things after nearly twenty years together."

Paul chuckled. "You're right. Sara bought new furniture while I was on tour. It took me two weeks to notice I was planted on a different sofa. I guess, after that much time together, we just start to take it for granted and only notice what we want to notice."

I leaned against the kitchen counter, glancing at the clock to see how much time I had before the boys would be home from school. "I think we assume things are running smoothly. And we have every reason to want to see them that way, but it makes it hard to recognize the things that've gone wrong until they're almost catastrophic."

Why did you call me?

"I'm sorry, Paulie, I know you didn't call to talk to me about marital troubles."

"I was in the studio with Seth Wiezel yesterday. It was the first time I'd seen him since he was in Atlanta, and he said he saw you and asked if I'd seen your paintings. Maybe I'll get you to do a poster for us sometime?"

Wow.

Butterflies did cartwheels in my stomach. Was Paul Sommers really asking me to do artwork for him?

"Yeah, sure. Just let me know what you want. I'd be happy to give it a shot."

"Oh shit! It's almost three. I have to get the girls! I'm sorry, Tierney, it was great to talk to you!"

"You, too, Paul!"

I assumed Seth had given him my number, which was fine.

Paul Sommers just called me.

You're having phone sex with Alex Wheeler.

Curiouser and curiouser.

I was flattered by Paul's suggestion that maybe I do something for Junkture. As much as I loved the band, it might be a unique way to give back a little bit of that love. I was getting my hopes up, though. I'd learned exactly how fickle and flighty rock stars could be. I wasn't getting excited about it unless he called with an actual request.

From: Tierney Cavanaugh Johnson
Date: January 17th 5:39 pm
To: Alex Wheeler
Subject: Paulie

Paul called me this afternoon. Completely out of the blue. I'm assuming he got my number from Seth and not from you. It was fine, just very odd.

Alex showed up on Saturday night, requesting a Skype chat.

Tierney   Where are you?

Alex   Home, hanging with Jack and Ginger. Amber's sick. Talia's out. How are you?

Tierney   Good! Bored.

Alex   Sam home?

Tierney   Yes, but working. Boys watching a movie.

Alex   I'm not an asshat.

Tierney   Your head is so far up your ass, you wear it like a crown. You're Princess Asshat!

Alex   Does it make you want to fuck a princess? ;)

Tierney   rock star princess

Alex   lol
So what the hell did Paul want?

Tierney   I still don't know. It was like he just called to chat.
Did you give him my number?

Alex   Nope.
Did you have phone sex with him?

Tierney   Ha! No, but 20YO Paul was the kind of guy I would've gone for in high school. His singer was too much of a pretty boy jackass :P

Alex   That's pretty boy asshat, thank you!

Tierney   Own it, Princess!

Alex   lol
So you had a crush on Paul?

Tierney   Strangely no.

Alex   Poor Paul Sommers. He doesn't know what he's missing

Tierney   You're the only rock star I get all whorey for, babycakes

Alex   I like it when you get all whorey for me, Buttercup

Tierney   mmmmmm do you?

There was a long, inopportune pause in the conversation.

Alex   aw fuck, buttercup! I gotta go. Amber's really sick.

Tierney   no problem.   Call me this week.   Hope she feels better!

He'd obviously sought me out as soon as he had some time alone. But his sick child had to take precedence, and he was gone again almost as quickly as he'd appeared. I was worked up and frustrated. I went back to my Saturday night on the couch with the boys, while Sam worked in the office.

I emailed him a day or two later. No response. Again, a couple days after that. Still no response. This went on for two weeks, and I was making myself crazy.

I kept replaying in my mind something he'd said to me early on, that if he got tired of talking to someone—friend, fan, whatever—he probably wouldn't actually tell them he was done, that he would just stop responding and let it fall away in its own time. It was part of the minutiae that was filed away in my detail-filled brain, along with virtually everything else that ever passed between us.

Time passed so strangely between us sometimes. It didn't seem to flow at the same speed as everything else around it. I knew it was just time, a constant, but the speed with which things transpired between us originally was still surprising. I had to really think about how long it took, the days over which it played out. There was constant contact, then not, then yes, then not. I hadn't expected to hear from him at all during the holidays, but then I did several times.

It was addictive to me, good or bad. I reveled in that time, when I had his attention. He had the innate ability to make me feel special to him, and I so wanted to believe in that. I wasn't sexually deprived at home, and Sam was making an effort to spend more time with me. But part of me was constantly tied up with Alex. Again, good or bad—I didn't know.

He was a charming, impulsive, distractible ass who could say the most unobtrusive things to me and have my undivided attention. Sometimes it took me days to come down from that and check back into the fact that he wasn't at my beck and call. I didn't begrudge him or Talia or anyone else that, certainly; it was just a side-effect of our initial, immersive bonding.

I needed him to be openly communicative with me. If he felt like he needed to sever ties with me, I hoped he would have the balls to tell me. I hoped it would never happen. Even if the sexting were to come to an end, I wouldn't want to stop talking to him or having him there. I adored Alex and genuinely hoped we would get the chance for an actual, physical hook-up. But I was willing to do whatever we needed that would work for either or both of us. I needed him not to leave me twisting in the wind if he found it too difficult.

I didn't want to seem like a simpering girl—it really wasn't who I was—but I emailed him once more, asking him to check in if he got a chance, to let me know he was okay. He didn't have to call, though he was welcome to do so, any time. I knew he was home and working. I reminded him again that I was there if he needed me, that it really was okay to have me as a friend.

The next night, I was asleep, deeply embedded in a fog of cold and flu medicine. My cell phone was plugged in on my nightstand. It startled me awake when it vibrated hard against the wood, lighting up the otherwise empty bedroom. It was Alex, and it was 12:51 in the morning.

"Hey," I answered groggily.

"Oh god, I'm sorry. I woke you." It sounded like he was driving.

Duh. It's almost one in the morning.

"Yeah, it's okay."

"I'm sorry. Go back to sleep. I'll call you tomorrow."

"Nonono. It's okay. I'm really sick. I have the flu."

"Yeah, your email said you were fevery. I just got over that shit. I know how bad it is. You need to sleep."

"Noooo. Are you okay?"

Why the fuck are you calling me at one in the morning?

"Yeah, I'm fine. I just got your message to check in and realized I hadn't talked to you. That email doesn't go straight to my phone, and I hadn't checked it in a few days. I'm sorry. Everything's fine. I called as soon as I could. Really, go back to sleep."

"But I want to talk to you." Even I could hear how awful I sounded.

"Buttercup, you need to rest. It's all good. I promise, I'll call you tomorrow."

"Okay. Goodnight."

"'Night. Bye."

I was surprised that he'd called. I was glad, but I wasn't expecting it. Especially not so late. I knew he was busy getting ready to go back out on the road. But he sounded genuinely... *concerned*? I didn't know what it was, but it was good from my feverish, sleepy perspective.

I was back asleep almost instantly. Sam hadn't come to bed yet and didn't hear the call.

Chapter 12

Valentine's Day was coming.

I *hate* Valentine's Day. On the surface, it seems like a sweet idea, a special day to tell your sweetheart that you love them. When you're a kid, Valentine's Day is all about the heart-shaped box of candy from your parents, and the class party. I remember making the Valentine's mailboxes at school every year. I always liked covering an old shoe box or a paper bag in handmade pink and red hearts and uneven paper doilies. Then on the day of the Valentine's party, everyone would walk around and drop their store-bought Valentine's into each other's boxes. There was no surprise; you knew you would give one to everyone in your class, and that everyone would give you one. Even the people you didn't like. It was like some weird, forced, social positive reinforcement.

And don't even get me started on what happens when you like a boy and he doesn't like you back, or vice versa. It's just creepy and a little degrading.

But the *real* dislike of the Hallmark Holiday started when I was eleven and my parents told me they were getting divorced, the night after Valentine's Day—which was also the night before my mother's birthday.

The next year, I started my period.

I was in high school the year I had chicken pox for Valentine's Day. Damien came to my house to visit me while I was home sick from school. He brought me a card filled with heart-shaped confetti, and a Mylar balloon. Then he got mad that I wouldn't have sex with him while I was running a 102.3 fever. He stormed out, and we didn't talk for two days.

There was the year when the apartment downstairs and over one from ours caught on fire in the middle of the night. Sam and I had company for the weekend, including two little girls who had to be rushed into the freezing Alabama night without shoes or a coat. Our cat got lost in the shuffle, though thankfully showed up unharmed. The guy who started the fire in the other apartment died.

There were two separate Valentine's Days when we and I had huge, blow-out fights that resulted in our not speaking for days on end. I left for three days during one of them. That was the same year I had to have minor surgery on Valentine's Day, the removal of a benign cyst that grew under my thick hair. I have a jagged two inch scar on the back of my head from that one.

There was one year that was okay: the year Tripp was born. He was actually born the day before. (If one more person told me to hold out just a few hours longer, I was going to punch them.) Of course, the day after he came home from the hospital—jaundiced and dehydrated—we were forced to huddle in our basement to escape a passing tornado. That was fun.

So the dreaded curse was looming. I never knew when exactly it would hit—a few days before or after—and I never knew what unexpected, uncomfortable drama it would bring. With all of the tension in the house around Christmas and New Year's, I was dreading the worst.

I decided to hope for the best. Maybe this would be the year we would break that curse.

I wanted to get something really special for Sam, something to show just how much I loved him.

For days, I waded through memories of happier times. I wandered nostalgically through our lengthy history, trying to find a place and time when we'd been the most content and in love, when we'd been the most drawn to each other. I remembered all the nights in our bed, when I thought my heart would burst from the joy and laughter, giggling breathlessly in the dark. There were the nights early in our relationship, when we would come home after work and drink or get high and lie together on the floor of our tiny apartment for hours, listening to music—old Red Hot Chili Peppers or Leonard Cohen or Junkture.

I laughed to myself about the year the blizzard unexpectedly hit Huntsville a few weeks after we moved in together, dumping upwards of eight inches of snow on the Rocket City. As soon as the weather had started to turn, Sam had taken me to the grocery store to stock up on junk food and beer and sickeningly fruity wine coolers. Neither of us thought to get firewood, but we were wasted enough to want to roast marshmallows. Sam opened the French doors to the small patio and spread the drifted snow apart, carving out a resting place for a can of Sterno. Stoned and a little drunk, we huddled together under a blanket on the floor, holding long, wooden skewers out the door and over the tiny fire, laughing at how good the hot, sticky marshmallows tasted, even with a hint of chemical smoke.

The last time I'd felt so close to him was a couple of summers before, during our last family vacation to Myrtle Beach. It was the first time we'd taken the children for such a long road trip, and it was hours and hours of MadLibs and the kid-friendly, alternative rock playlist I'd put together for the trip—songs that were okay for the kids but that weren't sung by cartoon characters.

Sam and the boys and I would sleep late and hit the beach upon rising, using our small boogie boards to maneuver the roaring Atlantic waves until Tripp and Ian were ready happily exhausted. Sam would work quietly on his computer while I read, waiting for the kids to wake from their nap and beg to be taken to the pool. After three days, Sam's broad, tanned shoulders ached from letting our sons use him as a human diving board, but he was all smiles and wry laughter as he dug through my suitcase for ibuprofen.

We found a local babysitter to keep the boys while we went out to dinner one night. It was the first time we'd ever been able to finagle a Date Night while on vacation. I chose a white skirt and tank top, new flip-flops and pretty pink lip gloss, for our walk to the Sea Captain's House, a few blocks from our condo.

We walked hand-in-hand to the oceanfront restaurant and waited for our table in the covered patio, listening to a local singer croon his best Jimmy Buffett. Sam ordered drinks for us and suggested we move outside to enjoy the view of the brilliant green-blue water.

I looked at Sam in the long, late sunlight. There was the boy I'd tumbled into love with on first sight, but there was also the man who worked his ass off to give me and our beautiful children an easy, uncomplicated life. His gray eyes still sparkled like they had when we were so young and giddy in our love. Now they were framed by thin laugh lines and crinkles from worry about the burdens of providing for our family. I could see the strong cheekbones and dark, thick brows that both boys had thankfully inherited from their father.

He looked at me and smiled brightly, quickly.

"You look beautiful," he'd told me, leaning in to kiss my neck.

"I look fat," I'd laughed.

"You look *beautiful*, Tierney. Your eyes are the same color as the ocean right now."

I blushed and smiled back.

We were ushered to an inside table and ordered a second and third round of fruity beach drinks to go with crab cakes and shrimp and grits. We shared each other's food, offering bites straight from our forks, not worrying to politely place a sample on the other's plate. We held hands across the table while we waited for dessert.

We strolled languidly along the beach and back toward Ocean Boulevard, hand-in-hand, stopping every few minutes to kiss and smile at each other.

"I love you," I'd murmured with each kiss. Every time I'd felt it, I said it before the moment escaped us.

We paid the sitter and checked on the boys. Standing in the doorway of their bedroom, we watched them sleep, their thin, tanned bodies entwined equally between cool, white sheets and their brother's legs.

"They're so pretty," I'd whispered in amazement.

"Like a pile of puppies," Sam had replied.

In our closed bedroom, Sam opened the glass door that led out to the secluded, ocean view balcony. Moonlight filtered through the vertical blinds, casting glowing lines across the bed. The night breeze off the ocean carried the roar of the high tide up to our seventh floor room.

I kicked my shoes into the closet and waited patiently by the bed for my husband.

"Thanks for dinner," I said quietly, my sunburned arms encircling Sam's waist. "I had a really nice time."

"Mmm-hmmm." He nuzzled against my neck, running his hands under the bottom of my long skirt. "Thank you for getting a sitter."

Methodically and full of love, we undressed each other, kissing each inch of newly exposed flesh as if it were the first time we'd seen each other naked. He slid my thin panties to the floor, his hands roaming across my ass. I self-consciously tensed when he touched my ample hips. During that first time, I'd been so worried about how I looked and if I would be a good lover for him. I was still not happy with my body, but I knew neither of us would leave that bed without coming. Sam was so gentle, and I pushed away the anxieties of my bodies and let myself feel him as he caressed me slowly.

Naked and stretched along each other, we kissed deeply. Our tongues did a perfect dance in the other's mouth, teasing and flicking, tasting of liquor and salt. My nipples were hard and pressed into his hot chest, heartbeats pounding against each other with their own rhyme and reason. Sam sucked my nipple into his mouth as he pushed his cock inside me. Even after so many years, he'd still felt perfectly fitted when he was in me, and I'd gasped at the feeling of *wholeness* when our bodies yielded fully to the other's.

We didn't talk. To say anything would've required us to stop kissing, and there was too much love for words to tell. He entwined his fingers in mine, holding my hands over my head, as he swayed against me, pulling and pushing us both to our orgasm. I hid my face against his shoulder, biting lightly as I cried out, the sounds of crashing waves and Sam's gasping moans mingling in the billowing wind.

We'd returned from vacation to the house and kids and Sam's ever-oppressing work schedule. For every media interview Sam did, or every meeting with a government agency or high-level executive, there were dozens of hours of prep—either at the office across town or in his home office, secluded away from me and the children. The pressure on him was constantly building, which could make him irritable and quick-tempered. If I made sure the house was ordered and the boys were settled, perhaps the domestic harmony would help lighten Sam's mood, at least until the beer could kick in and do the job.

But the trying exhausted me, and Sam worked longer and more intense hours. He barely had time to kiss the boys goodnight and tell us all goodbye the next morning. The higher his professional star climbed, the less light there was cast on me, and I was left to unsuredly grope my way through our dimming life.

I wanted to help us both remember that last vacation. I wanted to give him a reason to support my painting, to acknowledge that what I was doing was good. I went back to the art supply store to buy watercolors and pressed papers and a watercolor board.

"How's your painting going?" the sales guy asked me.

I looked at him, a little confused. "Fine...."

"Aren't you...," he started slowly. "Didn't you buy all new supplies a few weeks ago? Acrylics?"

I nodded and smiled, remembering that he'd been the one working that day. "I did! Yes, it's all... going pretty well, thanks."

"Well, we have in-store shows sometimes. You should send in pictures—" he handed me a postcard with information about their quarterly events "—so we can get some of your stuff included. We're always looking for new artists who'd like to share what they've been working on."

"Thank you!" I tucked the card into my purse, reminding myself to take some pictures.

I took my new paints and papers home. I marked off the margins on the hot pressed watercolor paper and stretched across the watercolor board, taping down the deckled edges. I prepped the paper with a damp sponge and let it dry overnight, while I sketched.

I searched my laptop for the photographs from vacation and found a picture taken from the bedroom balcony of the condo. The edge of the building and perfectly aligned rows of balcony rails projected over the ocean at sunrise. I drew the long, vertical edge of the stucco, the concrete floors and round railing caps jutting perpendicularly from the edifice. The thinner, square balusters were affixed solidly between the top and bottom rails, parallel to the building. The pattern repeated into the distance, the edges glowing with reflected morning sun.

Burnt umber and ultramarine blue mixed to create the shadow on the weatherworn facade. Cobalt blue and cadmium yellow for the deep, distant ocean that seemed motionless from afar. Waves roiled in burnt sienna and viridian, cascading frothily across light sands with a touch of yellow ochre.

For three days, I worked in the geometry of the picture. My shoulders strained against the minute detail. I let the laundry pile up, overflowing from the hampers onto the floor in each bedroom, pouring all of my excess energy into the lush and fluid memory of our happiest time.

I mounted the seascape in a driftwood frame I'd found the day before at an antiques store. The faded brown wood picked up the burnt undertones in the watercolors. I carefully wrapped it all in red tissue paper and tied it up neatly with a raffia bow.

I was excited about the painting. It was good, I could see that, but I also wanted Sam to love it. I wanted him to see that my painting again could be something we could both enjoy. I was eager to give him the present and struggled to keep my anxiousness at bay. Sam didn't seem to notice.

Before we could get to Valentine's Day, we had Tripp's birthday to celebrate. It had taken eighteen months of shots and pills, plus twenty-six hours of labor, to get my beautiful boy into the world.

Not even the tensions with Sam could keep me from celebrating my son.

We took the boys to Medieval Times for dinner and the show. They loved cheering for the evil Green Knight, and Tripp was thrilled when he was knighted by the king. It was fun and sweet, but Sam and I were distant. We sat at opposite ends of the children from each other, leaning across their young laps to pass napkins and help with their food.

"When did our baby get so *big*?" I asked as we walked across the parking lot toward the car. The boys bounded along the sidewalk, laughing in paper crowns as they sparred with light-up plastic swords.

"Genetics," Sam said. "They get that from you."

"How did the knights' swords *spark* like that when they hit each other?" Ian asked excitedly.

"*Magic*," Tripp assured him sarcastically, toying with the edge his souvenir photograph.

"There's no such thing as *magic*, Tripp! It's all tricks and lies! But I still wanna know how they made *fire* shoot off their sword like that."

"That's what she said," Sam quipped at me.

As we drove home in the dark, I listened to my sons giggle and recount every detail of the show—how the Red Knight was the best swordsman but how the Green Knight was just the coolest. I reached for Sam's hand, holding it in mine and resting it on his lap. He left it there for less than a minute before he squeezed my fingers and put his hand back on the steering wheel.

I woke early the next morning and made heart-shaped pancakes on Valentine's Day.

"These are the best pancakes ever!" Ian crowed, stuffing a syrupy forkful into his mouth.

I kissed his dark blond head. "I'm glad you like them, sweet pea."

"Can we open our candy?" Tripp begged. "Please? Just one piece before school?"

"It'll be one piece before school and one more after, then where will you be?" Sam joked. "Chocolate hearts are a gateway, Son."

I poured a cup of coffee for Sam and placed it next to his plate. "Happy Valentine's Day, baby."

"Happy Valentine's Day to you!" He reached up for a kiss. "I have to get something today. Can we do cards tonight?"

"Sure."

By six that night, dinner was set on the table, cards and Sam's gift sitting neatly to the side. The boys sat in front of their empty plates, their hungry faces expectant and waiting.

We hadn't heard from Sam.

"I guess Daddy's working late," I said. "He can eat when he gets home."

> ### Sam Johnson
> ### Feb 14th 6:15 PM
>
> **Are you on your way?   Dinner's ready.**
>
> ### Feb 14th 6:42 PM
>
> **Boys are finished eating. Showers then cards I guess. Trying to hold out until you're home.**

We finished dinner and cleaned the kitchen, the boys sharing the kid gossip from school that day. They each dug through their heart-decorated paper bags of class valentines, recycling anything that wasn't candy or a sticker or a temporary tattoo. They took long showers and brushed their teeth after *just one more!* piece of candy.

> ### Feb 14th 9:02 PM

Home in 15

By the time Sam came in, the boys had been in bed for an hour. I was lying in our bed, watching television in the dark. He pushed the bedroom door open and placed a vase of roses on my dresser.

"Happy Valentine's Day!" he said sweetly. He leaned across the bed to kiss me quickly.

"How was your day?" I asked.

"Okay. Sorry I'm late. There was an incident, and I was in the lab all day. Marketing came by around four and made me do a quick interview. By the time it was done, everyone was hungry, and they wanted to go to dinner."

You couldn't call? "So you've already eaten?"

"Yeah, sorry." He put away his things and changed into a t-shirt and shorts. "How were the boys?"

I stared at the television screen, mindlessly changing channels from my pillow. "They're fine." *They missed you.*

"Can I turn the lamp on?"

"Sure."

I propped myself against my pillow, sitting upright to see the card Sam handed to me.

"And these are for you." He moved the roses to my nightstand.

The *To My Wife on Valentine's Day* card was sweet. Store-bought, probably that evening, but signed ornately with a hand-written note about how much he loved me, how great a mom and partner I was.

"Thank you," I said, leaning toward him for a kiss. I gingerly pulled a deep red rose toward me and smelled the distinctive aroma that Sam knew I loved. "The roses are beautiful."

I flipped the blankets back and got up to retrieve his cards and gift from the kitchen.

"For you," I said, handing them to him.

Sam methodically opened the envelopes, careful to pull back the flaps in such a way that they didn't tear. *Happy Valentine's Day, Daddy!* *You're a Wonderful Husband*

"Thanks," he said after reading the cards.

"Open your gift."

He was as careful with the tissue paper as he'd been with the envelopes. He untaped the paper from the backing of the frame and flipped it over. He looked at it for a long moment, holding it out in front of him in assessment.

"Uh-huh," he intoned finally, "it's very nice."

"Do you know what it is?"

He studied it again. "Myrtle Beach? From the condo balcony?"

I smiled at nodded. "I thought it might look nice in your new office."

"I love it. Thank you."

He kissed me quickly and stood, putting the painting away in the bottom of his closet. "I'll take it in next week when I have time to hang it." He turned back to me, closing his closet door.

"If you don't like it...," I said tentatively.

"Tierney, *no. I love it.*"

"You're sure?"

"I promise. It's really beautiful. And you're right. It will look great in my office."

I knelt on the blankets and faced Sam, standing at the end of the bed.

"I love you," I said, kissing his neck.

"I love you, too," he murmured into my hair.

"I miss the beach." I flicked my tongue along his jawline.

"*Mmmm.* Me, too."

He kissed me gently, slowly, his tongue soft and cautious in my mouth. I snaked my own tongue precociously around his, tempting him to follow. He kissed me harder and pushed me back against the tousled sheets.

Sam dangled teasing kisses along my neck and stomach, toying with the edge of my panties. His warm hands pulled the front of my cami down, and my breasts splayed out in the lamplight. I rubbed them, kneading them into a sexier pose, pinching lightly at my own nipples. Sam watched me over the low mound of my belly, as he tugged at my panties with his teeth, pulling them off and dropping them to the floor.

"God, I love to watch you," he breathed hotly against me.

I held his gaze and twisted my nipples just a little, lifting my heavy breasts which strained against the tension.

"I love it when you see me," I hissed.

He licked at my pussy, a small flicker of panting before he dipped his tongue into the wetness. I arched my back, my hips pressing down and up, trying to find his mouth.

"Not yet," he teased.

He pushed my legs as far apart as he could, holding them down with his arms. Oh so slowly, he caressed me with his tongue, lapping slowly with wide, firm strokes. Sam nibbled at my clit and blew lightly, teasing me with just enough sensation to make me want more.

"I want you on my face," he said, grinning slyly.

He undressed quickly and slid up the middle of the bed, lying flat. I turned around and straddled his head and shoulders, facing away from him. I sucked in my belly, hoping neither of us would notice it in the naked distraction. Sam ran his hands up and down my back, mercifully avoiding my hips and ass, while I came face-to-face with his cock.

I leaned over him and took the head between my lips, swirling my tongue along the edge. He moaned and licked my dripping slit. I jacked his cock while I teased him with butterfly kisses from base to tip. He shoved his tongue inside me and fluttered it back and forth. I sucked farther down his cock, back up, and with more force. He dragged his tongue across my clit and licked me all the way up to my ass. I fondled his balls and took him down my throat, my tongue pulsing against his hot flesh. He took my clit in his mouth and sucked.

It became a race, a contest, to see who would cave, who could get the other one off first. But I could tell I was about to lose. I didn't care.

I stopped sucking and pressed my forehead against on his thigh, feeling the warmth and tautness of his muscles under the dark, sparse hair. I distractedly stroked his dick, forgetting to *try* to make him feel good. He knew I was caving. He spread my pussy lips wide and shoved his tongue all the way in me, raking it across my g-spot. My clit was twitching, so close to coming. I could feel the crazy spasms inside, and I wanted him to fuck me when I came.

"I need you in me," I panted.

"Come for me first," he mumbled against my mound and sucked my clit back into his mouth. He thrust two fingers inside me and rubbed the hard little ridge. I knew it was about to be big and messy.

"Oh fuck!" I whined. I had dropped his cock altogether, trying just to keep myself from crushing him when I came. Then the familiar tingle started right under my clit. "I'm gonna come, baby."

I writhed back and forth, riding his face. He pulled his fingers out of me and put his tongue back in, his lower lip hooked across my clit. He sucked one last time, and I jerked against him. My clit twitched, and I sat almost upright as my orgasm blasted through my body.

I moaned and ground against his mouth. When I tried to pull away, he pulled me back tighter, his arms locked around my thighs. He kept licking and sucking until I subsided and couldn't take any more.

I rolled carefully off of him and lay on the bed, luxuriating in the buzz still wafting through my body. He was on top of me immediately, his wet mouth on mine. I sucked his tongue that tasted like me and spread my legs to make room for him.

"In me. Now!" I said.

His arms on either side of me, I pulled my legs up and reached between us. I grabbed his cock and held it firmly, right at my opening. He teased us both, putting just the head in, pulling almost all of the way out, then back in a bit more. On the third pass he shoved his cock all the way into me, his balls slapping me in the ass. I cried out and wrapped my legs tighter around him.

And then, we just *fucked*. Hips slammed and legs rubbed and mouths sucked and kissed. We were sweaty and panting and couldn't get deep enough inside of each other.

For all the thousands of times we'd been naked with each other, I could *never* get over how *good* he felt inside me. I relished the crush of him—the weight, the heat, the incomparable comfort of how we molded around each other.

I pinched his nipples lightly and leaned up for a kiss.

He slammed against me, over and over. I watched him carefully in the low light, needing to see the tension and the effort in his face, that look of emotional carnality that proved how much *he* needed *me* in that moment. I pushed my hips up against him and squeezed his cock as hard as I could with my pussy. He gasped and his eyes flew open, looking into my eyes when he came, spurt after hot spurt inside me. I kept squeezing him until he was soft and spent. He rested on top of me for a moment, catching his breath.

"I love you," I said, kissing his neck, his cheek.

"I love you, too."

"Happy Valentine's Day, Sam."

He pushed up onto his forearms and looked into my eyes. "Happy Valentine's Day."

Chapter 13

One Friday afternoon, I was leaving the boys' school, having just finished part of an ongoing project for PTA. After four hours of paper folding and envelope stuffing and sorting it all into teachers' mailboxes, I was exhausted. I had almost three hours before the boys would come barreling through the front door, and I needed some time to clear the din of polite mom chit-chat from my head.

Driving home, I heard the *ding* of a text on my phone.

Alex Wheeler
Mar 8th   12:31 PM

Lost my skype contacts. Send me ur email addy again.

Driving. Can u call?

The phone rang almost immediately.

"Hey!"

"Hey, yourself. What's the address for your Skype account?"

I told him which one I thought it was.

"Yep, there you are. Where are you now?"

"I'm headed home from the school. Where are you?"

"In Austin. At the apartment."

Paul and Sara Sommers had moved their young family to Austin a few years after Junkture had become a staple of alternative rock radio. When the band was making enough money that they could be anywhere they truly *wanted* to live, Paul decided he wanted to move to Texas. That was just as the South by Southwest Music Festival was growing exponentially, driving the expansion of Austin's already eclectic music scene.

He refurbished an old recording studio that quickly became Junkture's home away from home. Even if they didn't record their albums there—choosing instead to record close to whatever big-name producer they'd hired—they used the studio, The Deck, for demos and rehearsals. *Persona Non Grata* had been recorded there, as Alex had explained to me, as a huge cost-cutting measure. They'd self-produced, letting Paulie mix the record, as he did for so many small artists in the Austin area.

Austin had also become home to band's record label, Indulgema Melodio. The guys had spent years under the major label system and were tired of the hassle. If they weren't battling the label for artistic control, they were battling each other, assigning blame over who'd made what side deal behind the others' backs. It had become ugly and regularly contentious by the time their last tour had ended, triggering the four-year hiatus.

After the four of them had time to breathe and enjoy their lives, they'd realized how much they missed their music. Working by themselves or with other artists hadn't felt the same as creating something so satisfying with their brothers. But the major labels weren't sure Junkture was still relevant to the current landscape of the music industry. They'd decided to leverage their years and knowledge of the business and do it all on their terms.

Paulie had also opened his own club in Austin, off of Sixth Street, called Flunky's. There was a small apartment upstairs from the bar, where the guys would stay when they came to work.

Alex had told me that Paul often crashed there when he and Sara were fighting.

"When did you get in?" I asked, turning into my neighborhood.

"Couple hours ago. We start rehearsals tomorrow before we leave for Europe next week. Paul wants to lay some new tracks, too. How close are you to naked?"

"I'll be home and declothed in a matter of minutes," I laughed. "Are you alone?"

"For now. Max is here, but he's asleep. Charlie's staying at Paulie's."

When the band traveled, they often paired off as Alex-and-Max and Paul-and-Charlie, especially when they had to share hotel rooms. Max was usually with Alex for afterhours partying. He was single, always prowling for pussy, and sometimes Alex lived a little vicariously through Max's conquests, the tiniest bit envious of that freedom to tap whatever he wanted.

I turned onto my street. "So you're just hanging out, all alone, while your bassist is sleeping in the other room?"

"Yup."

"Busy chatting up your other sexting friends while you waited for me?"

"I don't do this with anyone else." He sounded a little offended.

"Really?" I heard my voice get sweet and soft. I pulled my car into the driveway, thankful the housekeeper was already done for the day and gone.

"Yes, really. Why would you think that?"

"I don't know. I don't make assumptions."

"Tierney, no, I'm not doing this with anyone else. I'm so fucking busy. I hope you know I don't have *time* to do this with anyone else, and I call you every chance I get, as soon as I can. I just can't always contact you when I think about you."

My heart sang.

"What are you doing right now?" I asked, smiling to myself.

"Waiting for you to get naked."

"Are you trying to get me excited?"

"Yup."

"Are you going to let me finish this time?"

Alex chuckled. "Yup."

I came into the house and locked the door behind me. I sauntered down the hall to the bedroom, already excited about the prospect of some time with Alex.

"Hang on," I said. I put my phone on speaker and set it on the dresser. "I'm getting naked right now. And I got a new toy, by the way."

"You're making my dick hard, Buttercup. What did you get?"

I pulled my shirt over my head and tossed it to the floor. "It's a black bullet vibe. With a tiny wireless remote." I dropped the rest of my clothes and opened my dresser, retrieving the new toy from under a pile of panties at the back of the drawer.

"Here," I said, "listen." I hit the switch and held the small, egg-shaped toy near the phone. It buzzed quietly in my hand. I picked up the phone, taking it off speaker. "It's *very* quiet."

"Are you gonna use that with your husband?"

"Nope."

"Are you gonna use that with me?"

"Yep. The next time I see you, you get the remote."

I heard new background noises over the phone.

"What's that?" I asked.

"That's Max getting his lazy ass out of bed. *Are you up finally, you lazy fucker?*"

"Do you need me to let you go?" I was really horny and would probably have lost it if he'd left me hanging again.

"Nope. *Did you listen to that track I sent you?*"

"Are you gonna talk to me while I come, while you sit there with Max in the room?"

"Yup. *Yeah, I'm talking to Tierney Cavanaugh.*"

"*Hey, Tierney Cavanaugh!*" Max chimed from the background.

"Am I on speaker?"

"No. I have my earbuds. Hands free."

"So you're talking to me hands-free, and you want me to come for you, while you sit there and work with Max in the room?"

"Yes, please."

"That's hot, Alex."

"Yup. What are you doing right now? Tell me where those hands are."

"*Can he hear you?!*"

"Noooo. He has on headphones. *Hey, Max! Can you hear me?*" No response. "*Cavanaugh's fucking herself for me. Can you hear that?*" Nothing. "Get your fucking toy, Buttercup. Get the little bullet."

"Right now? For you?"

"Yep. Right now. And tell me *all* about it."

"Maybe I should just wait and let you see it in person," I tantalized.

"The next time you see me will probably be at a show."

"*Exactly*. I'll find you, before the show. There's no reason anyone would think anything about my being there early. I could be there for soundcheck. It wouldn't be surprising to anyone."

"Not at all."

"You'll get done, smile, come give me a hug. I can hug everyone hello and make my pleasantries. And none of them will know when I slip the little black remote into your hand. You'll look at me funny for half a second before you realize what it is and drop it into your pocket, a little flustered and excited."

Alex chuckled huskily.

"You want to push the button, but you're afraid someone will hear it. They're all so close right now," I whispered. "And as I walk ahead of you, trying my best to not attach myself to your hip, you'll reach in your pocket and try it out, just a quick, little push."

I pushed the tiny button again and held the vibrator near the phone.

"No one can hear it. It's really hard not to gasp or laugh when my pussy starts to vibrate. Even with the anticipation, the buzzing is unexpected. I'm dying to go into the bathroom and rub my clit."

I slid my hand between my legs.

"*Don't*," Alex ordered. "Leave your clit alone."

"But my panties are *soaked*."

"Good. But you can't come yet. I'm not gonna let you. I want you to feel that buzz for a while. Get worked up for when I fuck you."

I shoved the bullet inside myself and shivered against the vibrations.

"Just think about being on stage with the remote in your hand. I'll be out in the audience, right next to the stage. During the show, you're doing your best to not pay any more attention to me than to anyone else. But there are stolen glances and grins. Every time I see your hand go toward your pocket, I squeeze my pussy tight, just hoping you're about to push my button. Sometimes yes, sometimes no. It's a giant tease in front of a thousand people.

"And then... it's that riff that I love. The opening of 'Dollface'. *Will he or won't he?* Will I get the absolute, unadulterated joy of Alex *fucking* Wheeler singing my favorite song to me? Will I be sober enough to sing along? Will I be brave enough after Chicago?

"There you are, inches from my face, only the mic separating my mouth from yours. I'm trying to keep up with you, letting the energy of the melody pass from you to me and back again. Your eyes are locked on mine, intense, and I know if I look away right now, I'll lose it in front of everybody. I can taste your breath, you're so close, and it's taking everything I have not to put my tongue in your mouth. You laugh at me and flash that easy, broad smile. You kiss my cheek. As you turn toward the back of the stage, the vibrations start again."

I heard him sigh deeply. "That would be so *good*. I want to watch your face while you try to sing and come at the same time. I want you to feel your pussy throb in time to the bass and the drums. You're not coming yet, Buttercup."

"*Please...,*" I begged.

"You have to wait until the show's over."

"I have to push through the crowd. I need a drink. I know you'll want one, too. As I lean across the bar to order for us both, I feel the buzz again and grin. I know you're close enough to see me, and I make a point to shove my tits out just a little more as I grab the drinks and turn to find you.

"I give you your cup, trying to look you in the eye without blushing. It's hard to act normal with all these people around, when all I want to do is fuck you. You have fans to hug and things to sign and pictures to pose for. I make the rounds, chatting and smiling, while my nipples are so hard they're about to pop through my shirt."

"*God*, I want those in my mouth!"

"You text me to meet you in the bathroom. "

"*Yeahyeahyeah*."

"We both slip away, careful to look natural. You're pulling me inside before I can even get the door open all the way. The remote is in your hand, the bullet is vibrating like crazy, and I can't get my shirt off fast enough. We're both reaching under my skirt, trying to get my panties off. They're so wet, but I knew I'd be dripping everywhere without them. Boots on, skirt on, the lacy half bra with my hard, pink nipples exposed.

"Your pants are down, and your cock is hard and ready. I push your feet apart with my boot and go down in front of you. As much as I want you in my mouth, it's not time. I reach between my legs and pull the bullet out. It's creamy and slick, and I push it straight into your ass."

Alex moaned and gasped into the phone.

"I take the remote from you and stand up. I bend over and lean against the bathroom wall. My skirt is up, and your dick is in me before I can even catch my breath. You're pounding into me so hard, so fast. I'm squeezing your cock with my cunt as hard as I can, and I hit the little button to start the bullet vibrating in your ass."

I rubbed my clit furiously, the bullet buzzing steadily inside me.

"We fuck and fuck and fuck, and I'm trying not to scream out. I'm so close, so fucking close, goddamn I'm gonna come." My orgasm cascaded through me, and I cried out.

"*Beautiful*," he groaned as I came, screaming loudly into my empty house.

I heard muffled sounds in his background. "Talk to me," he whispered. "Talk me through it."

"Talk you through *what*?" I teased.

"I'm in the bathroom. I have to be quiet. I need to hear you."

"You need to hear me tell you how wet you make me when I come? While you jack your cock?"

He gasped hoarsely.

"You're still fucking and hard and your hands are so tight on my hips. You shove into me as deep as you can. I can feel your hot come inside me, and you're still fucking. I squeeze you tight from the inside, pulsing all around your cock, keeping it hard."

"*Fuck, make me come, Tierney!*"

"I pull off quick and drop to my knees on the bathroom floor. Your dick is coated in your come and mine. Glistening and throbbing, and you'll come again soon. In my mouth, fast, and *oh my god* you taste so good. The taste of my pussy on your cock is amazing. I want to suck you like candy. Down my throat and back out.

"You put your hands in my hair and fuck my mouth. The head of your cock is sliding against the roof of my mouth while my tongue laps along the shaft. Your ass is buzzing, and I wrap my hand around your balls. You try to pull out, but I have your cock all the way down my throat, and I'm sucking as hard as I think you can stand it.

"I look up at you. I want to watch your face when you come. And I want you to see your cock in my mouth, how I'm on my knees for you, your come running down my thighs. Hot spurts down my throat and your hands on my face as you fuck my mouth. You gasp and pull my head against you, and I grab the loop on the bullet and wiggle it while you're coming. Eye to eye as I suck you one last time. "

Alex caught his breath and panted quietly.

"*Oh my god!* You're so goddamn good at that! *Poor Paul Sommers.*"

I laughed throatily and stretched languidly in my bed. "Thanks. Only for you."

Getting dressed a few days later, I realized that all of my panties were just too damn big. I'd lost about forty-five pounds, which equated to roughly two pants sizes. My ass was still big, but my panties were sagging in all the wrong places.

I waited until Sam was home from work that night and told him I needed to go to the store. I spent a long time looking at underwear, trying to find something that was cute or pretty and didn't make me feel like a cow. I picked out a couple of new bras, too, to go with the new panties. I was in the dressing room when my phone rang.

Alex Wheeler

"I'm half-naked," I answered. "Let me call you right back."

I quickly chose several pairs in various shades of lacy and hurried to the cash register. I paid for my new undies and went out to my car. It was dark, almost eight o'clock. I moved my car to a more remote parking space at the far end of the lot, still under a street light, and called Alex.

"Why were you half-naked?"

"I was trying on bras. I had to buy new panties."

"So I called you while you were buying lingerie?"

"Yep."

"Where are you now?"

"In my car. In a mostly empty parking lot."

"What? Tierney, don't be stupid. Don't be somewhere that's not safe."

"I'm not, babycakes, I promise. I'm safely parked under a street light, traffic going by, doors locked. I promise."

"*Yeah, talking to Cavanaugh.*"

I heard a voice in the background. "*Tierney Cavanaugh?*"

"Hey, Max. He's so cute! I love him."

"So you want to fuck him now, too?" Alex teased. "*She says hi and that she wants to fuck you.* He says 'hi' back."

"No! Well, maybe. I don't know. I never really thought about it."

"I'm sure he'd be worth it. The boy's good with the girls, you know."

"Do you have personal knowledge of this assertion, Mr. Wheeler?"

"Only what I hear from the other hotel bed."

"I'll keep all of that in mind," I giggled. "It'll give my toy something new to think about."

"But," he breathed, "he could never make you... *whimper* like I could."

I roared with laughter. "I'm quite sure you could make me whimper. I've thought long and hard about that. Many, many times."

"*Whimper.* Make you *beg* me for it."

"Shit! All you gotta do is call me 'Buttercup'."

"But I like 'hot mess' better."

"'Buttercup' turns me on."

"'Hot mess' turns *me* on!"

Max was coming in and out of the room, and Alex wasn't able to delve right into me like he wanted. I didn't know how much he heard, how much he knew, and I really didn't care. The modified exhibitionism of it all turned me on.

They were getting ready to go to dinner with some business associates. We talked for a few minutes about what was going on with the tour dates. The band was leaving the next day for London, then on to shows in Germany, the Netherlands, and Paris.

"What time's your flight tomorrow?"

"Six o'clock."

"I'm so jealous. I miss my band. Can you call tomorrow before you leave?"

"*Doubtful*," he said slowly. "We have a ton of shit to do before we leave, thanks to Paulie. Motherfucker doesn't do half the shit he says he will, when he says he'll do it."

"My aloneness in the house tomorrow is questionable," I said. "I think Sam is working from home. The boys will be home around three. Call if you get time."

"If not, it'll be a couple of days before I can call you."

"*Bleh!* I really want to talk to you before you go. *No*, I really want to hear you come before you go."

"Oh, you are a hot mess, aren't you?"

"That's why you love me!" I trilled.

"You're hilarious!" Alex laughed. "Gotta go, though, Buttercup."

"Yep. Check in as soon as you can."

"Later."

"Bye."

I drove home, music blaring, silly smile spread across my face. I took the bag with my new, smaller panties into the house. Sam was working at his computer, and the boys were sleeping. I slipped out of my clothes and into new purple panties and a floral bandeau bra, lavender lace peeking around the edges.

"Yes or no?" I asked Sam, rocking sideways like a little girl with a secret.

"One sec," he said, finishing an email. *One, two, three, four, five.* "*Very* nice."

He swiveled toward me and stood from his chair. He wrapped his arms around my waist and kissed my neck. "How long are you gonna have this on?"

"That depends on how long it takes you to catch me," I squealed, running for the bedroom.

Chapter 14

On Friday night, I was insomnomaniacal. There was an amazing full moon, startlingly huge and brilliant. I'd seen it rising earlier in the evening, almost a harvest moon, pale yellow and so big on the horizon that it made me gasp and want to reach for it. As I came padding through the house in the dark toward the couch, the deep shadows in the office were shimmering at the edges from the moonlight in the windows. I caught myself wondering if the moon was as brilliant in London.

I hadn't been able to talk to Alex again before he left for Europe, and I missed him like crazy. I promised myself that I would play it calm and not contact him until I heard from him first. But I was thinking about him a *lot*. I had long, empty hours to fill, which were even more restless when the family was together on the weekend.

I wrapped myself in the blanket and plugged into my iPod, listening to the Princess Asshat playlist. Some of the songs were his. Most were songs that we both loved, or ones that took me back to conversations we'd had. They were things I listened to when I needed to be enveloped by the thought of him.

My body throbbed to the sound of his voice, pressing and pleading in the dark. I started the voice memo function on my phone, whispering everything I was doing, recording it for Alex a million miles away. I bit the blanket, muffling my cries as I came for him.

I emailed the file to him and tumbled, finally, into a deep sleep.

The next morning, there was a missed Skype request from him, sent an hour after I passed out, and an email.

From: Alex Wheeler
Sent: March 15th 4:17 AM
To: Tierney Cavanaugh Johnson
Subject: RE:

Jesus fucking christ! Amazing! Muah!

xoxo

Now I was definitely on Alex's mind.

Pictures from Europe started to show up on Facebook. The guys posing with fans. Blurry images of the band, taken on someone's cellphone. Paul and Charlie were in a few, but Max and Alex were most prominent, as usual. The gregarious twosome was obviously having fun and drinking a lot. I could tell from the fan pictures that they were all glad to be doing what they did best.

I spent the afternoon and evening at home with Sam and the boys. They were working and playing, while I was downstairs painting. I'd just finished cleaning my brushes and sat down to check my email.

There was a Skype chat request from Alex.

Tierney   Hey

Alex   Hey urself. What r u doing?

Tierney   Listening to 1965. John the Baptist might be the most perfect song EVER.

Alex   Agreed. I love Greg Dulli so much I'd let him fuck me.

Tierney   ;) How's London?

Alex   Good. Drunk.

Tierney   Of course you are.

Alex   Sam home?

Tierney   Yep. All of us are home.

Alex   Ok. I'll let you go then.

Tierney   :(It's okay. What's up?

Alex   Nuthin. Drunk. Wanted to talk to u.

Tierney   :) I'm sorry I'm not alone but we can still chat a bit.

How was the show?

But then he was gone. I knew his internet service might be spotty, especially if he was out and about. Now I was anxious, though. I wanted to talk to him, to see what he had to say about the message I'd sent the night before, to see how he was. I didn't know how long it would be before he could be in touch again.

Sitting at my desk, I went back to my email. Sam and the boys were in the office, piled up on the small sofa, laughing and playing ten feet from me. My cell phone rang, right next to my laptop.

Alex Wheeler

Oh fuck! This is gonna get weird!

"It's Alex," I said to Sam's questioning glance. I shrugged and answered. "Hello?"

"Goddamn, I need to talk to you." He was whispering, and it was hard to hear him.

"Hey! How's London?"

"You can't talk, can you?"

"No, not right now. Everything okay? Are you with Max?"

"Yeah, we're at the hotel. I'm watching porn."

"Oh, okay." My heart was pounding.

"Mmmmm, I need to talk to you," he whispered hoarsely. "I need you. Can you go somewhere and call me?"

I could hear the drunk, but I could also hear how worked up he was. The longing in his voice was brutal.

"Nope, we're just all hanging out at home tonight."

"*Fuck!* Okay, I'll go then. I'll call you tomorrow."

"Okay." *Fuck!* "You guys have fun. I'll talk to you later."

I clicked **END** and put the phone down.

"Alex and Max drunk calling from London," I tittered nervously to Sam.

I tried for a few more minutes to pay attention to my email. I was flustered. My head was spinning. I couldn't focus and kept rereading the same message over and over.

"I don't feel so hot," I said. "I think I'll go rest for a while in bed. Is that okay?"

"Yeah, sure. You okay?"

"Yeah, just feel kind of icky. Can you get the boys ready for bed when it's time?"

"Sure."

I grabbed my laptop and went into the bedroom. I settled onto the bed and sent Alex a Skype chat request.

Alex	Can you talk?
Tierney	Only chat. Is everything okay?
Alex	Yep. I'm so goddamn hard
Tierney	So you called to tell me you're watching porn?
Alex	No, I'm watching Max fuck some bird, this Brit chick.

Ohhhhh. I'd totally misunderstood.

Tierney	Is she hot?
Alex	So fucking hot! I wonder if she'd let me join them.
Tierney	Would Max?
Alex	I don't know. Should I ask?
Tierney	Do you really want to fuck her?
Alex	Yes. Maybe. I don't know. She's fucking hot. Hang on.

I sat there for a few minutes, waiting for him to come back.

Alex	Check ur email

In my inbox, there was a new message from him, with an attachment. It was a JPEG file, a shadowy picture of a half-naked brunette sitting atop some human form, which I assumed was Max. Even though her face was obscured in darkness, I could tell how amazing her body was.

Tierney	She is hot, you're right.
Alex	I think I want to fuck her. Just wanna come up behind her and stick it in her. Should I ask her first?
Tierney	Probably. But do you really want that? It's been eight years since you fucked someone else. Do you really want her to be the one you blow all that to hell for?

You're seriously going to drag me through these months and not let me be the one?!

Alex	Probably not. But I want to fuck someone. Where are you?
Tierney	Alone in my bed.
Alex	Can you leave and call me? Can you go to a hotel or something?
Tierney	Not really. It would be kind of hard to explain.
Alex	ARGH!
Tierney	I know you hate the typing, but it'll have to do if you want me right now.
Alex	I want to hear you fucking come for real. That message was amazing but I want to hear you for real.
Tierney	You're addicted to my dirty little mouth, aren't you?
Alex	Yup.
Tierney	Awww, do you miss me, Alex?
Alex	Yes. So bad.
Tierney	And you love my dirty mouth?

Alex   That mouth is divine!

Tierney   And do you love me?

He was drunk. I wasn't pressing this with him, now or maybe ever.

Alex   You know I do
I should've fucked you in Chicago.
I thought about it.

Tierney   You're such a liar!

Alex   Nope. Thought about taking you downstairs to one of those little rooms and bending you over a chair and fucking you right there.

Tierney   I probably would've let you, you know.

Alex   I thought you might.

Why? Because you thought the fat housewife might have a crush on you?

Tierney   If I'd thought for a second that you were into it, I would've fucked you before I left that club.

Alex   You should've.

Tierney   What was I supposed to say? Hey, Alex, I know we just met and we're both married and all, but I'd really like to fuck you right now.

Alex   Yes!
If you want something, Tierney, you need to ask for it! With me, Sam, whatever, you need to open ur fucking mouth and say what you want. Stop fucking dancing around ur life and be straightforward about what you want.

Tierney   It's not always that easy, and you know it.

Alex   Didn't say it was but we want what we want. Shouldn't feel guilty about it.
I want to fuck you.
It just is.
And the strange thing is that I don't feel bad or guilty about it. Not one damn bit.
We're animals. We want to fuck who we want to fuck.

Tierney   Ha! Right now, I want you to shut the fuck up and make me come.

Alex   Mmmmmm

We chatted for two hours. I was alone in the darkened bedroom, only the light from the laptop and the silent television. I didn't want to end the conversation when it was done, but he was tired—I was tired—and about to pass out. I knew Sam had gotten the boys to bed a while before, and I needed to check in with him, to make sure he wasn't suspicious.

"Are you okay?" he asked when I padded into the quiet office. He was sitting at his desk, checking email and perusing the internet.

"Yeah, I don't feel so good," I lied again. "My stomach is a mess. Chills."

"I thought you went to bed."

"I did for a while. Can't sleep now."

I took a melatonin and hoped to sleep through the night. I was awake again at three in the morning. I left Sam dozing peacefully in our bed and went to the couch, earbuds in, listening to my playlist.

I couldn't stop thinking about what had happened, about everything Alex had said during our lengthy chat.

When he said that he didn't feel guilty about this, I knew exactly what he meant. I felt the same. In my head, I knew the repercussions and the damage I could cause. But there was something I couldn't ignore and felt very, very strongly that I couldn't turn away from this until it got a chance at fruition. There was something I was supposed to be learning from this but I hadn't found it yet.

From: Tierney Cavanaugh Johnson
Date: March 16th 5:32 am
To: Alex Wheeler
Subject: truth in advertising

When I woke up at 3:00, I was (of course) thinking about last night. First, amazing. Lovelovelove you, Alex. (Don't get creeped out. I'm not going there.) But I told you early on I've never not loved my lovers, in some capacity. It's not *that* love, not right now, but I do adore you. It's easier to say I heart you to not blur that crazy line. And I don't just heart you because you're the only guy I've ever known who might really wear me out. There's so much about Alex the guy that just amazes me. I don't give a shit about your public persona with the exception that it's how we met and that it's your job. Your talents impress me, without question, but even that has nothing to do with rock star Alex. So the more I delve into you and immerse myself in you, the more blown away I am. The more I crave it. Blame yourself--you started it. :)

So for you to say that you wanted to fuck me in Chicago, it kind of blows me away. I'm pretty sure I don't fit the typical profile of the Alex Wheeler fuck buddy, good or bad. Had I had any inkling whatsoever that you were remotely open to the possibility (which I'm still taking with a grain of salt, knowing how drunk you were last night), I would have fucked you in that chair before I left. You do great, great things for me and my self-esteem, and I hope you know how much you and that mean to me. Really, I would do anything for you, ever. I try not to have expectations of you, except that you be honest with me, and I hope that your drunken talk isn't just bravado and sexual posturing in the heated moment. Because if you don't carry through on your promise to fuck me, repeatedly and in many different ways, I will lose my fucking mind.

Even right now, I'm so goddamn hot thinking about you fucking me silly and breathless that I can't think straight. I'm tired and horny and frustrated because I want to feel you. So if you're just the big talker and this goes nowhere, that will be the most heartbreaking part of it all. You could call it quits tomorrow for emotional and personal reasons, and I'd be hurt but okay. But if you just can't do it in reality, away from the phone and chat, I need you to break it off now. I'm emotionally and psychologically invested in this and can't bear the thought of it being completely ephemeral.

I'm going back to sleep now. Be sure this is what you want. There's no going back once we see each other. It's easy to say it's okay when you're thousands of miles apart and only on chat or even a phone call. If you don't have to see my face when I come for you, it still gives you the distance you need. As connected as I feel to you, I fully recognize that this may be no more than a really fulfilling fuck for you. I don't want that to be the case, obviously, but you are who you are. Please just take it all in and be sure it's what you want. I'm only getting off my pedestal for you. But for you, anything.

xox

Video was showing up on Facebook of Junkture doing a new song, "Whiskey Mouth". I didn't know it, didn't have it, hadn't heard it. They'd done a couple of unreleased tracks during the U.S. tour, but this wasn't one of them. The videos weren't great quality, though, and it was hard to tell much about the song.

"What is this song?" I asked Alex when he called briefly the next day.

"'Whiskey Mouth'? It's good. You'll love it. It's an outtake from the recording sessions for *Persona Non Grata*."

My relationship with Alex didn't entitle me to special treatment. I didn't know what those boundaries really were between me and him and the band, but I knew I didn't want to overstep them and ask for the track.

He called on Tuesday from Paris.

"Turn on your camera, so I can see you," he demanded after exchanging pleasantries.

"No! I look like shit right now."

"'*Look like shit*'," he scoffed. "Shut the fuck up. Stupid!"

"I do! I haven't had a shower. I'm a mess. I'm not turning on my fucking camera."

"You're so crazy!"

"Blech. What else is going on?"

"These three French chicks hit on me last night."

"Were they hot?"

"Yeah, they were. The girls here are unbelievably straightforward, Tierney. It's crazy! They're all," he dropped into his best French accent, "'*We're French, and these are our amazing egos, and we don't give a damn if you don't like us just how we are! We want what we want! Fuck you if you don't like it!*' It kind of reminds me of you. You should embrace your inner Frenchie and go with it. It's just bubbling under the surface."

"*Inner Frenchie!*" I sputtered, laughing breathlessly. "Did you fuck them?"

"No! They were like, '*Come on, it'll just be us. It'll be fun. We don't have to tell anyone. It's just sex. Fuck you if you don't like it!*' I told them I was flattered but I don't do that."

"*Awwww*. Do you only whore around with me, Alex?" I teased.

"You know I do. I'm sending you a file, by the way. Right now. It'll probably take a while. This fucking internet connection sucks. It's slow as shit."

"Oooooh, what is it?"

"Here, listen."

I heard a guitar intro, something new but it seemed a little familiar. *Whiskey Mouth!*

Your sins trickle like whiskey
From your dark amber pout
I don't care what's in your head
Only what's in your mouth

Your whiskey mouth spills lies
Across my anguished lips
Tongues tied and twisting
Crack a smile like a whip

We share ourselves
Our whiskey and sins
The sweet taste of your lies
The heat of your skin
Take out your flask
And pour out your heart

I promise I won't tell
What you whisper in the dark

"Oh my god! It's so good! I—"
"Will you shut up and listen?" He was adamant but sweet.
"Oka—"
"*Shhh! Shush!*"

Your love is a phone call at 2 a.m.
In the darkest place of your mourning
I love it when you're drunk
And I love the way you fuck
But no one can know I've come calling

You tease me and taunt me
And make me want you
Then you try to push me away
You opened this box
Then told me to stop
When you saw the sober light of day

We share ourselves
Our whiskey and sins
The sweet taste of your lies
The heat of your skin
Take out your flask
And pour out your heart
Promise me you won't tell
What I whisper in the dark

"It's so good! Thank you! Thank you for sending it to me."
"Yup."
"So you're not alone?"
"At the moment I am, but who knows how long that'll be?"
It wasn't long at all. Max came in, telling Alex about an argument Paul had with some guy at the venue. They were laughing about it, but I could only catch half the conversation.
"I gotta go, Buttercup. Can I call you tomorrow?"
"Of course."
"'Kay. Later."

"Bye."

I listened to the song again. And again. And again. It was amazing. There was something raw and pleading in Alex's voice. And the lyrics were a strange mirror of what was happening now, with me and Alex.

He'd gone out of his way to send the file to me, to make me listen to it while he sat on the tour bus, an ocean away. Did he see the irony of the song, or was he just sending me a spectacular, rare track from my favorite band? I couldn't think about it, and I wasn't about to ask.

I added it to the ever-growing playlist.

There wasn't a moment that I wasn't thinking about him. At dinner with Sam and the boys, getting the kids ready for school, in the midst of vivid, lucid dreams. He was *always* on my mind.

He was busy with work and the tour and family and life and couldn't be in our strange realm all the time. I was peevish and petulant when I couldn't get his immediate attention. I'd become increasingly dependent upon his awareness of me.

I was irritated with myself for feeling dark and vicious when Alex didn't respond to me quickly enough. It was making me outright bitchy. Unlike Alex, I was no damn good at compartmentalizing my emotions. I couldn't be that open and vulnerable with someone and not love them, at least a little. Part of me hoped we would have a night together, get it all of our systems, and walk away friends. Part of me wanted it over, so I could go on with my life. He took up an extraordinary amount of time and mental space, and it was exhausting, constantly waiting for him to focus his attention on me.

You're getting too close.

I was afraid that if I turned away from it, turned away from Alex, I would miss something huge. When I'd most needed to connected with *someone*, I'd found this amazing soul that spoke to me on so many levels. The sexual play with him was intense and intimate, and backing down from this thing now would mean never having freely open sex with him, never making crazy, passionate love to him just because it was easy and good.

The intense exploration thus far with Alex had changed how I saw myself and Sam, had brought our looming issues into glaring focus, and it wasn't fair of me to work out the problems of my marriage with another man. I felt guilty for having these strong sexual cravings for a man who wasn't my husband. I needed to talk to him, to tell him that I needed to end this thing between us. I hoped we could just stop with the sex and keep the rest of it, that we could still be friends. We'd barely started down this path, and it didn't seem too late to turn back.

I didn't want to regret anything, and it seemed likely there would be some kind of heartache no matter which way I turned.

From: Tierney Cavanaugh Johnson
Date: March 19th 11:52 AM
To: Alex Wheeler
Subject: Big crush

Not doing so hot. Call me when you get the chance.

I was pacing the office when my phone rang a couple of hours later. It didn't look like a Skype call. It looked like he'd phoned me from Germany.

"Hey."

"What's up, Buttercup?"

"Did you call from your phone? That'll cost you a fortune."

"It's my fucking phone! I can do what I want. What's wrong?"

I took a deep breath and *fell the fuck apart*.

"I don't know, Alex. I just, I started thinking about this. All of it. I don't know why you came into my life when you did. It doesn't even *matter* why!"

I was hysterical. I speed walked down the hall to the bedroom, pacing between the bed and the bathroom.

"I'm a *mess*, though! You never, ever promised me more than you were prepared to give, and I appreciate that—"

"Tierney, calm down! What happened? Nothing's happened!"

"I *know*, but it has! I can promise you Sam and Talia would *not* be happy to know what's happened so far. If they knew, Alex—"

"Where the fuck is this coming from? What *happened*?"

"I just, I thought about how *badly* I wanted to see you and then realized I can't. I won't. It might not ever happen. And it's making me fucking crazy! I don't like feeling like this, Alex! I don't like getting so excited to hear from you and then *not*! I don't—I don't know!"

"Okay. You're getting all possessive. This has to stop. It has to be over."

"That's not what I'm saying!"

"I *am*! This is not okay."

"I know it's not! I *hate* feeling like this!"

"You're being possessive and jealous, and I can't have that."

"No, I'm not! It's not that at all! I can't explain it! I'm just upset!"

"I can tell."

"*Fuck!* I just, I'm not, it's not coming out right. I don't want to lose you. I don't *want* to *not* be able to see this through. And it *sucks* that it won't be happening."

"It's unfortunate, that's for sure."

"I can't keep doing this. I can't keep feeling like this, Alex."

"I understand. Look, we'll just stop. *Now*. And I'm sure you'll email me about it."

"Don't be patronizing."

"I'm not! I'm sure you will. You're much clearer when you don't have to say it out loud. And I'm sure you'll email me to tell me what the fuck is going on. But *this* has to be over and done."

"I'm sorry." I wanted to cry but it wasn't coming.

"Me, too."

"I don't know what to say."

"Say goodbye."

"No.... I don't want it to be weird between us. If I run into you—"

"—and you will—"

"—I don't want it to be difficult, you know?"

"Tierney, it's okay. I'll see you when I see you—and I'm *sure* I will. It'll all be fine and won't be weird, I promise. But I have to go."

"Okay."

"Bye, Tierney."

"Bye."

I didn't want to hang up. I didn't want to let him go. I hadn't explained what I was feeling at all. Nothing that came out of my mouth was close to the truth of the emotion. But the emotion itself had come through, loud and clear, and I sounded like a crazy girl.

Tierney   It's over with A.

Seth   You broke it off?

Tierney   Ugly, ugly phone call. It's done.

Seth   I'm sorry. I know that must've sucked, but you know it's for the best.
I'm proud of you.

I wasn't. I wanted to throw up. I felt horrible. He'd just gotten the absolute worst possible impression of me, and there was nothing I could do to make it better.

I spent the next twenty-four hours in a daze. Nothing seemed real. Nothing felt real. I felt out of sync, by seconds, with everything and everyone around me.

From: Tierney Cavanaugh Johnson
Date: March 20th 7:02 pm
To: Alex Wheeler
Subject: yeah so now I'm writing

First, as I've told you before, I only want good things for you. I want your band to work and be successful so you can enjoy the process and not stress about every little detail, at least not any more than you would anyway. I want to be able to get the call or the email that Talia's pregnant and be nothing but happy and excited for you. For all three of you. I know how much you love Amber, and you'll be amazed at how much your heart expands to let an additional child into your world. And I _do_ want to be able to share in that joy with you, so please don't be afraid to tell me. I want to know that you're happy.

What I have loved most about this with you is that you were willing to open yourself to me, to find those deep places and take me there with you. Reciprocally, I loved that I could do the same and have that be celebrated. It makes me sad to know we're both facing that same repression again. Maybe that's what being a grown-up and being in a relationship is really about, you know? That compromise and finding a way to be happy and fulfilled through it.

You're absolutely right that it's unfortunate that it won't be what it could. Even now, while I'm typing, I'm trying to think of the best way to word it so that you know that I'm always open to the idea. (How's that for forward?) I can't imagine a day that I won't be attracted to you, when I won't crave you in every imaginable way. It's magnetic and it's overpowering. It's addictive, and I would do absolutely anything for you. I've told you that time and time again.

And what all of this tells me is that it's dangerous.

It's been hard for me from the beginning to step in and out of that place with you, the space that's always run parallel to my real life. I know that you separate the two, that you have always been able to segregate me from your day-to-day. That's consistently been a heart-wrenching thing for me, to know that I was never a priority. But when you were in that place with me, when I had your undivided attention and could delve completely into you, it was *amazing*, in part because I felt like I did matter and was important to you for a little while. You are giftedly charming, and you know it. You're one of the very few people who've ever been able to simultaneously unsettle me and put me at ease in a whole new place. It breaks my heart that I don't get to touch that anymore, not like I did.

I'm kicking myself, knowing if I'd just kept my mouth shut it wouldn't have gone down like this. But I also know that I was getting lost. I've spent so much time hoping and waiting for just a little bit of your attention. It's simpering, and it's not me. Even when I talked to you this afternoon, knowing full well what the answer needed to be, it hit me like a ton of bricks when you said it needed to stop. I still wanted nothing more than for you to blow some smoke in my face and calm me down and tell me it would all be fine, that you still wanted me to be available for you.

As much as I crave you, I could get completely obsessed in this and abandon every last shred of me to be what you want, when you want it. I won't be that girl for you or anyone else, and I know you wouldn't want that. I have to believe that you care enough to not want to see me go down that path because of what it would do to me, regardless of what difficulties it could pose for you.

You told me once that it would have to come to an end sometime, though it wasn't then. I have often thought about that, what the end game would be. Part of me was really hoping that I would see you, fuck you, get it all out of my system, and be able to move on and just be happy as your friend. But what I could never, ever come to terms with was how I would deal with Talia and Sam. You said earlier today that I shouldn't be freaking out because nothing's happened. You're right, sort of, but I know damn well that Sam would be incensed if he knew what had happened so far. Maybe I'm wrong, but I'm betting Talia would be unhappy about it, too. My point is, I've been on that side of the equation, and it sucks completely. Who the fuck am I to step into that?

I *love* knowing things about you that no one else knows, including Talia from what you've told me. It's sexy as hell. But today for the first time I felt a little dirty. And I've often worried who you were more concerned about when you admonished me to delete and clear everything, you or me.

The gist of it is, as much as I would turn myself upside down to have earth-shattering, volcanic sex with you, and as confidant as I am that it would be insanely incredible, I can't get there right now without going through some unpleasant emotional turmoil that neither of us is prepared to handle. If I could just spontaneously be alone with you, preferably drunk so I don't think very much, it would be monumentally wonderful. If I keep up the chat and the craziness that's been leading us there, I will lose my fucking mind.

I hopehopehope that you will still check in and call and let me know how you are and how the shows are and how writing is going. There's still something that clicked between us that wasn't just sexual. I don't want to lose that because I can't keep my heart out of your pants. :) I want to be able to adore you and heart you appropriately and openly, and not have it be strained because one of us is afraid I'm gonna flip out. (I'm not, btw. I'm okay right now, and I'll be fine in a few days.) I want to be to call you up and just check in to see how you are, and vice versa. I'm hopeful that if the sexual tension is pushed away, we can have as normal of a casual friendship as possible. And know that I really, truly am here for you any time you need me, no matter what it's about.

I love you, Alex Wheeler. You're amazing, but you're just not mine.

XOX

Tierney

Sam was working late, and the boys were asleep. I went downstairs to try to work out some of what I was feeling.

I flipped through a stack of primed canvases until I found a small one, six inches square. I found the small, fine brushes that I rarely ever used. I worked slowly and methodically, imagining the hurt coming from my body and into the paints themselves. I used the canvas to corral the pain, contain it into the smallest spaces possible. Hues of mauve and periwinkle blended with greys, a symphony of heartache and tears and melancholy. Swirls came from the outside *in*, converging in a tight, tiny spiraling circle. It was like all these weeks of *Alex* came together, consuming those few square inches.

When I finally stopped painting, it was almost two in the morning. I'd been working for hours and I hadn't noticed bodily cues, or that Sam had even come home.

I cleaned up my work space and my brushes, washed my face and hands. I went quietly into the kitchen and poured myself a shot of Jack Daniels. I downed it, and another. I slept a few hours and went to the park to walk.

I knew that last telephone conversation with him had to be as unsettling for him as it was for me. He sounded surprised and maybe a little hurt, though I was trying hard not to read too much into his tone. I hated that *that* was the last conversation we might ever have, especially after all the prior days of spectacular talk. And as much as I loved the Friday phone call when Max was there, and the amazing, brutally base chat from London, none of it was as special to me as the times he called just to talk.

I'd always known this thing between us would never go anywhere. I was careful to remind myself of that constantly. That didn't mean it wasn't extremely important to me. I felt awful. I didn't want it to be gone—him to be gone—and I was completely face-to-face with that. I wanted nothing more than for Alex to call me and tell me it was okay, that we just needed time to cool off and make sure my head was settled again.

I was rousing on Sunday night when I heard my phone vibrate on the nightstand.

From: Alex Wheeler
Date: February 28th 12:50 AM
To: Tierney Cavanaugh Johnson
Subject: Back in the USSA

Hey,

I've had a chance to mull over your thoughts in your email and I want you to know that I respect you 1000% for your straightforwardness and sincerity. I'm not good at this writing stuff so I'll keep it short and simple.

You are amazing, we will always be connected and I love you the same way you love me!

xoxo
A

Chapter 15

I didn't hear from Alex for weeks. It was okay that he wasn't ready to deal with me. I missed him, but I was still a little freaked out about what had happened.

Sam was scheduled to go to California, something for work, the first of April. My first reaction when he told me he'd be out of town was to let Alex know that Sam would be away. I knew it wouldn't matter, though. That part of our relationship was over. We were each going on with our respective lives, and my days of availability wouldn't matter to him.

In the days before Sam left for his trip, we were constantly in each other's faces. He was always working—easily sixty hours a week—and he was irritable and neglectful. If he spoke to me at all, he was often rude or dismissive. When we conversed, it was about the house or the children or scheduling plans. There was no intimate talk of any kind, and we weren't having sex again.

I tried to initiate it with him. I tried to be straightforward and tell him that I needed and wanted him. He ignored me. His response was always, "Maybe later." The night before he left, I tried again to engage him. He waited to come to bed until long after I'd fallen asleep while watching television. Like so many other nights, I roused at two in the morning, long enough to silence the electric murmuring of some infomercial.

"Can you spend some time with me before your flight?" I asked the next morning, wrapping my arms around his shoulders as he worked at his desk. The boys were gone to school, and he wasn't scheduled to leave the house until early afternoon.

"Maybe in a bit," he replied distractedly, typing at his computer.

I waited around for two hours. At first, I was patient, thinking he would stop working and come find me. As the hours wore on, I became more and more irritated at being dismissed again.

Maybe never came, and neither did I.

Livid and crying, I called Tessa five minutes after he left. "I hate that stupid motherfucker!"

"What happened?"

"He just left for San Diego. He'll be gone for three days. We haven't had sex in three *weeks*. So I tried to get him to come to bed last night, knowing he'd be gone. *No such luck*. I asked him to spend time with me this morning, after the boys went to school. He told me, 'Maybe in a bit,' and then *ignored* me until he kissed me bye on his way out the door."

"*Ouch*."

"I can't do this anymore, Tessa! I can't keep being ignored by this man! It's not fucking fair!"

"Is he drinking again?" she asked carefully.

"Not that I can tell. He's not bringing beer home. But it's like all that time he spent drinking before is now just spent on work. I know his job is hectic and stressful, but *goddammit!* just spend *thirty fucking minutes* with me! If I were a bad lay, maybe I'd understand it. But this pussy can pull a rabbit out of a hat—I'm worth half a fucking hour!"

Tessa cackled with sudden delight. "*Oh my god!* How do you do that? How can you be so *open* and *confident* in your sexual abilities?"

"Are you not? Do you not feel confident that you're good in bed?"

"With the right person," she replied. "I mean, I guess I'm so analytical, that I would have to add about a million caveats. Maybe you're mind-blowingly good with one person, but with another, you just don't click. And saying, 'I'm exceptionally good with you at this exact moment under these exact circumstances, but I might not be sexually compatible with the next person I happen to fuck,' somehow doesn't seem like the sexiest of bedroom talk, you know?"

I giggled at her. "Look, even at my fattest I knew I was a great fuck. Maybe it was *because* of that. I learned early on to work my body and use my sexuality to *my* advantage before anyone else could use it to theirs. Dave O'Shea used to call me 'Cleveland' in high school, because he said I could deep throat the entire city of Cleveland at once."

Tessa broke into her off-key, tone deaf rendition of "Cleveland Rocks".

"*Exactly!*"

Sam's ignoring of me wasn't new. It had gone on for at least a year before I'd started to realize what was happening. Just like when I was left at home alone for hours on end as a child and teenager, I'd habitually filled that empty time with television and food. Being sick for so many months had meant even more hours of doing nothing on the couch, which exacerbated the cycle.

When I started walking and tracking everything I did and ate through an app on my phone, I didn't watch so much television anymore. I funneled a lot of my emotions—anger, desperation, sadness, confusion—into my workouts and my painting. I'd cut out added sugar, except in my coffee. I happily ate complex carbs, mostly fruit and whole grains. I'd eaten sweets a grand total of seven times in six months, including through the holidays. Twice it triggered the crazy binges, once it made me horribly sick, and once just tasted bad. I didn't crave the sugar, and I didn't miss it. Late night snacks and binges rarely ever happened.

And it was paying off; I had lost sixty pounds by early April. I preferred to say I'd abandoned the weight, because I didn't intend to find it again. I joked that I'd abandoned a kindergartener's worth of ass in six months.

I posted a note about it on Facebook, letting friends and acquaintances know what was going on with me. Everyone was quick with congratulatory comments and questions about how and why I'd started losing the weight. It was one thing to talk with close friends about the process, about how I disliked my body. It was quite another to start giving specifics about it to just anyone. It laid bare a lot of old wounds and scars and made me feel really vulnerable, like I was thirteen years old again.

I felt I needed to be open about it. It was something I was going through, and I knew I wasn't alone. Part of my journey to reclaim myself included facing down some long-standing fears and misconceptions about myself, including what defined me as *worthwhile*.

I started to realize I had the strength and fortitude to take all of the things that scared me and hurt me and had made me so afraid to work at being my true, inner self, and *throw them away*. They may have led me to this place and time in my life, but they weren't who I was. I was determined not to let those fears control me or determine the size of my ass.

I caught Seth on chat early that morning, after I'd taken the boys to catch the school bus.

Tierney   60 pounds. Gone. From my ass.

Seth   Congrats! That's awesome!
                  Pretty soon you'll be at 100 and be tiny!

One hundred pounds? That seemed so daunting. It seemed so far away. I knew I could be there in another six months, but that still wouldn't quite put me at my total goal of one hundred and thirteen pounds. I was thrilled with sixty pounds, but there was still a long way to go.

To keep the total amount from feeling so overwhelming, I focused on a little bit of weight at a time. And every time Devin made me do another horrible medicine ball crunch or sixty seconds of planks, I would visualize that place and time I wanted to be, thinking of how I wanted to be just a little bit healthier when I got there.

My dad told me how proud he was of me. My mom joked that she hated me. Sam congratulated me when he called from California, but he was tired and could barely muster any excitement.

I saw my gynecologist for my yearly check-up.

"How's Sam with your weight loss?" Dr. Levin asked as we sat in his office, talking and revising my medical history before the pelvic exam.

I hadn't really thought about it. I was about the same size as I'd been when we got married, which was still a little larger than when we met. Could that be part of why he was so grouchy with me? Was he *unhappy* I wasn't so fat anymore?

"I don't know. Maybe... *huh*. Maybe not so good."

"I've seen that a lot. Men have a hard time when their partners are suddenly noticed. You look great, you're more confident, and now everyone is starting to see that. It's hard for couples sometimes."

He suggested I talk to a counselor. Maybe Sam would be willing to go along, too.

The night Sam was flying home, I was drunk and dancing to Junkture in the kitchen, alone while the boys slept, lip-syncing my way through the entire back catalog. I saw on Facebook that Alex was on the road again, back in Austin to write and record a couple of tracks at the Deck. I called him without thinking and without bothering to text him for permission.

He answered the phone on the third ring, laughing.

"I'm drunk and dancing and I've missed you and I wanted to talk to you!" I blurted, giggling and bouncing in place.

"You're so crazy!"

"Yep! That's why you love me! And I *am* the sweet, funny girl you love right now, not the crazy girl who lost her fucking mind."

"That's good to hear. How much have you had to drink?"

"A *lot*. My mouth is numb from the Jack."

I could hear his grin as he steered away from my numb mouth. "I saw your status update by the way, about your weight. That's awesome, Tierney. I'm happy for you."

"It's a very different body than the last time you saw me," I said confidently. "How's Austin? How's writing going?"

"Okay." He didn't sound thrilled. "They just... Paul spends so much time doing everything *but* what we say we're going to do. It drives me fucking crazy."

"How many tracks have you guys recorded?"

"*One*. Barely. They wanted to redo 'Whiskey Mouth'."

"*Why?* It's so damn good."

Alex sighed. "I don't fucking know. Paul wasn't happy with the original mix, and he got all excited about redoing it. *Fine. Whatever.* But then we don't start working for two hours, and we're all standing around doing nothing while he's doing some other bullshit that's got nothing to do with me."

"I'm sorry," I offered gently.

"Don't do that. Don't apologize. It's not your fault." He sounded a little irritated.

"I know it's not."

"Then don't say you're sorry when you haven't done anything wrong."

I decided to change the subject. "Where are you now?"

"At the apartment, about to crash. Recording for a couple of days, then we're going to Houston for this radio thing, some all-day festival. We play mid-morning for a bunch of drunks."

"When do you leave for that?"

"We leave Thursday, driving straight in overnight, doing the set on Friday morning, and staying in Houston for a show Saturday night."

"Well, if I don't talk to you before then, have a good show. Try not to let Paulie get to you. You get yourself all worked up over this shit, and you know the added tension doesn't help."

"Go pass out, you crazy girl. I gotta go to sleep. I'll call you soon."

"Yep! Heart you, Alex!"

"'Night, Buttercup."

It was quick and easy and pleasant. There was no expectation or pressure, just two friends who hadn't talked in a while.

I was dancing again in the kitchen, wearing only red panties and a black camisole, moving wet laundry from the washer to the dryer, flailing about to "Debris". Thrashing madly, my long, blond hair phwapped against my shoulders and back, my bare feet catching lightly on the kitchen floor. I spun around suddenly and opened my eyes to find Sam standing there, holding his suitcase and watching me warily.

I screamed like a little girl.

"I said 'hello'," he deadpanned.

Breathless with laughter, I kissed him hello. "I'm so glad you're home! How was your trip?"

"Fine. Let me through, so I can put my stuff away?"

I moved aside and let the man go through. I unplugged from my iPod and got ready for bed, flossing and brushing my teeth, combing my hair into soft, golden submission. I waited patiently in bed for my husband, while he unpacked his suitcase. Even though he hadn't made time for me, for us, before he left, I wanted to welcome him home with slow, languid love.

He didn't make the time when he got home, either.

I was past the point of hurt and angry. I felt like I was screaming for him to pay attention to me and he just didn't give a damn.

––––––––––––––––

The radio festival was being streamed live by the station that was hosting the event. Junkture was set to go on at ten in the morning, between a local band I didn't know and a national band I didn't like. I got the boys off to school and went to the park to walk. I listened to the set on my phone while I took a shower.

Alex Wheeler
April 5th 12:17 PM

How was the show? I listened to the stream.

It was good. Could you tell how tired we were?

Yeah, you sounded like you were struggling with those higher notes. Did you drive in this morning?

Yup. Drove all night, ate, went on. Fucking exhausted.

Where are you now?

Hotel. Watching porn. Where r u?

In my bed. Just took a shower. So I'm all warm and naked.

Mmmmm.

And you want to call me and tell me all about what you're watching, don't you? I know you do. You know you do.

I knew he was worried about what that would mean, if anything. I knew he was afraid of how I would be afterward. Would it start everything up again?

It took him an agonizingly long two minutes to call.

"What's happening?" I answered. "*Tell me.*"

"She's making him watch her take it in both ends," he breathed. "This guy is *pounding* her while she's sucking another one, and her husband's naked and jacking off while she's coming."

He was a little hoarse but engrossed and keyed up.

"Are you stroking your cock like he is?"

"Just like he is."

"Naked in the hotel bed, watching the girl take two guys, and you can't touch her?"

"*God*, I wanna fuck her so bad."

"Is that what you want, baby?" I purred. I leaned back against my pillow and rubbed my clit slowly. "You wanna watch me fuck two guys while you jack off?"

"Yes, please. *Oh god! I would love that!*"

"I'll make you wait. I'll make you watch me get off on some fat cock while I suck another one. You'll want it to be you so bad. But I won't let you. And I won't let you come, either."

He gasped and sighed into the phone, listening intently. "*Please....*"

"Not until they fuck me and come in me first. You have to *watch*, Alex. Keep your eyes on me. Watch my face, that look between pleasure and pain, with some guy's dick stretching my lips apart."

"I want that to be my dick."

"I know you do. Think about how good my mouth will feel on your cock, babycakes. My tongue is so soft and wet."

"Stick it down your throat."

"All eight inches? I can take it."

"I'll make you take it."

"You can't even touch me yet," I taunted. "*I am touching me*, but you can't. You just have to watch while I tweak my clit and get *fucked*."

"You're *killing* me."

"Do you wanna fuck me, baby?" I toyed coyly. "Do you wanna put your cock in me and see if I can take it?"

"*Yes....*"

"*Where*, Alex? Tell me *where* you want to put it."

"In that *beautiful* mouth, stretch that heart-shaped smile wide open."

"*Mmmm....*"

"I wanna fuck that delicious pussy after he fucks you."

I gasped, my fingers stroking furiously inside me.

"And I want to *fuck your ass*! I'm gonna bury my cock in you, Buttercup."

"It's *hot* and *tight*."

"I'm gonna fuck you harder and longer than they did. Grab your hips and *ride* your fucking ass."

"*Goddamn*, I'm gonna come!" I rasped.

"*Tell me, Tierney. Let me hear you come!*"

I closed my eyes and tucked the phone under my chin.

"*Fuck me, Alex. Fuck me hard. I wanna feel your balls slap against my ass while you pound me. Do it, baby! Come for me. Come in me!*"

I came hearing him groan against my words.

"Oh my god, you're so good at that!" he panted finally.

"And you've missed my dirty little mouth," I said, stretching languorously against my bed.

"You can't go all crazy on me again, Tierney," he said cautiously. "I can't do that again."

"I know, Alex. I won't."

We talked for a few minutes more, catching up on the last few weeks. I was elated when I hung up with him. We were okay. I felt confident that Alex and I could jump into what we did best and that I would be emotionally stable through it. I'd had some time to get my head on straight again, and Alex was willing to let me back in.

He texted me late that night.

Alex Wheeler
April 5th 10:52 PM

U around?

Yeah, what's up?

I left the hotel. Found this store close by. Watching this girl in a booth.

Tell me.

She looks like Annabelle. Oh my god, she looks so much like my exwife!

Whoa! Weird.

She's so goddamn hot! And she's
dancing in these fuckme heels.
I wanna fuck her
She's pointing at a hole in the wall

??

there's a dick. he's whispering for
me to suck him
she's nodding and rubbing her tits
against the glass
she wants me to suck this guy's
dick

Do you want to?

god i think i do
it's so dirty
suck   some   strange   dick   while
Annabelle watches

It was much like the things he told me about early on, the
intense sexual experiences he'd shared with Annabelle and never
revealed to Talia, adamant that she would never, ever understand
and would likely think much less of him if she knew what his heart
coveted.   It was all coming at me in broken text type, and I couldn't
be sure if it was real or fantasy. Either way, I was there, texting with
him through the whole process.

Fuck, I gotta get outta here!
I can't do this
What the fuck was I thinking?

Are you okay?

Yeah. I just gotta get out of here
right now!

Call me?

Nope. 2moro

I was awake at two in the morning, like I was so often. My brain was buzzing. I was a little worried about Alex after the texts. He seemed freaked out, but I didn't want to have misread what I couldn't hear. I didn't want to infer anything correctly.

I was worried about the way *he* had reacted, though. He knew in his heart that even the basest of his desires were perfectly natural. They were things he desperately wanted to explore again and further, but his head argued that they were demons to be vanquished. If he couldn't banish them outright, he would compartmentalize them, like so much else, and only let them out when he felt safe.

I was convinced that this was part of the reason he'd married Talia. From what I knew of her, she was sweet and refreshing when he met her, when he was still recovering from the break-up of his first marriage. She was much younger than he was and needed the regular father figure she'd missed as a child. He needed someone to give him a reason to never tap into his own shadowy vulgarities and self-recriminating shame again. I had no doubt that he loved her, but I felt strongly that he'd married her—at least in part—in the hope that she would save him from himself.

I wanted to talk to him, to make sure he really knew why he'd reacted the way he did. I wanted him to be able to be honest about it, both with me and himself. Especially himself. He needed to be able to understand why these deep impulses were so psychically upsetting to him sometimes, and I wasn't sure it wasn't part of the reason we were tossed together. He'd always called me his free sex therapist.

I wasn't freaked out by what he'd shared, neither the content nor the context. I was thrilled and turned on that he was in a place where he wanted to share with me. I'd been concerned that after everything that had happened between us, the wall he built between us in Europe would stay up. He was obviously willing to let me climb over again, knowing fully that there was nothing he could do that would freak me out so much that I wouldn't be there for him. I was my own kind of kinked, which was kindred with his kinked, and I hearted him so.

He called later the next morning, while I was out for a short, solo hike at Stone Mountain.

"I can't really talk. We're about to be driving again. But, look, I wasn't *really* there. It was fantasy, all of it. I was watching porn in my hotel, and there was this woman that reminded me of Annabelle. A *lot*."

He sounded unsettled. "I'm sure that was weird," I said evenly.

"It's... *whatever*. I just wanted to let you know it wasn't a big deal. It just made me remember her, and I was talking through it."

"That's fine. I'm glad you're okay. But all you had to do was tell me."

"I'm telling you now."

"I'm still worried about how you reacted to it."

"It's fine, Tierney. It was just some fantasy shit, and I was drunk. Very, very drunk."

"You could've told me that, Alex. You didn't have to lie to me about it. I would've still been there for you. All I've ever asked is that you be honest with me. Don't fucking lie to me."

"Goddamn! Calm down. It was just a fucking *fantasy*, Tierney!"

"I'm calm. I was calm before. I'm hiking and sitting by this lake talking to you."

"I gotta go."

"That's fine. Just remember that I will believe anything you tell me until I have reason otherwise. It's trusting and naive, I know, but that's how I am, good or bad. All I'm asking is that you tell me the truth."

"Okay. I gotta go. I'll call you later."

He was mad. His tone was polite but tense. As much as he could tell me the truths of me as he saw them, he *hated* it when I got all truthy with him. He denied it, again and again, but he withdrew every time I shared some insight about who and what I thought he was, especially if it was in direct opposition to how he presented himself. If I cut too close to the quick, he would shove me back into my compartment and file me away.

Chapter 16

The next night, Sam and I took the boys to dinner. It was School Night at a local pizza place, when the boys' elementary school would get a portion of the evening's proceeds. We had a really pleasant evening, laughing and enjoying some much-needed family time. Even when the boys were off in the arcade, Sam and I laughed and talked, enjoying each other's company like we hadn't in a while. We came home in time to get the kids bathed and ready for bed.

I sat on the edge of the boys' tub and turned on the water, feeling the temperature change from in-the-pipe cold to scalding hot, carefully adjusting the knobs until I found the warmth the boys liked best.

"Monkeys!" I called out. "Who's getting in first?"

I stepped down the hall toward our bedroom. Sam was standing at his dresser, emptying his pockets and getting ready to change out of his work clothes.

"Make sure they don't get water all over the fucking place again. I should be able to walk into my goddamn bathroom without sloshing across the rugs."

His tone was ugly and condescending, especially after we'd just had a great evening.

I started to walk away, to just let him rage and be done. But I *couldn't*. It was insulting and unnecessary, and I was tired of passively letting him yell at me whenever he felt like it, even—especially—when it wasn't about anything I'd done wrong.

"If I need your help, I'll ask for it!" I snapped. "Until then, don't talk to me like that in front of my fucking children."

I turned quickly from the bedroom doorway and stepped into the bathroom, leaning down to turn off the faucet. I heard pattering footsteps across and down the hall, an indication that both boys were headed toward the bathroom.

I turned toward the door as Sam stormed into my path. He was angry as hell.

"*Don't you ever speak to me like that in front of my children again!*" he bellowed. "*Who the fuck do you think you are?*"

He reached out and punched the door with the side of his fist, inches from my face. The door swung back, bouncing against the wall.

Out of the corner of my eye, I saw Tripp back into his room, directly across from us. I heard Ian's door shut quickly.

I clinched my jaw and glared at Sam defiantly. In truth, I was scared to death. He stared at me, seething, and stormed back to the bedroom.

I'd seen him mad many, many times. Once, early in our marriage, we were arguing, screaming at each other over something that seemed intractably huge at the time. Sam had followed me down the hall into the bedroom, yelling at me while I yelled back. I was aggressive and difficult, and I was egging him on. He pulled his hand back, as if to strike.

"*Do it!*" I'd dared him.

"*You do it!*" he'd yelled back. He spun on his heel and bounded from the room.

Sam had never, ever hit me. He knew all the details of my years with Damien, of all the times he'd threatened and hit and kicked me. Standing in front of that bathroom door, pointing my chin at Sam's anger, I was brought back immediately to one night in Damien's dorm room, when he'd been so angry with me that he'd picked me up by the neck and pinned me against his closet. His roommate came into the room seconds later to find Damien dangling me by the neck, three inches off the floor. He yelled at Damien to let go of me. It was still months before we finally broke up.

But I could suddenly see a pattern, of my pushing angrily when I felt threatened or hurt. Bad attention was better than no attention at all. It let me feel *something* other than dismissal. It didn't justify the behavior by the men in my life. It *did* make me question how my own nasty behavior could help drive some really ugly moments in my life.

I was upset by the exchange with Sam. I never really thought for a moment that he would hit me. He was aggressive, though, trying to assert his power over the situation. He knew damn well that it would frighten me, and he'd used that fear to make me submit to his control of the moment.

I emailed Alex late that night, bitching about what had happened. I was okay, I assured him. I wasn't hurt. He hadn't actually hit me. But I was mad as hell and was sick and fucking tired of all the bullshit with Sam. He obviously didn't like who and what I was, in any circumstances. Things were becoming untenable at home. I couldn't take much more.

Sam and I mostly ignored each other. I apologized the next day for being a bitch. He nodded and made some non-committal noise, turning his cold shoulder toward me again.

Deeply asleep the next night, I heard my cell phone ringing. It was down the hall, in the office. Normally it would be on my nightstand, but I'd left it syncing to my laptop when I'd fallen asleep watching television in bed. I glanced at the clock.

2:51 AM

I heard Sam move from his chair in the office, then back to it. He'd probably looked to see who was calling at that hour.

Who the fuck is calling me now?

I padded down the hall. My phone rang again.

Alex Wheeler

Fuck.

I unplugged the sync cable. "Oh, it's Alex." I feigned confusion. "He's probably drunk and forgot about the time difference."

I took my phone into the bathroom, turning off the ringer. It rang again immediately, silently vibrating in my hand.

"Hey."

"Are you okay?" He was driving. He sounded upset.

"Yeah, I was asleep."

"No! *Are you okay?!*" He was almost yelling at me.

"Yes, Alex, I'm fine."

"I just saw your email. This is not okay. You have to get him into counseling, Tierney. You have to get him help. Now."

"I know. Alex, really, I'm okay."

"*Goddamn it!* Are you sure?"

"Yes, I promise."

"Okay, look, I'm sorry. I know it's late. I'll let you go. I'll call you tomorrow and talk more about it then. I just wanted to make sure—"

"Yes, babycakes, I'm fine. I'm safe. I promise."

"Okay. I'll call you tomorrow."

"Okay. Bye."

It was sweet that he was concerned, but it was confusing, too. On the one hand, he was my friend, who was pushing me yet again to get my husband into counseling, to make things right between us. I knew he wanted me and Sam to be able to work through our problems and have a happy marriage again, for us and for our children. On the other hand, he was also my strange, unexpected lover, calling at three in the morning to make sure my husband hadn't hit me, to make sure I was safe.

Alex called the next morning, while I was at the gym. I went outside, pacing along the edge of the parking lot, while I talked to him.

"So what the fuck was he mad about?"

Standing in the shade of a decorative tree, I stared out across the wide open lot next to the gym. Small birds flitted between the weeds and rocks, as I went through the whole story again. I admitted that I was a bitch for no apparent reason. I admitted that it had scared me.

"But if I honestly thought for a second that he would hit me, I would get out of there. I would've left and called the police."

"Tierney, you *have* to get him into counseling."

"I don't think he'll go."

"Then go by yourself."

"And if he won't budge? If he won't work with me and try to fix this?"

"Then you know what you need to do."

"Alex," I said, "I don't know if I can do this. Is that fair, to him or my children?"

"Is it fair for him to be an asshole to you? It's not good for you, and it's sure as hell not good for your boys."

"God, Alex! I don't even know if I *want* to try to make this work. You know, I was so close to leaving in December—"

"I know—"

"—and I'm not sure it's not what I should've done. Fuck, it's so hard. I love him...."

"You're just not sure you want to be married to him."

"I'm not sure I want to be married at all."

"Tierney, you have to decide what's best for you, but I think you should try counseling with him. You owe him the chance to try."

Alex was advocating for my husband. He knew I loved Sam, but he also knew how unhappy I was. I didn't know if it was because he honestly thought it was the best place for me, or if he hoped it would keep the distance between us if I was happy again in my marriage.

"I've tried, Alex! I have busted my ass to make this work. It's so goddamn hard."

"I know, Buttercup. That's life."

I talked it over with Tessa later that afternoon. She agreed, somewhat grudgingly, that Alex was right. I needed to go to counseling, with or without Sam. Even if my husband refused to go, it would be beneficial for me to talk to someone, to work through these feelings of confusion about what I wanted out of my marriage and my life.

"You need to be careful with this thing with Alex, though," she warned. "I don't want you to let him dictate what you do with Sam."

"I'm not, Tess, I promise. He's the person I trust the most to be truthful with me, next to you. I don't know why. *No*, I *do* know why. He's just *that person*, who knew me from the moment we met. He can read me within seconds of answering the phone."

"I know why he's important to you," she said. "I just don't want him to become more important to you than he needs to be. I don't want you to get hurt."

I smiled. Even after almost twenty-five years, Tessa was still looking out for me.

"What if Sam refuses to go to counseling?" I asked. "What if he just won't do it?"

"Well... then you can put on your big girl panties and go by yourself. Maybe he'll follow, maybe he won't. But *you* need to do this for you, no matter what. You have so much shit in your head right now, and it would probably do you good just to have someone to help you sort all of that out."

"*What?*" I said, feigning incredulity. "You're tired of hearing all about my man troubles?"

Tessa laughed. "Oh, no! I love living your crazy-ass life vicariously, but I am hardly equipped to straighten out that big, blond jumble."

I steeled myself to talk to Sam that night after the boys went to bed. I was scared. I knew it had to happen, I knew why, and I wasn't scared of him or what he would do. I was frightened by the truth of it all, and it was making me tense. So many of our days started okay, then turned snippy and rude, then just distant, and I was unhappy like that. But then we'd have an amazing moment where we were totally together, though they were always fleeting. It made me sad, and I didn't know what I wanted.

If he refused to budge, to see where I was coming from, was it fair of me to ask him to leave? Was it fair of me to expect my life to stay virtually the same with the kids and to have him change his and move out? I knew that was simplistic. My biggest fear was that he would demand I give up my relationships with Alex and Seth and Junkture. He'd alluded to it before. I didn't know if I was willing to compromise any more than I already had for my marriage and it made me feel selfish and like I was headed for a failure no matter what.

Lying in bed with Sam that night, I turned toward him and propped myself on my pillow. It was uncharacteristic of me to wait until late, to start a heavy discussion right before bed. But there hadn't been time all day to mention it.

"I think we need to go to counseling," I said to Sam.

"That'll be expensive."

"The co-pay with the insurance is ten dollars a session,"

"But then it's on record. When it's filed with the insurance, it's part of *my* record. It could impact any kind of clearance or job I try to get later."

Seriously? That's more important to you than our marriage?

"We could find a counselor and pay out of pocket."

"I'm not paying for that shit."

"Well, I'm going. Whether or not you do, I need to see someone. Things are bad—with us, with me, with everything—and I need some help getting my head straightened out."

I lay back down on my side of the bed. We were silent for a minute, in the dark.

"Okay," he said finally, "I'll go, but only so I know I did everything possible. I want there to be a paper trail, showing that I tried."

That was a shitty reason to agree to go into marriage counseling, but at least he was agreeing.

I called the insurance company the next day. There was a lot of hoop jumping to get the referral, but I did it. I went through the lengthy list of available counselors, avoiding the ones who listed Christian- or faith-based counseling as one of their services. I didn't expect any marriage counselor to tell me it was okay to lie to my husband about my extra-marital fling, but I didn't want one who would outright judge me or tell me I was wrong to question monogamy as a basis for a relationship.

I scheduled the appointment with Janet for the following week.

———————————

Alex called on Friday, the day before his birthday.

"It feels like I haven't talked to you in forever. I feel disconnected from you," he said.

"You talked to me yesterday," I laughed.

"It's been too long." I couldn't help but smile to myself, sitting alone in a parking lot on a sunny afternoon.

"And I have news. I may be coming to Atlanta."

"*What?! Seriously?!*" I squealed.

I could hear the grin on his face.

"Yes, seriously! May sixth. There's a show planned, a private event."

"*Oh my god!* Come a day early!" My mouth was racing faster than my mind, for a change. "We could hang out and do nothing. *Pleasepleaseplease*, come to Atlanta a day early! It'll be a little bit of belated birthday fun!"

He was laughing at me. "I'll see. I'll think about it."

"I would just love some down time with you. Preferably alone, but I'd take Max if I had to. And I don't mean specifically sexual time, though you know how I feel about that."

"Yes, I do."

"*Besides*, it's almost your birthday! When I see you, I'll give you your gift. You can have your choice: a bottle of Scotch or a Scotch-Irish blonde."

He was laughing again. "You can't afford the Scotch I would want. It would cost more than you!"

"Asshat. I can do anything I goddamn well want. But if you'd rather have Scotch than the blonde, well... okay. I'll understand."

"I'll think about it. *All* of it, Buttercup."

"What are you doing for your birthday?" I asked.

"Working. I'm doing some vocals for this advertising thing for a friend. Talia has a party planned for me that night."

"I hope you have a really happy birthday, Alex!"

"Thank you. I have to go, though."
"It's all good, babycakes. Call me next week?"
"Yup."

From: Tierney Cavanaugh Johnson
Date: April 12th 3:05 am
To: Alex
Subject: Happy Birthday!

I'm so glad I got to talk to you today! Thanks for making the time, though I like to think you want it as much as I do sometimes. In fact, I know you do.

I *do* hope you have a wonderful and amazing birthday. You're a great guy, Alex Wheeler, and I'm really, unbelievably glad you fell into my life when you did.

I'm so excited I might get to see you in Atlanta! *I promise to behave.* I will even agree to *not* drink to excess if it means making you more comfortable. (I am fully aware of how I can get when I drink, thank you very much.)

I also promise to have no expectations. Look, you know how I feel about it. I can't have been any more straightforward (at your behest, I remind you!) about how amazing I think sex between us could be, on so many levels. You know all the reservations I have about putting myself out there to you like that, all of my issues and fears and self-doubt, and you've never, ever been anything but spectacular with me. All of that aside, you and this friendship mean more to me than that does or possibly ever could. If I have to choose, I choose to keep you, whatever way that works best. If you want whatever it is that we can make of this, it's yours. This ball's totally in your court, and I don't intend to mention it again.

Happywonderfulperfectamazingfantastic Birthday, Alex!

You have my love.

Tierney

———————————

Alex called again on Tuesday. I was in a store, trying on a dress. Yet again, half naked in a dressing room.

"You always know, don't you?" I teased.

"Maybe you're just always shopping," he countered.

"Ha! Maybe. I have to find a dress for Easter. We're going to Birmingham. It's also Sam's birthday. I have to look pretty."

"I'm sure you'll look great."

"How would you know? You haven't seen me in months. I'm not the same girl you saw in Chicago, Alex." I told him I'd call him right back. I quickly paid for the new dress and left the store, driving away toward home.

He answered on the first ring.

"Now... how was your birthday?" I asked

"It was great. Talia planned this party. I was supposed to be there at six, but I didn't get done in the studio until almost nine. It was good once I got there, though."

Three hours late. I'm betting she wasn't happy. "How was she about your being late?"

"Mad, but what could I do? I couldn't just *leave* where I was. But she gets mad about stuff, and I don't understand it. Like last night, she'd been out with some girlfriends. She came home around ten, and she wanted to have sex."

Great.

"I was already going to bed," he continued. "I had to be up this morning to drive to the studio."

"Yeah...."

"So she tells me she'll do all the work, to just lay there. I'm a really physical guy, especially when it comes to sex. If I'm there, I'm all there. What fun is that just *laying* there? She got really *mad*, about how I didn't want her."

"You rejected her."

"No, I didn't! I was tired and didn't want to just *lay* there. She went and cried in the bathroom. She never, ever lets me see her cry."

"No, I mean, from her perspective, you rejected her. Sometimes women need to be the one in control and feel some power from making their partner come. But if she was so angry...."

Don't say it, Tierney. You'll get all truthy on him, and he won't like it.

"What?" he pressed.

"Alex, it sounds like she's been... tempted. Like, something has tempted her, something she wanted and couldn't have. She needed to work through it, and you weren't there for her to do it."

"I'm sure she has. I know there was this guy that she used to date, right after we met. She was gone with him for, like, three days. I told her I didn't care. I just needed to know."

"No, babycakes, like... maybe something *recent* tempted her. She doesn't know what to do about it, and she was trying to reach out to you to make it better. You turned her down."

I could remember all the times I'd missed Alex and had gone to Sam for comfort. It wasn't that I would necessarily fantasize about Alex while I was in bed with Sam. It was more a matter of working through that unresolved energy. When Sam turned away from me, the lack of resolution often turned to downright frustration, which could make me angry and irritable.

Alex didn't say anything.

"Look, I could be wrong. I don't know Talia. I do know women, though. What would you do, if she came to you and said there was someone else she wanted to fuck?"

"I would be hurt, but I know it's natural. I know it's part of human beings to want to sleep with more than one person. It's not natural for most people to be monogamous."

"So why can't you tell her the same thing?"

"She really wouldn't get it. Look, she knows how I am. She knows if I'm out, I'm always sizing up everything going by, to see if I could tap it. It doesn't mean I'm trying to, but I'm always looking. It's just who I am."

"How is she about that?"

"She hates it, but she ignores it. That's why I don't tell her half the time, when I'm on the road and going out. I'll call and tell her I'm back in my hotel room for the night, but I'm really out at a bar or a strip club with Max."

"Alex! That's awful. Why can't you just tell her the truth?"

"Because she would question me, constantly, about who I'm with and what I'm doing."

"She doesn't trust you," I said.

"No, she trusts me," he replied. "She just knows how I am. Sometimes I have to lie to my wife to keep her happy. It's not perfect, but it's what I have to do."

You're lying to her, and you're lying to yourself.

But who the fuck was I to judge? I was lying to Sam all the time, keeping this *thing* with Alex from him. I would lie about why I'd talked to Alex that day, or what we'd talked about.

"Like, I know, when she sees us together—when she meets you—she'll know we've talked. She'll know we've had these intimate conversations."

"Why do you say that?" *Why do you think she and I will ever meet?*

"Because she knows me, and she'll *know* we've connected. It's hard to miss."

I knew he was probably right. The chemistry between us was palpable from the beginning. I didn't want to think about coming face-to-face with Talia.

"So are you coming to Atlanta? Do you know yet?"

"I don't know. It's still up in the air."

"Fuck!" I growled. "Just fly in for an afternoon. I'll meet you at the airport. We can fuck in the bathroom, and you can go on about your day!"

"*Buttercup,*" he chuckled, "I want this. I want *you*. But I don't wanna do it if I don't have the time to devote to it. It will take longer than twenty minutes."

"Yes, it will. I'm an amazing fucking lay, Alex Wheeler. It'll take *hours*."

"Uh-huh." His voice shifted into that sweet, sexy tone he used to work me up. "*Hours*, Buttercup. Buttercup. *Buttercup*."

"You're making me all warm and creamy, Alex! I'm driving, and you're killing me. All I'm gonna think about all afternoon is fucking you for five straight hours."

"At least. Maybe six."

"Asshat!"

"I'm not an asshat!" he laughed.

"Now I'm all... *wet*, and I know you're almost to the studio."

"Yup. It is what it is, Buttercup. Go home and take care of that, okay? You can tell me all about it when you talk to me next."

"Mmmm-hmmmm."

"I'll talk to you soon?"

"Yep. Love you, Alex."
"I love you, too."

_____

We had to go to Birmingham for the weekend. It was Easter, but it was also Sam's fortieth birthday. He wanted to spend the time with his mom and dad, with his sister and her family. We'd never not been at home for Easter, even when we lived in much closer proximity to the families.

Sam and I were barely speaking. My head was in a constant cloud, confused and balancing three different worlds. I was going through my days with the kids, being Mom and caregiver and doing all the things I normally would with them. I bought the stuff for their Easter baskets, prepped all of our things for a weekend away. There was part of me that was constantly thinking about everything with Sam—how we were going to get through this, how it would impact the children, how he and I might move forward, together or apart. And part of me was always with Alex. I was stressed and in a freefall in my own head.

Sam's family hadn't seen me since Christmas. I was smaller than I'd been during almost all of our relationship, and they'd never really known me at this size.

"You'd better watch out," his mom said, taking a picture of us with the boys. "Tierney's getting so skinny, and she looks so pretty. All the men are going to start looking at her."

She was sweet and joking, but Sam and I both felt the pressure of her words. She knew nothing of our marital problems, and neither of them knew the truth of my relationship with Alex. We pretended that things were perfectly fine.

I took a long walk with Sam's sister, Michelle, a few miles around the lake where his parents lived. She and I had never been close, even when we were classmates, but it was nice to check in with her for a while. We talked about our kids and parents and her work and Sam's constant workload.

"I'm at a place in my life where the work/life balance is really important," she said. "I'm not so driven by getting ahead at work anymore. I realize that it's just what I have to do until I can get home and be with my family."

"Maybe you should share that with your brother," I replied.

I had my first session with the counselor the next day, by myself.

I told Janet about my last few months, at least in part. I told her about the weight loss, the stress on my marriage, and my involvement with the rock stars. I shared a good bit about my painting and my progressive journey to find myself again. I was not forthcoming about the true nature of Alex and me.

I explained a great deal about the problems Sam and I had been having and how I thought all of my experiences had impacted him and us. I told her about the awful fight, when he'd hit the door and scared me.

"He sounds very controlling," she said, concerned.

I nodded in agreement. "I don't think he likes my doing things outside of him and his realm. I have all of these new interests that don't include him. He won't be happy again until I'm doing exactly what I was doing before, and I can't be happy like that."

"Do you still love him?"

"I do. Very much. I just don't know if I want to be married to him. I don't know if I want to be married to anyone."

Seth called as I was leaving Janet's office.

"How was therapy?" he asked.

"Hard. She thinks Sam is controlling. I told her I don't know if I even want to be married, Hammer."

"Wow. That's rough."

"Yeah, but it's true. I have to decide what I want. I have to let Sam decide if he's willing to let me have it and still be with me. But I doubt you called to talk about my therapy. What's up?"

"I did call just to check on you, but I also wanted to let you know that I'm launching my KickStarter campaign for the new record. It's going live tonight."

"Oh, that's exciting! You know I'll donate."

"Aw, that's sweet—thank you! But I wanted to call and invite you to my CD release show in May. It'll be here, in San Antonio. Everyone who donates gets a ticket to the show, but I'm calling my friends personally to invite them, even if they don't donate."

"*Seth*, that's... thank you. You know, Sam's getting this bonus in a couple of weeks, and he asked me what special thing I wanted. Maybe I want to come to San Antonio."

"That'd be great! Sam's invited, too."

"I said maybe *I* want to come to San Antonio."

Maybe Alex will want to come to San Antonio.

Seth's voice changed to bad TV announcer. "But *wait*, Tierney Cavanaugh Johnson! There's more!"

I giggled.

"I wanted to see if you'd be willing to do some artwork for the show poster," he said in his regular voice. "It's okay if you don't. You don't have to say yes."

"You want me to paint something for your CD release show poster?" I asked incredulously.

"Yeah, I do. I love the work I've seen you post online so far, and I would really like you to do something for me, if you have time. If you even *want* to."

"Seth," I replied, "I'm *touched* that you would ask. I would *love* to do this for you."

"Okay! Great! I'll email you some ideas, so you can get a feel for what I'm looking for.

Alex called that afternoon.

"How was the therapist? Did Sam go with you?"

"It was hard as hell, and no. He couldn't work it into his schedule."

"I'm sorry, Buttercup. I know it's hard. This will be good for you to work through this. I hope you guys can work all of this out."

I sighed, pacing the den while I listened to him. "And if we don't? What if he still refuses to get help?"

"Then you'll do what you have to do."

"My biggest fear with all of this is that you'll decide it's too much, that you'll decide you can't deal with all of this and decide to break contact with me."

"Tierney, I'm your *friend*. I won't step out of your life, ever, unless you ask me to. Your problems with Sam have nothing to do with me. They were there long before you and I ever met." He paused, doing something in the background. "Listen, Atlanta's been postponed."

My heart sank. *Of course it has.* "Why?"

"I don't know, something about the private event being moved to later in the summer. It was Max's thing. He was in charge of scheduling it. I just got an email about it this morning."

Fuck! "Great! One more goddamn thing to go wrong."

"I can't help it, Tierney. It is what it is." His tone turned cautioning and wary.

"I know that, Alex," I snapped. "I just... *nevermind*. I don't want to fight about it."

"There's nothing to fight about. I can't help it."

"I know. It's just coming down at once, all of this shit today, and I don't like it."

"Okay, well, I'll let you go then."

I didn't want to hang up. I was mad and irritated and frustrated about the whole thing. I wanted to see him and to get some kind of relief for this overbearing sexual tension. I wanted some time with Alex, in person, where I could see and feel him, even if it was completely platonic.

"Yep. I'll talk to you soon. You have my love."

My deep, abiding, complicated love.

When Sam asked about my visit with the therapist, I told him a little bit. I wasn't going into all of it. If he wanted to know, he could go with me and hear it for himself.

"I scheduled the next appointment for a week from Saturday. I can make arrangements for the boys to be covered, if you want to can go with me. I hope you will."

For months, I'd wanted him to fight for me. I wanted to feel his love for me, intensely, with no need to question it. No matter how damaged we were, I wanted him to see some reason to *try*, even if I couldn't see it myself.

"I will," he answered. "Just send me the meeting invite for my calendar."

His tone was tired and defeated, but there was something there that told me he was willing to put up a fight, just in case it actually helped.

─────────────

Sam and I were still politely passive with one another. We kept the household running smoothly and were able to communicate everything that was happening, logistically. I took the kids to school and doctors' appointments. I helped host a wildly-successful fundraising event for the school library. Sam was working and getting ready for a week-long conference in Las Vegas.

He left for his work trip, and it was just me and the boys at home for most of a week. Alex was home again but in the studio working on some demo tracks, and he was traveling an hour or more each way, every day. He would often call me in the morning, on his way to the studio. I was usually at the gym or just finishing up when he called. There was a lot of talk about my being hot and sweaty and taut.

He would also usually call at night, after I'd put the boys to bed. It was wonderful, cocooning myself on the big couch in the dark, talking to Alex again. It was so damn easy, telling him everything and nothing.

"You know why that is," he said matter-of-factly. I could hear quiet music murmuring around him in his car as he drove.

"Because we're so connected?" I offered teasingly. "It's the shared Irish blood."

He chuckled. "Yes, there is that!" His voice grew softer, more relaxed. "I didn't expect it, but you're important to me. I miss you when you're not there to talk to."

"I know. And I know it's scary for you. That you care. That I care."

"No, I'm not scared. Not of you," he said quietly. "There are all these things I've told you, my secrets and the stuff with Annabelle—"

"—that I'll never tell—"

"—I know that. That's why I told *you*. There are things you know about me that *no one* knows—not my wife, not my brothers, not Max, *no one*. Only you. I *trust* you."

"Why?" I asked gently. "Why did you trust me so quickly and so easily? You barely knew me."

"Because we've done this before," he answered. "We've been through a thousand lifetimes together. We've always known the other one. We just couldn't find each other."

I caught my breath. I was blown the fuck away.

"You're amazing, you know that?"

"No, I'm not."

"Yeah, you are. I was such a crazy fucking bitch to you. Alex, I'm sorry about that. I know I've emailed you an apology. I know you read it. But I'm so fucking sorry that I spun out on you like that. I promise, it won't ever happen again."

"It can't, Tierney. I can't do that with you again."

"I know. It was awful. I was so confused. I could *feel* how awful it was while I was talking to you, and I couldn't do anything about it."

"It was horrible. I was in Europe, and you were just freaking out, and I didn't know why."

"*I* didn't know why. You just have to remember that I'm always thinking—about you and this and my life—and sometimes I get overwhelmed."

"Sometimes you're a little overwhelming."

"I can't help it. I have all this energy, and a lot of it revolves around you."

"I know." He paused. "You're addicted."

"I am not!"

"You are. You get wrapped up and obsessive about things— your kids, your painting, your music. You get all worked up and excited and it spins out everywhere. It's beautiful but, yes, overwhelming. You have a very addictive personality."

"Maybe. But you use it to your advantage, don't you?"

"Sometimes," he snickered. "I'm almost home. I have to go. Can I call you tomorrow?"

"Of course!" *Awkward pause.* "I love you, Alex."

"I love you, too, Tierney."

I wasn't surprised by his telling me I was a bit overwhelming at times, though it hit me in a not-so-comfortable way. I'm loud and stubborn and demanding. I'm moody and overly sensitive sometimes. I can be obsessive and dogged and downright annoying.

But boiling me down to overwhelming.... That was like being told I was just too much.

It didn't stop Alex from calling the next night, or the next. He sent me a couple of tracks and asked for my thoughts.

"I trust your ears," he told me.

I didn't give him the same feedback he got from his musician friends. I'd had music training, albeit all through voice. I didn't play an instrument and didn't give a shit about how the guitars sounded or if the drums were too heavy or light. I was a music lover with unique tastes, and I listened for very different things than he or Paul or Seth did. I listened to the tracks and sent him my verbose responses, giving him feedback on what I did and didn't like about the lyrics, how I was naturally seeking out the harmonies.

I was deeply appreciative of his friendship, of the time he chose to spend with me, even when it wasn't sexual. *Especially* when it wasn't sexual. As much as I loved our intimate, naughty play, I was just as happy to talk to him about his work and my work and music and whatever else happened to come up in conversation. It reminded me that he cared on a completely different level, reminded me that I knew I got under his skin from time to time, even when I wasn't using my whorey little mouth to talk him through his own head.

Sam and I had our first joint session with the counselor, Janet. We talked about some of the same things she and I had touched on previously. We both admitted that our marriage was on some pretty jagged rocks and that we needed help. I did *not* say to Sam that I wasn't sure I wanted to be married.

"I don't understand why she wants to go and do all of these things by herself. I don't think her involvement with these musicians is good for her," Sam told Janet.

"Why is that?"

"It costs money, and it's not like she gets *paid* to do anything. It takes up a lot of time she could be doing something else."

"Like *what*?" I asked, turning toward him from my chair. "More laundry and dishes? More PTA meetings?"

"I don't know, Tierney. You've been painting again. It's really good."

"No one sees that, really. Sometimes my friends on Facebook see my stuff, but that's it. It's not like I'm out selling my paintings."

"Could you be?" Janet asked. "Is there some reason you couldn't be selling your work?"

I shook my head slowly, thinking about it. "I don't know. Maybe I could. It's hard as hell to break into an artist's market. I could probably *show* some things at a local small gallery, or maybe I could sell them online, but I will likely never make a ton of money doing this. And that's not *why* I do it anyway?"

"Why do you do it, then?"

"Because I enjoy it. Because it feels like a part of who I am. And there's nothing inherently wrong with having things that only I enjoy. Sam and the boys don't have to be a part of everything I do. I get to have some things that are just for me."

I paused, weighing the gravity of the moment. I kept my focus squarely on Janet, Sam hovering in the corner of my vision.

"Like, I got an offer to do a show poster for my friend Seth's CD release show," I said tenuously.

Sam started, moving in and out of my periphery.

"When?" he asked. Janet glanced at him. I couldn't tell if he was angry or just intrigued.

"He called a few days ago," I replied. "He asked me to do the artwork for his poster. He invited us to come to San Antonio for the show. In May."

"He invited *you*, I'm sure," Sam snapped.

I turned to face him. "He invited *both* of us. Would you *want* to go? You told me you were never going to a show again."

"Sam, do you not enjoy music as much as Tierney does?" Janet queried.

"I enjoy music. I just don't enjoy the loudness and the standing around and talking to people I don't know. I'd rather just stay home and listen to it when I want."

"But I don't want that!" I argued. "I *like* the loudness and the talking to fans. I *like* being in the middle of all that."

"You just saw him," Sam complained. "He was just here in December."

"I know, but this is the CD release show. He'll have the full band with him. And he wants me to do his poster."

"Would you be staying with Seth?"

"God, no! I'd stay at a hotel. I'd probably see Paul while I was there, too."

"I don't know, Tierney. There will be other shows. He'll be back in Atlanta soon enough, I'm sure."

"No!" I pressed. "It's a big deal. It's the release of *Maker*. That'll only happen once."

"Why does it matter to you? Why is this such a damn big deal?"

"Because Seth is my friend!" I argued. "It's a big deal for him, and I'd like to be there to support him. It would also be a good time to get away before the kids are home for the summer. You asked me what I wanted with the bonus money. I want this."

"Tierney, we have other financial obligations that need to be addressed first. I'd rather get those taken care of and make sure we have a clean slate before you go traveling again. Plane tickets and hotels and drinking in bars—it's not cheap, honey."

"I *know*, but I can find good deals on everything. I may have enough reward points to swing a free hotel. Besides, you *told* me I could get something. I'm not asking for ten thousand dollars, Sam. I'm asking for a weekend away to support my friend."

Sam looked at me for a moment, his face somewhere between disdain and wariness.

"Are there no other shows?"

I shook my head. "Not that I can make. He'll be heading north and west after that. It'll be the fall before he gets back toward Atlanta. He has a show in Chicago—I could see Tessa—but that's Memorial Day Weekend. Tripp has his fifth grade graduation on that Friday. You could go with me."

I tried to be sincere in my asking, but I really didn't want him to join me.

"I don't want to go. I don't understand why *you* want to go."

We were both silent.

"Sam, you don't seem enthused about this idea," Janet said.

"This trip she's talking about will take away resources from our family and only benefits her."

"Sometimes it's beneficial to both parties if one of the couple is having their individual needs met. There's nothing wrong with Tierney doing things that only make her happy."

I interjected, "I think the problem is that sometimes what *I* want is in direct opposition to what *he* wants. One of us has to win, and one of us has to lose. Neither of us wants to be the one to lose."

"It doesn't have to be a win or lose situation," Janet offered. "You both have to be willing to compromise, and sometimes that means one of you gets your way. If each partner is getting time and doing things for themselves, it can be rejuvenating, so they have renewed energy to bring to the marriage."

Janet was telling him to consider agreeing to the trip.

At home, I pushed harder against Sam, to get him to agree to let me go.

"I could really use the break right before summer starts and the boys are home all the time."

"Why the fuck is this so important to you?" Sam demanded

"Because it's the last time I'll get to see him for a while. He's my *friend*, and I want to support him. It's a big deal for him, I've been invited to participate, and I'd like to be able to do it. It's a good time, right before the boys are out of school. I can get away for a quick trip and be ready for the summer with them."

"It's just a concert, Tierney. There will be more shows."

"I don't know when they'll happen. I *want* to go!"

We argued about it for days. We tried our best to keep the tension away from the children.

I called my dad. "I need you to take the boys for the weekend."

"Everything okay?"

"No. Things are tense at home. Sam and I need some time alone."

Dad met me early on Saturday to get the children. He was taking them on an overnight gem mining trip in North Carolina. They'd be back on Sunday afternoon. Sam and I had thirty-six hours to sort this shit out.

I tried to engage him at home. Even if we weren't talking about the trip, we still had other issues that needed our attention. We needed to spend some *time* together.

But Sam and I were still playing tug about my wanting to go to San Antonio. I felt like he was backpedaling on a promise to do something special for me.

"I don't think San Antonio is a good idea," he told me.

"But I want to go. It's *important* to me. You *promised* me something special!"

"I thought you'd get something that would benefit both of us," he snapped. "I work hard for this fucking money, and I don't know if this is for you or for us." He took a deep breath and exhaled slowly. "I don't think the time is good, Tierney. I don't think you should go."

"I disagree."

"Why do you want to go so badly? I've never seen you so determined to do something! Is there something going on I should be worried about?"

"What the fuck are you talking about? What could possibly be going on?"

You know, Tierney.

"I don't know, but I don't like it. Not one damn bit!"

"Whatever. Fine, I won't go."

We argued for hours. Again. I was dogged and determined, selfishly thinking only of what I wanted, regardless of its impact on anyone else. He was being the great provider, lording his hard work over me, reminding me yet again that it was his hard-earned money. My contributions to the family as primary caregiver were all but ignored. I felt a huge amount of disdain coming from him when he reluctantly admitted to the magnitude of the work I did for the family.

Finally, I couldn't talk about it anymore. We were getting nowhere. He was tense and argumentative. I was pissed as hell and walking on eggshells. I stopped short of telling him he needed a drink.

"I'm going to walk," I said.

I wanted to see more of life than was visible from the end of my cul-de-sac. I wanted to be *going* and *doing* and *experiencing*. I loved Sam and the boys, but I felt certain I was worth more than my title of Mother-and-Wife afforded. I was trying to be true to this new sense of self I was finding, while trying to fulfill the obligations of home and family.

Seething, I headed to the park to walk it off. I was mad as hell, driving and listening to something harsh and angry, as loud as I could stand it.

I texted Alex, who called a few minutes later.

"Are you okay?" he asked

"No! I'm mad as fuck!" I turned my radio down, blaring Junkture's "Debris". "He *told* me to pick something I wanted! I want to go to Seth's show. I want some time away. I spend all goddamn day at home, doing everything for him and the boys, and it's not unreasonable to want something for myself!"

"Did you ask him if he wanted to go with you?"

"Yes! But I don't *want* him to go, Alex. I've done *nothing* just for me, for the last ten years. I've always been tied to the house and the kids and the whatever-the-fuck-else he needed me to do. We didn't even take a *vacation* until Tripp was a baby. I'm sick of it! I'm sick of always being what he needs me to be! I get to be *Tierney* sometimes, too!"

I pulled into a parking space and turned off the car.

"I don't get it, Alex. He gets away all the time. He travels for work several times a year."

"That's not the same, Buttercup, and you know it. Working travel isn't the same as doing it with your family."

"No, you're right. It's not. But I've been *nowhere*. I've done *nothing*. I *want* to go see Seth."

"Are you fucking him?"

What? I shook my head in bafflement. "What are you talking about?"

"Are you fucking Seth Wiezel? He's young and attractive, and you guys are friends."

"No! I'm not fucking Seth! He's my friend."

Would it matter to you if I were?

"You're starting to find yourself again. That's frightening and disorienting for Sam, I'm sure. Look, I'm not him, but it was a little scary when Talia started designing again and doing her own thing. She didn't *need* me for everything, which was good, but it feels a little emotionally threatening to be on the other side of that."

"Alex," I sighed, "Sam has taken care of me for years. Even when I couldn't do it myself. I don't care how boosting that's been to his *provider* persona; I can't let his emotional security dictate everything I do and don't do."

"Of course not."

I was quiet for a moment. I could hear muffled music in Alex's background.

"I *want* this, Alex."

He laughed. "Well, once you set your mind to something, you *will* get it. I know! You are the most determined person I know."

"Fuck you!"

"I'm not picking on you, Tierney." He sounded a little hurt but was keeping calm. "You are dogged when you want something. It's just who you are."

"I'm sorry. I'm not mad at you. I'm just mad."

"I know. It'll be okay. And I should probably tell you that Junkture's been added onto Seth's show."

"*What?*"

"Junkture is playing at Seth Wiezel's CD release show," Alex said deliberately.

"You'll be in San Antonio? For Seth's show? For the show he invited me to? That I'm doing the poster for?"

"*Yes.*"

Alex will be there.

"You'd better add the Junkture logo to the poster," he added.

"I, um, I just spent two days working with Seth on that artwork, finalizing the design. He didn't say anything about it."

"He might not have known about it. Paulie just told us a few minutes ago. Don't worry about *changing* it. I'm sure what you've done is great. You'll just have to add our logo. I'll tell Paul to email you."

"Okay...," I said slowly. *"You'll be in San Antonio?"*

"Yes, Tierney," Alex replied distractedly. "I.will.be.in.San.Antonio.for.Seth's.show. But I have to go. We're about to go into rehearsal."

"Thank you," I said as calmly as I could. "Really."

"Any time."

I plugged into my iPod and started walking.

I realized I sounded like a spoiled fucking brat, talking to Alex. Sam's reasons weren't all invalid. It was his condescending tone that sent me over the top. Five miles later, my head was a little clearer. I would've still been seething had I not talked to Alex when I did. I was always better when he blew a little smoke in my face.

Was there something inherently wrong that I was willing to trade the naughtiest of sexual favors for a little emotional validation?

Neither of us gets to make me feel like a whore, though, unless my panties are off.

And now there was the added, unexpected complication of Alex Wheeler *being* at that show.

Alex was right; I was *determined*. Somehow, I would find a way to make Sam understand that going to San Antonio would be good for me.

———————————

I went home and took a shower.

Sam came home late that evening, long after dark. I was watching television in bed.

"Tierney?" I turned to look at him, standing across the bedroom from me. "I just don't understand how this trip is more important to you than I am."

He was calm and sincere. He was hurting. I needed to make it better.

I stood and moved in front of him. "It's not more important to me than you are. Nothing is more important to me than you."

"If the boys or I were sick, would you go?"

"That depends on how sick you were." *An ear infection or a cold would not warrant a change of plans*, my practical Mom voice said.

"If I was in the *hospital*, would you go to San Antonio?"

"Of course not," I said evenly. "I would never leave you if you really needed me. I'm sorry. I see how much this is bothering you. Sam, *nothing* means more to me than you and our boys. You guys are my life. I love you. *You are my heart.*"

I reached up tentatively with one hand and touched his face gently. I pushed up on my tip-toes and kissed him gingerly.

"I love you," I whispered. "Forever and always and no matter what."

It was something we'd said to each other and the boys for years. A hand-painted decorative sign saying just that hung in our bedroom, across from the bed. It was often the first thing I saw when I woke.

And it was *true*. Sam and our life was more important to me than anything, including Alex Wheeler. But there was no denying how badly my heart wanted to go to Texas, to see this thing through.

He kissed me back, softly and sadly. He was searching for me, trying desperately to feel me there. As much as he'd backed away from our marriage over the years, I'd run just as quickly over the last six months. Counseling and talk and sex meant nothing if we couldn't *feel* one another.

Hands shaking, I unbuttoned his shirt. "I love you."

I was standing there, wearing only a camisole and panties. I was starting to get cold in the cool conditioned air. Looking him in the eye, I pulled my cami over my head. He watched as I stepped out of my panties.

I kissed his neck. "I need you."

I reached for his belt, unsure if he would let me continue. "I want you. More than anything. None of it means anything without you."

He kissed me hard, helping me with his unfastening and stripping. I pulled him back against our bed and wrapped my legs around his waist. I could tell immediately that I was wet and he was hard. He, licked at my lips, then kissed my neck, sucking on the spot that he knew would drive me crazy. I arched my hips against him urgently, pressing my pussy against him, and his cock was in me in the span of a breath.

I gasped as he pounded against me, over and over, like he was trying to bore his way into my soul. I felt him in a way I hadn't in a very long time. I pulled his mouth to mine and cried out when he came, slamming against me and making me come, too.

It had been so long, and we needed each other so badly, that we didn't stop. We were slower, less crucial, and more gentle. He lay down behind me, spooning, and I could feel his cock still hard along the crack of my ass. I pushed up on my elbow and craned my neck toward him, twisting into a kiss. I reached between my legs and grasped his dick, stroking it for a moment before slipping it back inside me.

Rhythmically, back and forth, I rocked my hips against his. He reached around with both hands, squeezing my tits. He rolled my hard nipple between his thumb and forefinger, just a little pinch, as he reached down with the other hand to rub my clit in the small, tight circles he knew would get me off.

He pummeled me from behind, stroking me harder and faster, until I wailed and collapsed in a contorted heap, my pussy fluttering him to orgasm.

We lay there for a long while, in the silence, waiting for calm breath to return.

"I want you to go on your trip," he said quietly afterward, holding me.

I snuggled against him. "No, it's fine. I can live without it."

"I know you can, but you're right, the timing is best. You need a break before the boys are home for the summer. It's fine, Tierney. I want you to go. I think you should go ahead and book your travel."

"No, you don't."

"Yes, I *do*. I just needed to know that I mattered more."

I pushed up on one elbow and turned to him in the dark. "Of course you do. You always did."

I kissed him again and pulled him back into more amazing sex. Again and again until it was time to get the children the next afternoon.

I was restless the week before my trip to Texas. I was ready to be *away*. I needed to *not* be the responsible one for a few days, not to have to worry about the little details that had been entirely my responsibility for ten years. Sam was a grown man and the boys' father; he could handle two days without me.

Sam worked late almost every night, leaving me with dark hours on my own. I knew he was still not thrilled with my going away for the weekend. I was doing my best to soothe his ego, and I didn't want to upset the tense detente we were sharing. Every time he would get upset about some small thing, bitching and railing for five minutes about minutiae, I would politely listen and patiently wait out the mini-tempest.

I filled my days with sweaty, heart-pumping walks and an extra couple of sessions with Devin. I wanted to look my absolute best by the time I got to Texas.

We had one more session with Janet before I left for my trip, on Thursday.

"Sam and I had a great week," I started. He was sitting in the chair next to mine. I reached over for his hand.

"I agreed that Tierney should go on her trip."

Janet looked surprised and questioning.

"I realized she needs the time away," he explained. "The kids will be home for summer soon, and it will be good for her to get away before that happens. We had a long talk about it. I needed her to remind me that I was most important to her."

Janet looked at me. "How do you feel about this?"

"I'm excited," I smiled. "I'm looking forward to it. But I won't go if he wants me to stay. I want to go and see my friends, but I need to make sure he's okay first."

"Honestly," Sam admitted, "I was afraid she was going there to sleep with someone else."

Whoa! Where the fuck did that come from?

"Are you?" Janet asked pointedly.

"No, of course not!" I turned to Sam. "I'm not going to Texas to sleep with anyone else. I love you. Only you."

I knew I was lying when I said it.

And I didn't feel bad about potentially sleeping with Alex. I felt bad that I was lying to Sam, but not enough to stop it or admit it. I was determined to see this thing through with Alex, no matter what. I *deserved* it. Fate had stepped in and forced us to see each other, and I couldn't tear my eyes away until I'd seen all that I could.

Sam went into the office after the session, and I headed to the gym. I did a full session with Devin but skipped my extra half hour of cardio. When I got back in my car, there was a voice mail from Alex.

"Call me if you get this in the next five minutes. I'm sorry I haven't talked to you in a few days. I've got, like, five minutes to tell you all the craaaazzzy shit that's happened."

I had one minute left to call.

"Hey, what's up?"

"Well, I'm sorry I haven't called. This *crazy* shit happened. I got an email on Sunday from my friend, Adrianne. I haven't talked to her in over a year, because she has this asshole husband. Well, she left him, and he hacked into her email, sending shit to everyone she knows. Adrianne changed her password and locked him out, but she let me know he was telling people I'd had an affair with her."

"*Ugh.*" *Did you?*

"The guy fucking emailed Talia, Tierney."

"*What?*"

"He emailed my wife and told her that I was cheating on her while I was on the road and that he had proof."

My heart started to pound.

"I'm not. You know I don't do that. And I *did* sleep with this woman, Adrianne, *years* ago, right after my divorce. It was a one-time thing. We knew it wasn't good for our friendship, so we didn't do it again. I had to tell Talia about it. She's already convinced I fucked this other friend of ours, Alana. I *didn't*, but Talia keeps bringing it up. It's making it uncomfortable when we see Alana and her boyfriend, who knows nothing ever happened."

"Yuck."

"It was fine. I mean, she doesn't like hearing about women I've slept with, but she was okay about it. She knows Adrianne. She knows there's nothing going on. I've told her a thousand times, if I were gonna cheat on her, it wouldn't be with someone she knows. I would have some road girlfriend in a city far away from her and just see her while I was on tour. I'd fuck her when I got to Chile or wherever. I wouldn't do it in my own backyard."

Is that what I was to Alex, some not-girlfriend in a faraway city? Someone he could fuck and never have to bring home? Was I just a kinky friend, his personal sex therapist like he always said?

I didn't know and wasn't sure I really wanted to.

"It just got me thinking about your husband and what he does," he went on. "He could get into your email any time and do the same thing."

"Or worse," I laughed.

"Yeah, no kidding. So I will talk to you and chat with you, but I'm not texting or emailing you anymore."

"Nothing? Ever?"

"Nothing like *that*. You know what I mean."

"I do. I mean, I don't think it's an issue, but I know why it would bother you so much. It's fine."

"Everything else okay?"

"Yep. Just leaving the gym. I fly into San Antonio tomorrow around one. I'll meet you at the venue." I paused. "You know, if you decide not to do this, it'll be okay."

"I know."

"I don't know what you're thinking about it all."

"I'm not. I'm not thinking about it."

Ouch. "Listen, I can bring the toys or not. I'm happy to. But, honestly, I don't want to do it if nothing's happening. I don't want to go through the trouble of packing all of that and getting it through security, if there's no reason."

"God, I don't know, Tierney!"

"I *know*, Alex. I just don't want it to be uncomfortable there if you decide you're not going through with it."

"You're making it uncomfortable now." He was plainly irritated.

"I'm not trying to."

"I know. Look, I'll just see you when you get there tomorrow, okay?"

"'Kay."

"Bye."

By the time the men got home that afternoon, my suitcase was packed, overstuffed with shoes and too many wardrobe choices. I didn't know what else I would be doing that weekend and wanted to make sure I had options for any occasion. I carefully chose everything I would take for the weekend, from the outfit Alex would first see me in when I arrived and what I'd change into for the show, to what I'd wear for Saturday afternoon hanging out and for Saturday night drinking. Cute panties and a new hot pink bra. Wonder Woman high tops and pink-glittered strappy heels.

I helped the boys with their homework and cooked dinner. I tried not to be too excited about leaving.

"Why do you have to go see your *boyfriend*?" Ian asked snarkily over dinner. It was a tone he'd picked up from Tripp, who'd imitated Sam.

I dropped my fork, clanging it loudly against my plate. "Seth Wiezel is *not* my boyfriend. He's just a very close friend who has a big event this weekend, and he invited me to be there to share in it with him, along with a couple hundred other people. *Please* stop referring to him as 'Mommy's Twenty-Year-Old Boyfriend'. Someone's going to hear that and get the wrong idea."

Sam and the boys looked back and forth at each other, looking bemused in their chiding. They knew me well enough to understand that I really was irritated, but they didn't think it was any different than farting at the kitchen table.

Sam and I got the boys showered and ready for bed.

We had perfect, crazy, horizon-expanding sex until we passed out.

Late in the night, I roused when my phone buzzed.

Alex Wheeler
May 24th 1:17 AM

Bring the goods

Chapter 17

I tossed the glass wand and the black vibrating bullet, with the wireless remote, into my bag. I hefted my suitcase into the back of my car and came back in to tell Sam goodbye.

I leaned over him in the dark bedroom.

"Baby, I'm leaving." I kissed him gently. "Thanks for letting me do this."

"Be safe. Have fun." Sam answered groggily, sinking immediately back toward slumber.

"I'll text you when I get there. Please get the boys to eat some fruit and vegetables this weekend," I reminded him sweetly.

The Afghan Whigs escorted me to the airport. *1965.*

A new security line opened as I got close to the checkpoint, and I was through the screening and on to the underground train to my concourse.

I was down seventy pounds. I'd seen Dr. Naland, my endocrinologist that week. I was off all of my hypertension medications, and I was only taking half of my original dose of metformin, for type 2 diabetes.

"Your diabetes is technically in remission," he told me. "your bloodwork is all *normal*, Tierney. The metformin is no longer a necessary, life-sustaining drug. It's a life-style maintenance drug now. You'll be able to come off of it soon, if you keep this up."

"When? What's the goal for when I can try life without it?"

"You're at a BMI of about thirty now. Somewhere between twenty-nine and twenty-seven, you should be able to drop it. Try it and see how you do."

"Your clothes are, like, little clothes now," one of my mom friends told me one morning during our walk.

There were still things I didn't like about my body. My hips were still too big, my thighs too dimpled, and my arms too flabby. I hated how my body looked naked, but I was starting to dig how it looked in clothes again.

No matter how unhappy I was about the aesthetics of my physical form, I was blown away by its capabilities. I could walk my hilly neighborhood and found it to be barely challenging, whereas six months before it had been downright daunting. I could walk five miles in the morning and not be so exhausted that I couldn't function.

I felt better than I'd ever felt in my life. I was two pounds over the weight on my driver's license. People told me all the time how great I looked, though I wondered if they really hadn't told me how bad I looked before. I was a normal, curvy girl.

After weaving my way through the bustle of Hartsfield-Jackson, I was disoriented in the smaller San Antonio International Airport. It wasn't small, just less congested than I was used to in Atlanta. Four men stopped to tell me how pretty I was. One of them gave me a, "How *you* doin'?", which made me giggle and blush.

I texted Alex, and Sam, that I'd landed in San Antonio and was catching a cab out to the venue. The forecast had originally called for showers, and I was afraid I'd be wandering around in the rain, wheeling my suitcase behind me. It seemed so Leonard Cohen. I was thankful the clouds were clearing by the time the cab dropped me off across the street from the Coda, a small club a few miles from the River Walk.

From the outside, it appeared to be a much smaller venue than I would've expected Junkture to play. It was an old, brick building, the facade plastered with peeling layers of years' worth of show posters, mostly from small and local bands.

Huh.

The rock stars hadn't arrived yet. I went across the street to get something nondescript to eat and kill some time before I saw them all. My stomach was a tangle of flutters, and I could barely eat my Chinese food.

Alex Wheeler
May 24th 3:17 PM

where r u?

Just finished eating. Where r u?

sushi, around the block

on my way

I went into the bathroom and brushed my teeth and my hair quickly. I freshened my lip gloss and my perfume. I was about to see Alex.

I stepped off the crosswalk and down the alley behind the club, I saw the poster.

It was pasted to a wooden pole, over layers of old, peeling posters and pictures of lost pets.

My poster.

Seth had told me he wanted something retro and modern, something whimsical but clean.

"Like Toulouse-Lautrec meets *2001:A Space Odyssey*?" I'd asked, jokingly.

"*Exactly!*"

I'd used an image of a modern Burlesque dancer, and another of a girl swinging on the moon. The image we settled on for the *Maker* show poster was of a mostly-nude girl nestled inside gearworks, one thigh-high-boot-clad leg dangling over the side.

The Junkture logo was just below Seth's name, added at the last minute when they'd announced they were appearing, like an afterthought.

"The poster looks great."

Startled out of my thoughts, I looked up.

"Hey, Charlie Taylor," I said casually. "Thanks!"

"Hey, Tierney! How are you?"

"I'm great!" He greeted me with a quick hug, all sweet and smiles as usual. "Trying to find Alex."

"Oh, yeah. I saw him with Max. I think they're getting sushi. Come on, I'll take you."

I pulled my suitcase behind me, following Charlie around the block, crowded with small restaurants and dark shops. I never would've found it on my own. I thanked him and opened the door, stepping inside and looking for Alex.

I didn't see him right away.

"I'm looking for some friends," I told the waitress. She pointed toward the back of the small restaurant, toward the sushi bar. They were sitting behind a partition and didn't see me come in.

I walked quietly behind them and stood there for a moment. It took them several seconds to stop their bantering and notice that I was right there.

Alex looked at me and shook his head quickly, startled both at my standing there and at my difference in six months. I was still purple-on-blond, still busty in a black t-shirt, but that was where so many of the similarities ended.

"Holy shit," he muttered, standing. "How are you?" He leaned in for a hug.

"I'm great," I smiled brightly. "Glad to see you guys."

Max stood and pulled me into a bear hug.

"Want something to eat?" Alex offered, popping edamame into his mouth.

I shook my head. "Nope. Thanks, though."

"Well, you look fantastic. How was your flight?"

"Thanks! It was good. I got hit on all through the airport. It was awesome."

I stood in the tiny, crowded restaurant, chatting with them while they finished eating.

"Come on. Let's go to the venue." They settled their check as I wheeled my suitcase back outside. Alex came out and reached for the handle.

"I can get it," I said.

"Just give me the damn suitcase," he argued.

We tromped back around the block to the Coda. They led me through a back door to the dressing rooms and stashed my suitcase under a table. We wandered through a maze of tiny hallways and doors until we got inside the almost-empty venue.

As I came through a side door, I spotted Paul, leaning against a pub table and checking his messages.

"Hey, Paulie!"

"Hey, Tierney! How are you?" He smiled and gave me a hug. "How do you like the club?"

It looked old and dark, like a hundred other bars I'd been inside.

"It's nice," I replied. "Smaller than I would've thought for Junkture."

"We played here a few times when we were young. The owner was a great guy, Jim, but he died last year. So I bought the fucking place."

"Wow!" I gasped. "Really?"

"Yep," he said proudly. "I'm what you might call an *entrepreneur* now, with two bars and a recording studio."

"Or a masochist," said a man's voice behind me. I giggled and turned quickly to see who was speaking.

"*Hammer!*"

I jumped at Seth, landing in a huge hug.

"I'm so glad to see you!" I beamed.

More hugs, more chit-chat. The techs, Anton and Corey and Ben, were finishing their load-in, getting ready for soundcheck. Seth and his band worked carefully around Junkture's equipment, setting up their gear. Max and Charlie ambled inside, and we all watched part of Seth's soundcheck. Alex was mostly quiet, watching the stage, as we stood around a pub table. Random people were moving past us, milling from one door to another. I nervously checked my messages and texted Sam that I was at the venue, safely with the band.

As Seth was finishing up, I turned to Alex. "What's on the setlist tonight?"

He shook his head. "I haven't seen it yet. Ask Max." Alex excused himself and headed backstage.

Max heard his name and looked me, eyebrow raised.

"Are you doing my song tonight? Are you playing 'Dollface'?"

He shook his head. "Nope."

"'Hot Mess'?"

He shook his head again. "We decided to do more old stuff tonight. Only a couple of songs from *Persona Non Grata*."

"I'm going to cry, you know. Big, fat, Amazonian, purple tears. Look for me during the show. I'll be crying."

Max laughed and winked at me.

"Alex said you guys did a rerecord of 'Whiskey Mouth'," I said tentatively.

"Yeah, it's good!" Paul replied, shifting excitedly from foot to foot. "And you've heard the original, right?"

"Alex sent it to me when you guys were in Europe." *Should I have said that?* "I hope that's okay. I won't share it with anyone. I just wanted to hear something better than bad YouTube videos shot on smug, European cell phones."

"It's fine," Paul answered. "I didn't realize you and Alex were close."

My heart skipped a beat. "We became friends after Atlanta. He's a great guy. I love him to death."

"He's an asshole," Paulie snickered. "I love him like a brother, but he's an asshole."

Max leaned forward as Paul got up to walk outside. "Don't listen to him. Too much togetherness, and Paul's on the rag."

Max sighed and growled under his breath. I shot him a questioning glance.

"They got into a fist fight."

I gasped and grabbed his arm. "About what?"

"We were working on a new song. It was something we started during the *Persona Non Grata* sessions, and Alex wanted to go back to it. Paulie was dicking around and wouldn't write the intro. Alex started yelling at him to write the fucking intro, and Paulie told him to go fuck himself, and Alex punched him."

"Holy shit!"

Max shrugged. "Nothin' new, I guess. It's hardly the first time those two have come to blows."

"So why do they still work together? Is it a man thing or a musician thing?"

"I don't know. I mean, men can just get mad and blow up and be done. And with musicians, sometimes you make the best music with the people you loathe the most. Doesn't mean you don't love to work with them."

Everyone moved to the small patio bar behind the Coda to kill time. The rainy weather was finally clearing, the late afternoon sun coming out in time for a Friday night street festival. I sat at a table with Max and Paul and Charlie, drinking Jack and Ginger. Glancing around, I didn't see Alex anywhere.

Alex Wheeler
May 24th 4:21 PM

where r u?

> **Patio with the guys. Where are you?**

dressing room

> **K. On my way.**

I found the right door and followed the exposed plumbing and conduit around toward the backstage bathrooms. I went past some old couches and a pool table but didn't see Alex anywhere. Pausing in front of a bathroom door, I was startled when it opened suddenly and Alex appeared in the doorway, close enough to me that I could feel his body heat.

"Hey—"

"Cavanaugh...," he said under his breath.

He didn't call me that often, but he was the only one who ever did. I knew I was "Cav" in his contact list—would sometimes see emails to me come with that name—and he always called me "Tierney Cavanaugh", with or without the "Johnson" when he referred to me. Cavanaugh was the part that was *me* and had *nothing* to do with Sam.

"Are you okay?" I asked softly. "I didn't know where you went."

He nodded. "Sushi's gone."

"*Ugh.* Please don't tell me you have food poisoning."

"No, I think it's gone before it got there. It tasted funny at the restaurant. No worries now."

I stepped back from the bathroom to let him past.

"Come on," he said quickly. "Let's get outta here."

He walked quickly toward the door, checking to make sure no one saw us. Everyone else was out back, so we cut through the club and out the front door. He stopped suddenly and turned toward the front doors, looking at something.

"What is it?"

He leaned back dramatically, shifting his weight to one leg. He cupped his chin in his finger and thumbing, considering....

The poster!

The front of the Coda was covered in them, large and small, color and back-and-white.

"Do you like it?" I almost whispered.

"It's *great*, doll. You did good."

I smiled at him. "I wasn't sure what... Seth wanted... I didn't know if it would be—"

Alex turned toward me and cocked his head chidingly. "Just say 'thank you', Tierney. You don't have to explain it or justify it. Accept the compliment graciously and go on."

"*Thank you*," I said sweetly, and then added a quick curtsy.

Alex chuckled and motioned for me to follow him. Companions often complain that I walk too damn fast on my long legs, but I was rushing to keep up with him.

We crossed the street and walked down half a block, ducking into another bar. The cold, compressed air felt shocking after the steamy warmth of the street. The place was half-full. Alex led us to stools at the bar.

"Do you guys have this drink, I think it was here, an Orange Crush?" he asked the bartender.

"Yeah! Orange vodka, triple sec, orange juice...?"

Alex smiled and nodded. "That's it. Lemme get two." He turned to me. "Is that okay?"

"Of course," I smiled at him. "Orange is my favorite."

He checked his phone, again.

"Here, look at this," he said, handing me his phone. "I need to beat this guy and can't see anything."

He wanted me to look at his "Word with Friends" game to see if I could win it for him.

He had one lone letter left, and there was nowhere to play it that would overcome his thirty-plus point deficit.

"You really only have this one play," I offered, handing it back. "There's no way to win it." He made the move and lost the game.

"So how much weight have you lost again?" he asked, putting his phone away.

"Seventy pounds," I said quickly. "It's a lot. I told you—" I looked down at myself, sitting "—it was a little different."

"Yeah, you look... *fantastic*. Really."

I smiled at him and sipped my drink through a tiny, red straw. "So Paulie said he bought the Coda?"

Alex snarled and drank. "*Motherfucker*," he mumbled under his breath. "Yeah, so, normally we wouldn't play such a small venue. I mean, the Coda was great twenty years ago, but it's a fucking *dive* now. Four hundred tickets, that's it! We would've sold two or three times that, *easy*, anywhere else. And we're not even getting our full fee for this show, because he owns the goddamn place!"

"I'm sorry...."

He shot me a wary glance.

"Okay, I'm *not* sorry. It's not my fault. But I *feel* for you— how's that?"

"Better," he winked.

Max and Seth came into the bar, sat on the other side of me from Alex, and ordered a beer. Some long-time fans in vintage Junkture t-shirts came up from behind us, shaking hands and smiling.

Alex made the introductions, but I couldn't remember anyone's name even five seconds later.

We turned back to our drinks.

"Seth!" Alex called. "What the hell is with that black eye, man?"

I looked down the bar to my friend. I hadn't even noticed the red and blue and yellow on the corner of his eye. It was fading but still visible. I'd been so busy paying attention to Alex that I didn't see it when Seth came in.

Seth cleared his throat. "Um, Megan kind of, um, punched me in the face?"

"*What?!*" the three of us yelped in unison.

Seth grinned sheepishly. "Yeah... she got really *mad* a couple of weeks ago. We were all at my apartment, hanging out and drinking and shit. One of my roommates said something about her being a snarky drunk bitch, and I didn't jump right in to defend her. She started yelling at me about how I'm the worst boyfriend ever, how if I were a real man I would punch my roommate in the fucking face. I told her she *was* being a snarky drunk bitch, so she punched *me* in the fucking face."

"Dude, your girlfriend is crazy," Alex said.

"Yeah, but she's *hot*," Max argued. "We'll put up with a lot of crazy for hot ass."

I threw my head back and roared with boisterous, half-drunk laughter. I grabbed Alex's arm, still laughing. He grinned and laughed at me, taking another sip of his drink. I patted his lower back, in natural proximity to my hand, without thinking a thing about it, and said something over my shoulder toward Max. Alex looked at me and half-smiled. Then he totally freaked. His eyes went wide, looking straight to me, then back toward them.

He stood suddenly and threw some cash on the bar.

"You!" he said, pointing at me. "*Water.* Only water. *For an hour.*" He looked toward Max and Seth. "Make sure she only drinks water for an hour." Looking back at me, "Keep an eye on them."

He bolted from the bar.

I'm a touchy girl. I talk with my hands, and that often involves *touching* the people I'm talking to, especially if I'm close with them. There was absolutely nothing out of the ordinary for me to have touched him when and in the way I did, and I was sure no one else would've thought anything of it.

Alex was upset, and *I* felt like a heel, even though I hadn't done anything wrong. I didn't know if anything was going to happen now, if he was even still speaking to me. I didn't know if I'd made the biggest mistake of my life, coming to Texas.

Max and Seth finished their beers, while I drank water. We talked as we walked back to the patio bar. I wasn't drunk, but I was feeling no pain.

Max ushered us along a cracked stone path toward the stone tiered terrace, shaded by Spanish oak. Paul and Charlie were laughing under a rainbow-striped umbrella. Seth flopped into the wrought iron chair closest to Paulie, while Max held another chair for me.

"Why didn't your husband come with you?" Max asked suddenly.

"Not his thing. I asked, but he didn't want to come. He's seen Junkture a thousand times. He doesn't know Seth." I shrugged

"Does he have to know Seth to know good music?" Paul said, feigning bafflement. "And it *is* damn good music. I know—I helped make it!"

I rolled my eyes at him, laughing. "Yes, Paulie, you're the world's best producer *and* guitarist."

In a bad Elvis voice he replied, "Thank you. Thank you very much."

"Sam's not a huge music person," I explained. "He likes what he likes, but he usually goes to concerts to make sure no one bothers me. He's great at keeping crowd surfers off of my head. Besides, I needed some time way."

I drank more water. I updated my Facebook status and took pictures of the guys.

Some other fans from out of town showed up. Lena was a friend of Alex's from Corpus Christi, and another long-time fan, George, had flown in from I forget where. I knew them from Facebook but had never met them.

"Has it been an hour yet?" I asked Max again.

He glanced at the time on his phone. "Fifteen more minutes."

Seth Wiezel
May 24th 6:48 PM

Let's go for a walk. I need some coffee.

> **K. Gimme a min to get something out of my suitcase.**
> **Meet you out front in 5.**

Seth waited while I went back to the dressing room. Alex was backstage, sprawled on an old sofa, earbuds in, eyes closed.

His pre-show nap.

I dragged my suitcase from under a table and unzipped it. I glanced around to make sure no one else could see me and pulled off my plain, black t-shirt quickly, stuffing it into my suitcase. I yanked my tight, black Junkture tee over my head and flipped my hair over and back, fluffing it. I was running low on cash, so I pulled another twenty from my reserve and stuck it in my pocket. As I reached into a zippered compartment in the suitcase, my hand bumped the toys, in their own zippered pouch.

I left the remote in the bag but stuck the black bullet in my pocket. I zipped up my suitcase and pushed it back under the worn folding table. Walking confidently from the room, I went straight past him, without giving him a second glance. In the bathroom, I quickly put in the bullet and left to find Seth.

> **Alex Wheeler**
> **May 24th 6:54 PM**
> **I have your remote if and when you want it.**

Seth and I walked around, killing time until he had to go on. We found a coffee shop and wandered through an old used bookstore. We caught up on all of our gossip. I was trying not to think about Alex.

Pacing ourselves through the rain-washed spring streets reminded me so much of teenaged evenings with girlfriends. We'd giggle and gasp at bawdy jokes, flirt with whatever boy happened to fall in our line of sight. And we were always smoking, cigarettes and smoke rings as equally enticing accessories. Even though I was with Seth, twenty years and a thousand miles away from those nights, it made me want to smoke.

"Give me a cigarette," I ordered.

"No."

"Yes, come on, give me a cigarette. Just one."

I'd quit smoking years before, when I first started trying to get pregnant with Tripp. Until I went through the saga of fertility treatments, quitting smoking had been the hardest thing I'd ever done. Usually I couldn't stand the smell or thought of one. Every so often, though, I would get a whiff of fresh smoke and think about how delicious that initial rush of nicotine would feel. I'd always said that I would start smoking again right away, if I ever had just one.

"Okay, but just *one*," Seth conceded.

I lit the cigarette, afraid it would make me cough and look like an idiot. Instead, the smoke hit my lungs, and I felt the same exhilarating relief I'd felt a million times before, like finally giving into a nic fit after spending hours with my non-smoking parents.

It was so damn good.

"So you and Alex are talking again," he said finally.

I hadn't told Seth that Alex and I were back in contact. He'd been very clear that he thought it best if Alex and I weren't having any kind of sexual relationship. I hadn't had the guts to tell him the truth, and it honestly wasn't any of his business.

"We are," I said. "I talked to him a few weeks ago, when he went to Austin."

"How was that?"

I nodded. "It was good. I'd missed him, you know."

"And did you have phone sex?" *Wallop!*

I looked at him and said nothing.

"Tierney, you *gots* to let him go."

"It's so hard, Hammer," I sighed. "He's just... he's that person.... Why does it bother you so much? I mean, I know you well enough to know you're not a judgmental prick. We are consenting adults."

He nodded, watching his feet as we walked. "You're right! You are! And I don't care *who* you fuck around with. You're a grown-up who can decide what's best for her."

"But there's Sam and Talia—"

"There is that, yes, but that's not even what bothers me so much." He thought for a moment. "I *get* how two people are just *attracted* to each other, so strongly that you almost wish it wasn't there, the attraction, because it *hurts* when you have to pull away."

"*Yes, exactly....*"

"*But*," he continued, "what bothers me most is that Alex Wheeler is a future version of myself, in a lot of ways. He's this musician with a wife and child, both of whom he adores. I *want* that one day. Maybe with Megan, maybe not. But I want that *family*. And that's one of the things I always respected about him—and Paul, too—how he made that work, even though he was on the road all the time. How he didn't give in to the groupies."

I winced. "But you *know* this has nothing to do with being a groupie. That's not at all why I'm attracted to him."

"Oh, I know! But I had a certain amount of respect for his commitment to that, and it's a little hard for me to see him in the same light, knowing what I know."

"I never meant for you to know, Seth," I said softly. "I never meant to drag you into this. I'm sorry."

"It's okay, Tierney. I'm not mad about that. And I'm your friend, no matter what."

"So why doesn't it bother you as much that *I'm* doing the same thing?"

Seth laughed mirthfully. "Because you're batshit crazy, and I would expect you to do the craziest fucking thing you could to turn your world upside down."

"Give me another cigarette," I said when we turned a corner.

"No, Tierney. No. Just one, that's what you said."

"Okay, so just *two*. I promise, no more."

I lit the second cigarette as we pulled headed back toward the venue. "How long has it been since you smoked?" Seth asked.

"Twelve years."

"*Twelve years?!* You fucking addict! I'm not giving you another one, so don't ask."

We made it back to the Coda just in time for Seth's set. I went out front, hoping to get close to the stage, but the small club was already packed. Half the people were congregating near the bar, so I was able to get as close as three people from the front, on the side in front of where Max would be later. It was the farthest back I'd ever been at a small Junkture show, and I didn't like it.

I met some other fans, people I'd made contact with through Facebook. They lived close enough that they could come out and support Seth. I also met Seth's very sweet parents, who gushed with pride at their son's accomplishment.

It was the first time I'd seen Seth play with his full band. Because of their other life commitments, he usually played solo when he traveled. It was a different sound, but the core of the Seth Wiezel brand was still there. His nerves got to him on the first song, though, and he flubbed the lyrics. He covered it smoothly and went on like nothing had happened. I was glad he got it over with early and could enjoy the rest of his show.

After his set, Seth went out front to sign some merch and do a meet-and-greet. Lena and George pushed their way through the crowd to join me. I only knew Lena from online. She was pleasant enough but didn't seem too happy when Alex made me message her about giving us a ride back to the hotel with them. George was one of Alex's constant groupie companions, traveling all over the world to see his shows. I tried to talk to them, but they were just *boring*, constantly trying to outdo each other with stories of *Who-Knows-Alex-Better*.

I bet I know things you don't.

I glanced around for Alex but didn't see him anywhere. I hadn't gotten a response to my text, and I hadn't heard from him in a couple of hours. He constantly checked his messages and would've seen it by then. I'd flown a thousand miles to see him; he knew exactly where I was.

He's uncertain.

Junkture came on, loud and rocking, as usual. Alex saw the group of us to the side and nodded in our direction. The crowd was receptive, and the set was great. But I was distracted, and I missed hearing my songs.

"Do you need me to give you a ride to the hotel?" Seth asked after the show.

"Nah, I'm gonna stay for a while. I'm getting a ride with Lena and George. But I'll see you Sunday for lunch."

Seth hugged me goodbye at the front of the Coda and left. I went back to the now-crowded dressing room. Alex was sitting on the couch, ten feet from me, talking to some girl.

"Hey, Cavanaugh! Get me that remote, will ya?"

I looked at him pointedly. He raised his eyebrow at me and bit his lower lip.

I caught my breath.

"Okay."

I reached into the silver pouch in my suitcase and retrieved the remote. It was small and black, part of a keychain. It looked like a key fob for any car. I tossed it to him and put my suitcase away.

He looked at the white buttons. "What does this do?"

I felt the first vibrations, intensely subtle. It was very quiet, and I knew no one would be able to hear it in that crowded room.

"Um, I think that's the power button."

He pushed the other button. The vibration changed.

"I think that one cycles through the options," I said.

The girl he'd been talking to asked, "What *is* that?"

He held up the remote, dangling from his fingers. "Tierney got it for me. It's this infrared thing, to help with the nerves in your hands or something." He looked pointedly at me. "How do I know if it's working?"

"I don't know if you'll feel it right away. You might not be able to tell until later."

> **Alex Wheeler**
> **May 24th 11:21 PM**
>> **I can promise you, it's working just fine.**

mmmm
I can't wait to get to the hotel
this build-up is fucking nuts!

> **yeah?**
> **whatcha gonna do?**

I'm gonna fuck u
and ur gonna love it

> **Ha! I'm sure I will!**
> **But it might be too much for you.**
> **I don't know if you can keep up.**

did u fuck Seth while u were gone
with him?

> **Nope.**
> **Would it matter?**
> **Would it bother you if I were fucking Seth Wiezel?**

Nope.

Well, I don't want to fuck Seth. I love him, but not like that. Besides, I'm a total fucking pillow princess. He'd never be able to take care of me. :P

LOL
pillow princess

I like this spot on my pedestal, thank you very much. I'm not coming down for just anyone.

you'll go down for me?

Uh-huh. All the way down my goddamn throat.

I don't think you can take it, you hot mess.

Call me Buttercup, and I'll take whatever you want.

anal needs loving

yours or mine?

both

Tease.

He hit the button and changed the vibration again, looking at me across the room.

For hours we moved around the Coda, together but not, waiting for load-out to finish so we could leave. We talked to Max and Corey and Ben. I stood patiently by while Alex talked to Lena and George about other fans, people they'd all known for a long time.

Alex cycled through the different vibrations, and I did my best to maintain focus.

Max passed me in the alley, on his way back to the patio bar. "I didn't see you crying," he said.

"That's because it was dark. One, lone purple tear slid down my face. Like that Indian who didn't like littering in the seventies."

Finally, Alex looked at me, standing in the alley under the orange glow of a street light.

"I think it's time to go. We need to get your stuff."

We were getting just a little bit closer.

Max, Alex, and I grabbed our bags from the dressing room, Alex lugging my suitcase and his backpack down the block to Lena's SUV. Lena and George were still politely laughing at each other's *Anecdotes of Alex*.

"I can't *stand* that guy," Alex whispered to me at the back of the car.

"But he's always coming to see you. He flew to London for the shows."

"I know. He's spent lots of money to come see us, but he always wants something in return. He's always asking me for stuff. It drives me fucking *crazy*!"

Alex loaded our bags into the back of the car.

"Shotgun," he called, opening the front passenger door.

Really?

"So I have to sit between these guys?" I asked.

"Mmmm-hmmm."

Alex settled into his seat and put on his seatbelt, checking messages and making fun of Lena's driving. I slid into the middle of the back seat between Max and George. Both of them leaned against their windows, trying to doze. I don't know how they didn't feel the constant buzzing of that vibrator across the back seat. Maybe they did and didn't know what it was. Maybe they were too nice to comment.

Alex Wheeler
May 25th 1:38 AM

how's that vibe?

it's making me wet

and sweet and creamy

I need to cum

you will
I'll make sure

Alex texted lewd things to me from the front seat, exactly what he planned to do with me when he got me to the hotel. I texted back in extreme detail *exactly* how that made me feel, trying to keep my screen from the guys' eyes.

He kept scanning through the satellite radio channels, trying to find something to listen to. As soon as a song he liked was over, he'd start scanning again.

"There! That one!" I squealed.

It was Soul Coughing's "Super Bon Bon"—one of my favorites. Alex was dancing in his seat, hands flailing about the cabin.

"You're the worst white guy car dancer ever, Wheeler."

He stopped mid-flail, the tiny, black remote dangling from his left hand. "I don't think this is working." He pushed the buttons, and the vibrations changed and intensified. "I think it's broken. Do you want it back?"

I smirked in the dark back seat. "No, no. Try it just a little bit longer and see what happens. I think it's working fine."

"What's that thing supposed to do anyway?" Lena asked.

Alex held it up and showed it to her. "It's supposed to send these vibrations through your nerves in your hand or something, intrared or some shit. It's supposed to feel good, but all it's doing is making my dick hard."

I laughed out loud in spite of myself. He pushed the buttons over and over and went back to dancing in his seat.

"Just valet your car," Alex instructed Lena as we got close to the hotel. She fussed, but he reminded her that it was almost two in the morning.

"Are we still drinking?" I asked.

"Yeah," he said. "We can hit the hotel bar."

Max thanked Lena for the ride and hugged us goodnight. "I'm gonna crash. I'll see you tomorrow." He grabbed his backpack and strolled across the lobby toward the elevators. Alex would be following him soon.

I went straight to the front desk to check in, which seemed to take forever, while Alex talked to Lena and George. I'd notified the hotel that it would be a very late check in. The others had come by on their way to the venue to get themselves situated.

I turned back toward the group and saw that the bar was closed. I looked at Alex.

"No more bar."

He shook his head, looking me in the eye. "I guess I'm going to my room."

I nodded, fidgeting with the two hotel key cards in my hand. "Oh! Can you take my *Persona Non Grata* vinyl now? To get everyone to sign it?"

I laid my suitcase on the wide, marble floor and unzipped it, pulling out a flat cardboard box. I zipped the bulging case closed again and walked over to Alex. I held out the thin package, one of the key cards stuck under my fingers. He took them from me and slipped the card into his pocket.

"Yep. I'll make sure everyone signs it this week."

"Thanks. I'll see you tomorrow for lunch?"

He nodded. "Yep."

I hugged him, careful not to hold on too long. I wished everyone a good night. I turned and went to the elevator and straight to my room. As the elevator rose the six stories, I texted him.

Alex Wheeler
May 25th 2:19 AM
607

Might b a while

Take your time

I really didn't know how long it would take him. I quickly brushed my hair and teeth, put on a cami and fresh panties. There was always a chance he wouldn't come at all, or that I would be asleep. I plugged in my laptop and started the Alex playlist, only the light from the computer screen illuminating the room.

May 25th 2:34 AM

I need you.

Max is still up.
C u tomorrow. Go to sleep.

The thought that we were *so close* was driving me crazy. We'd had all these months, talking and whispering and planning what it would be like. I knew he wanted it, wanted me, but it was a huge decision for each of us. Max was an easy excuse for him.

We were standing on the edge of a line that we could never uncross. I knew he wasn't sure if the time was right; I wasn't, either. But I also knew there would never be a *wrong* time for Alex and me.

I wanted to be understanding, but I almost cried.

Can't sleep with this throbbing.

Fuck urself to sleep.

With what?

Glass dildo?
This will help.

He texted a short video of him rubbing his beautiful cock for me.

Yes and yes.
So wet.

May 25th 3:17 AM

I can come fuck u with ur toys but I
can't stay long.

Yes please.

Be naked for me.

I tossed my clothes to the side of the bed and got under the sheets. I knew he wasn't sure if he wanted this, still, to fuck someone other than Talia. He was giving himself an out, and one for me, to just use the toys and not actually make the contact, make the penetration, and take on all the weight that act would entail.

And it would've been okay.

The room was a double, and I was lying on my stomach, half covered, on the bed farthest from the door. I was rereading the texts and watching the video when I heard the key card slip into the lock. I heard the end of the Afghan Whigs' "Neglekted" fade out.

I put my phone on the night stand and turned over, looking toward the doorway. I heard the click of the door closing and saw him come around the corner of the entryway. Even in the dim light and across the room, I could see how charged he was, how badly he wanted this. I could see the apprehension and the desire on his gorgeous face. He watched me from across the room, standing at the foot of the other bed, stripping down. He was naked and beautiful, and he crossed the room to me.

He looked toward my laptop, squinting to see what song was playing. I realized it was "Hot Mess".

It was mostly dark, and I was naked under those blankets like he wanted, like he asked me to be. I was so afraid to pull the covers back and let him in. It meant a lot of things to give another man access to my bed—any man, ever, but especially after so much time. For the first time, I was completely naked, broken down, in front of this man who knew me so well. It was strange and exciting. There was no way to hide anything in that moment, and I didn't want to. I didn't care that my thighs and belly were flabby still. Alex *knew* me— knew who I was and how I looked and how I badly I wanted us to be able to *consume* each other with shared sex—and I lost all inhibition.

Then he was on me and with me, and he obviously wanted me.

His tongue was strong and forceful and insistent in my mouth. I sucked his lips, nibbling, wanting to savor the sweet and smoky taste of him. His warm hands were on me in a second, and I reached for his hard cock. It felt so silky and unexpected in my hand, new and different.

"I can't stay," he whispered. He reached to the night stand for the glass wand.

"I know. It's okay."

Liar. Give him a reason to stay.

He looked me over, hands sliding along my thighs, my hips, my belly. He teasingly ran one finger along my slit. Moving down the bed, he knelt between my legs. My pussy was throbbing, and I writhed against the toy in his hand, pushing toward him. He leaned over me, kissing me again, while he pumped *our toy* in and out of me, deeper and deeper. His thumb brushed across my clit.

He dropped the glass wand next to us on the bed and stretched his lean frame over me. I felt a finger, two fingers, push deep inside my pussy. They were warm and just a little rough. I lost my breath as he used those long, amazing fingers to rub my G-spot with a pressing, come-hither crook of the finger. I couldn't move, it felt so good.

"I want your cock in me." I pulled him down to me, kissed him again, biting at his mouth. "*Wait!*"

He pushed onto his hands and looked me in the eye. Holding his gaze, I reached between us and pushed a finger between the hot, wet folds and inside myself. I brought the finger to his lips, and he hungrily sucked my wetness from my finger. I kissed him again, my finger still in his mouth and both of our tongues mingling around the taste of me.

"I want my cock in your ass," Alex hissed in my ear.

"*Do you?*" I teased, pulling my hips away from him.

"I don't think you can take it, you dirty girl."

"I can take anything you can give, babycakes."

He pumped his cock up and down the crack of my ass, toying between the two openings.

"Can I?" he whispered, looking me in the eye.

I met his gaze evenly in the blue-tinted shadows. I nodded. "I trust you."

He started to do it, nudging gently against my ass with the tip of his dick. I inhaled deeply and closed my eyes, waiting for the first moment of pain that I knew would subside in a breath.

But he stopped. I looked up and saw him watching me, blue eyes open and locked on my face. I ground my hips against him, just out of my reach, while he watched me. He looked entranced, interested, engaged. When I saw him watching me, it sent me spinning.

He kissed me deeply again, his tongue hot and searching.

He drove his long cock into my pussy and *fucked* me.

We did not use a condom.

I groaned and wrapped my legs around him as he slammed into me.

He was the first new lover I'd had in nineteen years, and he hit me in ways I wasn't used to. He leaned over me, and I laid my smooth legs along his ribcage, feeling his hot, smooth skin under my hands and my lips. His arms felt amazing, different, and I couldn't stop kissing him, anywhere I could reach. He sucked my hard nipple into his mouth, teasing it with his teeth and tongue.

"I'm gonna come soon," he breathed into my ear.

"Come in my pussy, baby," I whispered, just like he'd heard me so many times.

"*Mmmmm....* I wanna come inside you so bad." Alex looked down at me, still moving, his breath ragged. "Can I come in you?"

I sucked his mouth to mine and bit at his lip. "Yes, please. Fuck me harder and come for me."

He pounded into me, groaning and rasping against me in his orgasm. I etched my nails along his shoulders and back. I squeezed him tightly against me, inside and out, feeling his cock twitching and enveloped in my pussy. His hips moved more slowly, and he kissed me again.

"I can't stay."

"I want you to come again."

"It will take a while. I can't be gone long."

"But you're not leaving until I get your cock in my mouth," I growled.

He lay back on the bed, against the pillows, and I straddled his legs. I looked at his amazing body spread out in front of me. I realized he was putting his trust in mine, letting go so I could, too. It was a complicated, strangely-woven mix of faith and love and expectation that had brought us to this place, and I didn't want to disappoint either of us.

I heard the song change to Depeche Mode's "Lie to Me".

Ha!

He was still hard or hard again, it didn't matter.

You're the Golden Kitten for a reason.

I grasped the base of his cock and slowly felt the smooth, taut skin. I rubbed my hand over the head, silky and warm, and flicked my tongue along the underside of the shaft. I licked and sucked around his balls, sucking at the base of his cock gently, working my way up to the head. Swirling my tongue around the tip, fluttering and delicate, I sucked the head in, sucking down the shaft a little, then back up. Down a little further, then back, never letting go of the head, sucking on it for an extended moment every time. On the third pass, I took his whole cock down my throat and sucked with abandon, moving my head up and down, pulsing in the back of my throat while I moved my hand slowly. He tasted of him and me and of all the pent-up desire that had swelled for so long.

"*So good*," he uttered under his breath, his hands in my hair. "*So goddamn good!*"

I was so intent on remembering how he tasted and felt that I didn't think to look up, to watch his face while I held him in my mouth, doing what I do so well. I didn't want to stop. There were so many things I wanted to do to him, for him, for me—all the things we'd talked about for months, building up to this night—and there just wasn't *time*. I wanted to grab the glass dildo and fuck him with it, like I'd promised in lurid whisper so many times. But it was out of my reach, and I was afraid of what would happen if I stopped. I needed to feel him in me again, though, to let *him* feel how much I wanted him. He shifted on the bed, and I climbed on top of him.

Later, I would wish that I'd kissed him more.

There was a totally different kind of release when I was on top, completely in control of how everything felt. I rocked against him, barely moving my hips. I gripped at him from the inside, making sure we felt every inch of each other. He groaned and grasped at the sheets, his hands moving to my thighs, his fingers digging into the soft flesh. Clenching around him as tightly as I could, I felt his hips tense, reached behind me to feel his balls tighten.

"Come for me, Alex," I urged hotly against his neck. "Come in me again."

I barely moved but brought him back over that brink within moments.

I caught my breath and rolled off of him.

"Did you come?" he asked.

I looked at him, intent concern plain on his gorgeous face, and shook my head. "Nope, but I'm okay. I'll get it in a few minutes. I know you have to go."

He kissed me again. "*You* are an amazing woman."

I heard the first strains of "Whiskey Mouth". My heart stopped beating for a moment.

He jumped up and moved toward the bathroom. I heard the song over the sound of running water—Alex cleaning up after fucking a woman that wasn't his wife.

After fucking me.

"Here's your thing," he said, dropping the remote on the other bed.

"Thanks."

"I'll see you tomorrow."

I nodded, unsure of what to say. "Goodnight."

He kissed me once more, quick and hard. "'Night."

Alex was gone.

I lay there for a moment, uncertain. I felt exhilarated and confused. I'd just fucked Alex—for ten minutes. *Ten goddamn minutes!* It wasn't enough time for me to dive in and swim those dark, immersive waters, and it made me profoundly sad that it wasn't everything I wanted to give to him.

I got up and stopped the music. I couldn't bear to hear more. I padded into the bathroom, my bare feet shocked by the cold tile. I squinted against the sudden light and sat on the toilet. As I finished peeing, I opened my eyes and looked around the bathroom. My stuff—little bags of makeup and lotion and perfume and toothpaste— was already scattered across the marble counter.

Folded neatly across the edge of the sink, there was a wet washcloth, the one Alex used to clean up after he fucked me.

I looked down at the toilet paper and realized I was bleeding lightly.

I'd finished my period a couple of days before, thankful that I wasn't taking it with me for this weekend. I felt a little sore and crampy, but I was also exhausted, having been up for close to twenty-four hours. I cleaned up and went back to the bed, moving to the other side, away from the wet spot.

There was so much to think about, and I just couldn't face it. Not yet. I pushed Alex—and Sam—from my mind and passed out.

Chapter 18

Six hours later, I woke in the cold, dry hotel air. My sinuses were killing me, and I was freezing. My head throbbed lightly when I sat up. I turned the bedside lamp on and checked my messages. *Nothing*.

I was hungry. I couldn't remember having eaten anything since the Chinese food the previous afternoon. I started a quick cup of coffee in the room to hold me over until I could get out and scavenge.

The spray of the shower was strong and hot. I washed away all of the dirt and grime from the day before and felt refreshed. I drank my coffee in the bathroom while I put on my make-up. I grabbed fresh undies and a bra from the drawer, pulled my new black dress and sandals from the closet.

I opened the curtains for the day, bright sunlight streaming into the room. I turned back toward the bathroom and saw the blood on the sheets. The stain was light but huge. Obviously I'd bled more than I'd realized. I felt a little sore from being touched in ways I wasn't used to, but it was nothing that would've caused a ton of bleeding. I knew it was probably just wash-out from the end of my period, or maybe a small cyst had ruptured or something. I left the sheets exposed so housekeeping would change them when they came.

I walked out from the hotel and turned onto the wide walkways along the river. I knew there was a coffee shop nearby. I ordered a frittata and took my coffee to a small table. I ate slowly, trying to abate the nagging headache.

I was tired but didn't want to hole up in my hotel room. I spent a couple of hours exploring San Antonio. I walked over little bridges and through lushly landscaped mini-parks. I was impressed by the mix of modern and traditional, of historical and new.

I found a shady spot outside a coffee shop, sitting under a bright yellow umbrella. It was still early, but the River Walk was bustling already with people ready for the new day. I sketched the profile of a young woman sitting on a park bench, reading a book. The face of the sleeping baby, parked in his stroller at his parents' table next to mine. I hadn't expected to get much accomplished during my trip and was pleasantly surprised to find the time productive.

I realized it was almost two o'clock and time to meet up with Alex.

I stuffed my sketchbook into my bag and walked back to the hotel, through the dark wood and wrought-iron-trimmed lobby to the bar. I ordered water and waited at a pub table.

I saw him walk up to the streetside door. 2:10. *Late, as usual.*
"Hey."

"Hey," I smiled. "How are you?"

"Good. Hungry. How are you?"

"I'm okay."

The waitress came to see if we wanted a drink or food. Alex ordered a beer and lunch. I wasn't very hungry, but I needed to calm my nerves.

"Spicy Bloody Mary, please."

I wasn't sure if Alex would ever want to talk about what had happened, but I was pretty sure he wouldn't want to debrief right there in the Marriott bar.

He sighed and rubbed his hands through his hair, tired and nervous.

"It's strange," he said. "I have a hard time when I go home, after I've been gone for a while. I'm so used to *not* being there. *This* feels like home." He gestured around the bar. "A hotel fucking *bar* feels like home. That's fucked up."

I shrugged. "I guess it depends on what about it is comforting."

"It's what I'm used to. I know what to expect. If it's a hotel I'm at a lot, the staff knows and remembers me. Hell, one waitress in Boston was telling people, a couple of months ago, that I was fucking her when I came into town."

I looked at him, trying to keep my expression calm and even.

"I'm not. I wasn't. She was lying."

"Why?"

He shrugged. "I have no idea."

"You know I wouldn't really care, as long as I knew."

Liar?

"I know. But it was fucked up. I mean, I barely knew this girl. I was *nice* to her. Maybe I tipped her too much one time, I don't know. But all of that shit seems *normal* to me. It's hard going home and dealing with the day-in and day-out of that life."

"How does Talia deal with it?"

"She gets irritated with me. She thinks I can just step right back into her and Amber and their routine."

"But it takes you a little while to get re-acclimated."

He nodded at me. "Exactly. And I'm tired of it. Sometimes I just want to throw it all away and be done."

"So what do you do to expend that energy and come to terms with it?"

He thought about it for a moment. "I write. But there are some things I can't write about."

"Like what?"

He looked at me pointedly. "I can talk to you and text with you and come to you at three thirty in the morning, but I can never, ever write it down."

Max bounded through the door into the bar before I could respond. He joined us at the table, ordering his own food and drinks. I ordered another Bloody Mary.

"We're just talking about the worst parts of the travel," I explained.

Max stretched and yawned. "It's boring. It's tedious."

"Unless you're in a cool city you love," Alex added.

Max turned to Alex. "Before I forget, I'm going back to Austin on Sunday."

"*Are* you?" Alex held my gaze and took a sip of his drink.

You'll have the room to yourself.

"Is there a *girl* in Austin, Max?" I teased.

"There *is*." He grinned and blushed. "Elise. She's great. Sorry, continue. I didn't mean to interrupt."

I smiled at Max. "It's fine. I'm glad you met someone you like enough to travel to see. I think it's sweet that you'd go to a whole different city to see a girl you care about. She must be special."

"She is. She's a redhead."

I giggled at his happy grin. "So what do you want most now, for your career?" I asked Alex. "You've had hit songs and seen the world and sold millions of records. What will make you feel like you've succeeded?"

He thought about it for a moment. "I want to be acknowledged by my peers. By a mentor. I want someone *I* respect to say, 'This is good, Alex. Good job.'"

"So knowing you've written something good, or getting the feedback from the fans... not enough?"

"I think it's different when it comes from people you don't *expect* to like it. Especially when it's someone you look up to yourself." He shrugged.

"Hey," Max interjected suddenly. "We're going to the movies. You wanna go?"

We walked the few blocks to the movie theatre. They talked me into seeing some guycentric slapstick thing that I knew I would hate. I didn't care; I just wanted to be there with Alex.

I ended up sitting between the two of them. Having not slept much, having already had a two-drink lunch, I was sleepy. I drank my bottled water and fidgeted in my seat, trying to stay awake. Alex was so close in the chilly dark, and I wanted to lean my head on his shoulder, or convince him to give me his hoodie. I blinked for a long moment. When I opened my eyes, I realized I'd fallen asleep.

I hadn't missed anything in the movie.

"Oh! That was awful!" Alex said, stretching as he stood. The credits rolled across the screen as the house lights went up.

"I told you it would be."

Standing outside the movie theater, he looked at me in my short, black dress.

"You need a tan."

"I don't tan. I'm too Irish."

"*I'm* Irish," he pressed. "And I tan."

"You're *Black* Irish. I'm all red and blond. I don't tan. I'm pasty and tasty."

"What the fuck ar—"

"Don't listen to him," Max interjected. "Hell, I don't listen to anything he says unless we're on stage. I'm Irish and I don't tan, either."

We walked back to the hotel, firming up plans for drinking that night.

"Meet us at the bar around nine," Alex said.

It was almost six. That would give me a chance to take a nap and get ready.

"I'll be there, glittery heels and all."

I took a shower immediately, to give my hair plenty of time to dry. I lay on top of the bed, freshly made by housekeeping while I was out. I set the alarm on my phone for eight o'clock and was asleep almost instantly.

I woke just before the alarm. It was disorienting, waking in a room that was dark, except for the twinkle of city lights coming through the sheers. Turning the alarm off, I switched on a lamp and took a moment to wake up.

I spent a long time on my hair and make-up. I looked at myself a hundred times in the mirror, spinning slowly to make sure my pencil skirt and lacy camisole looked okay. The hot pink bra pushed my tits up beautifully and peeked out from behind the black lace. The pink glitter heels were perfect with my shiny pedicure.

I felt amazing in a way I hadn't felt in years. There had been days or nights when I felt pretty for a few hours, but never for the days on end I was feeling it now. I could look like total crap—sweats, no make-up, hair in a ponytail—and still *feel* prettier than I had a year before. I didn't really know what to do with this new *confidence* in myself.

I took a picture in the hotel mirror and texted it to Tessa and Jules and Frankie.

You look hot!

Hubba hubba!

Aw, you look so skinny!

At nine o'clock, exactly, I left my room.

The elevator dinged and the doors slid open. I took the few steps across the side of the lobby and turned right into the bar.

Alex was just coming through the streetside door, all the way across the bar from me.

He grinned broadly when he saw me. "You wore the shoes!" he laughed.

"I did. They're awesome."

Max came trailing behind. We all sat at the bar, drinking and eating dinner and watching baseball. I started with a double screwdriver.

"So you were in Chicago to see Tessa?" Alex asked. "When you came to the Double Door?"

"Yep. I fucking love that town. I love to go visit her."

"That's where my parents met," he said. "You wanna see where my dad lived before he met my mom?"

He reached into his pocket for his iPhone. He launched the Maps app and found the address quickly, showing me the street level view of the old building. It was a historic building near The Drake, and I'd passed by it dozens of times, driving around Chicago with Tessa.

He started to talk about his childhood, about moving around because of his father's work. He'd become accustomed to being uprooted at such an early age. It played a role in his natural wanderlust. As much as he complained about being on the road all the time, I knew he would never be happy if he were forever at home, either.

He told me all kinds of details about his family, about growing up with a mother who was, at times, overwhelmed by him and his three brothers. When he spoke of his father, who had died a few years before, his voice softened, a little sad and wistful. It was painful and obvious that he still missed his dad a great deal.

The things he told me weren't all secretive, but they were very personal. They weren't things you would share with just anyone on the street, though there was nothing untoward about any of it. Something about *how* he spoke, the look on his face when he talked of his past... it was all very *intimate*.

We decided to leave and go meet some other people Alex and Max knew.

The bar was crowded. We met up with a couple of people I knew by reputation and association, though we'd never met. Another screwdriver appeared in my hand without my asking. I gave Alex my credit card to start a tab.

Everyone was talking, mingling and laughing. Everyone was drinking.

I was getting drunker by the moment. I needed to pee. Carefully I navigated the steep, narrow stairs to the ladies room. I was so excited that I'd made it down, I almost cried when I realized I would have to go back up.

Alex was sitting in a chair by the fire when I got back.

"Where were you? You were gone forever."

I sat in a chair across from him, the glow of the fire like a halo around his dark curls. Someone handed me another screwdriver.

"Bathroom." I glanced around and realized we were alone for the first time that evening. "I need to say something."

He looked at me and nodded. He was apprehensive but attentive. I held his gaze in mine.

"I'm *sorry* about Europe, Alex. I'm sorry I lost my fucking mind. I know I've said it before, but I need to say it again, to your face. If you had told me everything you did that night coming home from the studio... if you had *told* me how and why I mattered to you... I *never* would've spun out of control like that."

He nodded, still watching me intently. He had that *look* on his face. He was listening, and he *cared* about what I was saying.

"I didn't know," I continued. "And all I could do was try and guess where you were and what you were thinking. It's like last night. I just didn't *know* what was in your head. I don't know if you know half the time.   But I *heart* you, Alex Wheeler.   Deeply. Inappropriately." I shrugged and smiled a little sadly. "I just do."

He was silent for a moment. I could hear the crackle of the flames behind him, feel their heat emanating all around us.

"*Thank you*," he said finally.

I smiled at him again, this time big and sweet. "I need another drink." Ice tinkled against the inside of my mostly-empty glass.

"You need water," he said. "Go find Max." He stood from the chair.

I shook my head. "I don't want to find Max."

"Tierney, go talk to Max." He turned and rushed away from the fire.

It's all fuzzy, the bits and pieces of that night. I found Max and Mike and Mike's girlfriend, sitting at the bar. I have no idea how long I talked to them. Someone else came up with another drink for me, a man I'd met but didn't know. Tom, maybe. He started telling me how it had been a long time since he'd broken up with his girlfriend, how long it had been since he'd gotten laid.

"I'm so fucking horny!" he complained.

Is he hitting on me?

I was too drunk to be sure.   It wouldn't have mattered anyway; all I could think about was getting Alex back to my hotel, to make up for everything that went wrong the night before.

I was sitting near the fire again in a small leather chair, with my legs crossed. Tom sat across from me, to my left. Alex appeared again, as if from behind a puff of smoke, and took the chair adjacent to mine, angled to my right.

When he sat down, the bottom of his thigh went right along the top of my pink glittered foot. I could feel his warmth through his jeans. I was curious what he would do. I made absolutely no attempt to move my foot or me or him. I left it alone. He stayed that way for a long time, talking to Tom. It took every ounce of self-restraint I could muster *not* to run with it, not to rub my foot along the inside of his thigh, to behave and to be still. Alex reached over, repeatedly, touching my knee and my bare thigh while talking, pulling me into the conversation.

I have no idea what the hell we were talking about. I could only watch him, thinking how much this was like the night before, at the bar near the Coda. But the tables were turned, and I knew goddamn well that it wasn't just me who was feeling this.

I was so drunk. I knew I couldn't take much more.

"Take me to close my tab," I said to Alex.

He walked me to the bar, where everyone was congregated in a small group. I signed the receipt and made sure I got my card back.

"Okay," I said, turning to Alex in front of everyone, "now I need to go back to my hotel room. And you're going with me!"

I didn't realize until the next afternoon how it sounded. I probably meant it in my heart, but it didn't come out *at all* like I intended. I knew I was too drunk to stumble back even half a block to the hotel, and I needed him to help navigate me and my heels along the cobblestone.

I was slow, stumbling toward the Marriott. "Are you coming up?" I called ahead to him.

"*No*. I'm not coming up to your room." He was terse.

"Please? Pretty please? You need to make sure I get there safely,"

"It's the *Marriott*, Tierney. What the fuck could possibly happen on the elevator? You'll be fine."

"Fine. Be that way."

I was mad and hurt. I was painfully inebriated.

I got into my room and texted him to call me. No response. I called. No answer. I left voicemail, asking him to call me.

I stripped down to my bra and panties and pulled the covers back on the bed.

Housekeeping hadn't changed the sheets.

The big smear of blood from the night before was still there, stark against the white cotton. I stood at the edge of the bed, paralyzed in drunken horror.

I'd fucked up and knew it. I was heartbroken. I dialed Alex's number again, confused and hurt.

"I need y-y-you-u to c-c-callll me," I sobbed to his voicemail. "I n-n-need to t-t-talk to you."

I curled myself along the edge of the bed, as far away from the blood as I could get. I faced the window, away from the room and the door where Alex had come just a night before. I cradled my phone in my hand and passed out.

It never occurred to me to sleep in the other bed.

5:41

Don't open your eyes. Way too early. Need to pee, bad.

I sank to the floor and crawled to the bathroom, to keep my head from pounding any sooner than necessary. Gray light was beginning to peek around the edges of the curtains.

I kept my eyes closed but turned on the bathroom light. I hoped they would be a little adjusted by the time I was done peeing. Not so much. My head was about to throb right off my damn neck. I squinted against the pain and felt around the counter until I found ibuprofen, knocking make-up containers and a can of hairspray clattering to the tile floor. I gulped down three pills with two glasses of water.

8:07

Go back to sleep. Too early. Sleep.

My biorhythms were off, and I just couldn't sleep anymore. I felt horrible. I slowly slid my feet over the side of the bed to the floor, pulling myself into a sitting position. My head pounded in time to my heartbeat.

I drank more water while I made a cup of coffee. Judging by the mascara and lipstick smeared down my face, I'd passed out without taking off my make-up. I used the make-up remover to get off as much as I could. I flossed and brushed my teeth, careful to scrape my tongue with the back of the brush.

I stood under the shower for a long time, letting the warm spray bounce off my weary body. I scrubbed away the last of the leftover make-up. I washed and conditioned the tangles out of my hair. By the time I dried off and put on fresh make-up and clean clothes, it was all of 9:15.

I messaged Seth that I had to check out by 11:00 and to come get me.

There was no way he was up yet. I packed everything into my suitcase, except my laptop, and sat down at the desk to check my email. I couldn't focus. I kept glancing back at the bloodstained sheet.

On one side of the bed was the stain, dark and old and ugly. On the other side was my pillow from last night, smeared with mascara and lipstick like a caricature of the Shroud of Turin.

And that bed... *that* was the place I'd blown my marriage to Hell.

Sam and I had been in a terrible place when the affair started with Alex. He was at least partially to blame for my having ever gotten to the place where I could even *consider* another man. But I'd asked to him to change, to stop drinking, to pay more attention to me. He'd obliged. Grudgingly at first, yes, but he eventually came around to the understanding that *we* could make our marriage better. All he needed to know was that I loved him the most, that I needed and respected him. That I would put him and us first, no matter what.

You're a goddamn liar, Tierney.

The one thing I asked Alex *never* to do, to lie to me, was exactly what I'd done to Sam. Withholding the truth of the affair was one thing. Having looked him in the face, time and again, and told him that nothing was going on, that I only loved and wanted him, *that* was the real crime.

And everything with Alex had changed in that bed. We'd finally crossed the boundary we'd pushed for so long, and it was *nothing* like it was supposed to have been. It was wonderful and awful.

I sat in that chair, staring at that bed, sobbing for an hour.

Alex Wheeler
May 26th 10:22 AM

> **I have to check out soon. Seth is supposed to meet me for food. Can I stash my stuff there later?**

Sure. I'm Skyping with Talia & Amber in a bit, though. You can't pop by until that's done.

> **K. Just text me and let me know when it's good?**

Yep.

> **Do you want any breakfast?**

Nope. I've got my coffee sugar, I'm good.

Seth Wiezel
May 26th 10:37 AM

I'll be there at 11:15 to get you.

> **Thanks. I'm starving. And hungover as fuck.**

    I couldn't stay in that room any longer. I washed away the streaks of tears and dug two more ibuprofen from my bag. I wheeled my suitcase and laptop bag into the long, carpeted hallway, wincing as the door clicked shut behind me.

    I checked out at the front desk, assuring the staff that the room and service were excellent. I still had half an hour. I found a comfortable chair in a quiet corner where I could watch for Seth. I mindlessly checked my messages until I saw his car drive up into the circle outside the lobby. I put my phone in my pocket and dragged my bags behind me through the double sliding doors. I opened the passenger door of Seth's car and threw my suitcase into the backseat. My laptop bag and I climbed into the front.

    "Good morning! How are you?"

    "Hungover. Don't yell."

    "*What?! I couldn't hear you!*" He turned up the volume on the radio.

    My entire body winced. "Asshole. I'm hungry. Feed me before I throw up in your car."

He drove me to a nearby diner, which he said he frequented quite often. Sunday morning at the diner was busy. We stood inside, waiting for a table for what seemed like forever. A waitress finally showed us to a booth in the back.

"How was your night?" Seth asked.

"I don't know. There was a lot of vodka. I'm not sure I'm not still drunk."

"Did you go out with Alex and Max?"

I nodded slowly. "Yeah, we went to some bar. Some other people were there. Mike. Tom. Fuck, I don't know."

The waitress came to take our order. I settled quickly on Belgian waffles and a Diet Coke.

I was quiet for a moment, trying to catch my breath around my pounding head and churning stomach. I was trying not to cry.

Seth was staring at me evenly. "*Tierney, did you sleep with Alex?*"

It wasn't really a question. It wasn't accusatory. He was incredulously stating a fact. Seth just *knew*.

I didn't say anything.

"You did! Oh my god! Please tell me you used a condom."

I still didn't say anything.

"*Tierney!*" he sighed, exasperated. "You know better than this!"

"I *know*, Hammer. It just... happened."

"It did *not* just happen." He paused, a little dramatically. "Well, honestly, it was inevitable. You two were bound to happen."

"Look, I bought condoms. They were right there. But I made the same decision I would've made with any other lover. I knew his past, knew his sexual history, and I made a judgment call. I trusted him enough to let him in without the condom. It's the same process I would've used with anyone else."

"I understand. I still think you're fucking stupid, but I get it." Seth coughed into his napkin. "Was it last night?"

"Nope. Friday, when we got here after the show. Last night... I don't know. I was a mouthy bitch. He wouldn't take my call at two this morning. I'm supposed to stash my stuff with him in a while, but I think I'll be surprised if he even talks to me after last night. All I want to do is go to sleep."

"How are you getting to the airport?"

"I don't know. Alex had said he would make sure I got there. He may make me walk."

I don't know what else we talked about. Every time he would say something, my head would pound harder. By the time my food arrived, I'd waited so long to eat that I could barely choke it down. I felt horrible.

Alex Wheeler
May 26th 12:34 PM

Come by any time
I'm working

We finished eating, and Seth drove me back to the hotel. I rolled my suitcase loudly through the lobby, lugging my heavy bag onto the elevator and dragging myself along.

Max was gone, back to Austin to see his new girlfriend. Seth knocked on the door.

Alex opened the door and ushered us in. He closed the door behind us and went back to the desk, earbuds in and looking at his MacBook. He pointed toward the corner, gesturing for me to put my stuff away. Finally he took the buds out and spoke.

"Good afternoon!"

"Uh-huh."

He smirked at me. "Feeling that good?"

"Yep. Thanks for letting me bring my stuff." I flopped into the chair across the desk from him.

He nodded and looked at me. "You look like you don't feel so hot."

"That's an understatement." I flopped in a chair across from him.

He got up and went to the wet bar, piddling with the glasses and I don't know what else. He and Seth talked guitars for a long time. I tried to make sense of it all, but it was like a verbal jackhammer.

Alex handed me a glass of water and sat back at the desk.

"Um, is it possible for me to crash here until it's time to go to the airport? I won't get in your way. I just need to sleep."

"Yeah, sure."

I tried to smile at him, but that hurt, too.

Seth said, "I gotta run. I've got some stuff to do on a project. Meeting with a colleague later."

I stood and hugged him. "Thanks for coming to get me."

"Any time. See ya, Alex." Seth lurched toward the hallway, closing the door behind him.

Here it comes. I sat back down and turned to face Alex.

His face was calm and reserved, but I could tell from the set of his jaw that he was mad. His pale, blue eyes were steely, forcing me to look at him. There was a lecture coming, and he was trying to hold it together and not yell at me.

"Do you know how much you had to drink last night?" he started.

I shook my head. *Ow.* "Not exactly. I know it was a lot."

"Your tab at the bar was a-hundred-and-twelve dollars."

"But two—"

"Two of those were mine, yes. But half your drinks were on Tom's tab. And that didn't include what you drank at the Marriott before we even got to the bar." He paused to let it sink it. "You were hammered. *Hammered.*"

"I know...."

"No, Tierney! You drank all the Stoli in the bar."

I looked at him. He had to be joking.

"*You drank all the Stoli in the bar.*"

"I did not!"

"*You drank all the fucking Stoli. in. the. bar.*"

"Alex, I'm sorry...."

"Tierney... you've been drinking a lot lately. Is there a problem?"

Honestly? The guy who passes out drunk every night on the road is asking me if I have a drinking problem?

"No, Alex. There's not a problem. I knew I was going out. I'm away from home for the weekend. I wanted to get drunk. I forget I can't drink as much as I used to. The seventy pounds makes a difference."

He nodded. "Look, these guys *know* me. I was with people I know, who know my wife. I see these people all the time. I have to be careful what I say and do around them. The more you drank last night, the bolder and more intense you got. I tried to get you to go talk to Max for a while and calm down, but you wouldn't."

"I didn't want to talk to Max."

"And then you asked me back to your hotel room in front of everyone."

"I did not!"

"You most certainly did!" Alex sat up and leaned across the desk. "You said, in front of everyone, that I should take you back to your room. I had to explain later that you were drunk, a fan from out of town. It was not pretty."

"I'm sorry. I didn't mean it like that. When I said it."

We didn't say anything for a moment.

"I knew you were mad," I started. "I tried to call you...."

He stood and crossed back toward the wet bar. "Yeah. What the fuck was that about? Why were you crying?"

"I was crying because I couldn't get ahold of you!" I snapped. I stepped across the crimson carpet to where he was. "I needed to talk to you. There was no one else."

"I told you. You can't freak out on me. I will cut the cord, Tierney. I will *cut the fucking cord*."

"It wasn't about freaking out on you! I was upset, and I needed to talk to my friend."

"Why were you so upset?" he pressed, a little sarcastically.

I rushed into an answer, unable to think ahead about what I was going to say. "I was upset, because I didn't get to come!"

He looked stunned, and a little hurt.

"No, that's not right." The words were stuck to my gummy tongue. "I was hoping we would meet up, fuck for hours, and get it all out of our system. I wanted it to be everything it was *supposed* to be. It wasn't. There wasn't enough time, for either of us. And I didn't come, so I didn't get *any* of it worked out."

I could still picture the stained bed, could still feel him inside of me. All of it rushed toward me at once, and I thought I was going to vomit.

"Tierney, I can't give you *resolution* with this!"

"I never thought you could!" I countered.

I was tripping over my own, enormous head, trying to explain myself to him. I wanted him to know that I wasn't disappointed in him, ever. Nothing was coming out right.

We were both quiet.

"I need to get a cab," I said finally. "For the airport."

"I have a car," he replied. "I'll take you."

"No, it's fine. I can get a cab."

"After that bar tab? No way."

"Are you sure you don't mind?" I was probably lucky he wasn't telling me to walk.

"Positive. Now, if you want to rest, you can lie down on the bed."

He pointed across the room. I looked at the bed where he'd been sleeping just a few hours before. It was made, though housekeeping hadn't yet come by. Everything in the room was orderly and meticulous—nothing like my hotel room had been.

If you hadn't been a stupid bitch, you'd be in that bed with him right now.

"Let me grab some stuff to take a shower. If you're cold, you can get the blanket or whatever."

I shook my head and sat on the edge of the bed, trying to take up as little space as possible. He gathered some clothes from the dresser.

"Get some rest, Tierney."

He went into the bathroom and closed the door.

We were alone in the room. Alex was so upset with me that he wouldn't even be naked in front of me, to get dressed or undressed for a shower. Barely two days after we'd slept together.

I didn't want to muss his bed. I didn't want him to have to sleep there that night, smelling me on his pillow and his sheets if he was so damn angry. I curled into the smallest ball possible, shivering with cold, and fell asleep on top of his quilt.

I woke a couple of hours later. I felt better, though still tired. Eyes still closed, I listened carefully to see if Alex was still there. I could hear music or the television, murmuring faintly across the room. I stood, dizzy, and took a deep breath.

"Hey," he said softly. "Feel better?"

I nodded. "I need more water. And some gum. Do you have any gum?"

He was standing by the desk, wearing the fresh clothes he'd pulled from the dresser earlier. He fished a piece of gum from the backpack at his bare feet and passed it to me.

"Thanks." I went to the sink and drank another three small cups of water. I started chewing the gum and crossed back to him, seated again at his computer. I motioned for him to stand.

"Are we okay?"

"Yeah, we're fine.

I stood directly in front of him, six inches from him, looking him straight in the eye.

"You're sure?"

"Yes. I'm sure. But if you go nuts on me again...."

I nodded. "I know, I know."

I pulled him to me for a hug. He looked at my mouth, probably trying to decide if my lipstick would rub off on him, and kissed me quickly.

"We'll be okay, you know," I said, turning away.

"You and Sam?"

Okay, we'll go with that. I nodded.

"God, I hope so!"

He grabbed his acoustic guitar and sat at the desk again.

"Listen to this for me."

He clicked on his MacBook and played part of a song I didn't know, though I recognized the voice immediately as Bruce Springsteen.

"*That*'s what I want, right there!" Alex sputtered. "There's something he's doing there with the lyrics, and I can't quite... *ugh!*" He played it again, listening intently. "I just want to channel Bruce Springsteen and write the next great American song."

"Well..," I started slowly, "he's a masterful storyteller, right?" Alex looked at me over his glasses, long fingers poised on guitar strings. "Part of it with him is that he moves the listener through the story slowly. You have a tendency to tell the story quickly and then extrapolate on it, on how it makes you feel. He's stepping slowly through the prose of the ballad."

Alex looked at me thoughtfully. He started to pick at his melody again, tossing words on top the notes, trying to find the right match of mood and word.

"*Fuck!*" he muttered under his breath. "Sometimes... sometimes I just wanna be done with all of it, you know? I just want the fucking spotlight off me, to tell the fans and the managers and the label and Paulie and everyone to just go fuck themselves. Talia says I should just pick up and go somewhere and take my guitar and tour around on my own."

"Where would you go?"

"I don't know. Ireland maybe. I love it there."

"And there's lots of whiskey," I smiled.

"There is that," he laughed. "I could just travel around western Europe and play what I wanted to and when and how and then come home to her and a house full of kids when I was tired of it. But sometimes... I don't even wanna do *that*."

"What would you do if you weren't a musician? Like, if you just *stopped*, right now. What would you do?"

He put his guitar down and thought about it for a moment. "I used to want to be a fireman, but now I'm too old. I like doing graphic work, designs. I would probably do that. My friend, Michael, is a manager and is always trying to get me to go in that direction."

"Would you want to? Be a manager?"

He screwed up his full lips and shook his head. "Not really. I mean, I *could* do it. I'd probably be good at it. It's just not what I want to do. If I quit *this*, I'm quitting all of it."

He was stressed and in a funk. So much of his life and his career weren't where and how he wanted it to be. It hadn't been for a long time, and he was having a hard time finding a way to see that it would be okay, that he would eventually be able to breathe a little easier. I wished I could give him an answer, to make his band and his life work the way he wanted them to.

Hell, I wish I had that for me.

Finally it was time to go. I stepped into my sandals and grabbed my suitcase. Alex held the door open and took the suitcase from me.

"I can get it," I protested.

"You never let people do things for you, do you?"

"I *let* people do things all the time. I just don't *expect* that other people will do things for me. I'm a princess, absolutely, but I wear my crown in the mud."

He laughed and held the elevator door for me.

"This is an awfully big suitcase for two days. How much shit did you bring?"

"I needed room for shoes and sex toys."

He laughed, loading me and my stuff into his rental car. He pulled out of the parking deck, away from the River Walk, onto the interstate. We talked about the Red Hot Chili Peppers and defensive driving and this car he used to have.

"I love him, you know," I said, out of the blue.

"I know you do. He loves you, too."

"I *want* to be with him. I realized how much I need him. When I can't sleep at three thirty in the morning, it's the feel of his *hand* on my hip that soothes me. I love how he's always the perfect temperature—hot or cold, doesn't matter, just what I need in that moment. He's funny and smart and... I love him."

Alex nodded but didn't say much.

I wanted to reach over and take his hand, hold it in mine for just a little while. I wanted to tell him to stop somewhere, anywhere, on the way to the airport to give us twenty minutes alone. We had no idea when we'd see each other again, and I didn't want more of our time to feel so wasted and irretrievable.

He pulled to the curb in the loading zone at the airport. Leaving the car idling, he unloaded my suitcase from the trunk.

"Thanks for the ride," I said, looking into his handsome face.

He nodded slowly. "You're welcome."

"I love you, Alex."

"I love you, too."

He kissed me quickly again and was gone.

I made it home late that night, exhausted.

"Did you have fun?" Sam asked.

I smiled and nodded. "I did. I had a great time! Thank you for letting me go."

"I'm glad. I missed you."

"I missed you, too, baby."

I brushed my teeth and snuggled next to him in our big bed.

As I drifted off to sleep, I realized something about the weekend: Alex never called me Buttercup. Not once. Not the whole weekend.

Yes, I loved him. It was complicated and deep and sometimes difficult, but it wasn't in a way that would ever make *us* impossible. I was very, very careful about how I let myself feel it.

I'm not in love with him, not like that, and I can't ever be.

It killed me to know that he cared, to know he cared deeply, but that he could never let that stand on its own merits. I had the freedom to say his name at home, to remark that I'd talked to him. We had a friendship, and I had no reason to hide that. But I didn't exist in his world, outside of his Junkture moments and his private thoughts.

I knew if I got the chance to go down that path with him again, I would do it in a heartbeat. Whether it was on the phone or text or Skype or even the imperfection of ten more minutes, I would take it. There was something unnamed that I got with him that I'd never gotten from anyone else. I had no real expectation that it would be there, but I was always going to be open to the idea of it, and of him.

No matter what, I would always be there for him.

I pushed it all out of my mind, again, and went to sleep.

Chapter 19

It was the last week of school for the boys before summer vacation. Our schedule was already filled with swim practice and class parties, plus Tripp's fifth grade graduation on Friday. Summer would start in earnest with the Memorial Day barbecue.

I called Tessa on Monday morning for the Rock Star Weekend debriefing. She'd known almost every detail of my relationship with Alex, with the exception of the secrets I promised to never divulge to anyone. It seemed only natural to tell her the truth of what had happened in Texas. I stepped through the two days and the emotions of it all, at least as far as I understood them in the confusing afterglow.

"Sorry to go on so long," I said after an hour.

"Nono! It's fine," she assured me. "I'm titillated and intrigued, frankly. It's not every day your best friend fucks a rock star."

"Great. You can live vicariously through me."

"Yup. No need for me to have a midlife crisis of my own. Mine wouldn't have been nearly as interesting anyway. I'm a little worried about you, though."

"Why?" I laughed. "Because I'm insane?"

"You know that I love you and I'm here for you no matter what," Tessa said carefully, "but I'm worried about the aftermath of all this. I've known you since you were fourteen years old. I was there when you met Sam, and I know firsthand that you've loved him your entire waking life. I'm just worried about how all of this is going to affect you down the line."

"What do you mean?"

"I have my own messy, complicated history. I made a lot of mistakes in how I treated Sean when Ed and I got together. Don't get me wrong—Ed and I are totally right for each other, but I still wish I'd handled things differently at that time. I wasn't very nice, and I've always felt guilty about how I handled Sean in all of that. I don't want you to have that same kind of guilt. It's not fun."

"But I *don't* feel guilty about this, Tessa. This was something that *had* to happen. I can't explain it. It's... I don't know, it's just so goddamn *complicated* with Alex. And with Sam. But this had nothing to do with Sam, as weird as that sounds. They're two separate things, really. And this thing with Alex... I guess it's over." I laughed derisively. "I gotta say, though... ten minutes was just... *ugh*."

"Yes! Ten minutes is *never* enough time. But if the sex was good—"

"Which it was, strangely."

"—then you'll do it again."

"I don't know about that." I sighed and ran my fingers through my hair, pacing the kitchen.

"Trust me. If the sex didn't suck the first time, it's hard *not* to do it again. I saw that on *House*. It must be true."

"*Oh my god!*" I gasped. "I banged a *rock star*!" I stopped. "I guess I can take that off my bucket list."

"Indeed! The question now is *what are you gonna do for an encore?*"

"Fuck if I know, but I'm betting it includes a *lot* of glitter! *And it's not lupus!*"

Tripp complained on Tuesday evening of a sore throat and headache. By Wednesday morning, we knew it was strep. He would miss the last two days of school before his graduation events.

I was busy with doctors' appointments and class parties. I was bored settling back into my life again after the brouhaha of the weekend. I didn't talk to Alex that week. I was trying to give him space and time to not be so angry with me. He probably had his own confusion and issues to deal with, after everything that happened.

On Friday morning, I couldn't stand it anymore. I knew he would be in and around St. Louis for the weekend. I was going to Birmingham on Sunday, for an overnight visit, and could conceivably catch a flight to meet him for a few hours and still be home to Atlanta in time for dinner on Monday.

From: Tierney Cavanaugh Johnson
Date: May 31st 6:44 AM
To: Alex Wheeler
Subject:

I really, really want to fly to St. Louis on Sunday evening, home early Monday, when I know I'm not expected anywhere. It's making me petulant and bratty.

From: Alex Wheeler
Date: May 31st 11:31 AM
To: Tierney Cavanaugh Johnson
Subject: RE:

Ha! Petulant & Bratty, awesome.

From: Tierney Cavanaugh Johnson
Date: May 31st 11:36 AM
To: Alex Wheeler
Subject: RE:
I still want to come and do inappropriate things. :)

From: Alex Wheeler
Date: May 31st 11:40 AM
To: Tierney Cavanaugh Johnson
Subject: RE:

I know u do.

From: Tierney Cavanaugh Johnson
Date: May 31st 12:10 PM
To: Alex Wheeler
Subject: RE:

Then let me. I can be there Sunday night, gone by dawn. Do this for both ot us.

From: Alex Wheeler
Date: May 31st 1:38 PM
To: Tierney Cavanaugh Johnson
Subject: RE:

You are an amazing woman Tierney and I am glad that i have you in my life.

I am still trying to figure out my head/feelings about what has transpired between us. I am tired and overused as well as lonely and really missing my family so its gonna take me a while before i can get back into my relationships with the people that i hold close to my heart. there is so much whirling around in my head and quite frankly i just want to throw everything away and be gone from this spot light. It's hot and consuming and I dont want it focused on me anymore.

I will figure things out and will eventually understand and accept myself again and hopefully all will be okay in my little world.

Thank you for everything you do/share with me, I truly appreciate our friendship but coming to St. Louis is probably not the best thing for you to do. I need to work out my nuts and bolts before i can relax and enjoy.

xoxo,

Alex

From: Tierney Cavanaugh Johnson
Date: May 31st 2:25 PM
To: Alex Wheeler
Subject: RE:

You blow me away, you know. I'm here when you need me, for anything, ever. No pressure. I'm your friend, above everything else. Let me be that and don't feel guilty about it.

I wasn't sure how you felt about what happened, or if you were even sure. You're such a compartmentalizer that I wasn't sure if it would have an impact, or if I was in it by myself. My own head is still spinning, obviously, but you know that. Believe me, I know full well the gravity and potential repercussions. But you're the only one I have to work through that with. I'll work the rest out in my painting. Above all else, it's been a spectacularly exquisite ride with you that I wouldn't undo for anything.

I'll do whatever I can to support any decisions you make about your life and your career. You matter to me, not the rock star. Whatever you need, if it's in my control, it's yours.

Take your time and find your peace. I hope you won't cut me out, will keep me in your loop. You're still my secret keeper, and that reciprocity is sacred.

I love you, Princess. Call me when you're ready.

Tierney

All of these emails went back and forth while I was with Sam and Tripp on Friday. We went to his graduation ceremony early. There were family events scheduled, but his strep made Tripp unable to participate in any of the outdoor Field Day events. We checked him out for the afternoon and took him to lunch and the electronics store, Sam and I laughing and happy together with our son. We came back for the class parade through the school, which we watched with Ian and his class, waving to all of the graduating fifth graders. It was hard to believe my baby was going to middle school.

I was happy spending time with my men. Sam and I were affectionate and smiling and happy, both with the boys and with each other.

But I was still consumed by thoughts of Alex.

We had a session with Janet on Saturday. I told her the same things about my trip that I'd told Sam—basically all of it, except having slept with Alex. We were smiling and holding hands and talked a lot about the children, if only because it didn't seem that *we* had anything pressing to deal with.

The start of summer meant going to the pool at least five days a week. I needed a new bathing suit. It turned out I also needed new shorts, as I'd gone from a size twenty-four to a size sixteen since the end of the last summer. I'd been putting it off, hoping to lose as much weight as possible before I had to make that trip to the mall. After the session with Janet, I jovially left the men at home early in the afternoon and went shopping.

I had to bite the bullet and go to Hell in search of proper summer attire.

Generally, for me, any excuse to go shopping is a good thing. I knew it would likely be difficult to find something that would make me happy, but I was up for the challenge. I'm a resourceful and savvy shopper under normal circumstances, and I was confident my luck would hold out.

I was so fucking wrong.

I made it through a couple of stores with very little luck. I did score a pair of shorts and some tank tops at the first store, nothing at the second. By the time I got to the third store, I was getting really anxious. I swear the stress was making me more and more bloated by the minute, as I stood under those fluorescent lights, jammed in the narrow aisle between overstuffed racks.

By the time I hit the third dressing room, I was in a full-blown panic. I texted Tessa for support and posted a Facebook status update, completely in an attempt to get someone to reach out and help calm my nerves.

Tierney Cavanaugh Johnson
June 1st

73 pounds and I'm about to cry bc I still can't find shorts or a bathing suit that don't make me gag.

Shorts and bathing suits are evil. You are beautiful!!!!!

With that kind of success, you can go naked!

ugh.. me neither! I have what I call "big thigh syndrome" my thighs are seriously out of whack with the rest of my body so shorts are ALWAYS tight in the thighs! YUK!! I'm about to start making my own

I think stores that sell clothes like those should have an in-house life coach that subtly makes us feel better about the process.

Listen I am a size 2 or 4 and I can't find shorts either! I am literally wearing shorts from 5 years ago because I hate every pair I try on so don't feel bad. Just go with light weight dresses. :-)

Bathing suits are a bitch at any size. Good luck!

I cry almost every time I'm forced to enter a dressing room, so I completely feel your pain. I've decided that the only way to combat it is to keep repeating "That's not what I really look like" the entire time I'm in there. That, or stores could introduce a policy of handing out Valium to every woman trying on summer clothing. (*Limit one per customer.)

I understand completely. I think there is an unwritten code that clothing designers follow which ensures that people who wear sizes above Large must have only choices in fabrics and cuts that accentuate their size. Plaids, horizontal stripes and gansta FUBU cut pants. I hate shopping for this reason.

After working for years in a shop that sold bathing suits and after seeing hundreds of women of all shapes and sizes try on suits, the one thing that I believe to be true in bathing suit shopping is this: figure out what you like about your body (everybody has at least ONE thing that doesn't make them cry about their body) and accentuate that. If it is your boobs, well, then find a suit that best outlines your bust and ignore the rest. If it is your hips, well, then find something that makes your eyes go for that shape and again, ignore the rest. Find something that YOU are comfortable in that makes your eyes directed to the spot that you want and be happy with that. Be confident in that you have much beauty to give - as you do.

I stood in the dressing room, treading those emotional waters and waiting for someone, anyone, to throw me a lifeline, and I cried. I looked at my body, seventy-three pounds lighter than it was just a few months ago, and I couldn't stand it. A great pair of jeans could contain the extra skin and extra movement; I wouldn't get the luxury of concealment in a swimsuit. All I could see were the ghastly thighs and the flabby arms, and I was disgusted and embarrassed.

That kind of self-disgust was nothing new. I'd felt it for years, like a fat little girl version of myself always hiding right behind my huge ass. Every time I turned to face it head-on, she ducked away, forcing me to turn 'round and 'round, trying to catch more than a glimpse of her.

Alex Wheeler
Jun 1st 3:47 PM
Remind me to breathe

breathe

in a dressing room crying, trying on bathing suits

281

I can overcome these body images issues, right?

Yes u can

I knew the amazing progress I'd made thus far. I knew I should've been proud of how far I'd come and of all the work I'd done. But I was still forty pounds from my goal—the numeric point at which I expected to feel comfortably healthy with my weight. Standing in that dressing room made me want to give up, to accept the futility of my battle, and to eat my way out of the fucking mall.

I couldn't battle myself again just because Alex, or anyone else, believed in me. Unless I could find a way to make peace with my personal, glaring imperfections and how I perceived them, I would never ever come to terms with my body.

I'd been so offended when Sam had suggested I just wanted to be young and thin, arguing that I wanted to be *me* and *healthy*. Part of being healthy had to include the acceptance of a pragmatic vision of my body. I wanted to be able to see what I thought of as *good* or *bad* about my body and recognize it as only *natural*.

I refused to give up that afternoon. I had better things to do than sit around on my ass, waiting for the sullen, taunting, fat little girl to get happy. I told her to stuff a cookie in her face and *shut the fuck up*. I got the hell out of that mall, where the temptation to allow myself to fail was so overwhelming.

I left and went elsewhere, and I did eventually find an acceptable suit and some shorts. I didn't love how I looked in them, but I could live with it.

We settled into our summer routine. Swim practice every morning, followed by a couple of hours of moms chatting poolside while the kids played. Lunch and showers and read-and-rest time, before an afternoon movie on the couch while Mom cooked dinner. Chlorine-soaked days blended together, but they were easy and much happier than they'd been a year before.

Alex called to check in one afternoon. He was back in L.A., done with tour dates and the tensions with the band, and he was glad to be home.

"How are you with everything?" I asked after a few minutes. "I don't know what you're thinking about it."

"I don't know. I'm not thinking about it."

"Listen, I wasn't very clear on Sunday about something."

"Hm?"

"When I said I didn't come, I could see that look on your face. I know it stung, and I didn't mean for it to. It wasn't because of you or anything you did wrong. I don't want you to think I didn't enjoy it. I *loved* every second of that with you, Alex. I wasn't disappointed in *you*, ever. It wasn't what it should've been. It wasn't long enough. I don't know if it ever could've been, honestly. But I didn't want to leave you with the impression that I was somehow *unhappy* about any of it, or unhappy with you. I wasn't."

"I know, Tierney. It's okay." I thought I heard the slightest bit of relief in his voice but didn't know if it was real.

"It sounds stupid as shit, but I hope it was... good? okay? for you...."

Seriously, Tierney? Did you just ask if it was good for him, too?

"Oh, yeah! It was great. And, no, it wasn't what it should've been, and I'm sorry about that."

"It's okay." *Liar.* "I know why. I'm not sorry about it happening. I don't regret it at all. Obviously I'd do it again in a heartbeat."

Alex chuckled. "I know. I'm not sorry, either."

"I have to go, though. The boys need Mom to do, you know, Mom stuff. I'll talk to you soon?"

"Yup."

"I love you, Alex Wheeler."

"Love you, too."

———————

Three nights later, I was at a swim meet with the boys. Normally Sam would join us early in the evening, in time to catch most of their events. Because Ian was usually finished long before his brother, Sam would take him home and get him ready for bed. I helped work the meet and had to stay until the end of the night.

On this particular evening, Sam was really late. I tried to call and text him to see where he was but got no response. Sometime after dark, he arrived. He looked tense and tired.

"You okay?" I asked, kissing him hello.

He half-nodded. "Yeah. Work."

He'd been working a lot of hours that week, spending long stretches of time in the computer lab at work, insulated from the outside world. He was investigating more high-profile incidents by Digital Freedom Front. The hacktivists had targeted public officials and websites again, flaunting their ability to gain access to protected information and take over sites. Sometimes the attacks were political in nature, though some of them seemed nonsensical. It had been all over the news for a week.

A few weeks prior, the same group had gone after a government/civilian task force. It had been kept hush-hush, but Sam and some of his colleagues had been targeted since that initial attack. He was internationally known for his previous work with some specific computer Trojans and cyber attacks. His expertise in information security was highly sought by clients and the government alike.

He was obviously pre-occupied and a little distant, but I didn't think much about it. The boys were both finished early that night. Sam took them home. I stayed to help clean up after the meet.

I came in around ten o'clock. I wasn't feeling well. The constriction in my throat and sinuses, the pressure on my glands, and the beginnings of extreme fatigue all pointed toward a sudden cold. Six summer hours on deck had left me sticky and tired. I went straight to the shower. I put on fresh pajamas and brushed my towel-dried hair. The boys were already asleep, and Sam was watching television.

The den was dark, except for the glow of the TV. He sat stoic, staring at the screen. He took a sip from the drink nestled between his legs. I realized it was a beer.

"Are we gonna talk about this?" I asked, settling onto the couch. He hadn't had a drink in almost six months. I wasn't surprised, though, knowing how stressful work had been for the last week. This was how the cycle always started.

"Talk about what?"

"Um, the beer you're drinking?"

He took a swig from the can. "I think we should talk about the nature of your relationship with Alex Wheeler."

My heart started to race. *Fight or flight.*

"Alex and I are friends. You know that." I tried to play it off, like I was confused that he was even asking.

"I think you guys talk about some things that most friends don't discuss. At least not friends who are married. To other people."

"Sam, there's nothing going on. Alex and I are *just friends*."

"Did you fuck him?"

"*What?*"

He looked straight at me and spat, "*Did you fuck him? In Texas? Did you fuck him?*"

"No! Absolutely not!"

Ohmygod, ohmygod, ohmygod! Stay calm. See what he knows.

"Where the hell is this coming from?"

He took another drink. "I was investigating these hacks, and I was logged into a server as one of my alter egos. I was looking through stores of data for anything that seemed out of the ordinary. I always look for certain keywords and string matches, including my name, your name, our email addresses. There was some shit in a directory that matched my server. The home server."

Calm down, Tierney. Keep your face calm.

"What was there?" I asked evenly.

"It was all stuff from *your* accounts. Emails and files. The most surprising was the video from Alex Wheeler, though. I like porn as much as the next guy, but I doubt his wife would like knowing he sent you those videos of his cock."

Oh fuck!

I said nothing. I looked at him steadily, jaw clinched. My head and throat were throbbing.

"But the chat logs!" he continued, turning to face me directly. "Those were totally unexpected. I didn't realize you talked to your friends about how wet your pussy could get."

I winced.

Sam was livid. The password for my email on Sam's server was too simple, and they were able to catch a file in an email packet. Eventually they'd gained access to much, much more.

I was still trying to play it cool. Yes, I admitted, Alex and I had some intense talks, even of a sexual nature, but nothing had happened. We argued until the early morning, when I finally felt so bad that I had to go to sleep.

I slept for nearly forty-six hours straight.

Every time I would try to wake up, my head would swirl, and I'd almost pass out again. I was congested and coughing badly, running a fever.

Late Saturday evening, I roused when Sam came into the bedroom.

"Just tell me," he said, glaring at me from the end of the bed, "did you fuck him?"

"No," I responded groggily, "I told you I didn't."

"I don't believe you! You *emailed* him that you wanted to sneak to St. Louis when I wouldn't know and be gone by dawn, to finish what you started! Was it as good as you hoped? Was it so good you had to go back and do it one more time?"

Oh fuck.

I looked at him, eyes wide and unsure of what to say.

"At least tell me you used a condom. Did you? *Did you at least use a condom?*"

I shook my head. "No, but—"

"We're done," he said. "I'm done with this. I'm moving out. I'm filing for divorce. You can repay me the money it's going to take to get your goddamn files back."

From: Tierney Cavanaugh Johnson
Date: June 15th 7:01 PM
To: Alex Wheeler
Subject: Ugh

Sam found out about my side project. It's exactly what you're thinking.

Things here are bad. As bad as they could possibly be. Worse than I could have imagined. I'm trying to mitigate damages, but it won't be easy. He's planning to file for divorce. There's way more to it than that. I can't explain via email.

From: Alex Wheeler
Date: June 15th 10:54 PM
To: Tierney Cavanaugh Johnson
Subject: **RE:** Ugh

Let's talk on Monday.

I wanted to go back to sleep, to hide from it all. I needed to do whatever Sam wanted. I didn't want to be without him. It had taken me months to realize how much I loved and wanted and needed him. I didn't want to lose that now. I went out to the deck, where Sam was drinking a beer and listening to music in the dark.

Shortly after we started counseling with Janet, Sam and I would find ourselves outside at night, after the boys went to bed. The spring weather was pleasant even after dark, and it was comfortable sitting together, talking about whatever. It had given us a safe arena in which to battle and air our grievances, whether with the other or with ourselves. Nothing was off limits, and we were allowed to be as honest as we could stand, with the agreement that the other wasn't supposed to hold that honesty against us. I'd dubbed them the Back Porch Sessions.

I sat in the chair next to Sam's and was quiet. I waited to see what he would say or do.

"When? When did it happen?"

"Which part?"

"You fucked him in San Antonio?"

I nodded.

"Any time before that?"

I shook my head.

"When did all of the other start?"

"After Chicago. Nothing happened *in* Chicago. It started a few days later."

Sam wanted the details.

It was awful, stepping through the relationship, beginning to end, and telling him how it had gone from a flirty text to the two of us naked, a thousand miles from home. I tried to spare his feelings as much as possible. I didn't know what he'd seen in the files and messages taken from my computer. I gave as little information as possible, still trying to cover my ass.

"And *why* didn't you use a condom? If you want to put yourself at risk, I don't give a shit, except that my children need their mother. But you put *me* at risk. I'm going in this week for a full battery of STD testing. I suggest you do the same."

"I'm not worried about an STD from him, but I understand why you need that."

"Then you're fucking stupid, Tierney. Do you honestly think you're special to him? Do you *honestly believe* he's not doing this with someone else? There's nothing special about you that would make you the only one he's fucking."

I did think I was the only one. Alex had told me time and again that there was no one else, other than Talia, and I completely trusted him on that. I wouldn't have let him put his dick in me if I didn't trust him, let alone have done it without a condom.

"Does she know?" he asked.

"Talia?" He nodded. "No. I don't think so."

"Do you think that's fair? Do you think it's fair to her not to know that her husband's been fucking around on her?"

"I don't know if it's fair or not. That's not my decision to make; that's up to Alex. He'll deny it, no matter what. I know he doesn't want her to know. I know he's afraid she would leave and take Amber if she found out."

"Maybe that's what should happen."

"Sam, this isn't my call to make, and it's not yours. This is up to Alex. They have their own issues, and no one else has the right to step into the middle of that."

"But it was okay for him to step into *our* marriage?" he hissed.

"He didn't! This had nothing to do with you or our marriage!"

He looked at me, aghast.

"It didn't," I pressed. "Yes, I was unhappy when it started. I was *miserable*. But Alex pushed me, time and again, to get you into counseling with me, to try to make this work. He wanted me to be happy *with you*."

Sam just stared at me.

"So what happens now?" I asked.

"I'm moving out. I don't know how long it will take. I'll start looking this week for a new place."

I nodded. "I don't want to tell the children or the families anything yet."

"Okay. That's probably best."

"I'm really sick. I need to go back to bed."

He nodded and opened another beer.

I slept a while longer, until sometime around dawn. I emailed Tessa to let her know what was going on. There was no point in trying to contact Alex before Monday.

The boys woke up a while later, asking about breakfast.

"And what about Daddy's present?" Tripp said.

Father's Day. The boys had picked out a DVD for him, *Green Lantern: Emerald Knights* on Blu-ray. Sam had loved Green Lantern since he was a kid, and this would be a great introduction to his favorite superhero for the boys, something new they could love together. I snuck into the bedroom, past sleeping Sam, and pulled the gift and cards from my closet. All of it had been signed and wrapped the day before Sam found out about Alex.

Sam got up late in the morning and took a shower, barely speaking to any of us. He saw his cards and gift on the table but didn't touch them. He quietly left the house, no explanation or indication of when he'd be back.

From: Tierney Cavanaugh Johnson
Sent: June 16th 2:00 PM
To: Sam Johnson
Subject:

I don't know where you are or when you'll see this. It may sit in your inbox for ages before you read it, or you could just outright delete it and never give me the chance. I am powerless right now, and I know that. I feel it deeply, believe me. Even sending you anything is a silly, silly thing to do, and I hope you don't use this to bite me in the ass later. I've got nothing else to lose right now; I'll take my chances.

I don't want this. I don't want to be apart, without you. I know it took me forever to realize that, to really comprehend how much a part of me you are, and always have been and always will be. I've said flippantly many times that I've loved you my entire waking life. I used to know what that meant, but I completely lost sight of it for a while. I feel like you did, too, but I'm not you and don't want to speak for you. I've had enough of trying to guess what's best for you.

What I know is that I love you utterly and completely. Not just because it's slipping away. I knew when I stood in front of you and told you all the ways and reasons that you meant everything to me. I'd been hurt for a very, very long time, and I didn't know or really care if you were hurting, too. When I finally realized, finally really *got* it, I knew it wasn't something that I wanted to lose. I knew I didn't want to be without you, ever.

I was so lost. And instead of curling up on the couch for three months like I'd done before, I fought back and let it all out, regardless of who was caught in my crossfire. There were days I absolutely did not want to be married, to anyone, let alone you. I was screaming inside for help to find my way. You couldn't or wouldn't hear me, as far as I could tell. I was hurt and angry and confused and more lost than ever for a while. No matter who told me I was getting out of control, I would deny it. I couldn't see it. By the time I did, it was so late. I was too far gone to know how to get back and only knew to move forward and let this cycle play out. I should've asked you for help instead of distance. I should've done a lot of things. I made the bad choice, time and again, and I know I can only be angry at myself for that.

I know you're hurting. Horribly. I can only imagine all the things that are in your heart and in your head. I barely know my own right now.

What I *do* know is that I will go to the ends of the Earth to try to make this work again. I won't be Orpheus, I won't look back, and I will traverse the depths of Hell to get back to you. I don't care what it takes, what has to happen.

I'm a flawed, scarred woman, without question. I have made some horrendous mistakes. I've been there with you when you've made your own and thought for sure we were finished. Maybe we've used up all of our lives, but I'm asking you to look deeply, one more time, and see if you can't find just the inkling of hope, just the tiniest glimmer of that spark, that would make you want to at least *try*.

I love you. I'm an idiot. And I'm sorry.

I tried to have a normal Sunday with the boys. I told them Daddy had to work, that he would be home later to see them. I moved his gift and cards to his dresser, so he would have to see and touch them when he came home.

I felt awful. Not just about what was happening with Sam, but also because I was so sick. I was chilled and feverish, and my lungs hurt like hell. At the very least, I knew had bronchitis.

Sam finally got back late that night. He'd gone into the office to avoid seeing me. I was curled up in bed, watching television, when he came in. I wasn't ignoring him, but I didn't have any intention of speaking to him until he spoke first. I was trying my best not to antagonize him.

I found him on the deck a while later. He was drinking and smoking a cigarette. He'd originally quit smoking even before I had.

"I'm really sick," I said quietly.

"Are you going to the doctor?"

I nodded. "I have to go tomorrow. Can you keep the boys?"

"Yep."

"Can I sit out here for a while?"

"Sure."

We were quiet for a long time. I started to cry.

"I'm sorry. I know that doesn't mean much, but I am."

"You lied to me. To my face. To our therapist."

"I know," I whispered.

"And you spent *my* money to go on this trip and fuck someone else!"

I didn't respond.

"I got your files back," he said finally.

"Okay."

I could only assume that he had, or was planning to, go through them all. If he hadn't already, he would see so much of the lascivious activity that had gone on between me and Alex. I didn't know what was there, and I was horribly afraid of what he would see.

"No, Tierney, it's not okay! I had to go out of state to cover my ass and Western Union five grand to a bunch of assholes I'm trying to help the TLA shut down! This is not okay!"

Sam went inside to get another beer. "Do you want a Xanax?" he asked gently when he returned. "It'll take the edge off."

I nodded and started to cry again. I followed him into the kitchen and took the proffered pill.

I went to the doctor the next morning. The cold that had come on so quickly on Thursday had turned into full-blown pneumonia. My lungs hurt, like I was trying to breathe through salt water. Two shots in the ass and three prescriptions.

Alex called while I was on my way home from the pharmacy.

"What the hell happened?" he asked.

I recounted coming home on Thursday, being asked about our relationship.

"Did you tell him it was just talk? That it meant nothing?"

"Of course I did! But he'd *seen* the emails between us. He had a Skype log of one of our first conversations, from November. My machine was hacked, Alex. He has stuff that *I* don't even have anymore."

"This is fucked up, Tierney. He set you up. He was watching you."

"No, I don't think so."

"He messaged me about Chicago. Did you know that?"

"What are you talking about?"

"He sent me a message, on Facebook, before you came to Chicago. He asked me to sing with you again, told me how much you'd loved it and shit. I didn't put the names together—you know, Johnson; you're always Cavanaugh when I think about you. He was watching to see what you did. The son of a bitch set you up!"

This was the first I'd ever heard of Sam contacting Alex. *Did he really intend to catch me in some trap?* I didn't think it was possible. I mean, it was *possible*; I just didn't think it had happened that way. Sure, Sam had felt the tension for months, had even suggested something undefined was going on. Nothing was going on before Chicago anyway, and he'd had no reason to monitor me or my accounts. Until now.

"Talia can't find out about the affair, Tierney."

It was the first time either of us had ever called it that.

"I know that, Alex. Look, I didn't want *him* to find out. I sure as fuck don't want you to have to go through this, too."

"Well," he sighed, "I knew what could happen. When I went to your hotel room in the middle of the night, I *knew* it might blow up in my face. I'll deal with it, if it comes to that, but I don't want it to. She will take Amber and *run*."

"I'm trying very hard to keep that from happening. I don't know what's coming. I'll let you know as I know."

"Okay. I guess let me know how you are. I'm sorry, Tierney. I'm sorry you're having to deal with this."

I knew he was worried about himself, but he seemed sincerely concerned for me.

"It sucks, you know? I thought we would be okay. I thought we were finally through the worst of everything."

"I know," Alex said gently. "You realized how much you loved him."

"Things were *so good*, they were so much better before I went to Texas. We were in such a good place. Like, we were *happy* again, like we hadn't been in a very long time."

"You didn't tell me. You didn't tell me things were better." His tone was suddenly reproachful.

Shit. "I know. I meant to, but then there just wasn't the opportunity, when I saw you." I paused. "I don't know why I didn't tell you."

"*I* know why you didn't tell me. You do, too."

I knew I could've made it happen, but I hadn't wanted to. I wasn't sure I'd even trusted that things were good. It was new and fragile, and it would cut me again if it broke. If I'd told Alex things were better, that Sam was happy and fucking me in new and unimaginable ways, he *never* would've crossed that line with me.

I went home and slept again. Sam made sure the boys were situated. I woke as they were going to bed. I tucked them in, kissed them goodnight, and went outside.

"I talked to Alex this afternoon," I told Sam.

"*Why?*" He was exasperated.

"He needed to know what was going on. He had a right to know his own life may be blown apart."

"Fuck him! Why does he have that right but I didn't?"

He was right. What was so special about Alex that I could consider his feelings over my husband's?

"It was just the right thing to do. He's afraid you're going to tell Talia."

"She deserves to know."

"I'm not arguing that with you. It's not my place or yours to tell her. That's Alex's decision."

"I think that's bullshit!"

I couldn't fight with him about it. I was so sick, and I needed to rest. I went back to the safety of my bed. Sam slept on the couch.

Chapter 20

Our first visit back to the therapist was brutal. Janet could tell immediately that we were not in a good place.

"I lied," I said to her matter-of-factly. "When I went to Texas, I slept with Alex Wheeler. I had an affair."

She glanced at Sam, then looked at me evenly. "One time doesn't necessarily constitute an affair."

"It was going on for months," I replied unabashedly. "There was an inappropriate relationship outside the bounds of my marriage for months before I ever had sex with him."

She took a deep breath. "Wow."

She asked Sam how he was handling it all. He shrugged. He was sad and shell-shocked and couldn't say much.

"An affair is a blow to the gut of a marriage," Janet said, looking from me to Sam. "Where do you want to go from here?"

We had a successful functional life together. We had history and two beautiful children. We loved each other, but would that be enough to get us through this?

Neither of us could answer her question.

"Tierney, you need to cut ties with him, with this other man. You can't continue to have contact with him, if you want to save your marriage."

I didn't *want* to end my relationship with Alex. Even if the sexual part of it was over, he was a close friend who knew me intimately. I needed him. I needed his guidance and support, especially now. Through my conversations with him, I'd learned so much about myself and the things I wanted out of life. Cutting him out would be like cutting out a piece of my heart.

But I didn't want to be without Sam. Ever. It wasn't just all the time and energy that had gone into our marriage. He was my best friend. He knew all of my stories and anecdotes and could still find something new to talk about with me, even though it felt like eons since we'd been consistent on our connecting. When we were putting the effort into each other, we were beautiful together. I didn't want to feel like all of those years had been wasted and blown apart by my own stupid choices.

Janet asked us not to make a decision about our future. She asked us to continue our talks on the deck and to see if we could find some common ground from which we might rebuild, something more personal than our past and our children.

All of our time on the deck before that night, all of the Back Porch Sessions, had revolved around how we felt about each other and what was happening to us *at that time*. That night, something shifted, almost imperceptibly.

For the next several weeks, we opened up every imaginable aspect of our relationship. We went back to the beginning—not just of our partnership but also of ourselves—and talked about virtually every relationship we'd ever had. There were so many things that each of us had just assumed the other knew, in part because we'd known each other so damn long. But there'd been years in our teens when we weren't in close contact, when what we knew of each other had been second-hand knowledge passed through India, and there were a lot of missing details.

It was especially strange to realize that there were parts of our sexual pasts that we'd somehow never clearly shared. While that might seem normal for most relationships, Sam and I were not like most couples. Neither of us had ever been especially reticent to reveal our experiences, either in general or specific. Sam was never likely to get upset or jealous if he heard about some kinky moment with another lover that I had really enjoyed.

I did, however, have a hard time hearing him talk about India, in part because I knew her side of their relationship very well. I was surprised by how different his take on moments in their relationship was from her explanations of the same experiences, years before.

"I worried for years that you had loved her more than you loved me," I admitted one night. I couldn't look at him when I said it. I kept my gaze trained on the darkness in the woods behind our house.

"*Why?* Why would you even think that? Didn't I tell you every day that I loved you? Couldn't you just believe that?"

"I believed you. I still do. But, Sam, you were so *broken* when you guys split. I kept waiting for you to come home and tell me that she'd called, that she wanted you back. I used to dream about it all the time."

"Tierney...."

I shook my head and looked toward him finally. "I *knew*, though, that you loved me more than you'd ever loved her, on the day that Tripp was born. You were so *happy*—with me, with the baby, with everything—and you kissed me in the delivery room like you'd never kissed me before. It wasn't like I thought you hadn't loved me until I birthed your child; it was just that *this* was something you and she had never shared. It was just *us*, and the proof of that was splotchy and slimy and perfectly wrapped in a hospital blanket."

Sam was quiet for a moment. "Tierney, I *never* loved *her* more than I loved *you*. Even when she and I were together, for those six years, the amount of love I had for her in my heart was *nothing* compared to the *hole* where you were missing."

"But you were so hurt when she...."

"When she cheated with someone else. When she fell in love with someone else and didn't tell me. Even though I'd told her I would be okay with her sleeping with someone else, as long as I knew."

Oh god.

"There's no way she could've told you," I said, somehow defending the ghost of my husband's ex-girlfriend and myself in the same breath.

"Why? Why couldn't she? She said she loved me and wanted to be with me for the rest of her life. Why couldn't she tell me that she was attracted to another man?"

"Because she didn't want to hurt you. She hoped it was just a sexual attraction, something that would just go away on its own. When it didn't dissipate, maybe giving in just a little bit would make it stop. But then she realized she had feelings for the other guy."

"I had a right to know. Her choices impacted me just as much as they impacted her and him."

"But it had nothing to do with you," I said very carefully.

"*How* did it have nothing to do with me? Either they fucked around behind my back and realized it would never work, in which case I probably never would've found out the truth, or they would fall in love and she would leave me. *How did that have nothing to do with me, Tierney?*"

I stroked my fingers through my hair, pulling it up, off my neck. "I'm not saying it wouldn't impact you either way, even if you'd never found out. But it didn't start because of you. You were nowhere in that equation. The attraction between them came out of the blue and seemed too powerful to ignore."

"But *I* am the one who got caught in that, aren't I? I'm the one who got to feel all the hurt and the anger, to feel the embarrassment of having been cheated on. I didn't get anything good out of that."

"If we're talking about India, it opened the door to me and our children. If we're talking about me, I don't know what good outcome will be revealed. But there *will* be one."

"*How*, Tierney? How can anything good come from this? From having my heart broken?"

"If nothing redeeming comes from this, it will have been an utter waste of time. There *has* to be a good lesson in all of this, something we're supposed to be learning."

"Yeah, I guess I'm learning that I'm a magnet for cheating women."

We had argued and talked and been emotionally truthful for weeks, and I had still shattered the last, fragile maxims of our relationship. Now there was nothing left to break, and it completely removed the pressure to protect—to protect the other's feelings, to protect our own egos, to protect *Us*.

For the most part, there was no impetus to be cruel to the other. Neither Sam nor I went out of our way to hurt the other one, most of the time. We could each be snarky and defensive and occasionally loud, but it was rare that we were ever overtly aggressive in our truthfulness. We would talk until we couldn't take any more. We'd go to sleep and wake up and do it all again the next night.

Sam was drinking every night again. At first, a couple of beers. Within a few days, it was at least a six pack every night. Sometimes more.

And we both started smoking again. One or two cigarettes a night, then half a pack a day. We wouldn't smoke at the house during the day, and the children had no idea it was happening at all.

We were very careful to keep all of this away from them. We were polite and cordial around them. Sam was working from home most of the time, constantly in view of me and everything I was doing. I would leave during the day and go to a nearby park, cycling through phone calls with Tessa and Seth, relaying everything that was happening and every conversation between me and Sam.

I was constantly reliving every moment of my life, over and over.

_____

At our next session, Janet asked me again to agree not to speak to Alex. In exchange, Sam would agree to stay through the end of the year. She wanted us to give each other six months to try to make it work.

Sam reluctantly agreed that I could call Alex to tell him what was happening.

"I can't talk to you anymore," I told him one afternoon in late June.

"You knew that was probably coming."

"I know, but it hurts. I don't *want* you to be gone. I don't *want* to not be able to talk to you when I need you. And I do need you. Sam is convinced that my having contact with you will lead to more of the same, that it'll turn into more chat and sexting and everything else. I told him I feel confident that *that* part of our relationship is over."

Alex scoffed.

"What? You don't think that's done?"

"I think it's over because it has to be, Tierney. I think it's necessary with what's gone on. But I am confident about it? Absolutely not."

I was stunned, sitting in the parking lot of the grocery store. He'd given me no indication whatsoever that he still thought of me in that way. As far as I'd been able to tell from our few, brief conversations since I'd returned from Texas, I was nowhere in his private thoughts.

"Hopefully I can check in with you in a few months and let you know how things are," I said quietly. "I'm sorry."

"It's okay. I can't blame him. I hate it for you, but I'll be okay. I just want you to be safe and happy. I hope you guys can work this out."

I called Tessa in tears.

"I had to tell Alex goodbye."

"I'm sorry. You know it's probably best, Tierney."

"No, I don't! It might be best for Sam, but it sucks for me. It's like cutting out a piece of my fucking heart! I need him, and I need Sam. The *worst* part is that I'm not sure it will even help. I'm not sure I won't end up losing them both."

"Do you love him, Tierney?"

"Yes, you know I do, but not like that. I just—"

"No!" she pressed. "*Do you love him? Do you love Alex Wheeler?*"

Did I? I thought about him all the time. I missed him when he wasn't there. I didn't think about or plan for a future with him, but it was hard as hell to imagine my life without him. He knew me like no one else did, both in scale and scope of knowledge.

"I don't know," I whispered.

"Oh, Tierney...."

"Yep. And now I have to go to the doctor for all these tests."

"But you used a condom, right?"

I was silent.

"Tierney! No!"

"I didn't think I needed to! I trust him." It sounded stupid even to me, no matter how much I believed what I was saying.

Tessa laid into me, lecturing me about safe sex like I was a teenager. "This is *not* okay. We always use a condom. *Always.* No matter what. You know this!"

"Yeah, but—"

"No! No 'but'. *Always.*"

My gynecologist said pretty much the exact same thing.

Dr. Levin was perched on a stool at the end of the exam table, where I waited anxiously, covered by a blue paper sheet.

"Tierney, what's up? Didn't we just do your check-up?"

I nodded. "Um, I had unprotected sex with a man who wasn't my husband." I could feel my throat stinging and tried to smile through the first tears.

"More than one man?"

I shook my head. "Uh-uh. Just the one."

"And *why* didn't you use a condom?"

"I know him extremely well. I made the same judgment call with him that I would've made with any partner. I knew his sexual history, felt I could trust him to be clean, and it's the same decision I would have to make with any new partner."

"But this was the first time you had intercourse?"

I nodded.

"You should've used a condom." I sighed. "Even if you're right and there was no reason for worry about disease, you've been relying on a vasectomy for birth control. When I did your endometrial ablation three years ago, we didn't tie your tubes. Now that you've lost so much weight, your hormones are getting back to normal and your cycles are more regular, right?"

I nodded.

"You could still get pregnant. It would be harder for an embryo to implant, but it *can* happen."

"If it did? What would the pregnancy be like?"

"*Horrific*. You probably wouldn't be able to go full term. It would likely be catastrophic to the fetus, and it just might kill you in the process. If you're going to have sex with someone else who hasn't had a vasectomy, you need to use birth control or get your tubes tied." He stood and pushed the call button for his nurse. "Have you had a period since this happened?"

I counted back. My last period had started a week before I went to Pennsylvania. I was well over twenty-eight days, but that wasn't necessarily abnormal for me. Although the symptoms of PCOS were subsiding slowly with the weight loss, I still wasn't having a regular cycle like most women.

"No, but I never know when my period's going to start. And I don't *feel* pregnant."

More stupidity coming out of my mouth.

Dr. Levin looked at me sarcastically. "We'll do a test. Just to be sure."

I slid down the table and hooked my heels into the stirrups, submitting to the pelvic exam and multiple swabs for pathology slides. I'd been vigilant for years about my annual exams. After all of the fertility treatments and two child births, I wasn't the least bit uncomfortable with opening wide and doing what needed to be done. But *this*... I felt *dirty*, like I had after the rape.

Dr. Levin worked as quickly as possible. I was grateful he was supportive and never made me feel *judged* about having slept with someone else.

I peed in a cup and waited in a chair in the lab. The nurse dipped a plastic stick into the urine and set a small timer. She took several vials of blood and said they'd call me in a few days with the test results.

"It's negative," she said, "but we'll do a blood test, too, just in case."

Of course it's negative. This isn't a fucking soap opera.

I went home to wait.

I was waiting for test results. I was waiting for Sam to decide what he wanted to do. I was waiting for Alex not to be in my head all the damn time.

My head was in much the same fog as the spring, before the trip. I moved mechanically through my day of laundry and dishes and cooking and children, into my long, intense nights with Sam. I was always thinking and worrying and talking about my marriage and my affair.

I was always wondering about Alex.

———————————

"Can you come to Birmingham for some girl time?" Jules asked when she called on Tuesday.

She knew nothing of the problems Sam and I were having. I'd been relying heavily on Tessa and Seth to help me work through my head. In the back of my mind, I was still hoping Sam and I would be able to work through our problems and that I would never have to tell anyone else.

"Maybe. I can check with Sam and see if there's anything going on. I take it you're coming to town?"

"Yeah, I'm bringing Jason to stay with my mom for a couple of weeks. He doesn't have a day camp those weeks, and I'm teaching a mini-session. Grandma was kind enough to agree to see her favorite grandson."

"He's her *only* grandson, Jules."

"Doesn't mean he's not her favorite. I tried to call Frankie to see if she had plans, but I can't get ahold of her. Have you talked to her?"

"Not in weeks. I get a text message from her occasionally, but it's always just very vague and mundane, letting me know she's still alive. I've tried to call and email her but haven't gotten a response. I think it depends on Jay and what his mood is like."

Frankie and Jay had been married for thirteen years. We'd all known Jay Luna since college, but they hadn't dated until much, much later. I always thought he was a great guy. As their marriage progressed, though, Frankie had become more and more isolated from her oldest friends. I knew she was active with her girls' friends' mothers, but it didn't seem that she had much contact with the people she'd known before Jay. Our own relationship could be sporadic, with long stretches of weeks or months between phone calls. But we always managed to pick up right where we'd left off, no matter how long it had been since we'd last talked.

"Hmmmm," Jules said, "he's just a controlling prick, isn't he?"

"Honestly, I don't know what he is, Julesy. I worry about her, but she says she's okay when it comes up. I'll try to message her and tell her we're getting together. Hopefully she'll make it."

I tried to call and text Frankie. I let her know we were meeting at the Oasis on Friday night for drinks and general girl debauchery. I got no response.

I told Sam that I wanted to go to Birmingham for the weekend.

"My dad says he'll keep the kids. I'll spend the night at his house."

"Why are you going? Is there a show?"

I shrugged. "I could use a night away. I'm restless and stressed and could just use the time with my girls."

I knew what I was asking. It sounded like other trips, other weekends. I'd been paralyzed for days, trapped at home with Sam and his anger. If we were going to move forward and ever get off that goddamn back porch, he would have to understand that I wasn't the same girl I'd been a year before. I still needed to see and do things, to have experiences to understand, in order to feel like *me*.

The boys and I drove to Birmingham the next morning, taking our time to stop at the state line for snacks and drinks and a bathroom break. They watched a movie in the car, while I drove, tuning out the animated voices and trying to quiet my own thoughts.

"How are things with you and Sam?" Dad asked after we'd settled in at his house.

"Not great. We're back in counseling. He's drinking again." *I'm a cheating whore.*

Dad offered his support but no advice and no judgment.

I was all dolled up, wearing the same ensemble and pink, glittery shoes that I'd worn in San Antonio, the night Max and Alex and I went drinking. I was happy and sassy, and I messaged Alex without thinking.

Tierney Cavanaugh Johnson
July 3rd 6:34 PM

It's Glittery Girl Night! My pink shoes and I are headed out with Frankie and Jules, and I was thinking about you. Things here are okay. Hope you're well!

I left Dad's house and headed toward Southside, near downtown. I plugged my iPod to the car stereo and hit shuffle. "Dollface" came on, totally random. I squealed with delight and sang along, the music so loud it hurt my ears. On the third repeat, I heard my phone chirp with a push notification from Facebook, as I was exiting the interstate. I pulled into the parking lot where I was supposed to meet Jules.

Alex Wheeler
July 3rd 6:58 PM

Woke up this morning to an email from your husband asking me not to have contact with you. It was awesome. Ciao.

I stopped the song on its fourth play. I couldn't breathe.
Sam had emailed Alex. As far as I knew, it was the first time they'd made contact. Was he trying to antagonize him? I'd already agreed not to have contact with him.
But you found out about it when you messaged him, didn't you?
I started to cry, in the dark parking lot.

Tierney Cavanaugh Johnson
July 3rd 7:07 PM

I was so happy just half an hour ago, listening to Dollface over and over. Now I'm sitting in a parking lot, bawling my eyes out. It's not fair. It's not right.

I hoped that I could ignore it all, just for a little while. Jules would be there any minute to pick me up, and I had to calm the fuck down. Maybe by the time the night was over, it would've worked itself out and no one would be upset with me.

Jules showed up a few minutes later, and I got into her car to go to the Oasis.

"Hey, Kitten!" she said, turning the music down as I slid into her passenger seat. "How are you?"

"I'm okay," I lied.

"Did you ever hear from Frankie?"

"Nope. I let her know when and where but got *nada* from her."

Jules caught me up on Steve and Jason. She asked how Sam and the boys were. I said nothing, still, about what had been happening.

Jules parked across the street from the bar. We could hear the local band playing inside as we showed the doorman our IDs.

"Thank you for carding me," Jules said to the grungy-but-cute twenty-something.

"We have to card everyone—"

"*No*," she flirted pointedly, "you just can't believe your big, brown eyes that two hot chicks like us could be over twenty, isn't that right?"

He winked at her and laughed. "I know. I was *shocked* that you were *twenty-eight*."

I laughed and pushed her inside the dark, smoky bar.

"God, Julesy! Sometimes I don't know if I want to *be* you or *fuck* you!"

"There's no reason you can't do both, Kitten!"

I settled onto a high pub stool at a side table, while Jules ordered our first round of Jack and Ginger. I checked my messages, but there was no response from Alex.

"So Steve brought home a cat," Jules said. She put our glasses, overfilled with ice and fizzy, amber sweetness, onto the table.

I knew Jules wasn't the biggest fan of cats. "Um, sweet...?"

"Not really. It's this mean, ratty-looking, long-haired thing. I'm not even sure it *is* a cat, but he *swears* that's what it is."

"So does it have a name?" I laughed.

"Yeah," she grinned. "I named it Merkin, 'cause what else would you call an ugly-ass fake pussy?"

I roared with breathless delight. "*Oh my god!* I have missed you! You are *so* not right."

"Don't throw stones, Miss Glass House. You're one twisted-up little fucker yourself."

"No kidding. You know, I've been going back through all this shit in my life, all my baggage. Honestly, it's kind of surprising that I've made it this far. Molestation, divorce, rape, Damien. And that's just before I turned eighteen. Do *normal* people have this much shit to carry around, Jules?"

"I don't know, Kitten. I don't know if I want to. I'm no better than you—I was sexually assaulted, I was beaten up by a boyfriend, and I was on my third marriage by the time I turned thirty. I'm no judge of normal, that's for damn sure. I tend to avoid people who have no wear. I find them dull and pathetic. I don't really meet many people our age without a few tread marks across 'em. Those are the black-and-white folks. You, me... we're the hazy grays. Sometimes I do feel darker than others, though."

"Instead of gray, can I be, like, *pewter*? That's *much* more interesting, with a little sparkle."

"*Shit*, Kitten! You are pewter with silver and platinum polka dots, leaving a trail of glitter everywhere you go!"

"Like a glitter slug?"

Jules thought for a moment, poised dramatically with her drink in her hand. "Can you still kill it with salt?"

"Only if there's a lime," I offered, toasting the air with my drink.

I was still giggling as Jules looked pensive, mulling some comment to fruition. "You and I have very similar histories, though certainly not identical. But what connects us is the *journey*, not the path. We all hit different road hazards. Some people limp down the road on flat tires, just hoping to find shelter. Some of us convert that wrecked piece of shit into a monster truck and blaze on down the trails, *Road Warrior* style. Everyone our age has damage, even if that damage is not having any mileage by the age of forty."

"Those are the dull and pathetic."

Jules nodded in agreement, eyes scanning the crowd. "But even the shelter seekers can appreciate the damage and applaud the road warriors. They get the vicarious victory."

"Sometimes I just need a detour, though, Jules. Maybe there'll be some unexpected beauty right around the bend; maybe there are just a bunch of ruts. But sometimes I *need* a little side trip down a dirt road, just to see what's there."

"There's nothing wrong with that, Kitten. Just be sure not to get stuck in a mud hole."

Jules glanced toward the door. "*Frankie!*" she called loudly. Half the crowd turned to see what was the matter.

Frankie stopped in her tracks and beamed at us with her girliest grin. Jules skipped over to her, hugging her and spinning her around.

"Hello, gorgeous!" Frankie cooed.

Jules motioned for the bartender to bring a third drink and ushered Frankie to our table.

"Yay! You made it!" I said excitedly.

"I wasn't sure I was gonna. I'm sorry I didn't get back to you. It's been a crazy week!"

"What's going on, Moonshine?"

Frankie took a deep breath, exasperated. She looked beautiful but tired. Her brilliant blue eyes were shadowed below, and her hair was pulled into the convenient Mom ponytail.

"Jay was being an *ass*," she started. "It's *summer*. The girls are out of school. *I* am out of school for two months. We should be able to sit around and do *nothing* once in a while, you know? But he has it in his head that we're home all the time, so we should be able to do *do* more."

"Like what?"

"He got upset with me last night because dinner wasn't ready when he got home at five thirty. Keep in mind, we don't normally eat during the school year until six thirty because of our schedule. *'But you're home now, Frankie, you could at least have dinner ready when I walk in the door!'* Fuck you, *twatwad*!"

"I never really thought of Jay as the fix-me-a-pot-pie-bitch type," I remarked.

Frankie shook her head at me. "He never has been. I don't know what the fuck is up with him. I asked him about going out tonight, to make sure he didn't have something else planned for us. He didn't, but he wouldn't agree to keep the girls. I had to take them to my sister's house for the night, just to be able to go out."

"What's Jay doing while you're out?"

"I have no idea, honestly. He was still at home, watching baseball, when I left. I haven't a *clue* what he was doing tonight." She finally hung her purse on the back of her seat and took a drink. "Enough about me! I haven't talked to you since you got back from San Antonio! How was your trip? Did you hang with the rock stars?"

I looked from Frankie to Jules and back again, and I started to cry.

I tried to hold it in. I'd been trying for an hour not to lose it, since I'd gotten the message from Alex. Jules and Frankie's faces fell into immediate worry.

"Kitten, what is it?"

"San Antonio was great. I got there, saw the rock stars, fucked Alex Wheeler, got drunk, pissed him off, came home, and Sam found out and wants a divorce."

I'd been careful not to discuss my relationship with Alex with anyone but Tessa and later Seth. Even Seth only knew a little bit. I knew Jules and Frankie wouldn't judge me, no matter how shocked I was sure they would be. Jules had been on both sides of relationship weirdness, and she would never tell me to do anything but to zealously protect my own heart. Frankie had her own tensions in her marriage and would understand completely why I'd been blinded by need of someone other than Sam.

They were stunned in their bafflement. I had told them nothing about Alex, nothing about what had been going on for months. I couldn't keep it in any longer. I started at the beginning, back to October and meeting at the Masquerade, the night in Montevallo, the night in Chicago, and all the nights after.

"You know," Jules said, "I wondered that night at your dad's, when you mentioned Alex. But it seemed pretty benign, so I didn't push it."

I nodded. "It'd been going on for weeks by then. And things with Sam have been *bad*. Long before Alex and not because of him. Alex had nothing to do with my marriage falling apart."

"Well, this can't have helped but push that along."

"Absolutely. But Sam had walked the fuck out long before I ever met Alex Wheeler."

Frankie thought for a moment. "Are you *sure* he wants a divorce?" she asked carefully. "I mean, has he filed for separation or anything?"

I shrugged. "I don't think he has. He says he's moving out, though. I don't know if or when. I don't know how the hell I'll get through this. How I'll get the *kids* through this."

"Do the boys know?"

I shook my head.

"Have you talked to Alex? Does he know?" Jules asked.

I nodded. "I got a message from him right before you got there to pick me up. Apparently Sam emailed him and asked him not to contact me again."

"*Eeek!* What did he say?"

"No idea. I haven't seen the message. And now Alex isn't responding to me."

"Will he do that? Will he drop contact with you because Sam asked him to?"

"Fuck if I know. I don't know why Princess Asshat does half the shit he does."

Jules caught the bartender's eye and ordered another round. "Doubles!" she called over the music.

"Oh, Kitten. I'm so sorry."

I smiled weakly at my friends, who looked back at me, mute. They had no idea what to say.

"Well, it just goes to show that sometimes you have no fucking clue what's really going on behind closed door," Frankie said. "Sometimes, it's like a tornado. You don't really know there's a problem until you *see* the shit start flying around."

The boys and I went back to Atlanta the next morning. We had plans to spend the Fourth of July as a family, watching fireworks from the seventy-second story of the Westin Hotel. The Sun Dial lounge, adjacent to the revolving Sun Dial restaurant, was hosting a family-friendly, gourmet, indoor cook-out. Mini-brats and sliders and housemade chips. All the cookies and lemonade the boys could stand. And we wouldn't have to fight the crowds or the swelter in Centennial Olympic Park. We would be in air conditioning, looking just below to the city's largest fireworks display.

The boys were giddy with excitement. They loved the ride in the great glass elevator on the outside of the hotel. We ate early in the evening, then wandered around downtown with the boys, walking slowly between rain showers from the hotel to Centennial Park and back. From so high up, we could see fresh summer storms firing up in the distance as nightfall approached. Lightning crackled across the sky as we watched a dozen different fireworks shows around the Atlanta metro.

"It's not pretty!" Tripp crowed. "It's awesome!"

It was hard not to remember that the Fourth of July was its own anniversary for Sam and me. It was the night we'd gotten engaged. Half-drunk and splayed in the middle of the floor of our tiny apartment, griping about eligibility for student loans for school in the fall, I'd suggested that it would be much easier to qualify if we got married.

"Okay, when?" Sam had asked from the couch.

"Two weeks from Friday."

"Okay."

When we'd woken the next morning, I'd turned to Sam and asked, "Are we really doing this?"

We were married on July 22nd. It was a month before I turned twenty-two, and Sam was twenty-three.

At the Westin, I tried to be affectionate with Sam, but not pushy, at least in front of the boys. He was curt and easily irritated, and he stymied my affection with cold distance.

That night, on the deck after the boys had gone to bed, I brought up his message to Alex.

"Look, I don't want to be mad about this for days. I don't want to seethe about this and just be angry. Did you email Alex?"

"Yes. I was going to tell you when you got home, but there wasn't time before we left to go downtown."

"Okay." I tried to stay calm. "What did you email him?"

"I just asked him to please give us space and time to try to heal, to not contact you and not to respond if you contacted him. Obviously he didn't respect my request. He didn't respond to me, either."

"Sam, I messaged him, just a hello to check in. He replied that he you'd asked him not to make contact, but he didn't say anything else."

"Why did you message him?" Sam demanded. "You said you weren't going to contact him again!"

Old habits and all that jazz.

"I don't know. I didn't mean to. I wasn't thinking about it and just did it. I'm sorry."

"Tierney, we can't move forward if you keep going back to him!"

"I'm sorry."

Sam was quiet for a moment. "I was going to tell you about it. You just found out before I could."

I had no right to be angry. He'd asked me—and I'd agreed—to stay away from the man I had an affair with. It seemed the logical, practical, caring thing to do, if I ever wanted my husband to forgive me and move on. But my message wasn't asking Alex to call me or fuck me or tell me he loved me. I just wanted to say hi to my friend.

Bullshit, Tierney.

Sam's emailing Alex, though, crossed some weird, imaginary boundary. Sam knew who Alex was, though they'd never met. He knew a little bit about him, from funny anecdotes and relaying of benign conversations I'd had with Alex. Alex knew substantially more about Sam, albeit almost all through me. There'd been so much effort to keep them apart, and Sam had stepped all over that.

"I can't keep doing this, Tierney."

I looked at him, sitting in his chair just a foot from mine. He might as well have been a mile away.

"I spent last night and this morning going over our financials. I tracked down paperwork and statements and made sure I had valid logins for all of our accounts. I'll need you to look at it and make sure I didn't miss anything. I have to get it done, so I can start looking for a rental house. I'm trying to find something affordable that's still in the school district. It'll make transporting the boys from house to house easier."

"I don't want this," I cried. "I don't want to be apart."

"You don't want to be married, either, Tierney."

"That's not true!" *Maybe it is.* "Is it really what you want? Do you *want* me to be without me? I'm a big girl. I *will* go on with my life. Are you gonna be able to handle watching me move on and find someone else and fall in love again?"

He was silent for a moment, drinking his beer. "No. Not especially. But I can't be your second choice. I can't live like that."

"You're not my second choice. You never were! I always wanted to be with you, even when things were at their worst." *Almost completely true.* "You've been my first choice since I was fourteen."

"Tierney, by the age we were married, virtually everyone is someone's second chance at love, romance, sex, or whatever. By 'second choice', I mean that priority wasn't given to me. Since late last year, I felt like no matter what I did—drink, not drink, spend time at work or home, with you or not—I wasn't making you happy. I couldn't. At least not happy enough to make you think of me and *us* as your priority."

"Bu—"

He raised his voice just enough to shut me down. "I feel cheated, in part, because you pursued me once, from Birmingham to Huntsville. But when you had the energy and desire to pursue someone or something different, you didn't direct that at me. You'd given up on that, even if there were plenty of signs that said you shouldn't have. Both of us said this was what we wanted. I feel like if you had taken that energy, especially the part of it you had when we were recovering, and directed it toward pursuing *us*, I would've been able to amplify it and return it. Instead you directed all of that energy away from me. It was time and money and attention that you turned away from us and spent it pursuing someone and something else that was much farther away and much less likely."

"Nothing was ever going to happen with him. I always knew there was no future with Alex."

"It was a long shot," Sam replied, "but you were closer to it than to me, even when we were closest."

He opened another beer.

We sat in silence for long minutes.

"You're absolutely right," I said eventually. "I hadn't been happy for a really long time. I didn't like you. I didn't *trust* you. And then something else was unexpectedly holding my attention. That something had set rules from the beginning, and I almost always knew where I stood with it. It didn't make me happy, per se, from the beginning, but kept me occupied and entertained."

Sam snorted derisively.

"It also dragged me through some heavy emotional and psychic bullshit, because it was obsessive and difficult and definitely addictive. When it was on, it was a huge high, but the come-down could be wretched and last for days."

"There's a fine line between addiction and love, Tierney."

"Yep, and it's hard to see it when you're in it. You didn't see the bad choices you made when you were drinking."

"But I *quit* drinking! For you and the boys! I *stopped*! We started counseling, and I thought we were having the best time of our marriage, maybe ever. It didn't matter what I did to try and make you happy. You went and fucked him anyway!"

"What did you *do*, Sam? I may have been tied up in your decision not to drink, but I fully believe it only happened because of what the boys said to my dad. And all quitting drinking did was take the smell of beer off your breath! All of that time and energy you had from not drinking went straight into your work! You were still a dick to us most of the time, especially to me, if you even paid attention to me. It felt masochistic to even try to reach out to you. If all I was getting was hurt or rejected, there was no sane reason for me to even fucking try!

"I quit pursuing you, yes," I continued, my words getting louder and echoing through the darkness. "You did the same! You had backed away from me and totally let go until I got in your face and demanded you go to counseling and try! I *begged* you to put up a fight—"

"I did fight, Tierney! I was fighting—"

"Your fight was to make *me* fight, Sam! You were passively pulling me back to you. You weren't coming after *us*; you were yelling for me to come back. I was yelling back for you to hold on, to give me a minute, but neither of us could hear the other."

"You went to Texas to *fuck another man*! You chose someone else!"

"No, I didn't!"

"*You didn't go fuck Alex Wheeler?*"

"Yes! Yes, Sam, I *knew* I would likely sleep with him when I went to San Antonio. I knew full well I was betraying you and our marriage when I did it."

"And I was never supposed to know!"

"*Exactly!* The risk and the gravity and the damage were worth it, when *I* was the only one who was supposed to get hurt! I was the only one who was ever supposed to carry the burden of my consequence."

"But you chose him, and I'm the one paying the consequence!"

"I didn't choose him over you! I chose *me* over anything and everything else. I was hurting and reeling and *dying* inside for months and maybe years, because I'd never, ever had anything that was mine *alone*—something bigger than me and outside of me that no one else had a say in how I did it. This was the *one time* in my adult life that I felt a moment of utterly selfish control. I could have something only because I wanted it. *And it wanted me back!* I met this challenge on solid ground that I'd never stood on before, and I was faced by someone else who fully understood all of those ramifications and didn't judge me any more than I judged him."

"If you had *told* me, Tierney, if you had just *said* there was something there that you wanted to explore—"

"What? You'd have done *what* with that? Told me it was okay? Told me to go fuck another man?"

Sam gripped his beer tighter in his fist. "I don't know! We'll never know. You didn't give me the chance to handle it. You just hid it from me!"

"The primary goal wasn't to hide it from you; it was to keep it to myself, where no one else could touch it. If was going to be damaged, it would be because Alex and I made the choices that led to that, not because someone else stepped in and took it from me."

If Sam was second to anyone, it wasn't to Alex—it was to *me*. I wasn't sure I would ever be able to totally overcome that. I am selfish and demanding, but that wasn't anything he hadn't always known. I still felt like I was drowning, though. I couldn't see around the bend, to tell where I was laying this path I was on, but I didn't feel like it was *my* path, to what was right for me. When I felt that fear, that instability, *that* was when I was most likely to get myself into trouble.

For months, when I'd felt like this, I would turn to Alex for advice. I may or may not have gotten answers, but he had the ability to talk me through my own head and calm me down to look for my own truths. Alex had always pushed and supported me to do what was best for me, above everything else, because I deserved to be happy and not feel perpetually like a martyr. He told me time and again that my doing what made me truly happy and fulfilled would, in turn, bring my children into a happier place, away from the difficulty and tension we'd all felt for so long. If that meant I was painting and away from Sam, so be it. But the real, best goal was to heal our marriage and be happy with my husband and my family while still painting and achieving my own, personal goals, whatever they might be. Never once did Alex suggest I do anything less than try my hardest to be *healthy*.

I wanted Sam to be able to do that, and I wished I knew how to tell him to do it. I knew Sam wanted to feel my energy being used on him and not feel like my time and emotion and effort were going elsewhere. I couldn't put all of my energy into him and us and not put some of it into *me*. I couldn't give away all of me and have nothing left to show, nothing with my stamp and my mark on it. That wasn't fair, and it was potentially unhealthy.

As long as I felt like I could talk to Sam and say what I was thinking, even if he didn't like it, I would keep talking and bringing my fear to him instead of Alex. The moment I felt like I was making him angry or judgmental or hurting him, I knew I would shut down, especially if I felt like my truthfulness was about to ricochet back toward me. Sam would have to decide if he could accept the risk of my getting all truthy and his hearing things he didn't like. I could turn to him or go elsewhere, but it had to come out, no matter what.

"I love you," I said, quietly crying. "I didn't want to hurt you. I don't want to keep hurting you."

"I need to be able to get over this," Sam said finally. "I need a break, a definitive date, to tie to it all being finished, a place to be able to move on *from*. Maybe we'll be apart and be able to find our way back to each other. I don't know. But I'm never going to know unless I do this."

"Okay. If this is what you need, I'll support it. Let me know what you need from me."

I stood from my chair and went into the house, straight down the hall to my bed.

Chapter 21

Sam informed me that he'd contacted a divorce attorney. It was probably a good idea for me to do the same. I found the name Tessa had gotten for me in December and made the call.

Elizabeth was very nice. During our initial phone conversation, she was supportive but no-nonsense. I was open about the affair, but I also made sure she knew Sam had a history of drinking problems.

"In Georgia," she explained, "adultery will only keep you from getting alimony. It doesn't impact division of assets or child support or custody. Judges don't really care about it, and they honestly don't want to hear it. With your husband's drinking, do you feel that you or your children are in danger?"

"No. He's a great, loving father. I mean, I wouldn't want to leave them alone with him if he were drunk. That would just be negligent on my part, as a parent. But he doesn't get out of control or abusive or anything when he's drinking."

"Well, it could become an issue if there were to be disagreement about custody. Unless he can show that you're an unfit mother—and the adultery doesn't make you unfit in the eyes of the court—then you'd likely get primary custody, with liberal visitation for Sam."

That was how my own parents had structured their custody arrangement, and I expected to have something similar. I'd been the boys' primary caregiver for their entire lives. There was no reason to think I wouldn't have them with me most of the time, alternating weekends and vacations and holidays with their dad.

"I would be happy to take your case, Tierney. I can email you the service agreement. You can return it to me with a two-thousand dollar retainer. Unless it becomes contentious, I think that would probably cover your entire divorce, though I can't guarantee it."

I didn't know how I was going to pay for this. Yes, it would have to eventually come out of marital funds, but I didn't want to create an unnecessary burden on our cash flow. Sam was trying to get the cash together to set up housekeeping elsewhere, which would take at least a couple thousand dollars. He would have his own attorney's fees, and I'd just cost him thousands of dollars for travel and the ransom to Digital Freedom Front. I knew I would likely have to trade marital assets to cover that debt.

I called my dad at work.

"Can you talk?" I asked.

"Yeah, what's up? Are you okay?"

"Not really." I started to choke up. "Um, Sam and I are separating. He's filing for divorce." I wasn't prepared to go into the details.

"I'm sorry, Tierney. I knew you guys were having problems."

"We've been in counseling for weeks. It's been a really long month." I swallowed, trying to stop the tears. "I'm calling 'cause I need money for a retainer. I got a referral for an attorney. She seems really nice and came highly recommended."

"How much do you need?"

"Two thousand dollars. I hate to even ask you, but I don't want to ask him to pay for it right now."

"You know you have every right to take the money from joint funds, right?"

"I know I can use our joint money, but I don't want to have to get into with him. He's trying to find a place to live, and that'll take cash."

"Just do what every other woman does," my dad joked. "Clear out the bank account before he can do anything!"

I didn't know if he was referencing my mom or my ex-stepmom, and I didn't care. I knew it was Dad's attempt at a little levity, but it irritated the shit out of me.

"I won't be that girl," I replied. "He's still my children's father, and I don't want to be a complete bitch about it."

Dad agreed to send me a check to cover the retainer. I stressed that I was not yet ready to tell anyone else in the family, including my mom. I wasn't ready to answer their questions and face their disappointment. I didn't want to hear my mother's judgmental tone.

Dr. Levin's office called almost as soon as I hung up with my dad.

"Tierney, all of your test results were negative. You're not pregnant, and there's no sign of an STD. Everything's fine."

I knew it would be.

From: Alex Wheeler
Date: July 9th 10:22 PM
To: Tierney Cavanaugh Johnson
Subject: u ok?

??

From: Tierney Cavanaugh Johnson
Date: July 9th 10:28 PM
To: Alex Wheeler
Subject: RE: u ok?

Not especially. I'm a crying mess right now.

From: Alex Wheeler
Date: July 9th 10:34 PM
To: Tierney Cavanaugh Johnson
Subject: RE: u ok?

Call me.

> "I have an email from Alex, checking on me. He wants me to call him."
> Sam nodded. "I sent him a message and told him you could probably use your friends right now."
> I was surprised. Sam had been adamant, again, that he didn't want me having contact with Alex. He'd reached out to him, again, without telling me, and it was a complete about-face from the last time, just a week before.
> I went into the bedroom and closed the door. I dialed Alex's number.
> "Hey, how are you?" he asked as he answered.
> "I've been better."
> "What happened?"
> "Sam is filing for divorce," I sniffled. "He's met with an attorney, and I've made contact with mine."
> "Jeez. I'm sorry, Tierney, but you knew it would likely come to this."

"I just don't know if I can do it, Alex. I don't know if I can start my fucking life over. The thought of doing it all again, of starting that search for someone and dating and all of that... it just makes me sick."

"Well, it's not like you gotta run right out and get remarried, Buttercup."

"I know, but I'm me, you know? I'm an almost-middle-aged mom of two with a fat ass and no job and doing *what* with her fucking life. Honestly, I can't imagine that I'll ever be happy again. Not right now."

"No, *stop*. Don't do that."

"Do what?"

"Don't let *this*, don't let the divorce make you feel *small*. You are an intelligent, attractive, amazing woman, and you will go on to have a great life, even if it's without Sam. You will take care of your boys, and you will be fine."

"Really?" I scoffed. "What the fuck am I gonna do, Alex? I didn't finish college. I haven't had a real job in ten years. How the fuck am I going to take care of my boys?"

"You'll *paint*, and you'll be *great*." I smiled a little to myself, hearing him. "As far as money goes, you'll be fine. You'll get half of his money, and he'll have to pay you to take care of his children."

"My attorney says I don't get alimony, if he files on grounds of adultery."

"Will he do that?"

"I don't know. He says he doesn't want to. He said that he's willing to file as irrevocably broken or whatever, as long as I don't try to screw him. He doesn't want there to be a public record of the adultery, in case the children go back looking for it later."

"I'm sorry. Is he drinking again?"

"Yep. All the time. Every night, and it's my fault."

"No," Alex admonished, "it's *not* your fault. He's a grown man, and he made the choice to drink again. You didn't make him."

"I might as well have. I fucking cheated and lied, again and again. *I* did that. *I* drove him back to the place where he wanted to drink again. That's my fucking fault."

Alex sighed into the phone. "I owe him an apology. I know I do. I can't email him, though. I'll have to see him face-to-face sometime and tell him I'm sorry and let him punch me in the fucking face."

"No...."

"Yeah, Tierney. I shouldn't have stepped into your marriage. I owe him that much."

"But this wasn't about him or my marriage, and you know it! This was about you and me, and it had nothing to do with him."

"Yep. I know. But I still owe him an apology. Man to man."

Really? And do I owe Talia the same? Maybe I would if she ever found out.

"As much as I hate to let you go, I'm fucking frazzled. I need to go to sleep and forget my fucking life for a while."

"Okay. Let me know how you are."

"I will. Thanks for calling." *I love you.*

"Bye."

"Bye."

That night I dreamed of Alex. I saw him in a dark room, little by a dark orange spotlight, in the corner. His hair was shorter than it had been in May, like it was the night I first met him. He was singing, his mouth moving half a second ahead of the sound. "Let Me Lie to You" by the Afghan Whigs, singing of shattered trust and deception.

All of this was happening less than two weeks before our seventeenth wedding anniversary.

Talking on the deck one night, I told Sam how I kept seeing us a gingerbread people, fallen flat and shattered into pieces.

"There's this red string, running from you to me. I'm wrapping it around the pieces, trying to put them back and bind us together, so we don't lose each other again."

"What's the string?" he asked.

"Hope? Love? I don't know."

"If you unravel the string, it will all fall apart again."

"Then we each have to hang onto our threads and not let go."

I wasn't even sure the red string would be strong enough to hold us together until we could heal. No matter how much we recovered from this, we would never be the same. There would be scars. Maybe they'd only be visible to us, but we would feel the pull against them for a long time, each time we tried to stretch or move.

I went to the craft store and bought an unfinished wooden frame, twelve inches square. I picked up two skeins of thin, tight red yarn, the kind that was unlikely to fray easily.

I spent an hour or two every day for a week, wrapping the yarn around and around the frame. I would watch television at the kitchen table while my wrist moved mechanically, pulling the yarn through the opening, around the wood, back through the opening, and pulling it taut, covering every bit of the wood. After I finished wrapping it in one direction, I wrapped it perpendicularly, creating a crosshatch pattern in the yarn. It took nearly ten hours to complete.

I planned to give it to Sam for our anniversary. Even though he said he wanted to separate, I could sense the waiver in his resolve. I hoped that I could push him, just a little, and get him to reconsider. There was a blank, gray wall in our bedroom. I planned to hang the frame there, in the center, with nothing inside. When the time came, I would tell him, we would choose the right picture to go inside. Together.

Even if Sam and I weren't able to find a way to reconcile, I wanted to be able to spend our last anniversary together. I expected to cry a lot, and I planned to get drunk. I didn't want the children to have to see any of that. I made plans to meet my dad on Saturday, the morning before the actual date, and bring the boys to him. I got back home around nine o'clock.

Sam was on the deck, halfway to drunk and listening to music. I smoked a cigarette with him and started drinking Jack and Ginger, as quickly as I could stomach. I changed the music to my own playlist of break-up and heartache songs, singing through my numb lips. I didn't care if I was off-key or if it bothered the neighbors. I just needed to sing and be sad with my husband.

I brought the red-wrapped frame outside and handed it to him, unceremoniously.

"I made it for you."

I didn't have to explain it.

Finally, close to midnight, I said, "I don't want to split up, Sam. You know that. I think it's fucking stupid. I love you, and you love me. We have a great life, here in this house, with our beautiful boys. If we did nothing else right in our lives, we made those two beautiful babies. And they were absolutely born out of our love. I think there's so much more that can happen for us, but we both have to be willing to work.

"Even if you don't want to be with me for the rest of your life, you should be with me tonight. It's our anniversary, and it could be our last. You should come to bed and be with your wife."

Sam looked at me in the tiki torch light. He said nothing.

"I'm going to lie down. You know where I'll be if you want me."

I waited for a while in the bed, lying in the dark and listening to the muffled music from outside. Sometime after midnight, I fell asleep.

I woke just after two when Sam got into the bed next to me. I turned my head toward him but said nothing. I could just make out his silhouette next to me.

He reached his hand for me.

I rolled toward him and kissed his mouth. He didn't kiss me back, but he didn't try to stop me. I kissed him again, moving my hand toward his face. I felt him wince in the dark. I snaked my tongue along the edge of his mouth, and he slowly parted his lips to let me in.

We hadn't been together in weeks. We took our time, kissing and touching and feeling each other. We spent long moments rediscovering the other—how we felt and tasted and aligned ourselves best.

We made love until we passed out. We woke mid-morning and did it again.

"Happy anniversary," I whispered, snuggling naked and against him.

He kissed the back of my neck and wrapped his arms around me.

"I'm hungry," I commented. "Would you like to take your wife to lunch?"

"I would. That would be nice."

I took a shower and picked a pretty dress to wear out with my husband. He was waiting for me on the deck, smoking a cigarette.

"You know," I started, "the boys won't be home until tomorrow afternoon. We could catch a flight and go somewhere—Atlantic City maybe?—and renew our vows. Just us. No one else."

He didn't say anything for a long while. "I don't think I'm ready, Tierney. I can't be sure yet, and I don't want to give either if us false hope."

For him, it was important to know he was okay enough to recommit to me. For me, I hoped that by making the public commitment, I would be okay with moving forward with him.

"It's okay," I said. "It was just a thought. When you're ready, know it's an option. Any time."

He nodded and stood to kiss me.

We went to a favorite Mexican restaurant for lunch. We split a pitcher of sangria, though I drank most of it.

"You look really pretty in that dress, by the way."

I smiled at him across the table. "Thank you, baby. I feel pretty."

"If we weren't sitting in this restaurant, I'd fuck you right now. On this table."

Hm! "You could take me home and do that."

"I might. But I think we have some errands to run."

I looked at him quizzically. He signed the check and stood, offering me his hand.

"What do we have to do?"

"You'll see."

We did go back to the house, briefly. He worked me up, and I thought for sure we were about to have sex on the kitchen counter. He reached under my skirt and pulled my panties off.

"Okay, let's go."

What? You're stopping now?! "Where are we going?"

"To buy an anniversary present."

"Can I have my panties back?"

"Nope."

I grinned evilly. "So you're taking your wife out in a pretty dress with no panties. To go shopping?"

He nodded innocently. "Yes."

He drove us to the toy store.

It was the same store I'd shopped in months before, looking for the glass wand for me and Alex. I didn't tell Sam. It was just a store, after all.

He walked me along each aisle, looking at everything. We touched and felt and played with everything that was open. We laughed at the improbable devices. I couldn't help but notice things I *knew* Alex would love.

We finally chose two new toys to add to our box. I was excited and offered to try them out on the drive home.

"No, Mrs. Johnson, you have to wait. We're not done yet."

He took me to finish real errands. Two more stores. Short summer dress and no panties. I was careful to keep my skirt down, careful to keep away from too many people in case someone bumped me the wrong way. I held tightly to the edges of my dress as we left the store, trying to keep the hot, summer breeze from giving me a Marilyn Monroe moment. He slid his hand under my skirt, careful not to let me expose too much while we were driving through Atlanta traffic.

"I don't need to get arrested," he said, pulling my skirt back down.

We fucked like animals when we got home. We got dressed near nightfall and went out for a while. We came home and did it all again. And again. There were new things—and new toys—we both wanted to try.

Sam and I were going to be okay.

―――――――――――

I was happy again, whirling through our life dizzily. I relished in the day-to-day with the boys, with Sam working from home most of the time. We couldn't stop touching each other at night. I found the cover of darkness freeing, loosening any sense of inhibition. I was regularly naked and exhibitive on the deck, late at night.

"You should get in touch with Alex," he said.

What?! "No. You don't want that."

"I do," he assured me. "I think you need him. I think he's good for your psyche. I just need to know what's going on and when."

"So now, after everything, you're saying it's *okay* for me to talk to Alex?" He nodded. "I don't know if I'm comfortable with that."

"Why?" He seemed surprised.

"Because I don't know if I can have a normal relationship with him. There's so much sexual tension between us. Even on the phone. Especially on the phone. I don't know if I can have regular conversations with him and not have them end up inappropriate."

"It's okay, Tierney. As long as I know what's going on, it's okay. As long as I know you love me and you're here with me, I'm okay with you and Alex talking. It's like I told you, and like I told India, as long as I *know* what's happening, I'm fine with it. There's no reason you can't have a potentially sexual relationship with another person. Neither of us believes in a moral or religious reason for monogamy."

He was dangling the forbidden fruit before me. Was it a trap? Was he testing me to see if I would bite?

I wanted to talk to Alex. I missed my friend. I missed our easy conversation and connection. But I also knew that I was a breath away from two fingers inside me if he called me Buttercup.

"No," I reiterated. "I can't do that to you."

Sam stood and pulled me to face him. "Tierney, I promise. It's okay. If you want to talk to him, if you need him in your life, I can handle it."

From: Tierney Cavanaugh Johnson
Date: August 4th 11:08 AM
To: Alex Wheeler
Subject:

Things here are much, much better. Sam has cleared me for contact. He's okay with my talking to you, no matter what. You know where to find me.

Alex Wheeler
Aug 4th 11:22 AM

yo

Hey!

can u talk?

"So what the hell happened now?"

I told him everything that had happened, how Sam and I had come to the understanding on our anniversary that we loved each other, no matter what. I explained that we had decided to hold off on any kind of divorce proceeding. Sam wasn't moving out, and I wasn't trying to plan a life without him.

"That's awesome, Tierney. I'm really happy for you. I hope you guys can work all of this out. Are you guys still in therapy?"

"No. After he told me he was filing, I didn't see a point in going back. I think we'll probably find a new therapist, someone who doesn't already know our problems. I think we both want a fresh start."

"But he says you can talk to me?"

"Yep. As long as he knows about it."

"This makes me uncomfortable," Alex said.

"Why? If you're not comfortable talking to me, that's an entirely different thing. I'll understand. But he's totally okay with it."

"No, of course I want to talk to you! I just don't trust this shift in attitude. It's pretty sudden."

"I think it's sincere, honestly. We've had hours and hours and hours of talk about everything. *Everything*. He gets that I need to be doing stuff on my own, just for me, and away from him and the boys. He said he knows that you're good for my psyche. But I told him I was a little afraid to talk to you."

Alex chuckled. "Why?"

"Because we both know it would take me five minutes to pull you back in. I could drop into that voice—" I shifted into the sexy tone "—and you can't resist it. If I moan and whisper in just the right way, we're back at it."

"You think so?" he mused.

"Uh-huh."

"You're crazy!" He was laughing, but he didn't deny it.

"That's why you love me!"

It was so easy to flirt with him. I could flip that switch inside myself, turn it on with one beat of my heart, and I was the naughty girl he'd first encountered.

"Maybe. But now I have to go work for a while."

"You have fun with that."

He laughed again. "Later, Buttercup."

And there it is!

I went home and told Sam immediately about the conversation.

"He can't resist you," he said. "It's hard to, I know."

"And what if he can't? What if it goes there again? Do you want me to stop?"

Sam shrugged. "You don't have to. As long as I know about it."

Alex Wheeler
Aug 4th 2:35 PM

Sam agrees that ten minutes was never enough time.

nope nowhere close

It would take hours. 5-6 at least.

at least. maybe days

I'm so tempted to tell you what I bought last weekend.

im tempted to tell u what im doing
right now

Call me?

I was sitting in my car, in the parking lot of the park, on a hot summer afternoon. It was mostly deserted, but a few people were kicking around a soccer ball on the field, in the distance. I answered on the first ring.

"Let me guess. European lesbian schoolgirl porn. And one of them has a strap-on."

"You know me well."

"Where are you?" I asked.

"Chicago."

"Are you gonna find some girl to fuck in the basement of the Double Door?"

"Only if she's you, Buttercup."

"Really?" I teased. "I have a hard time believing that. I think you'd be just as happy with one of those lesbian schoolgirls. Especially if she has a strap-on."

"The lesbian schoolgirl is *hot*, no doubt, and she makes my dick hard, but it's not her I thought about all those nights in my bunk on the bus. You *know* it's you I wanted to bend over that chair in the dressing room."

"Yeah?" I purred. "What would you do with me, Rock Star?"

He sighed deeply into the phone. "I'd put my foot between your boots and shove your legs apart. Then I'd yank your skirt up and *rip* your goddamn panties off."

"*Mmmm....*"

"Push two fingers in that hot, tight twat as deep as I could, then my thumb in your ass."

"Can I rub my clit while you're doing this?"

"*No, Buttercup, you cannot touch your clit!*"

"But it's so *swollen* and *hard*."

"Not as hard as my cock right now."

"You're killing me, Alex...." I squirmed in the front seat of my car, totally unable to do anything with the pounding heat between my legs.

"I bet that girl's strap-on is even harder."

"*Oooooh,* that would be *so good*, to watch her slam you from behind while you sucked my cock."

"Yeah? You wanna watch the pretty girl fuck me with her big, fake cock while you fuck my face?"

"*Yeahyeahyeah....*" His breathing was deep and uneven.

"And if I'm bent over the chair, I can reach between your legs and put my finger in your ass while your cock is down my throat. Two fingers, and you can think about her fucking you with that strap-on."

He groaned hard and gasped, and I knew he'd come, listening to me.

"Oh," I purred, "you've missed me."

"God, you know I have!" he breathed hoarsely, brutally sincere.

I grinned to myself. "You've missed my whorey little mouth."

He chuckled throatily. "Yep. But I've missed you, too."

"Goddamn! I'm in a fucking parking lot, talking to you while you get off. Yet again, there's no way I get to come! You owe me, Princess."

"Nope. Go home and get those new toys and tell me how they are. What did you get by the way?"

"*Oh!* A *lovely* new glass wand—it's all clear pink and curvy and bumpy and insanely good. And, um, a little pink butt plug."

"You've tried them both?"

"Shit, Princess, I was barely out of the parking lot of the store when I was checking them out."

"And Sam has seen them?"

"Yeah, he bought them for me. It's a completely different thing now. *All the damn time.* Anything I want. Everything I *ever* wanted to try. It's awesome!"

"It's about damn time!"

"No kidding."

We spent a couple of minutes, catching up on his work and my painting and the kids. I had to go home, though.

"Can I call you later?"

"I'll call you tomorrow. I'm working until late tonight."

"Okay. Check in when you can."

"Will do. Later, you hot mess."

I cackled and clicked **END**.

I waited until the children had gone to bed to tell Sam about the conversation.

"I didn't necessarily intend for it to happen," I explained. "It just kind of did."

"Did you ever get to come?"

I shook my head. "Nope."

"You should take care of that."

"Right here? Right now?"

Sam nodded.

I stood and moved my chair across from his, very close to him. I reached under my short skirt and pulled off my panties, tossing them to the side. I propped one foot on either of the arms of his metal chair and lifted my skirt. He watched me, closely, and I looked him straight in the eye when I came.

I hoped this newfound agreement between me and Sam and Alex would somehow bridge the gap between the two of them. They were both great men, about the same age, with similar interests, not the least of which was me. I was hopeful that they would be able to get over their weirdness and be able to forge an amiable relationship, even if they were never to be friends.

I wanted to be happy with Sam and still have Alex.

Chapter 22

Days later, Sam and I were sitting on the couch, just inches apart, watching television. Surfing channels, we stopped on some generic crime drama for a moment. The episode was set in San Antonio.

"That's the River Walk," I said, suddenly recognizing the flagstone walkway and brightly-colored umbrellas where the episode had been shot.

Sam stared at the television but said nothing.

Some unknown actor came on screen and said something unimportant. Tall, dark hair, fortyish. Very handsome with a little swagger.

"Is he your type?" Sam asked, pointing toward the screen with his beer.

I thought about it for a moment. I ran through my list of former loves and lovers, celebrity crushes, and schoolmate interests.

"I don't know if I have a type. Except I generally like brunettes. I think I've only ever dated one blond. I like men who are taller than I am. I guess he's as close to my type as anyone could get."

Sam sat there for a moment, staring at the television. He stood suddenly and went straight to the deck. *Fuck!* I stopped the show and followed him outside.

"Do you want to talk about this?" I offered a little wearily.

He shook his head. "Let's wait until tomorrow. I'm not sober, and I'd rather wait until I can fully be there to discuss it."

I was hoping the worst of the drama had passed. I finished watching the show by myself and went to bed.

Sam came into the bedroom moments later. He sat on the bed, propped against his own pillows.

"What are you thinking?" he asked. "What are you feeling right now?"

I'm thinking I don't want to do this tonight.

"I don't want to argue with you," I sighed. "Not tonight. I'm tired and want to go to sleep."

"It's okay, Tierney. I promise I won't pick a fight. I just want to know where you are."

Trust him?

"Okay," I started slowly, "You're all over the place, and I can never be sure of where I am in relation to that. I don't know if I can ever fully break from Alex like I know you really want. I am appreciative of your being willing to let me have him in my life, but I don't know if I can ever really be as honest with you about him as you need me to be."

He said nothing for a long time. In the dark, I wondered if he'd passed out.

"You *lied* to me, Tierney. You lied to me, so you could *cheat* on me with him. *Of course* I want him out of your life. I want him out of *both* of our lives. I can't kill him, no matter how much I want to some days. I thought I could handle you talking to him, even if it was more of the same, as long as I knew. The fact that you *want* to have anything to do with him shows how much more he means to you than I do. *He means more to you than our marriage!*"

"Sam, you promised—"

"Yeah, well, you promised a lot, too, Tierney! You promised to love me and only me—to fuck me and only me—*for the rest of your life!* You took *my* money—"

"*Our* money!"

"*My fucking money!* and used it to *fuck* another man, in another city, and somehow I'm supposed to be okay with that?"

Take it, Tierney. Close your fucking mouth and take it. He has every right to be mad. Shut the fuck up and let him yell.

"I thought for a while that you'd crippled me, emotionally. That I would never be able to get over this. But I was wrong. I *will* be happy again, but not until Alex is out of your life for good. I want him gone. Entirely!"

"*Oh my god!*" I yelled back, exasperated. "Not even two weeks ago you said you knew I needed him and to contact him. I said no, that I didn't think that was what you wanted. I *told* you it felt like a trap or a test! And now you're saying you want him gone again? I can't handle this!"

Sam turned toward me. I could make out the angle of his silhouette, the blue glow of dim nightlight glinting off his glasses.

"Tierney, let me prove to you that we can get past this and make it work. I want to work on this and be a family and be happy again. We can do this! But I need you to *not* talk to Alex, though. I know how hard you think that will be for you. I know how much you think you need him. But if we're going to really give this a chance, we need him out of our life. I can't move forward with you, if I feel like a part of you is still back there with him. I need to be able to focus on you and on us and know that you're doing the same."

It shouldn't have been a surprise. He'd been so back and forth with this for almost two months. It was time for him to change his mind again.

Have you ever really given him the chance? Have you ever let go of Alex long enough to let Sam come in?

Nope.

"I have to think about it," I said. "I don't know."

"What's there to think about?" he stormed. "You either want this or you don't. You want *me*, or you don't!"

"This is the complete opposite of where you were a week ago and the week before that and the week before *that.* I don't know where this is coming from, but I don't want to fight with you. I think I'm gonna go paint."

He laughed. "Your *painting. What a joke!*"

I looked at him.

"All those canvases downstairs, all that *mess.* You're not selling anything. You're not making the world a better place with your *art.* I wouldn't even call it *art.* It's just *crap.*"

"I'm sorry you think that," I said quietly. I didn't want to antagonize him further

"You put pictures of your crap online, and no one gives a shit about what you do. You should just throw all of that shit out while you can still keep some shred of dignity!"

"Someone cared," I retorted. "Seth had me do his poster."

"*That poster!*" Sam hissed. "Fuck Seth and fuck Junkture! He only got you to do it, because he knew you were fucking Alex Wheeler! You didn't even get paid for that. Seth didn't give a shit about your *art*—it was just a reason to appease the band."

"Thanks. That's so nice of you."

"What the fuck do you know about *nice*? You only know how to be nice to get what you want! I don't think you even *feel* what it means to *be* nice. You're a goddamn sociopath! You don't have any real emotions. You don't really *feel* anything. You just know how to pretend you have feelings and consideration for other people. *You're a sociopath!*"

"Okay, I don't know where the fuck this is coming from," I snapped, "but this is not okay! I'm not listening to this shit!"

"Of course you're not! Run away! Go to sleep or go fuck Alex!"

I stood to go to the den, leaving him in the angry bedroom.

"You'd think you'd want to stay and hear more. I'm talking about you, which is the only thing you care about in the least! You're a fucking narcissist. *You're a narcissistic sociopath!*"

"Fuck you! That's not true, and you know it!"

"Nope. And you know what else I know? You're a whore. Wait, no!" He feigned deep thought for a moment. "That would imply you actually get *paid* for what you do. You're just a slut!"

I'd had enough. I stormed from the bedroom and slammed the door behind me. I was incensed and exhausted. I shoved myself onto the couch and tried to go to sleep. But it wouldn't come. I lay there for hours, fuming in the dark.

Alex Wheeler
Aug 17th 1:42 AM
would you be better off without me in your life?

?? call me

I snuck down the hall and made sure Sam was passed out. I quietly unlocked the front door and went out to the carport. I unlocked my car and sat in the driver's seat, locking the door behind me.

"Cavanaugh! How are you?" It was hard to hear him over the din in his background.

"Where are you?" I was trying not to cry.

"*Max, where am I?* He says somewhere on Long Island. Drunk. I am duh-runk somewhere on Long Island."

"What time will you be back to your hotel?"

"I don't know. An hour maybe. What's wrong?"

"Sam is being a dick. He just started screaming at me, telling me I'm a whore and a sociopath."

The noise subsided just a little as he stepped away from his group. "Okay," he said calmly and evenly, "I can hear that you need to really talk. I'm really fucking drunk and with the guys, and it's really fucking loud in here. I want to be able to hear what you're telling me. Can I call you when I get back to the room?"

I need to talk to you now, you asshole! "Yeah. Okay."

I sat there, numb, staring into the deep shadows at the edges of our yard, hoping in the back of my mind that the Bogey Man would come and end this for all of us.

Alex texted me thirty minutes later that he was available to talk. He answered on the first ring.

"What happened?"

"Would it be easier for you if I weren't in your life and in your head?"

"No. Why are you asking?"

I recounted the story of Sam's outburst. I was raving, angry and animated and almost yelling at Alex.

"He called me a whore, Alex! Then he said I didn't make enough money to be a whore, that I was just a slut. He told me I shouldn't paint, that it was all crap, and that I should just throw it all away!"

"I'm sorry, Buttercup. I know that must've hurt, him saying that to you. You know he's just angry and lashing out."

"Do I? Maybe he's right. Maybe I'm just a talentless hack who shouldn't bother. Maybe I'm just that stupid cunt who cheated on her drunk husband."

"Tierney, no, don't do that. You know that's not true."

"No, I don't. I thought I did, but he hurt me. It was like he stuck his finger in every little crack in my facade and *pushed* as hard as he could until each one ripped open. I'm so sick of it all, Alex. I can't take any more of this. I just can't do it!"

"So are you ready to leave?"

"I can't stay like this. He's never going to be over this."

"Nope. He's not. I'm sorry." He paused and stretched. "Don't worry about it, though. I'll come down there soon and have sex with you."

I smiled and blushed in the dark. I couldn't help myself. "Will you?"

Completely different tone. What the fuck is that?

"Yep. But right now I gotta get some sleep. I have to be up and out by eight."

"Okay. Thanks for letting me vent."

"Any time. It'll be okay. Don't worry about it."

"'Kay. 'Night."

"'Night."

I recognized immediately that it was *fucked up* that I was flattered by his saying he would come and have sex with me. I was unloading about how my husband had intentionally wounded me in the worst possible ways, that I was so tired of it that I was ready, again, to end my marriage. And my attention shifted in a moment of flirt from Alex.

Why did *that* suddenly make me so happy?

Because you love him.

No, I don't. Not like that.

Yes, you do.

No....

Yes.

Oh fuck.

Could that possibly be true? Could I have really fallen in love with Alex?

I loved him, absolutely, and I always knew it wouldn't take much for that to change into something more. But we'd barely been in contact for weeks. When we had, we were almost always talking about my bullshit with Sam. It had only been the last few days that we'd been back in that place of sexual and intimate connection.

But I'd never stopped thinking about him. I still listened to the Alex playlist when I missed him. Sometimes I listened to it just so I *could* miss him. Every day I would see something and think, *Oh! I need to talk Alex about that!*

And I wasn't delusional about who he was. He was impulsive and stubborn and strangely exacting about certain things. A little OCD. He could be insecure and unreliable, though not intentionally. He compartmentalized the hell out of his life, especially when it came to me, and that made him often unavailable.

He was also charming and sweet and funny. He could read my mood within moments and was unbearably patient with me. He obviously thought about me when we weren't in contact. He was strongly attracted to me, even having started all of our flirtations when I was almost at my heaviest. He was honest and caring, and he missed me when I wasn't there.

And I loved him.

Rather, I was just on the *edge* of loving him, and I was a breath away from tumbling down that rabbit hole if he called me Buttercup.

I knew Alex had never meant to hurt me or drag me inside something that would tear and bite. He'd never wanted me to be so emotionally invested that I would need him or come to rely on him. He didn't want me to love him in any way other than distant adoration. But it had happened, and I cared. I needed someone, anyone, to care about, someone could at least pretend to care back. I'd desperately needed a *connection* to anyone, and what I'd found was someone there in the dark of night who could understand and accept and listen, someone with whom I had a deep, immediate connection that was felt both ways. I hadn't been able to let that drop even when I knew it was best for him and me and everyone else. It would never be Alex's hand on my hip in the middle of the night when I couldn't sleep. And I still couldn't let go, feeling how I did, and it was tearing my life apart at the seams.

Had I ever really given Sam a chance? I thought I had, especially in late April and early May, when I knew I wanted to make our marriage better. *Right before you slept with Alex.* I thought we would be okay after our anniversary. He *told* me it was all okay, that he was evolved and understanding that he might not always be able to fulfill my needs.

When he'd said that, I thought only of sexual fantasy, that maybe there was something I wanted to try that didn't or couldn't involve him. That didn't mean I'd have to exclude him from it, and I always expected he would be there with me, if I ever chose to explore those avenues. Maybe there was more to it. Maybe he knew he could never fill the space that Alex had consumed for so many months.

As much as I'd tried to keep my heart away from him, I'd given Alex a little piece of it. I hadn't meant to, but it had happened. And Alex was nowhere close to being able to care for that.

I went into my bathroom and closed the door. I washed my face and hands, brushed my teeth and hair. Put on some perfume and tried to feel normal. I stood in the bathroom doorway, my hand on the light switch, looking at Sam's sleeping form in our bed. I didn't want to go there, so close to Sam, while I was so angry and hurt and confused. I didn't want to go to him just because it was the only place I had to go.

Can I forget Alex and focus only on Sam? Can I forgive his awful words and the drinking and all the times he ignored and dismissed me?

I had to try.

I turned out the light and went into the den, to the couch, to the dark. No television or music or phone. Just me.

I retreated—from Alex, from Sam, from my heart. I was overwhelmed by all of the emotion and couldn't bear to face any of it. I sank into sleep as quickly as possible.

That night, I dreamed of Alex. Again, I dreamed of him singing "Let Me Lie to You" in the orange glow of a dark corner. Streams of tears were drying against my face as I woke, alone in the silence.

Chapter 23

My birthday was coming again, and Sam asked me, again, what I wanted. I didn't even bother to hope that he'd manage the perfect gift without my input. There was no way I was leaving either of us dangling in that delusion, given all of the miscommunications of the last year.

"Shoes," I told him. "*Purple* glittery shoes. Though I could probably use some new runners, too."

I love shoes. I don't have hundreds of pairs, but I do have more than I could ever possibly need. Some were bought to go with a specific outfit. Others were ordered just because they were pretty. Sam tolerated my collection of sequins and leather and velvet and had been more than willing to buy me a great pair of Wonder Woman high tops for a late Valentine's Day gift. It was *my birthday*, and this was what I wanted most of all.

My purple glittery t-strap heels arrived via overnight delivery on the morning of my birthday.

I was beside myself with joy, fastening the tiny rhinestone buckle around my ankle. I was careful not to break my ankle, prancing around the house in three-and-a-half inches of purple glittery goodness.

I went to the gym and ran some errands, my phone under constant barrage of calls and texts and Facebook notifications of birthday wishes. I choose FLIP Burger Boutique for dinner, a gourmet burger and shake shop owned by Richard Blaise of *Top Chef* fame. Sam, the boys, and I split fried pickles and sweet potato fries, along with lamb burgers and chicken-fried chicken burgers. I didn't ask for a birthday cake. Instead each of us ordered a different liquid nitrogen shake and passed them around, debating our favorite flavors.

At home, we got the boys ready for bed. I plugged my phone in to charge in the bedroom and went to join Sam in the den. We settled onto the couch for *Donnie Darko: The Director's Cut*. I can never watch it by myself. Frank the Bunny is the scariest damn anti-villain ever, and I often groggily see him lurking in the shadows of my bedroom at night. But it's a fuck-with-you, fantasy-in-reality type movie that I love, and it was my choice. I gasped and hid my eyes and grabbed onto Sam during all the scary parts.

As the movie was ending, I heard the ding of a text from across the house. I didn't care who it was. I wanted to spend time with my husband. I found my new purple shoes and dolled around the deck in them, wearing my pajamas.

I checked my Facebook messages one more time before bed. I had a hundred birthday wishes from friends and family. It made me happy to know so many people took just a moment of their day to wish me well.

A new post popped up on my wall, a happy birthday wish from Alex. It was sweet and silly and totally benign. Moments later, I realized there was also a message from him.

Alex Wheeler
August 27th 10:18 PM

Happy birthday Tierney

Tierney Cavanaugh Johnson
August 27th 11:34 PM

Wow! More than one message? I'm surprised, and it made me smile. Thank you! Hope you're well!

I shut down my computer and went to the bedroom. I looked at my phone to see who the earlier text was from.

Alex Wheeler
Aug 27th 10:34 PM

Happy birthday buttercup

The message took me completely by surprise. I hadn't expected to hear from him at all. I had no reason to think he knew when my birthday was, though I was sure seeing the messages from mutual friends on my Facebook had triggered his contact. I knew I would have to tell Sam that I'd heard from Alex, but I wasn't doing it right before bed.

I silenced my ringer as Sam came into the bedroom. I turned and smiled at him, across the room, as he closed the bedroom door. Watching him in the glow of the bedside lamp, I peeled off my clothes slowly. He clicked off the lamp and met me in the center of our bed.

We kissed deeply. His strong, warm hands touched every part of me, deliberate and tingling against my naked skin. He was excited and wanted me but patiently built my own excitement in all of my favorite ways. I pushed Alex out of my mind and gave myself over to my husband completely.

"Happy birthday, Mrs. Johnson," he breathed into my ear as I came.

I fell asleep almost immediately, happy and warm in Sam's arms.

But I woke around four in the morning, unable to go back to sleep. I was happy and content after such a wonderful day with my men. My mind was churning, running through all of the birthday wishes. Out of habit, I checked my silent phone in the dark.

There was a missed call and a voicemail from Seth, left at 3:30 in the morning.

I wrapped a blanket around me and went out to the deck. It was clear and beautiful in the wee hours. The neighborhood was quiet and still, and I could see a million stars over the trees and roofline. I put in my earbuds to hear the voicemail and listen to some music until I was ready to sleep.

> *Happy birthday to you!*
> *Happy birthday to you!*
> *Happy birthday, dear Tierney Cavanaugh Johnson!*
> *Happy birthday to you!*

I chuckled quietly to myself, listening to Seth drunkenly singing to my voicemail. He was the only one I hadn't heard from all day, and I was heartened that he'd noticed and made the call, giggling to himself as he tried to sing.

My Twitter app showed a couple of new messages, so I logged in to see what they were.

Alex Wheeler @Junkture:
@TierneyCavJ Happy Birthday Girlie!

Tierney Cavanaugh Johnson @TierneyCavJ:
@Junkture Thanks! It's been a great birthday!

There was also a direct message.

Alex Wheeler @Junkture:
@TierneyCavJ Happy birthday!

Tierney Cavanaugh Johnson @TierneyCavJ:
@Junkture Thank you! Wrapped in a blanket & listening to Dollface, watching Venus fly by the moon. Give the Princess my love & my big dimpled smile.

Five messages—what the fuck?
It was sweet that I'd heard from him at all, but five messages? *Seriously?* I didn't know what to think about that. For a man who didn't have room for me in his heart, he was making damn sure I knew he was thinking about me.

It made me a little uncomfortable.

I'd had a really wonderful day with Sam. For the first time in weeks, I really felt like we were on the verge of getting through everything and moving forward with our life. But hearing from Alex and responding to him so readily, without even thinking about it, made me question how ready I was to move on. I felt elated and a little bit dirty.

I managed to get back to sleep some time after five, curled safely against Sam.

I called Tessa the next morning.

"I heard from Alex."

"What did he say?"

"He was wishing me a happy birthday."

"Well, that's not so bad." She paused. "Did you tell Sam?"

"Not yet. I don't know what to do."

"Tierney, you have to tell him."

"Really? You think so?"

Of course you do.

"*Yes.* You *have* to tell him."

"Do I have to tell him there were five messages?"

"*What?*" She was stunned. "Alex sent you *five* birthday messages?"

"Yeah. I didn't really know what to think about that."

"That seems a little... excessive," Tessa replied. "You have to tell Sam, though. About all of them."

I flared my nostrils into the sunlight. I knew she was right, but I didn't want her to be.

"I don't want to," I complained. "He's going to be me mad as hell when he finds out."

"Probably, but he'll be madder if you don't tell him and he finds out. You gotta put your big girl panties on and deal with it, Tierney."

"Big girl panties suck."

"Yes. Yes, they do. But at least they're smaller than they used to be."

I waited until the boys were in bed and we were safely settled on the deck before I told him.

"I need to tell you something," I started. "I need you to listen and not be mad."

Sam took a sip from his beer. "Okay. What's up?"

"I heard from Alex. He sent me a message on Facebook, wishing me a happy birthday."

Even from three feet away, I could feel Sam tense up. "Is that all?"

I looked at him. "He posted it on my wall, and he sent me a private message. He also texted me." I looked down at my bare feet, hidden in shadow. "He also tweeted it and sent me a direct message on Twitter."

Sam took another sip. "So five messages?" I nodded. "Did you respond?"

I took a deep breath. "I sent him a message back on Facebook, thanking him."

"Is that all?"

Not quite. I nodded. "It wasn't a big deal. I didn't want you to be mad, but Tessa said I had to tell you. I mean, that's not *why* I'm telling you. You had a right to know."

Keep covering your ass, Tierney.

He was quiet for a while. I knew he was upset, and I couldn't blame him. I didn't *ask* Alex to reach out, and I hadn't expected it. It had made me happy, though, knowing I'd crossed his mind.

We didn't talk about it further. There wasn't much else to say, and neither of us felt like dragging anything out into the dim light. We went to bed, together, late that night.

I sent the children to school the next morning and went to the gym. When I stepped on the scale, I was thrilled to see my weight was dropping again, the loss having slowed dramatically over the summer. I was still careful about what I ate, and I was down ninety pounds.

I came home from my session with Devin and went into the bedroom to take a shower. I turned suddenly from the bathroom doorway, and my wedding band slipped off, dropping onto my dresser.

"Dude!" I exclaimed.

Sam peered questioningly around the corner from the hallway.

"My wedding band fell off."

It had been loose for weeks, and I'd stopped wearing my diamond anniversary band when it got too big in May.

"They need to be resized," I said, "but there's no point in doing it until I'm done with the weight loss."

Sam nodded but said nothing more. I dropped the ring into a small jewelry box and got in the shower.

The day went on like normal. I did laundry and dishes, cooked dinner, and got the boys ready for bed. I watched a little television while Sam worked. We finally convened on the deck late that night.

Sam seemed fine, calm and generally okay.

"How are you?" I asked.

"I'm okay," he replied quietly. He was silent for a long time, drinking a beer and smoking a cigarette. "So, you only sent Alex a message on Facebook?"

I looked at him. I knew damn well I'd sent a more personal response via Twitter, but I'd done it from my phone. It hadn't come from my computer, and I didn't think there was any way he would've known.

"You didn't tell him to give the princess your love and your big, dimpled smile?" The shadows between us filled with animosity.

"Sam...." What could I say? I'd absolutely done it and not told him. By withholding the whole truth, I'd lied again about Alex. I wasn't sure how he knew, but he did.

"You know," he continued, "you'd think you'd realize to turn off your wireless and just send that shit over 3G if you're going to do it. Really, I hoped you'd just delete it and not respond at all, but I guess that's too much to ask for."

Of course! My phone was on the network, and he was monitoring network activity. He was waiting for me to fuck up again.

"You have no right to go through my private messages!" I protested. "I didn't *mean* to respond the way I did, but you don't get to watch everything I do!"

"It's my network! I'll monitor it any way I see fit! Stop deflecting from the bigger problem, which is that you'll *never* be able to tell me the truth about you and Alex!"

"I've told you everything! Twice! I've been over every detail of our fucking relationship with you. There's nothing you don't know!"

"You won't tell me when you contact him. How many other times have you emailed him or texted him or called him and not told me, Tierney? How long will this go on? Do I have to worry about this for the rest of my fucking life?"

I shook my head. "No. I'm sorry. I don't want you to have to worry about it—there's nothing to worry about! I just—"

"You just can't stay away from him! You love him, and you can't leave it alone!"

He was right. I didn't mean for it to happen, but it was unbearably hard *not* to think about Alex and want to talk to him. I would think of a dozen things in a day that I needed to tell him and then be upset that I couldn't. I'd never intended to have things I wanted to keep from Sam, but Alex was part of *me*, not him, and I didn't want to share that.

Sam slept on the couch. We didn't talk at all the next day.

That afternoon, I was cooking dinner and helping the boys with their homework at the kitchen table. I walked into the office to check my messages. My computer was logged into Facebook, but I'd been away from it for a while.

Alex   halo

He'd sent the chat request five minutes before, while I was out of the room. I sat at my desk, staring at the screen, trying to decide if I could respond. I wanted to, badly, but I knew Sam would be livid if he found out. I was live on the network. I would have to tell him afterward. I couldn't *not* reply to Alex.

Tierney	hey Why are you visible for chat? you're never visible for chat
Alex	i don't know, just popped up fuckin facebook hows things?
Tierney	muddled
Alex	??
Tierney	how are you?
Alex	good, records sounding great u?
Tierney	You picked the wrong day to ask me. :)
Alex	:(
Tierney	In general, I'm well. I'm down 90 pounds I'm a kick-ass bruiser with damn good hair
Alex	kongrats
Tierney	:) thank you for my messages though it created a ginormous amount of fallout that's kicking my ass today
Alex	why
Tierney	because I responded the way I did
Alex	dummy u'll never learn

im chatting with like 20 hot chicks right now

Tierney   ha!
I'm doing some serious tongue biting

Alex   i'm asking for pics, think ill get any?

Tierney   of course you will

Alex   im kidding

Tierney   you don't do that, I know

Alex   I actually am kidding, just u

Tierney   :)
are you okay?
there are a thousand things I want to ask you

Alex   I'm good, busy but good. shoot

Tierney   I can't, I'm dying to, and I can't do it like this,
not right now.
I almost messaged you a dozen times today
but I didn't, for a dozen more reasons

Alex   k, understand
i'll let you go then

Tierney   :(
I want badly to ask you to call

Alex   dont

Tierney   my questions will bother me, for days
but I don't want to be hard for you

Alex   ?

Tierney   like why you sent me 5 messages....

knowing, *knowing* it would be crazy for me, good and bad
regardless of if or how he found out

Alex

wasn't sure which one you'd get
just wanted to let you know i was thinking about you on your birthday, all bases covered is my motto
i didn't think he'd find out
and a lot of people wished you happy birthday

Tierney

yes they did
and I don't think you were remotely malicious
I never thought that

Alex

not at all

Tierney

but it's shined a spotlight on the fact that I'm nowhere close to over this
and that I don't know that I'll ever be, because it's unfair and makes me irritable and sad and angry that it's not right
that it didn't go like it should have
and it makes me petulant

Alex

ok ok sorry doll, i'll let you alone

Tierney

and you don't want to
I don't want you to

Alex

I know you don't
I don't want to either, but it has to happen
I can't let you keep doing this

Tierney

it's not fair!
we meet, billions of people in the world and two people who were *supposed* to find each other *do*

and we can't do anything about it

Alex

ours to bear
lots of people have to turn away from the things they want to go back to unhappy relationships
happens every day

Tierney

that's why I'm angry
because I *know* you miss me
I *know* you don't want to
in a lot of ways and for a lot of reasons

Alex

got to, sorry to have caused you any stress, you should probably remove me from your friends list to make the cut easier

Tierney

this is why I didn't want to chat, why I wanted to talk, why I didn't message you
and why I didn't ask you to talk to me

Alex

you need to stop Tierney, its not going to get easier

Tierney

I don't want to be hard for you or for me, I swear
I just wish I knew that it would get easier, eventually

Alex

it will, gonna take a lot of time but it will

Tierney

and, look, I'm not obsessing about it, I'm working really hard to go on with my life
this is hard, Alex
I know you don't know what to say

Alex

i do and am going to
you've got to remove me from your life
now

Tierney   that doesn't take you away, and you know it

Alex   from everything that has my contact info

Tierney   is it so it's easier for me or for you?

Alex   you, i can compartmentalize a hell of a lot easier than you can
i'm asking you to do it Tierney, you have to

Tierney   yeah but at least I'm not afraid to feel it, it hurts like fucking hell, but I am whole-heartedly feeling every damn moment of it and always have

Alex   i know, thats why you're an amazing person
time to cut it Tierney
cut the rope

Tierney   you know damn well I'm more likely to hang myself with it than cut it :)

Alex   i know, that's why I'm going to remove myself from your life

Tierney   Alex, it doesn't matter if I delete every picture and burn my own CD's and everything else, you will always be there, you know you will, because we clicked from the beginning
and I don't mean that in some sinister way

Alex   i know
ours to bear

Tierney   tell me the truth before you go

Alex   its not going to make it easier Tierney

Tierney	I don't think it is, but I have to know I'm not crazy, that I didn't imagine it, that I didn't make it all up in my fucking blond head all of it, Alex, the fact that it ever happened You can be honest with me about so many things, and I wish for you most of all that you can find a way to be honest with yourself sometimes
Alex	you're not crazy, pushy and incredulous maybe but not crazy
Tierney	I'm selfish and obsessive and loud
Alex	yes
Tierney	and I'm curious and willing and emotional
Alex	all the above
Tierney	but you have to know how much you fed that
Alex	oh I know! I absolutely know!
Tierney	tell me why it mattered
Alex	why what mattered, the happy birthday, the phone calls, conversations? it doesn't matter! my feelings for you, your feelings for me they don't matter!
Tierney	don't say that! they do matter! just because it ever existed at all, it matters, Alex
Alex	of course it matters, doll LIFE matters!

but my wife and child, that's what matters
most

it has to
but things end
my first girlfriend broke my fucking heart
my ex-wife
I still LOVE her

Tierney

I know you do
and I know that I got under your skin in a
totally unexpected way, because it wasn't
one-sided

Alex

it's too much drama
we have to be done
in your life and out
you, me, Sam
I can't take the drama
I don't have time or room in my heart for this

say goodbye Tierney

Tierney

I don't fucking want to
I don't want to be angry at you

Alex

i can't help you with that
and if you are i am sorry

Tierney

I'm not angry, I'm saying I don't want to be
I don't want to be angry at you and let that be
the last time I talk to you, to make that what
pushes me out the door
so don't be a dick just to make me mad,
please

Alex

ok, but say goodbye, i've got to go

Tierney

go, but I won't
I'm not looking for you
I'm not waiting for you to pop up

but I'm not telling you goodbye again, either

Alex   Take care of yourself doll, you are the shit that killed Elvis! gnite

Tierney   asshat

And with that, Alex Wheeler promptly unfriended me on Facebook.

For the first time since it had all began, I wished I'd never met the son of a bitch.

Chapter 24

The next morning, I looked at the transcript of my chat with Alex, still sitting painfully in my Facebook messages. I copied the conversation and emailed it to Tessa. I called her and cried about how awful the phone conversation was.

"You know," she said carefully, "I haven't been privy to your conversations with Alex. I can't *hear* your tone or his like you can, but I have to tell you that you sounded a little bit like a crazy girl, when I was reading it."

She was right. I was out of my fucking mind half the time, thinking through the relationship. I'd been that way for months, and it had culminated in an unexpectedly desperate and weak attempt on my part *not* to let it drop. I didn't want Alex to be gone. I didn't want the attention and the affection to stop. I *knew* deep in my heart that I was right; he felt more than he would admit. It wasn't the end of the relationship in specific that was bothering me. I was infuriated by the principle of allowing something unique and special to fall away, and I was especially heartbroken that there was no grieving on his part about any of it. It made me feel like the previous nine months really hadn't mattered at all, as far as he was concerned.

Sam was quiet and distant all day, though we circled politely around each other in the house. That night, when we were finally alone, I told him about the chat with Alex. He had every right to know. I needed to talk about it, but I was afraid to tell him the truth. It would be hurtful, just hearing the words come from my mouth. And my heart stung every time I thought about Alex's words and reaction, the harshness of the conversation.

"He said I don't matter."

Sam looked at me quizzically.

"He said that it's too much drama, he can't deal with it."

"That's bullshit," Sam replied. "He loves the drama. He thrives on it."

I nodded. "He loves it when it's on his terms. This got out of his control, though, and he can't tolerate that."

He was quiet for a long moment, drinking a beer. "You know that's fucked up, right? He put you in this place, this compartment, and left you there."

"Yep. As long as he could take me out and look at me when he wanted, it was fine. When I started to seep in around the edges, it was too much." I shrugged. "It doesn't matter. He doesn't care. I don't matter to him."

"You're wrong," Sam replied. "He loves you."

I shook my head emphatically. "No. He doesn't. It was quite apparent that he doesn't give a shit, about me or any of it. I'm just a distraction and an emotional drain. I'm overwhelming."

"No, Tierney, he *loves* you. He might not like it, but he does."

"Then I guess he was right. It *doesn't* matter. It might as well have never happened." I stood and paced the deck by torchlight. "I'm sorry, you know. I'm sorry this keeps coming up, again and again. He's right, that it's too much drama. I'm sorry I dragged you through all of it and am dragging you through it again. Over and over, we keep rehashing this. I'm tired of it, too. I don't love pushing myself into this dark place, time and again. It's not fun for me. I can't imagine what it's like for you, and I'm sorry."

And I *was* sorry. I still didn't feel guilty about the affair. I didn't feel badly for having fallen for this other man; all of that still felt very outside of my control. But I felt horrible for having these issues resurface every few weeks, for constantly hurting Sam and making the pains of the past still feel so *present*. Every time we thought we'd finally made enough progress to see around the bend in our road, I found a way to throw an obstacle in our way.

Sam wanted me to be honest. He told me repeatedly that he would rather know what I was thinking and feeling than not. He would rather hear it directly from me than to try to filter through vague clues in my words and demeanor. But telling him these things, admitting them both to him and to myself, was incredibly difficult. I could tell Tessa or Jules or Frankie with no hesitation that I was hurting and confused, but telling Sam was like holding a cold, steel tip against his heart and waiting to see if I became angry enough to sink it.

———————————

Sam was attentive and affectionate and present, with me and with the boys. He was still drinking every night, but he was generally jovial and polite. He asked me constantly how I was, careful to listen when I needed to talk.

I didn't talk much, though. Getting back into the swing of school with the boys was difficult. Our schedule was different and busier than it had been in previous years. I'd barely had time over the summer to get into the gym twice a week, during my sessions with Devin. I was slowly building back toward five workouts a week.

Sam was trying to be patient with me, but I knew he was getting frustrated. I was moody and a little withdrawn. We weren't having sex.

Late one night on the deck, he asked me, "Do you want to talk about what's going on?"

I shrugged. "What do you mean?"

"Every time I ask you how you are, you shrug and tell me 'fine' or 'okay'. It's obvious you're not, Tierney."

"You're here all the time, Sam," I sighed. "You work from home almost every day. You *see* me constantly. I tell you everything I'm doing with the kids. You *know* how I am."

"Tierney," he replied gently, "I'm not trying to watch you like a hawk or insinuate myself into your separate life. But there's a distance again. Every time I try to initiate sex with you, you politely shoot me down."

"I'm *tired*, Sam."

"I'm not trying to push you. I just... I want to try to close that distance, but you retreat every time I do. My radar is *screaming*, because I sense a very different reaction from you toward me, especially in the last week. I don't ignore that feeling anymore."

I turned in my chair to face him directly.

"I miss the woman who would let me go shopping with her in a cute dress but without panties. I miss the woman who would go shopping for sex toys and blow a hundred bucks in five minutes. That woman who would wake me in the middle of the night and *mount* me, tell me how much she needed me, how the touch of my hands on her was sheer bliss." He paused. "What's changed, Tierney?"

I took a drag off my cigarette and put it out. "That woman is withdrawn and afraid and untrusting right now," I started slowly. "She's spinning in her own head, trying to come to terms with the last ten months of utter *freakshow* emotional turmoil. The last few weeks were especially upheaving, Sam—emotionally and sexually and psychologically.

"I was ready and resigned to the fact that we were splitting. I was *steeled* to go into the world a different woman with a whole new landscape of uphill battles, knowing that I would eventually get to the top and survive. But all these ups and downs over the last few weeks have dragged me by the hair, kicking and screaming, into some craziness in my head. Every time I thought I was on the edge of solid ground, that we were in the beginnings of a safe place, some nagging thing came along and threw me off kilter. I'm still a little apprehensive after being flung from one extreme to another over such a short period of time."

I stopped, giving him a chance to respond. He said nothing, watching me patiently and expectantly, waiting for me to let it all out.

I stood from the chair and started to pace the deck.

"I'm totally out of whack right now! I can't paint. I can't read. I can't focus on anything, because my head is in such a state of utter fucking *chaos*! I can see how I'm sliding back into that hellhole I dragged myself from, the place where I was bored and boring and uninterested in anything, where I was who and what everyone else expected me to be. I *hate* that girl, and I don't want to be her, and I'm fighting like hell *not* to be that again.

"I'm fighting to make the good choice—for you and me and our life—and to find some way to reconcile the three with each other. But I *have* to have some room to breathe, Sam. I *have* to have the time to explore my own head and find my way to the happy medium I can accept and embrace. I'm always slow to get there; you know that. And if you push me too hard, I am likely to lash out and swing back the other direction."

My voice began to quiver, and my hands trembled, the shaking moving quickly up my arms and through to the rest of my body.

Through clattering teeth, I cried. "I feel small and fragile, and I'm afraid to share it with you. I'm afraid of how you might take it or what you'll do with it. I'm afraid that being honest with you will slap me in the face. And I don't know how long it will be before I can let you in again. But I am *much* more than a sexual beast, even in the throes of sex. I fuck and I love at the same time, and it seems like only one or the other works at time, for me to keep my relationships honest and true. I'm *tired* of battling it, of battling myself. You can give me time and patience, or you can not. Sometimes, though, I just need a little vanilla to feel like a wanted, beautiful woman, and all I seem to get is a bunch of tutti fruitti."

Sam stood and walked across the deck to me, where I was leaning against the rail, sobbing quietly toward the dark woods. He slipped his arms on either side of me and placed his hands on the rail, his front against my back.

"Tierney," he said softly, "I'm afraid when you talk about spending time in your own head, you're really spending time in someone else's. I'm trying to be very cognizant of my response to that, to fight that instinct, for your sake and our sake. And I *get* what you're saying about not feeling like you can trust me or trust yourself. I hope that if you feel like you're about to make a mistake that will affect us, you would tell me in the *hope*—even if you can't trust it— that it would be better than not. We both need to shed the fallacy that ignorance is bliss, especially in our marriage."

I relaxed, just a little, and he turned me toward him.

"Help me understand what's going on with you and how I can and can't, or should and shouldn't, help you keep that hope alive."

I was *trying*, but it was so hard. I *wanted* a normal, happy life with Sam and our boys. I wanted to enjoy our life again. Every time I thought of Alex, I pushed him down into a deep, dark place in my heart where I didn't have to look at him.

I decided to try even harder to *be* with Sam. I did my best to be the funny, boisterous, sexy woman to whom he responded so well. It started to work, slowly, and things were okay again. Better than okay. I was in love with my husband.

My friend, Lisa, invited me to a fundraiser for Jerusalem House, an Atlanta shelter for people living with HIV and AIDS. It was a drag show at the Jungle, one of Atlanta's many great gay bars. I love drag—it's the epitome of Glittery Girl, even though all that glitters is not girl.

I got to dress up in something sexy, including my glittery pink shoes. Lisa and I laughed until we thought our sides would split. We cried when the emcee talked of close friends who had succumbed to the ravages of AIDS. It was a fantastic evening that included Lisa and I getting to simultaneously motorboat one of the performers during her number

When I came home that night, Sam was out on the deck. Tiki torches were lit, and he was listening to music.

"How was your evening?" he asked, smiling at me.

"Fantastic!" I cooed. I told him all about it, animated and excited. "I had so much fun! Thanks for keeping the kids."

"No problem! Do you want to listen to anything special?"

I wasn't sure what I wanted, but I was in the mood to dance. I scrolled through the artist list on my iPod until I found the Black Keys. I plugged into the speakers and started to wiggle.

It was hot and sticky, like virtually every other late summer night in Atlanta. I was still in my black lace camisole and pencil skirt. Careful not to get a heel stuck between the slats in the deck, I danced back and forth to "Howlin' for You" and slowly peeled my cami over my head and dropped it in Sam's lap. I reached behind me and unzipped my skirt. I turned deliberately away from him and slid the skirt down, bending over and moving my hips in time to the music. I stepped out of the fallen skirt and kept dancing, wearing a hot pink bra and panties and the pink glittery heels.

Sam watched me closely, sipping from his beer. I moved close, the smell of my gingery perfume rising in the heat. His hand slid up the back of my thigh. I threw him a sideways glance and grinned, dancing my way back across the deck. I unhooked my bra and tossed it on top of my skirt. I turned my back to him and made sure he saw the black mesh heart on my pink-clad ass. I glanced over my shoulder at him and blew a kiss. I peeled the panties off and added to them to the pile.

I danced back to him, wearing only the pink glittery heels.

I took the beer bottle from his hand and sipped, rolling the earthy taste of hops around my mouth. Placing one heeled foot on the arm of his chair, almost at his eye level, I slid the lip of the bottle inside myself. The brown glass was cold and slick against my hot skin. I handed it back to Sam, who drank greedily, watching me carefully as I replaced the bottle with my own long fingers.

Sam drained the last of the beer and reached to set the empty bottle on the low, metal table at his side.

"Give that to me," I said.

I quickly grabbed the other chair and sat directly across from Sam, planting one foot on each of the arms of his chair. Leaning back, I slowly pushed the neck of the beer bottle into my pussy, the condensation and my own wetness running down the crack of my ass. With my left hand, I held it in place, twisting and pulling it in and out, as I flicked my clit with my right hand.

Sam reached into shorts and freed his cock, stroking it while he watched me fuck myself with his beer bottle.

"It's better than the glass dildo," I said.

He lifted his hips and pulled his shorts down.

I rubbed furiously between my legs, the bottle pistoning me toward orgasm. Sam jacked his dick faster and faster, watching me as I writhed against the bottle and the chair.

"I'm gonna come," I moaned, my eyes locked on Sam's.

"Let it out," he urged.

I arched my back, pushing the neck of the bottle as deep as possible. My swollen muscles spasmed, contracting around the now-hot glass, intensifying the deep rumble of bliss spreading from my clit.

But I wasn't sated.

I gently dropped the sticky, wet bottle and heard it roll across the wooden boards of the deck. In one quick motion, I stood from my chair and turned my back to Sam as I pushed his hands away from his cock.

I balanced my weight on the balls of my feet, off the delicate pink heels, and held myself up with my newly-strengthened thighs. Up and down, my legs and ass straining deliciously with the effort, I fucked him there, in his chair, my hair slapping against my back and his thighs as I came again, biting my lip to keep from screaming out into the night.

Chapter 25

Things seemed sane and normal again. Sam and I were affectionate, smiling and kissing and cuddling all the time. We continued our talks on the deck. I was happy to spend time with him, but our sex life started to dwindle again. I was getting closer to the anniversary of my life exploding, and it was making me introspective and quiet.

Even though we weren't in counseling, we were still trying to work through our issues on our own. Part of what was still bothering us both was the sexual attraction between me and Alex. It wasn't him, specifically, that was concerning. I wasn't sure that I wanted to be sexually monogamous, going another nineteen years or longer sleeping with the same man. Sam was a fantastic lover, but he expressed his worry that he wouldn't be able to give me the different experiences I'd talked about with Alex.

"Mostly," he admitted, "I'm worried that you'll meet someone else again and keep it from me. I can't go through that again, Tierney. If you're not open and honest with me, I won't be able to take it. I won't survive it again."

"What happens if I meet someone and feel like I want to have sex with them? Am I just supposed to *tell* you, 'Hey, I met this guy and I want to fuck him!'?"

"Yes! It doesn't have to be those exact words, but I'll be okay with it as long as I know what's going on."

He'd said that before and then changed his position, and I wasn't sure I believed him. I *wanted* to, if for no other reason than it would give me the freedom to pursue other physical relationships if I found myself drawn to someone new. I wasn't looking for an excuse to fuck someone else; I just didn't want a hypothetical, unexpected attraction to derail my marriage again.

And I felt a little guilty, looking for permission not to be sexually monogamous. I'd always lived by the assertion that marriage meant fidelity—emotional and physical. I knew the worst part of my affair for Sam had been that I'd had feelings for someone else, though he was certainly still bothered by my having slept with Alex. But we were an unconventional couple who didn't think and act like most people we knew. Was it possible that we could renegotiate the terms of our marital contract to include safe sex with other partners?

How would I feel if Sam wanted to sleep with someone else? *I'd be fine with it.* Logically, there was no religious or moral impetus on my part that he be sexually faithful to me. Yes, I would want to know about it, though I wasn't sure if that was before or after and figured it would depend on the specific circumstances of the encounter. I knew, though, that multi-partnered and open relationships were often encumbered by unforeseen emotional traps. I wasn't sure how I would feel if he fell in love with someone else.

My four years with Damien had included a lot of breaking up and making up. While we were apart, he often tried to sleep with other women, though he never did to the best of my knowledge. He fully believed that, if he was attracted to someone else enough to want to go after it, he was okay to break up with me and pursue that other person. As long as we weren't together, his conscience was clear.

He'd never understood, even when I screamed at him during our last fights, that it was the *wanting* that was the real betrayal. I wasn't as upset that he hit on my friends as I was that he *wanted* to even try to hit on them, knowing that I loved him and telling me that he loved me.

I'd been on the other side of the betrayal, and I knew how badly it could hurt. And Damien's half-assed attempts to fuck some other chick were *nothing* compared to what I'd done to Sam.

Sam asked me to arrange for a babysitter, for Date Night. I did so readily, and he told me to wear something really sexy. I chose a tight red dress and black, lacy stockings. My favorite black velvet boots.

We drove to the Westin Peachtree Plaza, driving into downtown at sunset. Sam dropped me in front of the hotel while he went to park in a nearby deck. I stopped outside to smoke a cigarette. My ample cleavage garnered lots of attention on the side of Peachtree Street.

I rode the glass elevator up to the Sun Dial bar just before sunset, wondering if anyone who looked up from the street could see that I wasn't wearing panties. The last time I'd been there was the fourth of July, with Sam and the boys. I'd been in a dress then, too, but it had been a wholly different affair.

I exited the elevator on the seventy-second floor and took the stairs up to the lounge. From so high above the city, I could see the sun sliding below the farthest orange-blazing horizon. I walked all the way around the revolving, circular room until I found the bar.

"Screwdriver with Stoli, please," I smiled to the bartender.

He was cute, in his twenties, tall and thin, with a disheveled mop of dark brown waves. His long nose and strong cheekbones reminded me of Sam at that age.

"Are you joining someone? Should I start a tab?" He slid my drink across the bar to me.

I shook my head slowly, grinning. "No tab. We'll see."

He winked at me as he took my cash. I folded a sizable tip into his jar and went to find a lounge seat.

I sipped my drink, watching the last of the slanted autumn daylight slide down the steel and glass of downtown Atlanta. As the city sky turned to peppery twilight, Sam walked up to my low, leather seat.

"The bartender says you like Stoli." He offered me a second drink to replace my almost-finished first.

I grinned sideways and took the glass from him, stirring the liquid with the thin, red stick.

"Indeed I do. I hope you tipped him well for remembering."

"Indeed I did. Is this seat taken?" He gestured toward the one across the low table from me.

"It is now."

I sat up straight, my long legs pushing my knees up in front of me. I purposefully spread my legs slightly and crossed them, like Sharon Stone in *Basic Instinct*.

"Are we playing 'Lonely Business Man and the Hooker'?" I teased.

Sam raised his eyebrow at me. "I'm from out of town. I'm here on business."

He moved around to sit in the seat next to me. I giggled and caressed his knee.

"You look really *hot*," he whispered in my ear.

I blushed and grinned away from him. We ordered bar food and a couple more drinks.

"That bartender is cute," I remarked as our seats revolved past him again. "He reminds me of you when you were young."

"Are you gonna take him home?"

I laughed and shook my head. "Hardly. Though he is damn adorable."

"You could do it. I bet you could pick him up."

"*Great!* I'll stay here all night and wait for him to finish his shift and fuck him in the lobby bathroom."

"You can if you want to, you know. It'd be kind of hot."

Was he serious? I honestly couldn't tell.

"Another time maybe," I quipped.

By the time we finished sharing a burger and a quesadilla, I was four drinks into my evening.

"I'm a little drunk," I said as Sam pulled me to wobbly standing.

"*Already?*"

"I can't hold my liquor like I used to. It makes Mr. Stolichnaya very sad."

I stopped by the sleek, shiny bathroom before meeting Sam at the elevator. We rode back to lobby, as close together as we could get without offending other people in the car. We walked to the bank of elevators that led up to the rooms.

The hallway of the sixty-third floor was lushly quiet. Sam led me around the corner and down the deserted hall to our room, opening the door for me.

The chilled room was dimly lit by one lamp. Thin sheers and heavier drapes framed the gleaming city lights of Atlanta. I crossed to the floor-to-ceiling windows, curved slightly to make the outside wall of the round hotel, and opened the curtains fully.

Reflected in the glass, I saw Sam turn the bedside lamp off. He stepped up behind me and wrapped his arms around my waist, nuzzling against the side of my neck.

"You look amazing," he whispered into my ear.

"It'll be better like this," I said, pulling the flimsy red dress over my head and tossing it to a nearby chair.

I watched our shadowy silhouette echo against the glass as he reached his hand between my legs. He was hard behind me.

I turned my head and kissed him hard. Sam's hands did their warm roam of my body, lightly trailing from back to breast to belly. He pulled my bra down, freeing my breasts without bothering to unhook it. He stripped quickly. The foreplay had been going on for two hours; there was no need to delay.

He placed his hand on my back, bending me over and pushing me toward the glass. I pressed my arms against the window for support, and I could see the lights of Saturday night traffic creeping down Peachtree Street as he slid into me from behind. Sixty stories up and I was flying.

Legs shaking, we collapsed on top of the bed, gasping and kissing. Sam was on me again in an instant, barely slowing down after the first time.

"So you wanted to take the bartender home?" he murmured from between my thighs.

Eyes closed, I nodded against the pillow. "Maybe. Do you like that, baby? Does that turn you on?"

"*Mmmm-hmmm.*" He curled his arms around my thighs and pulled me closer to him. "The thought of you with another guy is *hot*."

We talked through the scenario, the parley aggrandized and colorful. At the very least, it was prurient fantasy. In the back of my distracted mind, there was the possibility it was passive negotiation of sexual freedom.

"*Oh my god!*" I panted as Sam crawled up next to me. I snuggled against him on his side, looking at me in the subtle light. "I love... *sex with you*."

I caught myself. I'd almost said, "I love hotel sex!" I was afraid it would remind him of what happened with Alex, and I didn't want either of us to spoil this night by thinking about *him*.

Sam laughed. "I'm sorry we have to leave so soon. There's not time to go again."

"Damn babysitter."

He nodded in agreement. "So inconvenient."

I went into the bathroom to straighten myself. Sitting on the toilet and peeing, I grabbed my phone and emailed Frankie.

Drunk and getting laid in the window of the Westin, 63 stories up— fucking awesome! Here's to hoping I'm too drunk to remember this tomorrow!

As I hit **SEND**, I noticed that it wasn't Frankie's email address in the **TO** field. It was *Alex*'s.

Ofuckohfuckohfuck! I need an UNSEND button!

His address was still the first one in my history, and my fat, drunk fingers had touched the wrong line.

I immediately emailed him a second message.

Sorry. That wasn't meant for you.

It wasn't the first time I'd sent him something by mistake. I would get in a hurry when replying to a text or email and hit the wrong thing. I'd done it the entire time I'd known him, and I didn't just do it with him.

I'll learn to use my fucking phone one day.

I would have to tell Sam, but I wasn't doing it then.

I was humming in the car on the way home.

"What song is that?"

"Twilight Singers. 'I'm Ready'. It's stuck in my head."

"Put it in."

I plugged my iPod into the MP3 jack and started *Dynamite Steps*. For once, it wasn't tied up with Alex.

"Goddamn, I love Greg Dulli."

"I don't get it but okay."

I laughed and sang and held Sam's hand as we drove home in time to relieve the babysitter.

"Thanks for a great night," I said as we climb into bed. My body was still buzzing, but my head was finally clearing.

"My pleasure!" Sam replied sleepily. He curled himself around me and settled into slumber.

I sucked it up the next morning and told him about the email. I explained quickly and with as little fanfare as possible.

"I didn't mean to do it. I meant to send it to Frankie. I'm sorry. I wanted you to know."

"Why would you send that to Frankie?"

"She and I had been talking about Date Night, that we were going to the Westin." I shrugged. "It's a girl thing. I would've told her the next time I talked to her anyway, but I was drunk and excited, and I couldn't wait."

He was quiet for a long moment.

"I appreciate your telling me, but I'm concerned it's a little more Freudian than you're giving it credit for being."

I smiled innocently. "I'm sure Freud would have a lot to say about it, but I swear it doesn't mean anything more than my fingers are too fat for an iPhone keyboard."

I'd made the mistake and been forthcoming. I didn't want to lend it any more emotional weight than it deserved. It had been totally unintentional, but it still struck me as funny.

Was Sam right? Was it a huge Freudian slip with subtle, dire meaning? What did it say about me that I was in the midst of amazing, mind-blowing sex with my husband and ended up telling my ex-lover about it?

At four thirty in the morning, Sam came into the bedroom and switched on his lamp.

"Tell me now, when did you change your Gmail password?"

Is he speaking English?

"What?" I asked groggily.

"You changed your Gmail password! When?"

Why is he asking me about my password?

"I changed my password after we found out my machine had been compromised. You knew that. Why are you waking me up to ask me this?"

"It's changed since then. You've changed it since then. I have a script set up to connect to all of our accounts regularly. It logs in and checks to make sure the account hasn't been changed. Yours has changed since the script ran last."

"Why the fuck are you monitoring my accounts? I didn't give you permission to do that!"

"It's my network!" he yelled. "This is my goddamn house! I will monitor any and all activity as I see fit!"

Sam had woken me up in the middle of the night to yell at me about the password to my private email having changed. This wasn't even my account on his server; this was for my account that was totally off his grid. I hadn't given him my password. If he had it, it was because he'd cracked it, and there was nothing I could ever do to stop that.

I didn't know how much he'd had to drink.

"This is bullshit! You woke me up in the middle of the night to yell at me about this? I haven't changed my password! Leave me alone!"

I tried to turn over and go to sleep. He left the room but came back a moment later, yelling my password at me. It was right except for one character that he wasn't making upper case. He'd written it down wrong when he cracked it.

"That's the password I had last, and now that's not working."

"That was *never* the password. It's wrong."

"Then tell me what it is!"

"Fuck off! Leave me the fuck alone!"

"No, Tierney, tell me the password. Tell me why you changed it. Was it to keep me from seeing when you emailed Alex?"

"I *told* you! It was an accident! I didn't *mean* to email Alex, I haven't changed my fucking password!"

I threw the blankets back and got up. I didn't want to argue in our room, right by the boys' bedrooms. I stomped down the hall toward the deck.

"I want to see the email," he hissed, trailing right behind me.

"I don't have it! I deleted it!"

"*How convenient,*" Sam remarked snidely.

"Oh my god! This is insane!"

"You'll never be done with him!"

I turned quickly and faced him, furious that he wouldn't leave me the fuck alone.

"*Goddammit! I didn't mean to message him!* His address was still in my history, and it was an *accident*! I can't help it!"

"I can make sure it never happens again."

Something minute in his tone shifted. Where he'd been enraged, he now sounded amused.

"What does that mean?" I asked calmly.

"If you really want to be rid of him in your life, I have a way to make that really easy for you."

"Meaning what?"

Feel him out. Stay calm.

"Meaning I can make it happen, if it's what you really want. It would be really easy."

"No, Sam, what the hell do you mean by that?"

He smiled. "I can make it impossible for you to *ever* talk to him again. If you think it will help, I can make that happen."

His tone was smug and intimidating. I stared at him.

"You need to tell me what the hell you're talking about."

He shook his head and smiled. "No. I don't. I'm only telling someone who trusts me enough to spend the rest of their life with me, to be *married* to me."

"I gotta tell you," I said, "that sounds threatening and ominous. I don't know what you're thinking, but you need to tell me now!"

"Nope. And there's nothing *threatening* about it," he scoffed. "Why would I take a stupid risk, when all I want is to be with you?"

He'd admitted that he was monitoring my email. I knew he'd previously checked my phone and text logs. Maybe he meant he would cut off my internet access or block emails or shut down my cell. Maybe he meant he would go to Talia and create a terrible rift.

He was irrational and erratic in his hurting. He was also regularly armed. I didn't want to think he would do something so stupid as to actually *harm* Alex, or me. The problem was that he was drinking all the time. He seemed less and less stable. This was way beyond angry and jealous; it was threatening and intentional.

"Besides," he taunted, "no one would ever catch me. I could fuck up his life—and Paul's and Max's and Charlie's just for spite—and absolutely *no one* would ever know it was me. I could show Digital Freedom Front a thing or two on how to *really* hack someone one's life apart."

"Paul and Max and Charlie had *nothing* to do with any of this! They didn't even know—"

"Then Alex fucking Wheeler should've thought of that before he *fucked* my wife!"

Oh my god.

If there was one thing Sam knew how to do, it was to find and manipulate information. He'd done dozens of interviews about large- and small-scale identity theft, and he had access to data that wasn't available to the general public. It would probably take him five minutes to destroy all of their lives.

I was sick, knowing my culpability in all of it. There was that whole "for better or for worse" thing, but I absolutely didn't trust him. I had no specific threat that made me think he would hurt me or the boys, but I was really worried he might go wonky at any time. I couldn't continue to place myself and my children in this increasingly deteriorating environment.

"I need to clear my head," I said finally. I wanted to get away from him for a little while.

"Fine. You have until ten o'clock tomorrow morning to give me an answer. You can tell me then if you've decided to be with me—and never speak of Alex Wheeler again—or if we're finished."

"I'm supposed to go to Birmingham—"

"Then I suggest you make a decision before you leave."

Sam was the one who'd left and walked out and was gone and done long before I'd known it. But then he was back, because I'd asked him to be and assured him and promised him. And I'd lied. I'd known what I was going to do before I did it. I planned and schedule and tricked to get the most selfish thing I could. Now he was watching my every move, every little thing I did, for signs of betrayal, for a reason to let me go and be able to blame me fully for it.

I knew what I'd done. I knew the potential repercussions when all of it started with Alex. I was dead inside then, done with my marriage and this life, and then something special and magical happened.

I was balancing tenuously, trying to figure out how to keep Sam calm and how to keep Alex safe. I was so goddamn mad at having ever been pushed to this god-awful place of walking the tightrope. I was trying desperately not to dangle for my fucking life.

Chapter 26

I woke early the next morning and threw some clothes and make-up into an overnight bag. I made coffee and breakfast for the boys, who were sprawled across each other on the couch, watching cartoons.

"I'm leaving," I said to a sleeping Sam, gently touching his arm.

"Okay."

"The boys are fed and watching television. I'll be home tomorrow afternoon."

"Where are you staying tonight?"

"At Frankie's."

"Be careful."

I didn't kiss him goodbye.

As much of an asshole as he'd been the night before, I knew Sam just needed to sleep off his aggression. I'd made an innocent mistake in emailing Alex. I was sure he would be mad for a few days and forget about it, like he always did.

I stopped for gas and a cup of coffee. The three-hour drive to Birmingham from our house wasn't a difficult one, but it was always much easier without the boys. I didn't have to worry about how loud my music was or if there were too many f-bombs to be kid-appropriate. I could just *drive* and lose myself in my music and my thoughts.

Jules had emailed me and Frankie two weeks before, asking us to come to the Barking Kudu to see her brother's band play. They had a half-hour set in the middle of the evening, one of half a dozen acts performing as a fundraiser for some local charity.

I hadn't seen Mac in years. Five years younger than Jules and I, he would sometimes come visit us when we were living together in Montevallo. He was this greasy, pimply, lanky kid who would ogle my tits until Jules punched him in the arm. He would always convince us to buy him beer and take him with us to some party, and then boast about how smooth he was with the college girls. I never once saw him actually *talk* to any college girl other than me or Jules, and he almost always ended up vomiting into some azaleas after three beers.

I'd packed a strapless, black corset top and my new, smaller jeans, but I knew my arms were too flabby to be on display, even in the darkness of a dive bar. I stopped at Brookwood Mall and found a black, ruched shrug in jersey knit that I really liked. There was no extra-large, though.

Try it. Maybe.

I tried on the large, and it fit perfectly.

I smiled to myself all the way back to my car, one small shopping bag dangling from my hand.

I couldn't remember having *ever* been able to wear a large. I was now a little smaller than I'd been when I started high school, and I was at least three inches taller than I'd been then. Almost no one who knew me had ever known me smaller than a size fourteen.

I had a quick lunch at O'Carr's, a deli I loved but only got to visit every few years when we had extra time during a trip to Birmingham. We were usually so busy running from family to family that we hardly ever had time to enjoy the city. I stopped at a nearby bookstore, Little Professor, and relished an hour of browsing that didn't include looking at a single children's book.

Frankie texted me to meet them at the bar at five. I still had a few hours to kill and needed to get ready. I called my mom to see if I could use her shower.

"Sure. Come on."

I hadn't seen her or been to her house in months. We talked at least a couple of times a week, but it was always just to check in and make sure the other was alive. I'd tell her about the boys' latest antics and assure her that Sam and I were each well.

I took a shower and settled onto the sofa in her den, across the coffee table from where she was nestled into her recliner with the dog. I wrapped myself in a blanket, feeling suddenly cold and not so well. I hoped I wasn't coming down with something. Mom and I caught up on family gossip and news and whatever ailment was bothering her that week.

"How's Sam?"

She knew things had been tense between us but had no idea about the truth of it all.

"He's good! It's been a long summer," I smiled. "You know, we were about five seconds away from filing for divorce. Things are much better."

"Can I tell you I'm not surprised?" she asked a little cautiously. "Based on some things you'd said and done."

I shrugged. "No matter. It's better now."

I hadn't delved into details of my marital problems with her, because I didn't want to hear *exactly* that kind of response. She could be so matter-of-fact about her views of a situation that she seemed judgmental and unsupportive. If I'd chosen to talk to her about it, I would've wanted her to simply ask what she could do to help. I would be *happy* if she would ever just *listen* and acknowledge that I was struggling with some emotional turmoil. That had rarely ever been the case with my mother, though, as she always had to chime in with her perceptions of the situation, usually accompanied by some anecdote of how she'd been through something similar. Somehow she always managed to turn it into something about her.

"How's Sam's dad?" she asked.

Sam's father had been bed-ridden for more than two years, his life debilitated by Alzheimer's. He was in relatively good physical health, but even that had been dwindling over the last few months. He was rarely lucid and didn't speak very often anymore. Sam's mother, who was fifteen years younger, spent almost all of her time caring for her husband. She'd refused to put him in a nursing home and was often physically and emotionally weary from the constant caregiving.

"About the same. I mean, it's not like he's going to get better. I just hate it, though, knowing was a smart, vibrant man he was when he was younger. Sam has hard days when I know he really misses being able to talk to his dad."

"It's going to be really hard for him when his dad dies, Tierney."

"I know."

Of course it is, lady!

"I know how it feels. I remember it well. He was your paw-paw, but he was my daddy."

He wasn't my paw-paw. He was my molester!

Was she really that deeply in denial?

Yeah. She was.

Facing the shortcomings of your parents as people, as plain old human beings, is undeniably part of coming into your own adulthood. It's sobering to see their faults, to see your own reflection in that retrospection, and I could barely imagine the horror of confronting the most deplorable deeds as something accountable to your earliest role models.   While I'd been faced with my mother's dismissal of my need to be protected and defended—also by father's temper and absence—I had no idea what it meant to know my parent violated my child in the most horrifying ways. But her neverending love for her father was an occasionally agitating source of vexation for me, especially when she obviously turned a blind eye to my own painful memories.

It wasn't like I didn't know she loved me. She would do whatever she could to help me, though I couldn't remember her ever being self-sacrificing in her support. My memories of my mother were often fuzzy and distant. There had been care and warmth and concern, but it was always pragmatic and she had assumed that I was able to take care of myself. Perhaps it had helped me become strong and independent, but I wished more than anything that I could remember having ever felt simply *comforted* by her care, rather than uncomfortable and waiting for her inevitable restraint.

I was learning not only from my faults and mistakes; I was learning how to parent, how *not* to parent, through my parents' missteps.

"I gotta get ready," I said.

Heavy, glitzy make-up and big hair, plus my new purple shoes, and I was off to see my friends.

By the time I got to Southside, I felt out of sorts. I was shivering with cold, though I didn't really feel feverish. Late September in the South is still quite hot, but I turned on the heat in my car, trying to abate the deep chill.

I pulled into a streetside parking space down the block from the Barking Kudu. The tan mini-van parked in front of me had a University of Montevallo student parking decal and a Girl Scouts of America bumper sticker. Frankie was sitting in the driver's seat, talking on her cell phone.

I got out and locked my car, dropping my keys into my tiny black purse. Walking up to her driver's side window, she held up a finger and motioned for me to hang on. She was nodding and listening, then arguing quietly into the phone. I couldn't hear the specifics, but her muffled tone was agitated and angry.

Finally she stepped out and rolled her eyes.

"Everything okay?" I asked, concerned.

She shook her head. "But it will be. How are you, pretty girl?"

"I'm cold," I said as I leaned in to hug her. "Kind of. I don't really *feel* cold, but I'm shivering like I'm freezing. I don't know what it is. I've been this way all afternoon."

"Let's hope it's not pneumonia again," she frowned, locking her car with a remote.

We went inside, straight to the bar, and order two shots of whiskey.

Frankie tossed hers back immediately. "Much better," she said, placing her empty glass on the dark, oak bar and ordering a second.

"What happened?"

She shook her freshly-highlighted locks and smiled innocently. "My husband is a twatwad. He's known for a week that I was going out with you guys. He also knows what happened. With Alex. He's been all weird all day, and I didn't know why. So he called me as I got off the interstate to ask me something about dinner for the girls. I'd *told* him there was lasagna in the fridge. All he had to do was pop it in the oven. So then he tells me not to drink after you tonight, because infidelity can be contagious."

"How the hell can infidelity be *catching*?" Jules drawled from behind us.

I spun quickly on my barstool. "Julesy!"

"Is there, like, a *virus* that makes people sleep with other people? Don't tell my first husband. It'll just make Kyle feel justified in having fucked a dozen other women."

Frankie and I laughed and ordered a shot for Jules.

"Where's Mac?"

"He should be here any minute."

I looked at Frankie. "Don't feel bad. Tessa said Ed is mad as hell at me."

"*Why?*"

I shrugged. "Because I cheated on Sam. He and Ed have been friends since they were twelve. They lived together in college. But I don't think Ed has even emailed him *once* to check and see how he is.

He tells Tessa that he feels awful for Sam, but he's not offered to be there for him. He told Tessa how he thought infidelity was just *the* worst thing a person could ever do in a marriage. I would argue that emotionally and sexually abandoning your partner is at least as bad."

Frankie nodded at me. "No shit."

"Well, I really think men are kinda programmed in a certain way," Jules said. "They react to things in a pretty uniform and predictable pattern, and they stick together. They have to *own* their pussy. Any threat to that perceived ownership is met with extreme hostility. For Ed and Jay, if it can happen to Sam, it can happen to them."

"You know what? If you don't want your wife to fuck someone else, you'd better make *damn* sure you're doing it yourself! He fucking *ignored* me for a year before I ever even met Alex. He wasn't *there*. I'm not blaming Sam for my choices—I'm the one who decided to let Alex put his dick in me. But Sam has his own culpability in the decline of our marriage, and I am fucking *tired* of asshats who think my falling for someone else is the worst possible thing I could've done to my husband. I can promise you, I could be a *lot* more vindictive than that!"

"But that's the real problem, isn't it?" Frankie interjected. "I mean, you *fucked* someone else. Okay. That's a problem. The *real* issue is that you *fell in love* with someone else."

"Who did you fall in love with?"

The three of us turned in unison.

"*You*, Mac," I deadpanned. "I fell in love with *you*."

"The moment you laid eyes on me?"

"Something like that."

I stood and hugged Mac, who was now tall enough to tower six inches over me. He picked me up and spun me around.

"You look *fabulous*, Tierney! You're a little tiny thing."

"No," I blushed, "I will *never* be a little tiny thing. But thank you for noticing. A girl needs a hot guy to sometimes tell her she's not too bad."

"Not too bad? *P-shaw!* You're a bombshell, precious! Now who did you fall in love with? Did Sam finally give you up?"

Jules slid down, so Mac could sit next to me. "No, Sam did not give me up, though believe me, he wanted to some days." Mac chuckled. "But... I had an affair. I fell in love with someone else."

Mac cocked his head and looked at me. "Well, I'm sorry it wasn't me, but it must've been someone special if you bothered to take the time for them."

"Thanks for not being a judgmental asshole, Mac."

He shrugged. "I might think differently if I were actually *married*, but that's precisely *why* I won't ever get married. There's too much pussy out there for me to be pettin' the same kitty for forty years."

"Okay, so tell me this," I started. "You're a *man*—"

"Why, yes. Yes, I am."

I winked at him. "We're just talking about how men, specifically how Frankie and Tessa's husbands are mad at me that I cheated on Sam. In their opinions, it seems to be the worst thing I could do. But Ed, specifically, was Sam's best friend for a really long time. As far as I know, he hasn't bothered to call or email Sam to check on him, even though he knows what's happened. It feels kind of hypocritical to me, like he'll be all indignant at what I've done but not enough to actually be there for his friend."

"Oh!" Mac replied. "I'm sure he won't! I mean, I wouldn't."

I looked at him quizzically. "*Why?*"

Mac picked up my glass and took a sip. "Because we're *men*. We barely like to deal with our own emotions, let alone anyone else's. And, more importantly, we don't want *someone else* all up in our shit. I mean, what's Ed supposed to say? 'Hey, man! How's that whole cheating thing going?' It would be like a red, hot poker right in the crotch. It's hard enough to feel like your masculinity has been eviscerated; you don't anyone else doing the flaying for you, no matter how well-intended they may be."

"That's fucked up," Frankie said. "Men suck."

"We do," Mac said smugly. "But you'll always keep coming back for more."

"Not me," Jules chimed. "If it doesn't work out with Steve, I'm done with men."

I leaned across Mac and touched Jules on the thigh. "I got a strap-on I can set you up with, *lovah!*"

Mac stuck his fingers in his ears and squeezed his eyes shut. "*Lalalalala! I can't hear you!*"

"So what the hell is this band you're playing in?" Frankie asked. "The last time I saw you, you were finishing up law school at Cumberland."

Mac nodded. "I did. Man, it's been a long time since I've seen you guys! I graduated, passed the bar, and I'm working as a mediator. I like to call myself a *facilitator*. I make things happen."

"So you call yourself a facilitator to sound badass?"

"No, I call myself that 'cause it sounds cooler to dumb chicks. I get so much more pussy that way." I poked him in the ribs. Hard. "No, I'm playing drums in this band with some guys from law school. We're called Cumberland Gorge."

"That's a *horrible* name!" I laughed.

"Yeah, but just saying I'm a drummer in a band—"

"Gets you more pussy?"

"*Exactly!* Women will do anything for a rock star."

Jules and Frankie and I looked at each other, shocked into silence for a moment, then roared with laughter.

"Don't I fucking know it!" I crowed.

"I gotta go unload and set up. Will you get me a beer?"

"Are you gonna throw it up if I pay for it?" Jules asked warily.

"There are no azaleas in here, so *no*."

We stuck around, talking and drinking, waiting for Cumberland Gorge to take the stage. They played all cover songs, but they were good. I was four drinks in by the time they started playing "Mantissa" to close their set.

It was Junkture's first big hit song, and it shouldn't have surprised me that a cover band would play it. But it startled me, sending me reeling into memories and thoughts of Alex.

"You okay?"

It was Jules with her arm wrapped around my waist.

I shook my head and smiled. "Not even close."

We stayed politely, watching Mac's band finish their set. The singer was okay, but he definitely wasn't Alex Wheeler.

The three of us went outside to the patio and ordered fresh drinks.

"I fucking *hate* Junkture," Jules sighed.

Frankie and I stared at her across the metal, mesh-topped table.

"Don't get me wrong. I really liked their first record, and I *love* Max. But it all sounded the same after that. It was all the same fucking song, over and over. I'm sure Alex is a great guy, but he needs some new goddamn lyrics. I mean, how many times can Alex Wheeler sing about being on his fucking knees?"

She wasn't wrong. It was part of what I'd told him in San Antonio, to look deep inside himself to write a great new song. When he was unsure or afraid of what he would find, he would always fall back on a comfortable set of imagery.

"I miss him, you know," I said finally.

"Have you talked to him at all?" Frankie asked gently, looking up from a text message.

"Nope. I want to, all the time. I get bored or I see some article about something that I know would interest him—or I hear one of his songs—and it makes me *crazy*, because I just want to *talk* to him. Just five minutes of his voice, knowing exactly why I'm telling him what I telling him. I miss that."

"Breakups suck," Jules said. "No matter which side of it you're on, they just fucking *suck*. And I know this is hard, because you don't want to not have Alex in your life. But the reality is, Alex is *married*. You are, therefore, a *fling*. Even if he cares deeply for you—and I can't see him *not* caring deeply for someone as wonderful as you—he is still married and that limits the level of intimacy you can have. *You* are still married and have two amazing kids. Walking with one foot in each world was throwing your world out of balance, Kitten. If you can salvage this marriage with Sam, it will take a firm decision on your part to cut that tie for good, even if that means Max and Paul and Junkture. Maybe even Seth. Any link to Alex. Otherwise, you're balancing on a razor's edge that just might split you right down the middle."

I started to cry, sitting in the sultry evening breeze. I hadn't even touched my drink. I felt sick and started to shake again.

Frankie excused herself to take a phone call.

"Sam is threatening to destroy Alex. Max, Paulie, whoever else he thinks has some modicum of blame in this."

"How?"

"I don't know specifically. He threatened to hack their lives apart."

"*Ugh.* That's no good, Tierney. He has a lot of ammunition and skills. I would imagine he could totally wreck their lives if he wanted to."

I nodded at her and gulped at my drink. "It wouldn't even be that hard for him."

"I'm betting he could be one badass motherfucker if you crossed him."

"Let's hope we never have to find out."

Frankie came back to the table, tears welling in her bright, blue eyes.

"Moonshine, what is it?"

"*Twatwad! Fuck!* I have to go home."

"Is everything okay?"

"No!" Frankie yelled. "My husband is a goddamn prick! I do *everything* in that house. I cook, I clean, I make sure the girls get their homework done and do their chores and go to Girl Scouts and soccer. I pay the bills. *And* I go to school full time. I asked for one night out, *one night!*, and he's giving me grief."

"What the fuck is he mad about now?" I asked. "Is it still because you're with me?"

She looked at me, refusing to answer directly. "He texted to remind me that I have to cover the nursery at church in the morning. Then he called to tell me that I would have to iron the girls' dresses before church, because he didn't know what I'd planned for them to wear. They're old enough to pick out their own fucking clothes!" She sighed, irritated and upset. "I just have to go home so he'll *stop*."

"I'm so sorry. I'm sorry I got you involved."

She shook her head and grabbed my hand. "*No.* Don't be. This is on Jay. I'm your friend, no matter what, and I would've been more upset if you hadn't told me you were going through all of this. He's just...."

"*A twatwad*?" Jules offered.

"An asshat?" I suggested.

"A total fucking dick," Frankie croaked. "I'm sorry, Tierney, do you have somewhere to stay?"

"Yeah, don't fret it. It's no problem."

She grabbed her purse quickly and hugged us both goodbye. "Tell Mac I said goodnight."

"I don't get that one," I said to Jules finally. "But who the fuck am I to judge? I'm in love with two men, neither of whom really wants me."

"Stop it, Kitten. I'm sure they both *want* you, but you know it isn't that simple. But Jay Luna... I'm worried about Frankie. I'm on my third marriage, and I can't tell you what works, but I am *damn* sure cutting your wife off from her friends will *not* be healthy for that marriage."

I stayed at the Barking Kudu with Jules and Mac and his bandmates, watching the other bands and drinking. I knew I had to drive, so I was pacing myself, but I was feeling no pain. Somehow karaoke started late in the evening, and I ended up on stage singing "Goodbye Earl" with Jules, who started yelling into the mic about how men shouldn't be assholes to their women.

Sam Johnson
Sep 30th   12:51 AM

Are you still at the bar?

>   **Yeah.   About to leave.   Going to my dad's.**

I thought you were staying with Frankie?

>   **Something came up.   I'll tell you when I talk to you.   I'm going to Dad's instead.**

Have you been drinking?

>   **Yes but I'm okay. I didn't drink too much.**

Are you sure you're ok to drive?

>   **Positive.   I promise.   I'll text you when I get to Dad's.**

I drove thirty minutes to my dad's house, careful to turn down the volume as I pulled into his driveway. One lamp was on in the den as I quietly unlocked the door. My dad was asleep in his recliner. I dropped my purse and shoes in his bedroom and quietly climbed the stairs to the den.

Sep 30th 1:36 AM

Are you still up?

Yes

I called Sam at home.

"Hey, sweetie! How are you?"

"Fine. How was the show? What happened with Frankie?"

"Show was good. Frankie and Jules said to tell you hi." I explained about Frankie's fight with Jay. "It's all good. I'm at Dad's. How are things there?"

"Everything here is fine. I'm just... I expected you to be with Frankie." He sounded angry.

"I couldn't help it," I said defensively. "I'm somewhere safe, it doesn't matter."

"We need to talk when you get home." He sounded sketchy and distracted.

I was alarmed. "What's wrong?"

"It's fine. It'll wait until you get home tomorrow."

"Sam, no, tell me now. It's just going to bug the shit out of me until you do. I won't sleep if I know there's something hanging over me. Tell me."

He took a breath. "Okay, but you have to give me a pass for telling you over the phone and not doing it in person."

Now I was really alarmed. Had he wrecked the car? Had the cat died? Were the children hurt?

No, he'd tell me that immediately.

The only thing I could imagine that would make him apprehensive to tell me over the phone would be if he'd slept with someone else. If he had, I knew it couldn't have happened since I'd left for Birmingham, almost twenty-four hours ago. He'd had the boys with him the entire time.

Could he have slept with someone else?

"Okay, done. Now tell me. You're freaking me out."

"I filed for divorce."

What the fuck? I hadn't seen that coming at all.

"*What? When?*"

"I got the call from my attorney this afternoon that it had been filed yesterday."

This afternoon?

That was when the shaking had started. I *knew* I didn't feel bad. I wasn't really cold; I was picking up on this weird, psychic tension from my husband.

"When did you tell them to file?" I demanded.

"On Monday, after your birthday."

I couldn't breathe. I was sitting alone in my dad's den at two in the morning, hearing that my husband had filed for divorce with absolutely no warning. I was almost two hundred miles from home, away from my bed and my children.

"*And you couldn't be bothered to fucking tell me?* Things were *better*!"

"You didn't tell me about the messages from Alex. There was still so much drama and excitement over all of that, and it just never stops. I need it to stop, Tierney."

"*Why the fuck didn't you tell me?*"

"I'm telling you now. I wanted to tell you when you were with Frankie, so you'd be with friends, but that didn't work out. I'm sorry, but remember you said you'd give me a pass for doing it over the phone."

"Okay," I conceded grudgingly, "I won't be angry for telling me over the phone. But *fuck you* for not goddamn telling me before I left town. *Fuck you!*"

"I know. I'm sorry. I didn't know what to say," he whispered.

I didn't understand. Yes, we'd had problems, for months. We were falling apart before I ever met Alex. We'd been up and down so many times, together and not, since he found out about the affair. Yet again, I thought we were up, together, and Sam was headed in a completely different direction.

"I'll be home tomorrow morning," I said.

"Okay. Be safe coming home."

"Yeah, whatever. Bye."

I hung up, hitting **END** as angrily as I could muster on an iPhone.

I sat there in an old, overstuffed chair, stunned. It was nearly three in the morning. I emailed Tessa and Frankie and Jules and Seth, short and simply that I was in Birmingham and Sam had just told me he'd filed for divorce.

I brushed my teeth and crashed on my dad's bed. He was asleep in his recliner in the den. I was thankful I didn't have to face him yet. My body passed out from exhaustion, but my brain never stopped churning.

I need to get home to my children.

————————————

I woke very early and went upstairs to take a shower. Dad was just waking in his chair when I came down, dressed and hair dripping everywhere. It was a little after seven.

"Up already?" he asked. "How was your night?"

"Fine. Yeah, I gotta head back to Atlanta."

"Already? Everything okay?"

"Not really. Apparently Sam decided to file for divorce."

Dad was taken aback. "I thought things were better."

"So did I. I gotta get home and find out what the fuck is going on."

"Do you need anything? Is there anything I can do?"

I shook my head. "Nope. I'll let you know what I find out."

I gathered my scattered things and tossed them back into my overnight bag.

I was just pulling out of his driveway when my phone dinged with a new text.

Seth Wiezel
September 30th 7:54 AM

Sorry I couldn't respond when you emailed me. I had a stripper sitting on my face.

It's okay.

I'm still up if you want to call.

K. Gimme five. I gotta stop to get coffee.

I pulled into the nearest gas station and got a large coffee, loading it with sugar and cream. I found a granola bar and some nuts, something moderately healthy from the convenience store. I also picked up a pack of cigarettes.   I paid and went outside to call Seth and smoke a cigarette.

"So he just told you over the phone?" he asked when he answered his phone.

"Yep." I told him the story, of how the night had gone with absolutely no warning of what was coming.   "I don't even really care that he waited to tell me until I was out of town. I mean, that's shitty and unexpected, but I guess there was never going to be a good time. What pisses me off is that he told his attorney to move on it days ago and didn't bother to tell me!"

"That's pretty fucked.   But, you know... maybe this was coming all along. You guys have been trying to hold onto something that's been broken for a while. Divorce sucks, but maybe it's the best thing for your family."

"Yeah, it might be.   I don't want to have to break my children's heart, Hammer."

"You guys will do what's best for your kids. You'll find a way to work together and make this as easy as possible for them. It sucks, I know, but they'll be fine, Tierney."

Seth and I talked for the first fifty miles of my drive. He was patient and honest with me, reminding me that lots of people had marriages that ended but that they were still able to go on and have happy lives.

Because I hadn't expected it emotionally, I wasn't sure how I was going to move forward. I'd had time over the summer to start to map out a plan for a new life, just in case it actually happened. Things between Sam and me had seemed so much better, and I'd stopped thinking about it.

But now, I had no choice. I had to start considering a life on my own.

Chapter 27

The boys greeted me when I got home, oblivious to what was happening between their parents. Sam was polite but terse. We got through the afternoon and into the evening with no incidents.

I thought we'd be able to go to the deck and talk through it, hoping in the back of my mind that he'd tell me he'd made the wrong choice. He'd been so erratic for weeks that I wouldn't have been surprised if he changed his mind again.

"So what's your plan?" I asked him.

"I'll start looking again for a place to live. Something close."

"How soon are you thinking you'll move out?"

He shrugged. "As soon as possible."

"It's not right," I complained. "There's no reason for this."

"I need a date, Tierney. There are all of these momentous dates—for when we got married, for when it happened, for when I found out—and I need a *new* one, for when it stopped. I don't know what happens after that. Maybe we can make it work, but I need a definitive date to start from."

Make it work?

"I'm confused. Are you thinking it's not the end? Are you thinking we'll be able to work these things out and start over after that?"

"I don't know. Maybe. I don't know what I'll want after I get some time and distance. Maybe it'll turn out to be the worst mistake possible, but it's something I need to do."

I didn't want him to hurt. Whether or not he was with me, I wanted him to be able to get over everything and move forward in his own head. I didn't want to be without him, though. We were irrevocably tied together because of our boys, but he was also my friend. He was my sounding board and my caretaker. I didn't want him to ever *not* be there.

"I want joint custody," he said.

"Of course you'll have joint legal custody. There's not any question about that. But the boys should stay with me. It's what they're used to."

"No, Tierney, my attorney says the trend in Georgia is for children to split their time equally between their parents."

I was immediately defensive and angered. How dare he try to take my children from me? Historically, he'd worked long hours with travel several times a year. I'd always been the one to handle getting the boys to and from school. He'd been to two teacher conferences ever and hadn't taken either of the boys to the pediatrician in years. I took care of almost *everything* for them and always had. It was my *job*.

"I'm not discussing this with you," I snapped. "I can't do it calmly. This is something we'll have to work out through our attorneys."

"But—"

"No! I'm not discussing it!" I abruptly went back inside.

Sam was right on my heels, jerking the back door open before I could let it slam shut.

"I've been willing to be fair about all of this, Tierney. I'm asking you to do the same."

I headed for the bedroom, while he drank his first beer of the night.

———————————

I called my attorney the next morning to let her know what was happening.

"Okay," she said, "I'll send you the financial affidavits you need to complete. You'll both have to do this. You need to fill this out, making your best guess as to what your expenses will be like *after* the divorce. Will you be staying in the house?"

"For now, yes, it looks that way."

"Okay, then you'll assume those expenses are roughly the same. Make adjustments to take Sam's costs out of your own. Are you planning to go back to work?"

"I think I'll have to. Neither of us wants the boys' standard of living to suffer, and I think I'll have to get a job to help cover that."

"Take a look at job listings and get a feel for what the going rate is for your skill set. Make a *reasonable* estimation for anticipated income and expenses."

I hadn't had a real job since before Tripp was born. I had no idea what I was worth on the open market. I'd been the boys' primary caregiver for their entire lives, and I still needed to be able to fulfill that role—both for me and for them. They would need as much consistency in their young lives as possible. Their schedules were staggered in such a way that I could only work part-time, unless I put them in afterschool childcare.

I didn't want to upend their life any more than necessary. They were smart, sensitive boys, and I was certain they would be able to adjust to whatever happened. I didn't want them to *have* to, though, and hoped we'd be able to keep their routines as similar as possible.

"It sucks, though," I said to Tessa when I called to complain, "because Tripp's school day starts later than Ian's. I can only work, like, nine-thirty until two-thirty. Almost no one is hiring for such limited hours."

"You should go back to school," she said. "Maybe you can get him to pay full support while you finish your degree."

"You sound like my dad," I replied.

"I still think you'd make a great attorney," she retorted.

She'd said this to me for years. I'd loved my job as a financial paraplanner, in part because I loved reviewing complicated estate documents and deferred compensation agreements. It was geeky, but it suited me.

"That will take forever. Besides, I don't want to have to go to court. If I could have a job where I just did documents all day, I'd be happy."

"That's a paralegal. You'd make a *great* paralegal, Tierney."

Huh. Maybe.

I hung up with her and made a mental note to look into it.

I didn't *want* to be working or going to school. The boys would only be boys for so long. Then what? I would still have to carry on with the next fifty years of my life, even if my life's purpose had already been fulfilled.

And what *was* my purpose? What good had come from my life? I hadn't finished college. Though I loved painting, I didn't have an amazing, fulfilling career. I'd irreparably damaged my marriage repeatedly, all in the hopes of trying to prove that *I* existed and was worthwhile to someone. Both Sam and Alex, the two people I cared most about in the world, had turned from me.

The only good thing I'd ever really done was to birth my sons. Had my destiny been fulfilled by the time I was thirty-two? Would I spend the next fifty years on this journey, constantly on this path toward *whatever*? I'd staunchly argued for months that it didn't matter where I was going, just that I was *going*. Did I even *deserve* to be journeying at all? Did I matter enough to the universe to do anything more than pass time until I died?

The drains of motherhood and womanhood and life were slowing their swirl, and it was a natural time to become introspective. With everything going on in my own life, all of it making me question whether I had any value to the world, I realized that, going forward, I could do anything—not because I was a grown-up with the freedom of choice, but because I was strong and had the capabilities to craft my existence into anything I wanted it to be.

For months, I'd been remembering who I was supposed to be; now it was time to *be*.

––––––––––––––

I could see the tentative beginnings of the structure of my new life. I didn't love it, but I could do anything for a couple of years. Making my children's lives as sane and normal as possible was my main priority. Whereas I'd spent years sacrificing my own wants and needs to care for them, I was ready and able to formulate a concrete plan for being content and confident in myself and my own abilities, while doing everything I could to keep them happy in the midst of so much imminent upheaval.

The one thing that would be missing was Sam. He would still be there, as my children's father, but that wasn't all that I wanted. I wanted to have him as a friend at the very least. We had a successful, functional life in our home with our boys, and I didn't want that to end. Pragmatically, it would be better financially and parentally if we were together. Emotionally, I needed him.

I spent hours going through our financial records. Sam emailed me the outline of our joint spending—everything from groceries to haircuts to magazine subscriptions. Some of the expenses would stay the same, even if he moved out; there would be no change to the mortgage or insurance. Some monthly expenses, such as groceries and utilities, would likely go down by as much as twenty-five percent without the fourth person in the household. But I would have to take on the added cost of health insurance for myself. While I was in substantially better health than I'd been in even a year before, I knew I'd likely have a hard time getting through underwriting for a preferred rate. I would lose my creditable coverage going from a group to an individual policy and might have to change healthcare providers. It was a daunting prospect.

I ran various scenarios in Excel, assuming I maintained my current standard of living, as well as reducing it to a reasonably bare bones minimum while still trying to keep the children's expectations in mind. Because we were upside down in our mortgage-to-home-value ratio, I was hopeful that I'd be able to refinance the house with a mortgage modification after the divorce was final and my income was substantially slashed. I looked at rental costs for the area, just in case I decided to be the one to vacate our current life.

I emailed Sam a copy of the spreadsheets, briefly explaining the details behind the comparisons. I told him of my concerns about the children and insurance, and I asked him to consider filing for a legal separation instead of divorce, if only to allow me to keep decent medical coverage until I finished school, if I decided to go that route.

He replied that he couldn't respond to any of it, that he would be happy to forward it to his attorney for comment.

We stopped talking, unless it was about what was happening in our routine life. We could cordially discuss the children's schedules, the bills that needed to be paid, and who had to be where and when, but there was little talk of Us.

It made me sad. I loved Sam. I could feel the hurt and sadness in him. Even though he was so close, he wouldn't let me reach out and comfort him.

But my heart was still tearing itself apart.

"I just wish I knew it wouldn't hurt forever," I cried one afternoon to Frankie, on the phone. I was in the parking lot of a nearby restaurant, picking up dinner for the family. "Alex is always fucking there. I wish I could see the day that he'll be gone, you know? I need to know I won't miss him, at least one day."

"I'm sorry, baby," she said gently. "The truth is, you'll always miss him. But it *will* get easier, Tierney. At night, when you're on your own in your head, picture him. Picture every detail of him that you can imagine. Slowly picture him fading away, starting at the bottom and working up. He won't be gone, ever, but he'll be a faded memory. Eventually."

I didn't want to forget him, though. I was still hurt and angry, at him but also at all of it just being *over.* I was swept up in the emotional injustice of it all, and it made me irritable.

But the truth was that he was gone. He was out of my life, no matter how badly I didn't want that. And I had to find a way to get over it, to get past it and move on. Sam and I were each planning our separate lives, and my new one wouldn't include Alex, either.

I was always a little on edge, and I was full of nervous energy again. I wasn't painting. I wasn't working. I wasn't playing. *What to do?* I could eat out of sheer stress and boredom, but that would've made me feel worse. Part of my ninety-plus-pound journey had been about teaching myself *not* to eat when I felt anything but hungry. I still had days when I wanted to stuff my belly with emotions, but I tried really hard not to give into that. It had taken a good long while of my kicking and screaming before I learned my lesson, before I realized how much better and different I could feel if I didn't feed my anxieties.

I was feeling antsy on Saturday afternoon, constantly thinking about food, so went to the park to walk. I plugged into my iPod with absolutely no idea what I wanted to listen to. I hit **SHUFFLE ALL SONGS** and started to walk.

It started okay. Murray Head, "One Night in Bangkok". Followed by Liz Phair's "Flower", which is not high energy but which I love inappropriately. Afghan Whigs followed by the Twilight Singers— double-teamed by Greg Dulli, *SWEET*! Then some Led Zeppelin, then the Beatles, neither of which I would've chosen, but I agreed with myself that I wouldn't change the song, no matter what.

"Hot Mess" was next. It was one of the songs that had helped propel me, day after day, when I started walking. I can remember exactly where I was the first ten times I heard it. A perfect fall breeze picked up and reminded me of exactly where I was standing at the other park the first day I did five miles, the day a very specific phone call and text from Alex sent me down a very different path that would eventually lead to so much more.

There was a strange poignancy that snuck up on me and almost dropped me to my knees. There would always be songs that would drop me back into some memory, unexpected and bittersweet, of the places and conversations and whatever, tied irreparably to my music. I wanted to stop in my tracks and cry. But I *couldn't*. I couldn't stop just because something reminded me of a moment that used to be mine. Those moments, those memories, were the path that brought me to *Here*, but they were from a place where I could never go back. They were from a lifetime that didn't even seem like mine anymore.

I kept walking, one purple-Nike-clad foot in front of the other, until the song was over and the iPod shuffled on to Van Morrison. "And It Stoned Me". The irony was palpable, but I pushed through it and waited for the next song, focusing on the rhythm of my stride. I felt the strength of me, of my body and my mind, propelling me forward, one step at a time along my path.

I tried to let the memories go, but it started me thinking about Alex and our months together. It hadn't ended at all like I'd hoped. Our last chat had been ugly and emotionally vicious, and that wasn't what I wanted. I cared about him deeply and didn't want to be angry at him for the rest of my life. I needed to be able to tell him that, to give him that anger and let him do with it what he would. I needed to uncork that bottle and make him drink it down.

"You're right," Jules said on the phone. "You have the right to tell him. He's gotten off pretty easy. You should be able to call him and tell him why you're angry."

"He won't take my call. He blocked me on Facebook. Asshole."

"Well, you knew that."

"That he's an asshole? Yeah. It's just one more reason I'm angry. There's so much animosity, and I need to find some closure. I know it'll bug the shit out of me until I get the chance to say what I need to say."

"So *call him*."

"No can do. He wouldn't take the call, and coming out of the blue would infuriate the shit out of him. And I'm sure he won't read anything I send him. There's not much else I can do."

"Will you be happy if you get a phone call with him? Would that give you the closure you need?"

"Probably not," I admitted. "So much of our relationship happened over the phone or text or email or Skype. It was always about making me fit into his schedule. I'm angry as hell at him for making me feel like I never mattered, and I don't really believe that's true. I want him to admit it, and the son of a bitch should have to look me at my face while it he does it."

"If anyone could get him to talk to you, it would be Mac. That's what he does best."

"Yeah, you let me know how that works out," I scoffed sarcastically.

I hoped that bitching about it would get it out of my system, but it didn't. I tried hard to put it out of my mind. If I started down the path of thinking through that conversation with Alex, of all the things I wanted and needed to say, it was one-sided and useless. I didn't really know how he would respond—though I was pretty sure I could guess—and I didn't want to get caught up in some crazy fantasy conversation. I took a Xanax and tried to sleep it off. All of the irritation and animosity was still there in the morning.

From: Tierney Cavanaugh Johnson
Date: October 15th 3:06 PM
Subject: Re: ugh
To: Seth Wiezel

Remind me it all gets better. Remind me to keep my head out of my ass and to get the fuck on with my life. Remind me there's a reason for the big girl panties.

Everything's fine, I just need to lash out. Just smile and nod and it will all be fine.

From: Seth Wiezel
Date: October 15th 4:44 PM
Subject: Re: ugh
To: Tierney Cavanaugh Johnson

You're telling yourself those things. Write an angry letter and delete it.

I was a big fan of writing and burning things to let them go. Maybe that would be helpful. I wasn't holding my breath.

That night, Sam sat with me on the deck while I drank Jack Daniels, two shots for every one of his beers. We were still living in the same house with our children and trying to be amiable with each other most of the time. We were listening to the entire Seth Wiezel catalog. "Maker" came on, and I started to dance.

Sam took a sip from his beer. "How are you?"

"Drunk." I shrugged. "I'm okay. Mad."

"Why are you mad?"

I opened up, unleashing my chagrin into the night and Sam.

"It's not right, you know? He should have to fucking deal with me! He helped make this mess."

"Have you talked to him?"

I shook my head and took a drag from my cigarette. "I haven't talked to him. I don't even have him in my contacts in my phone anymore."

"You should tell him."

"That's what Jules said. He won't listen. I don't have his number now, and I'm pretty sure he wouldn't take my call anyway."

"I can get him to listen to you. I have enough leverage to force his hand and make him listen."

No, that wouldn't be right.

If he was willing to talk with me, he had to do it because he wanted to. I was adamant that he couldn't come to that discussion with any more hatred or fear or distrust in his heart than was already there. I didn't want lip service; I wanted emotional resolution. I wanted the chance to really say goodbye in my heart and in my head, preferably eye to eye.

"You don't know unless you try, Tierney."

"I don't have his number," I repeated.

Sam went inside to get another beer while I scrolled through my iPod, looking for something else to listen to.

<ding>

It was a new text from Sam. It was Alex's phone number. He came back outside, bringing another drink for each of us.

"*No*," I said, "I'm not calling him. He doesn't want to hear from me. He doesn't *care* that I'm mad or hurt. I don't matter to him, remember?"

"That's bullshit! You *do* matter. Even if he doesn't want to hear from you that he's an asshole, you still have the right to tell him he hurt you."

"I don't want to fight with him."

Sam laughed sardonically. "Yes, you do. You're itchy, and you're looking for a fight."

He was right. I was mad and hurt, and I wanted to go off drunkenly on Alex for being a dick.

But I knew that being drunk and reactionary was never going to be effective.

I *hate* the feeling of being disregarded. I generally don't care if someone doesn't like me. I can deal with people being angry or upset with me, as long as there's the promise of communication regarding the problem. But to feel like I've been summarily dismissed, as though my feelings and I suddenly aren't worth the time and effort, is infuriating.

Throughout my life, there had been very specific moments of feeling emotionally exiled—by my mother's denial of my abuse, by father's absence due to work and divorce, by Damien's vindictive ignoring of me as punishment. Sam had subtly and overtly dismissed me in his own ways for the last couple of years. The sting of having my feelings pushed to the side was sometimes still strong, even when it seemed the drama was a lifetime ago. It took a brief second for me to remember my real and imagined transgressions and begin to question my inherent value. What was I worth to others if they could so easily turn away from me?

I knew there had been times when I'd been the cause or the catalyst for people withdrawing from my life, deciding that I was a liability to their own worth. The last couple of months with Alex were a prime example, and I knew I'd played my own part in driving him away. But to tell me suddenly that I can't do something has always been the *worst* possible way to get me to stop doing it. Taking away the toy I wanted most would make me ornery and unruly, and I tended to lash back in ways that were most likely to hurt *me* the most.

Like all the times before in my life, I needed to find resolution with Alex. I was stuck in the mire of overanalysis, picking apart the *woulda-coulda-shoulda* of the whole situation. I needed some kind of emotional detente to be able to move forward.

It was unlikely that I would ever get the chance. The bridge between us was rickety and unstable, and I'd just set it brilliantly ablaze.

I took another Xanax, on top of half a bottle of vodka, and passed out, no accord in sight.

––––––––––––––

That night, I dreamed of Montevallo.

It was dark as I crossed the old campus. I knew it was early morning, dark in the pre-dawn, by the birds chirping for their morning meal. The ground was hard and crunchy with frost as I ducked across the edge of the quad, my dream vision telescoping onto Bloch Hall, where I would have to exhibit my work for my senior show.

Have to finish one last piece to graduate. To move on to the life you've been living for twenty years.

I pulled the hood of my coat over my short hair, my ears stinging from the cold. I shoved my gloved hands deep into my pockets as I walked down the cobblestone street behind Tutwiler and Hanson Halls, where I'd lived giddy and boisterous with Jules. Fragmentary memories of dorm life filtered through wispy reverie, fleeting flashes filled with mixed emotions.

Can't focus on that now. Keep moving.

And then I found myself standing in front of the art facility on the back corner of campus.

The low, L-shaped building looked like an old elementary school, with a dozen doors on the outside leading into classrooms. Tucked into the crook of the L was a raku firing pit. I could smell the heat on the wind.

Fucking cold and windy. Some dumbass trying to fire something in the raku pits.

"You'll freeze your ass off out here," I said over my shoulder, as the phantom reached into the pit with his tongs.

He sighed and nodded, pulling a piece from the heat. "Yeah, I'm making up an incomplete from last semester. It has to be in tomorrow."

I nodded in understanding and wished him luck, unlocking the door to the studios. I stepped through the door and found it warm inside, too warm, sort of sticky. The smell of heat and paint, thinners and cleaners, was almost overwhelming. Sweet and slightly acrid.

I locked the door and unwrapped myself as I walked down the impossibly long and steep staircase toward my little spot in the building, my studio.

Everything was just as I had left it at the end of my sophomore year, when I just *quit*, so emotionally drained by school and Damien that I hadn't even bothered to go back and clean up my space or get my supplies. I tried to focus on the shadowy, shifting room and the barely-begun canvas, still resting on my old easel.

Where were you going with this?

Have to finish.

I awoke suddenly, remembering every minute detail of the dream, my heart pounding with still-drowsy anxiousness.

It was barely five in the morning. I crept straight downstairs. I grabbed an empty canvas and placed it trepidatiously on the easel.

I thought back to the guy in my dream, the student rushing to complete old work, just like I had been. I recalled the image, that guy and his raku, and started to work him out in charcoal. Not so much *him* but that moment when you aren't sure if the pottery will hold itself together. For something so hardy looking when cooled, raku could be surprisingly fragile and ornery when hot. It was very testy for a ceramic, but it was exciting to watch it form into a finished piece.

I spent a long time slowly drawing this figure, hair hanging down and obstructing most of his face, though the furrow of the brown was visible. His hands and forearms taut, holding the piece in the tongs. I could see the glazed design on the clay, the deep and vivid stains and crackling.

And there, I drew a craggy line from the lip of the vase downward through the neck, *a crack.*

All that time spent trying to make something right, to make something strong and perfect and lovely, and it was still falling apart, still broken.

And still beautiful with its imperfections.

Chapter 28

"Look," I started a few mornings later, after the boys had gone to school, "I get why you want to separate. I understand that you need to be able to start again. If that's truly what you want, I will do whatever I can to support that. But it's not what I want. I don't think it's best for any of us. What I really want most is to go back to counseling with you and to work through this myriad of issues, together. You're my heart. Our life is *here*, together in this house. I want you to consider if being apart is what you really want."

"I think it is," Sam replied softly, "but I'll think about it."

He was extra gentle with me that night, when we met on the deck. We didn't talk about anything pressing, didn't discuss my offer to still go to counseling, but just being together in the cool, evening breeze was pleasant and felt oddly nostalgic.

I went inside to watch television for a while before bed. My skin felt dry, and I went to get a bottle of lotion. I sat on the edge of the couch, facing the TV and the back door. The wooden door was open, the glass-fronted storm door closed, containing the cold air inside the house. Through the glass, I could see Sam's silhouette, glowing and shifting slightly in the flicker of the tiki torch.

I started with my lower legs, spreading the cold, white thickness along my shins and calves. I worked my way up to my thighs, spread wide toward the open room. I lotioned my arms, nonchalantly watching whatever was on the screen. I stood and pulled my cami over my head and dropped my panties to the floor. In my peripheral vision, I could tell that Sam was watching me from outside. I slowly and carefully slathered the lotion over my ass and belly, taking extra time on my breasts. I made sure every inch was well-rubbed-in.

The back door opened. "I can get your back, if you need help."

I looked at Sam for a long moment. "Okay."

Still standing, I turned my back toward him and handed him the pump bottle. I gathered my long, blond hair in my hands and pulled it over one shoulder.

He pumped a couple of squirts into his hands and rubbed them slowly, warming the thick lotion before spreading it, slowly and deeply, across my skin. His hands were warm and strong, and I was instantly turned on.

"There," he whispered, "I think that got it all." He handed the bottle back to me.

"Thanks!" I stepped quickly and nonchalantly back into my panties. I slipped back into the cotton camisole and put the lotion bottle away on a shelf. He disappeared into the kitchen for another beer, as I went back to watching television.

The next morning, after I returned from the gym, Sam asked suddenly if I'd like to have lunch with him.

"There's this French restaurant someone from work mentioned. I'd like to try it. Do you want to join me?"

"That would be lovely."

I took a shower and chose a long, black skirt and tight, aubergine shirt, adorned with small ruffles below the plunging neckline. My low, black heels made me a little taller than normal, though I still stood three inches shorter than Sam.

"You look beautiful," he told me as I stepped onto the deck.

"Thank you," I smiled.

Sam drove us to Violette for our 11:45 reservation. He valeted his car and walked me to the front door, holding it open for me. We followed the hostess to the back of the restaurant. Sam pulled out my chair for me, then seated himself on the long banquet across the intimate table from me.

We talked and laughed over quiche Lorraine. We shared each other's company and heavily-sauced French food. It was pleasant and easy and delicately loving. There was no hand-holding or overt flirting, but the attraction that had been between us for twenty-five years was obviously still there.

With more than an hour until the boys would begin their afternoon trail of book bags and shoes and sweaty little boy socks, I stripped down to my bra and panties and lay down on the bed. If Sam came in, fine. If not, I would delight in an impromptu catnap. Either way, I was planning to feel refreshed before the children came home.

And Sam did come into the bedroom. He lay down on his side of the bed, fully dressed and turned on his side, facing me. He scooted closer, still snuggled into his own pillow but close enough to me that I could see each of his individual lashes, lush and dark and long. *Just like the boys.*

"I think you're right," he said softly. "I think we should go back to counseling."

I turned over to face him, no more than six inches separating us.

"I think it's the right thing," I replied. "I think it's best for all of us."

"You looked beautiful today. You still look beautiful."

I gave him a small, blushing grin and shook my head against my pillow.

"Yes...."

He leaned in to kiss me. He was tentative at first, for just a moment, before he was stretched along the length of me, his tongue fully in my mouth. My hands shook as I unbuttoned his shirt and reached for his belt. He pulled me to sitting to unhook my bra and kiss that spot on my neck that he knows will always drive me crazy.

We made love, sweet and slow, in the filtered afternoon light, the house quiet except for the sounds of ragged breath and gasped moans.

We curled safely around each other and cuddled in that peace until it was time for the boys to come home.

————————

It felt like a fresh start. Sam and I had all this time at home during the day. He would work for a while, have lunch with me after I went to the gym, then work some more. Some afternoons we'd stop everything to meet for a while on our big bed, naked and open in the afternoon light. We were speaking to each other in gentle tones, careful and respectful of each other's needs. I felt comfort with Sam that I hadn't felt in a very long time.

In the midst of it all, I dropped below two hundred pounds for the first time since the eighth grade. I stood on the scale in the bathroom, naked and cold, and cried. Even I was surprised at how emotional I got about it. The next day, I hit the milestone of one hundred pounds of weight lost. I felt like I'd unstrapped an eighth grader from my ass and hit the ground running.

Friends and family were congratulatory and supportive. Sam told me how proud of me he was. I'd spent weeks looking online for the right pair of boots—without extra wide calves—and they arrived on the Day of 100. I took my giddy and incredulous self to the store and found that size twelve jeans fit the best, a size smaller again. I bought two pairs.

I called my mom to tell her my good news.

"I hate you!" she hissed jokingly

This was something I'd heard her say a lot over the previous year. Every time I would tell her I'd hit another weight loss milestone, she'd say it. Sometimes she was laughing, sometimes she wasn't.

And I knew she didn't really *hate* me. At least, I didn't think so. She was my mom. But she'd spent decades toying with her own yo-yo of thick and thin. I knew, rationally, that she was really irritated with herself and her own weight. It didn't matter. It stung.

"I went back to Weight Watchers this week," she told me.

"Really? Good for you." At least she was trying to practice with her yo-yo again.

"I figured if *you* can do this, then I can do it."

What the hell is that?!

How was I supposed to see that as encouraging or flattering? Was I so damaged and defective that I was the last person on Earth who could take on a life-transforming challenge and actually succeed? Did she think there was something inherently broken in me that this had somehow just happened, had been *easy* to accomplish and didn't require a *fuck*ton of work to do? I'd failed at a lot of things in my life, had walked away from hard work when I couldn't take the pressure, but this was something I was determined to complete successfully.

I'd spent years battling my body image issues, and I absolutely could not ignore my mother's role in that fight. It wasn't *all* her fault, certainly, but she'd never really given me the tools and support to trust my body and listen to its cues for hunger and nourishment. She was the central dancer in the chorus line that taught me to stuff my emotions into my stomach and hope that I could deal with it later.

Her aggressively passive support made me want to go through the closest drive-through. For years that had been my first reaction to any stressor, to find comfort in quick, easy food, often while I was alone and brooding. I'd worked hard to unlearn those habits, and I wasn't about to let her *laissez-faire* attitude sneak back in and bolster my own doubts. I'd just bought new, smaller jeans after losing a hundred fucking pounds!

I got off the phone with her and went home to slide my new-and-improved body into its fresh denim reward. I stood in the bathroom, looking at myself in the full-length mirror. Even seeing how different my body was, knowing all the amazing ways it had transformed in the last year, I was still unhappy. I had a little more weight to lose, certainly, but now I was also facing lots of loose skin. But I could see new tone in my arms, my belly, even in my hands. I also knew that I was *healthy* in a way I'd maybe never been, plainly obvious from the results of my blood work and the fact that I started my period on a 29-day cycle. The self-conscious girlie in me, though, was painfully aware of all of the glaring new imperfections, a direct result of the metamorphosis.

I jaunted downstairs and grabbed a sketch book and a couple of pencils. Back in the bathroom, I started to draw myself quickly, reminding myself of normal human proportions, of how many head lengths should make up the torso and the arm and leg length.

The shoulder line should be two head-widths for a woman, but you're you, Tierney. Make them broader.

But I was frustrated. Where I should have been able to see normal spacing on my own body, from nipples to belly button, from belly button to the apex of the blond triangle below, all I could see was *expanse*. I could *see* the normal proportions of the lean, toned musculature of my body, but they were distorted and felt amorphous.

I put away the sketches and pencils, and traded my new jeans for a pair of yoga pants.

"My ass is starting to look like a Shar-Pei puppy," I complained to Jules over the telephone. "There are these little *folds* and *wrinkles* where my ass and my thighs meet."

"Well, you knew that might happen, Kitten," she said gently. "You've seen enough *Lifetime* shows about fat people to know what happens when you lose a ton of weight."

"Yeah, but those people don't exercise like I do. I was hoping it would just go away. Kind of like I'm hoping my mom will just *go away*."

"Uh-oh. What happened now?"

I sighed. "She's a fucking bitch. I called to tell her about hitting a hundred pounds, and somehow it's all about her. I don't get it! It's like last time I was home, she started talking about my grandfather like *nothing ever happened*. He fucking *molested* me, lady! Don't fucking talk to me about him!"

"She's in denial, Tierney. For whatever reason, she can't wrap her head around the fact that her father molested you."

"That doesn't make it okay to just pretend it never happened!"

"No, sweetie," she soothed, "I'm not saying it does. But there's something in the South, something ingrained in the culture, to just ignore what you can't handle."

"But the pink elephant is always in the room!"

"Yes, but if you put enough lipstick on it, it's just a pretty pink elephant, and who doesn't like that?"

I should've been riding the high of my weight loss for days, but the conversation with my mom had made me cranky. I was short-tempered and withdrawn from Sam and the boys. My mood wore off on Sam quickly, and he was reactionary and ill with us, too.

He would be sweet one minute, then completely vicious the next. It was hard to fault him for his lashing out, and I felt like I just needed to take it, that it would pass one day. After everything I'd done to him and to us, I took his moodswings as part of my penitence.

I woke on Tuesday morning to a series of texts from Sam, drunkenly sent the night before while I was sleeping.

Sam Johnson
Oct 25th 11:33 PM

Do U get my mood the last cpl days? Whr wr U 1yr ago? Sad+angry, but happy I can at least see the ghost. 1025 almost over. B kind.

Oct 25th 2:44 AM

U broke his heart and got the best of him. YRU still angry? B kind.

Oct 25th 3:13 AM

I remember the first time we heard "Before We Start" together, live. Started to live as if it were our new

Theme. Haunted by the photo from
that Chicago show. B kind.

*What the fuck is he talking about? Where was I a year ago?
The Masquerade!*
It had been a year since that first Junkture show, which had
been the catalyst for so much upheaval. Our life had blossomed and
shriveled a dozen times since then. For me, the record itself was a
bigger influence than that show, but Sam was tracing it all back to
that night.
It was 5:30 in the morning when I saw his texts. He was still
awake, on the deck, smoking and surfing the internet on his laptop.
The boys weren't due up for another two hours. I was quiet as I went
outside, not wanting to disturb the misty peace.
"Why are you up?" he asked.
"Just woke up." *Why are you still up?* "Did you sleep at all?"
"Nah, I got an email about work when I was trying to come to
bed. Just wrapping that up."
I nodded and lit a cigarette. "I wish you wouldn't dwell on
this shit. It's no good for you."
Sam said nothing.
"I wish you had just come to bed with me."
"I couldn't," he replied softly. "I kept thinking about the
date—"
"A date *I* hadn't even thought about...."
"—and I couldn't wind down. Then the work email came." He
shrugged.
"Is there anything I can do?"
"Nope. I have to go into the office in a bit."
After you've been up all night?
I nodded. "And, look," I said, "I didn't break his heart."
Sam exhaled a long stream of smoke. "You did, Tierney,
whether or not you realized it."
"*How?* How the hell did I break his fucking heart?" *He's the
one who walked away from me.*
"You stepped out of the box."
"He doesn't care. That's apparent. It's fine. I'll be fine." I
stood and kissed Sam quickly on the lips. "I gotta go take a shower
and get ready."

    I was still walking in the early mornings and painting until the children got home.

    But my sessions with Devin were becoming more difficult. I'd had knee surgery when Tripp was a baby, after being diagnosed with chondromalacia—damage to the cartilage under the kneecap. There's a family history of misalignment of the patella with the thigh bone, and I'd inherited the problem. My excess weight and sedentary lifestyle hadn't helped.

    I was surprised when my knee started to bother me again. Having lost nearly a hundred pounds, I'd alleviated a substantial amount of the stress on my joints. The bulging discs that had been so problematic the year before were completely unbothersome now. It was frustrating that I was having unexpected and sudden knee pain, especially when Devin and I were so careful not to irritate it.

    I could tolerate walking or a recumbent bike, but the elliptical and anything weight-bearing were miserably uncomfortable. I spent a lot of time icing my knee and took ibuprofen around the clock. When an x-ray showed nothing obvious, my orthopedist order a check-in with physical therapy.

    I scheduled an appointment with the same therapist I'd used during my back pain.

    "Tierney! Oh my god! I almost didn't recognize you!"

    "Ninety-seven pounds," I replied. "But now my knee is a mess."

    After a lengthy evaluation, Beth determined that my medial quadriceps—the one running toward the inner thigh—wasn't as strong as the lateral and intermediate muscles, which were pulling my kneecap out of alignment. Any time I would bend it with or without weight, a tight, annoying pain would shoot under the patella. I started intensive physical therapy. I could continue to train with Devin, but I was given strict instructions about what exercises were forbidden.

    It was frustrating. I'd done everything right, and I was suddenly having this unanticipated complication.

    I shouldn't have been surprised. Like so much else in my previous few months, every time I said something was going to happen or not, it seemed like the absolute opposite occurred. I felt jinxed.

Devin and I changed my workouts and focused on the inner thighs, trying to build the muscles quickly without causing further pain. I did thigh lifts every day, whether or not I was on the weight machines. I stretched the hamstrings to loosen them up and let them release some of the tension on my thighs. I avoided anything I knew would irritate my knee further.

I was tired and in nagging pain again.

I was in bed, watching television and icing my knee, when Sam came to bed. I was half asleep when I felt him nuzzle against my side. He rested his hand on my belly and slowly started to trail his fingers toward my thighs.

"That feels nice, but it's probably not gonna get you anywhere tonight, baby." I kissed him on the forehead. I could smell the beer on his breath. "I'm tired, and my knee is killing me."

His hand stopped. He flipped the blankets back and stood up.

"You aren't attracted to me," he accused. "I'm not appealing to you."

"What the fuck are you talking about? That's not—"

"It is true! You're not sexually attracted to me at all anymore. You don't even fucking *like* me, so why would you want to have sex with me?"

"*I love you!* What the hell are you talking about? I've been tired, and my knee—"

"Just like before, isn't it? You're tired and in pain. Does this mean you'll be looking for someone else to fuck? Is that why you wanted to take the bartender home, at the Westin?"

Bite your tongue, Tierney.

"That's the only time you've been really turned on, when we were talking about your fucking another man. It's degrading! You can only get off if you're not thinking about me!"

"Sam, no! This is ridiculous!"

"You know what's ridiculous?" he hissed. "*This!*" He flailed his hands about, encompassing our entire life in his motion. "Sex with you used to be good. It was fucking *great*—until you went to Texas and fucked someone else! Now, it's just *boring!* It's not adventurous anymore. It's not thrilling anymore. It's just... it's just not the same. I guess you've had better, so now I'll never be good enough for you again!"

I jumped up from the bed to face him. "*Fuck you!* I'm offended by the accusation that I don't find you attractive. That's totally ridiculous! Just because I'm not in some *crazy fuck* mood, that doesn't mean I'm not interested.   I have never been anything but present and involved with you! If you don't like sex with me, you are free to find anyone else who will make you happy in bed, but don't blame that shit on me!"

He stared at me unblinking and walked out, slamming the bedroom door behind him.

My phone chirped to let me know there was new email.

One message in my inbox, from Mac.

---------- **Forwarded message** ----------

From: Alex Wheeler
Date: October 28th 11:20 PM
To: Mac Jordan
Subject: Re: Client's proposal

If your client wants to talk I will talk. Not sure what area you r speaking of, Portland till 2 or Nashville 4-6, but yes, if said client were to be in that area I would have a chat.

Sincerely,
A

On October 28th at 7:55 PM, Mac Jordan wrote:

Yes sir, the offer is absolutely sincere. As a facilitator, the goal is simply to overcome any logistical barriers, including your schedule, to effect a brief in-person meeting.

If the client were to be in that area during that time, would this be outside the realm of possibilities?

I don't require any details such as time or place, which would be between the two of you, but would appreciate only an indication of whether this is at all agreeable to you.

On October 28th at 2:02 PM, Alex Wheeler wrote:

Are u fucking serious? This is ridiculous. I don't need to fly to ATL for closure. If your "client" wants to speak to me "they" can do it over the phone.

I am available till the 2nd, in Portland, and Nashville from the 4-6 of this month after which point I will be unavailable to discuss anything until the new year.

I hope your "client" understands, if not that's unfortunate for them.

With all sincerity,
Alex

On October 28th at 2:43 AM, Mac Jordan wrote:

A,

My client, TCJ, seeks an opportunity to talk with you in person. I'm sorry I don't have specifics other than her request for "*a chance to talk face to face, where if we need to, I can yell at him and he can yell at me alone in a safe place... and exchange apologies and bring closure to some personal issues with no one else around*".

TCJ's desired outcome of the proposed meeting, as explained to me, are "*closure*" to personal issues resulting in "*no need to ever contact him personally again*".

If you agree to such a meeting, I offer the following as incentives at no charge to you:

- A first class or business class ticket on the airline(s) and flight(s) of your choice, on the day and time of your choice (for both arrival and departure), to and from the airport(s) of your choice.
- A one night stay at the hotel of your choice in a room/suite of your preference; should you choose to stay overnight.
- Cash up front, couriered to you beforehand, to cover meals, transportation, and reasonable out-of-pocket expenses.

Cost is no object, but these concessions all apply to a single 24-hour period.

Discretion and safety on everyone's part is paramount to myself and to TCJ. While TCJ would like to meet with you privately, I will cover the same costs for one other individual, if you choose so, as long as their primary role is your personal safety and security.

TCJ would prefer you fly into ATL (Hartsfield-Jackson Atlanta International Airport) and use an airport hotel. That would keep her costs low and, because ATL is a popular hub, provide some additional degree of discretion. You may take advantage of the visit as a stopover on another (pre-scheduled) trip as well. There is no minimum time requirement for the visit as long as objectives are met ("*it could take five minutes or five hours*" [TCJ]). However, the choice of day and times, airline, and destinations would ultimately be up to you.

There is no deadline for your response -- it's an open invitation.

If and when you want to take advantage of this offer, please contact me at this email address. One of my representatives will contact you via your method of choice (email, phone, etc.) to set up an itinerary.

Thank you for your thoughtful consideration.

> *What the fuck had Mac done?*
> I started to shake. Sam came back into the bedroom.
> He knew how I felt, knew that I wanted to have this talk with Alex and get some closure, to relieve the tension between us. When I had mused about it weeks before, while we were still on the definitive path of divorce, he said he understood and agreed that Alex owed me the confrontation.
> After what had just happened, though, there was no way in hell that Sam would support my seeing my former lover. But I had to tell him. He deserved to know about the messages from Mac, no matter how angry or hurt it made him.
> *He said he wants to know.*

I looked up at Sam in the dim glow of the television. "Alex says he's willing to talk to me."

The shaking became violent.

I showed him the message. "I didn't know Mac emailed him."

"So are you going? To meet him?"

"I don't know what to do about this."

It felt like a test or a trap, waiting for me to fall into the pit of temptation and doubt just to see if I would climb back out or dig in deeper.

"Well, as your friend, I know how important it is to you to do this. As someone more than your friend, I hate it. I think it's bullshit."

"Why? You knew how I felt, you offered to do the pushing for me."

"Yeah, if it meant you would get some closure, but I don't think you will. I think you're addicted to him and that it's just another way in for you."

I was stunned. This wasn't what he'd said before. His tone was getting more ragged and vehement by the moment.

"Did you honestly think I would be okay with your seeing the guy you fucked again? My worst fear is that you go there—"

"I know. Your worst fear is that I go there and fuck him again!"

"—and make me look like a sucker, like a chump! I know how unresolved this is for you. I know you *hate* how this ended with him, the least of which is because of me. You won't be happy until he makes you come! I'm not paying for you to travel and see the asshole who fucked my wife, just to have you do it again."

"Hush! Lower your damn voice before you wake the children!" I hissed.

"Well, let me be clear," Sam said, still yelling. "If you go to see him, we're through. We're absolutely done."

And there it is.

There was the ultimatum I knew would be coming again eventually. *It's him or me.*

I could choose to make amends with this man who would never, ever be back in my life, but about whom I cared deeply, or I could do one more thing to hold onto this degenerated marriage, in the vague hope that *somehow* we would survive this. Neither option made me terribly happy.

"Leave me alone. I'm going to sleep."

"Of course you are! It's what you do! When you don't want to deal with something, you retreat and run away from it. But you never come back and deal with it."

"Leave me the fuck alone!" I begged. "Please just get away from me. I'm tired and need to think."

"You won't be thinking," Sam snapped, "you'll be asleep!"

"Hopefully I'll get some rest and be able to think with a clear head. Now, *please* just leave me alone!"

"What's there to think about? You go and do this and get the closure you say you need, but it won't end. It's just another way into his life and to keep him in yours, and I'm the fixer, I'm your connection. Are you going to *really* let this be over, or will it just keep on? Will you really get the closure you need?"

"I don't know! That's my intent—"

"I don't wanna hear about intentions. I want to know what will happen!"

I gritted my teeth. "How the fuck can I know what will happen? Either I'll get what I need, and Alex and I get to go on and not be so goddamn mad at one another, or else we end up even madder and I want to punch him in the fucking face and never, ever see him again anyway!"

"So you can't guarantee you'll be done with him?" he challenged.

"I can't guarantee that about anything!" I was becoming more and more frustrated by the moment. "I can't guarantee I'll wake up tomorrow!"

"This is that important? It's as big a deal to you as whether or not the sun rises and sets?"

I rolled my eyes. "Oh my god! Leave me the fuck alone! Get the fuck away from me!" I pulled the blankets over my ears and turned away from him.

"That's what I need! I need you to *promise* me that you won't fuck him again. I need you to promise not to get your head completely wrapped around him again and that this will be over!"

"I can't make promises that I can't be sure I can make happen! I'm not going with the intention of fucking him! I don't plan to get my heart broken again! But I can't promise what I can't be sure of. I won't do that."

"It's what people do, Tierney! They promise things to make their significant others happy, even when they *know* they'll break those promises."

For Sam, promises were made to be broken. At the very least, there was always an implication of potential breakage, given enough time. On the other hand, I have always tried very hard not to make a promise unless I intended to defend it and do whatever it took to make it come to fruition—fully recognizing that sometimes shit happens and you just can't help it when things go awry.

Sam said something else while I covered my ears tightly and tried my best to ignore him. I grabbed my phone and went out to the deck. I read the message again. I didn't know what the fuck to do.

I decided to smoke one last cigarette, planning to be done the next day for good. Again. I was reading Mac's email again when I heard the storm door creak open. I assumed it was Sam and didn't look up.

"Mommy?"

I panicked. I couldn't help but exhale. I stuffed the smoldering cigarette into a flower pot.

"What do you need?" It was Tripp. It was dark out, and he wasn't wearing his glasses. I hoped he hadn't seen.

"I can't get to sleep."

"Okay, baby, go back in, and I'll be there in a minute."

He'd been prone to bouts of insomnia for his entire ten years. Occasionally I'd give him something to help him sleep. This, unfortunately, was one of those nights.

I hurried to the bedroom, where Sam was still awake.

"Tripp just came out while I was smoking a cigarette! Can you give him some melatonin?"

"Tell him to go back to bed and go to sleep."

I huffed and stomped into the bathroom. I brushed my teeth and washed my hands, sprayed some perfume on my hair. I got the small capsule for my son and told him to take it and go back to bed.

I calmed my heartbeat and settled into bed. I was about to drift off when I heard the bedroom door swish open across the carpet. I didn't hear steps right away and assumed it was the cat.

"What do you need, buddy?" Sam asked in the darkness.

"Nothing," Tripp whined, obviously upset. I could hear the tears in his voice. "I can't talk to you about it right now." He tromped dramatically down the hall toward his room.

"Go check on him," I urged.

"No, he's fine. He needs to go to sleep."

More eye-rolling on my part. I got out of bed and went into his room.

"Tripp, what's wrong?"

"Nothing," he sobbed. "I can't talk to you about it."

"Why? Tell me, sweetie. What's wrong. You can tell me anything."

"It's just, I thought I saw you... *smoking*," he whispered hoarsely. "I'm pretty sure that's what I saw."

"No, sweetie, it wasn't."

"That's what it looked like!" Even in the shadows of his lower bunk bed, I could see the upset on his young face.

"I know that's what it looked like," I tried my best to assure him. "Mommy had some incense, and it burns and makes smoke. I promise, it wasn't what you thought. It was dark, and you didn't have your glasses on. It's okay, I promise."

I am the worst fucking mother in the world.

I was overtly lying to my son to save my own ass. I'd done it before, all parents do, but never about something that I knew would bother him so much. He was so staunchly anti-tobacco, anti-drug, anti-alcohol. The school had certainly done its job in making him to never want *anyone* to try anything remotely illicit. I never, ever drank in front of him and usually did my best to keep the bottles out of sight. He didn't even know I'd ever smoked.

I finally fell asleep and woke the next morning to the same damn buzzing in my head. I got the boys off to school and ran some errands. My day was jaded with jitters and apprehension.

I was trying to listen to my gut, which said it was bad, a trap, the death knell for my time with Sam. But my heart was screaming that it was my last chance to see Alex and to make this right. My head didn't know what that meant and told me to go to sleep and ignore it. Instead, I headed to the park to walk. I had time to get in a couple of miles before dark, on the last warm, clear day forecasted for a while.

As usual, I plugged in my earbuds and chose the music for my pavement pounding. Afghan Whigs, *1965*.

Bad choice.

All I could hear was *him*, Alex, all over this record. I had listened to it hundreds of times in the years since its release. It was something I'd loved long before I ever met Alex, but now they were inextricably linked.

By the time I got to "Omerta", which blends seamlessly into "The Vampire Lanois", I was in tears, walking the last quarter mile of the winding track blurrily, eyes hidden from passers-by and the rising sun behind dark glasses.

On the one hand, I wanted to see Alex, to have this conversation. I needed to assure him that I would never, ever reveal those secrets I'd promised to keep, not to anyone. I wanted to be able to see him and tell him to his face, to *prove* to him that I could use my hard-to-find voice and actually *say* the things I had to say, rather than hide behind lengthy emails that he was barely attentive enough to read.

I needed to tell him that it was unfair that I was the one paying the price for everything, as far as I could see it. I was the one who was hurting so deeply, so intensely. I was the one who'd had to cut ties with innumerable fans and semi-friends, who couldn't explain her sudden withdrawal from their social network. I couldn't stand to see their pictures and videos and stories of him. I'd never been able to stomach their sycophantic love, simply on principal, but the constant flow of reminders that his life was going on happily were more than I could bear on a day-to-day basis.

I needed to yell at him for being so goddamn cruel, for having told me months earlier not to let a split with Sam make me feel small, then to have been the one to make me feel worthless and insignificant during that last conversation. I needed to remind him that he was a willing participant in every step of it, had encouraged me, and had seen exactly what would be coming, how I would react emotionally when this all came to an end. He'd chosen to ignore all of that, because the connection—and the sexual energy—were intense and consuming. I wanted to cry and tell him how angry I was that he'd *promised* me months earlier that he would never step out of my life unless I asked him to do so, but he did.

And he deserved the chance to yell back, to tell me how he'd warned me he'd have to cut the cord if I got too close. I was supposed to keep it all to myself, and he knew that I had failed, at least on some level. At the very least, Tessa and Sam and Mac knew, and that made me a liability. I was certain he would rip into me about how this was more drama, more turmoil, and that if I'd cared, I would let it go.

He would be right, about that and so much more. I knew there would likely be more, bad and good. I could imagine the topics of conversation, our respective responses to the other's accusations and revelations. But in the end, I hoped desperately that we would find a way to accept and understand the other, to acknowledge how sad it all was, and to have a chance to grieve it together, this ill-fated *thing* that had killed a very close friendship.

On the other hand, there was Sam. I'd spent months being selfish and demanding, doing everything I could to keep my secrets and make myself happy when I felt like no one else was trying. I'd lied, cheated, and stolen to get what I wanted, which had ended up being painfully disappointing and unresolved. I'd broken his heart, time and again.

But I'd also taken a lot of crap from him. He'd been vicious and cruel at times. He'd antagonized me repeatedly, especially if he'd been drinking. He'd accused me of being a narcissist and a sociopath, asking if I was incapable or just unwilling to ever admit that anyone else could be right, whether or not it meant I had to be wrong.

I couldn't see a day when he would trust me again, would stop questioning if I was distracted for a good reason or if I was thinking about Alex. He didn't see how I tried harder, every single day, to get over him, to let him go and not miss him so goddamn much. I knew the futility of letting my heart think of him for even a moment, and I struggled to keep it at bay. I knew the day would come when it wouldn't hurt so much, and it was generally getting a little easier every day. Some days were better than others. But I could see that Sam was having the same struggle, in his own way.

Sam didn't want me to see Alex or to talk to him. He firmly believed that I should go cold turkey and try to find my own peace in another way, elsewhere, quietly where neither of them had to deal with it head-on.

I was back to the dilemma of the summer; even if I did the right thing, made the right choice for everyone else, it wouldn't be the choice that could bring me any comfort, and I would very likely end up losing both of them anyway. My heart was steeling itself for a major blow. Again.

I was sure Alex didn't want to hear from me, even though he'd told Mac he would be willing to talk. I could tell from his email that the suggestion of getting together had infuriated him. He didn't want the contact, although I contended that owed me the opportunity to say what was in my heart.

This was the time to walk the talk, to put my big girl panties on and deal with it. I'd instigated so much drama over the previous year in my desperate attempt to reclaim myself. I'd been thoughtless and hurtful, to all three of us. As much as it hurt, I knew I had to do the right thing by these two men and not get my way.

But I still felt like I was drowning in my sorrow. There were days and moments when I missed Alex so badly, could feel him so acutely, that it made my heart ache. I knew there was no chance of mending that connection, of having him be able to reach out to me when he needed me, and vice versa. As much as I loved Sam, I felt like he was slipping farther and farther away, no matter what I did. The only way I would ever be able to assure him that I wasn't harboring secret thoughts of Alex was to have my own *Eternal Sunshine of a Spotless Mind* memory removal. I wished every single day that it was possible. As much as forgetting would hurt, remembering was so pointedly painful that it took my breath away, and Sam was tired of breathing life back into me.

I couldn't see any other logical outcome, other than *not* to go to Alex. If I went, it would break Sam's trust and shaky faith again, and we would undoubtedly be finished. And, after all was said and done, my heart would still be hurting, perhaps more broken than before.

I felt like my suffering in silence was the best thing I could do for each of them.

They'd both drawn their respective lines in the sand, one on each side of me—and all I could do was plod forward along the path they'd laid out, my feet sinking deeper and deeper with each step.

Chapter 29

The day of Halloween was warmer than normal for late October. As the school buses rolled through the neighborhood that afternoon, children burst forth up and down the street, raucous in their rambunctious expectation of trick-or-treating with their friends. The boys mapped out a plan for walking the neighborhood, reminding each other which houses gave out the best candy and which would just turn off their porch light and pretend they weren't home.

"I'll give you all of my Skittles for your Reese's Cups," Tripp said sweetly to his brother, knowing Ian preferred fruity candy over chocolate.

"Give me your Starburst, too, and it's a deal!"

Halloween was a memorable day for me, historically, filled with complicated, vivid milestones of youth that seem so *immediate* no matter how long and far you travel away from that time. Frankie and I had shared an unexpected, fucked-up Samhain twenty years before and would still giggle breathlessly about a sacrificial chicken. Jules and I had spent our first Halloween at Montevallo together, tripping on acid and squealing with unabashed delight at a guy in a stairwell who smiled at us with Fruit Stripe gum teeth.

Halloween was also the anniversary of the day that Sam and I had sex for the first time. We'd fooled around, come close before that night, but the actual deed didn't happen until late that evening, on the floor (and later in the bed) of his apartment. In the middle of the act, his estranged girlfriend, India—on a date with her new boyfriend—came banging on the door. She wanted to wish Sam a "Happy anniversary!" as it was also the arbitrary marker of the beginning of their time together.

It had been unexpected and violently, weirdly intrusive. I could remember lying in his bed, naked and suddenly alone under the blankets, listening to the strains of their conversation at the front door. I can still see exactly how the shadows of the room looked as I heard him tell her "Thank you" and "Goodnight".

I was simultaneously elated and sickened. She'd been my best friend. She and I had shared years' worth of craziness and synchronicity. All of that was being irrevocably damaged by the choices we made about sex and emotion. It made me mad that she *knew* what was likely going on inside that apartment, but she'd chosen to interrupt her own date, the new love she'd chosen over Sam, to remind him of the love they'd shared for six years.

But I was the one who knew the significance of that date for her, knowing that it was ultimately more significant for her than for him. I was the one who'd known without question that I would be sleeping with him on that date, trying my best to eradicate any thoughts of her and them, trying to reface the milestone.

And I did just that. He told her goodnight and came back to bed, with me.

Even though logistics hadn't always allowed Sam and me to be together on Halloween, I knew this year that I wanted to make a special effort to mark that date, especially given the extraordinary tensions of the last year.

"Are you ready to take me to bed?" I asked tentatively, a while after the children had brushed their teeth and washed the smears of sugar from their hands and faces, falling deep into a candy coma.

He wasn't. He was still *not* in my headspace.

"I think you need to see Alex," he said carefully, sitting on the deck. "I think this is exactly what you need to do, to try to get some closure. I know how you are, and you'll never be clear of this until you can tell it goodbye."

I was floored. It was a complete about-face from where we'd been just days before.

I shook my head. "I'm not going," I said. "I don't want to hurt you again, and I know this hurts you."

"Don't get me wrong. It'll be hard, and I'll probably ask you a dozen times *not* to do it. I hope I won't. But I think you need it."

"Sam...."

"*Tierney.* I can tell when you're somewhere else. I know how often you're arguing with him in your head. You deserve the chance to resolve this. It will bug the shit out of you until you make peace with it."

I didn't know whether or not I could trust him. It still felt like a trap, like he was testing me to see if I would jump at the chance to see Alex. I wanted to, certainly, but I wasn't swinging a-hundred-and-eighty degrees just to be knocked back again.

From: Tierney Cavanaugh Johnson
Date: October 31st 9:37 PM
To: Alex Wheeler
Subject: Nashville

I can be in Nashville Friday afternoon and evening, driving in after physical therapy. Can you meet? Where and when?

     He replied an hour later with his hotel and suggested meeting at the bar around 9 p.m. I was immediately apprehensive about drinking at a hotel with him. Sam was, too.

     "That's a potentially dangerous situation, Tierney. The two of you, where it's easy to go somewhere private and alone. Alcohol."

     "I won't be going to his room," I replied, a little offended. "I'm not stupid. And, *no*, I will *not* be drinking."

     "You say that now, but it's easy to happen when you're away from home and everything that matters."

     "Sam... I'm not going to sleep with him."

     I tried not to obsess about the conversation that was coming, about the fall-out after. It would either be what I needed it to be, or it wouldn't. Alex would give me the chance to say what was in my heart, or he would shut me down immediately. Either way, I was facing the end of the path, finally, and hoped to turn that corner and find my new way forward.

     I could've put it off until after the New Year. I thought about how that would give me time to lose more weight, to be closer to my physical goals before he saw me for the last time. But I also knew it would drag out everything, give me more time to stew about it.

     Sitting on the deck, the night before I left for Nashville, Sam asked, "Aren't you nervous?"

     "I'm a fucking wreck," I replied.

     "You don't seem it. You seem very calm."

     "I fully expect him to walk into that bar, to look at me and tell me to get it through my thick skull, to leave him the fuck alone."

     "He won't do that." Sam seemed very assured. "But what if he does?"

     I shrugged. "At least I'll have had the opportunity to *try*. I'll have given him the chance to say and ask what he needs to. He'll do with it what he will."

     "I'm really afraid of what will happen."

"I fully expect to be under surveillance the entire time," I scoffed. "I realize you could call your intelligence contacts in Nashville and have them keep an eye on me."

"No, I don't want to do that. I mean, I *want* to, but I'm not going to, as hard as it is to resist the urge."

"I don't want to hurt you again. I am fully aware of the trust you're placing in me, and I don't want to break that again."

We were *on*, we were connecting. I was in love with him, and I could feel his love for me. But the hurt constantly emanated from both of us. I tried, again, to get him to go to bed with me but he refused.

"I have to distance myself from this," he said quietly into the dark, "in case it goes badly. If you come home and something's happened... saying I will be unhappy is an understatement."

I didn't push him. I tried to keep it all to myself as much as possible.

The next morning, I reminded the boys to be very good for Daddy, to be on their best behavior while Mom was away visiting friends. I packed quietly, with as little fanfare as possible.

Sam and I talked briefly about my itinerary.

"I'll text you all along the way," I promised. "I'll let you know before and after. We can talk if you want, or not."

He nodded and hugged me close, kissing me quickly. "Let me know you're okay."

I loaded my suitcase and laptop bag into my car and drove away from home.

I spent the morning at physical therapy, getting the blessed ultrasound on my knee. Listening to the Princess Asshat playlist, I traveled to Nashville after lunch. Driving was particularly uncomfortable, sitting in the same position for so long. I stopped every hour or so, stretching my leg and chain smoking. I was hours early and probably ahead of his arrival, but I was carefully on the lookout for Alex everywhere I went.

Looking up the directions days before, the distance from my hotel to his appeared to be about a mile. In reality, it was two blocks. I could see his hotel from the parking lot of mine. I checked in and went straight for the shower. Road grime cleanly washed away, I dropped into a fitful nap, waking disoriented after dark.

Alone in the dark hotel room, my rousing thoughts jumped immediately to what was coming. With my eyes closed, all of the ghosts were *there*, surrounding and enveloping me, surging achingly through me over and over. I plugged in my earbuds and found Alex, found the pleading, eager energy of "Hot Mess" and "Dollface" and "Whiskey Mouth", and I came hard, lost in the raw and penetrating memories.

With a couple of hours to kill, I scrounged that area of Nashville for some semblance of healthy dinner. I spent an inordinate amount of time on my hair and make-up. I looked pretty. But when I smiled, I could see the deep crinkles around my eyes, another tell-tale sign of the weight loss. I knew how different I looked than even the last time he'd seen me, and I hoped to God that he wouldn't focus on the little sag in my neck or the new wrinkle on my forehead. I knew it was a ridiculously obsessive thought, like worrying about houseguests arriving when your house isn't spotless.

Sam Johnson
Nov 4th 8:55 PM
I ate. Leaving now. I'll text you when I'm back.

At 9:00 on the dot, I grabbed my little bag and the car keys and went out the side door of the hotel, closest to my room. His multi-storied, brightly-lit hotel stood on the hill above mine, like some beacon of impendment.

It was time to face Alex.

I parked and stomped confidently in my new black boots across the parking lot and through the lobby toward the bar. I didn't know who else would be there, though I knew he wasn't alone on this trip. As I rounded the corner, I could hear his voice over the strains of karaoke night.

He was sitting at the head of a table for eight, talking to someone directly to his right. Facing the door, he glanced up and did a double-take, mouth opened mid-sentence.

"You look fantastic!" He finished his sentence to his colleague and stood to greet me. "Really, wow! You look just fucking amazing!"

I met his broad smile with my own as he leaned in for a hug. It was close and tight, and we both held on just a little too long, saying so much in those few seconds. All of my fears that he would reject my attempts at resolution vanished. I knew he would listen to what I had to say, tell me what he needed me to hear, and that it would all be okay.

He introduced me to the guys I didn't know, and I greeted the ones I did, fans and friends and colleagues who lived close-by. He ushered me to the bar and ordered himself a beer.

"You want a drink?"

I hadn't planned to drink at all, told myself and Sam that I wouldn't be drinking with Alex, no matter what. I was shaking so badly I almost couldn't sit on the stool.

"Jack and Diet."

The bartender gave us our drinks, and Alex paid for the first round.

"So what's going on?"

"Well, I blew my knee again," I began.

"And I'm trying to find a job." I explained.

"*Plus* I'm thinking about going back to school—"

"Are you and Sam getting divorced?" Alex asked abruptly.

Finally.

I took a deep breath. "After you and I spoke, things went on like normal. It was tense, obviously. I was in Birmingham with Jules and Frankie. Sam texted me on the way to my dad's, to make sure I'd gotten there. I found out at two in the morning, while I was a hundred-and-eighty miles from home, that he'd filed for divorce two days after my birthday. By the time you and I chatted that day, he'd already told his attorney to move forward."

Alex was shocked. He didn't know what to say.

"We have since agreed to go back to counseling. Even if we don't make it, we'll have been through the whole process to try to heal this as best we can."

"So is it still pending?"

I shrugged. "He told his attorney to hold off."

"Does he know you're here?"

"Yeah, he knows." Alex turned toward me and glanced around the bar, as if he were looking for signs of Sam. "He's not here. He's in Atlanta."

"And what does he think?"

"He doesn't like it, but he knows why I need to do it. He knows there's no hope of my moving on with my life and in my head until I get the chance to bury this fucking ghost."

He looked pointedly at me, holding my gaze and saying nothing for a long moment. "You would blow your marriage apart for me."

And you wouldn't do anything to stop me.

I met his even gaze unflinchingly but didn't say anything.

"He's never going to get over this, you know," Alex said finally, matter-of-factly.

I nodded slowly. "I'm afraid of that."

"I'm afraid he's going to hurt you. He's a controlling prick, Tierney."

"Alex, he's really not." My voice sounded half-hearted in my own ears.

"He set you up! He was watching you from the beginning, waiting for you to fuck up. That's why he messaged *me* about Chicago. He knew who you were when he married you. He knew this would come."

I didn't agree with him completely, though we'd talked about it at length before. I wasn't sure Sam really *had* known who I was when we married. Hell, I didn't know if *I* had even really known.

"I don't think he set me up, not initially. Later, yes, absolutely he was watching to catch me."

I looked into his blue eyes. "I need you to know—" I reached out and touched his hand "—just let me say all this and then you can leave or yell at me or whatever—but I didn't know Mac emailed you. I could tell from your first response to him that you were mad as *fuck*, but I couldn't really tell from the second one. And I was surprised when you agreed to meet and talk, honestly. But I needed to say some things and give you the chance to do the same. My reasons are totally selfish—I know that—and I'm really appreciative of your doing this."

"Who the fuck *is* that guy? I thought it was you."

"No, it wasn't me. He's Jules' brother. He's a mediator in Birmingham. He just cares about me and wanted to help. I didn't think he'd actually contact you."

"That's why I was mad at first," he replied, "because I thought it was just you trying to make contact."

"Alex, look, you need to know...," I grasped his arm and looked him in the eye, "Alex, *never* would I tell your secrets. You have to know that—"

"I know, Tierney—"

"—those things you shared with me, especially about Annabelle, I will *never* tell them. Ever."

He turned slightly on his bar stool to face me. "I know that, Tierney. I wouldn't have shared those things, all of it, if I didn't know I could trust you."

"And even with everything going on... I'm still not telling him your secrets. I'm still taking flack for it, but I won't budge on this. He came so close to telling Talia, just a couple of months ago, and he thinks I'm still siding with you about all of it. It's not the specifics of it now so much as it's the principle."

"Tierney, I trust you. I don't know what I'll tell my wife if she ever finds out, but I'll deal with it if I have to."

You'll lie to her, like you always do.

We paused for a drink, and he continued. "I know it's unfair that you're dealing with all of this, that I'm not having the fallout that you do." I tossed my hair in mild protest. "It's true. It is. I *should* be dealing with this at home, but I'm not. Talia doesn't know about any of it, and it needs to stay that way. Honestly, I don't know if we'll make it. I hope we will, for Amber's sake. I want her to be able to grow up with a family. But Talia's tired of me, and I just don't know." He went on to explain about her business and how things hadn't gone according to plan. "It's been six months, and she still hasn't done what she's supposed to do. I can't babysit her and do this shit for her."

His friends were shifting and milling, talking about going downtown to see another musician friend play at a club. I waited patiently, chatting animatedly and politely, while he made next-day brunch plans and told them to go on without him. He was giving me the time I needed to tell him goodbye.

We ordered a second round. I felt the shift and jumped onto my next issue.

"Alex, after that last chat, I was so goddamn mad at you." He glanced sideways at me, questioningly, sipping his Stella. "Months ago, you promised me that you wouldn't step out of my life unless I asked you to, but you did." He started to say something, but I shut him down. "I *know* why you did, I get it, but it hurt like hell. I felt dismissed, and it was infuriating, after everything. And in the midst of it all, you told me not to let my marriage falling apart make me feel small. But *you* did that. *You*, in that last conversation, made me feel unimportant and insignificant."

I was surprised to see a hint of hurt on his beautiful face. He turned in his stool to face me again.

"I didn't mean to hurt you. It was hard, I was in the studio working, and all of this shit was going on...." He paused and looked at me pointedly. "I'm sorry it wasn't what it should've been. And I'm sorry it still can't be. Don't ever think you're unimportant or that you're insignificant to me. You're not. *You're not insignificant to me.* The respect and affection I have for you is enormous. And you're crazy if you think I don't want to fuck you right now. It's all I've thought about for three days." He held my green gaze in his pale blue one, biting his luscious lower lip.

My heart throbbed between my legs.

"Talia and I've been together for ten years, *ten years*, and I've never let anything touch me like that. That's the unspoken agreement, you know? I don't bring it home. I've never let anything get anywhere close to a relationship, and that's exactly what this was, *a relationship*. I miss you—*miss you!*—all the fucking time! And there will be certain days every year that I will *use* you." I grinned and blushed, in spite of myself. "But you have to let me go. We have to let this go."

"It's so hard," I sighed. "Some days, I'm good. I'm totally fine and feel like I'm inching forward. But other days... I can *feel* you so intensely... it knocks the breath out of me."

He nodded slowly in pointed agreement. "I know. It's because we're the same person. We have the same feelings and deviances and needs."

"You're ingrained in me. In every fiber of my being. You're never *not* there."

"I had all these things bottled up in me. I'd repressed them and pushed them down or forgotten them or whatever. And then I met you, and I could just let all that out."

"You always said I was like your sex therapist."

He smiled. "Exactly! I could've gone to a therapist and spent a bunch of money and told them my secrets, but instead I told you. And it was exciting, and it was so easy. Then it was *more*."

"I know it wasn't what you wanted, to get so close. You didn't want me to feel anything, and you didn't want to feel anything, either."

We were facing each other now, seated sideways on our stools, knees almost touching. "It's addictive," Alex said, "like a drug.

You have to have it. *It feels so good.* But you want something that's never going to happen," he smiled sadly.

"As much as you could compartmentalize it all and push it away, that left me to feel *all* of it, for *both* of us."

"I know," he said softly. "I'm sorry."

"Look," I said, "I know I did some crazy shit to keep me on your radar. It was manipulative."

He threw his head back and exploded with laughter.

"I'm a girl. We do that shit," I continued, smiling. "I'm sorry, though, and I have to release you from that. It's like my heart is a puzzle, you know? And there's a piece missing. You have it, it's yours. And maybe it belongs with you, but I think it's safer with me."

He laughed a little derisively. "That's the problem with you women!" He turned back toward his beer, sitting on the bar. I could hear the somewhat joking tone in his voice, though I knew he was making what he thought would be a valid point. "You want sex, but then there's all this *heart* tied up in it."

"That's how we're built! There's a reason for it. Oxytocin and neurotransmitters that get released!"

"Don't talk to me about brain shit," he joked. The bartender stopped in front of us. Alex pointed to my empty drink. "You want another one?"

Did I? I wasn't done. I had more to say, and I wasn't quite ready to tell him goodbye. Not yet. "Yeah. One more."

"This round's on the lady," Alex said to the bartender.

I reached into my small purse for some cash. "Is there a lady here?" I winked and grinned sideways at Alex.

"It's obvious the guy *loves* you, but Sam needs some intensive therapy, Tierney. You'll need to go through it together."

"I know," I admitted. "That's why we're going back into counseling."

"He's going to make you push it all down, everything you are and who you want to be. You'll have to suppress all of it. It's controlling, and you won't be happy. You *know* what you need to do."

It was so hard, hearing him voice all of my own fears and worries. And it was doubly painful, because as much as I wanted him to save me from it in that moment, to jump feet first into these unknown waters with me, I knew it was never going to happen. My friend, *my* Alex, was telling me the truth of me as he saw it, but my lover couldn't be the one to catch me if I dove off that cliff.

"As much as you want your family to work for Amber—and I know how much you love her—I want those same things for my boys. And the logistics of my life are such that this is where I am. I have to learn to live in those confines."

He looked at me again, holding my gaze harshly. "What's good for your boys is what's good for their *mother*. *You know what you need to do.*"

"And all of this you're saying to me, you know I could be telling you the exact same things, right?"

"Oh, absolutely I know!"

There it was. We were, yet again, two sides of the same coin, the same heads and tails forever chasing each other, never quite able to reach far enough over the edge to grab onto the other.

"You know, there are two things that still bother me."

He raised his eyebrow and sipped his beer.

"One, in San Antonio... that whole weekend... you never once called me 'Buttercup'."

He grinned at me. "You *love* that, don't you?"

I blushed.

"And you *are* a total buttercup, Tierney" he said softly. "Really, just lovely. All soft and pink, with a little blond on top." He bit his lip, and I felt the hot, wet need of him.

I blushed more deeply and cracked an unintended sexy smile. "And I get all over your face when you stick your nose in?"

He laughed and tried to say something in retort but sipped his beer instead. "What's the other thing? You said there were two."

I started to giggle nervously, trying to find the words that couldn't hide behind a phone call. "Okay, so, I *hate* the fact that you owe me something you promised repeatedly but never delivered on."

He looked puzzled.

"It involves your tongue and my vagina."

He glanced down at his hands. "I don't do that."

"You liar!"

He started to laugh again. "It's true! You can ask my wife."

Seriously, Princess?

"I used to!" he said, grinning self-consciously. "But I was dating this girl who wasn't really into it. I did it with Talia a couple of times, and she wasn't that into it, either. So I just... quit... doing it."

I was flabbergasted and looked at him intently, trying to make sense of what he was saying. "Are you *bad* at it?" I asked, after a long pause.

He turned red, smiling incredulously. "*Am I bad at it?*" He shrugged. "I don't know... maybe."

"Well, if it's any consolation, I secretly hate come in my mouth."

"Well, there you have it!" he laughed.

"Except I don't refuse to *do* it. I just don't *like* it."

We spent some time watching bad karaoke singers. Somehow we missed the end of the World Series, playing on the television over the bar. He was a sports fan, and I'd pulled him away from game seven. There were dozens of times when we started talking about something, nothing, details of our selves and our lives, but we were distracted by something else. It was like it always had been with him, easy to say anything and everything. I wanted to hear it all, but there just wasn't time. They were the small conversations that could've gone on for a lifetime.

It was almost midnight. I was finished with my drink, and so was he.

"Do you want another one?" he asked.

I looked at him, searching. The tension, the desire, was palpable. "I don't know. Do I?"

"I can't tell you if you want another drink, Tierney," he said quietly. "I would love to sit here and drink with you all night."

"But we can't."

"Because you need to tell me bye and go back to your hotel and never contact me again. You can't call me or text me or see me again. You can't come to shows."

"I know." I didn't want to do it. I knew this might be the last time I ever had the moment with him to myself. This could be the last time I saw him. I didn't want to believe it, but I knew in my head what he was asking. "I've had a lot to drink. I can't hold my liquor like I used to, you know."

"Your hotel is two blocks away?"

I nodded.

"Come on, I'll drive you."

I smiled at him and stood carefully from my stool. The bar was almost empty, one last karaoke singer on the tiny stage. I couldn't hear what he was singing over the sound of my own heartbeat in my ears.

I put on my jacket. I watched my feet as I walked toward the door of the bar, making sure I didn't trip over the threshold on the way to the parking lot, a step-and-a-half ahead of him.

"You're trying desperately not to look at my ass, aren't you?" I laughed over my shoulder.

"Every step of the way!"

I gave him the key and led him to my car. We sat quietly idling for a minute, letting the car warm up. It was so damn cold.

"You know," I said suddenly, "this afternoon, in the hotel... that was probably the last time I'll ever masturbate to your voice."

"You're amazing, Tierney," he laughed, shaking his head.

"I'm a force of goddamn nature!"

He chuckled and backed out of the parking space, turning toward my hotel. Even in that two minute drive, we bantered back and forth about the drive, which way to go, how I would've gone out the other side of the parking lot. It was more of the natural talk that had always flowed so easily between us. I directed him to park by the door closest to my room.

I pulled my room key from my wallet while he got out of the car. Waiting on the sidewalk, watching me through the windshield, he was shivering with no jacket. I got out and walked past him to the door, sliding my key card into the lock. He followed me inside and down the carpeted hallway, the few steps to my room.

He stepped into the room behind me. I dropped my bag and key on the counter and turned to him.

"Thanks for bringing me back. Thanks for meeting with me."

He looked me straight in the eye. "You need to text your husband and let him know that you're back in your room and safe."

Sam Johnson
Nov 4th 11:55 PM
Back in my room. I'm ok.

I looked up from my phone. He was looking down at the floor.

I wanted him to stay. I *wanted* to push him into the chair right behind him and straddle his lap and shove my tongue into his mouth. I wanted to take him to the big hotel bed and spend an hour trying to make up for what hadn't been right in San Antonio. My heart and my body desperately wanted to be naked with him, broken down and open, to come with my mouth pressed tightly against his warmth while he called me Buttercup one last time.

"I love you, Alex Wheeler."

Still looking down, he replied quickly, "I love you, too."

I came back to him and hugged him tightly.

"Be careful walking back."

"Be careful driving back. And don't contact me again," he laughed.

I rolled my eyes. "I know. I got it."

He kissed me quickly and walked out the door, gone into the cold night.

Chapter 30

Between the drinking and the being away from home, I didn't sleep for very long, about five hours, and was up before dawn. I dressed and went outside to smoke a cigarette. A deep fog had rolled off the Cumberland River into Nashville overnight. Where Alex's hotel should've been, there was only a deep mist blocking any signs of light.

I was tired and cold, but my head was clearer than it had felt in ages. I went back into my room and packed up my stuff. The hotel had breakfast in the lobby, so I grabbed some yogurt and a muffin, made a pot of coffee in the room.

Sam Johnson
Nov 5th 8:03 AM

I'm up and eating, leaving soon. I'm clear and good and okay. I'm bringing my heart home to you.

Glad ur OK. Be safe. Have fun!
Thanks for the txts. I love you.

I'm better than okay. I'm good like I haven't been in a long time. I love you deeply. Thank you for your patience and love.
I have a lot of work to do. WE have a lot of work to do. But I'm ready.

Good to hear. :)

Hands shaking, I deleted the Alex playlist from my phone. I quickly synced it to my computer and watched iTunes erase the silliest thing, the most poignant symbol of so much time and energy and emotion. I was okay for now, and I was ready to move on.

I drove away, stopped by the traffic light in front of his hotel. The fog was still thick and brilliantly white, and Alex was nowhere to be found.

———————————

Jules was expecting me by lunchtime. I'd told her I was coming to visit for the night, but I hadn't told her—or Tessa or Frankie—that I was planning to see Alex. I was afraid of what would happen, afraid that it would be either so ugly I never wanted to think of it again or so beautiful that I wanted to keep it all to myself. None of them would be thrilled that I was in contact with him, knowing how likely it was that I would be sad and crying for days afterward. I hadn't wanted the added pressure of their expectations, but I knew it was important that I share it with them after the fact.

I called Tessa first.

"I saw Alex last night in Nashville."

"*What the hell did you do that for?*"

I explained. I told her what and why and how. She didn't even ask if I'd fucked him.

"You sound okay," she said finally. "*No*, you sound better than okay. You sound *good*. I'm glad."

"I am, Tessa. I'm just... clear."

And I was. It wasn't like I thought I would wake up the next day and just be suddenly free of all the emotion and the pain. Finally, though, my heart could see that there would be a light at the end, even if I was still feeling blindly along the dank tunnel walls.

I tried to call Frankie but got no answer. I didn't leave a message.

I pulled into Jules' subdivision and wound past the jungle of almost-identical houses with their precise lawns browning for the coming winter. I hadn't been to her house in years, since just after she and Steve moved into it when Jason was a baby and she was a new faculty member at Middle Tennessee State. It looked the same, though, and no one else on the street would have both MTSU and University of Montevallo stickers on their cars.

"Tierney!"

Jason bounded toward my car. He was breathless and excited, bouncing from one foot to the other, blocking me from fully opening my car door. He looked just like a red-headed version of Jules, and I could see the same mischief in his grin.

"Jason! How's my favorite nine-year-old in the world?"

He giggled and took me by the grubby hand, my keys clasped awkwardly in my fist. "*Come on!* We made you something!"

I pushed the car door closed with my hip and locked it remotely. I let Jason drag me into the house, straight to the kitchen where Jules was taking fresh bread from the oven.

"Hey, Kitten!" She pulled a worn oven mitt from her hand and dropped it onto the marble countertop. "How are you?"

I hugged her, smelling her clean hair and the same perfume she'd worn as long as I'd known her.

"I'm good! Jason says you guys made something for me."

Jules chided her son with a sideways smile. "It was *supposed* to be a *surprise*!" She reached to tickle him, but Jason darted around the corner, giggling and watching to see if she would follow.

Jules lifted the lid from a domed cake plate, revealing chocolate cupcakes.

"Is that *cream cheese* icing?" I asked. "Jason, how did you know these are my *favorite*?"

"Mommy said so! She said not to tell you we didn't make the icing from scratch, though!"

I grabbed at my chest, feigning indignation. "Jules, am I not even worth *homemade* frosting? I'm hurt!"

Jason ran from the kitchen, down the hall toward his room. Jules glanced after him to make sure he was gone.

"Suck it, bitch!" she laughed. "How was your drive?"

"Short," I answered. I plopped myself onto a barstool at the counter. "I was in Nashville last night."

"*What?* Why didn't you—"

"I saw Alex."

"Oh my god." She sat on the stool next to me.

I went through the previous night's conversation with her, relaying the story as chronologically as possible.

"I knew for a week it was coming, but I couldn't tell you. I didn't want the added pressure of having to talk about it."

"I get that," she replied, "but if you hadn't told me after, I would've been *pissed*. And he just took you back to your hotel room and told you goodbye?"

"Yep."

"Nothing happened? Tierney, did anything happen?"

"No. Nothing happened."

"I'm proud of you."

I shrugged. "What's there to be proud of? I could either *not* fuck him and go home to Sam, or I could fuck him and not go home. And not going home is *not* an option."

"Did you *want* to fuck him? After everything?"

I looked at her incredulously. "Of course I did."

She looked baffled.

"Jules, I *love* him. My head, my heart, my body—they all *love* him. They *want* him. They want to *be* with him, and they probably always will."

"And what about Sam? What do your head and your heart and your body say about him?"

"They love him, too. Deeply."

"Do you love Alex more?"

I thought about it for a moment, trying to find the right words. "It's just... *different*. Where my love for Sam is deep and still and cool and pure, my love for Alex is torrential and flooding and hot... and a little bit shallow."

Jules said nothing, waiting for me to talk it out.

"It's like the kids book, *I Love You the Purplest*. Do you know this book?" She shook her dark head. "I've read it to the boys dozens of times. In the story, this mother is constantly asked by her two perfect little boys to compare them—to see which one dug the best worms or caught the best fish. When they ask her which one she loves more, she tells one that she loves him the reddest, the other that she loves him the bluest. She describes her love for each of them in these beautiful analogies of unique perfection. It's like *that*.

"I didn't *stop* loving Tripp when Ian was born, you know. I didn't suddenly love him any less because he had a brother. My capacity to love expanded and let another love into my heart. The same thing happened when I met Alex."

"Well, I don't love Steve less because we have Jason," she responded, "but I couldn't give Steve the same attention I gave him before we had to share our time with this other love."

I nodded at her. "You're right. There's only a finite amount of energy to expend on anyone or anything. It would be impossible for me to show Tripp all of the attention he got before Ian was born, but that doesn't mean I don't try my best to make him still feel special.

But where I can convince the boys to spend time *together* in Mommy's attention, there's no way in *hell* I'll ever get Sam and Alex in my orbit at the same time. Sam would kill Alex first."

Jules squinched her face and tilted her head, like she was trying to see me more clearly. "Would you want that? Would you want to split your time between them?"

"Would it be *ideal? No.* I want to be able to be with Sam, to live our life with the boys and be happy, to have him love me no matter what. But I would *love* to be able to have Alex from time to time, to call him just to check in whenever I wanted, and to see him every six months and *fuck* him, just between us."

"*Why?* Why would you be willing to have that little bit of him, if that were all you could have?"

"Because it's *that* intense, Jules. Because it's *that* goddamn good."

"You want to have your cake and eat it, too. *You little minx!*"

I nodded and reached toward the cake plate. "I want a dark chocolate cupcake with cream cheese frosting... and a little Alex Wheeler on top."

"Or bottom."

"Or from behind. *Especially* from behind." Jules giggled. "Oh *shit.* Now I'm gonna be thinking about that *all* day."

"Hell, Kitten," Jules laughed, "I'll be thinking about it, too."

Steve stayed home with Jason that night so Jules and I could go out. Dinner and drinks and late-night coffee at Waffle House. It wasn't exciting, but it was the girl time I needed, time to *not* think and *not* talk about Alex or Sam, time to drive and sing and reminisce about all the boys we'd once loved. Or at least slept with.

By midnight, I was collapsing under the weight of my bra and my make-up. Jules dragged my drunken ass back to her house. We put on pajamas and brushed our teeth and met up again in the guest bed. We lay in the dark, holding hands and giggle-whispering like we'd done so many nights in Montevallo.

"Can I tell you a something?" I slurred sleepily.

"Of course."

"Sometimes—not *all* the time, mind you, just *sometimes*—I think it would be easier if I were dead."

"*Kitten! Don't say that!*"

"It's not like I really *want* to die! I don't *want* to be dead. But the logistics of it all would be so much easier for everyone. Like, if I just weren't *there*. The *cost* of me is so much, Jules." I could smell and taste the whiskey on my breath.

"*How?* Those boys would miss you, Tierney. *I* would miss you. Sam, Tessa, Frankie... we'd all be lost without you."

I shook my head violently against the cool, crisp pillowcase. "You'd all miss me, yes, but that's not *logic*. That's not the expense of my life—the clothes and the food and the *expense* of being Tierney, the *price* everyone else has to pay for my choices. Sam, especially, would benefit from my not being there. Take the emotion out of it, and it's a logical conclusion."

Jules sat up in the dark and folded her legs under her, turned toward me. "Tierney," she said gently, "*why* would you even say that? You're amazing and beautiful and funny. Our lives are a thousandfold better because we *know* you."

I kissed her on the knee, because it was the part of her that was within my immediate reach. "Sometimes when I think about it, I'm selfish enough to realize that I don't want to die, that I want to be here to see my children grow into spectacular men."

I was quiet, deciding if I were really going to say what I was thinking. Jules waited for me to continue.

"But *then*," I said tentatively, "I think it would be best if *Sam* were the one to die. Do you know we don't even have life insurance, on me? There's no safety net for them if I died, and that wouldn't even really matter. I haven't had a real job in so long, I'm not worth much to life insurance companies. But Sam is heavily insured. The boys and I would be okay if something happened to him. I've thought about it a lot, like, how we'd survive, who I'd call first when the police come to tell me he's been killed in a drunken accident. Who I'd call at his company to claim survivor benefits and get his personal belongings from his office."

I looked up to Jules, the concern plain even in the shadows on her face. "Am I just *awful*? Am I just *horrible* for thinking about what my life would be life if Sam were dead?"

"Are you planning to kill him? *Of course not!* Look, Tierney, I've never, *ever* told anyone this, but I think the same things sometimes. I think about what would happen to me and Jason if Steve died. You're a parent; you can't *not* think about these things. In some ways, it's the responsible thing to do. But, *fuck*, Kitten—I'm *way* past the point of insurance! I've already planned how long I'd have to wait before I started dating again, and what kind of man I'd be looking for next. But that doesn't mean I want Steve to *die*. Thinking about it, though... that's something we *all* do, it's just that no one talks about it. Like masturbation."

"Are we just crazy?" I sighed.

Jules settled down under the blankets again, her forehead snuggled against my shoulder. "We are *batshit* crazy, Kitten. Both of us. But that's why we have each other."

Chapter 31

By the time I woke the next morning, Jules was in the kitchen with a fresh pot of coffee and blueberry muffins. Steve and Jason were outside, their mingled laughter drifting across the lawn and through the open kitchen window.

"How'd you sleep, Kitten?" Jules kissed me on the forehead as she handed me a cup of coffee. Two creams. Two sugars.

"Okay," I nodded. "Thanks for letting me crash here."

"Anytime. You know that."

We ate breakfast with her men. I asked Steve about his job search, and he asked me about my painting. Jason begged me to bring Tripp and Ian to visit soon. I took a quick shower and dressed. As I unzipped a pocket on the front of the suitcase, a small barcoded sticker fluttered to the floor.

It was the baggage claim sticker from my trip to San Antonio.

I took a deep breath and shoved it back into the pocket, zipping it closed.

I wheeled my suitcase through the house and out the front door to the small porch. There, lying in a beam of yellow to the side of the door, was a dead animal.

"Jules," I called carefully into the house, "I think you need to come here."

The dead animal opened one yellow eye and hissed at me.

Jules stepped onto the porch, looked at the pile of brown fur and then at me. She started to laugh.

"*That* is Merkin."

Merkin's fur was long and a spotty, filthy brown. Judging from his improbably flat face, he'd been bred to be a Persian. One of his short ears was missing a tiny notch of flesh at the top, scabbed with old blood. The other ear had been torn halfway off long ago. His tail was broken and bent a couple of inches from the tip.

"That is the *ugliest* cat I've ever seen in my life!"

He jumped up suddenly and arched his back, his matted fur puffing angrily. Because of the break in his tail, only the tip of it fluffed. He glared at us both with his one open eye and hissed again before leaping from the porch and running around the side of the house.

"He's no Golden Kitten, that's for sure," Jules sighed.

Jules and I stood in her driveway, leaning against my car. It was mid-morning, and the sun was already halfway up the sky, too bright and happy, reflecting off multi-paned, double-hung windows and car windshields.

"It looks like the sun on the morning you're going home from the beach," I remarked.

"When you're ready to be home but don't want to leave and go back to your real life?"

"Yep, just like that."

I dropped my bag into the trunk and hugged Jules goodbye. I was tired but okay.

Until I got into the car.

As soon as I put the key in the ignition, I started to cry. Right there, in the middle of the McKinnons' driveway. I tried my best to hold it in, hiding it from the smiling waves of my friend and her family. I was in the middle of nowhere, hundreds of miles from home, and all of the weight of how I'd gotten there came crashing down in an instant.

I started the car and drove down the street. I pulled out my phone, starting the iPod player. I cycled through the three most important songs, the most poignant, while I screamed all the way to the interstate. I tried to sing along, to keep my shaking voice in time to Alex's, but my throat closed around the words, strangling me with my sorrow. Tears streaming down my face, I could barely make out the lines on the lanes, and I was thankful the highway was mostly deserted on that Sunday morning.

My heart was being crushed under its own weight. Everything I'd been holding inside poured out in the cabin of my car, and there was nothing I could do to dam it up.

I cried myself out between Nashville and the Georgia state line, my agony building to crescendo with each mountainside my car would climb, then rushing away as huge tractor-trailers passed by me on the way down.

I merged onto I-285 outside of Atlanta, the Perimeter, as I got close to home.

We're on the road to nowhere....

Traffic came to sudden standstill, stopped by a wreck or weekend construction, as so often happens in Atlanta. I sat there in my car, waiting for the unknown obstruction to abate. I looked at the hundreds of cars stretched before and behind me, some with one, lone driver, others filled with families talking animatedly or ignoring one another, distracted by their individual electronic devices.

We all die alone. I will eventually die alone.

It won't matter who I do or don't love, who I do or don't have with me, when the time comes. It will matter if I love myself, if I am *with* me, when I die. Tomorrow or next year or ten years or fifty: the only person I ever, *truly* have to live with is *me*.

I don't want to live with regrets. I don't want unexplored opportunities. I spent so many years, holed up in my apartment or my life or my self, and there were so many other things I could or should have been doing. But all of those choices had led me to *here* and *now*, to do and see the things of the last year. In a sense of predestination, I'd never really had the choice *not* to look, and I couldn't unsee the things I'd witnessed and created. There had been a reason for all of it, and that reason was Alex.

I'd told him so many times, his role in my life was to help move me from one place to another. He was there to remind me who I'm supposed to be, helping me see my own worth when I absolutely couldn't. He delved into those dark, immersive waters and pulled me, gasping, to the surface. I'd been so numb from that cold, and he'd stayed with me, warming me until the numb wore off. But now, the pain was wearing back *on*, and he was gone.

Alex had told me, again, how he knew I was insecure, how he knew all the reasons I needed my surroundings to be a haven. It was part of what kept me with Sam, even when I felt like it was the worst place to be.

Looking at the ordered chaos around me on the interstate, I realized that, yes, I need to feel secure in my environment. I need to know that the things around me are staid and solid, allowing me to be tethered to them. But *me*... well, that's a different thing entirely.

I thrive on chaos. I am at my most productive when I'm under pressure. My creativity peaks in direct proportion to the upheaval in my life. And because I am driven to *understand* the experiences of my life, however mundane or profane, I will eventually dip my finger into the still waters and stir them, just a little, just to see what happens. If there's not enough excitement from outside forces, I will do whatever it takes to be excited, to be stimulated, to get a chance to understand something in a new and different way.

Sam, on the other hand, can handle the chaos, even though he will rail against it, loudly lashing out against the upheaval. For him, *I* am the tether point, the place he needs to be calm and staid, to help him find his way when everything seems to be crashing around him.

Our drives for security are in direct juxtaposition.

And it's not that either of us is wrong to feel the way we do. It's just who we *are*. It's our own lifetimes of experiences and influences that have led us to these personalities. On the surface, the two diametrically different needs should balance each other. They should be able to complete the whole.

For whatever reason, we'd come to a place and time in our lives when our basic schema were repelling us away from each other like similarly-polarized magnets.

———————————

I came home to my husband and my children, happy to see me. I was greeted with hugs and kisses and snuggles. I was immediately taken to see the new gadgets they'd gotten while I was away. We made it through dinner and baths and reading before tucking the boys into bed for the night.

Sam and I sat on the couch in the den. We were mostly quiet, chatting a bit about the superficialities of the weekend, about the drive through Tennessee and how Jules and Steve and Jason were doing.

Finally, gazing into the flames of the fire Sam had built for us, I asked, "Are we going to talk about the pink elephant?"

"If you'd like," he replied gently, sipping his beer. "I wasn't going to push you."

I went through the evening with Alex, step by step, as pragmatically as I could. I tried to stick to the chronological story, without embellishing it with my thoughts about everything.

There were a lot of details I didn't share. Lots of conversational things that mattered, to me, and didn't. I didn't talk about the karaoke, or the conversations with other people, or how he'd called me Buttercup again, *knowing* what it meant and did to me. I didn't tell Sam how hard it was *not* to drag Alex back to my hotel room or upstairs to his, from the moment that I saw him. And I wasn't totally forthcoming about the kiss goodbye.

When I said, again, that there were confidences Alex had shared with me, things I'd promised that I'd never tell, Sam's unspoken question hung dramatically over us: *Why can you keep those promises to him but break so many others to me?*

As I finally got around to sharing my epiphany about our drives for security, it was heartbreaking. We could both feel the opposition of our basic needs.

"If I want this to work, if I want this marriage to survive, I can't be like the kid in the candy store anymore," I said, staring off at the built-in bookshelves surrounding the fireplace. They were packed with books and pictures and pieces of artwork the boys had made in school—years of memories we'd all built together. "I can't expect to be able to dig my grubby little hands into the brightly-colored bins and take what I want, expecting someone else to clean it up, no matter how joyous the candy makes me. I realize that I can't do everything I want to do and still be in a successful relationship with someone else. I will have to compromise myself to make this work."

It seemed so simple, really: people compromise to make the people they love happy. But I knew, so painfully, that this wasn't about conceding on where to eat for dinner, or which curtains to buy for the bedroom. I would have to back down from the hill I'd been climbing for the last year, the one where I'd so confidently planted my Buttercup-adorned flag, if I had any hope of ever making Sam happy. And if I wanted him to feel secure, I would have to constantly be on guard, always cognizant of the need to brutally overpower my own impulses and desires, to push them back down into the frigid waters.

It was, again, in direct opposition to every belief about myself that I had achieved on this journey. I knew it, and so did he.

Sam said nothing for a long time. He finished his beer in silence. Finally he asked, "Did you go to his room?"

I shook my head. "I was only in the lobby or the bar at his hotel. And the bathroom."

"Did he come to your room?"

"I told you he did."

"Was the door closed?"

"I don't know. Yeah, maybe?"

"*Maybe?* Are you kidding me? I got the report yesterday. I know he was in your room, and I know how long the door was closed."

What? I was trying to make sense of what he was saying.

"It was hard to get your room bugged, with the last minute change in hotels. There wasn't much time."

Had I heard that right? Did he really have someone watching me and Alex in Nashville? And they followed me to my room? *And he tried to have my room bugged?*

I stared at him.

I'm done.

"Did you kiss him? Did you kiss him goodbye?"

I couldn't find the words to answer him. My voice and mind and heart were reeling. "I'm done."

"*Did you kiss him?* Just tell me. Did he come into your room and kiss you goodbye?"

"Yes, quickly." The kiss hadn't been a big deal. It wasn't a protracted make-out session. "I didn't fuck him."

"I didn't ask if you did. Why didn't you tell me he came into your room? When you were telling me what happened, why didn't you say that he came *inside* your room?"

"I *did* tell you! I told you he made sure I got in safely!"

"You told me he walked you to the outside door of the hotel and hugged you goodbye. You didn't tell me that you took him behind closed doors and kissed him!"

"*I'm done.*"

You know what you have to do.

"You just can't be truthful about him! Is this how it will always be? My having to drag the truth out of you?"

No, because I'm fucking done.

"I'm not doing this with you. I told you he walked me back to my room!"

"You told me you weren't going to be alone with him! You told me you weren't going to drink with him!"

I was appalled. I couldn't wrap my head around what he was saying. Sam had sent a private investigator, or some intelligence contact in Nashville, to *watch* me with Alex. Certainly, the thought had crossed my mind, but Sam had assured me that he wouldn't do it, to give me the chance to do the right thing, to make the good choice in the moment.

He'd been *waiting* and *expecting* me to fuck up. He'd sent me there, encouraging me to take the much-needed step toward closure, but he'd done everything in his power to catch me doing something wrong.

"Why can't you just tell me the truth when it comes to him?"

"You don't want to hear it! You don't want to hear the truth about how I feel!"

"Yes, I do! I want to know, so I can understand it and deal with it! But if you keep hiding it from me, I'll never know."

"Fine! I *love* him, and I *miss* him!" I lobbed the words at him, the emotional grenade hissing as it arced from my mouth.

"I know you do."

"And that will never be okay with you! You will never be okay with the fact that he's always there!"

"Tierney, I know he'll always be there. We have to find a way to not let it be an issue. That's why I have to know everything about the contact between you, so I can be prepared to handle it."

"No! You don't want there to be any contact. And there won't be, whether or not it's what makes you more comfortable. Alex is *gone* from my life!" My heart lurched with the pain.

I stomped out to the deck and lit a cigarette. Sam followed me and sat in the chair next to mine, opening another beer. We were silent for a few moments.

"I don't think it's unreasonable for one partner to demand that the other cut out contact with the person they cheated with. You know how I feel about it."

"Yeah, I do," I mumbled sarcastically. "We all know how you feel."

"Which is?"

"You know, Alex even thought it was fucked up. I told him that you had basically said it was okay for me to fuck other people, as long as you knew about it. *'Everyone except me?'* he said. *'That's fucked up, Tierney. You know how fucked up that is, right?'* And he's totally right!"

"Why is that fucked up? You have feelings for him, feelings that come between us. You lied, repeatedly, about your relationship."

"Yep."

There was nothing else to say about it. We'd been over it a thousand times, round and round and round. Hearing and saying the same words over and over, I could almost make out where we were in the cycle, like noticing the same on-lookers for the dozenth time while riding a carousel.

"Look," I said, "I can't help how I feel. Believe me, I have *tried* to make it not be there. It just *is*, and it always will be. I love him, and I miss him, and I will never *not want* him, but—"

I started to say that it didn't matter, that Alex wasn't coming back, that I would learn eventually to deal with that and not let it affect me so profoundly.

"Then we have nothing more to say," Sam interjected.

"Let me fini—"

"No. There's nothing else that matters. He will always be there."

I was tired, and it was getting late. I hadn't even wanted to have this conversation to begin with.

"Fine," I said finally. "I'm going to bed."

I was so tired and so cold, shaking violently against the stress. I tried to sleep, but my toes were almost numb, even between the flannel sheets and under two heavy quilts. I dozed fitfully until I finally got up to put on socks. And yoga pants. And a hoodie. And to turn up the heat.

It was early the next morning when I saw the email.

From: Sam Johnson
Sent: November 7th 1:25 AM
To: Tierney Cavanaugh Johnson
Subject: Forward from here

I'm hoping we can be realistic -- implying an honesty about actions regardless of feelings -- about where you and I go from here.

We are not marriage material now, even though we may have once been. More than ever, I am convinced that I will never again have that sacred connection with you that enables the total emotional investment upon which a lifetime of dedication through good and bad depends. Pretending that we have that connection is a lie and is destructive, much more so than being honest.

I would like to thank you for sparing me or showing respect for me by being honest in matters truly core to our marriage, but I cannot think of a single instance in the last year where that is deserved.

I wasn't about to respond. I took Ian to school and called Tessa. It was the ass crack of dawn in Chicago, but I knew she was usually up early to see Ed off before work.

"Sam sent a PI to watch me in Nashville. He tried to have my room bugged. I'm done."

"*What the fuck?*"

"Yeah, I don't know."

"He *encouraged* you to go. He said he knew how this was the right thing for you to do, but he totally tried to set you up to fail, to catch you when you did so he could prove you wrong."

"Yep."

"I hate to say it, Tierney, but I'm kind of not surprised. It's fucked up but not unexpected."

And she was right. When Alex and I left the hotel bar, walking toward my car, I did a quick glance around the bar, just to see if I could tell if anyone *might* be watching. I didn't see anything that made me obviously uneasy, though I knew quite well that it would never be that obvious. No investigator worth a tenth of their fee would be wearing a badge or pointing a camera toward their target.

I came home and got Tripp off to school, as well. I spent a bit of time looking online at rental listings in the area and decided to do a couple of drive-bys. I stopped at the park to smoke while I was out and called my dad.

"I'm moving out."

"Are you okay?"

"Yeah, I am. I'm mad as hell, but I'm fine."

"Well, I won't ask and pry. I'm here if you need to talk."

And then I told him the truth. Briefly. "Sam has the right to file for divorce on grounds of adultery. All that will do in the State of Georgia is keep me from getting alimony. I am well aware of the mistakes and horrible choices I've made, but I didn't get to that place alone. I'm a liar and a cheat, and he's a controlling alcoholic prick."

I told my dad about going to see Alex in Nashville. I told him how Sam was becoming more and more erratic in his drinking. He offered advice but never pushed or judged. Again, he told me to let him know if I needed anything, if there was any way he could help.

I had a couple of hours to kill before I had to go to the elementary school for a lengthy shift of volunteer time. I'd been so wrapped up with the family drama that I hadn't done any of my normally tireless service. I had intentionally distanced myself from school and PTA, in case there was a split. I wanted to steer clear of the Gossip Mill. I went back home. Sam was working in the dining room.

"I'll leave, I'm willing to be the one to move out, in exchange for the files and the agreement that you not do anything with them."

"Do what with them?"

"Tell Talia."

"No way. Not on your life. Alex was right; it's not fair that you're the only one dealing with this."

From: Tierney Cavanaugh Johnson
Date: November 7th 10:15 AM
To: Alex Wheeler
Subject:

There was a PI at the bar, who followed me back to my hotel. "It was hard to get your room bugged, with the sudden change in hotels. It wasn't much time." The impression I got was that there wasn't a bug, but what the fuck!

Because the rock star came into my room, with the door closed for even a moment, even though NOTHING happened except a hug and a quick kiss goodbye, because he wanted to make sure I got in safely at midnight in a strange town after I'd been drinking.... It's so fucked up.

I'm done. I'm looking for a new place to live today. I have Mom stuff, a placement test tomorrow for school, and an appointment to look at a house. Ian's birthday is in a few days.

Yes, I know what I have to do.

I didn't want to email him. After everything we'd talked about, after promising to keep my distance, I didn't want to go back on that and get in touch with him. I couldn't ask anyone else to do it, though, and I felt he deserved to know his privacy might have been invaded again.

From: Alex Wheeler
Date: November 7th 12:22 PM
To: Tierney Cavanaugh Johnson
Subject: Re:

keep me out of this Tierney, whatever you do, keep me out of this whole mess.
A

From: Tierney Cavanaugh Johnson
Date: November 7th 12:47 PM
To: Alex Wheeler
Subject:

I'm doing my best. I didn't want to email you, but you had a right to know. I'm afraid of what's coming next, and I'm busting my ass to keep it calm.

I knew he would be in a panic after seeing my email. I knew he was asking me to leave him in the dark, not to get him involved. I could do that. I had no delusion that I'd be able to rely on him now any more than I'd been able to weeks before. With his own life and his own issues and his own reality, Alex couldn't make the space for me any more, not now that it had touched him. He was able to be my friend as long as it was a secret he could shield from *himself.* As soon as it had threatened to impact him directly, outside of his immediate control, it was too harsh for him. I knew damn well that he had a hard time handling anything that didn't fit neatly into his compartments.

There was a strange calm inside me. It wasn't that I was resolved or at peace with any of it, with Sam or with Alex. I was somehow, unexpectedly, *okay* with where I was going. As much as I loved my home with my children and Sam and everything that worked so beautifully together, it was the natural and logical consequence that I was ready to move on. I didn't feel free or elated, simply... *destined.* Like there was no other way it could go.

I could make the choice to stay, to maintain the balance of the house for the boys and keep their logistical world as same as possible. I could make the choice to stay and fight with Sam over every little detail until a court finally settled our day-to-day issues. Or I could make the choice to vacate the place, the situation, that felt *not safe*.

I wasn't afraid Sam would physically hurt me, though my own history and knowledge of newsworthy events reminded me all the time of women who'd been harmed by their exes. We would continue to play this game of Emotional Damage One-upmanship, and it was futile. We were continually placing our X's and O's in the little boxes, trying to score but repeatedly blocking each other into a draw. I was tired of the most boring game in the world.

The cool, analytical Virgo knew exactly what I needed to do. She knew the plan, the steps I would need to take in order to find a home for myself and my children. She knew that she would continue to look for a part-time job, possibly enroll in school in January, and she would do her best to keep her children safe and happy and secure in the midst of the upheaval of their life. And she was very matter-of-fact about the whole thing.

That night, sitting on the deck, Sam played his X—on the side.

"I didn't have your room bugged. I'm not doing anything with the files. I deleted everything after the first of June. The rest of it is locked away."

What??

"I don't care if you tell Talia. I can't protect Alex, and I just don't care what you do with it."

"I'm not doing anything with it. I think it's best that she not know. She'll find out in her own way eventually, even if it doesn't have to do with you."

He went on, saying something about how it felt more in his control, knowing who knew and how they'd find out. I could tell he was trying to be diplomatic, to tell me he wasn't about to blow Alex's world to Hell, that he wasn't going after him just to come off like some vindictive dick.

But there was also the indication that he'd lied about the bugging, about the surveillance.

"But you still had someone watching me?"

He shook his head. "No. I bluffed. When you were telling me what happened in Nashville, I felt like there was more to it. It

447

sounded just like when you were telling me about him kissing you goodbye at the airport in Texas."

He'd lied about having me followed, just to see if I would fuck up and say something else. He was still trying to catch me in a lie. He was still trying to prove me wrong, no matter what.

His telling me the truth didn't really change anything. It didn't make me feel better about the whole thing, but it didn't make me feel worse, either. It was just one more X in opposition to my O.

Then Sam asked, "Are you still planning to go to the counselor with me on Friday?"

"Why would I do that?"

"So we can work on these problems."

What the fuck?

"You told me we aren't marriage material," I reminded him.

"We aren't, but that doesn't mean we can't be."

It was baffling. I honestly had no idea why he thought I'd want to waste the time and energy and money on that road. He knew I was making arrangements to view rental houses. He knew I was planning to move out as soon as I could get everything set.

"Why do you want to go to counseling?" I asked. "What good do you think it could possibly do?"

"We have huge issues that we don't have the tools and expertise to handle on our own. We're clients, paying for a service from a professional who's trained to help with such issues. I think getting insight into how we can communicate better and work through those issues is beneficial to us both, to all of us. It certainly can't hurt. I'm going, whether or not you go with me."

Our tables were turned from six months prior. He was now the one saying we needed help, and I was the one saying I didn't think it would matter.

And not once did he say, "I want to go because I think you and this are special enough that it's worth the time and energy. I want to go because I love you and want to make this work."

"I'm going to bed," I said.

"Okay. Is that a 'yes' or a 'no' or an 'I'll think about it'?"

I turned back toward him, sitting on the deck in the dark, and stepped inside the back door. I wanted to say it was a "fuck you" or a "go to Hell".

"It's an 'I don't know and I'll think about it'."

I went to bed. I heard him come into the bedroom shortly after me, but I stayed turned toward the wall, like I always went to sleep. I was almost out when I felt him get up. He rustled around in the dark and left. I heard the back door open moments later. I went to sleep.

I knew he was worried and conflicted, thinking about the prospect of breaking up the marriage and realigning the family. I'd been in his exact place twice before, on the other side of having my spouse preparing to leave. My love for him, my deep friendship of this really wonderful man, made me want to reach out and be a comfort to him. But the damaged lover was nowhere close to expressing empathy.

"I'll go with you to the counselor," I told him the next morning. "I'm not making any promises. I'm not promising to go again, or not to go again. I'm not saying I'm willing or unwilling to try. But I'll go with you tomorrow."

I was a bit ambivalent about the whole thing, and I was resolved to take the next few steps one at a time, methodically, until I had an undeniable decision about whether or not I was willing to stay and try once more.

Chapter 32

Sam and I met after lunch at the new counselor's office. He was standing on the front porch of the old house, one of many in the area that had been converted to commercial use.

I'd left the choice of the new counselor up to Sam. I'd chosen Janet, and that hadn't worked out well for us. I liked Dr. Hill immediately. He was friendly and personable. His office was eclectic, and he made a concerted effort to probe for specific issues and to listen to each of us equally.

"I don't really know the specifics of why you're here. Why don't one of you go ahead and jump in and tell me what's at heart of your seeking help."

I looked at Sam, who was quiet. Neither of us was sure who should start.

"Do you want me to address the pink elephant?" I asked.

"Sure."

I looked at Dr. Hill. "The quick answer is that I had an affair."

He nodded, non-judgmental. "When did it start and how long did it go on? Was it someone you both knew—a family friend, a co-worker...?"

"It started about a year ago. It ended, really, about three months ago, though I saw him last week." I paused and glanced at Sam. *Stoic.* "He's a singer in a band I liked, though I'd never met him until last year. He's a minor celebrity."

Dr. Hill looked at me, obviously not expecting *that* response.

"It's a story," I said sardonically.

We went through the quick history. Sam and I each added small details, while Dr. Hill took notes.

"Sam, how did you find out about the affair?"

Sam tried his best to be matter-of-fact about it. "I was targeted by a prominent hacking group that's been in the media." He gave more sensitive details about the string of incidents that led to his finding out in June.

"The files were put up for sale," I said.

"The files were put up for *ransom*," Sam corrected.

Dr. Hill looked at us.

"It's a story," I repeated.

We covered a lot in our first hour with Dr. Hill. We touched on our own reasons for going into counseling, what we thought our personal weaknesses were, within the confines of this marriage. We talked about our long, complicated history, including relationships prior to this one.

"You should be aware," I said to Dr. Hill, "that I have this *history*. I was molested as a child, my parents split when I was eleven, I was raped at sixteen—"

"*Whoa!*" He was looking at me like I was an alien. "Don't give me this as a laundry list. Slow down and tell me again." He grabbed his pen to take more notes.

I stepped back through the touchpoints, adding the four-year abusive relationship with Damien. "I'm sorry if I seem so... *okay* about it all. I understand the effect it's all had on me and how I view and handle relationships. But I've had so much time to deal with so much of it that I can be very nonchalant about it now."

"Can you? Do you think you've healed from a good bit of this? Do you feel like any of it's still lingering for you?"

"I've had time and energy to work through a lot of it and to let it go. My grandfather is dead. My rapist is dead. If there are any lingering issues, they have to do specifically with my mother."

Freud would be so proud.

"Why your mother?"

"Because the day I told her about my rape and about her father molesting me—Sam's ex-girlfriend was sitting there with me— she said, 'I thought something might have happened'. *So you thought your father was molesting your daughter, and you sent her back to that house, time and time again?* When I confronted her about it, a couple of years later while I was going through rape counseling, she said, 'It wasn't my fault! I didn't do anything wrong!', and I knew she would never get into it with me. Only recently did I find out that she didn't tell my father. She told him about the rape but not the molestation."

"Your parents were already divorced by this time?"

"Yes. My dad was livid."

"And you never confronted her about it again?"

I shook my head. "My grandmother is still alive—though there was some discussion once that maybe she knew what was going on. She's old, and she's in ill health. She says all the time what a great man my grandfather was, so I distance myself from it and bite my tongue. But she will die eventually, and I will have no reason to hold back any more. I won't have to care what my mom thinks, or my aunt or my uncle."

"Sam, how do you feel about this, about how Tierney has dealt with this and healed from this?"

"Honestly, I don't know how she's done it. I don't know how she's come to terms with everything. If it were me, I'd still be mad as hell and don't know how I'd ever be so calm about it all."

I could hear the anger in his voice. Not *at* me, but *for* me.

We went on to talk about more things, some between the two of us and some just for Sam.

We agreed that honest communication was a problem for us, especially when it came to me and Alex. We agreed that Sam wasn't the greatest at listening. We agreed that I have a strong tendency to be secretive, sometimes to my own detriment.

The session didn't feel productive, from the standpoint of giving us a specific direction or feeling like we'd put any issues to bed. But there certainly seemed to be a jumping-off point for us to start to heal.

Through it all, I was very careful not to roll my eyes or sigh or openly bite my tongue. I tried very hard to *hear* Sam. I tried very hard to give him an opportunity to speak and not bogart the session with talk of my personal drama. I made a point to acknowledge that he's a fantastic father who loves his children very much.

Yes, I admitted, I thought he loved me. I loved him. I married him because I loved him. Though I still wasn't sure if I was moving out or not.

"I can't advise you about that," Dr. Hill said. "That's something you have to work out for yourself."

Through the entire session, I never heard Sam say he loved me. He talked of times when he *had* loved me, but never of loving me *now*. He also didn't say that he was there to save this marriage, though neither did I.

"I think we should meet again, as soon as possible," Dr. Hill told us. "We'll start to lay out a plan for working on these issues, which we'll tackle in stages. You should consider maybe scheduling a couple of double sessions to give us more time to work at once."

We scheduled for Monday afternoon and left in our separate cars. I stopped on the way home and called Tessa to let her know what had happened. I met Sam outside, waiting for Ian to come home from school.

"I still haven't made a decision," I reiterated, "but I think it would take about two-thousand dollars a month for me to be able to move into the rental house. I sent over the application, though I really haven't decided. I still haven't found a job, and I won't qualify for student loans, not right now. I'm just letting you know where that line of thinking is."

Sam didn't say much, and the bus arrived shortly thereafter. Ian's birthday was coming up, and he was angling for a new bicycle. Our son had, in fact, let the air out of one of his tires and ridden over something, to blow the inner tube, knowing new tires were more expensive than a new bike.

"Were you planning to go tonight and look at bikes?" I asked.

"Yeah or tomorrow or something."

"Would you want to go tonight and take the boys to eat? I mean, I don't know, you know, with everything today how comfortable you are with that. I didn't know if you'd want to go out for dinner."

"I like dinner."

"I'm in the mood for tacos." *No, Tierney, don't jump ahead.* "I would like to go to dinner as a family, if you're willing. I would like to do that very much."

He nodded. "I would like that."

So we did. Tripp came home, and we piled into the car. Mexican and a trip to Toys R Us. Even with Ian spilling three separate things across the table, we had a lovely family dinner. Each of the boys found a great bike, and we made arrangements to pick them up. The drive home had lots of silly jokes, and I taught the kids the *Ren & Stimpy* "Log" jingle.

Late that night, after Sam returned from the Great Bicycle Load-up, I joined him on the deck for a few minutes. A small fire crackled in the new portable pit, and I spent long minutes staring into the flames, watching them dance and sizzle at the air around us. He was listening to the Grateful Dead—a band that had been one of his and India's favorites—and I finally couldn't stand it anymore.

"I'm going to lie in bed."

I fell asleep watching something on the DVR. Rousing when he came into the room for something, I clicked off the television and rolled over in the dark, dreaming almost instantly.

"I don't think I can afford two thousand dollars a month. I think it's unreasonable right now."

Huh? My groggy brain was having a hard time coming around.

"What?" I mumbled, trying to listen and still go back to sleep.

"I can't afford to pay two thousand dollars a month. I'm not paying for you to go do the things you want and just leave all of this here."

I glanced at the clock. 11:30

"Do we have to talk about this now? I was asleep."

"Well, you didn't give me much chance earlier! You just drop this in my lap, right before Ian gets home, and then we went out to dinner and I got the bikes."

"Sam, I was asleep. I'm not talking about this right now."

"There's no other time to talk about it! And you'd just gone to bed!"

"I was asleep!" I snapped. "I was *dreaming*!"

He stood there, a can of beer in his hand while he loomed across his side of the bed, yelling at me about money and my leaving. He was adamant that he wasn't giving me a dime of support until a judge ordered him to do so.

"I'm the one who works! I'm the one with a job! If you want to leave me and go live your life and do what you want, you're on your own!"

"What exactly did you think would happen when you were leaving in June, or—"

"I was going to—"

"Will you *please* let me finish my fucking sentence!"

"You were done! You paused—"

"I took a goddamn breath! That's not the same as being finished!"

We argued for fifteen minutes about his not letting me finish what I'm saying. "You said today that you need to work on *listening*. Then close your goddamn mouth and *listen* to what I'm saying. Wait until I'm fucking finished before you jump in with your response!"

We were getting louder. I asked him to close the bedroom door, so the children wouldn't hear. I was trying very hard to contain myself. I knew it was escalating to something very ugly.

"This is bullying! I'm not discussing this anymore tonight. Get the fuck away from me and let me go back to sleep!"

"No! I can—"

"Sam, this is verbally abusive. *Get the fuck away from me!*"

"Then call the fucking cops! What are you gonna tell them? That I'm *yelling* at you?" He took a drink from his beer. "I'm *yelling* because you're demanding I pay for your life after you fucked someone else!"

We went back and forth for another hour-and-a-half. He went on *ad nauseum* about how he wanted to go through counseling so he could figure out what went wrong with how he communicates.

"Everyone else who knows me says I'm laid-back and happy-go-lucky."

Who the fuck do you know that I don't? You're the most uptight SOB I've ever met in my life!

"I want to figure out what I did wrong," he explained, "what I'm doing wrong that makes it impossible to communicate with you."

"The other night, when I asked you why you wanted to go to counseling with me, you never once said it was because you love me and that this was special and worth saving!"

"Tierney, I'm not trying to save a marriage! I'm trying to find out what went wrong, so it doesn't happen again in the future!"

Then go to therapy by yourself, asshole.

"I'm done talking about this! I'm going back to sleep!"

"I want to be able to give you the things you want, the things you need, but I will have to compromise myself and never get what I want if I do what makes you happy!"

And he stopped. It was everything I'd been saying for six months, almost verbatim. The carousel had come halfway around the circle, and we were still riding, each of us watching the other pass by on our stylized, frozen horses, now in the same place where the other had just been.

"I have to think," he said, ragged and searching. In the dark bedroom, I could hear his confusion. He opened the bedroom door. "I'll be back."

"I'm going to sleep."

I turned over and pulled the blankets tighter around me. There was nothing else I could do for him. He had to come to this one all on his own.

———————————

Seth called the next afternoon, as I was wandering the mall, killing time by trying on new, smaller clothes.

"I can't talk long," he said.

"I know. You have a show. I'm about to pick up Ian from a birthday party anyway."

"So I wanted to tell you this, and it would take too long to text. There's this psychologist guy I was listening to on talk radio the other day. I forget his name. He's spent his whole career kind of specializing in marriages. He can take a couple and listen to them talk for fifteen minutes and predict with, like, ninety-three per cent accuracy whether or not they'll be together in ten years.

"So what he says is the biggest contributing factor is *contempt*. It's not criticism, you know, where one person says, 'Hey, I don't like the way you do things. You suck at taking care of the house while I work all day.' It's *contempt*, where that person says, 'I work all day, and you don't do anything. I do everything, and you do nothing.'

"It's really about loving the partner from a higher place. So Sam saying all that shit about being the man and being the breadwinner, it's just contemptuous. He definitely feels like his love for you is superior to your love for him."

Did he love me more than I loved him? Had he always?

Maybe.

Could that also be enough to make him feel superior to me in this relationship?

Possibly.

Yet again, the Hammer of Honesty was walloping me in the face. I always took what he told me with a grain of salt, in part because he'd never met Sam. They'd only ever had very limited, internet-based interaction. But the kid was a fucking genius and an old soul; he knew how to read people and situations better than most anyone I'd met in my life.

"Huh."

"I felt that way about Megan. That's part of why we didn't work."

Sam had always been smarter, stronger, more ambitious than I. He had almost always been the one to carry the brunt of our financial burden, which had undeniably taken a lot of time and energy away from our family. Because he was working in a field he loved, he was one of the few people I knew with a career that they found rewarding both financially and metaphysically. While working long hours might keep him from home and me and the children, he was generally able to find some other personal benefit from that effort.

I was forever the girl without a plan, perpetually twenty-two years old—which is just like being perpetually fifteen but able to drink in bars. I had half-heartedly tried to go back to school a couple of times, and I'd had various part-time jobs after the children were born, to help with finances but also to give me some kind of additional outlet. He'd spent so much time and energy taking care of me. Had he finally come to resent that completely?

He repeatedly said that he was my biggest fan, my most-spirited cheerleader. I wasn't sure if I'd ever quite seen that. Sometimes, yes, certainly I had felt his enthusiasm and support for whatever I was doing, but I don't know that there had been long stretches of time when I felt like he would support *me*, outside of *Sam-and-Tierney*, no matter what. I could easily pinpoint dozens of times when he'd been critical and harshly turned away from me and my plans.

For much of the last year, including during the session with Dr. Hill, Sam said he felt I didn't like him. In fact, he said, I hated him. There were *things* about him that I didn't like—something completely natural within any interpersonal relationship—but I generally found him to be a great guy. He was smart and funny and caring, and I never really doubted that he *loved* me.

Was it possible that *he* hated *me*? Did he unknowingly feel he was so superior to me, generally speaking, that it gave him permission to act the controlling prick?

––––––––––––––

We went back to counseling a few days later.

"Tell me some good things that happened over the weekend," Dr. Hill began.

Sam reached into his heavy backpack and pulled out a pad, glancing at his handwritten notes.

"We went out Friday night after we left your office. We had a great dinner with the boys. There were a few spills and mishaps, but the boys were really good. We had fun. Then we took them to pick out new bikes. I spent Saturday putting their bikes together. Tripp helped me, and we had a good talk."

"A talk?"

"Yeah, when there wasn't much for him to do, he would ask me questions," Sam explained. "Like, 'If you could erase one memory from your mind forever, what would you choose?'"

"Wow."

I nodded at Dr. Hill. "He's that kind of kid."

"What did you say to him?"

Sam said, "If I really had my choice, I would erase the last year from my memory, from existence, but I couldn't tell him that. So I told him I would forget about this wreck, a car accident, we had a few years ago. On Christmas Day."

"It was a bad accident?"

Sam and I took turns recounting the details. We'd been driving to Birmingham to see the family, the first Christmas after we moved to Atlanta. Sam and Tripp were in his car, while Tripp and I were in mine. Some asshole from Mississippi was speeding, in the rain, driving erratically, and was next to me. Sam pulled his car from behind mine, into the lane behind the asshole's Saturn. That guy slammed on his brakes, which caused Sam to do the same. I watched in abject horror while my husband and my six-year-old spun at sixty miles-per-hour and slammed into an embankment, then two trees.

I'd managed to call 911 from my cell and let them know where we were. Two ladies who'd witnessed the accident stopped and stayed with Ian, barely two and strapped happily into his car seat. By the time I got to Sam's car, it was resting against a fallen tree and sunken six inches into fresh mud. Tripp was hysterical in the back seat. A kind gentleman who had stopped when he saw the accident motioned to me that my son had a head injury.

"*Mommy! Make it all be a dream! Why can't this just be a horrible dream?*" Tripp had screamed. He was still in his booster seat, seatbelt holding him in place, with a substantial gash on the back of his dirty-blond head.

Sam had been moaning quietly in pain, barely able to move in the driver's seat.

I'd met them at the emergency room in Anniston, an hour outside Birmingham. My mom and stepdad had come immediately, as had my dad and uncles, followed shortly thereafter by my in-laws. I was able to hand Ian over to the family and stay with Tripp while he was x-rayed and examined. When the radiologist determined there was no concussion or neck injury, they were finally able to remove his cervical collar. He would need nine stitches in his scalp and would be sore for days.

"Mommy, my new Optimus Prime was in the car! It's gone now!"

I had no choice but to leave Sam in the care of the emergency room doctors. His own x-rays showed six broken ribs and a fractured pelvis. When he started having trouble breathing, the doctor realized a jagged rib had punctured his right lung. We had to wait for a surgeon to come in on Christmas Day to insert a chest tube.

My uncles took my boys to Birmingham. They were able to have some semblance of Christmas with the extended family, although neither Mommy nor Daddy were there.

Sam would spend eight all-expense-paid days in lovely historic Anniston, Alabama. My mom and stepdad were kind enough to cancel their own post-Christmas camping trip to keep the boys while I went back and forth between their house and the hospital.

The day after the accident, I went back to the scene to look for personal items. It was still wet and cold and rainy, as it had been for close to a week. I tromped through the muck and found most of Optimus Prime, partially in pieces.

I also drove the twenty miles to the junk yard where Sam's car had been towed. I needed to get all of his things from the car. I was shocked to see the damage.

The car was a Crown Victoria police interceptor. It was a white, road-worthy tank.

The suspension springs for the rear wheels had been knocked out of the car. They were covered in mud and resting in the back floorboards. The trunk of the car had taken the brunt of the trauma. It was pushed over, well past the mid-way point of the back seat. The back cushion and the bench of the rear seat had separated, leaving a gaping hole where they were supposed to meet.

Had Tripp not been in his flat-bottomed booster seat, which he was no longer legally required to use, he likely would've been pulled out through that gap in the seat, where there was no longer a trunk to speak of, and dragged under the rear passenger wheel of the car.

There were two other fatal accidents that day on the same stretch of interstate.

Sam came home with a walker. The insurance company ruled he was following too closely to the car in front of him for the conditions of the day. He was deemed partially negligent, and the asshole from Mississippi was never found.

"Does Tripp remember the accident?" Dr. Hill asked.

I nodded emphatically.

"Very clearly," Sam replied. "But he said he would wipe out the memory of Roceph shots," Sam concluded.

"He had chronic strep," I explained quickly to a baffled Dr. Hill. "The antibiotic shots were painful."

"So, what good things can you recount from the weekend?"

I thought about it. "Dinner was really good. I was happy when Sam agreed to go out for the family dinner." I thought more. "He was sweet to get the bikes and put them together. I know that took a lot of time and energy. But the big thing Sam is leaving out here is the fight we had Friday night."

I knew it wasn't another *good* thing and that I was defeating the purpose of the exercise, but it had to be addressed.

"Okay, what happened?"

I explained about the argument, about my issues with Sam saying he wasn't trying to save a marriage. I called him out for his attitude about money and being the breadwinner. I did not ask if he was just contemptuous of me.

We went cordially back and forth, discussing what had happened.

"Had you been drinking?" Dr. Hill looked to each of us.

I nodded and glanced at Sam pointedly.

"I had, yes," he admitted.

"I hadn't," I replied.

"Sam, I can tell that you want to get started, to get going on this process of healing. But sometimes it takes longer than we'd like. It's like if someone is brought into the emergency room and they need surgery, right away. Before you can take them to the operating room, you have to assess them and get them stable enough to move. You're barely in the process of stabilizing this. I can hear that you want to move forward and to do it quickly. You will have to be patient and learn to be in the moment, to let it comes as it comes."

I snickered and looked at Sam. "Dr. Hill just got all Krishnamurti on your ass."

"What do you mean by that?" Dr. Hill asked.

"Krishnamurti. *'Be here now.'*"

He nodded. "Yes, exactly. Let's see what we can do for you." *Uh-oh.* "Tierney, you get frustrated and have to find a way to let that out."

"I have a history of being an ugly, vindictive girl. I'm the girl who throws things, like cups and cabbages. I don't *want* to be that girl. So I try very hard to disengage until I am calm enough to deal with it. Sometimes, yes, that means I retreat and go away or go to sleep. Often times, I go to the gym. That's why I'm down a hundred and four pounds now."

Dr. Hill opened and closed his mouth. "Well, that's good that you've found some reasonable outlet for it. We don't want you throwing cabbages. But dealing with that frustration constructively in the moment is what will be most difficult for you. That's what you have to work on.

"Look, sometimes healing can take on very different forms. Sometimes we heal and are scarred but carry on very well. Sometimes we heal to death. It's like the story of the grouchy old man who pushed away everyone and everything in his life until he found out he was terminally ill. On his death bed, he had everyone he loved around him and had made peace with them. He could die happy. That's what I mean by 'heal to death'."

I don't know what Sam heard. And Dr. Hill wasn't outright saying he didn't think we would survive this. But there was a definite inference that Sam and I needed to come to terms with the fact that we would quite possibly *not* make it as a couple.

Chapter 33

The next couple of days were cordial. I spent some time painting, hiding away in the basement, while Sam was working from home. The logistics of the house were running as smoothly as possible.

I was coming down with another upper respiratory infection and crashed one night on the couch. Sam came into the room, standing behind the sofa and waiting for my attention.

"I picked up the paperwork from the attorney," he said quietly.

The divorce papers.

"Do you want to see them now or wait?"

It was late, and I didn't really want to deal with it, but I knew I wouldn't let it go. "You might as well give them to me now. I won't sleep, knowing it's lingering." I paused and stood up. "Can I expect to still be served, or is this your serving me?"

We hadn't really talked about it again. Obviously I knew he'd filed a couple months before, weeks after he'd originally seen his attorney to start the process of financial affidavits and disclosures.

"As soon as I hand them to you, it's service."

I nodded. "Then I guess you should just give them to me now."

I followed him into the dining room. He opened his bulky backpack and extracted a thick packet of papers, binder clipped together.

"There are tabs where you can sign."

I found my glasses and took the paperwork to the small sofa in the office. I always liked that spot to review things and read. I curled my feet under me and clicked the lamp on.

The settlement offer was bullshit. He was asking for joint legal and physical custody of the children—they would alternate weeks with us. He was asking to stay in the house, with a mortgage which was now under water, and would be required to have it refinanced as soon as possible. I would get half of one retirement account but was specifically excluded from another. Other substantial assets weren't addressed. He was offering me less than $1,000 a month in child support, adjusted in Georgia for the potential split custody.

He was suing on grounds that the marriage was irretrievably broken.

> **Jules McKinnon**
> **Nov 17th 10:21 PM**
> **I just got the most bullshit petition for divorce ever.**

Handed to you?

> **Yep**
> **He wants joint custody, $867 a month**
> **He wants to give me half his IRA, no 401k, no stock options, no bonus.**
> **I'm not signing this shit. This offer is insane.**
> **Oh and he gets the house.**

> **Dad**
> **Nov 17th 10:34 PM**
> **I just got served. His offer is crap.**
> **I'll call my atty in the morning to go see her.**

Let attorney handle it.

> **I will. But it's crap.**

I know and ur atty will offer him the other extreme of crap. Then work toward middle.

> **Well, I'm not discussing it with him.**

Let atty do talking is the best way

I will, just griping.

I know. It is tough.

Tessa called the next morning, as soon as she saw my email about the settlement offer.

"That's just insulting. That's ridiculous."

"I don't know what the fuck he's thinking! He's *never* been the one to take care of the boys. How does he think they'll do, being bounced from house to house every week? And I absolutely will *not* go for a week at a time without seeing my babies. He's *insane* if he thinks I'll let that happen! And this money thing... he's not screwing me on this. He doesn't get to put me in a goddamn hole. He doesn't get to punish me for the affair, over and over again. I put just as much time and energy into our life and our marriage as he did, and he doesn't get to walk away with everything just because I fucked someone else! *He walked the fuck away from me!*"

"Tierney, it will be okay. *You* will be okay. And you're right; he doesn't get to screw you out of what you're entitled to get from this marriage. You know that. Your *attorney* knows that. I'm just appalled that his attorney is being such a dick and starting from such an unreasonable place. You guys need to consider going into mediation rather than dragging this shit out from one attorney to another. You'll save yourselves a ton of money in fees if you start in the middle."

"I think Sam is determined to make this as hard on me as possible. He says he's not, but *this*—" I slammed the papers against my desk "—is ridiculous. There's nothing *fair* about this offer. If he wants a fight, I'll give him one. Yes, I had an affair, but I'm not the one who drinks myself to sleep every night! I'm not the one who got arrested for driving drunk and *still* kept drinking! I'm pretty damn sure that a family court judge will look far less favorably on *that* than on whether or not I let some other man put his dick in me."

I asked Sam to take the children out for a while that night, so I could do some things at home alone. I wanted to spend time going over the financial numbers, to be able to call Tessa or Jules to discuss it without having to leave my house. I didn't explain to Sam why I wanted them all gone. He didn't ask why but agreed.

He emailed me late that afternoon, before he left, with copies of the documents to support his financial affidavit. It was thoroughly detailed and annotated, but I saw a lot of problems with his assumptions, especially when it came to post-divorce spending and living expenses.

From: Tierney Cavanaugh Johnson
Sent: November 18th 7:52 PM
To: Sam Johnson
Subject: RE: Financial worksheets

As of right now, I am not planning to vacate the house, unless there's a dramatic change. I do not have the financial resources to do so at this time. I am neither agreeing nor refusing to do so in the future. Until my financial situation is stabilized, I cannot make a final plan of action.

In case there's any doubt, I am in no way approving this settlement offer. I don't want to argue with you, both for our sake and the children's, and I'm generally planning to let my attorney handle it, though I will absolutely not let her submit anything I haven't seen and approved. I would prefer to go through mediation rather than padding the coffers of our attorneys. It's still an option, so please consider it.

We can do this civilly, or we can make it a big mess. How this is handled will depend on both of us, and I believe you're willing to be pragmatic and fair-minded for the sake of the children.

Still congested and feeling generally terrible, I took an antihistamine. I fell asleep on the couch. rousing long enough to realize Sam had come home with the boys and was getting them ready for bed. I woke around one and walked through the office turn my computer off. I climbed into bed and started to settle back to sleep.

> I didn't hear Sam come into the bedroom until it was too late.
> "What did you do while I was gone with the boys?"
> "Stuff I needed to do," I sighed. It didn't matter what I'd done. It was my time alone. "I needed to check email and look at some files, go over some numbers."

"Well, I didn't know what you were doing. I didn't know if you talked to Alex."

"No, I haven't talked to him at all."

"Well, I don't know why you needed time. You get a lot of time alone when the kids are at school."

"You're working from home all the time now. I have the right to a little alone time in my own house. Can I please go to sleep now?"

"No! We need to talk about this!" Sam yelled.

I clinched my jaw and squeezed my eyes closed, hoping he would away. I could feel him standing there by the bed, watching me, waiting for me to engage him. I flipped the blankets back and jumped up, stomping through the dark house toward the deck.

"I won't tolerate your using the children as pawns against me!" he hissed as he swung the back door open.

"What the fuck are you talking about?"

"Your email! *'We can do this civilly, or we can make it a big mess. How this is handled will depend on both of us, and I believe you're willing to be pragmatic and fair-minded for the sake of the children.'* That's just you saying you'll try to take them or use them against me if you don't get what you want!"

"No, it's not! I didn't say that at all! In fact, I started to say 'I hope' but changed it to 'I believe'."

"I'll send the email to Tessa and Frankie and Jules and see what they say!"

"Be my guest! This is stupid!"

For forty minutes, he hurled insults and accusations at me as he finished off a six pack. He mixed a drink, presumably with my bottle of Jack Daniels, and kept at it. It was unbearably difficult, but I ignored him as best I could. I waited for him to finish his rant, to wear himself out like a tantruming toddler, but he was waltzing around his own arguments, delicately weaving a repetitive pattern of anger.

"Sam, *stop*," I pleaded. "You're talking in circles. This is going nowhere."

"I will say what I goddamn well want to say in my own home!"

"You don't have the right to harass me!" I yelled finally.

"I'm not harassing you! I'm just talking. Free speech! Are you saying I don't have the right to say what I want in my own house?"

"No, I'm saying you don't have the right to bully me and yell at me when I tell you to stop!"

"So leave! Go to bed!"

"I've been trying to go to bed for an hour!"

"And I've decided that Talia needs to know everything," he threatened. "I need you to be out of the house tomorrow, so I can email her. Alex, too!"

"Fine! Do whatever you want, Sam!"

He looked at me in mocking incredulity. "Are you saying I can do it now? That I can tell her?"

"I'm not saying you can or can't do anything! I don't care what you do! It's not as late there—call her right now!"

"No, tomorrow. I'm sending her everything. I'll send it to *The Washington Post*! And I *will* tell my attorney to file on grounds of adultery."

"Do what you want. I'm going to bed."

As I swung the back door open to go inside, I turned to look back at him.

"It doesn't matter what you tell Talia anyway. Alex will deny it outright. He will find a way to convince her that you're just the jealous, paranoid asshole husband of a fan he barely knows."

"You don't think he would admit it to her finally? Even if I sent her *everything*?"

"I don't think he would admit it even if you sent video of us having sex! He will *always* deny this. He will *always* lie to her. And he will *always* refuse to acknowledge me."

From: Sam Johnson
Sent: November 19th 6:46 AM
To: Tierney Cavanaugh Johnson
Subject: Does this sound like the right person?

She's fairly well hidden, even based on info from the Facebook profile you've visited, and based on that, I assume that the following is THE Talia:

He listed her address and phone number—Alex's address and phone number—and I knew immediately that it was the right Talia Wheeler. He went on to ask if she liked to have her hair done at a specific salon and to include a picture of their home, taken from the street.

It was creepy and stalkerish, but I knew it was *nothing* compared to what he could dig up if he really tried.

I didn't respond. I ignored Sam as I got the boys ready for school. As soon as they were safely away from the house, I went straight to the park to walk.

Would Sam go so far as to finally contact Talia and tell her what had happened?

Maybe.

He was mad enough, certainly, to do it. His life was falling apart, and he was bitter enough to destroy anyone else's. Collateral damage was sometimes a necessary evil, part of the calculated risk of destruction.

Not only was he willing to tell Talia and the rest of Alex's family, he was willing to tell *my* family. My dad was the only one who knew. My mom and my brother and my grandmothers and aunts and uncles—how would they react?

I don't care.

I knew they'd be disappointed, maybe even upset with me. I would have to defend myself, to explain why I had an affair, how Sam was a drunk asshole who'd emotionally abandoned me. Some of them would be sympathetic; others would be appalled.

But I didn't *care* about their reactions. I didn't *care* if they thought less of me after finding out. It wasn't their life or their choices. I'd stopped living up to their expectations years ago, long before I'd ever even met Sam. I'd always been the proverbial black sheep, and I was *happy* in that role. I would laugh it off when my grandmother warily eyed my choice in all-black clothing or my purple hair. In some ways, this might be exactly what they'd always expected from me.

"Maybe you should tell your mom before Sam can," Tessa advised. "This is a total bullshit power play on his part. The last power he has over you is telling Talia or your family or Facebook, God forbid. And while you say that you don't care if they know, you don't want to have to deal with your mom finding out about this from him."

She was right. I would eventually have to tell her about the divorce, though I hadn't decided if I would ever tell her about the affair. I knew she would be calm and wouldn't say anything to openly judge me. If she ever did, she would be matter-of-fact about her opinion and drop it once she knew I'd heard her. And I knew she and my stepdad would back me up, no matter what.

There was no way in hell I was letting Sam be the one to out me, though.

Big girl panties, Tierney.

She answered on the third ring. "Hello?"

"Hey. Are you where you can talk?"

"Yeah. What's up?"

"I'm calling to let you know that Sam served me with divorce papers a couple of nights ago. He has filed it as irreconcilable differences, but he's saying he will refile on grounds of adultery. He has every right to do so. I will not talk about the reasons for the divorce, and I will not discuss the details of the affair. Suffice it to say that there were a *lot* of issues in play before it ever started. I made a lot of choices and errors, and so did he. I'm only telling you this because he's threatening to go public with it. He says he intends to contact Alex and Talia today and tell Talia what happened."

"Who's Talia?"

"Alex's wife."

Mom was silent. It was so quiet I was afraid she'd hung up.

"What do you need me to do?" she asked finally, her voice even and slow.

I could tell she was worried, though she was trying not to let on. I knew her own belief system would be less than accepting of my having had an affair, but she'd also known there were problems long before this.

"Nothing," I replied, "but I appreciate it. I'm okay right now. I may need money eventually to get out of the house."

"Your grandmother's house is still empty. You can move in there, if you need it."

"I don't want to move back to Birmingham, Mom. The boys' life is here. So is mine. Their father is here, no matter what. But, look, I'm telling you this *strictly* in confidence. *No one* is to know about this—not your friends, not my aunt, and certainly not my grandmother. I'll deal with it when I'm ready."

"Can I tell Dan?"

"Yeah, of course. It's that whole *marital privilege* thing."

"Are you okay?"

"Yeah, *I am*. I'm fine. I've already dealt with the emotional stuff for the last six months. I'm over it. I'm sure I'll have days when it hits me and I lose it, but that's not today. He's being ridiculous and unreasonable, and he's drinking a lot, but I'm not worried about my safety or the boys'. I will get through this, and I will *thrive*."

"That's because you're Wonder Woman," Mom said.

"Yeah, well, I think I *forgot* that I was Wonder Woman for a very long time."

"Yep."

I'd just hung up with her when Seth called.

"What's happening?" He sounded jovial and easy.

"Oh, you picked the wrong day to ask!" I rounded the last curve in the asphalt path at the park.

"What's wrong?"

"Sam asked me to leave the house for a while, so he could email Alex and Talia. He says he's telling her today what happened."

"*What?*"

"He went fucking *nuts* at one this morning. He emailed me in the middle of the night, with their address and a picture of their apartment building, the name of the salon she uses."

"*Dude,* is Sam actually going to email Alex and Talia? *Seriously?*"

"Fuck if I know. He stayed up all night and drank a six-pack, plus half a bottle of Jack. He could do anything at this point. Sam's so up and down, I don't know if he'll even do it. It's all fucked up. He's going off his rocker."

"*Godfuckingdammit!* I feel like there's something I should do, but I pretty much can't."

I fished my keys from my pocket and unlocked my car door, sliding into the driver's seat. "I emailed Alex after Sam told me he had a private investigator in Nashville. He told me to keep him out of it no matter what. I love him, Hammer, but I can't protect him. I don't know what the fuck warning I could give him. Even if I emailed him, he's likely traveling for the holidays with Talia and Amber. I can't drop that on him like that. If Sam doesn't do anything, I'll have sent Alex into a panic for no reason. If he does, maybe the trip will delay Talia finding out. Alex knew all along this could be coming. But it's Sam's last power play. It may not happen."

"*Fuck,*" Seth muttered under his breath. "Well, I was calling with kind of good news. I don't know if it matters now."

"It matters. Tell me something good."

"I'm coming to Atlanta," he replied.

"When?" *Definitely good news!*

"Tomorrow. I have this buddy who wants me to record some vocals for him. I'm flying in tomorrow afternoon. I won't have much free time, but can you meet up this week?"

This would mean dealing with Sam to get out of the house, to keep the boys so I could see Seth.

Fuck him. He's their father. He can do this, and I deserve to be able to see my friend.

"I'll make it happen. Just let me know when you're free."

Chapter 34

"Seth is coming to Atlanta tomorrow," I started carefully that night. Sam and I were in the bedroom, changing clothes and settling in for the evening. "His schedule is pretty slammed, but he asked me to meet him for dinner this week."

"When?"

"Ian has that Thanksgiving performance at school on Monday. And you have a work dinner on Wednesday right? So I'll have to be available to keep the kids. So I guess I'll see him on Tuesday."

"Do I get to go?" he asked.

Seriously?

"I don't think that would be best."

Was he fucking serious? There was no way I was having dinner with Sam and Seth. I didn't think Seth would want to be anywhere near him, honestly. Seth was pissed as shit that Sam would be such a dick, knowing exactly what the fallout was likely to be. He saw Sam's threats, whether or not he intended to carry through, as vindictive and sad. And I sure as hell wasn't going to dinner with him.

"Why not?"

I wanted desperately to tell him that Seth probably thought he was a dick now, based on what I'd told him. Admittedly, it was a one-sided understanding, but I had tried very hard to relay facts with as little embellishment as possible.

"I just don't think it would be best given everything going on right now."

My post-walk half-caf was keeping me from being sleepy, so I decided to watch television instead. Just after midnight, Sam came into the bedroom and sat down on the bed, leaning against his pillows and the headboard, legs stretched nonchalantly before him.

Here we go.

"Are you guys planning something that I wouldn't be happy with?" he started.

"I am *not* discussing this with you—

"*Ah!* But you don't deny it!" His tone was argumentative and pressing.

I took a breath. "I am not having sex with Seth Wiezel. I am not in love with Seth Wiezel. I'm not remotely sexually attracted to Seth Wiezel. He is not remotely sexually attracted to me. We are friends and only friends and have only ever been friends—"

"But you don't want me around him at all? You have found a way to say, '*This is the only time he's got, and I want it. It's mine.*'"

"I can't help what his schedule is—"

"Yes, but, *but* we could both work it out. If he's got free time for anybody, we can both share that, and there's a—

"You've never met Seth!"

"—there's a reason that I want to go there and talk to him, and you're finding every reason under the sun why I shouldn't be there."

"You feel free to call or email him to ask him if he's free while he's in town. Why the fuck would you want to talk to him anyway?"

"I've never met him and would like to get to know your 'friend'. And he's only got one free time. That's what you told me, right?"

"No," I replied, "I can't go on Monday. I can't go on Wednesday 'cause you have dinner out with work."

"I'm not going to dinner with work. I would like to go there to dinner with him, with you, because I don't know—"

"*I* am not socializing with you!"

"You don't have to. I just want to be there, so after you're done socializing—or maybe even before—I can talk to him."

"Well, you can talk to him to find out if he's interested in that. Feel free to contact Seth. He'll be in town tomorrow." I glanced at the clock. 12:13. "He may or may not still be up. You could email him or call him, whatever you want to do. That's up to you and Seth. If Seth wants to engage you, he is more than welcome to do so!"

Sam made a face of exaggerated pensiveness. "I'm thinking about this reluctance of... me not being in the same place with you guys."

"Seth is my friend," I countered instead, carefully trying not to escalate the situation. *My friend.* "I'm not socializing with you."

"He knows me pretty well."

Huh?

"Seth doesn't know you from Adam's cat!"

"He's exchanged emails with me. We've talked on the phone while you've been on the phone together. We've been on video chat together."

Unless something had happened that I didn't know about, Seth and Sam had briefly seen each other once on a Skype call. That was the only time *I* had ever been on video conference with him. I could remember one time when Sam had relayed mundane info through me while I was on the telephone with Seth.

Let him think what he wants. Don't engage him. Don't antagonize him.

"M'kay."

"And now all of a sudden there's some secret—"

"There's nothing secret!"

"You've always said you wanted me to meet Seth, and now you don't want to socialize with me at all. I would just like to be there."

"You do *whatever* you need to do."

"Okay. Thanks for your permission."

"I'm not giving you permission to *do* or *not do* anything!"

"You said, '*Do whatever you need to do*'. That's permission."

"I'm not—again—I-I'm not going in a social environment with you. I'm not discussing my relationship, or lack of relationship, with Seth Wiezel any further with you."

Sam paused. "I'm pretty sure he's right up there with *Greg Dulli*, tied for second on your list of love interests. So, I think that while you're living here, that you're going to meet some man that you've said, '*I love him*', all that stuff you've ever said about him...."

"He's like my brother."

"I don't believe that at all—" I couldn't help but laugh! "—Alex was just a friend, I get it. You can say what you want about the relationship, but I know your feelings for him—" More inappropriate laughter. "—even if you don't."

"I have no feelings for Seth," I chortled.

"Yes, you do!"

"Look, Seth is my *friend*, and I *love* him. From *that* perspective and *that* perspective only. And if you think you're going to bully me into having or not having a relationship with a friend—*any* friend ever in my life—that's not going to happen."

"He's not. He's not a friend, see, that's a wall that you've built. You're saying, '*Just a friend, just a friend!*' There's a whole book in there called *NOT Just Friends*—"

"Yeah, you enjoy that book," I countered sarcastically. "I'll enjoy my dinner with Seth."

"And so will I."

"You will not be at the table at dinner with us."

"I'll still be there."

"Have fun with that."

Sam sat there in silence as I pretended to watch the late news.

"You need to tell me where you're having dinner, as soon as you decide," he ordered.

"I'm under *no* obligation to do so."

He took a sip from his beer. "I think you *should*."

I guffawed derisively.

"Unless we're separated," he continued, "unless you've moved out, and you don't have anything to do with the house and the kids, *then* you have no obligation to report where you are."

"I have no obligation even if we're *married* to report where I am."

"Oh, yes you do!" He waved his finger at me.

"Oh, no I don't! There is no such legal obligation!"

"No, not a legal obligation. How would you like if I just—"

My mind immediately starting counting all the times he'd just not come home. The first time was a few months after we moved to Atlanta. The children and I came home from an evening with our new neighbors, while he'd not answered any of my calls. Assuming he was working late, I was shocked when Tripp found Daddy passed out drunk in bed, his car nowhere to be seen.

I sat up in bed and faced him. "How many times have you just *not* come home?" I exploded. "Think back to all the times you stayed late at work, locked away in the lab with no cell service—or so you'd tell me at dawn when you finally called to check in! After I would call and text and email all fucking night, looking for you. *Fuck you!* How many times have *you* done that?"

"*No!* Not with a *woman* that I said I *loved*! '*You know, she's a genius, and she's brilliant, and I love her!*'"

"Okay."

Shut the fuck up. Don't engage him.

"You don't think there's an obligation to tell me?"

"You're drinking. You've been drinking for I don't know how long. I'm not having this conversation with you."

"That's always the cop-out with you! It has nothing to do with this. You use it as a cop-out and a defensive mechanism, as a way to build up walls between it, because I *really* know how you feel about him, and that if he said, '*Hey, Tierney, let's go fuck!*', you would do it in a heartbeat!"

"I would laugh in his face!"

"*You would do it in a heartbeat!*" he repeated.

"He couldn't even *say* those words to me without laughing! And I couldn't hear them without laughing!"

"Well, not *those* words, but you know what I mean. You're trying to find a time that I can't make it, because you want it to be alone time with him."

"No!" He was right about one thing; there was no way I was pinning Seth or me down to dinner with an asshole. "We can't do it on Monday because of the children. You have a work thing on Wednesday that you're supposed to be at, that you're now saying you're blowing off."

"Yeah. No! Yeah that's right. I never committed to it." *It's a dinner for senior staff and their spouses with the CTO. You better damn well have committed to it.* "I'm free, and I would like to go. If it's the only chance he's here, and that's the only chance I've got to talk to him about some things, I'll email him and see if he wants to meet. What if he says, '*Yes, I can meet with you and Sam both, at the same time*'? What would you say then?"

"I would say, '*You can meet with Sam when you want. I'm not socializing with Sam.*'"

It went on and on. I refused to be in a sociable situation with him. I wasn't having dinner with my estranged husband and my friend. Sam slung constant allegations of my wanting to have sex with Seth. It was *ludicrous*.

"You have filed for divorce," I reminded him.

"And you're still living here. We're not separated yet."

"It doesn't matter if I'm living here!"

"It does! I'm not bringing that stuff around. I'm not letting you go out. I'm not keeping the kids for you. You've got to arrange for kids, separate child support, separate living conditions, before you go out and do those things that require that kind of space."

"I will make arrangements for my children to be taken care of while I go to dinner with Seth."

"Okay. That's good. That'll free me up to meet with him then, too."

"You feel free to ask him about that."

"I'm sorry I'm spoiling your plans."

"You're not spoiling my plans! My plans are not gonna change. I'm going to enjoy my time with my friend, who I haven't seen in six months."

He stood and started to leave the room. He turned back in the doorway. "I know what you've said. I know how you react to questions about the relationship. It's a complete parallel, and...."

"First of all, I don't want to sleep with Seth. I'm not *remotely* sexually attracted to him. Not in the least. *And vice versa!*"

"No, not yet, but you're emotionally attracted to him. You have an emotional investment in him. He's your friend, and you talk about he's a genius and that you love him and stuff, and so those emotional things lead to that."

"I love Tessa, and she's a genius. I don't want to sleep with her, either."

"I'm sorry, there's a lot of people you can be emotionally attracted to, but I think that your preference for people is.... He's right up your alley, and I'm just a little suspicious of it."

"*Not remotely*. You can be suspicious of whatever you want."

"Forgive me if I don't believe any of your denials, but I know what I see, and I see you trying to arrange a time with him to get him *alone*, by yourself."

I chuckled openly, unable to stifle it any longer.

"And it wasn't about bringing me into the picture. That's about building walls between me and *him*, and opening windows between you and him. And that's exactly what happened with Alex. I see it exactly, it's the same pattern. It's well-documented and researched."

"You see what you think you wanna see."

"Those things are a warning sign, and if you don't see that kind of indicator...."

Sam was using the little knowledge he'd gleaned from his new self-help books to accuse me of starting an affair with Seth. He was adamant that he knew all about it, and that I should ask anyone else who might listen and look at it.

I was done. I stood and walked past him to go outside.

He followed me out to the deck. A moment later, "I've already emailed him to tell him my thoughts on it. I'll email him back and ask if him if it's okay if he's got time to meet with me, in that same time slot that he's got a chance to meet with you. I don't mean to spoil anything, but my intention is to spoil any potential *thing*."

I quit talking to him. There was nothing else to say. I was ready to go to bed and shut him out for a while. Just as I was falling asleep, I heard the email hit my phone.

From: Sam Johnson
Date: November 20th 12:40 AM
To: Seth Wiezel
CC: Tierney Cavanaugh Johnson
Subject: Meeting with Tierney

You should know that after Alex Wheeler, you and Greg Dulli are tied for second on her list of immediate love interests (that I'm aware of).

I've tried to invite myself along to her meetings with you while you're in ATL, but she's building walls to prevent that while simultaneously opening windows between you and her. She always finds a way to exclude me, both before and after divorce papers were served.

I would appreciate it if she limited these schemes until she moved out of the house. I know you're single and that your relationship with Tierney is generally good, and I really have little say in the matter at this point, but I would appreciate some restraint until the divorce is finalized and we are living separately. Apologies if I've read anything into anyone's intentions; I don't think my evaluation of Tierney's intentions are off-base at all. I've learned to get a good feel for these things lately.

From: Tierney Cavanaugh Johnson
Date: November 20th 7:10 AM
To: Seth Wiezel
Subject: Re: Meeting with Tierney

He's lost his fucking mind.

Let me be as clear to you as I was to him at midnight when he started this: I am not in love with you. I do not want to fuck you. While I think you are smart and funny and adorable, I am not remotely sexually or emotionally attracted to you in any way other than as my friend. I love you as my friend and only in that way.

I know you know all this. :)

I'm sorry, Hammer. I'm sorry he went nuts and dragged you in like this. Call me later and I'll tell you what happened last night.

And no, I don't want to fuck you!

It was unbearably tense in the house. I did my best to steer clear of Sam and his angry irrationale. I got through the day without incident, got the children ready for bed, and went into the bedroom to be alone.

From: Sam Johnson
Date: November 20th 8:57 PM
To: Seth Wiezel
CC: Tierney Cavanaugh Johnson
Subject: Meeting with Tierney

I apologize. I had been drinking. I took offense that I was excluded and read too much into it. I was also very disappointed, because I can't find any other time to meet you in person. What I read into everything was completely unfounded. The way I was thinking about it was confused, and the way I approached it with everyone was wrong.

I went out to the deck.

"I emailed Seth," Sam said. "I meant to send it *to* you, as well, but I *cc*'d you instead, accidentally. I'm sorry. I was wrong."

I didn't say anything. I didn't want to provoke him further.

"Can you listen to me for a minute?" he asked.

"I'll listen, but I'm not arguing with you."

"That's fine. That's good." He paused. "I was wrong to think what I did about you and Seth. I wasn't thinking about it clearly at all. There are things about it that are like everything else, and I was hurt that you were excluding me. It seems like you had been trying to keep me away from him since you met him. I can keep the kids for you to go to dinner with him. I won't intrude. I'm sorry about that.

"I'm sorry I kept arguing with you when you asked me to stop. You weren't asleep, but I know you were other nights. I'm sorry I didn't respect your request to leave you alone. I won't do that anymore. Sometimes, that's the only time we have to talk, after the kids are asleep, and you go to the bedroom to escape. If you ask me to stop, I will. And I won't follow you into another room and keep at it.

"But I have to feel safe and secure in my own home. The bedroom is a sanctuary, the one place I should be able to feel secure, no matter what. We should be able to talk about anything in there. And I will not stand for you to secretly record our private conversations in what should be the safest room in our house."

Busted.

Yes, I had recorded the previous night's conversation. When he'd come into the room, drinking and belligerent and still having not slept after Friday night's hours of fighting and craziness, I was a little afraid of what was coming. I knew he was being irrational in general, and I was afraid of what the specifics of that conversation would lead to. I had grabbed my phone and started the voice memo function.

Beyond that, I'd sent Tessa a copy of the recording. Honestly, I knew in the back of my mind that hearsay rules went out the window if something dire were to happen. If Sam went nuts and attacked, I wanted there to be a record of how crazy things had become. I told her to listen to it or not, her choice, but to file it away.

"I didn't do anything illegal," I said flatly.

"You're right. You didn't. But it's *wrong*, Tierney. I have to feel safe here."

"*I* have to feel safe here, too, Sam! I have every right to protect myself and my children."

"Did you feel *unsafe*?" He seemed bewildered and offended. "*How?*"

"*Yes!* Did I think you were *physically* going to hurt us? *No. Never.* Not them anyway. I know how much you love and cherish the boys. But you're creating such a volatile situation that it's becoming unstable, and there's *no way* I'm sitting idly for that. I *will not* tolerate feeling verbally attacked! You've been erratic for weeks, and I didn't know what the fuck you were gonna do. That's why I recorded it, in case something went wrong."

"You run away to the bedroom when you can't talk to me," he continued. "Avoiding it stifles opportunity for communication, regardless of whether the communication is constructive or a normal part of the healing process. If you run away from me, we can't address our issues."

"I *run away* from you when you're being a *dick*. It's the one safe place I have in this fucking house, and you don't even let me have that anymore! You follow me in there, you wake me up to *berate* me for whatever you think is wrong! I should be able to go into my fucking bedroom in peace!"

"You're right. The bedroom *should* be a sanctuary. Within those confines is an absolute expectation of *privacy*. It's the pinnacle of hypocrisy for you to say there are secrets exchanged with your affair partner that you'll never reveal on principle, to anyone, and then to record *exactly* what was said in confidence in *our* bedroom. We are still married. I've never told *anyone* the things we've said in there—not even my attorneys—and you emailed it to your best friend!"

"I felt *threatened*, Sam!" I reiterated. "And how the *fuck* do you even *know* I emailed Tessa? Are you *still* breaking into my email? Are you still watching everything I'm fucking doing?"

"I reserve the right to monitor anything on our computers and network, even if I don't always do it. I certainly *do* monitor what's sent in the clear over public networks, to and from *our* network, and I have every right to do so. There's no expectation of privacy there."

"I am not a child, Sam! I don't want or need you to monitor everything I do! I'm a fucking grown-up who can make her own goddamn choices, even if you don't like them!"

"*Your computer was hacked, Tierney!* Our entire network was vulnerable, and we lost five grand to an asshole hacker to get your goddamn files back! But I'm not monitoring your person-to-person verbal communications. And I'm certainly not recording them and sending them to other people!"

"Then stop making me feel unsafe in my own home! This is the one and only time I've done this, but you've harassed me in that room for months. You've woken me, time and again, from sleep to yell at me and question me and intimidate me. *It's not okay!*"

Sam was silent, nodding slowly toward his feet. "Okay. I understand that you feel threatened and sometimes need to retreat. I don't agree with it—it's never been my intention to make you feel that way—but that perception is of the receiver. I promise, if you ask me to stop, I will *stop*. I won't follow you into the house, certainly not into the bedroom, and keep talking to you. I won't try to *make* you address me when you can't. Can you please promise not to record our conversations?"

"I will do whatever I need to do to protect myself and my children."

"Tierney," he said quietly, "I promise, I would never hurt you or the boys."

"I don't know if you can promise that," I replied. "Your drinking is out of control."

"Yeah." He thought for a moment. "No, it's not my *drinking* that's out of control. It's my *behavior* when I drink that's out of control."

Can you really not hear yourself?

He was promising to leave me alone, but only if I did what he wanted. We were in no better place than we'd been days and weeks before.

———————————————

Seth Wiezel
Nov 21st 7:33 PM

We're slammed over here. I'm thinking the safest times to meet for me are either tonight or sometime in the morning before work.

Nov 21st 7:57 PM
I can come in an hour.
I gotta get the kids home and change and I'll be on my way.

"Seth just texted that he can only see me tonight or in the morning. I have kid stuff in the morning, so I'd like to meet him tonight. Is that okay?"

Sam and I were standing in the school gym, in the midst of a hundred first graders and their families. Ian and his classmates had just finished the annual Thanksgiving performance. Tripp was still sitting in his metal folding chair, earbuds in, mindlessly playing some game on his iPod.

Sam looked a little shocked. "Yeah, okay."

"I'm sorry," I said quickly, trying to explain to Sam and to locate my youngest son amongst a sea of Pilgrims and Indians. "This is his only time. I can't do it in the morning."

We went home, and I changed, put on make-up, brushed my hair. I debated dressing up—any excuse to wear my new boots—but I didn't need to impress Seth. He'd seen me hungover at my worst. He'd seen me on Skype in pajamas and glasses. There was no illusion to maintain with him. Jeans and a t-shirt.

He was staying at the Georgian Terrace, across the street from the Fox Theatre. I parked on a side street and texted him that I was there. As I jaywalked across Peachtree, I could see the silhouette of his unkempt curls on a bench outside the hotel.

"You look like half a person," he said, standing to hug me.

"Thanks. It's a little different than the last time you saw me."

We ended up at the Majestic Diner on East Ponce, drinking water and decaf and talking about everything. He gave me all the details on his project.

"This is a huge opportunity for you. I hope they're paying you well, but even if they're not, this is amazing for your resume."

We talked for hours. We drove around Midtown and stopped in Virginia Highlands for gas station coffee. We stopped at Atlantic Station to smoke. I tried to keep from dominating the conversation with more drivel about my marriage and my affair. I didn't want to keep going back to it, but something would come up and remind me about it all again.

I knew it was weird for Seth. He was my friend and wanted to support me, but my husband had come after him. And he knew Alex really well. He'd always been very open about the fact that he thought Alex and I were totally wrong to have cheated on our spouses.

"But it was inevitable," he said. "There's no way it *wasn't* going to happen."

"It's weird, you know," I said as I drove, the shadows in the car flashing rhythmically as passed under street lights, "you're married to someone who you love but who doesn't remotely fulfill your deepest sexual needs and desires—"

"Talia?"

I nodded. "And then you meet this busty, blond Amazon with a propensity for every kink you're into. Plus you connect as people and just *get* each other instantly. It's hard." Seth was silent but listening, knowing I needed to talk. "You know, in Nashville, sitting at the bar, he looked at me and said, '*You would blow your marriage apart for me*', and I thought, '*You wouldn't do anything to stop me*'."

"That's why Alex is an asshole," he replied.

We drove back toward his hotel, planning to walk around in the unseasonably warm night. I turned off of Peachtree onto Third Street.

"*Ooooh, Tierney! Did you see that?*"

I glanced back over my shoulder and saw a woman standing on the corner. She was dark, and even in shadow I could see that she was scantily clad. And that she had *amazing* legs.

"She's *hot*!" Seth cooed. "Do you think she's a hooker?"

"Maybe." I parked the car and turned off the engine. "I guess we'll see when we get closer."

"If she is, will you buy her for me? For my birthday?"

"I've got twenty bucks in my pocket. Whatever that'll get ya, it's all yours!"

"Just the tip!" he quipped.

As we approached the corner, the woman was yelling across Peachtree Street traffic at two homeless guys sitting on another corner. They were laughing, easy, talking about whatever.

"Yep, hooker," I said under my breath. Seth nodded.

"Excuse me?" she said as I glanced down the street. "Could I bum a cigarette from one of you?"

I reached toward my purse and looked up at the woman. Her legs were spectacular. And she was the ugliest, most horse-faced *man* I'd ever seen in my life.

I pulled a cigarette from my pack. Smiling broadly, I turned to Seth. "Give the lady a cigarette, Hammer."

Seth glanced from me to her, frozen in place. His face was a quickly morphing contrast of fascination and horror, intrigue and revulsion. I looked away to keep from laughing. He slowly handed the hooker a cigarette from his pack, never taking his eyes off of her.

She thanked us sweetly as we crossed the street, walking away casually. Halfway down the block, he finally breathed, "Tierney! That was a *man*! *Did you see that? It was a man!*"

I cackled breathlessly. "*Just the tip, Seth! Just the tip!*"

"*Oh, jeez!*"

"Have you ever?" I asked.

"Sex with a man? Nope. Doesn't interest me at all. I can't imagine waking up and thinking, '*Hm*, I think I'd like some dick this morning!'"

"Just because you eat eggs for breakfast every day, that doesn't mean you can't have a little sausage from time to time!"

Sam Johnson
Nov 15, 2011 12:09 AM

Babysitter calling. Where are you,
when will you be home?

"Just tell him you'll be home in thirty. I gotta go to bed anyway."

Sam had texted off and on all night. A dozen times, checking where I was, telling me about the kids being up. It was annoying and felt horrible. I hugged Seth goodnight, promising to see him again soon, and walked back to my car.

I missed the split at Peachtree and West Peachtree that should've taken me back to the interstate. It was late and dark. I should've just turned around and gone back the way I'd come, but I didn't. I just kept driving. I knew the road would eventually lead me somewhere familiar, and I'd be able to get home. But I didn't want to go home. I didn't want to face Sam and the drama and the tension and everything that had gone horribly wrong with me and him and us.

I wanted to keep driving forever, in the dark with just my iPod and my voice and my thoughts, with no one to tell me I was wrong or misguided or stupid.

Chapter 35

"So how have things gone since we saw each other last?"

Sam and I were sitting on the dark, striped sofa in Dr. Hill's office, facing him across the coffee table. He glanced back and forth between us, waiting for one of us to begin.

Sam started talking about the weekend. He admitted to arguing with me and being completely wrong in his insinuations about Seth and me. He tried to justify it all and explain it away. I was visibly seething.

Dr. Hill looked to me. "Tierney, what do *you* want to address today? What do you think is the most pressing issue to be addressed right now?"

I could've started in on Sam, about his irrational behavior. I could've tried to respond to each of his bullshit points about why it was okay that he'd been such a dick over the weekend.

"I want to talk about Sam's drinking."

I knew it would put him on the spot. I wanted someone else to hear both perspectives and tell me if I was wrong to be concerned that his drinking was unnecessarily impactful on our lives. I wanted someone to tell me I was right, to tell him that I was right, or to tell me to shut the fuck up about it.

Sam started talking. I interjected once, to mention what he'd said about it being his behavior when he's drinking that was out of control.

"I monitor my drinking very carefully," Sam explained. "I know how much I've had and when it's too much. I make sure I keep that under control."

Dr. Hill looked at him levelly. "So you feel you have control over it?"

"Yes, absolutely."

Does he honestly hear himself?

He started talking about his DUI. Yes, he'd been arrested, but it wasn't prosecuted.

"On *appeal*!" I stressed. "You were convicted at the city, and the county didn't process it *on appeal*."

"Because I went to the classes. I went to some substance abuse meetings."

"Compulsorily?" Dr. Hill asked. "As part of your case?"

"Yes. But I went to a few meetings here in Atlanta, right after we moved here."

What?

This was news to me. I'd never heard him mention having gone to a meeting here. The only ones I knew he'd gone to in Birmingham had been the ones he was required to attend.

"Why didn't you go back? Was there something about the meetings you didn't like?"

Sam was quiet, looking up toward the ceiling, as if he could pluck his thoughts straight from the crown molding.

"The meetings were sad," he said finally. "Not all of them, but the last one I went to... everyone seemed so depressed and bored and unhappy. They all seemed so *old* and *forlorn*."

"Not all meetings are that way, Sam. You said that yourself. I typically find that meetings and the participants seem that way if the observer comes into the environment already feeling that way himself. It's like if you think you'll see only scuzzy, old farts, the room will be filled with dirty trench coats when you get there."

Sam nodded. "It just seemed like there were so many people with *problems*, and they didn't seem to get better. I heard so many of them talk about how they'd relapsed, or how they'd lost everything and had to start over *again*."

"You're right; sometimes it is that way. But there are people who use community-based recovery programs successfully and from the beginning. Relapses happen, certainly, but they are not the rule of law for addiction. The most important step to beating substance abuse is finding the personal meaning of addiction. Abusers have to understand on a deep level what they're doing, to avoid becoming a chronic relapser.

"In my experience, the biggest indicator of whether or not someone will succeed in changing is whether or not they truly *want* to change. Right now, it sounds like you're just entering the *contemplation* stage, in the Stages of Change behavioral model. You're aware that there's likely a problem, and you're considering making a change, even if you don't want to admit it."

I glanced back and forth between them. Sam was processing what Dr. Hill was saying. I could see from the purse of his mouth that he was trying to form a response, but the words just weren't coming. Dr. Hill took his silence as opportunity to continue.

"Look, Sam: it's *normal* to feel afraid—of admitting addiction, of telling the people you love, and of failing at recovery. But there are people who do this every damn day. Addiction recovery *is* possible, but it's also *hard*. It takes a lot of work and a lot of courage, but it's worth the effort."

Sam nodded. "There's a meeting close to our house. I thought about going there, but I don't know...."

"So let's talk about this. What happens if you go?"

"I might run into someone I know."

"So?" Dr. Hill looked at Sam pointedly. "*So what?* Who is in a position to judge another person for seeking help? If you think you have something to lose by being seen at a meeting, remember this: *so does everyone else*. If they're willing to face that risk, so can you. Besides, how would anyone know it's you, unless they're in the meeting?"

"My car is pretty identifiable."

"Can you use Tierney's car?"

"She has a sticker on her car. Everyone knows it's her car."

I visibly struggled to keep from lashing out. Dr. Hill's kind, level gaze was boring holes in Sam. "Just breathe," he said evenly to me, from the corner of his eye. I nodded.

"I guess I could just walk. It's not very far."

"Yes, you could walk. There you go. And if it's an open meeting, your sheer presence isn't considered an acknowledgement that you have a problem."

Our time was up. We scheduled our next session and stepped outside. I told Sam I'd see him at home later and left, driving toward my attorney's office in Decatur.

I called Tessa to tell her what had happened.

"Did you listen to the recording?" I asked her finally. "If not, *don't*. Just file it away in case something happens."

"Honestly, I didn't. It made me feel kind of *icky*. I understand that you felt threatened, and I know why you did what you did, but I also understand that it's a huge personal violation for Sam. I don't think it would be morally right for me to listen to it. It would be like eavesdropping on an incredibly intimate conversation. *Icky*."

"I get it. I know why he feels the way he does. But if he goes crazy and kills me, just remember that you have it. I don't want O.J. to get away with it a second time."

Tessa burst forth with dark giggles. "You know, Sam's a *great* guy. He's smart and funny and generally just a cool guy to know. I *hate* to see him like this. And it may very well get worse, Tierney. I have several friends who've gone through this process, and it doesn't seem to matter how much or how little you fight, or even what you're fighting about. People who engage in litigation in this context tend to get caught up in a crazy spiral of self-destructive behavior, and I wouldn't wish that on either of you. Mutually assured destruction is not a good place to be."

"I know. It's getting crazier by the day."

I turned into the parking lot of my attorney's office.

"You guys need to think about mediation, Tierney. Versus divorce in a court setting, the outcome is about the same, in terms of percentages. The only thing different is the size of the pie. Don't waste your future, or your children's futures, on fucking attorneys' fees."

I waited in a small anteroom in an old wooden Victorian in Decatur. Elizabeth came in to greet me, shaking my hand and thanking me for coming in to discuss my case. She led me up a spiral, iron staircase to her office, overlooking an elementary school next door.

I sat quietly across the small conference table from her as she looked over the settlement offer from Sam's attorney. I tried to quiet my mind, my agitated heart, but all I could hear was the rushing of anger and apprehension.

"This agreement is a joke," she said finally. "*Why on earth* would he *exclude* assets you are clearly entitled to?"

"I don't think he knows what's in there," I explained. "I think Sam let his attorney handle it all. He told me the guy was a son of a bitch, and I think they're wanting him to push the adultery issue."

"But this is so far from where you'll end up. This is stupid."

We went over the agreement, paragraph by paragraph. We covered the financial affidavit and spending plans I'd prepared. We looked over Sam's version of the same data. She was shocked to see that we were so far apart in what each of us thought it would take to run an independent household.

"In Georgia," she explained, "adultery will only keep you from getting alimony. It doesn't impact child support or assets. He certainly can't *exclude* assets from the settlement. Now, when you go into negotiations, everything gets thrown into the pot. Each of you pulls something out, and you decide who gets it. You'll get your car, he'll get his. You'll get half of this, and he'll take half of that. If you want alimony for three years, maybe you could trade him both children as tax deductions for that period of time, to sweeten his pot. It's all a matter of give and take, Tierney, and you have to be prepared to do a little of both."

"What about mediation?" I asked. "Is there any benefit?"

Elizabeth nodded emphatically. "Especially looking at what his attorney has done. There's a lot of backhanded, unfair wrangling going on here, and I'm betting he will drag this out as long as he can. You would still need to take an attorney with you into mediation, but a mediator will let you *start* in the middle. They'll have already figured out what needs to be in the pot and what you can each have for yourselves, no matter what."

I left her office, fully prepared to go home to more of the same round-and-round talk, to explanations from Sam about why he was right about everything. I knew he would press me again about recording our conversations and protecting his privacy.

When I did get home, there was a piece of paper in my desk chair. It was a draft of a pseudo-legal document from Sam, promising to stop monitoring my emails and phone calls and network activity.

There was also an email from him, with meeting information for later that night. It was for an alcohol abuse meeting at The Program.

Was this for real? Did Sam just fucking get it?

During our session, Dr. Hill had called bullshit on him, in the nicest, calmest way possible. His demeanor outside the office was calm and nowhere close to the ranting lunatic I'd seen for days. Had Sam really just woken up to his life?

I'd just come upstairs from painting when Sam came home that night.

"How was your meeting?" I asked. I was washing brushes at the kitchen sink.

"It was hard. Really hard."

I didn't know what to say. All I could do was nod.

"I don't know what's going to happen to us," he said. "I know there's a lot of damage. I know how much damage has been done, especially by me. If it's too much for you to get past and move forward with me, I understand. I hope it's not. Either way, your friendship means more to me than anything else. I'd like to continue counseling to work through these issues and be able to go forward as friends, regardless of everything else.

"I filed for divorce for all the wrong reasons. I filed, because I was angry and hurt. I filed out of rage. Even if you file again tomorrow, I want your permission to drop the case. Even if you leave anyway, I think it's the right thing to do."

This was a complete turn-around from where we'd been just a day before. I'd never heard Sam like this. This wasn't lip service.

Everything just *stopped*. I wanted to believe him, and I was willing to give him the benefit of the doubt. If he wanted my support in getting better, in being healthy, I was more than willing to help him. This was something that needed to happen for him and for our children and for our family, whether or not he and I stayed together.

My mom asked to take the boys camping for the weekend, a getaway with the grandchildren before the holidays. They had plans to ride the Polar Express train to visit Santa. She wanted to take them to some Civil War battlefields, knowing Tripp shared her love of American history. After school, I packed their bags and loaded them up, winding through Friday afternoon Atlanta rush hour toward Chattanooga.

"You can stay here tonight," she urged. "We have plenty of room in the camper."

I didn't want to. She knew I wanted to go home. I wanted to see how Sam was without the children around to temper his emotions.

It was almost midnight when I got home, weary and emotionally drained from the days before.

There was a letter from Sam on my pillow:

I'm sorry I didn't accept your influence in our marriage. It's worse than that: I tried to repress it because I had a sense of what was right and wrong in any given situation, from the petty to the most important, based on a twisted perspective that was the result of years of rationalizing my behavior so that my selfishness would ultimately win out. I would have felt small and diminished for an unbearably long time, and that would have hurt terribly because it was caused by the person I loved most.

I unintentionally pigeon-holed you into a "nice, safe" primary role of wife and mother, and even when you excelled at that, I took a lot of that for granted and didn't give you all the credit you deserved. That would have left me with some part of who I am ultimately unfulfilled, some vital part unnourished in such a way that I would feel like I was dying, like trying get by with a working set of lungs but no heart. It would have made me feel desperate. I'm so sorry if I made you feel that way. I'm sorry that when I realized what I was doing, I was inept at correcting it.

I'm sorry I didn't express my fondness and admiration of you. Even when your depth, your complexity, your energy, your strength, your adaptability, and your intellect were something that amazed me, I restrained my praise. I did this because I was scared of change, especially good change, because I began to feel I couldn't deserve you, that you could do better than me, and I was afraid, so much so that it help create the conditions in which that fear became self-fulfilling. I became defensive and even attacked it. My approach eventually made things so bad that my praise wasn't even welcome, and rightfully so, because it eventually became empty reassurances linked to ulterior motives. I chose to wear blinders that narrowed my perspective of you so that I would see only what I wanted to protect my selfish world. I'm sorry that I didn't express my pride and appreciation adequately because I was threatened by how it might affect the balance of power. I'm also sorry for myself --that by doing that for so long, I denied myself so much of what makes you a beautiful, interesting person, and of so many rich experiences. I'm sorry I made it so you'd never know how dazzlingly wonderful I think you really are.

I'm sorry I lost touch with your life. I'm sorry I tried to compensate for what really caused the walls between our lives to rise up by sneaking around it and forcing or stealing my way back into it, resorting to interference to get your attention. Instead of dismantling the walls, I tried to smash them down, hurting everyone in the process. I want to be able to say that I know what stresses and joys you feel day-to-day, and I'm sorry I handled everything so ineptly until I eventually made it impossible. I would not want to connect with my spouse very often, or be honest about even mundane things, if all I thought it would bring were criticism, contempt, defensiveness, or stonewalling.

I'm sorry I didn't turn to you more, not so much in the case of stresses and negative emotions, but for the joys and the positive emotions in my life.

I'm sorry that I did things that made creating separate meaning in your and my lives so much more important than creating shared meaning in ours.

I'm sorry I didn't know how to solve my problems so that we could start solving ours. I'm sorry I made it so that you were coping with me, and I wasn't coping with anything, because then we couldn't focus on coping with the other big problems that come along when two intelligent, powerful personalities enter into a marriage. I'm sorry that I never had any clue of how to overcome gridlock between us on individual hopes, dreams, and personal goals.

I'm sorry I didn't listen as much as I talked. I'm sorry that when I did talk, I didn't talk to you as much as at you. I'm sorry I didn't say you're right when you were, or I'm wrong when I knew I was. I'm sorry that I never told you that I thought it was perfectly OK to fail. I'm sorry I didn't forgive you when you hurt me. I'm sorry I didn't tell you why I love you as much as I told you simply that I did. I'm sorry I didn't say thank you all the times I should have.

Finally, with each of the subjects of these apologies, however, I could find counterexamples, and in those counterexamples, hope.

I have generally behaved badly and thought bad things, but I'm not generally a bad person, at least not at heart or in all thoughts and actions. I think I have the capacity to empathize and understand the emotions of others; I have a desire to help with no expectations or *demands of repayment; I am perceptive and responsive to life's demands; I believe people are good and mean well by default and until they prove otherwise; I generally look for something good in everybody, even I have come to dislike them otherwise; I find other people interesting and can be a good listener; I can be trusting to a fault; I can be trustworthy; I am intelligent, and in some things, wise; I'm adept at examining myself, even if I am sometimes powerless to change; I am genuinely honest; I am ambitious; I am passionate; I can care deeply about others; I can be emotionally supportive, an advocate, and a cheerleader for those I care about; and I can feel love and being loved on the deepest, most abiding levels.*

All of these have been diminished or virtually killed off as my faults created spirals of negative emotions that required the building of protective emotional barriers and distance between what fed and enhanced these good qualities, and for so long! This is what I am sorry for above all else. But also I'm encouraged by a new perspective on why I should feel genuine regret and remorse, and the need to say I'm sorry for these things.

I stood next to the bed, reading and rereading his words. They were confusing at first. I couldn't make sense of what he was saying. Was it an apology, asking me not to leave? *No.* Was it an apology, then telling me all the ways I'd fucked up? *No.* Was there a caveat? *No.*

It was just an apology.

There was no blanket approach to it, either. He wasn't listing specific instances and grievances, but he was apologizing for every hurtful thing he'd ever done in our marriage. I knew some of it was for things that had happened over the last few weeks and months, but he was also digging back into hurts that had happened long before, throughout our relationship.

"Thank you," I whispered. My throat clinched around my tears.

"Thank you for telling Dr. Hill you wanted to talk about my drinking. Thank you for putting me on the spot when you did. I don't think I would've heard it that way, in any other place or time. I never heard it before, all the times you told me it needed to stop. I never understood when you said I was still an asshole when I wasn't drinking. I didn't understand, because I'm an alcoholic and a drunk, and I'm sorry."

I was so tired. I just wanted the safety and comfort of my bed, knowing my children were securely away from the drama of our house.

"I can't talk about it anymore tonight," I told him. "I need to go to sleep."

We brushed our teeth and stumbled into bed, well after midnight.

I snuggled down against my pillow, uncharacteristically facing his side of the bed. I was almost asleep when I felt the bed shift with his weight. Silence. Then a rustle of the sheets, and Sam's hand gingerly reached for mine, under the blankets.

I placed my palm gently in his.

In the dark, Sam held my hand. "Everything that happened, anything you think you did wrong... I forgive you."

I squeezed his hand tightly, and a silent tear rolled down the side of my face.

"I love you," he said quietly.

"I love you, too," I replied sleepily.

I was asleep almost instantly, Sam's hand warm against mine in the dark.

Chapter 36

Sam offered to meet my mom on Sunday, north of Atlanta to retrieve the children. I stayed home and took a nap. The next day, he gave me permission to tell Tessa and my parents about his going through the Program.

"Thank God!" Tessa exhaled. "That's such a relief! He needs this, Tierney. I'm thankful he agreed to stop this craziness."

"Yeah, me, too. It was different, Tessa. I've never heard him like this. Ever."

My mom was cautiously optimistic. "He was a completely different person yesterday, when he met us to get the boys. He was pleasant and calm and relaxed. He was almost... *contrite*, like he was a little broken. He didn't seem sad or anything. He was great with the boys. He let us pay for his lunch, which you know he *never* does."

"This whole thing has kicked his ass into gear. He totally had the lightbulb moment."

"Has he told his mother?"

"No, not yet. You can't tell anyone, by the way. He's given me permission to tell a couple of people, but this is not for public consumption. His mom has so much going on with his dad. I think he's afraid this will send him over the edge."

My mom reminded me that Sam was always welcome in her home, that she cared about him the same way she loved me and the boys.

"If he needs me, I'm here. I'm a trained chaplain. Anything he shares with me is confidential."

"I know," I replied. "I appreciate that. He will, too. I'll be sure to tell him."

My dad was relieved that Sam was seeking treatment. I knew he wouldn't betray our confidence and tell the rest of the family. Again, he offered his support without judgment.

At our next session with Dr. Hill, we told him everything that had happened since our last. We sat on the couch, and I held Sam's hand while he thanked Dr. Hill, and me, for making him hear what he'd refused to listen to for so long. I explained that I'd agreed to stay in counseling with him, to help our family, regardless of how our relationship ultimately resolved.

"I can't tell you how heartened this makes me," Dr. Hill said, a little awed by the changes between us from the week before. "It's wonderful to have the best session of my week first thing on Monday. *Thank you* for that, both of you."

Sam went to a meeting every night. When he came home, I would ask nonchalantly how it went. He always responded with a "good" or a "fine", and I never pressed him. I was happy and willing to be there and talk through anything with him, but I didn't want to push him to reveal more than he was comfortable sharing.

He seemed especially introspective after his meeting on Monday night.

"It was hard," he told me quietly, sitting on the bed. "I said it for the first time. The words. *I'm an alcoholic*."

I didn't congratulate him, and I wasn't happy. He was struggling, just beginning to come to terms with the gravity of what that word meant. It wasn't just that he had a drinking problem. The real addiction was in the pattern of behavior surrounding his misuse of alcohol and sometimes other sedating substances.

"I'm sorry. I know that must've been hard. Are you okay?"

He bobbed his head in slow response. "It was really hard."

"I'm proud of you," I said matter-of-factly. "You should be proud of yourself."

"There's nothing to be proud of."

"There's nothing to be *ashamed* of, either. You're taking responsibility for yourself and your actions, and you're consciously making the choice to make that better. I can only imagine how difficult that is."

I knew, to some degree, what it meant to tackle the demons that kept you coming back for inappropriate comfort. I'd done it for years with food. To a much lesser extent, I'd done it with sex and affection. They were similar battles but definitely different in their own way from what Sam was battling. Food and affection are life-sustaining, and it can be difficult to delineate between *use* and *overuse*. Alcohol isn't a necessity for life, though it lends itself to both physical and psychological dependency. I would never fully empathize with his specific addiction, but I could sympathize with the desire to blot out your world with an external crutch.

Sam and I were calm and kind to each other. We were polite and patient, with a new ease that we hadn't felt in months. We still had weighty issues to be resolved, but we were less burdened by each other than we'd been in ages.

The boys were out of school for the entire week of Thanksgiving. I'd already planned to go to Birmingham the night before, home the evening of. The boys would be going with me, but Sam was on call and had to stay in Atlanta, in case something happened that required a quick response from the office.

Thanksgiving was a blur of driving from house to house and trying to sneak in a couple of hours' worth of quality time with the families. Relatives who hadn't seen us in months were irritated that we couldn't stay longer and come to visit them. Having not been back for an extended visit for nearly a year, some family members were shocked when they saw me. I was thinner than they'd ever known me, and they told me repeatedly how fantastic I looked.

My mom offered to keep the boys through the long weekend. I missed Sam, and I couldn't wait to get home to see him. I snagged some leftovers of his favorite dishes and packed them in a small cooler. He'd gone to a lunchtime meeting, but my aunt's green bean casserole was better than anything he'd had at his Program luncheon.

For the first time in years, Sam and I went Black Friday shopping. We started just before midnight, standing in the long line wrapped around the shopping center. It was frigid, but neither of us cared. We talked and joked and flirted. We stayed close, rarely leaving each other's side, both inside the stores and out. After waiting in one line for nearly an hour, we realized the store only had one pair of the jeans I was looking for, in my new, smaller size. There was a forty-five minute wait to pay.

"Are you gonna be mad if I put these back and we leave?" I asked cautiously.

He smiled sweetly. "Not at all!"

"I'm sorry it was a waste of time."

"Don't be! I'm just happy to spend the time with you."

As tired as I was, I didn't intend to sleep with him. We were strained and weird, but he smelled so damn good in our bed next to me. His warmth radiated attempt and love, and I couldn't resist him. So much had happened in the previous month, the previous year, and it seemed like forever since we'd been together. It was sweet but awkward, cautiously finding each other in the aftermath of so much craziness. It was unspoken that making love didn't mean we were reconciled; it was just a familiar and affectionate connecting with the person we loved, no matter what.

We slept late the next morning. I painted for a few hours. He went to some meetings. We did not much of nothin' for two days. It was wonderful.

Late Saturday night, he handed me a disc.

"I think it's all here. That's all I could find anyway."

I looked at him, puzzled. *Tierney Cavanaugh Johnson:Emails & Files*

He'd just handed me everything that was gone—everything I'd deleted and everything he'd gone behind my back to delete for me.

I looked at him quizzically.

"Check and make sure it's all there," he said.

I took the CD to my computer and popped it in the drive.

There were texts and emails and Skype logs, pictures and videos and MP3's, mostly that had passed between me and Alex. Some of the files were things Sam had gone into my computer and copied, but there were many that had been deleted long before he ever found out about the affair. These were the ones the hacking group had caught in transmission. I hadn't seen some of them in close to a year.

I didn't know what to say. "*Thank you.*"

He nodded. "You know, it was really hard going back through all of that and looking at it again. But I was struck by something."

"Hm?"

"You had really difficult choices to make. There was so much going on, and sometimes you had to make a tough decision. I don't always like the choice you made, but I'm in awe of the strength and bravery you had to have to *make* those choices."

Wow.

I was speechless. I didn't want to elaborate on the ways in which he was right, or dismiss them as simple or unimportant.

"Thank you," I repeated.

It was all I could think of.

He stood to go out to the deck. He paused and turned back toward me. "I get why he was special to you," he said softly. "You're right that it was inevitable."

"I know it didn't make any sense. On the surface, he was *him*, and I was the fat, blond housewife." I shrugged. "It was illogical, but it happened."

Sam went outside for a last cigarette for the evening. I brushed my teeth and climbed into bed.

He joined me a few minutes later. "You know, I'm gonna call bullshit on something."

"What's that?"

"You said it didn't make any sense, you and Alex."

"It didn't," I scoffed.

"No, you're *wrong*. He saw that *something* in you, that spark, that was *special*, that you couldn't see and that I hadn't seen in a very long time. It was always there. He saw how amazing and beautiful you are and always were, even when you couldn't and I wouldn't. You're *amazing* and *beautiful*, Tierney. He was a lucky bastard that you cared. I know. I'm lucky, too. And I can't believe that he would never acknowledge your presence and influence in his life. If he would deny *you* in the face of *everything*, then he's an asshole who never deserved your affection. I can't understand how *anyone* would ever do something like that to *you*."

I knew how hard it was for Sam to say those things to me. He'd told me he forgave me for the affair, but to voice his understanding of why my lover had ever been attracted to me was something else entirely. He was admitting that he'd ignored me, that I had ignored *myself*, and that he had hurt both of us by letting another man be the one to pay me the attention I needed and deserved.

————————————

We went to therapy at least once a week. It wasn't easy and peaceful. We delved into our joint and separate sexual histories. We examined our respective parent and sibling relationships. Some days we left Dr. Hill's office with a sense of hopeful resolve that we could get through this, eventually. Some days we were left with more aching and sadness over the damage we'd each done.

Sam wanted me to make a commitment, to *choose* to move forward with him toward healing as a married couple. He was upset that I was wavering.

"Why do you think you're apprehensive?" Dr. Hill asked.

"Just a couple of weeks ago, we were spiraling out of control. We were at each other's throats. Sam was erratic and drinking all the time. I *want* to trust that he's better, that things between us are better, but I need the spiraling to *stop*. I need to be still and quiet for a while and let everything settle. If I make a decision right *now* to accept his sobriety as the new norm... it seems rash. I can't blindly trust that what he's telling me now is the ultimate truth. We've been too up and down to trust in it yet."

"I know we still have a lot of work to do," Sam interjected. "I want Tierney to commit to being willing to do the work, no matter what—"

Dr. Hill pointed at Sam. "You don't get that right now." He turned to me. "You need to *not* make a decision until the beginning of the year. You need to get through the holidays and let things settle for a while, you're absolutely right."

Sam seemed stunned that Dr. Hill hadn't immediately sided with him.

"Sam, you're still in the very early stages of recovery. While I understand that you feel better than you have in a very long time, you've barely started the process of establishing a secure sense of self without the alcohol. You've had a glimpse at the multitude of holes and traps that are lining your path to recovery, but there's a lot of *shit* that will come out while you work your program. It would be *dangerous* to accelerate your recovery just to save your marriage."

"I'm sorry," I told Sam in the parking lot after our session. "I know it's not what you wanted to hear."

"Tierney, it's okay. I understand. I guess I've had time to think about it in my own way, and I know this is what I want."

"I'm not saying it's not what *I* want. I just need time to be *still*."

There'd been so much emotional turmoil, for weeks. *Months.* So much going on with me and in me and around me. All the ups and downs had left me weary. The scales had been swinging wildly from one heavy weight to another, and I needed some time just to let them *stop*, to find a balance and let that *be*.

I'm a kinetic person, and I like to be constantly moving forward. And that kind of central balance is the kind of happy medium that feels so impossible to me. It usually takes me a long time to find what others call a happy place, where things are happening on both sides of the equation. I know that's how life is supposed to be, in the end, but staying in check is boring and unnatural for me.

So I had to make a conscious decision to be still. I had to make the concerted effort not to tip the scales in one direction or the other. I didn't know how to do that.

I didn't know how not to be in motion.

————————————

"Tierney, it's Paul Sommers. How are you?"

I hadn't talked to Paul in months. I'd not heard from him after my trip to San Antonio, but that wasn't surprising. I didn't know if Alex had told him about the affair, though I doubted it.

Why is Paul Sommers calling me?

The boys were at school for their last week before Christmas Break. Sam was at work. I stopped moving the wet laundry from the washer into the dryer and settled onto the small, blue sofa in the office.

"I'm good, Paulie! How are you?"

"Oh, I can't complain—if I did, no one would listen anyway."

I chuckled politely.

"Listen, I don't know if you've heard—maybe Alex told you—that Junkture is playing South by Southwest this year. In Austin?"

"Yes, I know where South-by is held, and no, I hadn't heard."

"Well, I really *loved* what you did for Seth's CD release show. The artwork for his poster?—"

"Thank you—"

"—and I'd like to ask you to do the same for Junkture."

Holy fuck.

"I know we talked about it a little bit earlier this year, about your maybe doing some artwork for us. We haven't really had any shows for most of the year, though. I'm sure you know that."

"Yeah." I still saw regular updates from their Facebook page, even if I wasn't friends with Alex.

He cleared his throat. "So we've been asked to do this party for a magazine. Actually, the party's happening at my bar, Flunky's. On that last Saturday of the music festival. Would you be interested in doing the poster?"

"Paulie, *wow*... I'm honored that you would ask."

"We were all in Austin recording a couple of weeks ago, when we got the offer for the party. We started talking about what needed to happen—the prep work and stuff—and Alex suggested you might be the ideal choice for this."

My heart stopped, and I caught my breath.

"You okay?" Paul asked, concerned at my sudden sound.

"Oh... yeah, sorry. I, um, dropped something."

"So do you think you'd want to do it? If you don't want to or don't have time—"

"*No!* Of course I want to! Are you *kidding* me?"

Alex asked for me.

Remember to breathe, Tierney.

"Did you guys have anything specific in mind? For the art? A theme? A style?"

"*Persona Non Grata* is still the current record, even though it'll have been out for a year-and-a-half by the time the show rolls around. You can start with that theme and see where it takes you, or you can try something else. You know that record, Tierney, and you know us, so I feel confident that you can find some inspiration for this."

"Thanks for the guidance, Paulie," I laughed.

"I'll check with the guys and email you anything they offer, but don't feel like you have to stay with that. Just be sure to send me proofs before you get too far into anything. I would hate for you to spend a lot of time on something that Alex decides he can't stand."

Wouldn't be the first time.

We talked for a few minutes longer, wished each other happy holidays, and hung up.

I paced the house, trying to make sense of what had just happened.

Paul Sommers called and asked you to do Junkture's show poster for South by Southwest.

"Holy shit!" Tessa exclaimed when I called her.

"No kidding!"

"No. *Seriously.* That's fucking *awesome*, Tierney!"

"Can I do this, Tessa? Can I *do* this? Can I be back in that?"

"Tierney," she admonished, "you don't have to be back *in* anything. You don't even have to have contact with Alex. You can go through Paul directly. It doesn't put you back in Alex's path."

"He asked for me. He told Paulie to ask me to do it."

"But Paul thinks Alex is an asshole. He wouldn't have asked if he didn't think you were the right artist for this. Neither of them would."

But *why* did Alex suggest *me*? They'd worked with dozens of graphic designers and artists over the years. They were fucking *Junkture*—artists all over the world would've given their eyeteeth for this opportunity.

Because you're good, Tierney.

In San Antonio, they'd all told me how much they liked Seth's show poster. And it *was* good, my artwork or not.

I would have to tell Sam, but I wasn't about to call him at work for this. It would wait until he got home and settled, until the boys were out of the line of fire, if it turned ugly. I wanted to do it— for my portfolio, for the experience, for the band I loved—but Sam could try to shut it down before it even got off the ground.

For the first time in months, I grabbed my iPod and found Junkture in my playlists. I would hear them on the radio sometimes, of course. Sometimes I could listen to it, sometimes not. The groupie and the mistress were often at odds when it came to hearing that music.

But this wasn't about Alex.

The whine of Paul's guitar against Max and Charlie's throbbing bass and drum. Alex's voice, smooth and then frictioned, even and slowly soaring and then coarse in seductive supplication.

The songs were all about women—messy, complicated women who were hiding something about their inherent selves from the larger world, keeping their secrets for themselves.

Ideas churned, quickly and fluidly. I grabbed my sketchbook and let them flood the pages.

I took a quick picture of my favorite on my phone and emailed it to Paul.

First inclination. Let me know what you think.

Just as I clicked **SEND**, I heard the front door unlock and open.

"Hello?" Sam called from the den.

"Hey," I answered, "I'm in the office."

I flipped my sketchbook closed and looked up at him. "You're home early. How was work?"

"Fine. It was slow, so I took the afternoon. I wanted to come home and see my beautiful wife." He kissed me, lingering. "Whatcha workin' on?"

"Well...."

Here we go.

"I got a call from Paul Sommers today."

Sam watched me with a calm, even gaze.

"Junkture's playing at South by Southwest, on the last Saturday. He asked me to do the artwork for the show poster."

He made a subtle face of surprise. "What did he say?"

"He said he really liked what I did with the poster for Seth's show. He'd seen some of my stuff online before, and had mentioned maybe having me do something, but you know how he is. Who knew if he would ever be serious about that, you know?"

Sam nodded.

"But he said... Alex suggested Paul ask me about doing the art."

"Did you talk to Alex?"

I shook my head. "Nope. I haven't talked to him since Nashville. I was as surprised as anyone."

"Why would you be surprised, Tierney?"

"*Sam*," I implored, a little irritated, "he didn't want to be in contact with me. And I'm a *nobody*. They could've had anyone do this for them."

"Well, he's not in contact with you, is he? If he'd wanted that, he would've emailed you or called you. But he knows what a good artist you are. You know their music. You know their tastes. And, honestly, maybe it's a peace offering."

I shrugged and stood from the sofa. I slid the sketchbook and pencils onto the top of my desk.

"I don't know," I said. "I sketched some stuff out after he called. I had an idea and wanted to see where it went. But if this makes you uncomfortable...."

Sam glanced down at the floor. "If it makes *me* uncomfortable, that's *my* issue. That's not yours. The question is how *you* feel about it, and whether or not you want to take on this project."

"I'm really intrigued," I admitted. "I mean, it's *Junkture* for God's sake! Even dismissing everything else, it's a huge band that I've loved forever, and they've asked *me* to do a show poster for one of the biggest music festivals in the world. For a magazine party. Thousands of people would see that poster. It could be a huge opportunity for me." I stopped, poised on the edge of another thought.

"But...?"

"But, there's... all of the other. It doesn't have to put me back in touch with him. It doesn't have to mean I'll talk to him or see him. It's a job."

"Are they paying you for it?"

"I don't know. Paul didn't even mention it. It almost doesn't matter."

"Well, it *does* matter. It's your time and effort—"

"No, I know it's *worth* something—don't get me wrong—but it's such a big chance, such an experience, that I would absolutely do it for free."

"Then I think it's settled."

"I can do it?" I looked at Sam questioningly.

He crossed the room to me and pulled me into a hug. "Of course you can do this. It's the right project, and you're doing it for the right reasons. I can't very well ask you *not* to do it."

"You *can*, if that's really what you want. If it's too much for you...."

Sam pulled back and smiled into my eyes. "*No.* This is something you have to do. You need to do. You *should* do."

"*Thank you*," I said, kissing him hard.

"Will you go to South by Southwest?"

I hadn't thought about it. The music lover in me had always wanted to go, just to see what it was like. The fan would love to see Junkture play there, especially at Flunky's. If Montevallo was like Mecca for groupies, Flunky's and the Deck were like Medina.

"I don't know. I mean, I would like to, but—"

"Then you should. You should go."

"Would you want to go with me? If I went? I mean, they would be playing on Saturday, but there would be other stuff going on for the days before. So many bands. We could catch a bunch of shows, maybe—"

"Probably not." He pulled away. "I don't really care about the music and the shows as much as you do—"

"I know, but—"

"—and I don't know how I'd do in that environment, with everyone there. I have so much coming up at work, and I wouldn't be able to get out there until Friday. Junkture's playing on Saturday, and we'll have to come home early on Sunday. I don't think it's worth the expense of having me come and not be able to really *do* anything but that show."

"There will be *lots* of stuff going on," I argued. "Bands will be playing all day long and on Friday night."

"No—"

"Then I won't go."

"Tierney, *no*. You *will* go, and you'll have a *great* time. Maybe you'll make some contacts and get some more projects. Think of it as a business trip."

Could I do that? Could I go to Austin and see them, see Junkture, see Alex, and try to hawk my services to other bands?

Maybe.

Sam glanced at his watch. "Time for the bus."

We walked outside, up the street to the school bus stop. It was chilly and breezy, but the sun was shining. I folded my arms around myself, trying to buffet my body against the sudden shifting winds.

"Here," Sam said.

He opened his coat and motioned me inside. I huddled against his body as he enveloped me in his warmth. I lay my head on his chest, listening to his heartbeat and his steady, even breathing until the school bus roared up the hill, bringing our normal life back home.

Paul emailed me early the next morning that they all loved the sketch for the poster.

This is fantastic! Go!

As soon as Sam and the boys were gone, I slipped into my Junkture t-shirt and a pair of panties. I pulled the shirt tight around me, clipping the back to account for the weight I'd lost since I'd last worn it in Texas. I took a couple of quick pictures that I printed out and carried them downstairs with me. I plugged my iPod into the portable speakers and turned the volume up as loud as I could stand it.

I set up my easel with a fresh smooth Bristol pad. The piece would be better as a drawing. I grabbed a fresh pencil and turned my creative eye inward.

Persona Non Grata. The unwelcome guest.
Can't see the face in full.
Favorite songs? 'Hot Mess', 'Dollface', 'Whiskey Mouth'.
Dark amber pout. The whiskey mouth.

I started at the face, from just above the lips, which were full and twisted slightly into a furtive smirk, chin tilted just away from the viewer. I followed the shape of my own slight grin—the line of the lips, the placement and proportion of mouth to chin. The graceful neck plunged into deep cleavage that was encased in a black t-shirt, just like mine in the picture, the Junkture logo emblazoned across her breasts.

Cover up the hurt and pretty up the mess.

Sitting, leaning back—comfortable in the *she* that's on display. Panties, no pants. Her hips curved round and luscious toward the floor and then into the long, akimbo stretch of her legs, their slight askew hiding and protecting her deepest secrets.

And his secrets, too.

I opened the flat tin of colored pencils and started to fill the sketch with shades—mostly blacks and grays with highlights of silver and pewter, space for white. Dark chrome yellow and light yellow glaze for the curling tendrils that framed her neck, with the lightest touches of pale geranium lake for lowlights.

Shoes?

The detail of the pink, glittery heels would be lost in the scale, and toes could look awkward and unappealing. Boots would be easy, but they needed to be sexy.

Black?
Pink.
Pretty little sparkles in the shining lights.
Metallic pink for the go-go boots.
Buttercup pink.

After four hours, I stepped back from the easel.

She wasn't me, but I was there. It was my mouth and my breasts and my sparkle. But she was every woman who'd ever loved a band, who'd ever let that music become so much a part of her life that she could live and die and be reborn in the total running time of an album. Her idea of Heaven was front row center.

Singing with the band.

Her secrets were hers, and it didn't matter if they were like yours. The empathy was in the *knowing*—that you were both shrouded in projected appearance, your confidences safely concealed beneath the enigmatic countenance and pretty, pink lipstick.

I spent two more days finalizing the piece.

"Tierney, it's... *really good*," Sam said. I'd brought him downstairs to see it before I emailed a picture to Paul.

"I know, with everything... but you were a fan...."

He nodded slowly, still looking at the drawing. "It's Junkture. Definitely. You did good, sweetie."

"What if they don't like it?"

"Then fuck 'em."

I took a couple of pictures and emailed them to Paulie. He called ten minutes later.

"Tierney! *Sensational!*"

My insides did a flip.

"Thanks, Paulie! I wasn't sure...."

"*No*, it's *superb*. It's almost like you know who Alex had in mind when he wrote this record."

I snickered to myself. "Yeah, I feel like I have a good idea of what Alex likes in a woman."

"Well, he was the first one to respond when I sent it to the band. He said it was perfect."

As much as I wanted to convince myself that taking on this project had nothing to do with Alex, I knew in my heart that there was a little part of me that wanted him to be proud of me. I wanted him to be able to really see me and my talents that had nothing to do with sex.

"Please, thank the guys for this opportunity. Really, it means a lot."

"It's our pleasure, Tierney. Go ahead and finish up the graphic work on the poster and send it to me when it's finished. We'll see it in Austin."

Chapter 37

The holidays were approaching again, and I didn't want a repeat of the previous year's morose celebrations. For the five years we'd been in Atlanta, we'd always traveled to Birmingham, either for Christmas Eve or Christmas Day. The rush had been hard enough when the boys were little and we were within half an hour of the entire family. Now that they were older, they wanted to be at home for Christmas, where they could stay in their pajamas and enjoy their new toys.

For the first time by choice, I wouldn't be at my grandparents' house with my dad's entire extended family, on Christmas morning. I'm the eldest of the seven granddaughters. My boys are the only great-grandchildren. Sam always complains that I have the loudest family in the world, that we get continually louder, trying to out-hear each other. It's usually spirited and filled with laughter, and some of my dearest memories are from Christmases with the Cavanaughs.

But *our* family needed to be at home, together. There had been so much turmoil for the last year, and there was still so much uncertainty about our collective future. Things between Sam and me were a thousandfold better than they'd been in ages, but we didn't know for sure what was coming. Sam and I had the unspoken understanding that this could be our last Christmas together as a family, and we wanted to make it as calm and wonderful for our children as possible.

"You have to do what's right for *your* family, Tierney," my dad advised. "We'll miss you, but we understand."

I half-expected to hear my mom gripe about not having the boys at her house for the holiday. "It's okay, Tierney. I understand completely."

We did agree to go over the weekend before, to see the families and the Karenas, who were flying into Birmingham for their annual holiday visit. I hadn't seen Tessa in a year. Although we talked nearly every day, I needed a hug from my best friend.

I spent Saturday shuffling the boys from grandparent to grandparent to open gifts and be as quickly gracious as possible. Sam needed some time with his parents and decided to take the boys to stay with his mother on Saturday night. I hadn't seen her since his birthday. I'd only talked to her by phone a couple of times since learning he'd told her about the affair. I wasn't ready to face whatever judgments she had waiting for me.

I planned to meet up with my beloved Cavanaugh cousins and some friends at Zydeco to see Wesley Cook, a musician I knew from Atlanta. We started drinking as soon as we got to the bar, laughing and squealing with delight when he covered "Laid" by James.

I was up early on Sunday morning. After a quick breakfast with my mom, we got ready to go see the Karenas.

I was tentative about seeing them, not because of Tessa but because of her husband, Ed. He was still pissed that I'd hurt Sam so badly, but he was also revolted by the entire concept of infidelity, finding it unimaginably cruel that anyone could ever betray their beloved in such a manner. He was upset about the principle and the specifics of the whole thing.

Sam was reticent to join us. He didn't know if he could face Tessa, knowing she knew everything that had happened. While the details had been relayed to her almost entirely through my voice, she was pragmatic and had never had any qualms about telling me I was acting crazy or stupid. She loved Sam and knew how much I truly loved him, and she was proud of him for getting into recovery when he did, if for no other reason than it was what *he* needed. He was afraid he wouldn't be able to look either of his friends in the eye, knowing they knew how badly we'd behaved.

There was no reason for either of us to worry. Ed smiled and hugged me, just like he did every time I saw him. Tessa was excited to see Sam, and the four of us spent a long time talking about physics and the kids and whatever geeky craziness came into our minds. It was just like we'd always been when we were together.

Tessa and I started talking about all of the loose skin I'd accumulated since losing the weight.

"It's a lot," I told her, pointing out my trouble spots through my clothes. "Like I told Jules, my ass is starting to look like a Shar-Pei puppy!"

"Okay, I gotta see it." She led me down the hallway to her parents' guest bedroom.

Closing the door behind us, she turned to face me. "Let me see."

I laughed and lifted my shirt. The top of my abs were pretty flat, but the trouble lay below. I unbuttoned my jeans and dropped them to my knees.

"See?" I said, grabbing the spare tire of Mommy bulge and dimpled skin. "It's *disgusting*."

"The bulge isn't that big. Can I touch it?"

"Sure."

She poked me gingerly in the belly. "Good grief! It's so hard under there!"

"That's my six-pack," I chuckled. "It's there. You just can't see it because of this soft-sided cooler."

"How are your boobs?"

I pulled my shirt over my head and unhooked my bra.

"Like this. I'm still between a C and a D cup, but now I'm almost a thirty-six band. I was a forty-two double-D even a year ago."

My breasts were still ample and nicely shaped, for the most part. But in the previous two weeks, it seemed the last five pounds had come almost exclusively from my chest.

"When I lie on my back, they're like little deflated soufflés."

I showed her the skin that hung from my arms. She was impressed with the thick, tight muscles that held up the bat wings.

"And then there's my thighs," I complained. I grabbed the loose skin and pulled it to the side, showing her how much thinner my thighs would be if it weren't there.

"Yeah, you should totally do that."

I'd busted my ass, literally, and I felt amazing. I was very comfortable with how I looked in clothes. But when I was *naked*, I was appalled by how different my body looked from how I felt at this new normal. There was an ever-growing disjoint between how I really looked and how I *imagined* I looked when I thought about it.

Ed's mom had lost a substantial amount of weight a few years before. She had opted to have the extra skin removed and told me it was one of the best things she ever did. I knew three other women who'd been through the same process, and none of them regretted the surgery, though they were all very forthcoming about the difficulty of the procedure and the recovery.

I tentatively planned to consult with some surgeons after the first of the year. First, I had to get through the holidays.

The week before Christmas was a blur of children and baking. Sam was gone to meetings every night for at least three hours. We were only able to catch up with each other late at night, after the boys were long asleep and I was almost there.

Sam told me that he would be at a late meeting on Christmas Eve.

"We're serving dinner to some homeless guys. There are a couple of special speakers. It's part of this thing about being a dignified, useful member of society while exercising compassion and understanding for my fellow man. Will you guys be okay if I go to that?"

"Of course!"

But I was a little irritated. He'd been gone and missed dinner with us the year before. Everything was so emotionally heightened this year, and I was trying not to see it as somehow *meaningful* or *important* that he would be away from us on Christmas Eve again. He assured me he'd be home in time to help stuff the stockings and play Late Night Santa.

He wasn't.

I had to set everything up by myself. He'd left late in the afternoon and didn't get home until after midnight. I texted him to be sure to get the Santa gifts from the basement before he went to bed.

We were up early Christmas morning and had a beautiful day with the boys. Although Tripp and Ian were almost four years apart in age, their interests had started to converge. It was the first time they were getting exactly the same gifts, not because it was easier but because they wanted the same things.

Sam and I had agreed to be low-key in our gift giving to each other. I got him a couple of DVDs and books, picked out some new shirts for him. He got me a new pair of purple running shoes and some earrings that I'd picked out.

Over breakfast, Sam and Tripp started talking about Russia, which led into an hour-long discussion of Georgian-Russian politics and Russian hackers, followed by talk of quantum physics. Ian and I were busy elsewhere, playing with programmable robots and his new table-top disco ball. There was no pressure to look at your stuff and hurry up 'cause we gotta go to Grandma's house. Everyone was relaxed and at ease, together.

I fell asleep, mid-morning, on the couch in front of a perfect fire, surrounded by my men, who were happily playing with their new toys. I woke after two hours and didn't want to move. I felt *content* in our house in a way I hadn't felt in years.

"There are a couple of meetings I'd like to go to tonight, if that's okay," Sam said. "The holidays are an especially bad time for alcoholics, you know? It's part of the celebrating, that you drink. Someone's supposed to talk about triggers and how to deal with them. I promise I won't be out as late as I was last night."

"Sure. We'll be here. Go and enjoy yourself."

I hid my irritation. It was a big holiday weekend, and I'd expected him to be with us for it. He was actively working his program with his new sponsor, who demanded he be an hour early for meetings and stay for small group chat afterward. As much as Sam needed to be actively in recovery, it was kind of the Program's dirty little secret that the time away from the family and in meetings made the alcoholic just as unavailable as the drinking had.

The difference was that he was away from us only in body. He checked in via text while he was gone, and he was emotionally present when he was home. He wasn't always happy when he came back to us, but he wasn't the sullen, inebriated asshole he'd been before. This was exactly what he needed to be doing, for all of us. When he was sober and healthy and happy in himself, the rest of us were relaxed and could enjoy him more than we had in a very long time.

But by Monday, I was especially distracted. There was less than a week until the New Year. When Sam had been pressing me to make a commitment, Dr. Hill had asked me to wait until after the holidays. My time was almost up.

Sam and I had been relatively happy during the previous six weeks. We had turned a huge corner, both together and separately. For months, we'd been working on communication, and I felt confident that there were few, if any, skeletons still to be rattled. If we were going to move forward, I had to make that choice and take those first, tenuous steps with him.

Is that really what you want?

I didn't want to be without him. I loved our home and our family and how comfortable I could be with him. I saw monumental changes in him and knew he was working diligently to be the man I could be proud to call mine, whether as husband or friend.

But there were still so damn many issues outstanding. I didn't know if I wanted to be sexually monogamous. I didn't know if I could promise to never have contact with Alex again, or even if that was still something Sam would demand. I wanted to be able to do things and see things and experience things, and I didn't necessarily want to do them all with Sam. He never told me I was wrong to want something, only to *hide* that wanting from him, no matter how much I thought it would hurt him to share it. It wasn't that I wanted to exclude him from my life, or even small parts of it; I just needed to be sure I would have the freedom to take the lessons I'd learned over the previous year and live my life. If I ignored all of that and turned away from my new understandings of my world and of myself, the efforts and growth and hurts of that year would've been futile.

Alex had kept me in a box, but within those confines I could expose myself totally, free to explore the ever-expanding boundaries of my soul without fear of judgment. If he couldn't handle what he saw, all he had to do was close the box. It was how he handled his own soul.

Part of me still missed him. While my connection with Sam grew stronger every day, the connection with Alex wasn't fading. I wasn't talking to him, but I still thought of him often. I still wanted to hear him laugh and make fun of my nervous stammering when I didn't know what to say. I wanted him to call me and tell me to go buy this CD because it's so damn good. Sometimes, I still wanted to hear him call me Buttercup.

But as much as Sam wasn't Alex, *Alex wasn't Sam*. Alex had almost never been there at two in the morning when I needed to cry. In fact, he tried to avoid that as much as possible. He had a hard time embracing my intensity and my boisterous demand to sometimes be the center of attention, especially if I needed the encouragement as I battled with my own self-esteem.

And I couldn't get past the *history* with Sam. He was my first love. No matter how many years we'd been together, it was about all the things that had happened in that time. It was the laughter until our sides hurt, the cow that peed all over our car as we drove to Nashville, or the day I sneezed grits all over the wall. It was the months of shots and pills and tests to get pregnant, and the voicemail I left him at work, crying for him to call me the afternoon I found out it had all finally worked. It was the nights of rocking colicky babies and all the mornings of feeding the annoying cat we'd had since before we were married.

It was the thick, long eyelashes and the gray eyes that watched me intently, no matter what I was doing. It was the graceful, warm hands that felt perfect against my skin, no matter when or where they touched me. It was all the times he'd refused to let me leave our bed until he'd made me come.

It's the fact that he loves me, no matter what, even after everything that had happened.

I told him I was ready to talk.

"Okay, we'll talk tonight after my meeting."

I waited patiently for him to come home, staying up long past the time I wanted to be asleep. I gave him time to come in and get settled before he sat down to hear what I needed to say.

"The holidays are almost over. It's almost the first of the year. Dr. Hill asked me to be still and not make a decision until... soon. I've been worried about it, worried about how to move forward with you. There are still so many things we have to work out. I don't know how to do that and how to start the process of negotiating what our marriage looks like going forward. But I can't do that alone.

"I've said time and again that I didn't want to be without you," I continued. "What I know now, for sure, is that I want to be *with* you, and that's a very different think than just not being without you. I'm ready to do this together, to start moving again, as a couple. This is where I'd like to start our next session with Dr. Hill."

Sam sat on the couch with me, quietly contemplating what I'd said.

"I told my sponsor tonight that I knew you wanted to talk when we I got home. I told him my worst fear was that you would tell me you were ready to make a commitment. And it's not that I don't want to be with you—I do! I'm scared that I can't make a decision that's right. Every decision I've ever made has been tainted and sometimes downright *wrong*, because I was drunk and they led me to this awful place where nothing I did was right. I'm afraid that any choice I make right now will be the wrong one."

I had no idea how to respond to him. Just a month before, Sam had been pushing me to commit, to make the decision to do this with him. Now he was telling me that *he* wasn't ready? I didn't know what to say.

"Wow.   Um, that wasn't what I expected to hear," I said slowly, my mind churning.   "I understand.   I want you to feel comfortable and ready." I paused. "I'm here. When you're ready."

Just don't wait too long.

I was glad his crazy carousel had slowed down, but it felt like he was hinting that he wanted to take another ride. Looking back, I know he was telling me he was afraid he would fall down from the dizziness if he stepped off the easy spinning.

"Can we talk more about this with Dr. Hill at our next session?" he asked.

"Yeah, sure. That would probably be best. I need to go to bed anyway."

Nonchalantly, I turned off the lights and went with him to get ready for bed. I needed to retreat into sleep for a while, though this time I took him with me into that temporary escape. I needed to let my pounding heart rest, but I was choosing to find my respite next to my husband.

———————————

I went to the endocrinologist for my semi-annual check-up the next day.

"I was at a conference in Chicago last week," Dr. Naland started, as he came into the room, "and I probably mentioned you a dozen times."

"Why?" I laughed

He turned the in-room computer monitor toward me. "Six months ago, you were on half of your original metformin dose. Your total cholesterol was at 179. Now, forty pounds later, and on *no* medicine, your cholesterol is down to 151. Your triglycerides dropped from 121 to 79. Your bad cholesterol is down, but so is your good cholesterol. I expect to see that a little bit with fat loss, and it's still okay. Your Hemoglobin A1c, which is a marker for how controlled your blood sugar is, was at 5.5 on half your meds. That's perfect. It dropped to 5.4 on *no meds*.

"I'm at patient ten thousand, and I can count on both hands the number of patients who've done what you've done, Tierney. It *can* be done, but most people don't want to do it. I can't tell you how proud I am of what you've accomplished."

"I gotta say, I'm really proud of myself. I've worked really hard to get this far. I have another eight pounds to my goal weight, but I may drop that another ten to allow for maintenance calories and any regain that comes with that. I'm really more concerned about my body fat percentage now. I'm at thirty and want to be at about twenty-four. That's another four to five months, if I do it at the same rate I have been."

"Well, I think that's the smart way to think about it." He clicked on the screen to update my medical record. "Yeah, we're just taking this diabetes diagnosis off completely. You are definitely no longer diabetic."

I was giddy and glowing. I was off that nightmare of medicine, and I felt better physically than I had in years. But I was still worried about what was coming with Sam.

Sam went to his meetings on New Year's Eve. The boys were determined to stay up until midnight, and it was the first year we agreed to let them.

"Mom and Dad may be asleep," I'd said when they asked, winking at Sam, "but you guys can stay up all night if you want. Just don't come a-knockin' a midnight."

He and I had been apart for New Year's Eve the year before, and I was determined to not only kiss my husband at midnight but to be making love with him at the witching hour, to lay waste to my lingering superstitions and set an entirely new tone for the new year. Regardless of the momentousness of the night, it had been nearly two weeks since we'd been together, because of meetings and holidays and mild illness. I was getting a little worried.

Sam came home around ten that night, as the boys and I were just starting to watch *Peter and the Wolf*. I had very fond memories of a book-and-record of this story, of spending hours as a child with my little turntable, listening to Prokofiev's layered music and turning the brightly colored pages when the record beeped. Both boys were learning to play new instruments, and I was sure they would love the story and the music as much as I had.

But Sam went straight to the kitchen for a snack. The boys followed, begging for their own cinnamon toast with Daddy. He told them they had to eat it in the kitchen. I paused the movie and padded into the kitchen to take a Xanax.

"We just started watching a movie," I complained politely. Sam didn't seem to hear me over the cacophony of little boy excitement. "I guess we can watch it later."

As they were wiping away the last of their crumbs, Sam offered to take them outside to shoot off fireworks in the cul-de-sac.

"Yes!" they squealed in unison. They ran to put on shoes and jackets.

I could've joined them. I was more than welcome to go outside and blow up brightly-colored cardboard tubes. I felt slighted, though. Nevermind that I'd been with the boys for hours while he was gone, or that I was doing something with them. He swooped in and took over, changing our plan without even consulting me. They were his children, too, and he wanted to spend time with them. He didn't seem to want to spend the time with me.

"Wake me up before midnight," I said to Sam. "Make sure you kiss me when the clock strikes."

He smiled and nodded and kissed me before going out with the boys.

I went to sleep.

They woke me moments before the ball dropped in Times Square. We all piled onto the couch together and counted down with the announcer on TV. As *Happy New Year!* flashed across the television, I kissed my husband, sweet and soft and loving.

"*Ew*, do you guys have to do that in public?" Tripp complained.

We laughed and hugged our babies, wishing them a happy new year. We shooed them quickly to brush their teeth and get into bed, so we could be alone.

But Sam was tired. He was emotionally worn after an intense meeting, and it was late. As we lay in the dark, I didn't know if he was planning to cross the expanse of bed to find me.

"Not to be so crass, but are we going to have New Year's Eve sex?" I asked.

"I'm tired, and my head is hurting," he said gently. "I'm sorry. But it'll still be January first tomorrow."

Seriously?

I clinched my teeth and squeezed my eyes shut. *One... two... three....*

"But I *do* love you," he said sleepily.

I wanted to punch him in the fucking face.

I turned over in a mild huff and went to sleep.

We all slept late into the morning. After breakfast, I was still feeling out of sorts and told Sam I was going to the park to walk.

"Six Mile Sunday. I'll be back in a little while."

I was still seething from the night before. I thought I'd been pretty clear about wanting to set a new tone for us for 2012. I was hurt and frightened when he turned me down. As badly as I wanted to go into this new year together, doing our best to obliterate the last, there was no way I was reaching out from the hurt to convince him to be with me. When he didn't reach out, either, it felt like unadulterated rejection. I wasn't willing to degrade myself and beg for his attention, no matter how minute. If he didn't want me, fine, *fuck him*. I felt an ever-growing distance between the two of us again, and it scared the hell out of me.

Though there was a different reason, we were back in this cycle of Sam being gone until late, coming home by the time I was so tired that I needed to sleep for the next day's routine. It didn't matter that he was doing it for all the right reasons. I was growing more and more bitter that his regular absence meant I was forced to take on virtually all of the burden of the house and the children, plus some of the emotional turmoil of his recovery. My life was headed back to being all laid out in the light of day, full of laundry and dishes and minutiae that could only be resolved during business hours. I didn't like feeling that there was an expectation that I would make sure everything was taken care of. I would always try to make sure that happened, no matter what, but sometimes I needed a little extra effort, a little extra help, from him.

No one could tell us how long it might be before he wasn't at nightly meetings. His recovery was a one-day-at-a-time thing, but I was ready to move and be kinetic again. While I wasn't responsible for his recovery, it didn't get to stop me indefinitely, too. Sam wasn't ready to move yet, and I didn't know how to reconcile his needs with mine. Whereas I'd had an arbitrary deadline of "after the holidays", there was nothing like that for him. His recovery could, and probably would, take a lifetime. I couldn't wait on the sidelines of that forever, watching him get better while I got fat and boring again.

I couldn't make plans for going back to school full time. When I'd first expressed the interest, Sam had made it very clear that between work and the Program, he couldn't be expected to be responsible for the children if I had a night class. Spring break and summer vacation would be coming soon, which would mean I had to be available to keep the children during the day.

And what of my supposed trip to South by Southwest? Sam knew I wanted to go to Austin in March and have the experience of being in a new city, far from home, engulfed in new and well-loved music. I knew he was a little apprehensive about my seeing Alex again, a thousand miles from home. I hadn't heard from Alex, but I couldn't imagine he would be terribly comfortable with my being there, either. I thought about all of the people who had no relevance to him who would get to be there when he was, people he didn't give a damn about who would be getting his attention. And there was the issue of the poster and the art I'd spent hours bringing to fruition for Junkture; I wanted to be there to see it on display, even if no one else saw it. It made me mad and felt very, very unfair.

I quit walking after three-and-a-half miles. I was wasted and didn't see the point. It was great that I'd lost all this weight and gotten healthy, but now I was encumbered with all of this extra skin. I didn't know why I had even scheduled plastic surgery consults. I had no real expectation that Sam would help pay for it. He told me I was beautiful no matter what and but didn't seem to see the point or potential benefit. I didn't think he would ever help me come up with the tens-of-thousands of dollars I would need to get rid of my fat girl baggage. It was unimportant, of no benefit or use to him, so it wouldn't be worth his time or effort or understanding, especially after I'd already cost him so much.

I still didn't feel like talking. I didn't feel like opening and moving my mouth enough to actually use my words. But my girl heart was determined to talk to its BFF. It was a holiday, though, and I wasn't sure if she'd be home.

"Hello?" she answered.

"Hey."

"Hey. How are you?" She sounded concerned.

"Not good."

Tessa and I talked for an hour. I told her everything that was bothering me, about Christmas and New Year's and Sam's recovery, unleashing a torrent of soul-rendering self-pity.

"Have you talked to Sam about any of this?"

"Not really," I replied. "He was at a meeting, and I was asleep." I started to cry again.

"Okay. It sucks that Sam is gone so much, but you know why he's doing this. He's doing it for you and your children and for himself. He's doing it to make your life better, and he has to be healthy to do that."

"I know."

"So you're going to *paint*. You'll miss him while he's gone, but you can use that time productively and create something new and beautiful that *only you* can create. You're going to take the pain and the hurt and let it out on your canvas. And you're going to find a way to get your art out, into the world."

I wanted to believe her. I needed so badly for someone to push me, hard, in the right direction. And there was no one in the world that I trusted more than I trusted Tessa.

Tessa had been the first one to know about Alex. She was there with me when the seeds were sown and watered with vodka. She listened to my highs and lows, cheered me on and encouraged me, and had no qualms about telling me I was being a dumbass. If anyone knew what I needed to do when even I couldn't see it, it was Tessa.

"Okay," I conceded. I felt the tiniest bit of immediate relief. "Thanks for letting me talk this out."

"Of course. That's what I'm here for. I'm just glad I was here to take the call."

"Me, too. I love you."

"I love you, too."

Later in the week, we met with Dr. Hill.

"How were your holidays?" he asked.

I explained about Sam being gone for Christmas Eve and New Year's Eve, how I felt guilty for being upset that he was gone, as well as Sam's trepidation about making a choice to commit.

"I missed so much with my wife and my children, and I want to be able to spend as much time with them as possible," Sam expressed. "It's really frustrating when my sponsor demands that I be there for three hours each night. I'm missing everything I'm working hard *not* to miss."

"You need to talk with your sponsor about this," Dr. Hill advised. "Make sure he knows the strain this is putting on you. It won't go on forever, but there's no way to know for sure how long it will go on.

"Tierney, how are you handling all of this?"

I shrugged and tried to smile. "It's hard. He's just as physically unavailable as he was before. Now he's emotionally here, though. If I was concerned about it before, it's obvious now how much more aware he is of me and of us, after these last few days. I'll do what I gotta do to help him get through this."

In the last ten minutes, Sam said suddenly that he would like to talk about the divorce filing.

Looking toward Dr. Hill, he said, "I don't know what to do about this. I don't know if it needs to be amended or refiled." He glanced toward me. "I don't want to make assumptions for you."

Is he saying he wants to go ahead with the divorce?

I was stunned. Dr. Hill looked baffled. I dropped Sam's hand suddenly and turned toward him on the sofa.

"As far as I knew, you wanted to dismiss the case. You *told* me that's what you wanted!"

Calmly, Dr. Hill interjected. "Are you saying you still want to proceed with the divorce?"

I was still reeling, staring at him, slightly agape. "You *told* me," I sputtered, "that you thought it was the morally right thing to do, that you'd filed out of anger and rage and that you wanted to dismiss the case, even if I refiled the next day! If you think it's the right thing to do, no matter what, then you should do it."

Sam looked at me confused. "Uh! No!" He shook his head emphatically at me and at Dr. Hill. "No, I want to drop it! I just didn't want to make assumptions for you."

"But I *told* you I want to be with you! You're the one who said they were uneasy."

"I'm not uneasy about being with you, Tierney! I'm just unsure of how we agree to take on our life."

"Okay," Dr. Hill soothed, "you guys need to spend some time talking and thinking about what issues you think may be problematic going forward. You don't have to come to any decisions. It will give us a place to start working from next time."

We scheduled our next session and left.

In the parking lot, Sam turned to me. "I'm sorry. None of that came out right. I don't want to pursue the divorce. I want to drop it. I just want to make sure that's okay with you."

"Of course it is. Both because it's what you said you thought was right and because I didn't think that was where we were headed. I'm sorry. I'm rattled. You threw me."

"I'm sorry. No, I promise, I'll call my attorney today to start the paperwork."

It took another two weeks, but we received notification from the court that the judge had approved Sam's request to dismiss the case without prejudice.

I emailed my attorney to let her know we'd decided not to pursue separation.

"Best of luck to you both!" she wrote.

Sam and I were sitting on the deck the next morning.

"I just don't know where we are on big issues," I explained. "I don't know how to move forward, not knowing where you are. It's like I'm in my bubble of all possible outcomes, and you're in yours, and all I can do is bang around inside this bubble until you give me some idea of how to merge the two."

"Like what? Give me an example."

"Like Alex, for one. That's one of our biggest issues. I don't know if you're at one extreme of not wanting me to ever be in contact with him again, to the other extreme of it's okay for me to see him every six months and have sex with him and go on about our life."

"I know how I feel right *now*," Sam replied, "but I don't know how I'll feel about some things until we're in the moment, faced with them.

"What I *do* know is that I have three priorities of what will make me happy. First and most important is that *you* are happy and healthy. Whatever you want, whatever you need, to be happy in a healthy way, I will do whatever I can to support that.

"Second, I want to raise our boys to be happy and healthy men and enjoy that process *with you*.

"Third, I want *us* to be happy and healthy, to be able to communicate what we need and not have every difference be an intractable issue.

"If all of those things come together, then *I* am able to be happy and content."

———————————

After I finished the artwork for the Junkture poster, I went back to painting for me. I'd been painting regularly again, more still-lifes and acrylic recreations of old photographs. But now that I was almost at my goal weight, it was time to look at my body one more time.

I waited for a quiet morning without Sam and the boys at home. Like I had a year before, I took my phone into the bathroom and stripped quickly, pajamas piled on top of the bathroom scale. When I'd done this last, I was down thirty pounds from my heaviest weight. Now, I'd abandoned *another* seventy-eight pounds.

I examined my reflection in the full-length mirror again. I saw myself, but I also saw the old me, how I'd looked a year ago and how I'd looked even before that. Each iteration of me cascaded before my mind's eye simultaneously, the past and present converging in an infinite loop of reflections.

Where before I'd looked fat, now I looked athletic. Hips and thighs were substantially smaller. The thick, healthy muscles were well-defined and shapely but hidden beneath skin that was dimpled and sagging in ways that time would never correct. The breasts weren't as heavy or round, now held lower than ever before by puckering stretch marks. My nipples were still strawberry gum drop pink, still reacted quickly to my touch.

I took new photographs and transferred them to my laptop. I compared them to the older pictures, and I was startled by the difference. Like so many fat people, I'd never liked to have my picture taken. It was usually me with the camera in hand. The best pictures I could find were of me eighty pounds before, just at the beginning of my journey to reclaim myself.

It really was as stark a contrast as I remembered. And it was a *realistic* comparison I'd made in my mind. I could see the thin girl peeking out from underneath the excess, the remaining baggage, and I wanted to give her a chance to *be*. I could see Tierney in that girl, but I had to really look for her around the eyes. She looked unhappy and uncomfortable in her own damn skin, even if she had great purple-on-blond hair.

But she and I had jumped down this rabbit hole together, no idea where we were going. We laid the path of our choosing, never sure of where it was leading but always willing to follow it, no matter the destination.

My search for my *self* had led me down an incomparably twisted and tumultuous path, knowing there were profound lessons to be learned along the way. I hadn't known where I was going or where I would end up. For me, it was loud and raucous and wrought with tumultuous exploration.

It's never about the destination. It's all about the journey.

And it finally hit me: my ultimate destination was *Me*.

I chose the best of the new pictures, the one most angled and composed like the fatter image I'd chosen to paint last time. I tacked the printed version to the wall behind my easel. I didn't need to do a gesture drawing; I knew exactly how to do what I wanted.

I deliberately mixed the paint colors, remembering the minute errors I'd made in palette choice the last time. I carefully drew the outline of my new, still-imperfect body.

You're not so fat now, Tierney.

I reminded myself to be genuine and guileless, to reflect the transformed shape as accurately as possible. I was calm, not as agitated as I'd been before, now comfortable with confronting my body and my form even when I didn't like what I saw. There was realistic beauty in my body, and I was confident that I could transfer that from my mind to the canvas.

Although I was veracious in conveying my body, I was genuinely unhappy with the new form. It didn't matter that I could do fifty sit-ups with a twenty-five pound disc weight on my belly, or that I had made the elliptical trainer my bitch. Even when I was telling myself and everyone else that I was losing weight for health reasons, there had always been an aspect of sheer *vanity* to my efforts. I wanted, just once in my life, to see myself as *beautiful*.

I scheduled consults with four surgeons but loved the second one so much I canceled the last two. She and I were about the same age and had grown up on the same stomping grounds. We clicked immediately, and she was very highly recommended. Body reconstruction was her specialty.

As I stood naked before her and her full-length mirror, she took all kinds of measurements. She showed me exactly where she thought she would make incisions and how the procedures would go.

There would be a massive abdominoplasty, a tummy tuck, that would wrap around to my back to take the excess skin from my hips. The scar would be hidden by even a bikini. The Mommy bulge and my bothersome hips would be gone, and the lift would tighten up my ass. Scars for the brachioplasty to remove the wobbling skin under my arms, my bat wings, would run from my elbow to my arm pit. She would make a series of cuts on my breasts, called a lollipop incision, to do a lift and augmentation. It would bring the breasts back to their original position and restore the fullness I'd lost going from a 42DD to a 36D. She wanted to do liposuction on my thighs at the same time she did the body lift, to prep them for later removing the jiggly, loose skin.

It would mean two or three procedures.

"We can't do them all at one time," she explained. "Your lymphatic system will freak out if we do the body lift and the thigh lift at the same time. You'll have to wait six months between those. But we could do your upper body work in the middle, or you could combine it with the medial thigh work."

I'd originally thought it would be late spring before I would be able to start the work. The more I thought about it, the more I wanted to start as soon as possible.

"It would be awesome," I told Sam one morning after the boys were at school, "to be able to get the first surgery out of the way now. Six months later, I could do the rest and go into my fortieth birthday with an entirely new body. All of my fat girl baggage would be gone by Tierney Day.

"I know you think I'm being ridiculous. I know it doesn't matter to you, all this skin and sagging. But it bothers me, and I hope you'll at least consider trying to work with me on this."

"Tierney, I understand why It bothers you. No, it doesn't bother me. Quite the contrary! I think you're gorgeous and beautiful no matter what. Having lost all of this weight, your confidence is higher than I've ever seen it. And that's beautiful unto itself. I can only imagine how much more confident you'll be after this. My concern is that someone...."

"*Say it.*"

"*Someone* will come back. *Someone* will realize that you were amazing *before* the surgery, but now... after that...."

I stood from the couch and walked around to face Sam.

"Listen to me. Anyone who would come to me and say, 'You were pretty great when you were fat, but now that you're skinny and hot, *now* I want you!', that person wouldn't be worth my time of day.

You of *all* people know my issues, know why my weight was a problem and how it happened and what it means for me to conquer this. *No one* can *ever* rival that, Sam. No one can ever understand it the way that you can, and that means more to me—that you *get* it— than almost anything else in the world."

He kissed me hard. "Wait right here."

He turned through the kitchen and down the hall. I heard him moving around in the back of the house but didn't know what he was doing.

"Close your eyes!" he called from the bedroom.

I did as he asked and waited as I heard him coming back into the den. He kissed me again and slipped something over my head. *A blindfold!*

He took me by the hands and led me to the very center of the open den. He slipped my shirt over my head and dropped my yoga pants to the floor.

"You're beautiful, Tierney. Your face...." He caressed my cheek.

"Your neck...." He kissed that spot I love, the pressure point of utter bliss, right by my collar bone.

He reached behind me and unhooked my bra, tossing it aside. "Your voluptuous breasts.... They are... beautiful!" He sucked my nipple into his mouth, and I bit my lip, clasping my hands anxiously behind my back.

Sam ran his fingers along my ribs and down my hips, peeling my panties away. "The curve of your stomach...," he ran his palm along the Mommy bulge, the part I hated the most, "...how it goes so lusciously down to that delicious pussy."

He tucked his fingers inside me, and I gasped, his other arm steadying me as I stumbled backwards. He pushed me back toward the couch and knelt in front of me, grabbing me forcefully by the hips and pulling me forward until my ass hung just off the edge of the cushions.

The soft blindfold shifted above my line of sight. I could've opened my eyes to watch him, to see him, but I needed to let him do this. I needed to let him show me what he loved, in his own way.

He spread me open, pressing his palms against the folds of skin, holding me tightly how he wanted. I felt the tip of his cock yearning into me, and he pushed hard, fucking me there in the bright afternoon, telling me all the while that I was lovely and gorgeous and beautiful. I came with his mouth on mine and my fingers curled into his soft hair.

While I really wanted to start my surgeries as soon as possible, I didn't think we'd be able to afford it so quickly. Sam had a plan. He moved some things around, and we were able to pay for my body lift and lipo almost immediately.

I scheduled the surgery for February first.

———————————

Sam was unexpectedly called away to investigate a top secret hacking incident, the weekend before my surgery. I was getting more and more stressed, knowing what was looming ahead for the next few weeks. I quit smoking and was irritable and agitated.

He missed his flight home from Los Angeles, just twelve hours before I was supposed to leave for the surgery center. A power substation near the airport blew and took out all of the traffic lights for miles. We texted back and forth, furiously trying to get him on a flight that would land in Atlanta before noon the next day. I found a redeye leaving at 10:55 PST.

Sam Johnson
Jan 31st 5:45 PM

I am first on standby

> **Ok. Worst case scenario is you meet me at the surgery center. It's okay. Just breathe.**

Thanks :)

> **I loooooooooove you**

I love you. Sorry for the snafu. Not what you need right now...

> **As long as you're there when I wake up, it's okay. It'll be an adventure!**

I had the boys' favorite babysitter come to spend the night with us. She would be there to help with them in the morning, back when they got home from school. Sam and I were both relieved to have someone close and trustworthy taking care of them while we were across town for so long.

Because Sam wasn't there, I had the sitter help me with an arts and crafts project. I spread a sheet of white paper, cut from a long roll, onto the kitchen floor. Anna traced the outline of my pre-surgery body, carefully running the pencil along my almost-naked form. I wanted to be able to remember what it looked like before I altered it irreparably.

"I'll do this between each procedure," I explained to her as I lay on the hard floor. "I'll do it one more time after I heal from the last surgery. I'll be able to see them all lined up together, layered in different colors."

I took what would be my last shower for a week. I wouldn't be able to bathe or wash my long hair until after my first post-op appointment, when the first bandages would be removed. I ran my hands across my bulging, lumpy belly and hips, up and down my flabby thighs, and under my neck—everywhere that would be addressed by my surgeon the next morning. I felt all of the years of physical baggage one last time.

I stood under the warm spray, my hand on my belly, talking to my body. "We're going in for surgery tomorrow," I told her, out loud. "It's going to hurt, and you're going to be scared. It's not an assault. We're *choosing* to do this. We're choosing to let the past go, to let the bad habits die and fall away. You'll be under for a long time tomorrow, asleep. Remember everything that led us to this point and *let it go*."

Sam landed just before six the next morning. He rushed home, took a shower, and drove me to the surgery center across town. He stayed with me in pre-op, laughing at me after I'd had my Versed shot and tried to sing "I Wanna Be Sedated", half a second behind every note. He took pictures of my Sharpie-covered body.

"I look like a topographical map!" I joked in slight slur.

My surgery lasted seven hours. I spent the night at the surgery center and went home the next day. Percocet every four hours kept most of the pain away, but not all. I felt like I'd been hit by a truck. I was sorer and in more discomfort than I'd been after either of my childbirths.

The surgeon told us she took about five pounds, including fourteen inches of skin.

"Fourteen inches, five pounds!" Like a baby.

And in some ways it was like birthing another baby. It took time and effort to get her here. I cut her, almost literally, from my loins. *I* may have been a pretty baby and pretty little girl, but *she* started to grow into something hideous and ugly, born from trauma and miscare. I named her Medusa. Like Perseus, I took my mirrored shield and slayed that fucking monster.

Sam was spectacular through the entire ordeal. He took meticulous care of me, making sure I ate and drank and took my medicine. He slept on the couch next to my recliner, close-by if I needed even the most minute thing. He rubbed my swollen feet and emptied my four drain tubes. When the narcotics wreaked havoc on my system, he took me to the emergency room for an unexpected catheter.

The last of the drain tubes came out on Valentine's Day. He promptly took me to the mall and bought me two-hundred dollars' worth of lingerie. It was the first year I didn't feel like I'd been taunted by the Valentine's Day curse.

But, just like every other time I thought my life had settled and that I was on solid ground, something shifted.

The Valentine's Day curse was coming—it was just delayed.

Chapter 38

I received an unexpected email from Indulgema Melodio, inviting me to a private signing party for Seth Wiezel. The label was finally flourishing, and there was money to hire Paulie's protégé. The show would be happening on the Monday before South by Southwest—two days before I was scheduled to fly to Austin.

It was happening in San Antonio, at the Coda.

"I'm sorry I didn't tell you before," Seth called to tell me. "I couldn't say anything to *anyone*, even my parents, until the deal was inked. I hope you're not mad."

"Of course not! I'm so happy for you! You know I'll be there if I can."

I forwarded the message to Sam.

"You should go with me!" I told him excitedly. "We could go out on Monday. You could come home on Tuesday, and I could go on to Austin. It would be so much fun!"

"It sounds great," Sam said. "It's a good opportunity to see Seth."

"I was kind of surprised to get the invite, honestly."

"But Seth's your friend. You were there for his CD release. Of course he would want you there!"

"I know, but...."

"It's *obvious* this is for you," Sam continued. "You were there to support him early on. But I think, for me, the timing is bad. You should still go and have fun. Between your surgery and my trip to California, the boys have been tag-team parented and baby-sat a lot lately. I don't know that I would be able to relax and enjoy *anything*, between worrying about the boys and worrying about Alex."

"The boys will be fine!" I interjected. "They liked going with my parents for that weekend after the surgery. I was with them the entire time you were in L.A. They're old enough to have Mom and Dad both gone for a day."

"I know. The part of me that really wants to go with you says it's not a big issue. But another part of me knows I'm going to need help and meetings while you're in Austin, and travel is always stressful for me anyway. I would feel a little guilty about leaving them without a parent, and I think it would bother me the entire time. I think it's easier for *me* if I don't go. Just make sure Anna's available to keep the boys, so I can go to some meetings while you're gone."

I didn't like the idea of missing Seth's party. This opportunity wouldn't come again, but I needed to support Sam.

"Then I'll decline. We won't go."

Sam shook his head. "No, *you* should go. It sounds awesome, you know you have to go, and I know you'll love it."

I wanted to go to San Antonio and support my friend. I was looking forward to my five days in Texas, on my own, and this would be an added bonus. It would be easy enough to change my flight and get a rental car and drive over to Austin. I scrounged online for a hotel. There were a few options, but the best, most convenient choice was the Marriott.

I was apprehensive about being there again. There was no way to avoid the reminders of Alex and everything that had happened when I stepped right back into the same place. It would be ten months later, and I wasn't the same girl who'd checked into the hotel that night. I told myself that I was stronger and smarter and wiser than I'd been in May.

And as far as I knew, Alex wouldn't even be there.

I was finally cleared for light cardio and took to the treadmill three weeks after my body lift. I was surprised at how much the core muscles were engaged with virtually everything I did. The day before surgery, I'd been able to walk five miles at a four-mile-per-hour pace with no problem. Three weeks later, thirty minutes at three-miles-per-hour sent me home to take a two-hour nap.

The abdominal muscles were still sore and swollen, but it was getting better every day. I was sent home in a double layer of compression garments to help the skin retract and hold its shape after surgery. I was allowed to drop the outer layer and found that the other one was getting too loose. So were my old jeans.

Looking at my naked body in the bathroom mirror, I was still shocked to see how *flat* my belly was. I couldn't remember a time in my life when there wasn't a little bulge there. More than the flatness, I was surprised by the definition. My surgeon had told me that she could see the six-pack abs under the skin when she tightened them. Now that the swelling was beginning to subside, I could plainly see the outline of the muscles under newly-taut skin. My hip bones protruded where they'd only been buried under fat before.

The strangest part of all was my belly button. The incision was made just above my pubic bone, running almost all the way around my body, along my hips and toward my lower back. No one even bothered to count how many stitches there were. The surgeon removed six inches of skin *up* from the front incision, which meant I had to get a whole new belly button.

I *liked* my old belly button. It was ridiculously deep—I'd often put a marble in it just for decoration—and quite lovely. The new one was well-crafted, new skin stretched across and through the original opening. It was pretty but seemed strange and foreign. And your belly button is one of the first body parts you *make*. Any parent knows it's a big deal when their baby finds their belly button. It's a sweet, intimate part of a child.

"But I gave you that belly button!" my mom whined, half-joking.

"It's the same one," I told her. "It's just been renovated."

I went shopping for new jeans the week before my trip. My weight was a little less than it had been the morning of surgery, but my clothes were definitely getting too big. Even with the extra layer of girdle, I kept having to pull my jeans up past the point where Medusa used to live. At the mall, I had to stop and buy a belt just to get through the day.

"I don't need a bag," I told the sales girl. "Just take the tag off, and I'll put it on now."

When I was so heavy, I mostly shopped at the plus size stores. In the last few years, more and more stores and designers had begun offering plus size departments, but for years there were only a few Fat Girl shops from which to choose. The clothes were often ill-fitting on my Amazonian frame—pants and sleeves too short, shirts too tight across my broad shoulders and very ample breasts.

I was almost overwhelmed with all of the new options available to me for buying clothes. I could find something I liked in almost any store I passed. My thinner body was the key to opening the floodgates of normal-sized clothes. If I tried something on and didn't love everything about the way it fit or looked, I didn't have to buy it. I would almost certainly find something else within a few minutes of looking elsewhere.

I tried on twenty-two pairs of jeans before I found the new, smaller ones that I liked the best. I called Tessa and my mom to tell them I'd shrunk again. It was the smallest size I could remember having ever worn.

"Size ten!" I squealed to Mom on the phone.

"I hate you!"

Sting!

"Wow," I replied calmly, "that's really supportive, Mom. Thanks."

"Well, I don't *really*," she countered nervously. "I'm proud of you. But I hate you right now."

"Okay. I gotta go. I'll talk to you later."

I didn't go off on her. I was mildly hurt and angry by her comments, though I wasn't the least bit surprised. It was, sadly, more of what I'd come to expect from her. The difference was I'd finally had the courage to *say* something about it, to call her out on her backhanded support.

I got home from shopping and checked my email. There was another message from Indulgema Melodio about Seth's party.

Junkture would be playing at the event.

Having not played together in public for nine months, they were gathering in Texas for rehearsals ahead of South by Southwest. They were using Seth's event as a private dress rehearsal for the weekend show.

Sam was in Texas on business. It was a command performance for the president of the company, to clean up someone else's mistake. There'd been a potentially damaging error and subsequent breach, and it would impact the company's stock price dramatically if it wasn't remedied quickly. Sam had been tapped to be the one to fix it.

He was on his way home, flying somewhere between Houston and Atlanta, when I got the news.

Alex will be in San Antonio.

Tessa was quiet when I called to tell her. She said nothing for a moment, long enough for me to think something was wrong with the phone, and then she burst into raucous laughter.

"I'm sorry," she gasped, "but if you don't laugh about it, you'll stick your head in the oven or something, and you're too pretty to be Sylvia Plath."

"There's no other way this could've gone," I giggled morosely. "Honestly, this is the universe's way of giving me a giant-ass raspberry. With my luck, they'll check me into the same hotel room."

"*Of course* they will. Really, Tierney, your life is *implausibly* tragicomedy, but I'd much rather watch from a distance than live your craziness."

It was like a weird, cosmic do-over had just been dropped in my lap. I would be in San Antonio, at the same hotel, with Alex in my immediate proximity.

If it had just been Seth's event, there was no reason to think Alex would be there. He wasn't likely to travel early for the show, leaving Talia and Amber any longer than necessary. Paul would be there, definitely, and maybe Max and Charlie. I hadn't seen any of them since May, since before everything had exploded. I'd been looking forward to having the chance to see them and put any initial discomfort behind me before being confronted by Alex in Austin.

I had to tell Sam, and I expected him to freak out. I knew he wouldn't be comfortable with my going, and I couldn't blame him. I was ready to give up the trip, or to have him come with me. Either way, it wasn't going to be what we had originally anticipated.

He didn't get home until late that evening. We hadn't seen each other in a week, and I wasn't ruining our first night back together with talk of Alex Wheeler. I waited until the boys were gone to school the next morning to let him know what had happened.

"I forwarded an email to you," I started, "that I got yesterday afternoon. Um, Junkture's going to play Seth's signing party."

Sam leveled his gaze at his feet.

"I didn't know. When we agreed I'd go and I booked this trip, I had *no* idea he would be there. I didn't tell you last night, because I didn't want to hit you with that as soon as you got home." He nodded. "I *swear* I had no idea, Sam. So either you can go *with* me, or I can just *not* go. I'm okay with it, either way. Really. I mean, I want to be there for Seth, but this wasn't what I had in mind for next week."

Sam was quiet for a long minute.

"I think you should go," he said finally.

Really? "Then you should go with me." *Please.*

"I don't see why his being there should change our plans. This is still a special opportunity for you, Tierney. His being there shouldn't change that."

He was actively using what he'd learned through the Program. We'd talked a lot over the previous few months about how fighting Fate had created all of this extra tension in our lives, how sometimes you just had to let out-of-your-control things happen and not try to change their outcomes. Fate was again forcing me to see what it thought I needed to see, and there was a lesson to be learned somewhere in this bubbling quagmire.

It was settled. I would still go to San Antonio on Monday, then on to Austin on Wednesday for five days. It was the longest I would have been away from home and the kids, on my own in a strange city. It was a little scary. Could I handle this—being out of my natural territory, close to Alex, and not screw something up?

Yes, you can. You know what you have to do.

They were Alex's words from months before, but it was *my* voice I was hearing. I was hearing myself, reminding me that I had the knowledge and tools and wisdom to do this. I was strong enough and brave enough to confront these fears directly and to conquer them in a way that would make others proud, but also myself.

Put your big girl panties on and deal with it.

All of the lessons of the previous eighteen months were about to be tested. Trusting myself and my ability to direct my life. Speaking up and saying what I wanted and how I felt. Letting the grown-up Tierney not be controlled by the scared little girls inside.

My bravado was wearing thin.

As the date got closer and closer, I was feeling more and more agitated. I wasn't sure Alex would even talk to me. I didn't have any reason to think he would outright ignore me, but there was always that possibility, given everything that had happened. I didn't know if he'd even been back to Texas since May, though I knew he'd seen Paul and Max and Charlie since then. It would be a tense situation, and he could react by being a dick to me. It was unlikely but not out of the realm of possibility.

The other thing making me hesitate was the overwhelming sexual tension between Alex and me. It had been hard as hell in October to turn away from that. We'd both felt it from the moment we saw each other—probably from the time we'd agreed to meet— and I knew damn well it would always be there. I hadn't gone to

Nashville with the intention of sleeping with Alex, and I wasn't planning to do it again in San Antonio. But there was no way I wouldn't feel the physical desire when I saw him, whether or not my heart would want to entertain the thought.

"I got your back," Seth told me.

"You'll be busy, Hammer. I can't be glued to your side all night. Maybe I should just not come. Maybe it's best for everyone if I stay away from this."

"Tierney, stop being a pussy and pack your fucking bag! Nothing's going to happen. If Alex is a dick to you to try to distance himself from it, he'll just look like a posturing, egomaniacal prick. Just *come* and *have fun*!"

Sam was going to nightly meetings, and I was painting. I did my best to stay distracted from what was coming.

We saw Dr. Hill for the first time in two months on the Friday before my trip. We caught him up quickly on my surgery and recovery, how things had been between us since our last session. In general, we were doing very well. We were intimate and communicating and enjoying each other.

"But I'm worried about this trip Tierney's taking," Sam admitted. "When we first talked about her going to South by Southwest, I was supposed to go with her. It was expensive for her to be gone, and I wasn't going to be able to get there until the weekend, which would've meant a lot more expense. I decided not to go. She was determined to go to Austin, so I made it happen. Then this opportunity came up for her to go to San Antonio again. Now that I know *he's* going to be there, I'm just not comfortable with it."

"I offered, repeatedly, *not* to go!" I argued. "I tried to get you to come *with* me! Besides, he'll be there in Austin for the show on Saturday. You knew that the entire time."

"I know, but it's different in San Antonio. It's the same place, the same circumstances, and that voice inside me that I didn't listen to last year, the one that told me something was wrong, is *screaming* at me again that this isn't right.

"I'm worried because we haven't been in counseling in a while, and we haven't had a chance to talk about these lingering issues between us. There are all these things we still haven't come to an agreement on, about how to go forward from here. It doesn't make me feel very confident about Tierney going back to this situation when I know these huge things are still unresolved."

There it was. We'd still not addressed whether or not we were moving forward as sexually monogamous, and he was worried about my seeing Alex with that hanging over us. Sam knew what that sexual tension was like—he was there the night we first came face-to-face—and he'd seen the gory details of our relationship over and over.

"What will you do to stay connected while you're apart?" Dr. Hill asked, looking at me.

"We text a lot while we're apart. More than just what's going on in our day. We can't always talk, so we send a lot of messages back and forth when one of us is traveling." I shrugged. "We try to talk on the phone every day, but it doesn't always work out that way."

"What about a talisman?" he suggested. "What if you gave each other something to hang on to while you're apart? Then you'd give it back when you reunite."

I liked the idea. It would be something tangible to hang on to if I felt unsure or scared.

Sam didn't seem moved by the thought. Dr. Hill sensed his hesitation.

"I'll also suggest that you each write the other one a letter before you leave. Something heartfelt and personal. Neither of you gets to open it until the next day, or later that evening while Tierney's at this event. Do you think that would work?"

Sam and I had been able to open up and share a lot of difficult things when we emailed each other during emotionally charged periods. I knew immediately that I wouldn't email him or type the letter. I would take the time to handwrite it and tell him everything I needed him to know.

"I think that would be okay," Sam agreed cautiously.

But I was still upset about his mentioning the money for the trip. Yes, we'd talked about the added expense of his flying to Austin, but the hotel was paid for no matter what. Changing my flight to San Antonio was cheap, and I had enough credit card reward points to cover two nights at the hotel and a rental car to get me to Austin. As far as I was concerned, money had never been a determining factor in his decision not to go with me. It had always boiled down to the boys, and whether or not he wanted to put himself in an emotionally-charged situation in such close proximity to alcohol.

We left Dr. Hill's office and went on about the business of our day. We didn't see much of each other until that night, after he got home from his meeting.

"Are you okay?" Sam asked me on the deck.

"Not really. I feel like you threw me under the bus at Dr. Hill's today."

"*How*? What did I do?"

"You kept talking about the money and the cost. You made it sound like I demanded to go and that you didn't have a choice, that somehow I twisted your arm into letting me go. That's not how it was at all! And as far as not working on some of our big issues, I pushed you for the last month to schedule a session. I asked you over and over to look at your schedule."

"I know it's my fault we didn't get back after your surgery. I'm sorry if it seemed like I was griping about the money. That's not what I was saying at all. I was trying to explain that I'm really worried about this trip, Tierney. It's so much like last year, when you were telling me how important it was for you to go, how you couldn't live without it. It's the same place, the same hotel, the same people. I don't see what's changed."

"*I*'ve changed, Sam! I'm not the same girl that planned to go to Texas and do what I did! I'm stronger and smarter and just not the fucking same!"

He said nothing. He didn't argue that I was wrong, but he also didn't assure me that I was right.

"I don't think it's a good idea," he said flatly.

I stood up suddenly, pacing the deck. "This is *bullshit*! I *knew* it was a trick! I *knew* you would do something like this!"

"Like *what*? What am I doing?"

"You're freaking out, and I don't have a choice but *not* to go! *Fine*! I will cancel my goddamn trip to make you happy. The whole thing! But don't you *dare* ever mention the money of this to me again! I don't want to hear one goddamn word about how it cost you two thousand dollars for nothing!"

I turned to go inside. I was angry and starting to shake, but I didn't want to retreat. I wanted him to assure me that he believed in me and that he knew it would be okay, no matter how scared he was. I wanted him to say that he trusted me to do this. I was unsure enough of myself and needed to feel his support.

"No! I'm not saying you shouldn't go to Austin! You *should*."

"That makes no fucking sense, Sam! He'll still be in Austin. I'll still see him there."

"You don't have to talk to him."

"*What*? Of course I have to talk to him! That would be unconscionably rude to just ignore him in front of a thousand people. He may just ignore me anyway."

"He won't. You two will always be pulled into each other's orbits. You have the same interests and shared circles. No matter how far apart you are, there will always be something that brings you back to the other's proximity."

"I'm not so sure!" I laughed derisively. "But this trip has nothing to do with him. I want to see Seth. This is a big deal for him. And I would like to see my band, definitely. Alex or not, that's been my favorite music for twenty years. And I want the chance to prove I can do this. To prove it to myself and to you. I *can* do this, Sam, and if I don't take this opportunity, I'll never know."

"There will be other opportunities, Tierney. You'll get another one on Saturday. But *this* situation.... You can't go into it and promise me nothing will happen."

He knew I wouldn't promise him anything unless I could be sure about what would happen. I was having a hard enough time convincing *myself* I was sure I'd be okay. I didn't have the strength to pacify Sam.

I started to cry. "I can't deal with this right now. I'm *choosing* to retreat and ignore this until I can calm down. I'm going to bed." I jerked the back door open and stormed down the hall.

I had to decide something pretty quickly. *Am I going or not?* Sam wouldn't be happy if I went. I wouldn't be happy if I stayed, but I didn't want to upset him needlessly. I was pissed that he was waiting until the last minute to voice these concerns, especially after we'd discussed it when it first came up. I offered repeatedly and honestly not to go, and he'd shut me down at every turn.

I wasn't sure that I could take the weight of my choices flying in the face of what Sam wanted and making him so uncomfortable. Hadn't I done enough damage? Was it best if I stayed away? Most importantly, I didn't want my actions or inactions to impact Sam's sobriety. I was tired of feeling unsure of myself and my choices because of how others might react to them.

It felt, again, like it would be so much easier and safer if I retreated into my old shell. I didn't like feeling that way, but I couldn't be the one to hurt Sam again. I would rather fuck myself up than put him through all of that again.

I was too upset and too tired to make a rash decision and decided to sleep on it.

I padded back down the hall, still crying, and found Sam sitting on the sofa, watching television.

"Look," I started, "I'm upset. I'm angry. But it doesn't mean I don't want to talk to you. I don't want you to sleep on the couch or not come to bed. I don't want to wake up in the morning and not talk to you."

"I don't feel like doing that," he said gently.

"Okay. Then come to bed soon and hold me."

He nodded, and I kissed him goodnight.

Chapter 39

Frankie called the next morning as I was leaving the gym. I sat on a curb at the far end of the parking lot, luxuriating in the warm sun and quiet breeze.

"Francesca! I was afraid you'd fallen off the face of the Earth!"

"I might as well have," she laughed. "Spring Break started yesterday, so I finally have a chance to breathe. I'm sorry I haven't called in ages. Tell me what's going on. How are things with Sam?"

I made a non-committal grunt and started to laugh. "Settle in, Moonshine. There's so much that's happened."

It took half an hour to catch her up on the *Happenings of Tierney*. I told her about Sam's erratic behavior—

"*Ugh!*"

—and about my trip to Nashville—

"*Did you fuck him? How was Jules?*"

—about my surgery—

"*I saw the pictures of your new belly button! Awesome!*"

—and about the trip to Texas, including all of the brouhaha over seeing Alex in San Antonio again.

"He's so afraid that I'll be pulled back into Alex's orbit," I said. "That's already happened."

"Yeah, and you guys collided all over the fucking galaxy."

"True, but I'm doing my damnedest to turn all of that ethereal debris into something beautiful, you know?"

Frankie asked, "Tierney, what are you afraid of? Honestly? Take Sam out of it for a second, and tell me what you're really scared of."

I sighed, gazing across the mostly-empty suburban parking lot. "I'm afraid of what happens when I see him. I'm afraid the scared little girl inside of me who needs that attention and that approval will come squealing to the forefront, you know? The *grown-up me* has got this; she can totally see him and be comfortable in her big girl panties. It's the *teenaged me*, with her rainbow hair and sexy black boots that will be tempted."

"Is that what you want?" she pressed. "To be tempted and to fuck him again?"

"No. *I don't know.* I mean, I don't *want* to go to that place. The emotional fallout of coming back from that again would kill me. But my vagina wants what my vagina wants. I can't help how it feels when it sees him."

Frankie giggled. "Okay, here's what you do. *Talk to yourself.* Put your hand on your heart and *tell* that scared girl that you're handling it. Remind her that you're a grown-ass woman and you can handle seeing an old lover and maintaining your strength and beauty in this. Touch your heart and tell yourself these things. It will help. I promise."

"You might be right," I said flatly, "but I think it's the things I tell myself with my hand on my vagina that get me into trouble."

I was afraid that I wasn't really as strong and brave as I led everyone, including myself, to believe. I was scared the *Pretense of Tierney* wouldn't be formidable enough to keep the attraction to the rock star at bay. But deep down, I *knew* I could do this. My head was questioning it, but my heart was absolutely confident in its resolute ability not to let Alex's sheer presence spin me out of control again.

Sam and I didn't discuss it again that day. Anna was coming to babysit the boys so we could get in a Date Night before I left town. I wanted to enjoy our evening, no matter what it entailed. We could tackle this other issue tomorrow.

Date Night turned out to be ribs and guns. I wore a new drop-waist black sweater dress and three-inch heels. We stopped at Sam's favorite barbecue place, and I made a point to order the messiest, manliest thing on the menu. I was a hot mess, dolled up and covered in spicy sauce, licking my fingers clean in the middle of the restaurant.

He took me to his favorite indoor gun range. I hadn't shot a gun in almost twenty years, since I'd taken a shooting class as my P.E. credit in college. Sam went to the range regularly and brought his Glock and his AR-10 rifle for us to shoot, plus a small revolver that had belonged to his dad. He rented a .22 semi-automatic for me to try.

No one was more surprised than he was when my first ten rounds were all within a space of the center of the target.

"Nice group," he said slowly, "*Really nice.* And your fourth bullet went right through your third hole."

I shot dead center on the X with his .40.

"You totally would've killed that guy," he laughed after he saw my four shots with the assault rifle. Three to the head, one to the chest.

All while wearing heels and heavy pink lip gloss.

We went home and *fucked.* It wasn't long, and it wasn't romantic, but it may very well have been *the* best sex ever of our relationship. I felt good about leaving town with things like this.

While he was gone to his meeting on Sunday night, I packed my bag for my trip the next morning. I chose a new purple t-shirt dress and my boots for the San Antonio show. I packed my pink elephant t-shirt and jeans for the day after, just in case I did end up seeing Alex. The thought of being the pink elephant in the room made me laugh to myself.

I found the talismans I wanted to leave and to take. I had an old penny that I'd found on the ground one afternoon in a parking lot. It had been dropped and run over so many times that it was almost indistinguishable as currency. It was rough and scarred from the friction, the shiny finish almost completely worn away. Only tiny splinters of copper still shone along the edges, now worn and jagged in its abandon.

Sam had a hematite ring that had been his before he and I were a couple. It had been in my jewelry box for years, sitting and doing nothing. But hematite has the mystical properties of grounding and protection. Supposedly it makes us feel safe and secure, endowing us with courage and strength. I still wasn't wearing a wedding band—neither was he—but I wanted to take this and wear it while I was away from home.

I also sat down after the boys went to bed and wrote a letter to my husband. I reminded him that I loved him, that I was thankful for him and our life, and that I didn't ever want to do anything to screw that up again.

You are my breath. You and our life are my reason for everything.

I promise to think of you before I act.

I promise not to do anything that won't make you proud of me.

I promise not to do anything that won't make me proud of myself.

I promise to bring my heart home to you.

I sealed the letter in an envelope and tucked it into my nightstand until later.

Sam came home about ten o'clock. I was sitting on the deck, listening to the warm evening.

"How was your meeting?" I asked.

"Good. How are things here?"

"Fine."

"So you've decided to go? I see you packed your bag."

I nodded. "I was waiting for you to get home to talk about it."

I planned to tell him how I knew I could be a big girl and do this, how I trusted myself to go safely into this situation and enjoy it and come out whole. I wanted to explain the talismans I chose and to give him the letter, to be opened just before I was supposed to leave the hotel for the venue. I wanted to take him to bed and make love to him and sleep curled next to him until it was time to go.

"I think it's a stupid idea for you to do this, Tierney," he said evenly. "I don't just think it's a bad idea; I think it's a *terrible* idea. I think it's dangerous for you and for us if you go into this situation."

I stared at him in the moonlight.

"I don't think you should go," he reiterated.

I was silent for a moment.

"You tell me *now*, twelve hours before I'm supposed to be on a plane, that you think I shouldn't go? What the fuck?"

"I tried to tell you Friday that I was having a hard time with it. My insides are screaming at me that it's bad, that you shouldn't do it."

"Your insides don't get to dictate how I live my life! What are you so afraid of? That I'll fuck him? *I'm not going to fuck him!* I'm not going to get sucked into the emotion of him again!"

"I don't think you can help it, Tierney. I don't think you can be in his orbit without getting sucked in."

In the peppery light, Sam had the same poise, the same expression he'd had so many times over the summer. I saw the same condescending look, heard the same tone in his voice. When he popped open a can of Diet Mountain Dew, it might has well have been Budweiser.

All the time I'd been telling myself that I was strong enough to do this, I'd assumed I had Sam's support. Even when I knew he was struggling with the situation, I thought it was because he was being reminded of what had happened. Of course I understood the irony of it! There was no way I couldn't see it. But at least I knew I had Sam there to bolster me if I felt my own resolve faltering. I thought he would hold me up, no matter what, and remind me that I was strong and brave.

If he, of all people, couldn't see that I was capable and able to handle this, then how could I possibly see that in myself?

"This is *your* fear talking, Sam! Not mine! I can do this!"

"I can't help how I feel, Tierney. My feelings are mine, just like yours are your own. I don't think you're ready to be in this situation. It's like if I parked outside a liquor store to make a quick phone call and someone walked up and handed me a six-pack. I didn't *go* there for it; it just happened. It must not be in my control."

I was about to explode. My head was beginning to throb, and my heartbeat was racing. "Take your pseudo-Zen steps and shove them up your goddamn ass!"

"Oh," Sam said, finally looking at me, "I see how much respect you have for me and this."

"This is bullshit!"

"I knew you'd react like this."

"*Excuse me?*"

"I knew you'd be angry, and you'd probably demand to go anyway. Then you'd refuse to go."

"How dare you?!"

"It's your pattern, Tierney. It's how you always do this."

"So now I'm so simplistic and easy to figure out that you know everything I'm going to do and say? *Fuck you! Go to Hell!*"

I stormed into the house and to my bathroom. I was shaking violently, standing in front of the mirror and looking at the dark rage on my face.

"You're a worthless piece of trash," I said to my reflection. "You're a cunt-ass whore. You will never be worth the time or money anyone puts into you. You should quit trying, you useless piece of crap. You should just go be an unhappy fat girl and shut the fuck up!"

All of this, I said out loud. I felt the words come from my mouth, in my harshest voice, and right back into my ears and my heart.

I called Seth, shaking.

"I was all set, Hammer! I knew the challenge would be to see Alex and not turn back into that girl I was a year ago. If I fall back in that hole, I have to climb back out of it, and I refuse to do that again. He doesn't think I can do it! For all of his talk of forgiveness and love and support, I'm only worth the affection and support I can garner with a mouth full of cock! Every bad instinct I've ever had about myself just came right back at me in his condescending look!"

"Tierney, that's not true, and you know Sam doesn't really believe that! He's hurt and afraid and insecure about your going. That's natural. But you're doing this for *you*. Alex is staying out at Tom's. There's *no way* anything can happen."

"It doesn't matter,' I said. "I'm too stupid and weak to even be in the same goddamn town as him."

"Shut up! That's not true!"

"Apparently I want to put myself back in Alex's *presence* in the vain hope that he will fuck me and suddenly be willing to openly love me."

"Dude, you didn't even know he was gonna be there!"

"Doesn't matter, Seth. It doesn't matter that I'm not that same girl, or that I thought for a second that I could be a big girl and enjoy the band I've loved the most for twenty years. Fuck! I offered *repeatedly* not to go! Before *and* after I found out he'd be there."

Seth sighed into the phone, unsure of what to say next.

"I'm a stupid whore, Hammer," I continued. "For all of his bullshit talk of not letting Alex have the power over me, he still thinks I'm just a weak, simpering slut who will bend over on sight. I can refuse to go and be a resentful child who's been bullied into the choice, or I can be a fucking fatass, angry housewife who fell for an emotionally damaged and unavailable rock star. Either way, he's out money and I'm fucked."

I rocked myself to sleep, curled into a ball on the edge of the bed. Sam slept on the couch.

———————————

When I woke shortly before dawn, I was hopeful that Sam would acquiesce and agree to my going. I needed to leave around 8:30 to make my flight. I took a shower and got ready, did my hair and make-up. Looking at myself in the mirror, I could see what Alex had seen in me, what Sam said had always been there. I looked tall and beautiful. It was more than the defined collarbone and chiseled jaw, more than the long blond hair and bright green eyes. I could *see* the confidence, both in my new, svelter body and radiating from the inside.

You look pretty, Tierney.

I put my bag in the car and went to pick up breakfast for the boys while everyone was still asleep.

Sam was rousing as I came back into the house.

"There's breakfast on the counter for the children," I said from across the den.

"So you're going?"

"I think I should. It's your fear that's trying to hold me back, Sam. I'm not going to sleep with him. I'm going to support Seth and to enjoy this special opportunity."

"This is stupid, Tierney." He was getting angry. "This is a fucking mistake. If you go, you'll be setting us back a very long way."

"Are you saying I shouldn't come home if I go?"

"No! I'm not saying that! But when you get home, there will be a *lot* of problems."

My choices would be at the center of our problems, again. All of the weight and blame of our relationship was being shoved back onto my broad shoulders.

My keys were still in my hand. I threw them at him from across the room. "*Fuck you!*" I screamed as they landed in the floor, six inches from him.

I bounded across the carpet and picked them up. Throwing them again, they keys landed squarely against his chest with a tinkling thud.

"*Fuck you!*"

He jumped up, and I sprinted down the hall to the bedroom. I grabbed the sealed letter from my nightstand and ran back to the den.

"I wrote you a fucking letter like I was supposed to!" I screamed. "Here's your goddamn letter!" I threw it at him, watching it flutter flaccidly to the floor.

"*Get out!*" he yelled back. He grabbed the phone. "Leave! Get the fuck out of the house before I call the police!"

"It's my goddamn house, too! Fuck you!"

"You're enraged and threw something at me and hit me with it! Get out, or I will have the police escort you out. The kids don't need to see that!"

I wanted to stand my ground and have it out with him, but the boys would be up soon. I didn't want them to bear witness to this anger.

"*Fine!*" I grabbed my keys again and opened the front door.

"Don't come home until you're calm! And call me before you come back."

I fled. I went to the park and called Tessa, crying hysterically.

"He's a dick! I fucking hate him!"

"Where is this coming from, Tierney?" She sounded as confused and exasperated as I felt. "I mean, he *knew* days ago that this was coming. Why did he wait until the last minute to do this?"

"He said that the more he thought about it, the more it bothered him. He tried to apologize for waiting until the last minute, but it was crap. I'm so fucking mad."

"I'm so sorry. I know you were looking forward to this show."

"It's not the show that I'm upset about, you know? I mean, I *am*. It's a really special setting to see Seth and see Junkture, and I was *invited* to this, after everything that happened. But, whatever, I'll get over it. I'm upset because he has absolutely no faith in me. None! Not as his wife or as a woman or as a fucking human being. I can't be a big girl and make a good choice, as far as he's concerned."

I sat on the curb at the park, rocking back and forth and crying.

I'm supposed to be driving to the airport right now.

And I debated, seriously, going anyway. He was already mad as hell. How much worse could it get?

A lot.

I was afraid he would file for divorce again and use it against me, somehow, to try to prove I was an unfit, abandoning mother. Or he would do something to prove that I slept with Alex while I was away and file on grounds of adultery.

Or worse, he'll start drinking again.

How the hell did his drinking become the central focus of my life? How long could I be expected to let his fear and his sickness control my choices? It wasn't fair, but I knew I could never have lived with myself if he got so angry that he tossed away his sobriety over this.

I called to tell him I was coming home.

"I'm going to wash my face and put on my pajamas and go to bed. I don't want you to talk to me. I don't want anyone to bother me. Tell the kids I'm sick, I don't care. But leave me the fuck alone."

The boys were sitting around the kitchen table, eating the breakfast I'd gotten for them. They said hi and smiled. I kissed them on their sweet, beautiful heads and went to the bedroom, closing the door.

I sat in the middle of the bed, rocking back and forth and slamming my knuckles together, shaking. I tried curling into a fetal position but couldn't find comfort.

I felt like I would do better to be fat and unhealthy and unhappy and *numb* again, if it meant not having to feel and know what was there. I was back in exactly the same goddamn place I'd been a year before—except I knew more and my heart wanted more and hurt more than it maybe ever had in its sad, complicated life. I wanted to scream and break things and run the fuck away from home and never look back. I wanted the previous eighteen months ripped out of my fucking head so it would be quiet.

I'm painting, for what?

For my own, sad amusement.

It seemed grandiose and useless. Great, a few people sometimes saw pictures of my work. *Big goddamn deal.* I looked again at those pictures, the images I kept with me on my phone, and felt like I sucked and that I just shouldn't do it. I couldn't see any talent, no potential reward. It didn't matter that painting felt like an inherent part of me.

I wasn't making my mark on anything or anyone. I couldn't see that I ever had or ever would achieve anything, with the exception of bringing my boys into the world. I'd been right in the summer when I'd said that my value was bankrupted up when I birthed my children. The point to my whole fucking life was made by the time I was thirty-two. I was a thorn in everyone's side.

I'm just a thorn.

I cried until I fell back asleep.

I woke again around 10:30.

I'm supposed to be on the plane right now.

Seth Wiezel
Mar 13th 10:34 AM

I'm not coming. I'm not going to sxsw. I fucking hate him.

He bullied me into canceling. He threw me out after I threw my keys at him and screamed fuck you.

That fucking sucks Tierney. That isn't fair....

It's not I'm in bed bawling.
He set me up. He lied to me for months that he loved and believed in me.
He gutted me. It's his payback.

What do you mean?

He never forgave me or intended to trust me.
He lied when he said I was wonderful and amazing to him.
He set me up and kicked me down.

How many paybacks does this man get?

I didn't even see this coming.
I was an idiot to trust him.

From: Tierney Cavanaugh Johnson
Date: March 13th 11:08 AM
Subject:
To: Sam Johnson

You hurt me more than anyone ever has. Ever in my whole life. My entire world just came crashing down around me. All of your talk of love and support and trust and all of it was a lie. I think you want to be okay with everything but you aren't and never will be. You'll never be okay with me. I gutted you and now it's time for retribution.

Fuck you for making me feel small and worthless. Fuck you for not having the balls to tell me a week ago and two weeks and two months ago that I was delusional to think we'd ever get through this. Fuck you for making me believe in me and you and us. Fuck you for shoving me back into that dark place where I will never be good enough to deserve any love that isn't attached to a cock. And fuck me for letting you back in when everything screamed at me that I shouldn't, that I'd trusted you one too many times already.

Your fear and your sickness are still controlling you and me and us and always will. I let you do this and I'm awful and stupid and I hate you for letting me believe for moment that I wasn't. I hate you for setting me up and kicking me the fuck down, time and again. I hate you for pretending that you believe in me when you never did. I hate you for pushing me back to hide in my bed because I'm too hurt and afraid to do anything but lie here and shake.

I thought I had you there, you told me I did, and it was a lie. You lied to me that you loved me and that I was amazing and special. The real tragedy is that I was stupid enough to believe you and I didn't see it coming. There's your goddamn revenge. There's your fucking payback for everything I did that you told me you forgave me for. I wanted so badly to believe you that I let it all be real when it never was. I'm sorry I ever fucking trusted you again. I'm sorry I decided to believe anything I thought I felt from you.

I'm sure you'll say none of it was the case, that I'm just spoiled and selfish and stupid and acting how you thought I would. Fuck you for pushing me back into how you wanted me to be, where it was safe and easy for you to feel good about being in control.

You broke my fucking heart. I'm sure it'll never be even for you, you'll always feel like it's never enough to punish me. Fuck you. Fuck you. Fuck you!

And fuck me for loving you.

I fell asleep on the bed and woke after dark.

9:00

The house was quiet. Sam's side of the bed radiated cold.

He's been gone a while. Go back to sleep.

11:07

I lay in my bed, staring into the shadows at the corner of the ceiling and the wall. There was nothing especially exciting about that spot; it just happened to be in my line of vision, and I was too sad to decide to look elsewhere.

The aching was still there, like a crushing weight where my heart was supposed to be.

I loved Sam. I wanted to be with him. Even when I'd thought we were splitting, I'd had this resolve that I would be okay, that I would get through it. I'd even picked out a beautiful new bed, planning colors for new sheets and blankets and trying to remember where I'd gotten the pillows I loved so much. There'd been a strange elation from knowing something *new* and *different* was coming. I couldn't see that now. I couldn't see what our marriage might look like going forward, good or bad, and it was horribly, terribly unsettling. There was more uncertainty than ever.

All I knew to do was to quit—to quit painting, to quit the idea that I was worth any effort. I would just be there and make sure the things Sam and the boys needs were seen to. He needed me to support his recovery, and I would do everything I could handle. There was no reason for me to expect a life outside of that. I never should've opened my eyes and thought for a moment that I was worthy of love or attention or anything other than what everyone else thought I needed to survive.

I don't deserve it.

I'm not worth it.

I felt like the useless, fat, worthless girl who couldn't keep her head on straight that I was before. All I did was cost other people so much—money, pain, wasted energy—and everyone would be better off without that. Anything I'd ever wanted seemed stupid and unattainable. I was done bashing by head and my heart against everyone else and trying to get the things I stupidly thought would make me happy.

I'd had to consciously choose to be with Sam and to work forward past all of the fears and doubts, through all of the bullshit we'd done to each other. I had to find the place in my heart to forgive him and to forgive myself for months and years of neglecting us and me and him. I did that. I found that there was something inside me that was lovable and worthwhile and had value, and I was wrong.

He made the little bit I could see in myself that was defensible as nothing, as worth less than the loads of laundry and dishes I could do in a day. And I let him do it. I let myself believe that he was telling me the truth, that I was of value to him, and I wasn't. I hadn't been in a very long time. He held onto me because he needed it to stop his spinning, and he made me need it, too. I let him do that. I let him lie to me and get inside me again when I knew it was the worst thing possible for me. That was all on me. It was my cycle of needing to be loved and lighting under the guise of affection.

Alex was right. Sam was never getting over this. He would never accept me and support me for who I was, because it flew in the face of everything he needed to feel supported. His fear and his sickness would never *not* control my choices.

I felt back where I was a year before. My heart was broken like it never had been, and my immediate, reactionary thoughts were that I needed Alex. I wanted a safe place, for just a moment, somewhere soft and nebulous that wouldn't hurt me back.

But I knew damn well he wouldn't be there if I reached out. He couldn't. It wasn't fair to Talia or Sam, to either of our families, for him to be my support, no matter how badly I was hurting. He was the pressure point, the catalyst, and it wasn't healthy for any of us if we truly wanted to heal and move on.

I knew that if I reached for him, he would shove me back in that goddamn box with everything else he didn't want to see. I wasn't an old shirt or some shitty CD. I was a fucking person with everything ugly and beautiful and complicated that entailed. I could do stupid shit and make mistakes, and I could love and hate and get hurt when other people were as careless with me as I was with myself.

I needed someone who knew me to say, "I know you're hurting, and I know why, and I'm sorry, and you'll be okay somehow even if you can't see it."

Mostly I wanted to hear Alex say, "I'm sorry for knowing I would let you break your own fucking heart and just not giving a shit."

But it was never going to happen.

And *that* was the remaining lesson I had to learn from Alex, to trust my inner strength and believe in my own power to succeed, no matter what I was doing. It had always been there, just like he and Sam said, but I hadn't been able to feel that inner flame in such a long time. By the time I could see it again, my spark had flared into an inferno, singeing everything around me and threatening to turn my world into a wasteland. Now it was a controlled burn, able to help and harm equally, but at my discretion.

11:27

Sam was sitting on the deck, smoking a cigarette, listening to the Doors' *Strange Days.* It was *our* record, the one we'd listened to together, over and over, lying together in the dark and the burgeoning of our relationship.

I wrapped myself in a blanket and went outside to join him.

"Just tell me one thing," I said defiantly.

"What?"

"Did you do it on purpose? Did you set this up, intentionally *plan* to pull this trip out from under me at the last second?"

"No, Tierney, of course not." He was adamant but didn't sound angry or insincere.

"You had every right to feel what you did about the trip. I *know* why the circumstances of San Antonio made you uncomfortable. But how you handled it...."

"I *tried* to tell you. I knew you would be upset, no matter what."

"I'm not upset because you asked me not to go. I *hate* that I missed Seth's show, but it's not the end of my world. It's *how* you did it. Waiting until the last minute. And your *tone*, Sam.... It felt like you just turned your back on me."

"*How?*"

"You said you didn't think I could *do* it. All this time, all these months, I've been *fighting* to feel tall and beautiful and brave, and you took that away! I thought I had your support, but it was just rickety facade that couldn't bear the weight of us. All the progress I thought we'd made toward being able to be ourselves and bring that to this relationship was just a lie."

I started to cry.

"I *needed* your trust and faith and belief, and I thought I had it. But you snatched that away, and you took my own trust and faith and belief in *myself* with it. It almost doesn't matter if you intended to hurt me or not. If it wasn't malicious, it was negligent, and I don't even have the alcohol to put some of the culpability on, to help mitigate the damages."

Sam exhaled a long stream of smoke. "Tierney, you *are* tall and brave and beautiful. And wonderful and special—"

"I believed you every time you told me that. But all of those things that make me *Tierney* are the things you can't *stand*—my love of music and my painting and my desire to understand the experience of my *life*. You said for months that you thought I really hated you. I know exactly how you felt. I think you *want* to look at me and love me, and you can as long as I'm within the bounds of what's acceptable to you. But the seeds of everything in me that flourished were also the seeds of everything you *hate* about me, everything that scares you and makes you hope I'll be quiet and soft."

Sam bent in front of me, his knees pressing against the cold, wooden planks of the deck. He was just below my eye level, trying to grasp my hands through the tightly-cocooned blanket.

"Tierney, *listen* to me. You *are* special and wonderful, and I *don't* hate you. I *love* you. Deeply. I always have and always will. And you have *blossomed* into a remarkable woman—more than even I ever thought possible. You're strong and confident and a *spectacle* that I am honored to behold. You're a force of nature, undoubtedly, and that is scary as hell some days.

"I promise, I *swear*, I wasn't trying to hurt you. I'm sorry if my tone wasn't as gentle for you as maybe it should've been. I was scared and didn't know how else to say what was in my head and in my heart. I *want* you to be *you*. I *want* you to be that amazing creature, and I want to be able to enjoy that. I don't want either of us to hide from it."

I pulled my hands from the blanket and held his. "I'm sorry that I hurt you, saying what I did, that you'd hurt me more than anyone ever. I know it was brutal."

I wasn't apologizing for feeling it, or even for actually *saying* it, just for having laid such hurtful emotion on him.

"It was wrenching," he replied quietly. "I really didn't mean to hurt you, Tierney. I knew you'd be upset and disappointed, but I wasn't trying to punish you. I wasn't trying to make you feel badly about yourself. I love you, and I believe in you, really. I just couldn't...."

I nodded, shushing him. "I know. And I'm still hurt. And we still have a ton of work to do with Dr. Hill."

"This set us back a lot, I know."

"You're right. It did. But I'm still here. *We*'re still here. No one's threatening to leave. No one *wants* to leave. And that's a very different place than we were in a year ago, Sam."

He rubbed my hands for warmth and comfort.

"I want to go to Austin," I croaked toward my lap. "I want to go to South by Southwest and get away from here for a few days. I want to *see* my poster outside the venue. I still want to have that experience."

"I think you should," he replied. "Really, I do. I think you should go and have fun and still see Junkture like you'd planned."

I should've been able to see them tonight. Right now.

Sam ducked his head and looked up into my face, forcing me to see him. "*Go and own that fucking town.*"

"Okay then. I'm going to Austin."

Chapter 40

I rearranged my flight again and flew to Austin on Wednesday morning as planned. There was an unspoken agreement that Sam and I wouldn't talk again about what had happened until we went to counseling after I got back from Texas. Sam was cordial, kissing me goodbye and telling me to check in when I got there.

The Austin airport was smaller than I'd imagined, but that meant it was easy to navigate. It was packed with people coming into town for South by Southwest. I spent more time standing in line for a cab than I did for baggage claim.

I went straight to the hotel, where my ass-freezing room was ready, thankfully. Otherwise I would've been dragging my stuff around Austin all day like some sad, tourist hobo.

Sam Johnson
Mar 15th 12:35 PM
> **Room 108. Gonna unpack and go downtown.**

Ok. Glad you're there safely. I'm very excited about it, and for you!
Have a blast!

I unpacked quickly and freshened up before catching the shuttle to the Convention Center, at the heart of the festival. I checked in at registration and got my music badge, which would grant me access to discussion panels and registrant-only shows. I'd also get quicker entrance to venues for parties and showcases. I wasn't planning to sit in on a panel until mid-afternoon, so I wandered the blocks closest to the Convention Center, to start to get a feel for how Austin was laid out. I ended up catching sets by bands I knew and bands I didn't, bands I loved and some who just sucked. I found the Registrant's Lounge for my free Tito's-and-Monster-Lemonade.

And for every band, there were a dozen posters. Big, small, color, black-and-white. It looked like every square inch of Austin's trash cans and light poles and brick walls were overlaid with information about the hundreds of shows going on around town. But I didn't see *my* poster anywhere.

I posted on Facebook, asking people to let me know of acts I should catch while I was there. I had a pretty thorough list of shows, provided by SXSW, but there were so damn many things going on at once. It was impossible to keep them all straight. When I looked over the schedule for the weekend, there were as many as eight acts playing simultaneously that I *really* wanted to see.

I wandered around, just feeling everything out. I wanted to see everything at once, but I knew I needed to pace myself. My surgeon had cleared me for the travel, and there were no limitations on my activity, but I was still healing, still swollen and puffy and a little sore.

Apprehensive about what was to come, I texted Alex.

> **I'm in Austin. When are you guys getting here? I don't want to wander around for the next three days, looking over my shoulder for you.**

He replied to tell me they'd be there on Friday afternoon, the day before the show at Flunky's, Paulie's club. They'd decided to stay in San Antonio for a couple of days to catch some smaller acts and avoid the crush of South-by.

Honestly, I was a little relieved. I could relax and enjoy my time without fear of running into him in the middle of a crowded street. I wasn't looking for him around each corner, scanning the crowds for his face. I was on my own and content.

I spent the first two days walking around Austin, miles and miles, and it felt amazing. It was fantastic to be so kinetic again. As nervous as I was about being on my own in a strange city, I relied on that inner spark of courage, the one I'd been too numb to feel for far too long, and I thrived on the constant cacophony of South by Southwest. Every bar and club had a band playing from noon until the early morning hours, plus the stages and tents set up around town for parties and showcases. There were street musicians on virtually every corner. The only place to hide from the music was in my own head, and my thoughts rushed in time to the pace of my body.

I would meet people, standing in line or walking, and they would ask me if I was a musician.

"No," I would say, a little tentatively, "I'm an artist."

"Really? What medium do you work in?"

"I'm a painter. Mostly acrylics, but sometimes I do oil or watercolor. And I did a poster for South-by."

"*Really?*"

I would nod and smile self-consciously. "For Junkture. At Flunky's. On Saturday."

Sometimes, if the person I was talking to was young, they wouldn't really know who Junkture was. Occasionally, someone would make a face that let me know they didn't really like Junkture. But usually the other person was *impressed*.

And because so many of those other people were musicians themselves, it gave me a chance to hand out some of my new calling cards, with the image from the Junkture poster on one side, my name and phone number and new website on the other.

I met and talked to all of these amazing people every day, but I loved the solitude of being by myself, free to light from corner to corner without worrying that I was altering someone else's agenda. It let me soak in the experience in a completely different way than if I'd been with Sam or Tessa or anyone. And I slept soundly in the big, cold bed, all by myself.

There were a lot of bands I wanted to catch, but there were just too damn many playing at the same time to see them all. Many of the shows were so crowded that it was incredibly difficult to get in the door to see the set. But you can often hear it all from outside. And it's cool to stand there, surrounded by the mayhem and the smells and laughter from everywhere, hearing some song you may or may not know, from some band that you may or may not love. I had to enjoy each moment while I could, though, because something else was going to come quickly along and distract my from that moment, plunging me headlong into the next.

I sat in on lots of the daytime panels. Sometimes, the panels were just an excuse to sit still for an hour in the air conditioning. I was in one of those sessions when I got an email from SXSW that I'd won one of the lottery tickets to see Bruce Springsteen that night at the Moody Theatre. There would be less than three thousand people in attendance, and there were no plus-ones.

I called Tessa to tell her.

"He's doing the keynote speech in a little while. I should probably go, huh?"

"Well, *yeah*, it's the Boss. Fan or not, that's not something you're likely to be able to see again. Tell him 'hi' for me."

"Sure! I'll just jump up and yell, 'Hey, Bruce? Tessa sends her love!'"

Tessa laughed into the phone. "And he'll be like, 'Hugs and kisses to my bestie!' Bruce and I are just like that, you know."

I settled into the room at the Convention Center with a couple thousand other people to hear what Bruce Springsteen had to say about the craft and business of music.

He was funny and self-deprecating, talking about the music that had influenced him and why. He talked about the unmitigated, abject sadness of Roy Orbison's songs, the genius of Bob Dylan, and the importance of the Sex Pistols. When he launched into an acoustic breakdown of "We Gotta Get Out of This Place", I was overjoyed. I have a deep, abiding love of Eric Burdon, and Bruce readily admitted to ripping off the Animals for his own work.

But Bruce also touched on something, briefly, that stuck with me all day, about the emotional depths of these artists. He referred to the Animals as being ugly and emotionally frightening, so different from their British Invasion counterparts, and I pondered this everywhere I went that day.

Great music is emotionally frightening. There's something in the lyrics and music that can take your very soul to the precipice of despair and fear and love and joy in ways that you're not just *hearing* but *experiencing* as you delve into that song. The gravity of the emotion is so overwhelming that it *hurts* to take yourself there for that three or four minutes, but it's so good that you want to go back there over and over—whether it's a repeat on your iPod or CD player, or rewinding your cassette tape while you drive to school, or even resetting the needle on your record.

There are lots of songs with boundless emotion that simply *look* at something and comment on it. They aren't great because they don't make you *ache* to be in that moment with the singer. If the artist is afraid to look at that part of themselves, if they compartmentalize themselves in such a way that even *they* can't face it, they'll never find the truths they need to take their audience to that unforgivingly beautiful place.

It was why Alex would never be able to accomplish what he wanted most. He would never truly channel the depths of Bruce Springsteen, or any of his other music heroes, and find unanticipated approval from a mentor. He was too afraid to face his own truths, to dump the contents of his innumerable boxes onto the ground and really sift through himself. He would never create his own legacy of Great American Song, because he was too goddamn scared to be honest with anyone, especially with Alex Wheeler.

And I knew it was where he needed to go, because it was where *I* needed to go, in my painting. My best pieces were the ones wrought with emotions, the ones that exhausted me and made me cry when I was finished. They were the ones I could look at in the days after and both love them because of their beauty, and fear them because of the dark fathoms I'd had to traverse to find them.

I did go that night to see Bruce Springsteen and the E Street Band. It was strangely intimate, even with his huge musical entourage. What impressed me most was that it wasn't a show so much as it was Bruce and his friends having a party on stage, inviting the audience inside that inner circle.

I was ready to feel that same intimacy with my band. With Junkture.

———————

Friday morning came way too early. I dragged myself toward a shower and breakfast before catching a shuttle downtown. I hit one panel and a Day Stage set and decided, "Screw it! Go catch some bands!"

I wandered for a while, listening and watching. I was surprised to realize I was ravenous. I'd barely eaten since I'd gotten there, so caught up in everything that was going on around me.

I also decided to drink. Never a beer girl, a friend of Seth's had introduced me to a raspberry Lambic on Thursday night. With the exception of a couple of beers at the Ginger Man, I hadn't really had a drink. Lunch was Tex-Mex and a free second round from a hot bartender. Jack and Ginger and I danced our way down Sixth Street until I was happily drunk. I went back to the hotel to take a shower and sleep it off before I went out to face the music.

I'd just woken from my nap when my phone dinged with a text from Alex.

catching a quick set at the bayou
lounge at 7

Is he inviting me to join him?
He wouldn't have sent me the info if he didn't want me to know. He had every excuse and reason to wait to see me until the next night at Flunky's.

I put on my make-up and dried my hair, opting to let it hang straight, now halfway down my back and at least four inches longer than when I'd last seen Alex. I tried on three different outfits, unsure of how I wanted to look. I decided on a flouncy black skirt and leggings, a black crocheted shrug, and a gray t-shirt, *Persona Non Grata* embellished across my tits like a label or a badge of honor.

I waited for the shuttle, fidgety and checking messages.

When I'd seen Alex in November, we'd agreed it would be the last time. Even when he'd told me I couldn't come to shows, that he wouldn't see me again, I wasn't sure. My head had said *maybe*, but my gut said *no*. My heart had refused to take a stance at all, too afraid of thinking that far forward. I hadn't seen Max or Paul or Charlie at all since that last Junkture show at the Coda, the night Alex and I slept together. Not only had everything come to a head since that night, I'd lost another forty-five pounds and had the first surgery. I didn't look, or feel, remotely like the same girl who'd rolled her suitcase down the sidewalk in San Antonio, searching for the rock star.

I landed downtown and walked the few blocks from the Convention Center to Sixth Street. It was still overflowing with the afternoon revelers, gearing up for a long night of drinking and music. I walked into the Bayou Lounge just before seven o'clock.

Like most of the clubs along Sixth, it's a long, narrow strip of club, the bar along one side and the stage at the end. I wanted a drink, just one, to help steady my nerves. I ordered a Jack and Ginger, deciding it was too soon to start mixing liquors, and drank it quickly through the stirrer. I felt the sudden flush of alcohol on my neck, the warmth spreading through my belly like a little surge of confidence. I dropped the white, plastic cup into the closest trashcan and looked up as Alex and Max walked through the side door.

I stopped in my tracks, just a few feet from them. Alex was carrying a cable and a guitar case.

He took three steps toward me and glanced at me quickly. "Hi," he said, walking past me toward the bar.

"Um, hi."

Max looked toward the stage, then toward Alex and shrugged. "How are you?" he asked, beaming.

"I'm fabulous, Max. How are you?"

He pulled me into a deep, strong hug. "I'm good! You look great!"

I smiled at him. "Thank you!"

He motioned for me to hang on and jaunted to catch up with Alex. I stepped over, more out of the way of the stage, as Alex and Max walked toward it.

Max flashed me two fingers and mouthed, "Two songs."

There'd been no mention of an acoustic set on the Junkture Facebook page or from their Twitter account. There was nothing on the bar's schedule, taped to the door.

Alex and Max plugged in cables and check-check-one-two-one-two'd into their mics.

The bar owner stepped up to the stage. "Ladies and gentlemen, we have a *really* special treat. At the last minute, these guys agreed to come and do a couple of songs for us. They'll be playing tomorrow night at Flunky's, and since you have to miss that show because you'll be *here* for our showcase... give it up for Junkture!"

The crowd of fifty or so people whooped and hollered their approval. They probably would've screamed the same way if the guys had asked if they loved Hitler, as drunk and excited as all of Sixth Street was. But Alex looked the tiniest bit relieved to feel that support.

Max was playing the acoustic guitar. He was a bassist, so it stood to reason that he was perfectly capable of strumming a few chords. It was something I'd never seen him do. Alex often played the guitar and sang for a couple of songs during shows. I was guessing that he'd brought Max along as a buffer.

He started with "Give up the Ghost". Very few people were singing along, but around the room, lips were mouthing the words along to Alex's gritty voice—mine included. Halfway through the second verse he looked at me intently, squinting just a little. But he wasn't looking at my face. As he broke into a grin, I realized he'd notice my t-shirt, knowing damn well why I'd chosen *that* as the message for the evening.

The crowd clapped and whistled politely. Alex asked everyone to sing along to the next song. It was an acoustic version of "Mantissa". It was undeniably their biggest hit. Almost twenty years later, it still sounded as fresh and brutal as it had when I'd first heard it and fallen in love with Junkture. I sang along, just like everyone else. The emotional depth was there, the reckless abandon that he'd been able to tap so long ago in his brash youth. Alex was more than capable of writing a great song, if only he would allow himself the freedom to do it.

The song ended, and Alex thanked everyone. Max quickly wrapped up the cables and packed Alex's guitar, heading out the side door. I stepped outside behind him, while Alex talked to the bar owner one more time.

"So you guys stayed in San Antonio?" I asked.

"Yeah. It sucks. Fucking Paulie."

I giggled. "I gotta say I'm not surprised."

"No kidding. Alex and I are gonna be in Atlanta next month. We'll have to get together for a drink while we're there."

Huh?

"Why are you coming to Atlanta?"

"Our manager, Lee, asked Alex to go check out some band. It's someone Alex knows, but Lee wants to come down and see them. They're playing in Buford. I'm gonna drive over for the show and meet him."

"Call me. We'll go hang out at the Mall of Georgia. We can be old mall rats together."

Max smiled sideways and nodded. "*That* is a plan, Tierney Cavanaugh!"

Alex came through the door, looking warily at us. "You ready? Are you walking with us to the bar, Tierney?"

"Is that okay?"

Alex nodded. "Sure."

I forgot how fast he walked, and I had to push myself to keep up with him. "How are you?"

"I'm good. Stressed."

"I'm sorry. If it's because of me. I don't want to stress you."

"No, you're not my stress, doll," he said distractedly. "So what's going on? How was Springsteen?"

I told him about the show and about the keynote. "This whole thing of emotional fright in songs... you need to go online and watch this keynote address, Alex. He stepped through this acoustic version of this song and said he'd ripped off the Animals for every song he'd ever written."

Alex glanced at me sideways as we crossed the block. "*Really?*"

"Yeah. You should go listen to the Animals and then Bruce and see what you hear. I thought of you immediately, after everything you were trying to do when you were writing last year. It made me look at my painting in a different way, too."

"How's your painting going?"

"Good! I talked to a couple of local coffee shops and restaurants. They're letting me put some stuff up for sale. Tessa suggested I put some things out on Etsy and see if I can sell them. Paul says you asked about having me do the poster."

He glanced toward me and nodded. "I hope that was okay."

I smiled. "It was... surprising, but definitely okay. Thank you. That was a huge opportunity for me."

"The artwork is *fantastic*, Tierney. Really. You should be very proud of yourself." He paused awkwardly. "I hope Sam is proud of it, too."

"He is, in his own way. He doesn't say much about it. It's hard for him, but he agreed that it was the right project for me."

He nodded. "So you're still with him? How is he? Is he here?"

"He's in Atlanta. He lied about having me followed in Nashville."

"Of course he did."

"I didn't know at the time. Things were *awful* at home. Everything was so crazy. It got so bad Tessa had to step in and tell us both to cut it the fuck out and get into counseling and mediation. It was rough."

"Wow."

"Yeah, but we were in a session with our counselor a couple of weeks later. It's a new counselor, who we both really love. I said I wanted to talk about Sam's drinking. He'd told me over the weekend that his drinking wasn't out of control, it was his behavior when he was drinking that was so horrible."

Alex sighed derisively.

"Yeah, it was fucked up. But he *heard* how fucked up it was, and he started recovery that night."

"Did he check into rehab or—"

"Nono, Program meetings. But he's there almost every day. He stopped drinking."

"Tierney, that's huge. I'm glad for you both."

"Yeah me, too. He came to me a few days later and apologized for having stepped out of our marriage, for having ignored and dismissed me for so long, and for ever having put me in a position that I would feel like turning to another man. He told me he forgives me for anything I think I've done. And it doesn't feel like lip service, Alex. It doesn't feel at all like he was just telling me what he thought I needed to hear."

"That's *amazing*."

I shrugged. "He freaked out that you were gonna be in San Antonio. I was supposed to be there."

"Paulie said you were on the list, that you'd RSVP'd, but you never showed."

"It was bad, Alex. I just... no, you know what? Let's just say it was bad and leave it at that."

Max was half a block ahead of us, and Alex slowed his pace mercifully. My sore abs could work a little less hard for the last three blocks.

"Does he know, by the way?" I asked.

"Max? No. He doesn't know."

I smirked mirthfully. "I think you're an *idiot* if you believe that. There's no way he doesn't."

"Well, I haven't *told* him. And honestly, he would never say anything about it. It's my business."

I could just make out the bright red Flunky's sign down the street.

"Do you have time to talk?" Alex asked.

I nodded, my heart pounding with nervousness and exertion. "I have all the time in the world."

We crossed the last street to the venue. The streets were crowded with revelers and festival-goers, and the "One In, One Out" rule left badge-holders and random fans waiting patiently to enter as soon as someone else moved on to another show. He led me to a back entrance, in an alley behind the club.

"Let me drop my stuff upstairs."

"I'll wait here."

I leaned against the old brick wall, watching the changing light of the quickly shadowing alleyway. The smells of South by Southwest—stale beer and sweat and souring trash—were becoming overwhelming, having simmered in the Texas heat all day. I was thankful when Alex's tall frame pushed through the heavy metal door, even though his consternation was obvious.

"You wanna walk?" he asked.

"Yes, please, but you have to slow down. My abs were so sore the first day here, but the constant motion has been fantastic."

He looked puzzled. "Why were you sore?"

I stopped suddenly in the middle of the street. "*Oh!* You haven't seen!"

I grabbed him by the arm and turned him toward me. I pulled my shirt up, to just below my bra. His eyes widened at the sight of my flat belly and new belly button.

"It's still healing," I explained, pointing to the red circle of new skin. "But you know what was there before...."

He nodded and bit his lower lip. "*Wow.*"

I smiled at him. "And my abs are *tight*!" I pounded against them like a taut drum and dropped my shirt, motioning him forward again. "It's fabulous."

"That's crazy, Tierney. When did you do it?"

We walked side by side, inches apart but never touching. We both looked down at our feet or watched the flow of people around us.

"February first. That was the first procedure. They did my stomach and hips first, and some lipo. I'll do my arms and new boobs in the spring, then my thighs last, in the summer. I'm a size smaller now than when you saw me in Nashville. I may settle in even a size smaller than that, when it's all said and done."

"Wow! As tall as you are, that'll be... *wow.*"

I laughed, knowing he was probably picturing it in detail. "Yes. It will be. I hope!"

We crossed another street, moving away from the crowds, toward the Convention Center.

"I was scared to death before the first surgery. It was the longest I'd ever been under anesthesia. Honestly, it hurt like hell. A few days after the surgery, I was in so much pain that I questioned whether I had maimed myself irreparably. In a way, I did, but I'm glad I did it."

"Tierney, after all the pain you've been through in the last year... that was *nothing*."

"I'm still healing. Two more surgeries. I've really just begun this *process* of bringing my image of me out of my mind's eye and into my mirror. And I will *always* be a curvy girl. I'll never have a swimsuit model body, and I'm perfectly okay with that. I will still have stretch marks and cellulite and imperfections, you know? The scars are long, but they'll fade. And those bags of skin were so much *baggage*, of heartache and self-loathing. I exchanged all of that for scars that are permanent signs of *healing*.

"Alex, I had to learn from you to open my mouth and use my voice and *say* what I was feeling, not to hide behind an email or a text. That was a huge lesson, and I thank you for that. But... everything started with you when I was almost at my heaviest. You know how I am about my body and how unbearably difficult it was to open up to you about all of my body image issues. To be naked with you, it was...." I blushed, just a little.

"I know," he said gently.

"Never once did you make me feel inferior or lacking because of my body." My eyes started to water. "Now I'm gonna cry.... *Thank you*," my voice cracked, "for never making me feel anything *less* than beautiful. It means a lot. More than you will ever know, and I needed to thank you personally for that."

Alex was quiet for a long moment. "Thank you. And you're... welcome.... It's not... it's what any decent human being would do."

I could hear from his tone, he didn't get it. He didn't fully understand how much his acceptance of me, inside and out, had bolstered my confidence when I needed it the most. Alex knew *me* and why *I* would need that, but he couldn't see how anyone would ever not just be kind about that, especially with someone they cared about. "It's not, Alex. My ex dug at me all the time, knowing how it would make me feel. Sam has done it a couple of times, *never* intentionally, but it's happened."

"*Wow*...." He couldn't imagine it.

"It just... *thank you*."

"You're welcome, Buttercup."

I smiled sideways at him.

"How's Amber?" I asked.

"She's *great*!"

"And Talia? How is she?" It seemed only polite.

"Good." He was less enthusiastic. "Busy. Really busy. But good."

"Everything's okay?"

"Yep."

"So how are *you*? Really?"

"I'm good. We went back into the studio."

"How are things with Paul?"

I saw Alex shrug from the corner of my eye. "Fine, I guess. It's me and it's Paulie"

There were still people milling about the outside of the Convention Center. People were getting on and off shuttle vans, flagging down pedi-cabs, and walking toward surrounding venues. But we found a deserted corner and sat on thick, marble benches, facing each other.

I settled my back against the brick wall. "You know, you were the catalyst for so much...."

"That Junkture record was the catalyst," he laughed.

"I'm happy that you were able to get back that part of your soul that was missing," he continued. "I'm thankful and grateful to have been a part of that. But it's like I told you before, you—we— weren't looking for something different; we were looking for what was missing."

He was right. I'd been willing to go down that path with him because I was so unhappy with Sam. I felt ignored and insignificant to my husband, and I needed to feel something, *anything*, that resembled real affection. What had Alex been missing with Talia?

There was the sex, certainly. He had needed a safe place to work out the sexual desires that he'd repressed and ignored for so long. But there was more to it than that. He'd needed to feel adored and accepted. He'd needed someone who didn't know all of his anecdotes and history who could see him in a new way and be fascinated. He had needed to feel flattered, as a man.

"I was dying—*dying*—inside before I met you. I was *nothing* of what I am now."

"All those things you are, you were all of that before you ever met me," he argued. "That was always there!"

"You were the first person to see it, Alex. All of it. *I* couldn't see who or what I was until you reminded me who I was supposed to be."

"*Are you that insecure?*" he scoffed jokingly.

"You know that I am! You *know* how fragile my self-esteem is!"

"You know, you're the *stupidest* fucking smart person I know! You don't think, *then* you think, then you *overthink*."

I shrugged dramatically, flipping my palms open with a flourish and a grin. "It's who I am. And I'm not apologizing for that."

"I don't want you to apologize for who you are, Tierney. I never did."

"I know that *now*, but all I could see for so long was that I was a problem—for you, for me, for Sam. *I* am not the problem. *My choices* are sometimes a problem, but not even always to me."

"You don't have to be sorry, Buttercup."

"No, I do. We make choices, we do things, and there's always an equal-and-opposite reaction. Even the best things, the most selfless choices, can have bad effects. And when I make a mistake, I need to own up to that and admit it. So I am. I'm apologizing for those missteps. But great and wonderful things can come from missteps, as well."

"There's always a rock that causes the ripple."

"*Exactly.* I'm sorry for all the times I was complicating and confusing for you. There were times when I called out to you, when I drew you back in, that weren't fair to you, and I'm really sorry for that. It was wrong of me to be confounding. It was selfish, and I *do* owe you an apology for that. But I am *done* apologizing for who and what I am. I've done that for my entire life, and I'm just not doing it anymore. So I won't say I'm sorry for being loud and brash and needy and overwhelming. It's who I am, and I am *unapologetic* for that.

"And I'm *not* sorry about what happened, Alex, and I probably will never be. My lack of remorse is still a problem for Sam, and I can't help it. I feel bad that I *hurt* him. I feel bad that I lied and kept secrets when he asked me not to. But I'm *not* sorry that I met you, or that this thing with you happened... or that I loved you."

The sun was sinking behind the buildings, but we were both still hiding behind dark sunglasses. I could just make out the shape of his eyes, watching me intently and patiently.

"You were so angry with me," he said, "for boxing you away and compartmentalizing you, especially during that chat after your birthday."

I nodded.

"I shouldn't have done it that way," he continued. "I shouldn't have done that to you, treated you that way, and I'm sorry for that. I'm sorry for *hurting* you like that. It wasn't how I should've handled it.

"The truth is, I should've shut this thing down before we ever got to the Marriott. I should've been bold enough and strong enough to never have gone that far with you." He glanced down at his long fingers, fidgeting aimlessly with his wedding band. "I don't know.... Maybe I should've made sure it happened the way it was supposed to, to get it all out. Maybe that would've been the end of it. Maybe not, I don't know."

He looked at me, considering.

"You have all this shit bottled up inside you, Alex. There's all this fucking baggage. That was part of what worked between us, you know? It was a safe place to let all of that out. But you don't. You keep everything so packed away. You need to be able to dump all of that shit out in the floor into a big pile and sift through what matters and why you're hanging onto it. More than anything, I want you to be able to look at all of that in the light of day and come to peace with it. With *yourself*."

He leaned back against the wall and stretched his long legs before him. I pulled my knees up to my chest, crossing my ankles and wrapping my arms around my legs, facing him directly.

"It's so hard, you know? Even now, all these months later, there are all these *reminders*. I'll drive through an intersection and think, 'Oh, I was talking to Alex that day he called from Detroit,' or I'll drive by some parking lot and remember sitting there in my car, having phone sex with you."

He chuckled and blushed just a little. "Those don't go away."

"*Fuck*, I know! It's just so goddamn *pervasive*! It's bad enough when you come on the radio, but then there are all of these things that shouldn't be tied to you, shit I loved before I ever even *knew* you. Like, I was on the plane and wanted to listen to music. I thought, 'Okay! Afghan Whigs are my favorite road trip music!' I couldn't do it, Alex. I *tried* to listen to *1965*, and I *just couldn't fucking do it!*"

"What did you listen to instead?" he asked curiously.

"The Doors. And I fucking love Jim Morrison—I'd tell you all to go to hell and fuck his *ghost* if it appeared right here—but that was the only safe thing I could find that didn't make me think of you, and even *I* was sick of it after four hours. Some days, it's *impossible* to find a safe place from you." He was still watching me, and I felt emotionally brave. "And I *miss* you. Still. *Every fucking day.*"

"That doesn't go away," he almost whispered.

You told me it would. You told me it would get easier, that it would take a lot of time.

"Do you miss me?" I asked suddenly, almost challenging. I looked him as close to in the eye as I could, wanting to watch his face while he answered. "Do you still miss me?"

He nodded. "I do. Yes."

"If you had *died*, there would've been some definitive reason that our friendship had ended. Unfortunately, it was simply a matter of a friendship that overstepped into something much different. Those emotions made it hard to focus on the more pressing, more important parts of life, so it had to be cut out. We didn't cut away something bad; it felt like we excised something good and necessary, and it was painful. I *miss* being able to call you and just *talk* to you. I miss my friend."

"I owe Sam an apology, I know that. That'll probably be years from now, after I've had time to deal with it all myself." He looked up at me. "I would love nothing more than for him to be *okay* with you having contact with me, for us to be able to have that connection. And if he ever is, you reach out to me—you call me or email me, and I'm there."

"I don't know if he'll ever be okay with that," I said sadly. "And it hurts."

"I know. And it's funny, you know, Talia will call out to me from the other room, to tell me to come look at something, and I'm always afraid that Sam has emailed her with what happened."

I shook my head. "I don't think he will. You know, though, you've never asked me not to tell her."

"Not to tell Talia? I never would," he said matter-of-factly. "I don't want her to find out, but I would never ask that of you. Things are hard at home. We have all of these issues, and we should probably get help for them. We're going through all this shit...." He looked skyward and shook the thought from his dark head. "I have so many things I need to work out. Hell, *I* should probably get help with all of it. But I can't take it to her. I can't give her the things that worry me and bother me."

"*Why*, Alex?"

"Because I get to keep some things for myself! I don't *have* to share everything with my wife."

Is that what I was? Something you didn't have to share?

"After San Antonio... you've never told me where you were with all of this, in your head and in your heart. We've been 'round and 'round with what was in *my* messed-up head and where you were in relation to that, but you've never told me how you felt."

"And I never will."

"Why?"

He looked at me directly, confident in his resolution. "Because it's *mine*, and no one else's."

And it hit me. *Hard.* All of the times he'd told me how he compartmentalized me away, like everything else, it wasn't because of *me*. It was because of *him.* I'd always thought it was a defense mechanism for him to keep me from intruding, to be able to make sense of me and keep me at a safe distance. If he could ignore me, he didn't have to feel me and the repercussions of what I was feeling. If he could ignore it, maybe it wouldn't happen, maybe it would take away the power from those feelings and make them less significant than I felt they were.

"You feel everything so intensely," I said slowly, "so deeply, when you let yourself. I knew for months, and I know now, that you felt more than you wanted to admit. I never *once* saw the possibility that you might have been afraid to feel the *reciprocity* of me, of my feelings. I *never* thought that I could be of such emotional import that it was hard for you to accept your own feelings, not just mine. I knew your feelings were *there*; I just didn't think they mattered to you.

"You didn't want to know that I loved you—fuck *I* didn't want to know! But it never once entered my mind that I was more than an inconvenience to you. My own lagging self-esteem makes it hard for me to imagine that I can be of any real effect on another person unless it involves sex. But that *someone*, especially someone like *you*, could feel more for me than arousal... that seemed absurd."

Alex was listening intently, saying nothing.

I continued. "I know how much it hurt me to feel so much for you and not be able to explore that fully. It seemed *unfair* and terrible. I imagined you to feel only annoyance and resentment at feeling anything more for me. I wanted to know that there was a moment, *just once*, when you let it out and said, 'You know what? This tiny part of me loves her and that's okay. I can feel that and it's good and I'm not mad about it.'"

I reached across to him and clasped his hand. "Alex, I never thought it would *hurt* you to have that moment, to know it had to be packed away again when it was over. Even right now, my thick, fucking head is screaming at me not to be arrogant and not to give myself too much credit. It's hard to imagine I could ever be special enough to make someone else's heart *hurt* because they missed me. As badly as I wanted that from you, I never really thought it could be there."

"It's there, Tierney," he murmured, almost inaudibly. "It's always there and when I least expect it."

"Alex Wheeler... you never fail to astonish me."

He flashed an easy, broad smile. "I'm not...."

"You *are*. Look, I don't love a lot of people. I don't *like* a lot of people, and all these people in my life have really hurt me over the years. I have *reasons* to be wary of letting people in. When I do, and especially when I choose to let them in far enough to *love* them, they're special. You are a very rare breed of human being that I both *like* and *love*, and not just because I have to." I tucked my hair behind my ear. "That's why I get so mad about it all. That's why it feels so unfair. I don't want that to have been a waste of my energy."

Alex sat up, leaning forward on his knees. The late sunlight slid behind his glasses, and I could see his blue eyes through the dark amber lenses.

"Talia's that way. I mean, she has a hard time letting people in. She doesn't love easily. Even though she tells me all the time that she loves me more... I don't... I know it's not true."

The same way Sam knows he probably loves me more.

"But there are people you will *always* love more than you love your spouse," he said.

Huh?

"Your children," he continued.

Okay, maybe.

"Your parents," he offered.

Not even remotely.

He tilted his head and looked me in the eye. "Just... *people*." He paused, holding my gaze. "But I love Talia—I do—"

"I *know* you do," I said gently. I touched his warm hand. "I never questioned that."

"And I *adore* my daughter!"

I smiled at him. "*That*, right there! That look and that tone of voice. When you talk about her, every time you talk about her, I can *feel* how much you love her. That's how I knew you weren't just a great guy, that you were a really great *man*. That's one of the first things that drew me to you, honestly."

"I can't do anything to disappoint her, Tierney. God knows I'll have so many things to answer for one day." He glanced up toward the sky. "But I don't want that to be one of them. I don't want to do anything that ever makes her life difficult or makes her resent me. I have so many things I still want to say to my dad, so many things I'm angry about, and I don't want Amber to ever feel that way."

"Alex, the best thing you can do is find peace in yourself. Take the good and bad consequences of your actions and *learn* from them and *move the fuck on*. Modeling that behavior for your child is the best way to make you worthy of her pride, to show her how to be the human being you would want her to be."

The sun was setting, about to disappear entirely for the night.

"Come on," he said, standing to stretch, "let's go get a drink."

He reached his hand to me and pulled me to my feet. He started to turn toward the street, but I held his arm.

"Wait. I have one more question."

He stood with his back against the shadows, tilting his head expectantly. His curls were short again, like they were when I'd first met him. There was the same scraggly-but-sexy facial hair, flecked with gray. There were small crinkles and laugh lines around the edges of his eyes that I'd never noticed, and I thought that they suited him beautifully.

I looked up at him through a tangle of blond, wisping golden around my face in the dying afternoon glow.

"When you die, will you say you've been in love exactly *six* times?"

Alex looked at me directly, peering through the safety of dark sunglasses. "At the end of my life, I don't know what that number will be. I hope that's too long from now to guess. But if I had to answer today, I would still say five. I would say five, but I would whisper six in my heart, because that's where it belongs, where it's only mine and no one else's."

Remember to breathe, Tierney.

I reached up and touched his face, cupping his cheek, feeling his warmth against my palm. I stopped my thumb from running across his full lips, the luscious lips I so desperately wanted to feel against my own.

"I love you, Alex Wheeler." He said nothing, just looked at me evenly. "Good or bad, I do."

"I know. And I thank you for that, for your love and your caring."

"I don't know what you know about me. I don't know if you really know when my birthday is, or what my kids' names are, or even what color my eyes are—without looking. But what I *do* know is that you are *special*, you are *significant* to me, and I will *always* love you."

He clasped my hand in his, holding it against his cheek for just a moment too long. "Don't go all Whitney Houston on me, Buttercup."

I cracked a smile and glanced down at my tits. "I'm *way* more Dolly Parton than Whitney, Princess!"

He laughed the easy laugh I loved and gently dropped my hand, turning back toward the passing crowds.

"Come on," he said, "let's go find a drink."

————————

For the first time in days, I slept late. I woke after ten. I got a quick breakfast at the hotel and called Sam to check in.

Yes, I was fine. *Yes*, I was having a good time. Tell the boys I miss them. I love you, too.

I called Tessa to tell her everything that had happened.

Tessa said, "It makes me sad. It's just kind of tragic in its own way."

"Like Romeo and Juliet?" I scoffed.

"Kind of. It's a cautionary tale, right?"

"*Fuck that!* Romeo was a dumbass. They both were. But he was a fucking putz, right from the beginning."

"You see my point."

I got off the shuttle bus outside the Convention Center and started toward the banks of doors to go inside for a cup of coffee. But I stopped, my eye caught by a flash of pink.

A cute-but-greasy guy, young and shaggy, was reaching as high as he could, up one of the huge marble support columns under the portico. He was smoothing a piece of paper over layers of more paper.

The entire column was covered in my poster.

There were dozens of the girl in her buttercup pink boots, taking up every available space the guy's arms could reach. Pasted in long columns, overlapping in asymmetrical rows, there she was.

I stepped slowly toward the display.

"Good morning," the guy said.

I nodded, still staring wide-eyed at her.

"She is *hot*! Drawing or not. I think that's the best poster I've seen the whole festival."

I looked at him. "Really?"

He nodded. "I've been doing this for two weeks. Every morning. I've seen them all."

"Th-that's my poster," I stammered. "I did that."

"*Really?*"

I beamed giddily. "*Yeah. I did that!*"

I spent the early afternoon watching bands and walking from day party to day party. Alex texted me that they were going to the Deck to record a little bit. He told me to meet him at the back door of Flunky's at 8:00.

I was punctual, as usual, in my Junklure t-shirt and new, smaller jeans. I was also wearing a pair of black cheeky panties with the words *Big Girl* rhinestoned across my ass. The crowd was wrapped around the block toward the back door.

"I can't walk anyone inside," he said carefully, halfway leaning out the doorway. "It's not our party. It's the magazine's showcase. I'm sorry."

"It's okay. I'll see you inside."

"George is here somewhere. Lena. Some others,"

"Oh *god*! Don't make me hang with them. Please!"

Alex burst into laughter. "I can't help it, Buttercup. Just ignore them."

"They're so... *bleh!* I can't even deal with them online."

"That's because they're a bunch of bitches and buffoons."

"Ain't that the truth...."

He smiled at me once more. "I'll see you in a bit."

He walked through the back door, and I turned back toward the front.

I had my music badge, plus a special pass for quick, first admittance into the venue. It was the most expensive ticket for any Junkture show, ever. I was inside as soon as the doors opened. I stood with George, who hugged me hello, and Lena, who ignored me completely. I saw some other fans I knew, talked and chatted about the possible setlist and the excitement of South by Southwest. None of them knew the truth of what had happened, and I was careful not to say something stupid. I planted myself just in front of where Paul would be playing, where I'd stood as a fan for years. The show was free and open to the public, and they were turning away people at the door.

We watched the opening band, who'd been chosen by the party's sponsor to play the event. I didn't know them, but they were good, thanking Seth and Junkture and the magazine for inviting them to play.

Seth and his band came on next. He grinned as soon as he saw me. He'd called me earlier to tell me that he wouldn't be at the venue until the last minute, that he had to turn around and drive back to San Antonio that night.

"Is there a *girl* involved here, Seth?" I'd joked.

"*Maybe.*"

"Are you *sure* she's a girl?"

"*Just the tip, Tierney! Just the tip!*"

Seth's set was great, and I was so proud of my friend, who'd worked so hard to get what he wanted in his life. He deserved the record contract and the adoration of this crowd, and I was happy and honored that he wanted to share it with me.

The VIP area was upstairs, overlooking the stage and the floor and the bar, which had swelled with fans. While Ben and Corey and the other techs readied the stage, I looked toward those high shadows, searching for Alex. There was no sign of him.

The setlist was taped to the stage floor in front of me. It was a mix of old and new. "Hot Mess" wasn't there, but "Dollface" was. There was a new song, "Runnin' Late", listed as the first of the two-song encore. "Give up the Ghost" would be last.

It was too much to hope that I'd finally get to see and hear "Whiskey Mouth" live, but I'd never really expected they would do it. It was such an emotionally-charged song, given everything that had happened, given the significance of the song. As much as the groupie in me wanted to hear it, I wasn't sure my heart could take it.

Then my groupie love took to the stage. Not only did they play "Dollface", they opened the set with it. *It was my song.* Even without the attachment to Alex, it was my favorite. I loved it long before my path intertwined with theirs, and it was still one of those songs that could sweep me away to a deeply, personally happy place, every single time I heard it.

But Alex didn't sing it with me. I didn't blame him. He was unlikely to sing an opening song with a fan anyway, and Max and Charlie and Paulie were all *right* there, in view of everything. Then there was "Mantissa" again. Not the slower, acoustic version he'd sung at the Bayou Lounge the night before, but the full-band, screaming, rocking version that had rocketed their career so long ago. He moved through the crowd, holding out his mic to fan after fan, letting them have a moment of the song.

They ended the set with "Debris", then exited for the short break before the encore. The house lights were down, and the crowd was screaming. Thin, high whistles pierced the dark, squealing past the muffled ringing in my ears.

They came back to the stage, one by one—Charlie, then Max, then Paulie, and finally Alex.

"We wanna thank everyone for coming out tonight to see us at Flunky's!" Alex yelled to the crowd. "The owner's a real asshole, but we can't do much about it!"

Paulie laughed and pretended to shoot him with his guitar.

"We have a new song. It'll be on an upcoming record, hopefully out this fall."

He stepped back from his mic, waiting for Paul to play through the guitar intro. He wandered next to the amps at the back of the stage, his hips moving in time to the music. He took a sip from his cup and came back, singing:

> *He stood you on your feet*
> *And then dropped you to your knees*
> *Deafened by the sound of his fury*
> *Take your happy pill*

And feel his hand on your head
This is your life, baby,
Don't worry

In the dark
You call for him
Hear the echo of your voice
On your mark
It's all for him
Feel the echo of your choice

So young to be somebody's wife
Twenty years later, you're runnin' late for your life
He gave you a shiny, silver-plated dream
And hung you in his frame of mind
The monster in your bed
Is better than the demons in his head
And you're afraid now
You've run out of time

It was hard to make out the lyrics over the crowd and the loud bass. But I watched Alex's mouth, trying to catch every word.

It was so close to home. He'd said he'd never write about what had happened between us, and this wasn't a song about fucking a crazy girl in the middle of the night. It wasn't about falling in love with someone else. But it sounded like me, like my life, but my life was like that of so many other women I knew.

Is this song about me?

I couldn't think about it. I couldn't take my heart to the place where he might've actually written about me. It was too much to consider.

Not here. Not now. Not in front of so many people.
Go back to it later, when you're all alone.

It was a beautiful song, and the crowd seemed to love it.

Alex glanced down at his setlist and turned to Paul.

"I don't wanna play that. Do you wanna play that?"

Paul looked down at the floor and shrugged. He shook his head.

"Let's not play that."

Alex bounded sideways toward Paulie and whispered in his ear. Paul nodded and smiled. He fingers strained against the guitar strings, and in the first chord, I knew the song.

Whiskey Mouth.

Some of the crowd knew the song. The ones who didn't were the ones who didn't realize Junkture had ever had a career past their second record. The hardcore fans had obviously pulled it up on YouTube, from the Europe shows. I wasn't the only one singing along.

Alex avoided my eye, shaking hands and waving to other fans in the crowd.

Finally, he stopped in front of me, singing the beginning of the last verse. He looked at me, his mouth still moving in time to the lyrics.

Are we doing this? he asked with a raised eyebrow.

We are! I answered with a grin.

He held the microphone down to me for the last chorus:

We share ourselves
Our whiskey and sins
The sweet taste of your lies
The heat of your skin
Take out your flask
And pour out your heart
Promise you won't tell
What I whisper in the dark

We were locked, eye-to-eye. Just the microphone separated my mouth from his. I could taste his breath and feel his heat, and for just that moment, he was *my* Alex again.

Junkture took a bow, and the crowd cheered. The house lights came up, and I pushed my way to the bar for a drink. I downed a bottle of water and ordered a Jack and Ginger. I drank it quickly, glancing toward the VIP booth to see if Alex was there. I couldn't see him. I talked to a couple of fans for a few minutes and walked toward the front door, to step outside and get some fresh air.

"Tierney!"

I turned toward the sound of my name. At the end of the bar, in a corner, stood Paul Sommers. He was obviously drunk and talking to a female fan. She shot me a quick, pouty look, telling me I was intruding. I didn't care.

"Holy shit!" he exclaimed, stepping out toward me. "Look at you!"

"Nah, I look at me all the time. I don't need to see it."

He reached for a hug, big and close. "*Holy shit!* Charlie said to me after the show, 'I think that skinny girl is Tierney.' I said, 'No, there's no way!'" Paulie grabbed me by the arms and looked into my face, his hazel eyes bright and intoxicated. "*You were standing right in front of me for the entire set, and I didn't even realize it was you!*"

I laughed and blushed, giddy with the left-handed compliment.

"Wait!" he said, taking me by the hand. "I have to dance you!" He held my hand, pushing me back a couple of steps. "Dance, beautiful! Dance for me!"

I spun in place, over and over, slowly and then faster, laughing and exuberant.

"*Just beautiful!*" he breathed. "*Beautiful!*"

I looked up toward the VIP booth again. I could see bodies milling in the shadows but could only make out the form of Charlie, watching us intently from above.

"Charlie Taylor!" I yelled. I pointed straight at him. "Come down here!"

He nodded half-heartedly and waved. Max walked out of the door at the bottom of the stairs, toward the stage. Ben and Corey were busy breaking down the equipment, beginning the tedious load-out.

I hugged Paul one more time and excused myself to tell Max goodnight.

He was crouched at the front of the stage, untaping cables from the floor. "Do you have time for a drink?" he asked.

I shook my head. "I have an early flight. You can buy me a drink in Atlanta."

I beamed at him as he jumped down from the stage. "Yep. I'll call you when I get to town. We'll own that fucking mall." I hugged him once more and kissed him on the cheek.

Charlie walked up and asked Max if he'd seen Evan.

"Hi, Charlie," I said tentatively. "Great show!"

"Hi, Tierney. How are you? Great job on the poster, by the way. That kicked ass. If I were into chicks, I'd totally be into that one."

"How's the baby?" I asked.

He smiled his perfect drummer smile. "He's good. Perfect. Into everything."

"Glad to hear it! Have a safe trip home, okay?"

More smiles, more hugs. I turned to walk away.

I still hadn't seen Alex, and it was time for me to go. I texted him one last time.

Come tell me goodbye before I have to leave.

I waited for two minutes but didn't get a response from him. *Screw it*. I was turning to leave, to walk the ten blocks back to my shuttle, when he came through the backstage door.

He stopped to shake a couple of hands and tell a couple of people goodbye. He looked at me across the mostly empty bar and nodded his chin toward me. *Give me just a minute.*

I watched him in the dim light He was still the tall, sexy rock star I'd loved from afar for twenty years, but he was also the tired, insecure man who'd shared his secrets with me, who'd opened both my heart and his in the most unexpected ways.

He walked toward me, motioning for me to walk with him, outside. There were people everywhere around us, but no one was so close that they could hear what we were saying.

"Call me when you come to Atlanta," I said quietly.

"I can't do that, Tierney."

I rolled my eyes. "Don't be weird, Alex. It's okay."

"No, I can't do that. I can see you in other cities," he motioned around us, "but I can't do that there. I can't do that to Sam."

"Alex," I smiled tiredly, "I just want you to be able to see me, in a totally normal way and place, and say, 'Wow, there's the big, blond Amazon that I used to care about—'" *that I still care about* "'—and *goddamn!* I'm happy to hear her loudass laugh and see those dimples!'"

He smiled, shaking his head a little sadly. "I can't.... It would be like pissing in his backyard. I wouldn't want it done to me."

I shrugged. "You do what you need to do." I reached up and hugged him once more, feeling his warmth and strength in the cooling night air. "I love you, Wheeler."

"I know, Tierney," he sighed. "I love you, too." He pulled back and looked at me. "Go catch your shuttle. And text your husband and let him know you're safe and okay."

I nodded. "Safe travels, babycakes."

I turned from him and walked into the crowds of late night Austin.

I was a block away from my shuttle bus, exhausted and sweaty but elated, when my phone dinged with a text from Alex.

August 27th
Ian & Tripp
Blue

Yes. Yes. What the fuck is he talking about?
My eyes!

They're green, Princess.

I dropped my phone into my purse and grinned to myself, eyes ahead, moving rhythmically forward into the night.

Acknowledgements

Persona Non Grata was undoubtedly a labor of love, and I never would have been able to do this without an incomparable cast and crew, whose support and encouragement helped bring this project to fruition.

Hannah Lankford, Alan Clarke (The Entertainment Law Group) Cheri Pizarro (Ground Pounder Graphics), Cheryl Porter, Mary Catherine Lee (Mary Catherine's Salon), Christine Brandigi-Clark (Photos by Digi)—all of you made my life easier, giving me the tools I needed to get this done, both logistically and emotionally.

Corey Bishop, thank you for knowing *exactly* what I had in mind, and for walking miles and miles and miles with me.

Susan Cadley and Amy Alderman, thank you for helping me bring what was scared and hiding to the beautiful forefront of my life.

Adam Taylor, you are a fucking genius, and there's always a twenty in my pocket, just in case you need it.

My deepest thanks go to my editor, Leigh Partington, for making me cry and doubt my abilities when I needed it most, and in the kindest, gentlest ways imaginable.

My inner circle of readers—Becky Laney, Sandra Chang, Danielle Turberville, Angie Curtis, and Kim Cunningham—you are the most surprising and unlikely group of women, who all said, "You know what? It's okay when sex makes you blush." Thanks for reading and rereading and rereading.

Kristi Weldon, Morgan Chatham, and Amanda Chandler, you're my sisters from other misters, and I'll still love you when we make it all the way to eighty.

Tiffany Lopez, who has been there for me every minute of every day—before, during, and after—you are the other half of my girlie heart. It doesn't beat without you.

To Absolem, the mirror of my obstacles, thank you for showing me exactly how complicated the character of Alex Wheeler really was.

To Trey and Patrick, my beautiful boys, you are the best thing Mommy has ever done. Thank you for patiently entertaining yourselves when I needed to work. I hope you will one day understand why this was so important to me, and that you have something that means as much to you. I've decided to keep you both forever.

To Don, who will be DH forever and always and no matter what, your strength of support amazed even me. *Thank you* for giving me what I needed to be able to do this.

To all of the rock stars who have turned my heart upside down for as long as I can remember, thank you for baring a bit of your souls to your fans. Your words and music have been the soundtrack of my life and of Tierney's life.

And to my fans who have waited very patiently while I worked through revision after revision, *thank you* for reading my words at MuchnessandLight.com. *Thank you* for putting up with my song lyrics and talk of glitter. And *thank you* for sticking with me. Your support means more to me than you will ever know.

StephQJ
September 2012

For a list of songs that helped to inspire *Persona Non Grata*, visit www.junkture.com.

www.ingramcontent.com/pod-product-compliance
Lightning Source LLC
Chambersburg PA
CBHW061504020726
47502CB00006B/1931